THE SOCIETY

I0562687

JENNIFER WORD

EMP PUBLISHING
Atchison, Kansas

THE SOCIETY
Book One: Genesis
Book Two: Transcription
Book Three: Regeneration

ISBN: 978-0-9980860-3-3

The Society Book One: Genesis was originally published by Stony Meadow Publishing, March 30, 2012 © 2010 Jennifer Word
The Society Book Two: Transcription was originally published by Stony Meadow Publishing, March 26, 2013 © 2010 Jennifer Word
The Society Book One: Genesis, 2nd edition was published by EMP Publishing, October 27, 2015 © 2010 Jennifer Word

Printed in the United States of America

To H.G., My Best Friend, and My Special. Thanks.

I will praise thee; for I am fearfully and wonderfully made: marvellous are thy works; and that my soul knoweth right well.

—Psalm 139:14

I know in my heart that man is good. That what is right will always eventually triumph. And there is purpose and worth to each and every life.

—Ronald Wilson Reagan

Book One:
GENESIS

1

Jessica Wembly was attacked at three o'clock on a Wednesday afternoon. Unlocking her apartment door, she stepped inside, kicking it closed behind her.

Did she smell after shave? She felt her body tense. *Behind you, behind you!* She turned to look, doubting her thoughts. A figure previously hidden by the open door darted from the shadows. *A man.*

He held something in his hand—a white cloth. She jumped back as he lunged, causing the man to stumble, falling to his knees.

Jessica turned to run, heading toward her bedroom. He reached out and grabbed her ankle, wrenching his arm back. Her feet flew out from beneath her. She threw her arms out to cushion the fall, but the impact was still enough to drive the breath from her lungs. Her shoulder blades and upper arms absorbed most of the shock. She felt a sharp pain, already growing sore.

She kicked her feet wildly, trying to dislodge his grip on her ankle. He held her tight enough to stop the circulation to her foot, which had already grown numb.

The man pulled her back. On their stomachs, they swam across the carpet in a strange dance of malice and survival. He made progress, slowly inching up Jessica's calf, grasping her right knee. She screamed, the weight of his body pinning her legs to the floor.

She reached back and raked her fingernails across his cheek, sinking her nails in deep. She relished the warm pulse of blood over her fingers.

The man howled, rage and hurt seeming only to make him stronger. He released her left leg and grabbed her wrist, dragging it away from his face. Jessica shrieked as he twisted her arm behind her back, pinning her down. The muscles in her shoulder screamed in agony.

She was pinned; paralyzed and helpless.

The man's hand lifted from her knee. Jessica vaguely registered him fumbling for something on the floor. A second later, the man launched his body forward, releasing both her pinned leg and arm. He had his full weight on top of her, his torso and legs pinning her whole body to the floor.

She turned her head sideways and screamed, the last breath leaving her lungs. His hand curled around her face, the white cloth he'd retrieved clamping over her nose and mouth.

"Hel…!!" Jessica cried out, before the cloth sealed her mouth.

She smelled something dull and chemical. She tried not to breathe any of the poisoned air, but instinct overrode reason. Her lungs empty and burning, she gasped, drinking down greedy, tainted breaths. She felt drunk, the world swimming.

As Jessica Wembly breathed in again, the world grew dark. Her last thoughts were sad, lamenting the loss of a life barely lived.

***

From black, the world became dark gray, lightening by degrees. She was moving, floating in a warm ocean. As she regained consciousness, she realized it was the steady swaying of her body in the back seat of a car.

She lay on the seat. Pulling herself upright, a dull pain throbbed through her shoulders, arms, and neck, her muscles stiff and sore. A migraine pounded behind her eyes. She felt as if she might be sick, swallowing back waves of nausea.

She looked at the driver, realizing it was the man who had attacked her. He was dressed all in black. The car reminded her of a police squad unit—a thick glass barrier between her and the driver—three parallel slats in the glass, a quarter inch thick, their only means of communication.

Jessica looked at the man in the rearview mirror. He wore sunglasses, but she could see the ragged marks her nails had grooved into his left cheek. She briefly caught sight of her own reflection; almond eyes haunted beneath with dark circles. Her dark-brown, shoulder-length hair was plastered to the sides of her cheeks with sweat; her body's reaction to the chloroform and the attack. She smelled of musky perspiration, her white t-shirt clinging to her damp underarms. Her jeans felt moist and claustrophobic, hugging her skin. Her usually pale complexion appeared even more drained, making the dark circles underneath her eyes more prominent. She dropped her gaze away from her dour reflection.

Jessica looked out the window, trying to discern where the man was taking her. She couldn't have been unconscious for long—her apartment was in West Santa Monica—she immediately recognized where they were upon seeing the ocean. They were driving up PCH, through Malibu.

She tried to tamp down the rising panic, but the sinking sensation in the pit of her stomach refused to let go. She looked out at the ocean, watching as sparkles of gold danced over the dark blue sea. She stared at the seagulls flying over the water and felt as if she were dreaming. She wasn't dead yet. The man had attacked her but hadn't killed her. She wasn't even handcuffed. Where was he taking her?

Jessica spoke, her voice sounding faint and distant.

"Where are you taking me?"

He didn't answer. She saw him flinch, however. Perhaps it was a slight jump at the unexpected sound of her voice? Jessica wasn't certain. She asked again.

"Where are you taking me?"

"Ma'am, it would be best if you didn't talk."

She felt shock at the quiet register of the man's voice, including his seeming manners. She detected a slight southern lilt. A dozen conflicting thoughts raced in her head. What did this man want with her? Why had he kidnapped her? Where was he taking her? One overrode the others, its urgency making her breath hitch and heart race.

"Are you going to kill me?"

Jessica fought hard not to cry. He looked at her in the rearview mirror, and despite his sunglasses, she thought she saw a faint tremor beneath the mask of shadows.

"What are you going to do to me?"

"Ma'am, please don't speak anymore."

"Why are you doing this?!"

Jessica sobbed, burying her face in her hands. She folded herself forward until her hands touched her knees. He said nothing, only looked at her in the mirror. *He's young*, she thought, despite her tears and panic. She tried to calm down again, sitting up, wiping the tears away.

"Please, just tell me. Are you going to kill me?"

He continued glancing between her and the road but remained silent. She gave up on any answer and went back to looking out the window. She tried pulling on the door handle and slumped back defeated in her seat when she discovered it to be locked from the inside.

"No."

She looked at him in the mirror, trying to read his face. He looked forward and continued driving. She wasn't certain if he'd spoken at all.

"Are you a serial killer?"

He shifted in his seat, looking uncomfortable. "No, I'm *not* a serial killer."

She thought he sounded offended. "Then what are you going to do to me?"

"I'm not a serial killer. I work for the government. They tell me to do things, and I do them."

"The *government*?" Jessica sat upright, stunned rigid. *The man must be crazy.* "The government told you to kidnap me?"

"I'm not kidnapping you," he said, shaking his head.

"Yes, you are. You're taking me someplace against my will, that's called kidnapping. You attacked me in my own apartment! You drugged me!"

9

"You attacked me, too," he said. "Jeezus."

He touched the scratches on his cheek, his voice sullen, like that of a three-year-old. He muttered under his breath, Jessica catching only every other word.

"Ridiculous... should have... no warning... her file... tranquilizer... fucking Taser... the others."

"What are you saying?" she screamed. "Talk to me. This can't be *legal*. The government can't just kidnap people like this. Who do you work for?"

"I can't tell you that."

"Why not?"

"Because I don't know," he said, his voice growing quiet again.

"What? What do you mean, you don't *know?*"

"Why are you focusing on these mundane details?"

"What the hell are you talking about? How is wanting to know what branch of the government is *kidnapping* me *mundane?*"

"Well, instead of wanting to know who, I'd be asking myself *why.*"

Jessica stared at the man, thinking about what he'd said. He was right. Why would the government want to kidnap her? She was *no one.* She worked in a mall, baking cookies. She lived in a tiny apartment. She made twelve hundred dollars a month. She paid her rent each month on time and didn't even own a car. She walked to work every day, at six-thirty in the morning, in the dark. She lived on leftover cookie dough for breakfast, cheap Chinese noodles for lunch, and sandwiches or cereal for dinner. She was twenty-four years old and had no real future planned. What could the government possibly want with *her?*

Jessica pondered all of this while watching the million-dollar beach houses drift by. They passed through Malibu, continuing north up PCH. *Nothing is up here*, she thought. Where was he taking her? Then, suddenly, she thought she knew.

"We're going to the base, aren't we? At Port Hueneme?"

"I can't say."

"So, *why* does the government want to talk to me?"

She decided that even if the man was lying or making up some crazy story, she would play along and see where it took her.

"I don't know."

"What *do* you know?" She fixed her gaze on him, through the rearview mirror.

"Nothing."

She stared at him, her face ashen and pleading. Finally, he seemed to relent.

"You're calmer than most of the others," he led.

"The others?" Jessica frowned.

"I only take orders," the man said. "I do what they tell me, no questions asked. I don't even know who I work for, only that it's an agency with no name, and my boss has a boss."

"And you've done this before, to other people?"

"I get a file," he shrugged. "It tells me all about the person... Photos, surveillance, their work schedules, who their neighbors are, who their friends are. Everything I need to know to pick them up. That's what I do. I get them in my car and transport them."

"To where?"

"A secure facility on the base."

"So, I'm right, you're taking me to The Point."

"Everything's done in pieces," he said, shaking his head. "Whoever you are, the government's been watching you a *long* time."

"But I haven't done anything," Jessica said. "I'm a good person. Why would they even bother with me?"

"I don't know what they want with any of you. You all seem like perfectly normal people to me," he said. "I don't know what they do with you. Lock you up, maybe? Who knows? I just transport you, that's all."

"So, you don't know if I'll be killed, do you?"

"If they wanted you dead, you'd be dead," the man said. "They have men for that, too. They want you for *something*, I just don't know what. All I know is, I bring people to the base, and from there, they disappear."

"Christ, how can you do this?!" Jessica felt panic again.

"It's my job."

"You're a criminal!" she screamed. She angrily kicked the back of the man's seat, throwing a fit.

"Ma'am, stop that, please."

"Stop calling me Ma'am!" Jessica shrieked. "For all you know, they torture people on that base. Did you ever think about that? They could be killing innocent people, and you're a part of that. You are a serial killer. You are!"

"No, I'm not!"

Clearly upset, he settled down in his seat and continued driving. When Jessica attempted to speak to him again, he didn't answer. He never spoke to her again.

They continued north on PCH and eventually turned off, onto a side road. They were somewhere north of Malibu and Trancas, but south of Oxnard. They continued down side roads, through farmland, until they came to a guarded gate obscured by trees. A soldier with an automatic trotted up to the car. The driver rolled down his window.

"Bravo-Charlie, Alpha-Alpha."

"Bravo-Alpha-Alpha," the soldier replied, trotting back to the security booth, activating the gate.

"Where are we? This isn't Port Hueneme, is it? This isn't the base!" Jessica screamed.

The man continued ignoring her. They drove past the gate. Barbed wire surrounded everything. Although it appeared to be an orchard of citrus trees they now drove through, it surely wasn't. Eventually, they came to an opening in the trees.

In the middle of a dirt clearing, a low, tan building loomed, seeming to go on for miles. The building disappeared into the trees, creating the illusion of being immense. She thought she saw shadows across the building's façade, cast by the trees, until it dawned on her that the building was painted that way. *Camouflaged.* She leaned her head against the window, looking at the ominously obscured structure. *No windows.*

The car came to a stop. Two men stood in the clearing. The driver got out and shook hands with them. Both wore suits. The driver spoke to one of them, briefly. She saw him reach up and touch the scratches on his face, then shrug and throw his arms out to his sides. Then he walked away, never looking back. He disappeared into a tall stand of citrus trees. Jessica never saw him again.

The two men walked over to the car. One held back, while the other opened Jessica's door. She shrunk back, looking at him in fear. He appeared to be middle-aged, perhaps in his late-thirties, with a slightly receding head of salt-and-pepper hair, although it was still more chestnut than gray. The other man looked to be in his early forties, with a full head of dark-blond hair. Both were clearly fit; well built, their postures rigid and identical, like soldiers standing to attention.

The salt-and-pepper-haired man looked at Jessica for several moments. His eyes were a piercing shade of blue, his face stern, but when he spoke, his voice sounded surprisingly gentle.

"Please, Ms. Wembly, if you'll come with me, everything will be explained shortly. I assure you, we mean you no harm."

"Why am I here?" she demanded, not moving. Although her heart still pounded in her chest, she immediately regained her composure—an unnoticed reaction to this man's seeming sincerity.

"I promise you, all your questions will be answered."

"Yeah, right," Jessica said. "If I come with you, I'm sure I'll be tortured to death slowly, then buried in an unmarked grave somewhere out in those stupid trees."

The man looked at her with amusement. A small smile played at his lips.

"Why would we do that?" he asked. "Ms. Wembly, think about it. Why would we waste our time and resources to bring you here, if we were merely going to kill you? What would be the purpose?"

"I'm not sure, but if you aren't going to hurt me, why all the lies? Why all the secrecy?" she challenged. "I was attacked in my own home. I thought I was going to be murdered." Jessica started to cry. She felt ashamed of herself, but she couldn't help it.

"Ms. Wembly, I'm sorry about the physical struggle you had to endure. It was never our intent for you to experience that. I'm sure it must have been very frightening. Agent Fielding was supposed to render you unconscious before you knew what was happening. He failed in that regard, and for that, I'm sorry. If it's any consolation, you're the first person to put up such a fight. No agent has ever been injured during an acquisition before. You've proven to be quite the firecracker."

She thought he looked at her with something like respect. His tone of voice also seemed to match this assessment.

"Why am I here?" she repeated, her tone less combative.

"All of this will be explained, I promise you."

Jessica looked at him, then over his shoulder at the other man. The second man smiled, waving sheepishly.

She frowned. *What the hell is going on here?* She reluctantly realized she didn't have much choice but to get out of the car and follow these men. She was on some sort of secure military base, somewhere in Southern California, and no one knew she was there. She lived alone, and no one was going to look for her. She was, for all intents and purposes, completely anonymous and unimportant; the type of person who could go missing for days before anyone noticed she was gone.

Jessica sighed and slowly got out of the car, her legs shaking. She followed the two men without further complaint.

2

The blond-haired man punched a code into a keypad, then pulled the door open. A loud buzzing came from the door-frame. Once inside the first door, she followed both men down a short corridor. They turned a corner and arrived at another door. The same man entered another code. Again, the door opened, this time silently.

Once past the second door, Jessica followed the two men down a much longer corridor, with several unmarked doors on either side. She took note of the cameras mounted near the ceiling, every ten feet or so along the hallway. They turned several times, eventually arriving at an unmarked door on the left. The place was a maze; white and featureless, as though designed to disorient those inside.

The older man stepped forward, removing a key from his pants pocket and unlocked the door. Jessica thought it was strange that the first two doors had electronic locks, yet this one was a simple key-lock. She stood just behind the man, noting how tall he was.

She was led into a small, white room, with a rectangular white table in the middle. There were cameras in here too, in each corner of the ceiling. Two metal chairs sat on either side of the table, which contained a manila folder, a small stack of red plastic cups and a pitcher of water. Salt-and-Pepper motioned for her to sit in the chair in front of the table, while he walked around and sat in the chair behind. The blond-haired man closed the door and stood in front of it; a human barrier.

Jessica sat down in the chair, looking across at Salt-and-Pepper, who sat staring back at her. She folded her arms, angry and defiant. The man smiled at her and reached for a plastic cup. He filled it with water then set it in front of her. He poured himself a cup of water as well and set the pitcher back down.

"Have some water, Jessica. I'm sure you must be parched," he said. "Chloroform dries the mouth."

She looked at him and shook her head. "Sure, so you can poison me?"

"Now, why would I do that?" The man smiled. "You really are a firecracker, aren't you? Not very trusting. Again, if I wanted you dead, why would I go to all the trouble of bringing you here?"

He continued smiling, his expression all friendly concern. Jessica couldn't help noticing how good-looking he was. His cheekbones looked like they were chiseled from stone, his brilliant blue eyes flashed with electricity. For some reason, however, he made Jessica think of Jekyll & Hyde. She was afraid of him.

"Besides," he said, lifting his cup, "if the water was poisoned, how could I drink from the same pitcher?"

He drank deeply from his cup then set it back down on the table. His eyes never left hers. She looked at his cup then eyed her own warily.

"Anyhow, it's your choice." He extended his hand to her, indicating he wanted her to shake it.

"My name is Doctor Milbron," he said. "If you like, however, you can simply call me Dr. M. Everybody else does."

Jessica refused to shake Dr. M.'s hand. He smiled again, lacing his fingers together in his lap, sitting back in his chair.

"I brought you here to tell you something," he said. "Something fantastic. Something you most likely won't believe, at first."

Dr. M. sat forward again, opening the manila folder on the table, leafing through several papers.

"This is your life, Jessica. Everything about you, from your blood type, to all your most favorite foods, to the first day you started your period. Don't ask how we know that," he said, as she opened her mouth to speak. "Trust me, you don't want to know."

Dr. M. closed the file and set it aside. Then he leaned forward even more, resting his arms on the table.

"Let me start by explaining that I am a doctor of genetics."

She opened her mouth to speak again, and Dr. M. silenced her by holding up his hand.

"I will now tell you, in a roundabout way, why you are here. You won't believe a word, beyond the basics, and a lot of it will simply be beyond your understanding."

She reached nervously for her cup of water and drank. She felt extremely thirsty. She drained the cup and set it down as he looked on. He smiled at her and continued talking. As predicted, she didn't believe a single word of what he said, beyond the first few minutes.

"There was this little thing that got started back in 1990, *the Human Genome Project*. It involved hundreds of scientists from different organizations worldwide. I was one of those scientists.

"At the end of the project, we'd managed to map the entire human genome. However, we also discovered genes with polymorphisms.

"These polymorphisms became the focus of my team. I was tapped to head the project. My work on polymorphisms is what turned everything into what it is today. Do you know what polymorphism means?"

Jessica shook her head. Dr. M. nodded.

"It is from the Greek word *poly*, meaning *multiple*, and *morph*, meaning *form*. In terms of genetics, it simply describes the multiple forms of a single gene that can exist in an individual or among a group of individuals.

"You see, it all comes down to genes, really, Jessica. Good genes and bad. And then there are *different* genes, which is why you are here. Are you following me so far?"

Dr. M. stared at her for several long moments. She realized he meant for her to answer him. She frowned and then shook her head. She wasn't exactly certain yet what he was trying to tell her.

"I think after everything I've been through, I deserve to be told why I'm here," she said.

Dr. M. smiled at Jessica, but it looked forced. The light in his eyes faltered.

"There are several types of polymorphisms found. One type is known as a *pseudogene,* a gene that appears to have gone dormant, serving no further genetic purpose."

He looked at Jessica, who stared blankly back. Then she reached her hand up to her mouth and faked a yawn. This time Dr. M. looked clearly perturbed. His smile quickly faded. He looked anxious, almost desperate to impress.

"About point-one percent of the world's population has a deviant pseudogene. That was my discovery, back in 1993. That is what changed everything, Jessica. The discovery of a pseudogene that other humans simply don't have. An extra gene. One gene. That's all. A small difference, barely detectable.

"It's very rare, but on average, about one-in-one-hundred-thousand people has this extra gene. In 1994, I began my work on it. I was tapped by a sector of the government that I cannot name, to try and figure out what the deviant gene is meant to do.

"It took me months to come up with an answer. The deviant gene was dormant, useless. The only way I could possibly learn what its function was, would be to activate it somehow."

Dr. M. smiled at Jessica again. He had a crazed look in his eyes now, making her feel uneasy. Her mind felt a bit clouded. She no longer felt afraid, however. She still did not know why she was there, but she no longer worried she would be murdered. Her head felt woozy. Dr. M. went on talking.

"I had to find a way to cause a non-coding genetic sequence to code; trying to figure out how to activate the dormant pseudogene. I eventually discovered that ingestion of a specific enzyme activates the gene, which in turn, does very interesting things to the human body.

"When activated, the gene seems to regulate body temperature, thermal output, and brain functioning on a synaptic level. It also seems to have some sort of function regarding the energy output of cells inside the human body. And just as there are many different combinations of genes, which in any individual, makes them unique, the deviant pseudogene, when activated, manifests itself within each human in varying ways. Does this make sense to you, Jessica?"

She looked at the doctor, panic coursing through her. She felt dizzy and blinked several times, trying to focus.

"Ah, you're beginning to figure things out, aren't you, Jessica? Pushing past the boring science jargon. Do you want to know what enzyme activates *your* deviant pseudogene? It's called Photinus Pyralis Luciferase, but I simply refer to it as Luci, for short. In liquid form, it is clear, odorless and tasteless. We abstract the enzyme from the abdomens of fireflies. It's one of the main enzymes, when mixed with a few others, that causes them to glow. Bioluminescence, it's called. In humans, Luci has a decidedly different effect.

"I couldn't put it in the water, obviously, since I also drank from the pitcher, but the plastic cup you drank from was coated with it, and when I poured the water into the cup, the Luci was reconstituted, or dissolved into the liquid you drank."

Jessica stood, feeling disoriented. She backed up against the wall, looking toward the door. Blond guy stood, looking straight ahead of him, as if completely unaware of what took place.

"You poisoned me?!" she shrieked. The room distorted around her, slowly whirling.

"No, Jessica. I merely introduced an enzyme into your system. Once it passes into your digestive tract and enters your blood stream, you'll notice some changes in your body. You may feel warmer, at times downright hot or feverish. You may feel dizzy, as though you are floating, a slight loss of equilibrium. Most of these symptoms will pass. Other than that, I cannot tell you what will happen. We'll just have to wait and see. The first effects are generally felt within a half-hour of ingesting the enzyme."

Her breathing came in short, heavy bursts. The doctor regarded her with pity.

"Sit down, Jessica. There's no reason to panic. If you sit down, I can finish explaining to you why you are here. Aren't you the least bit interested in knowing how we found you? That's a good one, as well."

She slowly walked back to her chair and sat, deflated. Her head swam, her feet felt as though they weren't even touching the floor. She listened to Dr. M. in a complete daze.

"We discovered, while mapping the human genome, that, for some reason, everyone with the pseudogene is born precisely five weeks early—specifically in week thirty-five of gestation. This gave us a pretty good starting place for identifying other transgenics, or simply transgens, as we call them.

"A transgenic, in case you are wondering, is simply an organism into which a new gene or set of genes has been transferred. In this case, the pseudogene has been transferred into you, Jessica. You see, it is *very* rare—so rare, it cannot be by *accident.* Your gene holds all the markers of biomedical tampering. There is now indisputable proof, with the discovery of the deviant pseudogene, that tampering has been done to humanity. Simply put, Jessica, you were designed, on a genetic level, and we still don't know how.

"If you're wondering exactly what to expect, well, I can't tell you that. We'll just have to wait and see."

Dr. M. stood and gestured casually toward the blond guy still standing in front of the door.

"Mr. Gees will show you to your room. There will be a few standard outfits there, including some blue pajamas. I suggest you make your toilet, then go to sleep. You'll find you have everything you need to be comfortable.

"Get a good night's rest, Jessica. Tomorrow will be the first day of your new life."

Jessica stood up as Dr. M. motioned her toward the door. She swayed on her feet.

"What if you're wrong? What if I can't do anything? You probably made a mistake."

"No, I doubt that," Dr. M. said, smiling. "I think you're simply in shock. It's common. The initial effects of Luci can be overwhelming."

"This feels like a dream," she said, as Mr. Gees opened the door. "I'm floating," she smiled.

"That's normal, Jessica. I'll see you tomorrow." The doctor smiled back.

"See ya," she waved.

***

Mr. Gees led Jessica on what felt like a dozen turns down various corridors and white hallways, eventually putting his hand on her shoulder to steady her. He opened a door and let her into another white room. There was a bed in the far-right corner—white sheets with a light, cream-yellow cotton blanket. A door on the far-left opened onto an en-suite bathroom—a cream-yellow counter and sink, with another door leading to a closet-sized space containing a toilet and tub. Back in the main room, against the left-hand wall stood a wooden four-drawer dresser, along with a small, round table and one wooden chair near the door. No windows.

Mr. Gees cleared his throat. "Your clothes are in the dresser," he said. "If you need anything, just press this button here on the wall."

She turned and looked at the red button and intercom on the wall to the left of the door. Then she walked over to the bed and fell into it. She was asleep in moments. She didn't hear Mr. Gees leave the room, or the door as it clicked, locking her in.

***

When Jessica woke refreshed the next morning, she still had the strange sensation of floating several inches above the ground. She lay in bed for a time, staring at the blank, white ceiling; the events of the previous day flooding back to her.

Sitting up, swinging herself out of bed, she frowned at her feet. She'd fallen asleep with her shoes on. She toed each one off at the heel and then did the same with her socks, frowning even harder at her feet. They were touching the floor; she could feel the cool, Berber carpet against her soles, but the floor itself suddenly appeared to drop away, leaving her dangling over a nightmare precipice. She jumped back, huddling in the corner of the bed, against the wall, her heart hammering. After several moments, she inched forward and peered over the edge. Solid floor.

Jessica snapped her head up, glaring directly into the camera in the left corner. Dr. M. was probably observing her at that very moment, like a rat in a cage, she figured.

She turned her focus back to her surroundings. Slowly, she stood up from the bed, realizing she needed to pee. She quickly walked into the back room, where a variety of toiletries had been set out for use: A toothbrush, complete with favored brand of toothpaste; a bottle of face lotion, again, the same brand she used at home. Opening a drawer, she found several types of makeup, including her brand of mascara. Everything she kept in her bathroom at home.

Heading into the small cubicle housing the toilet and bathtub, she shut the door. There was no lock, but also no camera, as far as she could tell.

She inspected the toilet, wondering if there was a camera inside. "Surely, they can't be that sick," she whispered. Then she sat down and peed.

While sitting on the toilet, she saw that bottles of the shampoo and conditioner she used at home sat on the edge of the bathtub, along with her brand of razors. She sighed.

Finished, she walked back into the main room. A glass of water waited on the round table. She didn't remember seeing it there before, but didn't much care, realizing upon sight of it that she felt cloyingly thirsty. Picking up the glass of water, she eyed it suspiciously. Setting it back down, she walked directly in front of the left corner camera and threw two middle fingers at it before retreating to the bathroom. There, she turned on the sink faucet, gulping desperately, directly from the tap.

Returning to the main room, she sat back down on the bed, the last, lingering vertigo thankfully passing. Holding her hands up before her face, she frowned, turning them from front to back. They prickled with pins and needles, as though falling asleep. A sudden, sharp pang in her belly distracted her from the sensation, along with the realization that she hadn't eaten in almost twenty-four hours. She looked up at the camera, lost and uncertain.

"Um… I'm hungry."

No response. She waited a few more moments then decided to try the intercom on the wall. Pressing the red button, she waited for a faint crackle of static to disperse before speaking.

"Hello?"

She pushed the button then released it quickly. Then pushed it again, keeping it depressed while she spoke.

"He—… hello?"

A brief pause, a slight click; then an unfamiliar male voice echoed around the room. He sounded high-pitched, Jessica thought, almost like an adolescent.

"Yes?"

"Um… I'm hungry."

"Are you ready to leave your room?"

"Yes," then, under her breath, "let me out of this prison hole."

"I will unlock your door, Jessica. Once in the hallway, simply say the word *cafeteria* and follow the red arrows."

"Red arrows?"

A faint click sounded from the direction of the door. *God, I haven't even had a chance to change my clothes!* Opening the door, she stepped out into the hallway.

Everything was white, the fluorescent lights overhead buzzing loudly. She looked left, then right, confused.

"What arrows? I don't see anything." Then, recalling the voice's instruction, she sighed the word: "Cafeteria."

A large red arrow instantly appeared on the wall before her. She walked over and touched it. *Like magic.* New arrows appeared as she followed their directions. How this was even possible she couldn't imagine. It seemed dreamily like something from a science fiction novel.

Eventually, the arrows led her to a white door, where they simply stopped. Another light clicking indicated that the door had somehow unlocked itself.

Jessica opened the door. She gasped at the sudden color that flooded her senses. As she walked inside, the door closed behind her, its lock clicking, sealing her in.

She stood in a rectangular room. The right-hand wall, however, contained floor-to-ceiling glass windows, revealing a large courtyard. She saw hummingbirds flitting around several trees, and birds-of-paradise lined the glass near the ground. She stared out the windows for several minutes, smiling.

The rest of the room contained several, round white tables and green chairs, with walls painted a light yellow. There was a counter to her left with a drink station, like in restaurants. She walked past the soda taps and grabbed a tall, red plastic cup, filling it with orange juice, then turned and walked over to the wall opposite the courtyard. This side contained one small panel of glass, the size of a car window.

She stared in wonder at a much larger cafeteria on the other side of the glass and saw roughly a half dozen people sitting at round tables. Some of them looked up at her in wonder. She felt embarrassed; on display. She quickly moved away from the glass and looked in the baskets on the counter to the right. One contained various kinds of bagels, another had sourdough bread rolls and English muffins. There was a four-slot toaster and a basket with small tins of single-serve butter, with various flavors of jam; single-serve boxes of cereal, bowls, silverware, and a tall pitcher of milk.

"Hello, Jessica."

She started almost out of her skin, turning to find Dr. M. smiling at her. He chuckled.

"I didn't mean to startle you. How are you feeling?"

"Like I'm in the Twilight Zone… with the nicest Motel 6 continental breakfast spread I've ever seen." She glanced sideways at him. "Everything just feels… *off.*"

"Well, that's to be expected. This is all very unusual, I'm certain. Why don't you fix yourself a plate, or bowl, and sit down with me? We can talk while you eat."

"Yeah, right. I bet all this stuff is contaminated with that… whatever you gave me yesterday."

"Luci? No. Amazingly, it only takes one small dose to do the trick, if you can believe that. Less than half an ounce, in fact."

Jessica watched warily as Dr. M. sat down at the nearest table. She turned back to the food baskets and selected an English muffin. She imagined the doctor's eyes, boring red-hot holes through her back. She toasted her muffin then grabbed some butter and jam along with a butter knife. She carried her plate and orange juice to the table, reluctantly sitting down across from Dr. M. She ate slowly, eyeing him the entire time. He stared back at her, smiling.

"You're hungry," he finally said, after several minutes, when Jessica was nearly finished with her muffin. "That's totally normal. You'll find you're hungry more often now. Your abilities will require a larger intake of calories, and depending on what you can do, you may burn a little or a lot more than you did before. Suffice it to say, there are no overweight transgens in this facility."

Jessica stared at him, her dark eyes full of hatred, then looked over at the glass that provided a view of the larger cafeteria. Several sets of eyes looked back. Unsettled, she returned her attention to the doctor, who glanced over his shoulder.

"The members of The Society. Some of them, anyhow. You'll be able to interact with them in a few days. Today, you'll remain isolated. It's strict protocol. We do this with every new arrival."

"The Society?" Jessica frowned.

"That's what we call it, since that's what it is. A small collection of people with unique abilities. There are over a dozen people in this facility. The transgens have formed their own culture within the compound. There are the popular people, and the not-so-popular," the doctor chuckled. "It's an exciting day for us, Jessica. Once you've finished your breakfast, I'll ask that you return to your room and change into the clothes that have been provided for you. There are socks and underwear, and yes, they're all the right size. We're very good at knowing certain things, you see."

"But I still don't understand," she said. "You're just throwing all these terms at me. Luci, psycho-genes, The Society. I still have absolutely no clue what the heck is going on around here!"

Jessica rubbed her hands together. They stung as though *burning* with her rage. Dr. M. scooted his chair closer and lowered his voice to a whisper.

"Stay calm, Jessica. I didn't explain certain things to you yesterday because I didn't want to overwhelm you. Besides, it wouldn't have done any good to dump a lot of information on you while you were suffering from the initial effects of the Luci. Also, it's not psycho-gene," Dr. M. laughed, shaking his head. "It's *pseudogene,* and the scientific explanations are really mundane at this point.

"The Society is simply comprised of other people like you—people with a deviant pseudogene that I've activated using Luci. They each have a unique ability. That's all."

Jessica scoffed, shaking her head. She sat back in her chair, crossing her arms and glared at the doctor. He continued talking unperturbed.

"One person we've activated can float. He hasn't flown quite yet, but floating has been observed. We've got a woman here who can boil water without a stove, another who can blow things up, but only if the object is less than ten percent water. Don't ask me why. There's still too much we don't understand.

"There's a man here who can read minds—*very* unnerving. There's another young woman, about your age, who can put her hands through solid objects. Although, *only* her hands, it seems."

"Do you have the invisible man here, too? What about Kitty Pride?"

"No, we don't have her," Dr. M. smiled, ignoring the quip. "I told you this would be difficult for you to believe. This isn't the X-Men, Jessica, or Heroes. This is… something else. The next step for humanity, perhaps? We simply don't know. What we do know is that people like you can do things most people cannot. What you'll be able to do, remains to be discovered."

"I can't do anything," she said.

"Well, that remains to be seen. Once you've changed your clothes, and showered, perhaps, then we can get on with our day. You'll be instructed to follow the arrows into a testing room."

"And then what? You poke and prod me? Shove me full of needles?"

"No, Jessica," Dr. M. said, his tone sounding hurt. "We'll ask you a series of questions about how you're feeling, to describe any physical symptoms you've been experiencing. That's day one. On day two, we'll begin showing you a series of picture cards to try and evoke an emotional response. You see, a transgen's abilities are often manifested through an emotional trigger. It helps the ability to surface. Once you're aware of whatever it is you can do, you can learn to make it happen at will, with training."

"Training?"

"As I've said, Jessica, there's a lot of information to process. I don't think it's wise for me to try and relay everything to you at once. For now, I suggest you go back to your room and change, so we can begin your testing. I can explain more to you afterwards, if you feel ready to hear it."

"And what if I refuse? What if I just decide not to cooperate?"

"You can do that, if you choose. However, we can also choose simply not to open your door. We can choose to keep you locked in your room, with only water to drink. Let's see how long that lasts, hmm?"

"And you call yourself a nice person?"

"I never claimed to be nice, Jessica."

"I hate you," she seethed, glowering.

"Well, that's too bad. But, it doesn't really affect me one way or the other. I have a job to do, and I'll continue doing it, regardless of how you feel toward me. I'm a scientist."

"And that justifies everything you do, right?"

"No, it doesn't. However, I am being closely watched by some very important people in our government, and they expect results. I merely take orders, Jessica, like everyone else around here. Including you."

"I don't take orders," she said.

"You will." He sounded sad, rather than threatening. "One way or another, you will."

The doctor stood and left the cafeteria, but not before reminding her to return to her room. Jessica watched him leave, then, not knowing what else to do, she went back to the window.

They all looked so *normal*. A few sat together, sometimes laughing or smiling. Most sat alone. A couple walked by holding hands. The bearded man had grayish-white hair, appearing much older than the woman. The woman, a pretty brunette, looked to be in her late twenties. A few people looked back at Jessica. Another, much younger-looking, bearded man, perhaps in his mid-thirties, sat alone. He briefly glanced up at her, then went back to reading a book. Another young man, this one obviously in his early twenties, also sat alone. He looked over, smiled and waved.

"The Society," she whispered. She did not wave back.

Eventually, she left the small cafeteria, but not before eating another muffin and a bowl of cereal. The door of the room clicked open for her when she stood in front of it. In the hallway, she did as Dr. M. had instructed, and said, "My room," then followed the red arrows, which now appeared on the opposite wall. Once back in the room, she lay on her bed, the tears finally coming, hot and stinging. After the sadness, anger surged. She felt so helpless, so trapped. The white walls seemed to close in around her. She'd never been claustrophobic before, but suddenly, she felt as if she couldn't breathe. Her response to the sudden panic was more anger.

She sat up, pulling her pillow from behind her back and hugged it in her arms, pulling her knees up to her chest, huddling in the corner of the bed. So much unfamiliar emotion, she felt as though she might burst with it. Then her hands started to burn again, this time much more fiercely; enough to *hurt*.

She frowned, looking at her palms. still *so angry*; needing to vent somehow. She felt like ripping her pillow to shreds. Instead, she pulled it up to throw it, the heat in her hands surging, the blood boiling to plasma in her veins.

She threw the pillow, and everything slowed down, as if her life were a movie being played in slow motion. She saw every detail in protracted time. The pillow exploded, showering white feathers around the room. At the same time, the dresser against the far wall slid across the floor with a loud scraping noise, wedging into the corner next to the door with such force, it shattered. The table rocked sideways and fell, taking the chair with it. All of this was followed by total darkness, as the lights in the ceiling went out. Jessica gasped, as heated air rushed over her face.

She sat in pitch darkness, breathing heavily, in shock. *What the hell just happened?* An alarm sounded dully out in the hallway, in syncopation to her heart hammering in her chest. She slowly stood, feeling her way toward the door, in the dark, delicately stepping around, then lightly tripping over debris.

It took a few seconds of fumbling to find the knob on her door. It gave effortlessly, and she found herself standing in the hallway, the lights blinking on and off. The alarm sounded much louder out in the hall, and the faltering bursts of light spilled into her darkened room. She saw the bits and pieces of her shattered dresser and stared in confused shock, then turned, stunned to see a man in a white coat running toward her from around the corner. Before she even realized what was happening, she felt a sharp, stabbing pain in her torso. Her entire body lit on fire; her muscles tightened, then went limp, as she slipped from consciousness.

3

She woke in another white room. She lay on her side in an unfamiliar bed, facing the wall. Her shoulders ached fiercely. She tried moving her arms, finding them bound together at the wrist, zip-tied. Rolling onto her back, wincing at the pain in her shoulders, she found Dr. M. sitting in a chair, watching her intently. He had a clipboard in his hands, taking notes of some kind. At least, that's what she presumed. If she'd been able to see from the doctor's perspective, she'd have seen a sketch of herself lying in bed.

"Ah, awake at last."

"Why am I handcuffed?"

"For your own protection, as well as mine."

She sat up and set her feet on the floor, staring at Dr. M., feeling dazed.

"What did you do to me?"

"Well, it's not pretty, but we had to Taser you."

"You *Tased* me?!"

"We couldn't risk getting close enough to inject a sedative, now could we? You blew up your room, knocking out the power to the surveillance cameras, and all the electrical equipment wired for lockdown. Incidentally, the circuit boards on the cameras are fried. The only thing I know of that can do that is an EMP."

"An EMP?"

"Electromagnetic pulse. There are two kinds of pulses, Jessica, nuclear and non-nuclear. You're not a nuclear weapon. That would be physically impossible, not to mention extremely hazardous to your own health. However, it appears that the ability you've developed is the biological equivalent to an explosively pumped flux compression wave. You generated an NNEMP, *non-nuclear electromagnetic pulse.* It's amazing."

"How's that even possible?"

"An EMP is a burst of electromagnetic energy that results from fluctuating magnetic fields, a high-intensity, short-duration burst of electromagnetic energy. Somehow, you were able to generate and control it."

"I didn't have control, I didn't even know it was going to happen."

"Well, that's how these things usually occur. It's always a surprise the first time an ability presents itself. Transgens don't come stamped with an ability on their genes. We never know what we're going to get."

"Stop calling me that." Jessica snapped.

"What, a transgen? I'm sorry, does it offend you?"

"Yes. I'm a person, like you or anybody else."

"No," Dr. M. laughed. "You're not. That should be apparent by now."

"This isn't funny." She glowered at him.

"No, it's not." Dr. M. seemed somber, but she received the impression that he merely patronized her. If she didn't know better, she'd swear the doctor seemed excited.

"I still don't understand what happened. All the furniture flew into pieces."

"Yes, as I said, you also produced a compression wave, it's a side effect of the EMP, which is why the dresser slid across the room and fell apart, and your pillow was ripped to shreds. If someone had been in the room with you, they most likely would have been liquefied."

Jessica's eyes widened in horror. Dr. M. continued, not seeming to notice her reaction.

"Compression waves also generate high temperatures. If a person weren't crushed to death, they'd likely have been burned alive."

"But that can't be. I was in the room, and I'm fine."

"Yes, that's most interesting, isn't it? We're still puzzling over that one. It could be that the burst was directed outward, away from you, and that shielded you from harm. When we inspected your room, however, we found that your bed sheets were singed brown. All except where you were sitting. It's almost as if you were shielded somehow; just long enough to escape the hottest blasts. How long after your burst was it before you left the room?"

"I left right after it went dark."

"Are you sure about that? Exactly how long do you think it was from the time you did your little trick, until you came out into the hallway?"

"I don't know, maybe, a minute?" she frowned.

"Try four."

"Four minutes? No, that's impossible. I got up almost right after it went dark."

"I'm sure you did, in your mind. However, outside the shield, nearly four minutes had passed."

"What are you talking about?!" Jessica grew more and more agitated. She perspired lightly and felt dizzy.

"What I'm trying to tell you, Jessica, is that you seem to have created some sort of time-accelerating force field around yourself at the same time you created the pulse."

"This is impossible," she shook her head violently. "You're crazy! People can't do things like this, they just can't. You must think I'm totally stupid!"

"No, Jessica. I think you're quite amazing. You can do *astounding* things. Do you realize that? Every transgen in this facility is special. And then there's you."

"Stop calling me that! You're crazy!"

"No, just in awe. Every person in here is special, Jessica, but even among the special, you stand out."

"If I'm so special, why am I handcuffed. Untie me!"

"I'm afraid I can't do that until I'm certain you're calm. We can't risk another unplanned burst. How were you feeling right before it happened? Were you angry?" He flipped to a new page and held his clipboard and pen at the ready.

"Not as pissed as I am right now." She glared him down.

"So, you were angry," Dr. M. stated, jotting it down. He had no reaction to Jessica's violent looks or boiling tone. "Why were you angry?"

"Are you mental?! *Why* am I angry? You've locked me up in a prison, to mess with, like a lab rat!"

"So, you were thinking about *me*?" He jotted again.

"What?!" She shook her head, frustrated. "No, it wasn't *you*." She sighed. "I was just feeling trapped. Claustrophobic, like I couldn't do anything to help myself."

"So, you were feeling angry and *helpless*. Is that right?" More scribbling.

"Yes," she hissed.

"Were you thinking of anyone? Anyone at all?"

"No, why?"

"Are you sure?"

"Yes, I'm sure! What is this?"

"Could you make yourself feel that way again?"

"What? What the hell is *wrong* with you?"

"You must be able to do it again, Jessica."

"No." She daggered a look at him, laced with hot defiance.

"We have to figure out a trigger, Jessica. Then you need to train and condition yourself to perform at will, without it."

"*No*," she repeated. He seemed to miss the poison zeal of her rebellion.

"Now, Jessica, I don't want to be cruel, but I will if I have to." He gave her a warning, yet reluctant glance.

"So… what? You're going to *torture* me, is that it?" She threw him a challenging look.

"I don't want to." His voice grew low and almost humane for the first time in the conversation. "But if you don't learn to cooperate, I won't have any choice."

"You can't do anything to me," she sneered.

Dr. M. sighed in resignation. He looked disappointed, and was that sadness on his face? She couldn't be certain.

"Amazing abilities, short term memory." He stood up, making for the exit. Glancing back at her over his shoulder, he smiled sadly, before easing the door shut behind him.

***

The room was small, about the size of her other bedroom, minus the en-suite bathroom. Other than the bed, which was identical to hers, the room was empty. She'd been told she would be staying in a new room while her old one was repaired and cleaned up, but that was clearly just a trick to lure and lock her in this glorified closet space. She'd known something was off, as her hands remained zip-tied behind her back. She'd told herself it was simply a safety measure on their part while walking her to her new room, but before she realized the true reality, she was inside this room, and the door had clicked, locking her in all alone, still handcuffed.

Jessica didn't move, trying to remain calm. Her mind spun, offering up unwelcome observations. *No bathroom, no red intercom button.* No windows, nothing but herself.

Her stomach audibly grumbled, twisting and writhing with hunger. She looked up at the camera in the left corner of the ceiling and started to cry, despite herself. Surely Dr. M. wouldn't keep her in here for too long, would he?

"Hello?"

She stood and walked to the camera. "Can you hear me?"

She waited several minutes, growing angry, then turned her back to the camera to flip it her middle finger.

"You won't break me!"

She kicked the nearest wall then stumbled back to the bed, lying down. Rolling over, she placed her back to the camera and stared at the wall, exhausted by hunger and raw fury. She was asleep in less than a minute.

***

Jessica had no idea how long she'd slept. It felt like at least ten hours, but it could have also been only two.

She sat up, wincing as her belly cramped with hunger. Her bladder followed suit, causing her to curse the full glass of orange juice she'd enjoyed at breakfast however long ago.

"Jeezus."

She winced again as the urge to pee intensified. Even if there was a toilet in the room, her hands were still tied behind her.

Her stomach growled again, twisting and turning as though intent on tearing itself loose. Her mouth felt as dry as her stomach did empty. Tears sprung up in her eyes. She lay down in bed again, staring up at the white ceiling, trying to will herself back to sleep, but could not.

When she finally sat up again, she felt dizzy and light-headed. She attempted to stand, and quickly sat again. She felt close to passing out. She cried as her bladder pricked anew, this time much more urgently. She looked up at the camera, scowling through her tears.

"Screw you!"

She slowly stood up, waves of dizziness threatening to drag her down into oblivion. After a few moments of uncertain stillness, the dizziness slowly subsided. Facing the corner of the room, she tried moving her hands around her left side. With great discomfort, she managed to get her left hand as far as her hip. She stretched her fingers as far as she could, wrists bent, until every muscle in both hands ached, the tendons standing out as taught cords beneath her skin. With all her concentration, her fingertips still fell several inches short of her jeans button and zipper.

She cried out in frustration, stomping her feet, swinging violently back and forth, then quickly stopped as a new wave of dizziness overtook her. She slid down the wall to sitting, breathing heavily. After a few moments, she sighed, silently crying as she conceded to her bladder's demands. She couldn't help it. Her entire groin section suddenly soaked in a hot bath of urine.

She lurched forward before the expanding puddle reached the lower half of her jeans. Walking away on her knees, she propped herself against the bed frame, humiliated and ashamed.

After a few minutes, the warmth of the urine began to fade, leaving her sitting in cold, wet jeans. The smell alone was enough to make her feel nauseated.

She sat this way for hours, muddling through increasingly painful hunger cramps. The aches slowly escalated throughout her body, every joint and muscle eventually singing its own dirge of agony.

***

Jessica woke several hours later, still against the bed frame. She felt grateful she'd managed to sleep at all. Movement caused her to cry out, every muscle in her body throbbing.

She itched maddeningly, her now dry jeans stiff and coarse against her skin. She felt like crying but couldn't, far too dehydrated for tears to come. Her mouth as dry as sandpaper; she found it impossible to so much as swallow. For some reason, this depressed her more than anything else. Moaning in utter misery, she found her efforts to stand thwarted, sinking back down to the floor.

She felt so hungry, her stomach didn't even hurt anymore, instead becoming a solid, dead lump in her abdomen. She'd grown so weak now, she had trouble concentrating. Even thoughts seemed to seep and snarl in their usual channels like drying sewage. All she could do was *feel*, fomenting in helplessness and defeat.

She lost consciousness, her eyes rolling back in their sockets. All she felt now was a vague sensation of floating, falling; as though she were little more than a feather bullied by conflicting breezes.

"I'm dead," she whispered. "I'm dead."

***

Jessica woke in another white room. There were monitors along the wall to her right, next to her bed, an IV in the back of her right hand. Oxygen tubes trailed from her nostrils. She felt like a semi had run her over. She stirred in her bed feebly, realizing that at the very least, she was no longer handcuffed, her arms laying limp at her sides. She glanced to her left, away from the monitors, taking in the rest of the room. To her dismay, she saw Dr. M. sitting in a chair near her bed, casually reading a magazine. He looked up at her and smiled.

"You're awake. *Good*. You almost died on us."

"You almost killed me." Her voice, barely above a whisper, sounded alarmingly weak, as it cracked.

"No, and believe me, that was never my intention. I only wanted to find a way to help you cooperate. But you're different than most, Jessica, and my mistake nearly cost me. I'm not joking when I say you nearly died."

"How long was I in that room?"

"About sixteen hours."

She stared at him in disbelief, blinking several times, tears pricking her eyes. "That's not even a whole day."

"Yes, but I imagine it felt much longer to you. That's the whole point. I've had people in that room for barely over two days, supplying water, of course, who refused to believe they were there for any less than a week. It's a head trick, and very effective at inducing cooperative behavior. Normally, it's not a problem, health-wise. With you, however, it was a dangerous gamble, and for that, I'm truly sorry."

"How could I almost die after less than a day?"

"According to Nurse Charles, your body was utterly depleted. You remember I mentioned how you would be hungry more often? Normally, even a transgen with a considerable gift can still go at least a day without food or water. However, your gift is *unique*. We've estimated that your little trick probably depleted you of about seven thousand calories in the space of a few minutes. You're not that large to begin with. I'm sorry. By the time we realized your condition, you were extremely dehydrated and malnourished. You lost eight pounds in twenty-four hours. We've managed to nurse you back to health, but it's been three days."

"Three days?"

"You were in a coma for the first forty-eight hours, and asleep for most of today. We will need to monitor you very carefully from this point on. Your diet will be strictly managed, and training will begin *very* slowly. We need to find an equilibrium between your performance and your health management. I would think that two, maybe three times a week is your limit. And you'll need to maintain a daily diet of at least four to five thousand calories, permanently. We don't want to risk another incident like this one. You're our most important transgen."

"I told you to stop calling me that."

"What, *transgen*?"

"Yes."

"I'm sorry, it's just what I call your kind."

"*My kind*? What the hell are you talking about? You talk about me and whoever else you've got locked up in here like we're freaks, as if we're not normal."

"You aren't."

She stared at the doctor for several long moments. He simply smiled back.

"Whatever this thing is that I can do now," her voice shook, "it's all *your* fault. *You* did this to me. I'd still be *normal* if you had just *left me alone*."

"You were never normal," Dr. M. said. "Although you appear to be one hundred percent human on the outside, that one alien gene makes you… different."

"*Alien*?" she frowned at the doctor, sounding horrified.

"That's right, Jessica. Your deviant pseudogene cannot be found in any other life form on this planet. However, all other genes in the non-coding sequences are found in every other life form. We were all made from the same *stardust,* so to speak. But *your* gene is not biologic to life on Earth. We may all be made from the same dust as everything else, but you and the rest of The Society have something extra—something *unearthly.* Technically, you may not even qualify as human, on a genetic level."

"What are you saying? Of course, I'm *human!*"

"It depends on what definition you use. Of the one-in-one-hundred-thousand people who carry the gene, only one-in-a-million is a person we can effectively make disappear. Most transgens we find have families. We only bring people here who have little to no family, or family they don't communicate with. You, for example, are an only child, whose mother is an alcoholic and your stepfather isn't exactly the nicest of sorts, is he?"

"Shut up."

"Many of the people in here are an only child. A few have at least one parent in prison. None of you had any close friends. I wonder if the gene influences that, somehow? Many of you seem to be decidedly... *anti-social.*"

"You better hope I don't develop the power to blow up your head," she whispered, tears filling her eyes. "Whatever you may think of me, it doesn't give you the right to lock me up in a room and starve me to death!"

"Well, I didn't have much of a choice, did I? You see, Jessica, it's really a no-brainer. You can live here comfortably, in a nice, clean room, with a *toilet.*"

Dr. M. emphasized the word toilet, shooting her a look of accusation. She blushed and looked away, embarrassed and ashamed.

"You can eat wonderful foods and never feel hungry. Sleep in as much as you want. You can have a wonderful life, and never experience any kind of physical discomfort ever again. All you must do is use your ability a few times a week, in a controlled setting. That isn't so bad, is it? It's your choice, but if it were *me*, I'd have no trouble deciding."

"Easy to say, when *you're* in *control.*"

"I'd love to be able to do what you can do," Dr. M. said, sounding more emotional than usual. He leaned forward in his chair. His breathing had changed, coming in deeper, more passionate bursts.

"I may be smart, I may even be termed a genius by some, but in the end, I'm just a normal human being, like so many others. There are other smart people. There are even other geniuses. I'm not unique. But you, Jessica, you can do something that no one else alive can do. If it were *me*? I'd want to show it off. I'd want to *perform.* I'd feel *so alive*, if I could do what you can do, so *powerful.* I wish you would be more grateful for the position you're in."

"What position? How can I possibly feel powerful, when I have no control over my life?"

"You *do* have power, Jessica—the power to *choose.* And if you're smart, you'll choose the right thing. If you cooperate with me, I can make you into the most powerful human being that has ever lived."

"I'll never have power, not so long as I'm your puppet."

"You can choose to look at it that way, or you can choose to take advantage of the situation. So many people would love to be in your shoes. Utterly taken care of, with no more financial burdens or monetary worries, and free room and board for the rest of your life, all for the price of blowing a few things up. How much fun is that?"

"You call this fun? Being tortured? You tried to kill me! You've stolen my life from me!"

The doctor ignored her last remark, only addressing the first part.

"That was never my intention, as I've told you. It was a mistake that will never happen again. Living here can be either enjoyable, or decidedly not enjoyable. There are other ways to persuade you that you do *not* want to discover."

"So… basically, my choice is that I have no choice."

"Now you're getting smarter," Dr. M. said, smiling.

Jessica stared at him for a long time. Inside her head, she weighed all her options, searching for a way to turn the situation to her benefit.

She raised her hands up to her face, turning her palms inward, taking everything in. Then she set them back down in her lap, smiling lightly. For now, she'd play along. She realized her newfound ability just might be her only way out. If it was strong enough to land her in this situation, maybe it could also get her out.

"Fine, then." She offered the doctor a winning and mischievous grin. "Let's begin."

4

Several more days passed before Dr. M. felt confident that Jessica would not be a danger to the other members of The Society. Two days after she was released from the medical lab, she returned to her room, which had been repaired. Although, in the back of her mind, she wondered if that were true, or if she might not simply have been given a different, but identical room. She couldn't tell from her path down the various, all-white hallways, whether she returned to the same doorway as before or not.

The clothes she'd arrived in were long gone, having been removed from her body while unconscious. She now wore standard issue, light blue pants and a shirt of the same color, resembling nursing scrubs. The pants had an adjustable drawstring waist. She wore white socks and light gray slip-on shoes.

As the days passed, Jessica noticed that the dirty clothes she took to folding and placing on top of her dresser were gone when she returned from her shower trips into the bathroom, replaced by clean, neatly folded clothes inside her drawers.

She stayed in her room for three days, only leaving to eat in the small cafeteria. Several times a day, she was instructed to go into the hallway, say the word 'lab' and follow the arrows into a small, white room, where Dr. M. waited behind a heavy glass barrier.

For hours at a time, he showed her flashcards of different things, including pictures of her stepfather and her mother, which shocked her. The card's subjects ranged from images that made her angry, to ones that made her sad; pictures of dead dogs and cats run over in the road, bunnies that had lost their fur from having products tested on them.

Mostly, Dr. M. tried to make her mad. When the images did not make her angry, he said cruel things to her instead, all from behind his window. He chastised her, told her she was stupid, ignorant, useless. None of it made Jessica angry—it merely annoyed her. Even when she did become angry, it quickly passed, instead of building like it had before.

After several days of this, it stopped, and Jessica was left to sit in her room for hours at a time, bored to tears. She was provided with magazines to read, which appeared on the table while she showered or used the toilet. A deck of cards appeared at another point, and she played solitaire for several hours one evening, until she could stand it no more, and went to bed.

One small relief was the clock that appeared on the dresser. With no windows, it was impossible to tell if it were day or night, unless she went to the cafeteria to look out into the courtyard, but the clock relieved this anxiety somewhat. A quick trip to view the courtyard on the morning the clock first appeared gave her enough confidence to assume the time in the a.m. was probably accurate.

On day five, Dr. M.'s voice came through the intercom, first thing in the morning. He sounded extremely pleasant. In fact, Dr. M. began acting nice to Jessica the moment she decided to cooperate.

"Jessica, I think it is now safe for you to enter the large cafeteria, if you'd like. If you don't feel ready, that's fine. Just say the word 'cafeteria' like you always do. The arrows will lead you to the larger room now."

She got out of bed and walked over to the intercom, pushing the red button.

"Hello?"

"Yes?" said Dr. M.

"Um… will there be people in there?"

"I assume so."

"How many?"

"I'm not sure, would you like me to check? If you're not ready to socialize, I completely understand."

"You're not worried I might hurt someone?"

"No, you seem completely stable to me. Unless you think you might get angry?"

"Why would I get angry?"

"Who knows? But we've discussed this. If you feel your anger rising, simply leave, return to your room, if you need to. We've been working on this, so far without a great deal of success. Believe me, if I can't so much as raise a cross word from you, I doubt anyone in the cafeteria will."

"Well, if you're sure."

"Only *you* can be sure, Jessica. Remember—if you start to feel strange, or have any doubts, just return to your room. Okay?"

"Okay." She wished she felt as sure as she sounded.

Out in the hallway, she followed the red arrows until she came to a white door. It looked like all the others, but she knew this one was different. How long had it been since she'd interacted with anyone except Dr. M.? Far too long to sustain what few social skills she'd managed to develop. Breathing deeply, she stepped forward and opened the door.

There were only a few people inside that early in the morning, one of them familiar—the young man who'd waved at her on day one. He looked at her now, and waved again, smiling. She smiled awkwardly and waved back, glancing around self-consciously.

She went to the food station on the far-left and fixed herself a bagel. When she turned around, a young woman stood behind her, closer than Jessica found comfortable. She was a pretty Latina, roughly the same height as Jessica, with dark hair and even darker eyes—squinting with a shrewd, angry look.

"So, you're the new girl, huh?"

"Um... I guess so," she said. She looked around, uncertain and uncomfortable.

"Yeah, well, you don't look so tough to me."

"Um... Okay."

Jessica walked away, instinctively heading toward the table where the young man sat. The girl followed her for several steps, then halted, still talking.

"Yeah, you ain't so tough!" she yelled.

The few people in the room turned to look at her and Jessica, and she lowered her head, quickly heading to the table. She sat down, keeping her head low, picking at her bagel.

"Hi," the man said, his voice quiet, seemingly shy.

"Hey," she replied, barely making eye contact.

"She ain't so tough!" the girl yelled again, to no one in particular, and seeming satisfied, headed back to her table on the other side of the room.

Over the young man's shoulder, Jessica saw a strange-looking, middle-aged man staring at her from the next table. He looked to be in his early fifties, head cocked to one side, smile broken and crooked. *A face only a Mother could love.* He waved at her, wiggling each finger on his hand in a manner that made her skin crawl. She went back to eating her bagel, keeping her head down, eyes fixed on the table. After a few minutes of eating in silence, she began to relax, sitting up in her chair. The young man finally spoke again.

"My name's Aaron."

"I'm Jessica."

"Yeah, I know."

She looked up at him, her eyes questioning. He smiled gently at her. He looked to be about her age; dark blond hair, bright blue eyes and light skin. Cute, but there was also a *needy* quality to him, she thought.

"Dr. M. told everyone about you. Apparently, you're extra special. We were all instructed not to do anything that might make you *angry.* That got everyone curious."

"So, if no one's supposed to make me angry, what's up with aggressor-chick?"

"Alma?" Aaron shrugged and shook his head. "That's just her style. She likes to do things people tell her not to. She's a *Rebel*." His eyes widened dramatically, but he offered a friendly grin.

"A rebel?" Jessica looked over to the table where Alma sat. Alma glowered at her. Jessica smiled, amused.

"Heh, sounds like my kinda girl."

"No," Aaron laughed. "She's not anyone's kinda girl. She doesn't have friends."

"Yeah?"

She looked at Aaron, feeling decidedly more comfortable now. She glanced over his shoulder, to see the strange man still staring at her, still smiling. She nodded at Aaron, indicating to the man behind him.

"What's up with him?"

Aaron looked over his shoulder at the man. He turned back to Jessica, rolling his eyes, and lowered his voice.

"Oh, God. That's Hanley. Just ignore him."

"Why does he keep staring at me?"

"Who knows? He does that sometimes. He's... sort of the resident weirdo, you know?"

"Seriously?" Jessica laughed, covering her mouth.

"Why is that funny?"

"Nothing, it's just... aren't we *all* kind of the resident weirdos?"

"Yeah, we're all kinda weird, I guess," Aaron said. "But he's plain old crazy."

"Why?"

"Well, for starters, he's not all there in the head, if you know what I mean?"

"No, not really."

"Oh, okay. Well, he says he can communicate with *aliens*."

"Aliens," Jessica stated.

"Yep."

"Wow."

"Yeah. On top of that, he says he talks to them all the time, and that they're gonna come and rescue him from this place. Oh, but get this— Only when the time is *right*."

"What?" she laughed.

"Yeah. Says he's 'telepathic'. Talks to the 'aliens' all the time."

Aaron made quotation marks with his fingers while saying this.

"Maybe he can."

"What, talk to aliens?"

"No, communicate telepathically. Dr. M. said there was someone in here who could read minds?"

"Oh, no, that's Martin. He's over there," Aaron pointed to a man with his back turned to them, sitting at a table on the far side of the room.

On cue, Martin glanced over his shoulder, looking at Jessica momentarily, before turning back around. Feeling unsettled, somewhat paranoid, she turned her attention back to Aaron, who had never stopped talking.

"Hanley's not telepathic. He says he is, but no one's ever seen any proof of it. Says he's waiting for *the right one,* whatever that means."

"Weird," she said.

"Yeah, like I said."

Aaron grew quiet. He looked at her, then back down at the table. She smiled, amused by his shyness.

"So," he said. "What can you do?"

"What do you mean?"

"Your ability. The reason we're not supposed to make you angry. What can you do?"

"Oh," Jessica said, faltering. "I-I'm not really sure."

"It must be something good."

"Good?"

"We've only been told a few times not to make someone angry. The last time was Rachel, and she's not allowed in here anymore. They've got her in isolation."

"Rachel?"

"Yeah, Rachel Harley. Now *that's* a story."

"Tell me," she said, looking at Aaron intently.

"Well... Rachel can boil water without using a pot—that's her ability. It's not just water, though. Dr. M. says she's capable of heating any liquid to over four hundred degrees. She can also boil the blood in a man's veins. It's not very pretty."

"She killed someone?"

"A technician," Aaron nodded, looking extremely nervous. "What a way to go, huh? Rumor has it there was blood everywhere. It... like... boiled out of every orifice."

Jessica closed her eyes, her stomach flip-flopping. She put her bagel down, stifling the urge to vomit. Aaron seemed not to notice.

"Needless to say, she's no longer allowed to socialize with anyone in The Society. They keep her locked away, on her own."

"What about the other woman, the one who can blow things up?" Jessica asked.

"Dr. M. told you about her?" Aaron looked baffled. "Well, she seems to only be able to affect things when she's really angry. They work hard to piss her off that much, she's usually really sweet and kind. Her name's Jenny. She's with Malcolm."

"Malcolm?" Jessica frowned.

"Yeah, he's the white-haired guy with the beard. They're not here right now, but they're always together, always holding hands."

Jessica nodded. She remembered seeing them on her first day.

"So, what can you do?" Aaron asked again.

"What can *you* do?" she asked him, quickly turning the subject back onto him.

"Me? Nothing special," he said. "I can, sort of... affect plants. It's *so* not cool. The only reason I'm still in here is to keep me quiet, I guess. Guess they figure if they set me free, I'll run and tell. I'm not useful to them."

"What do you mean, affect plants?"

"Um, well. I can make them change color."

"Change color?"

"Yeah," Aaron said, blushing. "I affect the chlorophyll, somehow. I don't understand science. Dr. M. tried to explain it to me, but I don't even remember anything he said. I don't care, it's useless anyway."

"I don't get it."

Aaron looked at her, blushing more deeply. Then he smiled and stood up.

"Come on, I'll show you."

"I'm still hungry."

"We'll come right back. Just come with me for a few minutes. Please?"

"Okay," she said. "Where?"

Aaron just smiled.

Jessica stood and followed him. Alma glared at her as they passed. She babbled nervously as they exited the cafeteria. "There's no plants in this place... Um... Aaron? Where's the plants?"

***

"Atrium."

A red arrow appeared on the wall. Aaron and Jessica followed the directions, him playing tour guide.

"There's a recreation room with TV's and a pool table, we have a gym, a library; *thousands* of books. You can even request DVD's... Oh! There's an orchard too, so you can be out in the sun. We call it *the Atrium,* although it's outdoors. You can basically do whatever you want—sleep in every morning—eat whatever foods you feel like, read, socialize. They don't even discriminate against romantic attachments.

You don't have to work, or deal with bosses, or traffic, or any of that nonsense."

"Wait, you sound like you're trying to sell me on this place, just like Dr. M." Jessica shook her head. "I don't understand these hallways, it's so disorienting."

"Yeah, they make everything look the same. That way, no one can memorize their way through any of the hallways. I mean, they all look the same, and they keep turning around and around, this way and that. It's maddening. You just say the name of where you want to go and follow the arrows."

"That's insane."

"They do everything they can to make sure no one can escape. The doors only unlock when you stand in front of them—everything's on camera—it's a good system for them. You can't even open a door unless they want you to."

"I can," she said.

Aaron looked at her, confused. She saw the questioning look on his face and sighed.

"It's called an EMP, according to Dr. M.—*Electromagnetic Pulse.* It affects electronics, like the doors. I've only done it once so far, but it shut everything down—the lights, the door locks—even the cameras."

"Seriously?"

"Yeah," she nodded. "I knocked the power out completely inside my room. My door was open. I walked out in the hallway and the lights were still on, but all messed up. Next thing I know, some guy is running at me with a Taser."

"Man," he shook his head. "They like to do that."

"Yeah. And as far as I know, EMP won't affect those. And they really hurt."

"Man," Aaron said again, shaking his head.

They followed the arrows around a final corner, before stopping outside another identical door.

"One other fun fact." Aaron turned to her, looking grave. "Another safeguard, I guess—only two people are allowed in the Atrium at any time. If there's more than two people standing here, or anywhere near here, the door won't open."

A faint click sounded. Aaron turned the knob and Jessica found herself outdoors, surrounded by fragrant flowers and trees, buzzing bees, large Monarch butterflies and hummingbirds zooming high above her head. They walked down a dirt path spotted with orange trees, quickly swallowed up by the foliage. She glanced behind, to see the tan, camouflaged building already obscured.

"No cameras here," she mused.

"Don't be too sure," Aaron said, pointing up.

She peered up into the trees, barely making out a black camera high up in a branch. As they walked by, she saw it move, tracking them.

"Motion activated," Aaron said in disgust. "Trust me, there's nowhere in this place where they can't see you."

"What about sound?"

"Sound?"

"Yeah, can they hear us?"

"Don't know," Aaron said, sounding thoughtful. "Never thought about that one before."

He brought them to a halt in a small meadow clearing where wild sunflowers grew in profusion all around. Aaron took Jessica's hand—the unexpected contact startling—her first instinct to pull away. She did her utmost to smother it, allowing Aaron to lead her into the forest of flowers. He brought them to a halt in a space where they stood with a single sunflower sprouting between them, its radiant head exactly at eye level. She looked at him, waiting. He released her hand and touched the yellow-orange petals with the tips of two fingers. She watched in amazement as the flame-colored petals flushed a light, bluish-green.

"Oh… It's beautiful," she sighed.

Aaron reached across and touched another sunflower next to her shoulder. It turned purplish-pink. He blushed, picking it, and handed it to her.

"It's totally useless," he shrugged.

"No, it's not. You know, it takes days to do this with flowers? They have to stick them in water with dye and wait for the plants to suck it up."

"Yeah, well, Dr. M. isn't too impressed. I don't even train or perform anymore. I just live here, taking up space."

"I haven't trained yet, at all," she said. "I mean, I was, but then it just stopped."

Aaron looked at her in surprise.

"Really? Why? I would think with what you can do, he'd have you training around the clock."

"He's pretty up front with me about things," Jessica said. "They can't get me to do it again. And anyway, Dr. M. says they can't test me the normal way. I'll break all their sensory machines, or something. He's trying to put together a *safer* way for me to train. He said it would need to be outdoors, away from the facility."

"Seriously?"

"Yeah, and I can only train a few days a week. I guess I burn, like, seven thousand calories each time I do my thing. I'd literally starve to death in hours if I did it too often."

"Sheesh. Man, I can do this all day," Aaron said, touching another flower and turning it tan and white. "Don't even break a sweat. Not much energy to it, I guess."

"Well, I think it's cool," she said, smiling. Then she frowned. "So, that Hanley guy…"

Aaron frowned. "What about him?"

"If he isn't telepathic, what can he do?"

"Oh, that really chaps my behind," Aaron said, blushing. "The guy's a nutcase, but his ability is sort of cool—he can melt metal."

"Really?"

"Yeah. They make him melt junk all week long. Dr. M. apparently never gets tired of seeing it."

"What about that Alma girl? What can she do?"

"Her? She can put her hands through things."

"Wait, she's *that* lady? The transparent-hands lady?"

"Yeah, you've heard of her?"

"Dr. M. told me about her."

"Really?" Aaron frowned momentarily, then continued. "Well, my theory is that she's so pissed about her ability, she's just angry all the time. I mean, no offense, but that's even more useless than what I can do. I mean, what can you do with transparent hands?" He laughed.

"No wonder she's so angry all the time," Jessica laughed back.

"Yeah, she really hates you. She hates Hanley, too. She hates anyone that can do anything, really."

"What about you?"

"Me? Nah, she doesn't care about what I can do."

"No, I mean, do you feel the same way Alma does… about me?"

"You mean, do I hate you?" Aaron asked.

"Yeah."

"No. No, I don't hate you at all. I think you're pretty neat, actually."

"Neat?" Jessica giggled.

"Well, I mean, cool."

They walked back toward the building.

"No arrows out here," she said, sounding thoughtful. "What's to stop someone from just walking off into the hills? There's only a few cameras in the trees."

"Yeah, but you can't escape. If you keep going in any direction away from the building, you'll come to a really tall fence."

"So?"

"So, it's covered on top with barbed wire, and it's electrified."

"So, we get Hanley out here to melt the fence."

Aaron stopped walking and stared at her.

"Not gonna happen."

"Why not?"

"Please, you think no one's tried to escape before? You think you're the first one to try and come up with a plan?"

"Someone has?"

"Yeah, Alma and that Harley chick. She boiled a technician while trying to escape. Alma tried to get a group together to break out. Suffice it to say, it didn't work."

"Wait, that's what happened with Rachel Harley?"

"Yeah."

"But, if Hanley can melt the fence—"

"He's not allowed outdoors," Aaron interrupted. "You think they haven't thought of everything? They *know* he could melt the fence, so he's kept inside. Forget the two people only rule, the door won't even open for him if he's alone, *and*—no arrows will show him the way to the Atrium. There's no way to get out, Jessica."

"Nonsense, there's always a way."

"Not nonsense—no matter what you think you can do, trust me—they've got a plan for it. I mean, look; a simple Taser is all it takes to stop you. So, woo hoo! You can turn off the power, so what? There's no way out."

"Thanks for the support," she said, stomping down the dirt path, back toward the facility.

"Look, I'm not trying to piss you off, okay?" He grabbed her shoulder, stopping her in her tracks, though his grip was gentle. "I just don't want you getting your hopes up. Trust me, if there was a way out of here, someone would have done it by now."

"How long have you been in here?"

"Four years," he said, looking at the ground.

"Four years?!"

"You think I haven't tried to figure a way out of here?"

"I've been in here for less than two weeks, and I feel like I'm losing my mind."

"Yeah, well, now you understand Hanley. He's been here for over a decade."

"He's been here for *ten years*?"

Aaron nodded. Jessica looked at him in shock.

"What about Alma?"

"I don't know. I guess she came here about a year ago."

"Jeezus," Jessica said. "I can't live here for the rest of my life. *I can't.*"

"You'll get used to it," he said.

She glared at Aaron in anger and disgust. "No, I won't," she said, and walked away.

5

For the next few days, Jessica avoided Aaron, who ate alone. Hanley continued staring at her, and Alma took to bumping into her and laughing. Jessica tried to ignore her.

The first morning after her fight with Aaron, she sat alone at breakfast, until a man came over and stood before her table. He looked to be in his late thirties, handsome in a rugged kind of way—brown hair, deep brown eyes—a grin that could charm angels out of their halos. He introduced himself as Martin, the man Aaron had pointed out the day before. She hadn't noticed how handsome he was from so far away. *Delicious.*

"Delicious…?" He mulled this over, smiling. "I'm not sure anyone's ever called me *that* before."

He sat down, winking at her, still smiling. She blushed deeply and tried to recover herself. She suddenly felt more naked than she'd ever been in her life, recalling his ability.

"Wh—Who are you?" she stammered.

"Martin," he repeated. "But you already knew that. Aaron pointed me out to you yesterday. And yeah, I am cuter close up." He winked again, his playful grin widening.

"What? I didn't think that," she said, blushing, looking away. She saw Aaron looking at her. He quickly looked away again. She rolled her eyes.

"He means well," Martin said. "He really only wanted to keep you from getting hurt, not dash your hopes."

"You know, it's not nice to snoop around in people's heads."

"I can't really help it, Jess," Martin sighed. "I hear this stuff as if people are saying it out loud. *Screaming* it, in fact."

"Why did you call me Jess?"

"It's what you prefer, isn't it?"

"Only with my friends." She glared at him.

"Well, I'm not your enemy, that's for sure. That would be Dr. M."

"He's not so bad."

"That's not true and you know it," he said, looking down at the table. "Oh, and by the way, I wouldn't think so poorly of Hanley. Remember, I can read minds."

"What does that mean?"

"Only that you shouldn't take everything at face value. And no matter what Aaron says, you shouldn't lose hope. He means well, but like most people inside this place, he has no idea what's going on."

Martin smiled, standing up to leave.

"Wait, you're leaving? I thought we were becoming friends?" Jess hated herself for the blatant panic in her voice.

Martin sat back down, his expression inscrutable. He spoke very low.

"We are friends, Jess, but trust me, you don't want to be obvious about that. It gives Dr. M. too much to work with. That's number one. Some people listen to me on that, others don't. Number two—even if it was safe for us to be friends openly—most people find it unnerving to be around me anyway, knowing I can read their every thought. I don't have friends in here, at least, not that many."

"I'm sorry," she said, meaning it.

"I know." His gentle smile made Jess melt, her heart beating just a little faster. *He is so cute.* She blushed, and so did he.

"You see? That right there is what drives most people away."

"Well, maybe I'm not like most people."

Martin's smile faded. He stood up again, looking away. Then he leaned back down, speaking quickly.

"I'm sorry, Jess, I like you, I really do, but…" He looked at her with sympathy. "If you know what's good for you, you'll steer clear of everyone. Trust me, Dr. M. will find a way to use it against you if you get too close to anyone in here."

"Then why did you even bother talking to me?" She felt angry now, at both herself and Martin. She still couldn't control her basic thoughts, and he now hung only inches from her face. *God, he smells good.* Martin sighed, answering her question.

"To introduce myself, so we know each other. There will come a time, Jess, when everything makes sense."

"Well, you're making no sense *now*, you know that?"

Even in the depths of her frustration, she couldn't deny her attraction to him, or her confused desperation. She wanted him to leave, but she also needed a friend, especially with Aaron and her on the outs for the time being.

"We are friends, Jess. Now you know me. And at some point, you'll be grateful we talked. Just remember what I said, okay?"

"Whatever."

Martin leaned in again, putting his face very close to hers. She could feel his breath on her skin. He smelled incredible. She didn't care if he heard that.

"Be careful who you get close to in here," he breathed.

"This isn't fair, and you know it," she said. "You're playing me."

"I have to. I can hear everyone's thoughts. If you're going to trust anyone, it should be me, right?"

"I guess," she shrugged.

"Why would I lie?"

"I don't know."

"I wouldn't. Hanley knows things. He tells me. He says you're going to help us get out of here. We're gonna need you. We're *all* gonna need you. Just be careful about making friends in here."

Martin looked desperate, his face so close to hers, they were almost kissing. He pulled slightly away and looked in her eyes.

"Now I'm going to leave and make a small scene, for the benefit of the cameras, okay? Trust me, Dr. M. is watching. He needs to think we don't get along, or things could get bad. And, Jess? No matter how nice he is, don't hang out with Aaron too much, okay? It's better not to have any obvious friends in here, like I said."

Jess sighed in exasperation as Martin stood, sauntering backwards, looking smug. He smiled and shrugged.

"You're not my type!" he said loudly, causing several people to turn and look at them both. Jess slouched down in her chair, turning red. Martin walked away, chuckling.

"Get over it," he said, sitting down at his own table, alone.

Jess looked over at Aaron, who sat with his profile to her. She could see he was upset, his cheeks high with color. She looked over at Hanley, who only smiled and nodded. She looked away in disgust, and saw Alma sitting at a table of her own, snickering. Jess stood up, chair scraping, and quickly walked out of the cafeteria.

***

Jess's training resumed three days after she began to socialize. It consisted of Dr. M.'s voice talking to her through a headset, while she sat in a chair in a meadow, surrounded by trees. It wasn't the same meadow Aaron had taken her to, but another one of the facility's outdoor areas.

Dr. M. tried provoking her temper in multiple ways—bringing up her stepfather, her drunken mother, insulting her intelligence, and so on— but nothing worked. He reiterated that she was trapped, stuck in the facility, with no way out. At one point, Jessica became mildly annoyed.

"This is counterproductive to our relationship."

"How so?" Dr. M. said, his voice distant and tinny through her headset.

"Well, suppose at some point you succeed in pissing me off and I blow something up? Then I'll associate that anger with you and won't trust you anymore."

"You already don't trust me," he said. "And since when did you become an expert in psychology?"

"I'm just saying… if you want our relationship to remain healthy, you should have a technician speak to me on here."

Silence for several moments. Jessica felt like she'd won a small victory in making the good Doctor think twice about his methods.

"If I find a trigger to your ability, Jessica—I *want* it to be through *my* voice—not some technician's."

"Wow, how arrogant."

"I prefer to think of it as authoritative."

"Yeah, exactly," Jessica smirked, shaking her head.

She didn't know it, but Dr. M. smiled too.

***

For an entire week, she trained daily, never growing angry enough to repeat her performance. She began to wonder if her gift was gone. She hadn't spoken to Aaron in several days.

She went to the cafeteria on the eighth morning since being allowed to roam freely, to find the atmosphere decidedly different—much more quiet than usual. She glanced around while toasting an English muffin. She'd been eating a steady diet of four thousand calories a day, food being brought to her room by a technician in the evenings.

Jessica could eat whatever she chose in the cafeteria, but in the evenings, she was instructed to also eat what they brought her. She realized every bite she took in the cafeteria was being monitored, to make certain she consumed enough calories.

The food brought to her room was always something she liked, which never failed to creep her out. Just how much did they know about her? When they brought her favorite ice cream one night, she merely sighed and lapped it up.

The rest of the cafeteria's denizens talked lowly, whispering, many of them glancing at the small observation window on the far side. She finished fixing her breakfast, then carried her tray over to the window, setting it down on the nearest table.

Her heart skipped a beat as she looked through the window and saw a stranger inside the smaller room. It was an older black man, perhaps around his mid-thirties, dressed in jeans and a baseball shirt with maroon sleeves. He glanced nervously over at Jessica then looked away. She felt sorry for him, remembering how lost and confused she'd felt when she first arrived.

Her heart skipped again, as Dr. M. entered the room, sitting down to speak to the man. His lips moved, but she couldn't hear what he said.

"Guess you're no longer the flavor of the week, Chica."

Jessica jumped, turning to find Alma behind her, looking smug.

She attempted to negotiate her way around, but Alma simply shifted to stand in front of her again, so close Jessica could feel her breath against her face. They danced this way for several moments, before Jessica sighed in defeat.

"Oh, someone's getting *mad*," Alma sang. "Not that it matters. Word is, you can't do your thing. Know how I know? A little birdie told me you need lots of food for energy."

Jess looked over at Aaron, who looked down, blushing guiltily. She sighed again, glaring back at Alma.

"I know you ain't doing nothing. I mean, look at you, girl. You getting *fat*!"

She felt her anger rising. Again, she attempted to skirt around Alma, but the woman continued blocking her path. Jess's hands curled into fists, her nails biting into the palms as she attempted to calm down.

"Yeah, you a little fatty now, ain't you?"

Alma laughed. Heat burned in the palms of Jess's hands. She no longer felt the sharp cut of her nails piercing skin. She felt trapped, helpless, and now her anger seethed.

No.

She tried to swallow the rising panic, failing. Her attention strayed to Aaron, who watched her with open concern. Hanley sat staring at her from the corner, as he had been all week. She realized he was smiling. *Crazy, you've lost your mind. What are you smiling about?*

"Please, move," Jessica whispered, her voice shaking.

"*Move*? What, you think you can tell me what to do? Oh, no, bitch. You walked in here thinking you was so amazing, right? I been here a lot longer than you, and no one tells *me* what to do. Especially some skanky-ass bitch like *you*!"

Alma shoved Jess's shoulder, making her step back. Anger surged up inside her, no stopping it now. *Leave the room. Leave the room!* She looked around, helplessly, her eyes traveling to Aaron, then Hanley, finally finding Martin. Their eyes locked, the lethal emotion swirling around her head suddenly filling his like a bullhorn. *Get them out Martin, get them out now*!

"Everybody RUN!"

The room immediately fell dead silent, everyone looking first at Martin, then back at Jess and Alma.

"Do what he says," Jessica strangled out, her voice barely above a whisper.

A man sitting at the nearest table saw the look on Jess's face. For a moment, she locked eyes on the bearded stranger, who lowered his book and stared back at her. *God love him, he understands!* Rising, he ran for the door. Several people followed suit, chairs scraping, but Alma remained.

"Bitch, *please*, don't make a scene. You can't do nothing. You just act like you special, but you ain't."

Alma pushed Jess again. She fell back another step, no longer tense, instead, loose and boneless as a rag doll. Alma stepped back, folding her arms across her chest in defiance.

Jess didn't know what happened next, only vaguely aware that everyone had left the room, Aaron being the last to leave, dragging Hanley with him. She and Alma were alone.

Jess stepped forward and grabbed Alma by the hand. Alma tried to yank herself free, but Jess held on tight. Alma cried out in pain, as several bones in her hand audibly snapped. Jess yanked Alma forward, to her side, shoulder-to-shoulder, then released her broken hand to step directly in front of her. Alma's back now rested against Jess's. For the briefest, oddest moment, Alma's sight lined up with the window into the smaller cafeteria, where she saw Dr. M. suddenly stand, leaving the black stranger sitting alone in confusion, as the doctor ran, quickly exiting the room. She didn't see or hear anything that happened next. When she looked around seconds later, the cafeteria had been obliterated.

Alma stumbled away from Jess, her eyes large and bulging. She held her broken left hand limply with the other, tears streaking her cheeks. She stumbled backwards a few shaky steps, fumbling, then turned and ran from the room.

The door already stood wide open. Several people inside leaned against the wall, staring, including Aaron and Hanley. The bearded man who'd been the first to run, also stood there, gazing at her with an odd, knowing look in his eyes. A friendly smile played upon his lips. Martin appeared briefly, his eyes full of tears, then disappeared. Others filed in, staring at Jess in amazement. She tried to warn Aaron away with her eyes as he approached.

"Don't come any closer," she said, starting to cry. "I don't want to hurt you."

Aaron didn't listen. Hanley followed, still smiling wildly. Aaron stopped directly in front of her.

"How did you do that? Where did you go?"

"What are you talking about?" she asked, her voice cracking with emotion.

"You and Alma disappeared... And then you were... just there again."

"How long?"

"What?"

"How long were we gone?"

"I'm not sure. Everyone ran out into the hallway, then we heard this huge explosion." He paused, clearly still shaken by events. "When we looked inside, the cafeteria was wrecked, but you and Alma were gone."

"Why didn't you go find *help*?" Jessica gasped, doing her best to contain her frustration. Aaron retreated a step. "How could we? No one could go anywhere without the arrows. They went down with the lights."

Aaron shrugged, saying nothing else. The silence stretched out, unnerving, interminably long. Hanley stepped forward then, speaking to Jessica for the very first time.

"That was freakin' awesome!"

Jess and Aaron both jumped at his sudden outburst. She peered around Hanley to assess the damage she'd inflicted upon the cafeteria. All the tables had been hurled to the far side. Most were in pieces, as well as the chairs. The food stations were gone, thick dust floating in the air, slowly settling. The far wall stood heavily cracked, large pieces of plaster torn loose, some still falling away.

"How long?" she asked again.

"I'd say you were gone a good three to four minutes," Hanley said, still smiling crazily.

"You were gone, and then, you were just there again," Aaron repeated, bewildered.

"All right, that's enough, you two."

Aaron and Hanley turned to find Doctor M. standing a few feet away, his arms crossed over his chest. They looked at one another, unsure of what to do.

"Well, go on, you two—*get*. There are technicians in the hallway that will lead you back to your rooms. Those locks are still working."

Aaron and Hanley slowly retreated. Hanley still smiled, Aaron glanced sympathetically over his shoulder. Jess returned his gaze for a second or two before turning her eyes to the ground. Dr. M. did not speak again until they were out of the room. When he did, his voice came out surprisingly gentle. Jess began to cry.

"Alma's being looked at in medical," he said. "I don't know for certain, but I'm guessing you broke a few bones in her hand. It didn't look too pretty."

Jess's legs collapsed beneath her. She felt weak, crumbling to the floor before the doctor could even try catching her. Dr. M.'s voice sounded genuinely concerned.

"Are you feeling weak, Jess? Let's get you to medical as well and get some nutrients in you. I'd have you fix a plate to eat, but…" He glanced around at the cafeteria and chuckled.

Jess felt too shaky to stand. After a few feeble attempts, to her shock, Dr. M. picked her up in his arms and carried her out of the room. Too tired to protest, she laid her head on the doctor's shoulder before passing out.

6

Jessica awoke in a medical bed, an IV in her hand. *This looks familiar.* Dr. M. sat nearby, watching her with fondness.

"Please don't look at me that way."

"What way?"

"Like you're proud of me. Like I did something *good.*"

"But you did do something good, Jessica. Before this morning, I was beginning to worry we'd never find a trigger for your power, but thanks to Martin—"

"Martin?"

"Yes. I believe you talked with him yesterday?"

"Yeah, so?"

"Sometimes I find his skills to be very useful. Along with immediate thoughts, he can sometimes pick up on things you have no idea about. He's the one that told me a little shoving and name-calling would do the trick. That, and calling you *fat.*"

"He told you that?"

"Yes, he did. And I instructed Alma to push you around a little bit. There was no script, however. That was entirely her creation."

"Is she okay?"

"You broke metacarpal bones one and five in her left hand, if that means anything to you."

"Will that give her permanent damage?"

"No. The fractures will heal just fine in about five to six weeks, with a cast." Dr. M. smiled.

"This isn't funny! I could have really hurt someone."

"Yes, I'm aware of that. And you did blow up the cafeteria. I have staff working overtime on repairs while serving over a dozen transgens meals in their rooms. Luckily, we have abundant resources at this facility. The cafeteria should be repaired in less than two days."

"Am I going to be isolated now?" Jess's eyes welled. "Like Rachel Harley?"

"Why would you think that?" Dr. M. seemed upset. He sat up and leaned forward in his chair. "Who told you about Rachel Harley?"

"That doesn't matter. They told me she killed a man while trying to escape."

"You don't know the whole story," the doctor said, sounding sad. "But I don't think isolation will be necessary in your case. I'm fairly certain my warning of 'don't make her angry' will be heavily heeded from this point on." Dr. M. laughed. "And I doubt that Alma will ever bother you again."

"I could have killed her."

"Well, that's the most interesting part of this whole catastrophe. You should have killed Alma, but she's fine, isn't she? I also have three witnesses who've told me that both of you simply vanished, only to reappear several minutes later. And just as with your bed, there was debris all over the floor, except in one spot, in a circular area, right where you and Alma were standing."

Jess stared at Dr. M. in disbelief. She shook her head.

"This is impossible. None of this is happening."

"You generated a force field around both yourself and Alma. What's more, both you and Alma traveled forward in time, approximately three minutes and forty-eight seconds—ample time for the air to cool and the debris particles to settle. The people near the door had to wait a few minutes to even enter the room. They saw you and Alma appear out of thin air."

"How come I'm not going to be isolated? Aren't I dangerous?"

"Not unless you get angry again, and I doubt that will happen. In truth, I anticipated an event like this. If I couldn't make you angry, I hoped someone else might."

"You knew this might happen, and you let me be around people anyway? What if I'd killed Alma, instead of shielding her?"

"But you didn't, did you?"

"But I could have!" Jess screamed. "How could you put me at risk of becoming a murderer?"

Jess glared at Dr. M. in disgust. She didn't want to admit it, but she'd begun to trust him on some strange level. In the time they'd spent together in her training exercises, she'd spoken more with him than anyone else in The Society. She had to remind herself that despite his outward appearance of kindness and concern, it was only for his own selfish purposes. She looked away, feeling ashamed.

"Anyway, it all turned out well enough. We now know what makes you angry. It's not merely *helplessness,* but also being forced into the role of *victim.* That's what I've been missing all this time."

The doctor continued speaking, but his voice had lost its conviction. Jess kept her face turned away from him. Eventually, he trailed off, silence descending. He looked down at the floor, seemingly ashamed, but she didn't see. After several minutes, he spoke again, his words shocking her.

"I'm not a bad person, Jess. I know you'll never believe that, but it's true. I'm just an ordinary man, operating under extraordinary circumstances. I know all about what it's like to be different. You want different? Try being a ten-year-old in high school. By the time I kissed a girl for the first time, I was on my second doctorate. Suffice it to say, the kiss didn't go very well."

He paused then, as if waiting for a reply from her. When he didn't get anything, he continued.

"I spent my childhood being told I was special by grownups and called a freak by my peers. Most of them were probably just jealous, but I didn't realize that back then, and even if I had, I wouldn't have cared. I just wanted to *fit in*, Jess. All my life, growing up, all I wanted was to fit in. Eventually, I realized that just wasn't possible."

She turned and looked at him, frowning. This time, she saw that he looked sad. He briefly made eye contact, then continued talking to her, while looking away, as if he were talking to the floor.

"When I started my work on the Human Genome Project, I was put into a position of authority. No one ridiculed me. That seems like a hundred years ago, now, although it was only fifteen. I was young, then. I'm not anymore. But it started out as a project that I thought was going to help the world, by revolutionizing medicine and how we fought diseases. I thought I'd find cures to every major ailment that plagued man." He laughed. "I wasn't ridiculed by my peers, instead I was *exalted.* I was the king of everything."

He shook his head, sighing heavily. Jess's head swam with confusion.

"Then, I discovered the deviant pseudogene, and I was a *God.* Imagine: My own top-secret project that not even the private sector knew about. And the discovery of the enzyme? That should have taken decades. I figured it out in *months.*"

Finally, he looked at her again.

"But all that time, Jess, I still thought I was doing *good.* I was discovering, exploring, trying to uncover secrets that would benefit all of humanity. I never dreamed back then, that I'd be doing what I'm doing now."

How much of this was genuine, and how much just a play act for her benefit, Jess wondered? He looked at her, and she felt sympathy. She didn't want to, but she did.

"By the time I realized what the government wanted of me, it was too late. They used me, and my genius, just like I use you and your abilities. I can be persuaded as well, Jess."

Finally, she spoke. "Don't call me Jess, only my friends get to call me that."

He nodded, then sat back in his chair, deflated.

"It was the *power*, Jessica. I can admit that. By the time the project became what it is, I couldn't stand to have it taken away from me. Who else could handle all of this? Oh, I'm sure they'd find someone. I'm not the only person on the planet with a high I.Q." He paused briefly, seeming to make a joke. "A *very* high I.Q. But if the project was in someone else's hands, I'd never know anything about it ever again. If I walked away, I'd be relegated to some lab to study stem cells or do further research on alternate chemical bonds."

"Don't bother," Jess interrupted, eyeing him suspiciously. "Don't bother trying to be my friend. You figured out how to trigger my ability. Fine. How is this going to help?"

"You leave that to me, Jessica," Dr. M. said. "I'll figure something out. At any rate, we won't need a trigger for too long. Trust me, once you adjust to using your ability, you'll get better and better at calling it up at will. At some point, you'll be able to use your power with no trigger at all. You'll have complete control."

"Yeah, if it doesn't kill me. I thought if I had a carefully controlled diet, I wouldn't get sick like this again?"

"Well, there are factors I failed to take into consideration. Not to mention your show today was somewhat unexpected. You're on your period, Jessica?"

She nodded, blushing. Dr. M. smiled.

"There's no reason to be embarrassed, Jessica, it's a completely normal bodily function for a female. However, it does mean the iron in your blood is lower than normal. Also, your display this morning packed a larger wallop than the last time, perhaps because you were shielding Alma as well. Or, your ability may still be developing. We'll need to adjust your caloric intake again, and make sure you get more daily iron."

"I don't want to increase my calories unless I'm going to be able to start using my ability at least a few times a week," she interrupted him.

"Why?"

"Because I'm sort of… gaining weight."

"I see," Dr. M. said, amused. "Does your personal appearance concern you?"

"I don't want to be *huge*. You said there are no fat people in The Society. I don't want to be the only fat one in here. Alma said I was fat."

"Then we'll need to get you performing soon, won't we?"

Jess nodded. "But it's true, then?"

"What?"

"I'm fat? I said that Alma said I was fat, and you didn't say that I wasn't."

She stared in disbelief, as Dr. M. covered his mouth, attempting to hide a smile. He looked like he struggled not to laugh.

"It's not funny!"

"I never said it was."

"Then don't laugh at me!"

"I didn't mean to laugh, I—"

"I'm not vain, you know." *Why does he look so amused?*

"Sure, you are, but that's okay." He cleared his throat and sat more upright, seeming to fall back into 'the doctor' mode. "You have every right to be vain. You're a very pretty woman, Jessica. Things in The Society function just as they do in the larger world. There are young men in this facility. Young men like... Aaron, perhaps? Or Martin?"

"What? Ew. I hate Martin. And, no way. I don't like Aaron like *that*."

"Why not? He seems to like you."

"No. No way. We're not doing this. We are not going to sit here talking like you're my dad, now."

"What? Ew. I'm definitely not your—"

"Well, whatever," she interrupted, completely missing his offended tone. "We're not sitting here talking like we're best friends or something. We're *not* friends, you got that? So just *shut up.*"

Dr. M. said nothing—only smiled and nodded his head. If she didn't know any better, however, she'd have sworn that he looked a bit hurt.

***

Over the next several weeks, Jess trained, this time without a headset. The day following the cafeteria's destruction, a technician showed up in the meadow, looking decidedly nervous. He ordered her to stand from her chair. When she did, he shoved her on the shoulder, just as Alma had. Jessica felt sorry for him. The young man looked utterly terrified. After several days of this tactic yielding no results, a young woman approached her, radiating fury.

"*Bitch.*"

Jessica stared at her in surprise, not getting up from her chair. The woman drew close enough to make her more than a little uncomfortable, deliberately invading her personal space.

"I'm talking to you, *bitch*. Get out of that chair and get outta here!"

Jessica stood up, but the woman put both hands on her shoulders and shoved her back down. Jess tried to tamp down the rising anger, but the woman kept yelling.

"Hey *fatty,* get outta that chair, you, fat-ass bitch. You ain't nothing! You ain't so tough. I can kick your ass, candy-cunt bitch! Ugly fat-ass!"

"Shut up. And watch your filthy mouth!"

Jessica stood and shoved the woman backward. The technician's eyes momentarily lost focus. Jess realized she listened to Dr. M. give orders on her headset. She didn't care; the anger had surfaced and continued to grow. Instead of trying to control or constrict it, she did just the opposite—letting go of all control—allowing her emotions free reign.

"Yeah, you! Fat-ass bitch!"

The woman continued her tough act. Then she caught the look in Jess's eyes and began backing away. Jess barely held on long enough to warn the technician.

"Run," was all she managed to choke out, raising her hands, palm up, towards the woman.

All the fire went out of the technician's eyes. She immediately turned tail and fled. Jess tried to hold back a moment longer. In the back of her mind, she prayed the woman had run far enough away, but this thought felt so vague, she wasn't fully aware of it.

The woman managed to run half a football field's length before Jess let go, releasing the pulse. The immense compression wave knocked citrus trees lining the clearing flat.

Jess didn't see the woman go down, swept up as she was in her time-insulating bubble. When it burst, the world merely blinking momentarily back into solidity, and Dr. M. stood before her. Jess craned her neck, attempting to see around him, but he moved to block her view. Despite his efforts, she saw the technician being lifted onto a gurney and carried out of the clearing by two medical staff. Jess began to cry.

Dr. M.'s arm encircled her shoulders, gently turning her around as he walked her back into the building. Once inside, he led her back to her room. She made no attempt to resist the tears.

Infinitely grateful for her bed, she laid down with every intention of sleeping. However, Dr. M. didn't leave. He pulled up the only chair in her room and sat only a foot away. She kept her back to him, facing the wall.

"You're a good person, Jess."

"Don't call me that, only my friends get to call me that and you're *not* my friend."

"As you've said. I'm sorry you're so upset."

"No, you're not," she spat. "You wanted me to hurt her! You wanted me to pulse, and I did, so now you're happy. All you care about is what I can do. You don't give a shit about me, so stop *pretending*!" It was the first time in long while that she'd used such a heavy swear word, but she didn't care.

"I do care about you, Jess. That's why this is all so difficult for me.

I'm not supposed to care. I'm only supposed to get results."

"What the hell are you talking about?"

"Rachel Harley," Dr. M. said, his voice so soft, she barely heard him. As he continued speaking, she sat up in bed, her knees pulled up to her chin, and listened.

"Two years ago, I had orders to take Rachel to Kandahar, Afghanistan. I did. The military had been tracking an Al Qaeda cell that they thought was hiding out there. The leader of the cell grew up in this little town, that's all I knew. They were hoping to isolate them all in one building with a surprise attack, get them cornered. And they did. But the cell chose a school at the end of the street to hide in. Our troops couldn't go in. They surrounded the school. But the terrorists had chosen it, knowing our forces wouldn't open fire; they had no way of knowing how many people were in there. And every now and again, one of our soldiers got picked off by their snipers."

"Why are you telling me this?"

The doctor ignored her.

"I got the order to bring Rachel in. The soldiers were ordered to move back, to a safe distance. Rachel could boil anything, even through walls, up to fifty feet. I walked her into position, and she performed. Even I didn't know who was in the building, or how many.

"Afterwards, the soldiers went in, did a sweep, but a group had been hiding in a classroom in the far-east corner, just out of Rachel's range. Three soldiers were killed before the terrorists were overpowered and taken down, but not everyone was killed. I was ordered to release Rachel into the building. She had headphones on, so she could hear my voice, but nothing else.

"I was surrounded by men with guns, Jess. In my position, you do what you're told, end of story. I ordered Rachel to perform. The soldiers put her in place, then left. She was alone in the building. Even I didn't know what was going to happen. I told her to release a small *heat;* a term we both came up with for what she does, just like your *pulse*, and she did."

The doctor paused, struggling. He swallowed several times, and Jess frowned. He didn't look at her, instead focused on the floor. As he continued, she closed her eyes, her stomach flopping with queasiness. At the same time, she noted how the doctor's voice cracked. *He can't be faking that. He can't.*

"There were two women, three children in the room, along with the leader of the cell. The women were his wife and mother. The three children were his. I didn't find that out until later."

He shook his head and sighed.

"Rachel was never supposed to see what she did. When it happened, I didn't even know why she was so hysterical, at first. Then I found out. She was inconsolable. There was nothing I could do. Her mind cracked, only I didn't realize how bad it was."

"What?" Jess didn't understand, feeling lost, but he ignored her.

"She was so used to taking orders, she did whatever anyone told her, after that. She was broken, only I didn't understand. Unfortunately, part of your conditioning process means that some of you are more vulnerable to doing everything you're told, not just by me. It's a small price to pay."

"I don't understand what you're talking about."

"I didn't want to hurt Rachel," the doctor said. "And I don't want to hurt you. But, don't you see? I have no other choice. I take orders, Jess. That's all I do."

"What about that woman? The technician. Did I kill her?" Jess began to shake and cry all over again.

"No. She's being treated for first-degree burns over parts of her arms and neck, some pretty good scrapes and bruises, and some of her hair was singed, no broken bones though, so all in all, the technician got off pretty lucky."

Jess said nothing in response. The doctor stood to leave.

"This doesn't make us friends, you know?" Jess stared hard at the doctor. "Just because you've told me some of your secrets. We're not friends."

Dr. M. nodded and opened the door. He walked out with his head bowed.

***

Jess's training improved from that point on. Over a span of six weeks, Dr. M. conditioned her to summon anger and rage at will. No more technicians were used.

Her powers became tamed, utterly under her control. Soon enough, she stopped consciously experiencing the anger and outrage necessary to evoke them, instead manifesting her abilities with the same natural, instinctive and unconscious ease as breathing. She began to feel empowered, just as Dr. M. had told her she would.

During this time, she continued eating in the cafeteria, and began socializing in the rec room, watching TV and playing pool with Aaron. She resumed talking to him partly in attempt to upset Martin, since he'd specifically told her not to socialize with Aaron. Martin's betrayal still burned. She doubted it'd cool any time soon. Socializing with Aaron was initially just a way of making her hurt plain, but the more she did so, the more she genuinely came to enjoy his company.

Occasionally, Hanley sat down next to Jess while she watched TV. He never said anything, only smiled at her with his crooked teeth. Jess decided he was crazy, but harmless. She even began to feel fond of him, in a strange way; like a stray puppy that always followed her around.

***

Her first day back in the cafeteria, she nodded to the bearded mystery man who'd been the first to run from her unscheduled 'performance'. She'd never spoken to him. He was quiet and always had his face in a book. He looked foreign, skin a light olive, with dark-brown, shoulder-length, shaggy hair, tucked behind his ears, and a short-cropped beard and mustache. He was young, perhaps in his late twenties or early thirties, Jess figured. She knew his name was Jesus. Looking at him her first day back, she couldn't help but wonder if his look was intentional to the name or not. She smiled, shaking her head as she sat with Aaron for a meal.

"Who is that Jesus guy? Do you know him?"

"Yeah," Aaron said, then laughed because she'd pronounced the man's name wrong. He quickly corrected her. "It's pronounced Hey-Zoos."

"Hey, zoos?"

"Yeah, you know, like *Jee-zus*? As in Christ? That's how you're supposed to pronounce it. Not Jee-zus. Hey-Zoos."

"Yeah, I get it. Is that why he looks like that? Because of his name? He's trying to be funny or something?"

"I don't know, he looked like that the first day he got here. His name is actually Matt or something. But he told everyone to call him Jesus. That's not his real name, but that's what people call him."

"Why?"

"Heh, because he can walk on water," Aaron smiled.

"Really?"

"Yeah. If you want to get all scientific, I guess he changes the molecular structure on the surface of the water, making it solid, or something."

"Huh."

"What?"

"Maybe *Jee-zus* was a transgen, you think?"

Aaron looked at Jess for a moment, wide-eyed. Then they both broke out laughing. Neither of them knew it, but Martin smiled as well, his back to them at a far table.

Alma sat at another table, her left hand in a cast up to her elbow and roped in a sling. Jess looked at her, attempting to smile, but Alma looked away.

"She hates me."

"Well, you did try to kill her."

"No, I didn't. If anything, I saved her life."

"The only reason you had to save her life was because you lost your temper to begin with."

"I only lost my temper because she pushed me and called me fat," Jess said, her voice rising.

"You could have just walked away."

"What? I tried, you saw. She wouldn't let me."

"Yeah, I guess," Aaron said. Jess stared at him for several moments, her cheeks coloring.

"Are you trying to make me angry?"

Aaron looked at Jess, his face frozen like a deer caught in headlights. He swallowed audibly, growing nervous.

"Um… no."

"Good."

She glanced briefly at Hanley, who sat smiling at her. She shook her head and went back to eating her sandwich.

***

A few days after returning to the cafeteria, Jess met the black man she'd seen through the observation glass. He no longer wore jeans and a baseball shirt, but the same light blue scrubs everyone else dressed in. He seemed quiet, keeping to himself, much like Jess had on her first day being socially exposed. She was cautious about approaching him, knowing only too well how freaked out he must be, but she had grown used to not eating alone, and he was the only person in the cafeteria at the time, save for Alma, who hated her, and creepy Hanley.

"Hi," she said. "Do you mind if I sit down with you?"

The man didn't speak, only shook his head, eating.

"My name's Jessica. What's yours?"

"Earl."

"Hey, Earl."

They ate in silence for several minutes while Jess watched him. She judged him to be in his late thirties, but she didn't ask. He seemed sketchy and shy, but his eyes held an aloof awareness, like a trapped animal looking for escape.

"It's an adjustment, I know," she finally said. "I mean, I've only been here a few weeks, myself."

Earl looked up at Jess, surprised. She smiled at him gently.

"It's scary how fast you get used to it. I mean, I haven't even really thought about my old life." She frowned. "It's kind of weird—terrifying, actually. You see that guy?"

Jess pointed to Hanley, who sat in the corner, stalking her, per usual. Hanley saw her pointing at him and waved, his smile never fading.

"Weird," Jess whispered. "Anyway, supposedly he's been here for ten years."

Earl looked at Jess in shock, then over at Hanley, who still simply smiled. Hanley waved again, nodding. Earl looked back at Jess, clearly panicked.

"And that girl over there?" She pointed to Alma. "She's been here over a year. This friend of mine? Aaron? He's been here four years."

"I won't be here inside a month," Earl said, speaking for the first time. His voice was low, thick and rich, but friendly.

"Why not?"

"I ain't staying here longer than I have to. Once I get control of what I can do, I'm outta here."

"What can you do?"

"I can walk through walls," Earl smiled. It was contagious.

Jess smiled back. "How do they keep you in your room?"

"Don't think they thought that far ahead, yet. For now, I can't do it at will," he shook his head. "But they gonna train me," he laughed. "You believe that? Think they can turn me into a circus monkey or some stupid bullshit. Shiiiit, they should know better, smart as they are. Once I learn to do it at will, I'm gonna walk right on outta here."

Earl smiled at Jess again. It was like the sun breaking through dark clouds. That was the start of her plan.

***

A week later, Jess walked in the Atrium with Aaron. She'd asked him to go with her, telling him she wanted to see him use his ability again. It was apparent to her by this point that Aaron had a crush on her. When she told him that she liked watching him change the flowers, he immediately agreed.

Once out in the field, Jess looked around, scanning for cameras. She didn't see any, and in the middle of a field of flowers, she felt confident they couldn't be heard. Aaron was turning a sunflower blue and lavender, when Jess spoke.

"I'm getting out of here."

Aaron looked at her, smiling, and nodded. He obviously wasn't taking her statement seriously. She reached her hand out and touched his. He blushed and looked down.

"I'm serious, Aaron. I'm leaving here, and I want you to come with me. All of you."

"Who?" he frowned.

"Everyone it will take to get out."

"You can't get out, Jess, I told you. Everyone who's ever tried has failed and ended up in isolation."

"Well, that's gonna change."

"How?"

"Look, you told me several weeks ago, that Alma once tried to escape? Got a group together?"

"Yeah."

"Why'd it fail?"

"Because you just can't get out, *that's* why."

"What happened?"

"Alma made friends with Rachel Harley. She also got Malcolm and Jenny involved. Malcolm can float, remember? I guess if he's holding someone's hand, they can float, too. Alma wanted Rachel with her, for insurance. So, if someone tried to stop them, Rachel would help."

"You mean kill someone?"

"Yeah. Alma's power can't kill anyone. It's useless, remember? Plus, Alma's not capable of that, but she didn't seem to have any problem convincing Rachel to do it. Rachel's kind of... easily influenced. She didn't have a lot of friends, only Hanley... and Alma was one of the first people to really talk to her. I think Alma made her feel special, you know? Plus, she told Rachel she could get her out, and Rachel was in."

Jess stared at Aaron with wide eyes. Then she shook her head.

"So, *that's* what he meant."

"What?"

"Nothing. The plan, why didn't it work?"

"The four of them started 'floating' over the fence, each holding onto Malcolm's hands in a little circle, or something. You know, so they were all connected? They made it over, but there were technicians waiting. They see everything, Jess. Rachel killed one of them, before getting Tased. There were too many of them, you see?"

"So, how come this Malcolm guy doesn't just escape on his own?"

"He won't go anywhere without Jenny," Aaron said. "And he's not allowed outside now, after what happened."

"Okay, so forget floating over the fence. We can get Hanley out here to melt it."

"He's not allowed outside either, remember?"

"Okay, but I can short circuit the doors with my pulse and sneak

Hanley out, right?"

"Wrong, you're not listening to me, Jess. It won't work."

"Why not?"

"Because the only way to get out of here is to kill a lot of people," Aaron said, tears filling his eyes. He sighed heavily and continued.

"Look, you're right, okay? If someone really wanted out, they could probably find a way. But the only way is to kill people. And I don't know about you, but even if my ability enabled me to take a life, I don't think I could. Could you?"

"No," Jess said, her voice faltering. "I burned that lady and felt horrible."

"What?"

"Nothing."

Aaron shook his head.

"Most of the people in here who might be able to escape, they just aren't capable of killing anyone. Escaping is bad, Jess. You'll only end up in isolation like Rachel Harley. Then I'll never see you again."

Aaron blushed and stared at the ground. Jess didn't say anything.

"And besides... taking a life made her go crazy. Once you kill someone in here, I don't think they're willing to take any chances."

"I could have killed Alma, and Dr. M. indicated he still wouldn't have locked me up."

"Yeah, but Alma's one of us," Aaron said. "If you killed a technician, it would be a different story. And if you killed a technician while trying to escape, then all bets would be off, no matter how much the doctor likes you."

"What does that mean?"

"Nothing, just... it's no secret he likes you. You're his favorite. You're like, friends, or whatever."

"We're *not* friends, I *hate* him."

"You sure act as if you like him."

"Yeah, *act* being the key word. What's wrong with you, anyway? Are you jealous or something?"

"No," he said, his tone weak and unconvincing. Jess gave him a stern look, but her eyes remained soft.

"I've been playing along from the beginning. Dr. M. is so damned arrogant, he thinks his little act of friendliness will fool me. God! The man is so caught up in himself he doesn't believe he could ever be wrong. But he *is*, because he's playing with fire. He's amassing all these people with abilities, creating the perfect storm."

Aaron looked at Jess with interest now.

"All these people," Jess continued. "If we could *organize* them, with all their different powers, there's no way they could stop us."

"They'd kill us if it ever came down to it. Dr. M. may not believe we could pull it off, but if we did, he'd stop us any way he could. If that means killing us, he'll do it."

She nodded. "Still, there's got to be a way."

"And if some of us got away, then what? Where would we go, how would we hide? I have no money, no wallet, no ID. Shoot, Jess... I came here when I was eighteen, straight from foster care. I never even held a job. I couldn't make it on the outside, and besides, you know if anyone ever escaped, their face would be on every news channel in the country. Dr. M. would make sure of that."

Jess was shocked by the small wealth of personal information he'd just offered up about himself. Aaron continued, oblivious to her reaction.

"I've thought about all of this, Jess. I've had the time to think it through, in every way. There is no life outside of here, at least not one that would be any better."

"But, I can't just give up. It's the only thing that's gotten me through, so far."

"I'm sorry, Jess," Aaron said. "But, it's not so bad, is it? At least you're not alone. You have me."

Jess scoffed. She stared at Aaron for several, long moments, before leaving him standing alone amongst the flowers.

7

Jess sat in the rec room watching television one afternoon while Hanley sat next to her on the couch. Suddenly, he leaned over and spoke.

"Don't give up hope." He no longer smiled.

She frowned, then looked at the television again, ignoring him. He followed suit but continued talking.

"You're plan's a good one, Jess. You're just short one person."

"What are you talking about?"

Hanley smiled. Then he sang his reply to her. "She's here."

"Who?"

"The last rung in the ladder."

"What the hell does that mean?"

Jess turned and stared at Hanley, hoping to get more information out of him, but he would not speak again. He only stared at the TV, smiling crazily, once more. Eventually, she got up and left the room. As she did so, she spotted Martin, watching her from the corner. She turned away from him and left.

***

The next afternoon, Jess and Aaron ate lunch in silence, when Hanley suddenly pointed to the observation glass. Jess glanced over, curious, and frowned. She looked back at Hanley, who nodded and smiled, giving her a thumbs-up.

"That guy is completely nuts," she said, standing up to look at the window.

"I told you," Aaron said, his mouth full of food.

When Jess walked over to the glass, she gasped. Inside, she saw a young girl, who looked about ten-years-old.

"It's a child!"

Everyone looked at Jess in surprise, the room erupting into loud whispers and exclamations. Several people jumped up to look through the window, including Alma, who kept her distance from Jess. People looked at each other in shock. Jess turned, addressing no one in particular.

"They can't put a child in here, can they?"

"Looks like they have," Alma said, her eyes shifting nervously to Jess.

"But that's just *wrong.*"

"Like Dr. M. cares about right and wrong," Jesus said, looking at Jess in despair.

She'd spoken to him a few times, by then, and invited him to play pool with her and Aaron at one point. He'd refused, but in a friendly way. Jesus was a reader and spent most of his time in the library.

Jess walked back to her table and sat down, dejected. Aaron tried to comfort her.

"How could they put a child in here? What about her family?"

"Maybe she's an orphan, like I was?" Aaron offered.

"It wouldn't matter. Putting a child in here…" Jess shook her head.

"What are you gonna do about it?" Hanley asked.

Jess and Aaron turned to see Hanley standing at his table. He walked over and sat down across from them, at their table. He didn't smile.

"She's the key to this whole thing."

"What are you talking about?" Jess sighed.

"Just ignore him, Jess, the man's crazy," Aaron said, but she wasn't listening.

"She's the one we've been waiting for." Hanley went on.

"Who?" Jess asked.

"The little girl," Hanley said. "My friends told me."

"What friends?" Aaron snorted.

"My friends up there," Hanley pointed up.

"You have friends in the ceiling," Jess deadpanned. Aaron snorted laughter.

"Not in the ceiling, you *morons*, out in *space*."

Aaron and Jess looked at each other. Aaron shrugged, stifling his laughter and shook his head. Hanley continued speaking, ignoring the kid.

"Yeah, I know what the two of you think of me—you, and everyone else in this joint. Well, except for Martin. I also know that you, my dear, are dying to escape from this hell hole. So am I, and it's taken me ten years of waiting. Only now, my time's up. You think *you're* patient, *plant-boy*, because you've been here four years? No one's more patient than me."

Hanley settled back in his chair, arms across his chest, a smug, satisfied grin plastered on his face. Jess leaned forward, her tone serious.

"How did you know I wanted to escape?"

"Please, I'm friends with Martin." Hanley scowled.

"Yeah, right," Aaron said.

"Oh, yeah? See Alma over there? She's a lesbian. Did you know? If she wasn't so busy hating your ass, she'd probably have a thing for you."

Hanley pointed to Jess. Next, he motioned towards Jesus, then Earl.

"Jesus has a tiny crush on Alma, poor schmuck. He doesn't stand a chance. Earl, there, thinks he's just gonna walk on outta here, and he's planning on doing it sometime next week. And you, *flower-king*, are so gone over this little lady, you'd probably be willing to kill for her, despite your lack of gusto." Hanley finished by thumbing his hand toward Jess.

She frowned, looking toward Aaron, who now blushed madly. He quickly looked down at the table, all but confirming Hanley's statements. She put her hand on his arm and he flinched away.

"Aaron," she said, surprised.

Aaron hastily stood, his chair scraping so loudly, half the cafeteria grimaced, as if nails had been scraped down a chalkboard. Blushing madly, he walked out of the room. Jess watched him go, then turned back to Hanley, furious now. She leveled a look at him that let him know she was not pleased with his magical show-and-tell.

"Oops," was all Hanley said, lacking any genuine tone of remorse.

"Is all of that true?"

"He walked away, didn't he?"

"Why do you always act so weird?"

"They told me to," Hanley said, pointing up again.

"The aliens."

Jess sat back in her chair. Now it was her turn to smugly cross her arms.

Hanley nodded, looking Jess straight in the eyes. His honest tone unnerved her.

"They know every single one of us. As soon as we're activated with the Luci, something inside our heads, that your genius Doctor hasn't even detected, sends out some signal. They know who we all are and exactly what it is we can do, including you." He pointed at her face. "And they've been waiting."

"For what?"

"For all the right pieces to come together. All the right people, with all the right abilities."

"The aliens," Jess said again, her voice louder now, unable to hide her skepticism.

"Shhh! Keep your voice down!" Hanley whispered. "Yeah, the aliens. Look, there are mics in the cameras. If it looks like anyone's getting too excited, or saying something interesting, our good Doctor sometimes takes notice. Then he turns up the volume, or sometimes confronts you on what you were talking about. And if he thinks you're not being honest, he likes to lock you up in a room with no food for a couple of days."

Jess fidgeted, suddenly scared. Hanley had hit a chord.

"Just act normal, like I'm regular old bugging you, and we can talk like normal people. Now, as I was saying—"

"If they know we're here, why don't they just break us out? Can't they do that?" She raised a defiant eyebrow of victory at him.

"Well, that's the tricky part, see? Our friends up there… they're sort of… pacifists."

"Pacifists?"

"Yeah, it means they're non-aggressive. In *all* ways."

"I know what a pacifist is," she spat, sounding highly offended. "How would rescuing us from here be aggressive?"

"Are you kidding me? This place is surrounded, and I don't just mean the trees and electric fences. There's a whole other perimeter surrounding the facility—guards with machine guns and itchy trigger fingers. Your boyfriend's right, no one's getting out of here. Dr. M.'s got things locked down nice and tight. Even if we got past the fence, *which I would melt.*" Hanley delivered this revelation in a melodramatic tone that caused Jess to smile, despite herself. Hanley smiled back.

"Yeah, I know about your hatchling plans. Even if we all got through the Atrium door—and got everyone past the fence—there'd be hundreds of soldiers with guns surrounding everyone. The Graylings can't do anything to harm anyone. It's against their nature."

"The *what*-lings?"

"Graylings. That's what they call themselves. To us, at least."

"Little gray men, *right*," she toyed with him. "Of course."

"No, no—they're tall, apparently. Real skinny, and super-smart. The other hybrids call them Graylings." He shrugged.

"The hybrids?" Jess frowned.

"Yeah, the ones in the ship, hiding behind the sun," Hanley said, his tone all matter-of-fact.

Jess sighed, rubbing her temples. Hanley continued, not noticing.

"You see, it all began a couple of hundred years ago: The Graylings were super advanced, but they didn't have any weapons. They had amazing amounts of technology at their fingertips, but none of it was used for defense. They're a completely non-aggressive species— literally incapable of hurting anything. They couldn't even throw a punch to defend themselves, if it came down to it. The concept of war is completely alien to them, no pun intended.

"So, this totally aggressive race, which they call the Bailon, comes to their planet—they attack the Graylings with all this mass weaponry— try to take over their planet for their own use. The Graylings died in mass numbers and were almost completely wiped out. A few thousand of them escaped in this massive ship, because they have spectacular technology. They ran, see?"

"Uh-huh." Jess was more convinced than ever that Hanley was mad.

"They traveled for decades and decades, and eventually entered our solar system. On Earth, they found life they'd never seen before. And in Humans, they found something unique. While studying us, they found they could alter us—give us abilities. Just one gene in the right place, and—Whammo!" Hanley clapped and yelled.

Jess jumped, then recovered herself. "I thought you said to keep your voice down?" she grumbled.

Hanley ignored her. He'd brought his plate of food over when he sat down. He picked up the sandwich on his plate and finished telling his story with a full mouth.

"It took several more decades to perfect it. To find people. It doesn't work on everyone, you know? You have to have the right DNA sequence."

"No kidding, we won the lottery," Jess fumed. "But what does any of this have to do with us?" She didn't believe any of Hanley's story, but the part about escaping nagged at her.

"They can't aggress, see? But Humans? Humans are the most aggressive, murdering animals on the planet. But we've also got intelligence. And with their help, we've got super talents. They had it all planned. They can't aggress, but we can. So, they planned to collect a race of beings to take back to their home planet and clean house. Problem solved. They get their planet back, they don't kill anybody, and the Bailon are sent packing. Or wiped out—either way. In us, they found a way to fight their war, without actually fighting."

"Then why are we locked up in here?"

"'Cause Dr. M. discovered our little gene and figured out how to activate it before the Graylings could get to any of us. By the time they realized what was happening, it was too late. The facility was built, transgens started being collected, and the Graylings were caught in a bind. They need some of us, but they can't break us out of here, for the same reason they can't just go blow up all those damn Bailon."

"Well, why not? I mean, if you have to, then you have to. I don't want to, but I could easily punch somebody in the face to defend myself."

"Right, *you* can. If your brain tells your hand to make a fist, your hand makes a fist. If your brain orders your arm to swing that fist and smash it into somebody's face, your arm will comply. But what if you told your arm to swing, and it wouldn't move? What if the synapses in your brain that needed to fire for the order to reach your arm, simply wouldn't fire? You'd be literally, physically incapable of throwing that punch, hmm?"

"But…" Jess trailed off, shaking her head.

"Don't understand it?" Hanley shrugged. "Try this—some dogs *allow* their masters to beat them relentlessly—and don't ever bite back. They could if they wanted to, but they don't. The Graylings *can't*. See the difference? You could walk right up to one of them and literally beat them to death, and they won't ever raise an arm against you. They can't. How sad is that?"

"Pretty darn sad," Jess said. "*If* it were true."

"It is," Hanley said. "You still don't get it, do you? You think they have a choice? You think because you can decide to fight, they can, too?"

She nodded emphatically. Hanley nodded back knowingly, and offered a sad smile, tapping his temple.

"Listen to me, Jess, and try to understand, th—"

"But I am listening, Hanley," she interrupted. "It just doesn't make any sense."

Hanley sighed patiently. "You're hearing me Jess, but you're not *listening*. You're not listening to understand. *Hear me*—You may never be able to understand why, or how, but I'm telling you, the Graylings simply cannot fight. You've gotta try and wrap your head around that, despite what *you* can or would be able to do. They're them, and we're us. They can't do what we can do, and they need what we can do. We're their only hope—and Dr. M.'s got us all incarcerated—putting the Graylings into yet another bind. But they've waited this long. Another decade? No problem. Eventually, enough of us would be activated that if we put our talents together, we could break *ourselves* out. Once we're out… the Graylings will pick us all up and take us away from this God forsaken planet."

"You're crazy, Hanley," Jess said, rubbing her temples again.

Hanley looked at Jess and smiled.

"I'm *not* crazy. And that little girl in there? Her name's Sarah. She's the one we've been waiting for. Know what she can do? She can make pacifists out of anyone she wants. Like flipping a switch. Once she gets control of it, we can walk right past all those soldiers with guns, and they'll simply wave us goodbye."

Jess stared hard at Hanley for several moments, hope growing inside. Finally, she was able to speak, her voice barely steady.

"Is that true?"

Jess's face was steeped in desperation. Hanley dragged his chair right next to hers, took both her hands in his, and she didn't pull away.

"It's true. If you're willing to blow a hole in this place, get some doors open, I can take down the fences. With Sarah's help, we can walk everyone out of here. Earl needs to do some snooping around, find out which doors have people locked up inside. We need to find Rachel. I'm not leaving her behind."

"Okay, okay," Jess sighed. "Just excepting the fact that I don't believe any of this alien junk. Supposing I believe you can get us all out of here. Aaron's right, we'd all be on the run. They'd catch us, eventua—"

"You have to believe *all* of it," Hanley interrupted. "Because if you don't, we're never getting out of here. No one's gonna come and rescue us, Jess. It's up to us to get ourselves outta here. The world doesn't care about us. They don't even know who we are. If they did, they'd all turn their backs on us, because we're different. We're freaks."

"I'm not a freak," Jess said.

"To the world, you are. With the things we can do? People would be afraid of us, Jess. They won't fight for us, for our rights. Our own government has us locked away. And are you telling me you'd rather stay in here, instead of fighting for your freedom? Staying in here is a one-way ticket to Murder Ville, for you. It's only a matter of time before Dr. M. takes you out in the field. He'll want you to do your thing, say it's another exercise—put you on a mountain top, maybe. Only, what you won't know is that a plane carrying a foreign diplomat is flying just beyond your sight, on the other side. You'll do your thing, and bam! Bye-bye, birdie."

"No, that's not possible. Dr. M. would never do that to me."

"He wouldn't? What do you think you're in here for, huh? To *amuse* Dr. Milbron? Has he blindfolded you yet?"

"What are you talking about?" Her eyes prickled with tears, already disturbed. She remembered—how could she forget?—how she'd sensed a duality in the doctor her very first day inside the facility. She'd thought of him as Jekyll and Hyde. Fully remembering now, her arms broke out in gooseflesh as Hanley continued talking.

"That's what he does—starts asking you to wear a blindfold while performing. Says it's a *trust exercise*. He did it to Rachel. She believed him. She'd gotten so used to wearing the blindfold in her exercises, she didn't question it. He took her outside the facility. They put her on a plane, then walked her into some room. She couldn't hear anything, had those damn headphones on. The only thing she could hear was Dr. M.'s voice. He told her to do her thing, and she did." Hanley shook his head, disgusted. "Then, they started walking her out again. One of the technician's—or so she thought, turned out they were soldiers—but anyway, one of their shoulders brushed against her head, and the blindfold slipped. And she saw…"

Hanley looked like he was going to be sick. He wasn't eating anymore.

"She told me later that she was in what looked like a classroom. The people had fallen out of their chairs, onto the floor. When she saw the tiny feet sticking out from in front of the desk she'd been standing behind, and she saw the children's shoes… that's when she started screaming."

"Kandahar," Jess whispered. "So, that's what happened. What he meant, when he said she *saw*."

"What?"

"Nothing," Jess shook her head. Dismissing her thoughts of the doctor on day one, she advocated for him. "Look, it wasn't his fault. Dr. M. was only taking orders."

"Jeezus, you're defending that guy?!"

"Shh! Hanley! What happened to keeping our voices down?" Jess dropped her voice to a whisper. "Look, I'm not defending, I'm just saying, he's not as bad as you think. He feels really bad about Rachel. He told me so."

"Jeezus, Jess. He's *playing* you. Just like he did with Rachel. He's just trying to get on your good side, so you'll trust him. Believe me, Dr. M. doesn't care about you. All he does is play mind games. You'll see. It's only a matter of time before he tries to manipulate you, too. Just like Rachel. She trusted him and look where it got her. He turned her into a mass murderer, and eventually, a catatonic zombie, hidden away. Hell, for all I know, she's not even here anymore. She may not even be alive. She could be dead."

Hanley's voice cracked, his eyes filling with tears. "That's all he does, Jess. Doctor M. He *kills* people. You understand that? He kills them. And if he doesn't kill them, he makes *you* kill them. He'll make you kill people, Jess."

"It won't happen." She shook her head.

"No? He'll find a way. He's already planning it. You know… Aaron's of no real use to him. What he can do can't help the doctor at all. But he knows you two are friends, and he knows you care about Aaron. He's going to use that to his benefit. You should've listened to Martin when he told you not to make any friends."

"He knows I can't kill anyone," Jess said. "He'd never make me hurt anyone."

"Really?" Hanley stared at Jess long and hard. Then he tapped his temple again, shrugged his shoulders, and indicated towards Martin, who sat at another table with his back to them. "Martin says different."

Jess sighed. "Martin's a regular old snitch, isn't he? Likes to gossip," Jess snapped.

Hanley continued talking, ignoring her remarks.

"Don't be so naïve, Jess. When push comes to shove, the good Doctor figures you'll do anything he asks, to save Aaron's life."

"No," Jess said, her voice trembling. "No, you're lying. You couldn't possibly know that."

"No?" Hanley looked past Jess and smiled weakly at Martin's back. Then he looked back at her.

"Alma is coming over. She's going to apologize to you for being so mean. Been planning it a few days, now."

"Yeah, right. Alma hates me. She would never come and talk to me."

"She wants to be friends." Hanley shrugged. "Thinks you can help her."

A few moments later, Jess turned at the sound of a woman clearing her throat.

"Hey," Alma said.

"Hi."

"Well, uh, look... I just wanted to say I'm sorry, you know? For pushing you around? They told me to do it. And that I was hoping we could... like... get along?"

"Uh-huh." Jess just frowned at Alma, feeling stunned, at a loss for words.

"Well, gotta go. Ladies..." Hanley bowed. "See you later, Jess."

She watched Hanley walk away, completely confused and overwhelmed. She looked back at Alma, who nervously fidgeted her feet and glanced sideways at her.

"Want to sit down?" Jess sighed, resigning. Alma hesitated, acting as if Jess might lunge at her any moment.

"Seriously, it's okay. I've got a handle on it now."

Alma sat, though the look of a wild animal about to bolt never left her eyes.

"So," Jess said. "I know this is going to sound strange, but I'd like you to tell me all about your failed escape plan last year."

"I don't..." Alma faltered, but Jess could see from the look in her eyes that she did understand.

"Look, there's no point in lying to me. I know everything, so just save us both the time and breath, and tell me what I want to know."

Alma writhed, clearly uncomfortable with this, but eventually capitulated, relaying the entire escape plan to Jess. When she had finished talking, Jess returned the courtesy by filling her in on everything Hanley had just said. When she'd finished, Alma stared at her, then over at Hanley, who now sat with Earl, talking and waving his arms excitedly.

Both women watched as Earl and Hanley stood up together, crossed the floor, and sat down at Jesus's table. Then the two women looked back at each other and turned around to face the table, putting their backs squarely to the remaining scene. Jess leaned in closer to Alma, their foreheads nearly touching. Already, Alma had grown comfortable enough with Jess, this didn't faze her one bit, despite acting as if she thought Jess might blow her to pieces just minutes before. The transformation was lost on both women, wrapped up in circumstances as they were.

"So, what are your thoughts?" Jess asked.

"Hanley's crazier than a bat shitting on a Unicorn," Alma said. Jess frowned but also smiled. "But if he says that little girl can get us past all those soldiers, we might just have a fighting chance," she finished.

"Yeah, but how can we trust him? Surely alie-," Jess caught herself before finishing the word, sighing heavily. It was simply too ludicrous. She redirected her question.

"How does Hanley know about the little girl?"

"Are you kidding me?" Alma stared at Jess. "The same way I knew to push you and call you fat. Martin hears every thought, and he's more than happy to pass tips on to Dr. M. But in this case, we get a sneak peek, using Martin's snitching talents, into Dr. M's head, instead. Forget whatever psycho explanation Hanley gave you, it's just nut-job talk, because he's crazy. But Martin obviously heard Dr. M.'s thoughts and knows what the little girl can do. Martin told Hanley, not no dumb *aliens*. And while Hanley may be crazy, it takes insanity to even think about getting out of here. Especially after seeing how badly *my* plan went."

Jess nodded, firmly impressed by Alma's concise summation, not to mention her obvious guilt over the botched escape plan involving Rachel Harley. She had her own quick flash of guilt, realizing she'd underestimated Alma's intelligence, as well as unfairly judging her morality and conscience on the matter.

"So, you trust Hanley?"

"Hell, no. But I want outta here. I don't believe his crazy stories, but I'm willing to trust his *plan*. Don't you want outta here, Jessica?"

Jess nodded. The two women spent the rest of their meal eating in peaceful silence, their former hostilities already utterly washed away. That was the day that Alma and Jess became lifelong friends.

8

After lunch, where Aaron remained suspiciously absent, Jess sat watching TV. She hadn't seen Aaron since he ran out of the cafeteria. She figured he was hiding. Hanley wasn't there either, but as she sat staring at the television, Martin sat down, so close, their shoulders touched. *He's so warm*, she thought, then felt mad at herself for still finding him attractive, despite his deceit. *He may be a liar, but he still smells amazing.* She rolled her eyes and sighed heavily, cursing her uncontrolled thoughts, and the fact that he could hear them as if she'd said everything out loud.

"Look, Jess... I'm sorry, okay?"

"For what?" She refused to look at him.

"For telling Dr. M. your trigger. It's not like I had any choice."

"No?" She turned to look him in the eyes, her stare glassy and cold.

"No."

His voice shook. Once again, his face was so close to hers, she could feel his breath. She felt herself softening and fought to resist. Martin smiled again.

"Do you have to sit so close," she whispered.

"Yes," he whispered back.

"Why?"

"Because, I don't want anyone to hear me."

"Oh." Her ego was instantly deflated. She couldn't help but feel disappointed.

"I did what I had to do," Martin said. He took a deep breath and exhaled. "If I didn't, Dr. M. would kill my wife."

Jess pulled away, a look of complete shock on her face. Martin had tears in his eyes.

"Your *wife*? What are you talking about?"

"What, you think the doctor only makes runaways and orphans disappear? Wake up, Jess. Not everyone in here is an only child, or someone who won't be missed. Some of us were actually taken from our families."

"No," Jess said. "And stop peeking inside my head."

"I'm sorry. But some of the missing person stories you see on the news? They're not all *missing*. I'll bet a lot of them are in places like this."

Jess didn't know what to say.

"Some of the people in here have families," Martin repeated. "I do what Doctor M. tells me to, and my wife lives. Alma does what he tells her to, and her sister lives."

"Alma's..." Jess trailed off.

"Now you know why she was so desperate to escape. Desperate enough, she was willing to dupe Rachel into killing, if need be. Until you've been that low, you can't even begin to imagine what you might be willing to do, in your desperation to grasp onto anything, even the slightest sliver of hope. Sometimes you find yourself doing things that don't even feel like a choice." Martin suddenly choked up. He took a moment to compose himself, before going on. "In a fight for survival, where it's life or death, and not even your own, but someone else... someone you love more than anything in the world, even yourself... there is no choice. *That's* desperation. That's when you become someone you never thought you could be." He hung his head in shame.

"I'm so sorry," Jess said, and she genuinely meant every word. Without thinking, she'd already forgiven Martin for everything, before he even finished speaking.

"I know."

"So, is it true, then, what Hanley said about the little girl?"

Martin nodded.

"And the other stuff," Jess began slowly. "You'd know. Hanley's crazy, right?"

"Yes, and no," Martin said, moving even closer, whispering lower. She had to lean her ear right up to his mouth to hear him.

"I read minds, Jess," Martin said. "I'm not psychic. I only know what people are thinking. I can't hear any aliens. Hanley says he's talking to them. All I hear are Hanley's thoughts. I can't tell you if any of what he says is true. All I can tell you is that *he* believes it. He's not lying."

"And you can't tell if he's insane? If his mind is just... broken?"

She pulled away to look at him, but he leaned forward till their foreheads touched, and she reciprocated. By this point, however, she no longer felt physically aroused in any manner, although, she briefly wondered if her breath smelled bad. Martin smiled.

"It's fine," he chuckled. "Hanley's mind isn't broken. He believes what he says, one hundred percent. He's as honest as they come. He's not insane."

"Honest? Not insane? Those aren't answers, Martin. He believes *aliens* made us, and they want to come and take us away," she rasped, her whisper growing louder. "We're gambling all our lives on a guy who sounds crazy!"

"Shh," Martin warned. Then he smiled again.

"Crazy can sometimes be beautiful, too, Jess. There are worse kinds of crazy than what Hanley's talking about. I mean, setting aside your skepticism, and looking at his story from a different point of view, you begin to let in something that's truly amazing, even if it *is* completely fetched."

"What do you mean?"

"If you listen to what Hanley's really trying to say, it's gorgeous, Jess. What he's telling us? It's beautiful, if you let it in."

Jess shook her head. "Let what in, Martin? What is Hanley saying, in all his crazy talk, that could possibly be considered anything other than nuts, let alone *beautiful*?" she scoffed, but he quickly cut her off.

"That we were made for a purpose."

She stared at him, stunned. His simple statement caught her completely off-guard. Martin didn't skip a beat, launching immediately forward.

"A purpose that, if you really look at it, makes us heroes, Jess... *Saviors*. Not freaks. I mean... it's a nice thought," he sighed. "A beautiful idea."

Martin's focus drifted, his eyes tearing up. He smiled at Jess, the tears making his eyes shine. He quickly blinked them away. *Heh, just like a man*, she thought, *too tough to actually cry*. Then she felt bad for thinking her thoughts, again. She sighed and nodded. She even found herself tearing up a bit, she couldn't help it. But she still didn't believe Hanley, and she summed up Martin's beliefs as simple desperation to try and make sense out of everything he'd already been through. A sort of coping mechanism of sorts, she reasoned. Martin sighed, resigning himself to her continued logical reasoning and skepticism.

"Regardless, Hanley's right about the little girl. I've heard it in the doctor's thoughts. Crazy or not, he's actually got a pretty decent escape plan."

"Wait, you mean, you didn't tell Hanley about the little girl? If you didn't tell him, then how did he—?"

"Jess," he whispered, closing his eyes.

"What?"

"I'm sorry, the doctor's watching and getting suspicious, forgive me."

"What?"

Before she realized what was happening, Martin leaned in and kissed her gently on the lips. She resisted at first, but even if her mind rebelled, her body did not. She kissed him back. They stayed that way for several moments, until Martin pulled away. He sat for a moment, as if listening to something Jess couldn't hear.

"He thinks we like each other," he whispered, sounding sad. "Thanks."

A tear slipped down his cheek.

"I'm sorry," Jess said, seeing the sadness in Martin's face, and shocked at seeing him cry. "Martin, I would never..." she faltered, feeling infinitely guilty. "I mean, I didn't—"

"No." He smiled weakly. "It's okay. He's not watching anymore, so it worked. No interrogation of this conversation. Unfortunately, there will still be consequences."

"What do you mean?"

"Nothing," Martin said again, still sounding sad, although, Jess didn't understand why.

"How many people know about Hanley's plan?" she asked, eager to steer away from the kissing incident.

"Me, you. He told Earl, you told Alma. Jesus knows as well."

"That's it?"

"That's it. We need to tell Aaron. Malcolm and Jenny should be given a heads-up, too."

Jess nodded. Martin looked at her in concern.

"Talk to Hanley some more. He can help you deal with what's coming. You know... he's got it way more together than anyone gives him credit for."

Martin stood and walked out of the room. Jess watched him go, feeling more lost than she'd ever been in her life.

***

Late that afternoon, Jess arrived at her usual training session, just before dinner. She always trained in the orchard, although the trees were flattened and black by that point, most of them crumbled to ash. What began as a beautiful, green, citrus grove was now a blackened, decimated crescent of destruction that fanned out in front of Jess for over the length of a football field.

Dr. M. had assured her several weeks earlier, that, although the compression wave's heat only affected things physically to that distance, the EMP continued traveling much further. If she wanted to, he told her that day, she could knock out all power and electronic equipment for over a mile, in whatever direction she faced.

"Take out the right power grid, and you'd get what they call the *waterfall effect*. In the right place, at the right time, you could take out the power to the entire Eastern seaboard."

"Why would I ever want to do that?" Jess replied, attempting to sound uninterested.

"I don't know," Dr. M. laughed, shrugging. "But it must be nice, having that feeling? Knowing you hold that kind of power at your fingertips?"

"Not really." She had resigned herself, long ago, that no matter how 'friendly' they got along with one another, she would never give the doctor as much as an inch of satisfaction. And she would never call him her friend.

"That's my firecracker," the doctor had smiled.

Now, as Dr. M. approached her in the blackened field, Jess was surprised. The last few weeks of training, she'd been able to use her powers without the help of a technician, or the good Doctor himself. She'd simply gone out into the orchard, what was left of it, and sent out a pulse. Then she went back inside, as Dr. M. instructed her to, and they discussed her progress. Today, he held something in his hand, smiling.

"Hello, Jessica." He sounded too cheerful by far.

"What's going on?"

"Well, you're progressing very well." He reached her and stopped. "Performing independently, without a technician or trigger."

Jessica nodded, attempting to seem disinterested, despite the frantic pounding of her heart.

"It's time to move on to your next level of training," Dr. M. continued. "It's called a trust exercise. Have you ever played one of those?"

"No, not really."

"That's too bad, it can be very exhilarating. A real *rush.*"

Dr. M. stared at Jess for several moments, and she stared back. Neither spoke—at a standoff—until the doctor finally broke the silence.

"Well, we're going to play a trust game today." Dr. M. held the blindfold out to her.

He shook the material, indicating he wanted her to take it. She didn't move, glaring in defiance.

"Take the blindfold, Jessica. It won't bite you," the doctor said.

"No."

"Now, I know it may seem scary, at first," Dr. M. said, his voice chiding. "But that's why it's called an *exercise.* Trust is difficult. It takes time to build. But the first step is putting on the blindfold, Jessica."

"*No.*"

"Why not?"

"Why do I even need to do some stupid trust exercise, anyway? I can already pulse without a trigger. What more training do I need?"

An odd smile played at the corners of Dr. M.'s lips. The hand holding the blindfold slowly lowered.

"You're right, Jessica. Your training has progressed nicely, and much faster than even I had anticipated."

She frowned.

"And I realized, what with you being a little firecracker and all, that you most likely would refuse to do this exercise. Unfortunately for you, without it, we have to jump to the next exercise."

He paused, his eyes cold and calculating. When he spoke next, Jess's blood froze.

"It has come to my attention that you and Aaron have gotten rather close."

"No, not really."

Her response came far too quickly. Dr. M. smiled.

"I encourage friendships in The Society. It makes the days go by quicker, doesn't it? Look, Jessica, you may be young, you may even be naïve, but there comes a time when everyone must grow up. That day for you is *today*. Do you understand what I'm talking about?"

"No," her voice trembled. She felt like she was dreaming.

"I think you do."

She hated the sound of his voice. Jess wanted to obliterate him on the spot, to leave him little more than a burn mark on the ground, ashes in the air.

"You knew this day would come, and I knew you would not go willingly. I know you so well, Jess."

"You don't know me at all," she spat. "And don't call me that!"

"I know you well enough. I know that if I want to, I can get you to do what I ask."

"No," Jess said. "I told you—I don't take orders."

"Not even to save Aaron's life?"

"You wouldn't do that."

"I wouldn't? Really? What use is Aaron to me, hmm? Tell me, Jessica. Do you really think I want to spend all day long staring at rainbow-colored flowers? Aaron is useless to me. Except when it comes to you."

"Kill him, see if I care." It was a pathetic attempt at apathy, and she knew it.

Dr. M. offered a snide, disbelieving smile.

"You *would* care. We both know that. And if you don't, well, maybe next time I'd take aim at our dear Martin."

"I hate you." Tears of anger welled up in her eyes but did not fall. "I hate you so much. You're nothing but a filthy liar."

"How so?" the doctor asked. He did not smile.

"You pretended to care about me!" Jess screamed. "You tried to tell me you're not a bad man, but you are. You've got a little girl in here, you bastard!"

"Sarah?" The doctor sounded disturbed. "That's right. But you think you know everything, Jessica? You don't. Let me tell you about that little girl. Her parents *died* last week in a car accident. A drunk driver. Sarah was at home with the babysitter. She was an only child, with no extended family. No surviving relatives. All she had was her parents, and now they're gone. She would have spent the rest of her childhood being bandied around one foster home and the next. So, I took her in."

"You're lying!" She shook her head, yelling. "I don't believe a word you say. You don't care about anyone. I bet you had her parents killed. I bet you *knew* there were children in that school when you sent Rachel Harley in there!"

These statements caught the doctor off-guard. He stepped backward, in shock, stumbling, nearly losing his balance. His face blanched, his mouth falling open. He stared at Jess with what appeared to be genuine pain in his eyes. *It's an act, I know it is!* She refused to believe this man felt anything like remorse. She fought back her natural compassion and tendency to reciprocate, biting back tears, in shame and anger. Recomposing herself, she rallied to the doctor's tear-filled eyes with a look of fired vitriol, offering a sneer of a smile, all but challenging him to prove her wrong.

"Is that what you believe, Jessica? Is that what you think of me?"

"Yes," she spat.

"I'm telling you the truth, Jess."

"Don't call me that! You're a liar. I know it."

"What do you think you know?"

"What about Alma's sister?"

"You know about her?" he didn't sound surprised.

"What about Martin's wife?"

"You know about *her?*" This time his voice sounded startled. He shook his head. "It wasn't my choice to use that threat."

"Shut up!" Jess yelled, and she spat in the doctor's face.

A long silence passed between them. Dr. M. slowly wiped her spittle from his cheek, looking shocked and dejected. Then a slow fire sparked and kindled in his eyes. Jess shrank away from him, but he stepped forward, grabbing her arm, gesturing wildly at the surrounding orchard.

"Look at this place! I have given you *everything*, Jessica. Look at what you've done! I brought you here, granted you unimaginable powers, and all you can do is spit in my face?! Free room and board, friends to keep you company, you can have anything you want!"

"Except freedom!"

Something in his eyes broke. His voice sounded pleading.

"Freedom? What is that, Jess, huh? Tell me, because I'd sure as hell love to know. What is freedom? The chance to work in the mall? Never own a car, barely afford your rent each month? Is freedom walking by a bum every day and never once giving him a single dollar?"

She flinched, looking confused.

"I told you I know everything about you, Jess. Things you probably never realized about yourself. You stand there and judge me, when you have no clue what it's like to be in *my* shoes, to face the decisions *I've* had to make. I don't know you, right? But you think you know *me*? Go ahead and tell yourself you're a good person, but you're no better than anyone else, including me."

The doctor's voice suddenly changed, from pleading to angry, in a heartbeat.

"You have power at your fingertips, and you can't even appreciate that. You sure as hell didn't appreciate your own life. You never aspired to be anything. The best you could do was bake cookies. Well, bravo!"

Dr. M. clapped, his face flushed with rage.

"You were *nothing* before you came here. If anything, I've given you more freedom here than you ever could have had in your old, miserable, useless life."

Jess started to cry out loud, the tears spilling down her cheeks. She crumpled to the ground, her legs buckling beneath her. Dr. M. threw his head up and looked at the sky in exasperation, then stooped down next to her.

"Cry all you want, Jessica, it won't help. You will do what I ask of you, because you *do* care about the people inside this facility. You don't want to hurt anyone, but it's easier to hurt someone you'll never meet than watch someone you care about suffer in pain, isn't that right? So... try this one on for size... You do what I tell you from now on, without arguing—or I'll bring Martin's wife here, and have her killed in front of him, while I make you watch—and he'll *know* exactly who it was that caused it all to happen."

Jess looked up at Dr. M. in horror and disbelief.

"Play time is over, Jess. No more games."

"Please don't do this to me," she sobbed.

The doctor looked away briefly, then back down at her.

"I don't think you fully understand the pressure I'm under, Jess—to perform, to *produce*. Nor the danger, believe it or not, that *you*, and everyone else inside this facility is in. And just as you can be persuaded to succeed, so can I. I have been heavily persuaded over the years, in various ways. You have no idea wh—"

"Shut up."

Dr. M. attempted one more time to console her, stooping to place his hand on her shoulder. She pushed it away.

He stood, sighing, and threw the blindfold down on the ground in front of her before stalking away, leaving her alone in the decimated orchard. She couldn't move to stand, only pulled her knees up to her chest and hugged herself, rocking back and forth, as the sun began to set.

9

That evening, Jess went to the cafeteria later than usual—almost ten o'clock at night, despite the fact she was starving. She didn't want to run into anyone she knew.

She was relieved to see that there were only three people in the cafeteria. Jesus was there, and Malcolm and Jenny sat together at another table. Jess had heard so much about them but had never talked to them. They kept to themselves.

She went to the hotplates and loaded up on fettuccini with chicken, and a couple of pieces of garlic toast. She sat down at a table by herself. After a few minutes, Jesus came and sat with her.

She'd learned through previous conversations that although Jesus was a legal citizen, his mother had immigrated from Venezuela in the mid-sixties. Jesus had inherited his mother's accent. Somehow, Jess felt the foreign-sounding dialect only added to his adopted persona. She ignored him and kept eating.

"I listened to Hanley," he said. "I think he's crazy, but, maybe he can get us out of here."

Jesus grew quiet, looking over his shoulder at the couple at the table several yards from them. He smiled.

"It must be nice, having family inside here."

"Family?"

Jess frowned, looking at him, then over at Malcolm and Jenny. Jesus saw her confusion.

"You didn't know? Malcolm and Jenny are father and daughter."

"Father and daughter?" Jess continued to frown. She was suddenly embarrassed for having thought they were a couple.

"Yeah. It's unusual for more than one person in a family to have the gene, I guess, but there they are. I guess they were special."

"Malcolm can float, right?"

"Yeah, and Jenny can blow things up."

Jess nodded and looked at them again.

"Wow, father and daughter. I thought they were a couple." She laughed, shaking her head, blushing. "And they both have powers..." she mused.

"Yeah. Makes you wonder, at least, I do. Could my father walk on water?"

"Huh," Jess mused. "So, to your father, you're missing?"

"No. My dad left before I was even born. And my mother is dead now, but she raised me without my dad. She was all I had. She raised me all alone then she got sick and died. That was two years ago."

"I'm sorry."

"That's okay. What about you, who did you leave behind?"

"Just my mother and my stepfather."

"Do you think they miss you?"

"I doubt it. I hadn't spoken to my mother in over four years. I left when I was eighteen and never looked back."

"That's sad," Jesus mused. "I loved my mother so much. When she died, I took it bad. Pulled away from any friends I had, which wasn't too many. Where I came from, the bad part of the city, you're not cool if you like to read."

"You do spend a lot of time in the library." Jess smiled. She didn't even think to ask him what city he'd come from.

"Yeah, well, I was always that way, you know? You don't like to read?"

"Sure, I do, it's just… I guess I never really do."

"Then you don't like to read."

"Yes, I do."

"No," he said. "If you like doing something, then you do it."

"Well…" Jess didn't know what to say in response to that.

"You should try to read more. It's a great way to *escape*." His voice reduced to a subtle whisper.

"You don't have to talk in code, Jesus. I know what you're talking about. As long as we don't talk too loud, I don't think the camera mics can pick us up."

Jesus nodded.

"What do you think about everything?" she asked.

"I don't know. Hanley says we can get out of here. It sounds like a good plan."

"Yeah, but do you think he's crazy?"

"What does it matter?"

"How can you even ask that? Are you willing to break out of here and risk everything on the word of a loony?"

"What choice do I have? It's either that, or stay here, forever."

"But if Hanley's wrong, or just plain crazy, we'll be walking targets."

"Not with the girl."

"If she can really do what Hanley says she can, then maybe we'll escape here without a bullet ever flying. But if Hanley's crazy, we're dead, Jesus. Have you listened to some of the junk he's been spewing? If there's no ship waiting to whisk us away from here, which, no offense, sounds like a fairy tale ending to me, then we'll be sitting ducks. You're telling me that little girl can keep us safe every day, every hour? That's impossible. If we run, and there's no one waiting to rescue us, we're screwed, Jesus."

"Better free and dead, than alive and chained."

She recoiled. "You mean that?"

Jesus nodded, then smiled. "What if Hanley *is* right, have you ever thought about that?"

"Hanley can't be right."

"Why not?"

"Because, if he is, everything I believe in will be gone."

"I don't follow you."

"Dr. M. said the gene was put into us, that we were *made*. It's hard enough for me to accept that. If there really are aliens out there, waiting for us, then… then…"

Jess's chin quivered, and she teared up, not even aware, as Jesus looked on sympathetically, his own eyes tearing up in reaction. He suffered from the same reciprocal compassion that she contained.

"Then there's no God," she whispered.

A tear finally brimmed over and silently slipped down her cheek. She swiped at it, almost angrily, but she also seemed embarrassed and bitter.

"That's not true," Jesus said, his voice soothing and gentle. "Maybe this is all part of God's plan? Maybe it's fate, and He is in control of it all?"

"You're just trying to rationalize."

"So, what if I am? It doesn't mean I'm not right. Right?"

"It doesn't mean you're not wrong, either."

"All this craziness is going on around you," Jesus laughed, "and you want to get into a theological debate?"

"Why is that funny?"

"It just is. If you want to believe in God, Jess, *believe in God*. Nothing that happens, nothing you learn, can ever take that away. Whether you believe there are aliens out there or not shouldn't matter. Even if there are, that doesn't take your God away."

"It doesn't?"

"The only thing that can take your God away, Jess, is *you*."

"This, coming from a man named *Jesus*. Is that supposed to be an omen?"

"Only if you want it to be. But, aliens or no, I believe Hanley is right about the girl. And I believe in choice."

"Choice?" Jess frowned.

"If we choose to try and escape, we might be killed. But even if we do, we'll be choosing it. Here, there's no choice. Eventually, we will all be forced to kill, or be killed. I'd rather die trying to win my freedom than stay here, locked away. This is no kind of life. Is staying here worth living for, Jess? If it means killing people?"

"You wanna bring God into this, Jesus? Why would God allow this, huh? Why isn't He protecting us?"

"Maybe He is, by providing a way for us to escape."

"So, now you believe that Hanley's crazy plan is part of God's design? You're crazier than he is!"

"Perhaps. You have to decide if this is all a plan, or just random."

"I used to believe that *nothing's* random."

"Well there's your answer, then."

"Just like that?"

"Just like that," Jesus smiled. "At any rate, we *need* you. If you don't go with us, you'll be choosing for everyone else. Do you want to be the one responsible for keeping everyone in this place, just because you're afraid?"

"I'm not afraid."

"Sure, you are, and so is everyone else. But we all *believe*. We feel it deep down inside, don't you? That whatever's outside these walls, we were not meant to be locked up inside them."

Jess fell silent, thinking. Jesus watched her closely.

"You know, I also read the Bible," he said. "With a name like mine, how could I not? I was raised Catholic."

"I thought Jesus was your nickname?"

"It is, because of my ability, but in my old life? My name was Matthew. Matthias, in fact, but it's still a biblical name, however you pronounce it. I remember a part of Scripture I read, once, when I was fifteen. I never forgot it: *When I was a child, I talked like a child, I thought like a child, I reasoned like a child. When I became a man, I put childish ways behind me.*"

Jesus shook his head, smiling.

"I thought I understood that Scripture, about not being a child anymore. I thought it was about growing up. Now I know the true meaning of those words—it's not about growing up, Jess—it's about finding *purpose*. First Corinthians, it's all about love, and hope, and believing that you have a purpose. If you believe your purpose is to be here, then stay. Otherwise, *come with us.*"

"*And now these three remain: faith, hope and love. But the greatest of these is love*," Jess said, a tear slipping down her cheek.

"What?"

"That's the last line in your Scripture."

"There is no love inside here, save for the people you care about, Jess. I believe Hanley, and I believe we all have a purpose. What do *you* believe?"

"I know I don't want to be forced to kill anyone, and if I stay here, that will happen."

"Then you'll come?" Jesus looked hopeful.

"Yes," she said, wiping another tear away.

"And you'll be all right with your God?"

"He's yours too, Jesus. We both read the same Bible."

"Yes, but God is someone different in each person's mind. Your God is not mine. He belongs only to you. Remember... No one can ever take that away."

Jess smiled and nodded. Jesus relaxed, smiling. Then he laughed.

"What?" she asked.

Jesus chuckled. "I guess you do read, after all."

***

The next morning, at breakfast, Jess looked for Aaron, but he wasn't there. She felt a brief flutter of panic, recalling what Dr. M. had said: *What use is he to me?* Martin passed by, speaking quickly.

"Aaron's fine, he's just too embarrassed to see you. Hanley wants to talk."

He sat in the corner, at his usual table. On the way, she saw Jesus, who gave her a warm smile, then went back to the book he was reading. Alma saw Jess and immediately got up and followed, sitting down next to her, across from Hanley.

"Oh, great," Hanley said, sounding amicable. "Hey, Alma. So... does she know?" Hanley asked, leaning towards Jess.

"I'm right here, Hanley." Alma rolled her eyes.

"She knows," Jess said.

"Yeah, aliens, whatever, I don't care. All I care about is getting outta here. If you have a way to do that, I'm in. Anything to see my sister."

"That's no problem," Hanley said. "We can pick her up on our way out. Your sister and Martin's wife. Deal?"

Hanley was so matter-of-fact, Alma and Jess stared at him, not knowing how to respond. Alma audibly swallowed as her eyes filled with tears.

"You'll make sure I can get to her?"

"Yep," Hanley smiled warmly. "It's all part of the plan."

"The plan to get out of here," Jess said, attempting to steer the conversation back to reality.

Hanley nodded. Alma nodded back.

"Then I'm in," she said, wiping her tears away.

"Great," Hanley's smile stiffened. "That's great to hear, Alma. Um, but I kind of need to talk to Jess… alone."

Hanley stared at Alma for several long moments, before she responded.

"Oh, right. Okay. Well, see you later then, Jessica?"

"Sure," Jess said. "And, you can call me Jess, if you want to."

"Oh," Alma smiled, blushing. "Cool. Bye."

Hanley smiled and waved after Alma, wiggling his fingers. Then he rolled his eyes, turning back to Jess.

"Is she lezzing out on me?"

"How should I know? I can't read her mind. I only know what Martin tells me."

Jess glanced over at Martin's table. As usual, he had his back to everyone. Despite this, he raised his right hand and gave a thumbs-up to what appeared to be no one.

"Oh, God, she *is*?"

Martin gave Jess a resounding thumbs-up, thrusting his hand even higher into the air. His shoulders shook. Jess looked back at Hanley, bewildered.

"Is he laughing at me?"

"It would appear so."

"Well, it's not funny, *either of you.*"

"You don't have to raise your voice, he can hear you just fine. The poor bastard can't help it. He picks up on everything, even from other rooms. Sometimes from the other side of the building."

"Really?" Jess glanced back over at Martin, who nodded emphatically.

"That sucks," she said. Martin nodded even harder.

"Yep, it sure does," Hanley said. "He hears every thought anyone ever has, including when he's having a particularly bad hair day."

They both looked over at Martin, who raised his right hand again, flipping them off. They both broke out in wild laughter.

"He's so vain," Hanley laughed, tears in his eyes.

"Well, so am I," Jess said, shaking her head. "I mean, it took him telling Dr. M. that if Alma called me 'fat', I'd pulse."

"Seriously? I thought you did that because she pushed you?"

"No, it was the 'fat' thing."

"Huh." Hanley looked Jess up and down. "I'll try and keep that in mind. And by the way, you're not fat."

"Thank you. And not anymore, I'm not. Not now that I'm pulsing several times a week."

"I'm not even going to point out the sexual innuendos one could infer from that statement."

"*Hanley!*"

Jess turned red. He broke out in gales of laughter, and she soon followed. On the other side of the room, Martin laughed as well.

A few minutes later, after all three of them recovered, Hanley asked Jess to take a walk with him.

"Where are we going?"

"You'll see."

***

Out in the hallway, Hanley raised one devious eyebrow, and said, "*My* courtyard." They both followed the red arrows to a door. Hanley opened it, and Jess found herself in a courtyard filled with beautiful, flowering trees and bushes. It was large, surrounded on all four sides by the building. Jess recognized it, seeing the tall panels of glass on one side, as the courtyard outside the small cafeteria.

"I thought you weren't allowed outside."

"I'm not. They're afraid I'd melt the fence. This isn't outside—it's a courtyard—a nice little playpen they built especially for me, so I could still see the sun, occasionally."

"They built this for you?"

"Yep. You're forgetting I've been here a long time, Jess."

"I'm sorry."

"It's okay. I've gotten used to it. Some of it, anyhow. It definitely got better once they started allowing people to mingle."

"What do you mean?"

"I've been here since the beginning. At first, they didn't allow anyone to interact. They kept everyone in separate rooms, completely cut off. But they found that after a while, we weren't faring too well. People need other people, Jess. Without human interaction…" he shook his head. "Well, we need friends, people to talk to. We need people we can relate to. So, they changed things, invented the groundwork for The Society. Unfortunately, it has some negative aspects as well."

"Why are we here?"

"I want to talk to you about a few things. What do you say we sit down?"

"Okay."

They both sat down on the grass. Hanley looked at Jess with concern.

"It can't be that bad," she said.

"It might be, it might not. I'm not sure how you'll take it."

"Then, just say it."

"Okay. I know about what happened between you and the doctor the other day."

"If Martin told you—"

"Martin didn't tell me anything. I know because I've been here since the beginning, and I know how this show goes. What Dr. M. told you, you'd better believe."

"What? I don't understand."

"Sarah's our way out of here, without getting shot," Hanley said. "But she's new here, and she's a kid. She's not gonna have any amount of control over her powers for a while, and I'm talking months, here."

"Okay, so?"

Hanley looked at Jess with tears in his eyes.

"Well, *what*?"

"Dr. M.'s ready to start sending you out into the field."

Jess grew quiet, remembering what the doctor had said about Martin's wife.

"If I don't do what he tells me to, he said he'll kill Martin's wife, and probably Aaron, too."

"I know, Jess. I know what Dr. M. told you, because Martin knows. He knows about the threat against his wife. Dr. M.'s used that one on me before, too."

"He's sent you out into the field?"

"Jess, I've been here for ten years, remember? I've been going out in the field for so long, I don't even remember all the things I've done."

"He makes you kill people?"

Hanley grew quiet then, hanging his head. He began to sob. Jess put her hand on his back, trying to console him.

"Hanley, I'm sorry."

After several minutes, Hanley stopped crying and spoke to her again.

"It's hard, Jess… making that choice. *Choice*… what a laugh. There's no choice. He gets you in here, with this small group of people. *The Society,* he calls it. I hate that. And he knows you'll end up caring about them. How can you not? These people in here? They're all you have. You end up loving them like they're your family. So, when it comes to making a choice between taking orders from the doctor, or watching a friend die, what else are you supposed to do?

"It doesn't make it any easier to live with, though. You do it to save your friends, then you can't even look them in the eye. You feel bitter towards them, and it's not *their* fault. Your head, it starts going in circles. You start thinking you can escape, or maybe Dr. M. isn't serious, maybe he's just bluffing. So, you decide to call him on it."

"Hanley, what are you talking about?" Jess whispered. Hanley grew very quiet then, and in the silence, Jess felt a chill creep over her. He looked down at the ground as he spoke.

"I was in here two years. Then this woman came. Young, beautiful. I was younger then, too. She could rearrange molecules. If you broke a plate, she could fix it. Or, she could take a person apart, one tiny piece at a time. She was *powerful*. I loved her, and she loved me. Dr. M. saw that, and he used it. He wanted me to melt a car, in a motorcade. Not here; in some foreign country. I don't even know where. I wore the blindfold, you see? I didn't want to do it. I didn't want to be the one responsible. I didn't want to kill anyone.

"He said he'd kill her... *Angelique*. I decided he would never really do that, considering what she could do. She had a sister, though. She loved her sister so much, talked about her all the time. It killed her to be locked up in this place. Just like Alma, come to think of it."

Hanley shook his head.

"Dr. M. said he'd kill Angelique if I didn't do what he said. He never said anything about her sister. They flew me there, put me into position, and I did nothing.

"When I got back, Dr. M. was so angry he took me and Angelique into a room. There was a large window, and on the other side, was a room, with this girl, maybe about nineteen-years-old. Angelique started screaming. It was her sister. And a technician, or somebody, walked right up to that girl, and shot her in the head. They killed her, right in front of Angelique's eyes. And it was *my* fault."

"Jeezus," Jess whispered. "That wasn't fair. He didn't tell you he'd do that."

"No, but I should have known," Hanley said. "I knew he would never kill Angelique, but I just—I just didn't realize..."

He hung his head and fell quiet for several moments before continuing. "Angelique was beyond consoling. She was completely despondent. Then, one day, in the hallway, I saw her just standing there, with this look on her face. She saw me, and smiled, said she'd found a way *out*. I didn't know what she was talking about... then I watched her take herself apart, piece by piece..."

"Oh my God... Hanley... I'm so sorry."

"So am I," he said, smiling through his tears. "It hurts, knowing you've killed people. But trust me, Jess, it's ten times harder to live with the death of a friend in here. You're never free of it. And Dr. M. doesn't always play by the rules. He doesn't always tell you who he might kill if you don't cooperate. Sometimes he doesn't even give you that chance."

"But it cost him, too," Jess said, sounding angry. "He lost Angelique. He made a mistake."

"Did he? He got me to do whatever he asked, from that day on."

They sat in silence for several minutes. Then Hanley sighed.

"Do what he tells you, Jess, and don't cross him. If he tells you he'll kill Martin's wife, he means it. And when he tells you he doesn't care about Aaron at all, he means that, too."

"Why are you telling me this? We're getting out of here, remember? No one has to kill anyone ever again."

"I'm telling you because of Sarah. We can't leave till she's ready. Dr. M.'s ready to start using you *now*."

Jess sat looking at Hanley, her eyes wide. Hanley looked back, sadness filling his own.

"You're about to change in ways no one should ever have to. I wish I could get us all out of here before that ever happens, but I can't. I know what kind of ugliness you'll have to face, and it kills me."

"Hanley" Jess was barely able to strain out a whisper.

"I *see* you, Jess, how *pure* you are, how naïve. In just a few short days, you're going to lose all of that."

"What's so good about being naïve? It makes me stupid."

"No, it doesn't. It's part of who you are, wanting to believe the best in people, finding it impossible to believe anyone could really be so *cruel*. But they are, and you need to realize that. Not the way I did, I hope."

"I know Dr. M. is evil," Jess said. "I can see it in his eyes."

"Living with blood on your hands, though, Jess… you'll be different. I *know* you will. Just like I was, and so many people in here. You'll pull away, like everyone else.

"Why do you think so many people eat alone? Why do you think it is you haven't even met or spoken to Malcolm or Jenny? No one wants to risk getting close to anyone.

"Dr. M. relishes the fact that Aaron glommed onto you so quick. It gives him more ammunition to use. And Aaron's never had to face what a lot of us have. His power isn't useful. The only reason he's still here is because he'll try to make friends with anyone new, who doesn't know any better. He has no clue, and neither do any of the newbies that come into this place. Aaron's lonely and Dr. M. knows that. All I can do is sit and watch it happen."

"I'll be okay, Hanley."

"No, you won't. You're about to go down the rabbit hole," Hanley smiled weakly. "I just need you to know before it happens: There is *hope*. It won't be forever, and certainly not ten years.

"When I first went down that dark path, I had no hope. As far as I know, I was the first person in here. The Graylings didn't even contact me until after Angelique. Even then, they couldn't tell me how long before I'd get out. They need us *all*, Jess. And they can't risk any of us getting killed while trying to escape. They certainly can't attack any of the guards."

"Hanley, please."

"Fine," Hanley said. "You don't believe. No one does. I'm not crazy, Jess. We *can* get out of here."

She looked at Hanley with sympathy. Martin had told her that Hanley believed everything he said. At least now she understood why.

10

Hanley and Jess sat in the courtyard for a while longer, then parted ways. Jess returned to her room, wanting to be alone.

After a while, however, she grew anxious to talk to Aaron. She'd been avoiding him up till now, to give him space, but she needed to see him.

She left her room and stood in the hallway.

"Aaron's room."

The red arrows lit her way. She'd been to his room before, but only a few times. No one really hung out in each other's rooms. There was nothing to do in them, and they all looked identical.

Jess reached his door and knocked. No answer. She knocked again. Still nothing. She knocked a final time, and then, just as she turned to leave, the door opened. Aaron looked down at the floor.

"Hey," he said.

"Hey. I haven't seen you. A lot has happened. Can we talk?"

"Um, I guess."

"Okay, but I could really use some fresh air. The Atrium?"

"Sure."

As they followed the arrows, Jess couldn't help but bring up the elephant in the room.

"I didn't know you felt that way," she began awkwardly, "about me. I'm sorry."

"You knew I liked you."

"Yeah, I did, but... I didn't know how much."

"Hanley made it sound worse than it is."

"Worse? Is it bad?"

Aaron stopped walking and sighed, looking away from her. Her heart broke for him.

"Aaron, I'm sorry, okay?"

"For what, not feeling the same way? It's okay, I understand."

"No, you don't. It's not that I wouldn't like you, it's just, in here, with everything that's going on? I can't even think about liking someone. My head's too crazy."

"That's a lie, and you know it."

"What?"

"You like Martin."

"No, I don't, he's married."

"Yes, you do," Aaron said, not even fazed by Jess's comment about Martin being married.

"No, I *don't*."

"Then why did I see the two of you kissing, huh?"

Jess sighed and closed her eyes. *He saw that?* She couldn't explain that to him inside the building. She grabbed his arm and started to walk again, following the arrows, but Aaron pulled his arm out of her hand.

"Forget it, I'm done with this."

"Aaron, wait!"

Her tone caused Aaron to stop in his tracks. He turned and saw she was on the verge of tears.

"I need to talk to you," she said, her voice trembling even more. "Please."

"Okay," he said, after a short pause.

They reached the Atrium door and walked out into the field. There, where she knew it was safe to talk, she told Aaron everything that had happened after he left the table the morning before, including what happened in her training exercise with Dr. M., and the threats on Aaron and Martin's wife.

She told him what Martin had said about Hanley, and that Dr. M. had seen them talking, and that was why he'd kissed her.

Aaron seemed skeptical at first. He noticeably relaxed, however, as she continued explaining about Martin; the look on his face, the tears in his eyes, and how much he clearly loved his wife. She then told him about her conversation with Jesus, and that she'd reached her decision to cooperate in whatever escape plan was being cooked up. Finally, she told him about Hanley. She struggled with this part, as she felt the conversation with Hanley was personal, perhaps even meant to be confidential, but she *needed* to talk to someone about it, and Aaron was her best friend. Aaron listened to it all, without saying a single word. When she had finished, he still said nothing.

"Well?"

"Well, what?"

"What do you think?"

"I think, if we can all get out of here, great," he shrugged.

"You believe Hanley?"

"No. I think your base fears are dead on. He told you he never heard from these Graylings until after Angelique, right? And you suspect that, perhaps, the stress of Angelique's death somehow caused a mental breakdown?"

"I think there's a good chance," she nodded. "If he's crazy, he wouldn't know it himself. He'd believe it. Who knows, maybe he really does hear voices? That doesn't mean there are aliens. I mean, telling him they'll come and get him? What, so he can escape? It's all so fantastical. I think believing is the only thing that's gotten him through all these years. And Martin can only tell if Hanley believes what he's saying. That doesn't make it true."

"But, he was right about the girl, Sarah. How did Hanley know about her?"

"I don't know. Martin probably told him. He tells Hanley everything he learns. Martin would have heard it from Dr. M's head, I'm sure."

"So, you don't believe we'll be rescued?"

"No, of course not." She closed her eyes and sighed. "But, next week, I'll become a murderer. And I'll have to live with that, for obvious reasons. I don't want to see you hurt, or Martin, either."

"So, you're still planning on leaving here, with everyone else?"

"I'd rather die out there than stay here and go crazy like Hanley, killing people for that maniac-bastard doctor."

"Okay, so, the whole alien thing is a moot point, right?"

"Wrong. I'm okay with leaving, but you aren't. You said so yourself."

"Don't assume so much, Jess."

"So, you'll come?"

"Hey," he shrugged and smiled. "Maybe I can see the ocean again before I die."

"It's not funny, Aaron. If you come with us, we're on the run, just like you said."

Aaron shrugged again, looking Jess dead in the eye. She frowned.

"I don't get it. Last time I told you I was leaving, you tried to talk me out of it. You said it was impossible."

"Last time, the plan wouldn't work," Aaron said. "This time, with Sarah to keep the guns at bay? Yeah, I think we actually have a chance."

"But you said you didn't want to be on the run, that there was no life outside. Now you're willing to go, knowing we'll be hunted down and probably killed? I don't understand."

"Then, why did you bring me out here, Jess?"

"I wanted you to know, for one thing," she said. "And to give you a chance to change your mind."

"Or maybe you were hoping that I'd change yours," he smiled gently down at her. "But I won't do that, Jess. I would never ask you to spend years killing people, simply to keep me alive. If you've made up your mind, I'm not going to try and change it. So… I have to ask… why have you assumed that with a plan to escape, I'd turn the chance down?"

"I wasn't certain if you'd believe Hanley. That changes your whole outlook on the situation, doesn't it?"

"No. Either way, you're going, right? You've accepted that there's no rescue, and you still want a shot at your freedom, if only for a day, right?"

"Yes." She closed her eyes.

"Then, I'm going with you, Jess. No matter what. You say you're probably going to kill someone next week, because you care about me that much. You won't let me be killed. I'd tell you to just let me die, Jess, don't become a murderer, but you wouldn't listen, would you?"

"Aaron—"

"No, Jess. I know it's not just me, I know you want to save Martin from any pain, either. But still... you're going to do something so terrible, so that I can live? Of course, I'm coming with you. The sacrifice you're about to make for me... if I then stay here, locked up, what will that have been for? I'm coming with you, Jess. I care about you too much to let you face this alone."

Jess looked at Aaron and saw the look in his eyes. He was clearly in love with her, and although she cared about him (Dr. M.'s threat could never have been so effective otherwise), she knew she didn't love him back the same way he loved her. He was incredibly loyal, and the best friend she'd ever had, but, even still, friendship was all she felt for him. She was beginning to hate herself for it. As the conversation continued, she felt sick with herself.

"Aaron, you can't go for that reason. You'll *die*, don't you understand?"

"Yeah, Jess, I do. I don't think *you* understand. I'd rather die *with* you, then be here without you."

Aaron's words broke Jess's heart. She'd never had anyone care for her in such a way. She'd had a few idiot boyfriends over the years, but none of them ever seemed to care about her. Yet, suddenly, here was Aaron, standing right in front of her, willing to risk death, to go where she went. If she couldn't love him, she must be made of stone, she reasoned. She'd slept with a few of those jerk boyfriends, even, when she knew they didn't love her, and she certainly wasn't in love with them. But she knew she loved Aaron, and even if that love for him was only as a friend, it was still much more than she'd felt for men she'd laid down in bed with. *Maybe if I just give it a chance, the feelings will come?* she reasoned in her head. *If I just engage with him in that way, surely, I'll start to feel more?*

But she didn't get the chance to reason any further. Aaron kissed her then, and in her guilt, she let him. Her mind reeled but she did not rebuke his advance.

Eventually, she pulled away, and tried to smile. She felt overwhelmed. Again, she reasoned with herself that, perhaps, if she gave it enough time, she'd feel the way he felt. He took her hand, and again, she let him. They walked, holding hands, back into the facility. For all intents and purposes, they appeared to be a couple.

That was the beginning of 'Jess and Aaron'. They didn't hide it from anyone. Dr. M. had already made it clear that he would kill Aaron if she didn't follow his orders. He knew she cared for Aaron. Whether it was as a friend, or eventually more, either way, she didn't want to lose his companionship, and she had already resigned herself to doing the doctor's bidding, so there was no reason to hide.

***

The next few days, Aaron and Jess were inseparable, and she tried to be as happy as he was. They held hands everywhere they went, took long walks in the Atrium, and kissed for hours. Aaron never left her side, except when it was time to sleep, and one night, they even slept in the same bed together, though sleep was all they did.

Jess thought about her last session with the doctor often.

Aaron tried to comfort her as best he could, but Jess's anxiety began to build after the first few days, overpowering the distraction of his love for her.

***

The doctor called for her three days later. She was in Aaron's room. They'd just returned from breakfast. Aaron excused himself to use the bathroom, and as soon as he'd left the room, Jess heard Dr. M.'s voice over the intercom.

"Jessica, leave Aaron's room and go out into the hallway. Follow the arrows."

Jess sat for a moment, stunned. She hadn't expected to hear Dr. M. on Aaron's intercom, addressing her. She stood quickly, her heart pounding. She left Aaron's room, following the arrows for what felt like forever. Eventually, she came to a room and opened the door.

Inside, Dr. M. stood waiting. He greeted her with a warm smile that made Jess feel as if she'd just entered a party, the host eagerly showing her in.

"Good morning, Jessica. How are you feeling?"

"Fine," she said.

"Good, *good.*"

He handed her a gray coat. She took it and held it, looking at him with an empty stare.

"It's cool outside this morning, Jess. Heavy fog, too. Fall's quickly approaching."

"Where are we going?"

"I can't tell you that. Just follow me, and don't speak."

She followed the doctor and looked on in amazement as he tapped the back wall, revealing a door that had been invisible up till that point.

Once through the door, she followed him down a bizarre, green brick corridor. They passed through another door, and her heart skipped a beat. They were outside, and once they rounded the building, she could see that they stood in the same dirt courtyard she'd arrived in on her first day. She looked back at the entrance, and saw the door she'd last walked through, what felt to her like eons ago.

A black sedan waited, just like the one agent Fielding had brought her in. She followed Dr. M. without saying a word, her heart rate still elevated. Mr. Gees waited by the car, whom she also hadn't seen since she first arrived. She was shocked when he opened the passenger door, motioning for her to get in. She looked over at Dr. M. He smiled and nodded.

Mr. Gees got into the driver's seat, and Dr. M. disappeared into the trees. As the car started, Jess buckled her seatbelt, disoriented and confused.

"Where is Dr. M. going? He's not coming?"

She was shocked at how dependent she felt, as if she were a two-year-old in a strange place, who had suddenly been separated from her parent—clingy and lost. Mr. Gees smiled.

"He's coming in a separate car. He'll meet us at the hangar."

"We're going on a plane?"

She was surprised when Mr. Gees nodded. She'd expected either no response, or a shut-down chide, like, "I can't tell you that."

She felt numb as the car began to move, looking back, realizing she'd just walked out of the building she'd been held prisoner in for the last several months.

As they drove, she felt nauseated and disgusted with herself, realizing she'd complied with their orders without a single argument. But then, Dr. M.'s threats echoed in her mind.

She'd already resigned herself to this. Even so, she was shocked at just how easy it was for her to simply go along with everything.

They arrived at a military gate after only a few minutes and were let through after Mr. Gees spoke to the guard.

The car drove a short distance around the base, until they pulled into a large hangar. Mr. Gees got out, then opened Jess's door. She realized she hadn't even bothered trying to open it herself. *Probably locked anyway.*

As she stepped out of the car, a second black sedan pulled up. She saw Dr. M. get out. He quickly walked over and greeted her, smiling. It made Jess sick, especially considering the relief she experienced at seeing him. She followed the doctor to a waiting plane and up the stairs to board.

11

Jess swooned beneath a wave of nostalgia at the 'new-car' smell of the plane's interior. The seats were large, dark leather, arranged in groups of four, with a table in the middle. There were two groups of these, one on either side of the plane.

It made Jess think of old fantasies of what first class might look like. She could see, from the number of seats, that the plane was designed to carry only a few passengers—eight at most—the level of comfort they'd obviously enjoy, the reserve of diplomats or rock stars.

She was instructed by Dr. M. to sit in an aisle seat on the right side of the plane, facing forward, toward the cockpit. Then he disappeared.

After a few minutes of twiddling her thumbs, Jess grew restless. She leaned over to look out the window. Dr. M. quickly reappeared. He leaned across her from the aisle and pulled the shade down. Then he took the seat directly across from her, not making eye contact.

The plane took off almost immediately after. Jess closed her eyes. She'd never been on a plane before. While they were still ascending, Dr. M. spoke.

"It won't crash, Jess. You're too important for that to happen."

She opened her eyes and saw that he held a magazine, his hands trembling. *What in the hell does* **he** *have to be nervous about?* She closed her eyes again, attempting to ignore her fears. After several minutes, the plane finally leveled out, and she began to relax.

"Where are we going?"

"You know I can't tell you that."

"Well, can you at least tell me how long we'll be flying?"

"Seven hours," he said, matter-of-factly. She was surprised.

After about an hour of sitting in silence, the doctor got up. About fifteen minutes later, he reappeared from the back of the plane with a steaming plate of food. She dug into it as if she hadn't eaten in days. She was starving. Dr. M. watched her with amusement.

"Good, eat. You'll need your energy."

Jess finished eating, sated. The doctor left again and took her plate away, bringing back a tall glass of root beer, her favorite. She drank half of it down, then set it on the table in front of her.

"Why are you being so open with me?" she asked.

"What do you mean? You have no idea where we're going, or what you're to do once we get there. If that seems open to you..." he shrugged.

"But, you didn't blindfold me. I sat in the front seat of the car, and—"

"I don't need to blindfold you, Jessica. I already have your compliance, we both know that."

"I guess I just expected something different, is all."

"Like what?"

"I don't know. Men with guns, a huge escort of soldiers, *something*. Not you, and Mr. Gees, and… and… magazines."

The doctor laughed, then got up from his seat across from her and ordered Jess to move over to the window. Once she'd moved, he sat in her old seat, next to her. She looked at him awkwardly, feeling both uncomfortable, yet, strangely relieved as well.

"It's an odd experience, your first time out, Jessica. I realize that. Everything feels strange. You're probably experiencing a great deal of anxiety, just being out of the facility, am I right?"

He looked at her, smiling.

Jess nodded, confused and embarrassed. She didn't want to need the doctor, but she couldn't do this without him.

"What once felt like a prison to you, is now your home," he continued. "And even though you view it as a cage, when you've been there for a certain amount of time, even leaving a cage can cause great distress. It's for this reason that many criminals in prison are repeat offenders. They get so used to prison, they can't deal with life on the outside. They prefer captivity to freedom. It's the same with animals in zoos. Ever noticed how a lot of the fences look so low and flimsy?"

"I'm not an animal," Jess said. "Or a criminal."

"I'm merely trying to tell you that what you're feeling and experiencing is perfectly natural."

He grew quiet. She sat looking straight forward, not making eye contact. When he spoke again, it startled her, making her jump. Dr. M. chuckled briefly as he talked, and she gave him a dirty look.

"You're probably also feeling some very confused emotions towards me, am I right? That you only feel secure when I'm around?"

That was exactly how she felt, though it filled her with shame to admit.

She looked away again, toward the shuttered window flap. She felt the overwhelming urge to cling to him, to embrace him and not let go. At the same time, she also wished she could slap his face hard enough to leave a hand-shaped bruise.

"It's called Stockholm Syndrome. It's when the person being held captive becomes dependent on their captor and begins to identify with them. They begin to feel as if their captor is protecting them, instead of holding them against their will. It's a coping mechanism, perfectly natural in your situation, Jess."

"You're really defining it for me?" The bitterness in her voice was as sharp as a razor blade.

In her indignation, she didn't even realize she'd allowed the doctor to call her Jess without complaint. This had happened several times, in fact, but she'd missed it. He smiled at her again, and it confused her even more.

"I'm not a monster, Jess, and you're far too smart for me to keep you in the dark. I have great respect for you. I want to be up front, share things with you. And, whether you believe me or not, I don't ever want to force you to do things with horrific threats."

"Then, why do you?"

"To make the assignments I'll take you on like this. No blindfolds, no lies. It's much easier this way, isn't it?"

"No, not considering what you had to do to get us to this point."

"Us?" He raised an eyebrow, but still smiled.

"You know what I mean."

"Yes, I do, but it's okay if you don't hate me, Jess. No one said you had to."

"But if I wasn't so docile, you'd have a gun to Aaron's head, right?"

"We don't have to even think about that, so long as you cooperate."

"You sound relieved," she sneered.

"Because I am."

He sighed again and looked at Jess with such *honesty* it drove her crazy. She knew he was only lying to her, yet she found herself wanting to trust him, wanting it as much as she hated herself for it.

"You actually have the nerve to sit there and tell me you're relieved, when I know what you did to Angelique?"

She looked at the doctor and saw complete horror come over him. Then, his face crumbled in utter sadness.

"I'm not a bad person, Jess." It was barely a whisper.

"You're not? You don't think it makes you a bad person, shooting Angelique's sister in front of her face? Just because Hanley wouldn't do what you wanted?" Jess yelled with all her might now. "You killed her sister, and then you caused her to kill herself!"

"He told you about that?" Dr. M.'s voice shook. "I'm surprised... When that happened, Hanley was nearly destroyed."

"Why did you do it?"

"Because I had to, Jessica. The project was new, and I was under extraordinary pressure to perform. I got to keep my baby, so to speak, but I still had to take orders, whether you choose to believe that or not. Don't shake your head, just *listen to me.*

"I take orders, Jess. Where we're going today, do you think I just made up our itinerary? No, of course not. It came to me. I was told where we're going, and what you're supposed to do, what I'm supposed to *make* you do. And if I don't, the project will go to someone else. If I ever fail to perform, I'm out. And believe me, Jess, whoever takes my place will not be as kind."

"You call yourself kind? You're a *murderer!*"

"I have never killed anyone in my life, Jess. Do you hear me?"

"You're being serious?!"

"Yes!"

"Angelique *disintegrated* herself, to get away from *you*, and all the pain you bring. You want to keep trying to explain things to me? Well let me explain something to *you*, Doctor Milbron. You have *murdered people*. Who knows how many? You killed Angelique, even if she took her own life. It was because of what you did to her sister!"

"I never shot her sister!"

He appeared visibly shaken. His hands flexed into fists, his breath quickening. She instinctively shrunk away, upon seeing his fists. He took several moments to compose himself and regain control of his breathing, before speaking again, this time, in a much calmer manner than she would have expected.

"If Hanley told you the whole story, then you know it was a technician that did that. Technician, hell, they're trained soldiers, Jess. They are way more dangerous than I am, than you could ever *think* I am. They'll kill anyone they're ordered to."

"But *you* ordered them to!"

Dr. M. shook his head. "When Hanley failed to perform, I was ordered to entice him in any way I could. I was new to the project then, and Hanley was my first field assignment. I was told by a team of psychologists that a threat of that level was the only way to appeal to compliance.

"Hanley's not a killer, most of you aren't. I can't bribe you with money, I can't give you things. What can I offer you that would get you to follow orders, hmm? Think about it. I was told to make a threat, and I did it. I would never have killed Angelique, of course I wouldn't. I'm not a soldier Jess, I'm just a lackey scientist. But Hanley had no other family, or anyone he cared about. She was the only thing I could use. It was an empty threat, however, and he knew it. But when he wouldn't perform, when they flew him all the way to his destination, and he wouldn't do what he was *supposed* to, they came down on me so hard... they threatened to take over everything. There were threats to me as well."

Jess shook her head. "You were afraid to lose your baby, poor you," she spat. "It was early on, you should have just walked away."

"You're not hearing me, Jess. I told you, you're not the only one being controlled here."

"Lies! Excuses! Mind games!"

"I wouldn't lie to you, Jess!"

"I don't believe you!"

"Damnit, Jess, will you listen to me, *they killed my father!*"

Everything went silent. Jess's world stopped. She shook her head, trying to wake up. The blood rushed in her ears. When the pulsating cacophony finally subsided, she realized to her dawning horror that the doctor was sobbing, his face in his hands. Before she could even think, she placed her hand gently on his shoulder and he desperately grabbed onto it, still covering his face with his other hand. She leaned her head on his shoulder and silently cried with him, their interlaced hands falling to seat-level between them.

They stayed this way for over ten minutes before the worst of the doctor's sobs subsided. It took another several minutes before he finally quieted, seemingly done crying. She'd never heard a man cry that way before in her life. Even Hanley hadn't cried like this. She hadn't even known it to be possible. And unlike any of the doctor's other attempts to communicate with her on a more humane level, this time, she did not doubt his sincerity in the slightest. No one could ever cry in such a manner, so prolonged. She felt his entire body shaking in agony as she kept her head upon his shoulder. *This is real,* she thought. *This isn't an act, this is really him.* Her eyes were still closed when he finally spoke again.

"Much like Hanley, I didn't believe their threats, at first. I refused to even threaten Hanley with killing Angelique, I didn't want to use threats like that, to force anyone to follow my orders. I wanted to do it by befriending them, gaining their trust. But there was no way. I mean... how? For God's sake, we were kidnapping people and locking them away. Turning them into freaks of nature, then forcing them to do the most heinous things imaginable," he gasped. "But it was already too late. I thought I was the king of everything, remember?" He looked at her in pain and desperation. She nodded, giving him what she hoped was a comforting look. He nodded back, sniffling.

"I told you, Jess. By the time I realized what was really happening, and what I had somehow signed onto, it was too late. I knew too much. I either ran the whole thing, or they'd kill me. And once I was running everything, I had to do everything they told me, or they'd kill *my* family. And they did..." he started crying again.

"Don't," she said. "Just don't talk about it anymore. You don't have to."

"You'll never understand, not unless I do, Jess." He gave her a pained look. "I lost my father. They showed me what they could do, and how far they were willing to go," he hitched. "And suddenly, I was threatening Hanley, with the life of Angelique. If I didn't… it was to be my mother next."

Jess closed her eyes, crying again. She'd never seen a grown man cry before, save for Hanley, only recently, but she'd never seen anyone, male or female, cry like this in her whole life. Her heart broke open for the doctor in unspeakable ways, letting all the anger out that she'd been holding inside against him, and all the vitriol, hatred and doubt. Everything dark inside her that she'd ever felt towards this man, now suddenly drained away in an instant. All she felt for him now was compassion and to her shocked amazement, love. In a single moment, what she'd previously believed to be impossible happened. He became her friend.

"I called them on their bluff, and they showed me," he said. "I threatened Hanley. They owned me. But Hanley then made the same mistake that I had. He had to be punished. I had to regain control. My mother was next. I received orders to make good on the threat of a life being lost for his lack of compliance, and it had to be a life he would care about. I couldn't kill Angelique, so they brought her sister in. It wasn't *my* idea Jess, you have to believe that."

She nodded, but he didn't see.

"It's the truth, I swear to you."

"I believe you," she whispered, shaking her head. "But, if you were just taking orders, Martin would know, wouldn't he? He hasn't said anything to me about any of this. He told me you were a terrible man."

"Martin wasn't in the facility then, Jess. This was eight years ago. He's only been there eighteen months. And trust me… something like that… the only way to move on, or even function afterwards, is to bury it away and try never to think about it ever again. So, I didn't. You all needed to fear me, anyway, or I couldn't be effective with the project. I had to become a monster. I had to bury everything I ever was, never think about any of it again, and become horrible Dr. M. I guess I must have succeeded pretty well, if Martin doesn't know any of it. What a gift."

He sounded so bitter, so hateful of himself. And although Jess was still reeling from the sudden turn of events and perceptions—even feelings—she immediately offered her comfort.

"Don't do that to yourself." She grabbed his chin and turned his face to look directly at her. "Do you hear me? Don't do that. Don't hate yourself, *please*."

"Ask me anything you want to know, and I'll tell you," was all he offered back.

She frowned. "What about Martin's wife? Does she even know what happened to him?"

"No, of course not. He went out for cigarettes one night and never returned. She filed a missing person's report, and every night, she waits for him to come home, or the phone to ring, telling her they found him."

"That's so awful," she said, then regretted it. "Oh, I didn't mean—"

"It's okay, Jess. I deserve much more than that. It *is* awful, and so am I. I tried to tell you. I've been trying to tell you... I just didn't know how, and I wasn't ready..."

She frowned at his last words, but he didn't speak again. Several minutes passed in silence before Jess spoke again.

"I don't know how I'm supposed to... *be* around you now." She frowned again.

"You must be surprised by how you feel today, I can only imagine."

"It's just a syndrome, like you said." But it was at that very moment that they both realized she still held his hand. She quickly pulled hers away.

"I think it's more than that, Jess. We've become friends, whether you care to admit that or not."

Jess shook her head, reeling all over again. She felt guilty for what she said next.

"How do I know you're not just playing some stupid game right now, telling me lies?"

"I'm not playing *anything*, I swear to you, Jess. What would it take for you to believe me?"

"You act as if you care about whether I like you or not. Is that what you want? You want me to *like* you?"

"Maybe I do. It's not easy, going through your entire life being teased, taunted, and then *hated*. And then to never have anyone you can talk to or tell, about anything. About any of the pain."

"You want me to *care* about you?" She said this so gently, it wasn't an accusation. She simply needed to hear him say it. But she knew already that she loved him.

"No, I'm not a stupid man. I know you'll never truly care about me."

"I didn't ask what you know, I asked you what you *want*."

She looked at the doctor and he looked right back. Then he leaned forward and kissed her on the lips. It was short and platonic, over in a moment. Then he sat back and looked down at his hands.

She stared at him in complete disbelief. Despite her sudden new revelation of feelings, she hadn't expected him to kiss her at that moment. Her mind went into overdrive. As short as the kiss had been, she hadn't resisted. And unlike with Aaron, where she had to talk herself *into* a romantic situation, here, with the doctor, she tried to reason her way *out* of it, allowing doubt about this man to return with a vengeance. Dr. M. remained quiet for several moments before finally speaking again.

"You know, that's the first time I've kissed a woman in five years," he laughed. "I last kissed a lady technician, and then they changed all the techs I had contact with to men. Guess they don't want me getting distracted. Hell, I live and sleep at the facility just like the rest of you."

He blushed beneath her scrutiny. She balked in disbelief.

"You didn't know? I'm just as much a prisoner as the rest of The Society. I live, eat, sleep and breathe this project. It's my whole life, and right now, that means that *you're* my whole life."

"I think *you* have a syndrome," she said numbly, looking away.

She looked back when she felt his hand over hers. He held it gently.

"Please stop," she said.

"Okay." He let go. "But I'm not a bad man, Jess. I guess I just needed you to know that."

"I still don't believe it," she said, this time not regretting saying so. *He's just playing mind games, like Martin said.* "Not after how cruel you've been. To me and everyone else."

"Well, that actually hurts me."

"It's all a game, isn't it? Some sort of trick? While I'm vulnerable with this Stocks... Stocks-home..."

"Stockholm Syndrome," he chuckled. "It's the name of the city where Patty Hears—"

"Whatever," she cut him off. "You're trying to take advantage of me. Everything you say could be a total lie."

"I'm sure you believe that, despite the fact I'm putting myself in a very vulnerable position. It shifts the dynamic of power, and that's not a good thing for me."

"Then why tell me everything you have?"

"Because I'm tired," he sighed. "Maybe I don't think I can keep doing this for very much longer."

"You don't?" She didn't know what to believe.

He looked down at his hands again, and she saw that they were, indeed, trembling, the same way they had been earlier, when he held the magazine.

She frowned, realizing that he'd been nervous before ever broaching any of this conversation with her. She looked at the doctor and saw a lonely, defeated man, full to overflowing with regrets. In a moment of pure sympathy, she spoke without thinking.

"If you could find a way out, would you take it?"

She looked at him with desperation and he looked back into her eyes with an equal longing of burning intensity.

"Yes," he breathed, leaning over and kissing her again, this time for much longer.

This time, the kiss was anything but platonic. There was an energy and a heat to his kiss, and Jess felt a tightness and tingling in the pit of her stomach, helpless to stop the seemingly autonomic response of her body.

And, again, she didn't resist. Her mind was a jumble of conflicting thoughts and emotions. Aaron flitted through her head, and Martin, Hanley; even Rachel, whom she'd never met. She felt so lost and alone, even with Aaron and all her new friends. She felt utterly vulnerable, and this whirlwind of feelings she suddenly had for this horrible man, who now seemed like a victim, could not possibly be real.

Even her feelings for Aaron, which remained platonic, despite her attempt to force a romantic passion inside of her to bloom, and her desperate clinging to him the last few days, were also probably the result of her emotional vulnerability, she reasoned. She finally pulled away. The doctor let her. He continued holding her hand, however. *So warm.* He looked in her eyes, not letting her look away.

"If you had a way out, would you take me with you?" He kept his eyes locked on hers, filled with desperation and longing. "Take me with you, Jess."

"Wh—where?" she stuttered.

"You *know* where."

Could he know about their plans to escape? Or was it all a trick to try and confirm something he'd only suspected? It'd been a miracle that they'd kept it from him this long.

"Okay, I'll make this easier for you, Jess," he continued, his voice not losing its tenderness.

"I know. I know *everything.*"

She pulled away, yanking her hand out of his. He continued speaking, his voice urgent and honest, although, she could not bring herself to believe in him.

"I know what Hanley told you, about the aliens—the plan to use Sarah—your plans to escape, once she has her ability under control."

Jess looked back at him, all her hopes of escape lost, broken in moments. Her eyes filled with tears that quickly spilled down her cheeks. The doctor surprised her by gently wiping them away.

"All these years, I've done what I had to," he said. "And just like you, I had no way out, Jess. Until *you* came."

"How could you know," she cried. "Martin said you couldn't hear us."

"There are mics in the tables that I didn't know about. An operation like this, you think they don't have it down to an exact science?"

"Then, why did you let Alma try to escape? With Rachel, and—" she shuddered, her tears and panic making it difficult to speak.

"The mics were put into place *after* that incident. I was put on leave, temporarily, and they reconstructed things, without my knowledge. Someone else listens to those recordings. If I had no knowledge of it, Martin couldn't know either. It was a *safeguard*."

"When did you find out?" She frowned.

"Yesterday. The audio was supplied to me yesterday."

"And now?"

The doctor sighed. She still saw no trace of malice in his face.

"Now, everything has changed. Now there's a way out—for *all* of us."

12

"You want to *go*?"

"Of course, Jess. There's no life here for *me* in The Society, either. I thought I was helping mankind, but I ended up losing everything, Jess, including myself. And it turns out I'm just a stupid lackey who takes orders from higher up. And there's always a higher up, no matter how high you go. Power is just an illusion. I never had it, not even with you. Because no matter how smart I am, no matter what threats I make, I can't change your mind. I can't change how you feel about me."

"You were going to kill Martin's wife, you would have killed Aaron. Martin read that. How can you expect me to believe you're suddenly a good person now, when a day ago, you were willing to hurt the people I love?"

"I'm not the same person now, Jess. I told you that. I've *changed*."

"In one day?" Her voice trembled, rising.

"Is that so hard to believe? I just explained to you how I became a monster in only one day, Jess. Doesn't that prove anything to you? Believe me, the world can change in a day. Your whole life can change in an hour. Hell, it did! Life can change in a minute, even, Jess. Why can't you let go of the stubborn definitions you hold on everything, over *everyone,* and see that?"

"I don't know what to believe. I don't know what to think."

"Stop thinking, Jess, and tell me what you *feel*. Do you feel that I'm telling you the truth? Do you believe that I want out of that damn place just as much as you? Look at me, Jess! Believe me!"

"You're going to ruin everything, for everyone," she cried. "You want to stop us."

"No, Jess, I don't. I only want to go with you."

"You don't *believe* Hanley, do you?"

He nodded his head.

"Do you have proof?" she asked, searching his eyes, suddenly afraid that he did.

"No," he laughed. "How scientific is that? How genius? But do you remember me telling you how your deviant pseudogene couldn't just happen by accident? And how I told you its existence is proof that you were made?"

Jess nodded, feeling light-headed.

"Well, we wondered how the gene got there," the doctor laughed. "I think Hanley's 'friends' are the explanation." The doctor made quotation marks with his hands, much like Aaron, or even Hanley had done in the past. Jess shook her head again, as the doctor continued.

"So, yeah, Jess, I believe."

"But you're a scientist," she said, numbly. "You're a genius."

"Yes."

"You expect me to believe that you're willing to risk your whole life, your future and everything you've worked so hard to maintain, on the word of Hanley? He's crazy and what's worse, you *made* him that way!"

"That was never my intention, I'm *not* a bad man, Jess."

"Stop saying that, you always say that!"

"Because it's true! It's true, Jess. I want out, and this is the only way. And it's more than I could have ever hoped for. I wanted to help mankind, but this is what mankind has made me into—a killer, a manipulator—a cruel, unfeeling man that you hate so much, you can't even look me in the eye. But I'm tired of the lies. I want out! But just like you, there's no way out if I remain in this world. There's nowhere for me to go, nowhere for me to hide. Up until yesterday, I thought I was trapped, to live this miserable life forever. All that's changed. *I've* changed. Believe me, Jess."

"How?"

"I don't know," he said. "You can ask Martin when we return. He'll read me as soon as I get back to the facility. Then you'll know."

"Just like I believed in him when he didn't even know the tables were mic'd?"

"What will it take for you to believe in me, Jess?"

"I don't know. Proof."

"There is no proof, Jess. You'll deny it all, anything I try to use to prove myself to you, even Martin. What do you *feel*?"

"Confused."

He quickly leaned over, pulling her chin to bring her face to his, and kissed her lips again. His warm breath on her face, the gentle touch of his lips made her want to melt into his arms. He pulled away again, locked on her eyes.

"What do you feel now?"

"Doubt," she said. "How can I ever possibly believe in you?"

"Sometimes, Jess, you just have to go on faith."

She frowned. "That's what Jesus said."

He laughed. "I won't even point out the ridiculous irony in that one."

She surprised herself by laughing. He smiled at her again.

"What about Aaron?" She frowned.

"What about him?"

"You kissed me."

"You kissed me back." He blushed.

"But... I hate you."

"And up until yesterday, I was going to kill Aaron if you didn't do whatever I told you. Today, I'm jealous as all hell of Aaron, flying you on a bogus assignment, kissing you, and asking you if you'll please let me run away with you and your friends, to go live in space with the 'aliens'."

Again, he made quotation marks and Jess laughed. Then she frowned.

"It's a bogus assignment?"

"Well, technically, it *is* a mission, but I told them you weren't ready for anything too grand. Originally, you were going to fry the mainframe computers of a secret military sect in Afghanistan. Now? We're going to knock out a few converter towers in Nepal. Don't ask why. All I can tell you is that you won't be killing anyone, and some U.S. hostages will be coming home very soon, to some very relieved families.

"Sometimes, I really do help mankind out, a little. Very few missions are this way, but it's the only thing that's gotten me through the last ten years."

Without thought, she took his hand in hers, interlacing their fingers. He looked surprised.

"Everything's going to change now, isn't it?" she asked.

"Yes. But you won't be able to convince anyone that I'm not a bad man. You've barely been in the facility for half a year and look how difficult it was for you to change your mind."

"I didn't change my mind."

"You didn't?" He pulled his hand up, which she still held. "What's this then?"

"A consolation."

"Oh."

"So, you believe Hanley's telling the truth? You actually believe— You, The Genius—that there are aliens?"

"You don't?"

"Changing my mind about *you* is one thing, but that? *No.*"

"You really are stubborn, aren't you? You have super-powers, Jess. It's not much more of a leap, is it?"

She gave him a look, eyebrows raised. He sighed.

"Okay, for you I guess it is. But the Evil Doctor is now willing to run away with you, and you still believe we're just going to hide out somewhere, lay low?"

"I don't know."

"Sure, you do. You changed your mind about me, Jess. Why not that, too?"

"One small step at a time. Besides, I told you, I didn't change my mind. You don't know me," she said. "Just because you have a huge file about me doesn't mean you know me."

"That's not how I know you, Jess. I know you because I must, if you've changed me this way."

"How am I supposed to go back to the facility, after this? What am I supposed to tell Aaron? Or anyone, for that matter? What if someone else is listening in? Maybe there are mics here, on the plane?!"

"No, there aren't."

"How do you know?"

"I checked for bugs," he said, looking glum.

"But, who's flying the plane? Maybe the pilot—"

"I know this plane like the back of my hand, Jess. I also know the government. An operation like this, they don't want the left hand knowing what the right hand is doing. The controls on this plane don't allow the pilot to hear anything inside this cabin. He's a low-level Air Force Cadet, filling his hours to earn his stripes. His job is to fly the plane and take us wherever orders tell him to, no questions asked. He doesn't know anything about the facility, transgens, The Society, the pseudogene, nothing. He's just a pilot."

She sighed closing her eyes, nodding. Then she took a deep breath, leveling him with her eyes.

"What about us? We just go back to the facility after all this has gone on, and what, pretend nothing happened? I pretend I still hate you, and you just act like Evil Dr. M.?"

"I'll have to put on a very convincing act, Jess," he sighed. "I'll have to lock you up when we get back. You won't be allowed to have contact with anyone."

"Then how can I organize our escape?"

"You won't," he said. "I'll have to do that."

"No one will believe you. And you can't go kissing everyone in there."

"Martin will believe me," he laughed. "It's nice to see you can still keep a sense of humor in all of this."

"What other choice do I have?"

The doctor didn't speak for a few moments. He seemed to be mulling something over.

"I know you don't feel the same way about me," he finally said. "Just like Aaron knows, too, that you don't feel the same for him as he feels for you."

"How—" But he held up his hand to silence her.

"You clung to him because you needed him, and now you're doing the same with me. I know that, Jess. Don't think I don't."

"I… I don't know what I think," she said. "Or feel."

"Exactly. So, don't think I'm holding you to anything, okay?"

"You really care?"

"Yes, I really do. But I'm not going to kiss you anymore. I want you to trust me, and I know that won't happen for a very long time. If everything works out the way I'm hoping, both of us are going to have some adjusting to do. Not least of which, for *you*, will be re-ordering how you view everything in your belief system. There won't be any energy left to feel anything, for anyone. This all seems acutely real to you now, but at some point, it will be just a dream."

"I'll remember."

"Yes, but you probably won't feel the same as you do now. Your feelings for Aaron have already changed, haven't they?"

She thought he sounded hopeful. She nodded, ashamed. "I wasn't using him," she said. "And I'm not using you."

He laughed. She shook her head.

***

"I'll be locked away, and Martin will work with you at convincing the others?" Jess asked.

"Yes, and as far as my superiors go, I'll be handling the situation. Diffusing it, so to speak. They trust me now, Jess. The only reason they hid the microphones from me was as a safety measure with Martin. He keeps everyone on their toes. They believe I want to keep you all there just as badly as they do."

"Wait. Your mother… will they still kill her, then? If you disobey them, and when they find out?" she sounded genuinely concerned, and although she didn't know it, his heart filled with warmth, and hope.

"I appreciate the concern, Jess, but my mother died last year. Natural causes." He shot her a reassuring look. "Although, she spent the last seven years of her life as a widow, because of me."

"Not because of you," she said. "It was the ones who threatened you, right?"

He shrugged, unwilling to reprieve himself.

"Who *are* they?"

"Does it matter?"

He saw from her expression that it mattered to her.

"Fine—my boss's name is General Levin. I answer to him."

"And you're certain they're not listening now?"

"I checked for bugs, remember?"

"And they don't believe in the aliens?"

"It's being explained as psychosis on Hanley's part, and the rest of you are so desperate to escape, that doesn't matter. All they're concerned with is that a group of people with abilities appears to be banding together to plan an escape. The aliens are a moot point."

"Everyone keeps saying that."

"Some things bear repeating. In the meantime, of course, I'm to train Sarah, as much as she can handle. Her gift is very useful, as you already know. She could command entire armies to lay down their weapons, and that's something my superiors are very eager to develop.

"I'll be working around the clock with Sarah. She's to have no contact with anyone else. With you locked away, and her isolated, the plan falls apart. No one can escape from the building without your talents, or Sarah's."

"They could all just go out into the Atrium, have Hanley melt the fence."

"You're forgetting already, Jess. The Atrium door won't open if more than two people are within even one hundred feet. The only way to override that, as the controls for that door aren't located inside the main facility, would be to cut the building's power, and *that* room *is* inside the facility. But we'd need your ability to knock out the power. And there are still other protocols you don't know about, Jess. Martin knows. That's why he knows we need Sarah. Without Sarah, we don't leave.

"As for you, we'll need you to disable all the doors. I can show you exactly where to pulse to knock out all the power in the building. The arrows won't work then, but I can lead the way, if I can gain everyone's trust."

"Then we don't need Hanley to melt the fences."

"The fences are run on a different power grid from the building," he shook his head. "We'll still need him, too. Hanley, you, and Sarah. The rest are just tagging along."

"They're my *friends.*"

"I know," he said, taking her hand in his.

"I thought you said you weren't going to do that anymore."

"I said I wouldn't kiss you again."

"Oh."

They discussed their plans for the rest of the plane ride. Jess's head swam from the incredible change of events. She couldn't believe she was sitting on a plane now planning her escape from the facility with the very man who had first put her there.

***

When they reached their destination, Dr. M. ushered Jess into the back seat of a waiting car that had a chauffeur, then got in himself, taking the seat next to her, in back. It was an older, beat-up looking beige car, nothing like the shiny black sedans from back at the facility. She grew increasingly nervous as they drove through the streets of what seemed to be a small village. The doctor took her hand and held it for the rest of the drive.

They drew to a halt somewhere on the outskirts of the village, where humble abodes gave way to sparse forest encroachments, and a small, concrete building stood alone. Dr. M. whispered in Jess's ear, instructing her on what to do. She got out of the car, breathing deeply, her heart pounding. The car turned around and backed up to a safe distance, leaving her alone.

Dr. M. got out of the car (now faced away from Jess) and watched with anticipation. The driver still faced forward in his seat, directed to only look forward, no matter what. These were his orders, and the car did not even contain a rearview mirror.

Jess walked up to the building until she stood only three feet from the walls. She took a deep breath and mustered every ounce of concentration she had, which, given the events of the last several hours, wasn't much.

This was different from pulsing in the orchard. That had become so easy to her, she barely even had to think. Here, outside of the controlled environment, she was suddenly afraid nothing would happen.

She closed her eyes, trying to gather her thoughts. As the doctor had taught her, she recalled the states of frustration and *fury* under which her powers had originally kindled. The familiar tingling in her palms waxed and waned, until finally, the prickling of embers blossomed into the now familiar inferno of heat that always felt as though her hands had caught fire.

All the while, Dr. M. watched, his heart hammering against the walls of his chest.

***

All at once, Jess let go, releasing the pulse. The building was immediately obliterated, the hillside behind catching fire.

Dr. M. squinted, trying to see through the clouds of dust, debris, and smoke that filled the air, but he knew that Jess wasn't there. She wouldn't appear for another three minutes, forty-eight seconds.

Normally, he would have had the presence of mind to time it on his watch, but he'd been preoccupied—filled with awe for her, as he always was.

As the minutes passed, he waited, the time interminable, wondering if it was as tortuous for her, in whatever other space and state she found herself in.

**

Then, in an instant, she was there. The debris had already settled enough, he caught sight of her the moment she came back. He ran to her, and he knew that he loved her. She would never love him back, he felt certain, but at that moment, he didn't care. He just needed to get to her.

He reached her, and she turned to face him. She stood before him, visibly depleted, dark circles beneath her sunken eyes, face blanched, lips paler than normal. She wasn't the only one drained, but she was not in any state to notice his anguish or exhaustion.

Jess allowed herself to collapse into the doctor's arms. She couldn't recall ever feeling so weak. She'd expended so much energy dealing with the tumult of emotions and stress she'd rode here, she could now barely stand.

The doctor carried her back to the car in his arms. Once inside, she collapsed against his chest and he held her that way until they reached the hangar.

On the plane, Jess was immediately given food and water. Then she laid down to sleep.

**

The doctor allowed her to sleep through the descent to spare her any further anxiety. When she woke, she found her head resting in his lap. He looked down at her, gently stroking her cheek, brushing hair from her face.

"We're here, Jess. We've landed."

"You're a different man." She reached up to touch his face, smiling sleepily.

"I'll have to go back to pretending, once we're off this plane."

"I know."

"No, you don't. I'll have to hide my feelings for you, which means you'll have to do the same."

Regardless of her feelings for him—so overwhelming, they could smother her like a swamp, if she let them—she knew the escape effort was impotent without him. If any of them had a hope of freedom, she had to trust him, which meant pretending to feel nothing for him.

She sat up, leaned forward, and kissed him. It didn't last long—he pulled away, clearly confused.

"Why did you do that?"

"All this time, you've been trying to make me change my mind about you, and when I do, you question it?"

"Only when it makes no sense."

"So, blame it on Stockholm Syndrome."

"You've been through too much, Jess. You're too fragile. I won't take advantage of that."

"Why not? You've already hurt me enough. What's a little more?" Her words came out sounding far more brutal than she'd intended.

"It's not *you* I'm worried about."

Suddenly, he was a small boy—an awkward adolescent. She saw the fear in his eyes and realization flooded her. He was afraid of getting hurt by *her*. Jess finally believed in him—if it had all been a ruse, he'd never have taken it this far.

She stood up and steadied herself, preparing to disembark. As she headed for the exit, he stopped her with a hand on her shoulder. He stood behind her, gently speaking into her ear. She closed her eyes.

"We'll enter the facility by the side door, then walk back to the same room where we met. I'll instruct you to leave and follow the arrows back to your room.

"Once you enter your room, Jess, you won't be able to leave. The door won't open for you anymore.

"You'll be there day and night, with no one to talk to, and worst of all for you, you'll have no way of knowing what's going on outside.

"You'll still pulse, of course, out in the orchard, to keep your strength up, and to maintain your equilibrium. In the hallways, the arrows will take you in such a way that you won't ever see anyone.

"I'll still instruct you when it's time to go to the orchard, but other than that, I won't be able to have any contact with you at all. You'll only hear my voice on the intercom."

"*Why?*" She tried to swallow back the waxing desperation, but it was akin to telling herself she wouldn't vomit after a night of Tequila. She turned to face him as he continued explaining plans.

"I... I don't think I can be around you without my true feelings for you showing," he said. "And it wouldn't make sense, anyhow. In isolation, you shouldn't need contact with me. You don't need me there with you, anymore, to pulse. The next time I see you, it will be when it's time for you to go back out into the field, and I can't guarantee that the next assignment will be as easy as this one."

"This was *easy?*"

"Unfortunately, yes. But I can't keep shielding you from the tough assignments forever. If I do, it will look suspicious. I must appear completely neutral. If anyone suspects that I'm emotionally compromised, I'll be gone."

"I don't want to be alone."

"I *know*. But I'll make sure you have things to help you pass the time. Rachel does. Your own TV, any books you want, a DVD player."

"For how long?"

"I don't know."

"We can't do it without Sarah. They know that, so why isolate me, too?"

"Because they don't want to take any chances. And it's what I've been ordered to do." He shrugged, pain clearly showing in his eyes. "I'm sorry, Jess, but it won't be forever, try to remember that. I'm going to get you out of here. I'm going to get *all* of us out of here."

He took her hand and squeezed it, then leaned forward till his forehead touched hers. They both closed their eyes, enjoying the simple, yet powerful intimacy of the contact.

"Can you do this?"

She nodded. They headed towards the exit, this time with Dr. M. leading the way. Just before they reached the door, Jess stopped short. The doctor turned to her, clearly concerned.

"Are you not ready?"

"No, it's not that. I just need to ask you one thing before we go."

"What?"

"What's your first name?"

He smiled at her, his eyes softening, and if Jess had ever seen happiness flood a man's face, it was in that moment.

"Ben."

***

Jess did as she was instructed, never once daring to so much as look at the doctor... at *Ben*.

It was easier than she'd expected, consenting to be sealed away like some plague carrier. She tried the doorknob in her room, after hearing the seal click shut. As expected, it refused to budge. She was a prisoner again.

She'd returned almost twenty-four hours after leaving. Just twenty-four hours, yet, it was another world from yesterday. It felt as if yesterday had happened years before. Ben was right, everything could change in just one day.

She felt guilty about Aaron, whom she no longer had any romantic feelings for, and truly never had. Then again, she mused, they'd only been a couple for three days before she left on her first mission. Surely,

Aaron couldn't be too upset about a lost romance that only lasted such a short duration of time, could he?

Then she thought about Dr. M. She still felt shock over having feelings for him, and even more so that, unlike with Aaron, her emotions concerning the doctor were decidedly romantic. The shock was akin to trauma, and yet, it quickly subsided to feelings of euphoria, comfort, and giddiness, at the simple picturing of his face, the memory of his warm hand enveloping hers, their fingers intertwined. Thoughts of his soft, gentle kisses upon her lips made her sigh, and she giggled.

She lay down on her bed, lacing her fingers behind her head on the pillow, and stared up at the ceiling. She ran the events of the last twenty-four hours through her head, in disbelief. When she got to the part where the doctor had first kissed her, her heart rate sped up, and she smiled.

"Ben," she whispered.

13

The first day was the easiest, to Jess's surprise. By the end of the fourth day, however, she began to feel stir crazy, and no amount of reading, watching TV, or playing solitaire would relieve it. She took showers for an hour at a time, and even spent one afternoon putting on ridiculous amounts of makeup, then simply danced around her room, eventually working herself into wild gyrations that ended in a dizzy collapse upon her bed, out of breath. It occurred to her that she could quite easily go insane if she had to live like this for too long. As to how long that would be…

She thought about Rachel, and how long she'd been in isolation. Worse, Rachel had killed a man. Jess couldn't imagine being trapped inside these walls with that kind of guilt seething in her skull. She didn't know how sanity could survive it. Yet, they needed Rachel. Both Martin and Hanley had been emphatic on the point that they would not leave her behind.

If Rachel's mind had been broken from killing one technician, how could anyone now expect her to simply be okay with escaping the facility with the doctor who had terrorized her? But if Hanley wanted Rachel, then they'd bring her.

Jess spent hours trying to figure out how the escape would work. Would Ben come to her room one day and announce it was time? How would they carry out their plans? He said he'd be able to instruct her on where to pulse, to shut down power to the facility. But what then? How would everyone else know when it was time? How would they get to Sarah, and Rachel, while gathering everyone else together?

It drove her crazy not knowing what was going on with her friends. She wondered what they knew, while simultaneously worrying that Aaron would find out about her and Ben.

Of course, to everyone else, he was still Dr. M. She had difficulty even thinking of him by this old title. She laughed to herself, realizing how bizarre it all was.

Ben had told her how hard it would be to live in isolation. She felt irritation that he knew her mind so well. *Well, that is his job, you know.* There was something both exciting and utterly terrifying to her, that anyone could know her very thoughts, understand her mental workings so intimately.

A technician now brought all her meals. It was the only time every day when she saw another person. She noticed during the first visit that the technician wore a Taser loose on his belt. He eyed her warily. Was this the same guy who'd Tased her before?

She glared at him and said, "Boo!" He jumped. She laughed, and he put his right hand on his hip, caressing the Taser while giving her a snide smile.

She quickly stopped laughing and the technician left the room. She stuck her tongue out after he left. *Definitely the same man.* Oh well, at least he might be a source of entertainment.

On day three, Ben's voice came over the intercom about an hour after she'd finished breakfast. He instructed her to leave her room and follow the arrows. Despite Ben's information that it would no longer be operable for them to converse, she couldn't keep herself from trying the intercom.

"Hello?"

Silence. The door opened with little effort, the arrows directing her along paths and corridors she wasn't familiar with. The walk gave her opportunity to wonder whether Ben would be waiting for her at the end, though part of her knew it wasn't likely. He'd told her how it would be from here on out: Perfunctory pulses in the orchard, then a return to isolation. She grew angry with herself for even hoping otherwise.

She entered the orchard through a different door than usual, several yards from the one she was used to. Her spirits fell, despite herself, at the realization that she was here for nothing more than the usual exercise. It was all over in moments, though several minutes had gone by in the world outside her time-insulating bubble. In the seeming seconds since she finished pulsing, she exited the orchard, following the arrows back to her room. Closing the door felt less like being sealed inside a cell this time, and more like a tomb.

On the table there sat a steaming helping of clam chowder in a bread bowl, a strawberry shake, and a baked potato buried beneath a heap of garnishes. They were all among her favorite foods. She felt ravenous and fell to eating immediately. Even so, she barely tasted the food, its volume doing little to fill the emptiness pulsing at her core.

She lived this way, going to the orchard every three days, for another two weeks. Each day, she felt more and more detached from everything. She began to imagine that it had all been a dream. Perhaps she'd never met anyone in the facility. Maybe she had always only ever been in her room. She even began to believe that Dr. M. was still simply Dr. M., that she'd imagined the entire exchange that took place between them on the plane.

At night, she dreamed about the aliens, having horrific nightmares. This started in the second week.

She dreamed one night—the worst—that Ben came to her room, telling her it was time to go, but when she followed him out into the hallway, it was green brick like the one he'd taken her down on her assignment. There were no doors anywhere, and they walked and walked for hours.

Finally, they came to a door where the brick corridor simply ended. Ben turned, taking her hands in his.

"They're behind that door, Jess." He kissed her tenderly on the lips and motioned for her to go. On the wall next to the door was an intercom with a red button, and as she stood in front of it, a man's tinny, high-pitched voice emitted. It was the same voice from her first day in the facility.

"Just say the words, 'There Is No God' and you can be free."

Jess turned back to Ben, pleading.

"Please don't make me say that."

He kissed her again, this time more aggressively, then spun her around, hissing in her ear.

"All you have to do is what I tell you, Jessica. That's not so difficult, is it? *Just do it.*"

She turned to him, sobbing, and he backed away, his eyes so cold.

"Please, Ben," she sobbed. "Don't make me do this."

"Who's Ben?"

Jess watched in horror as Dr. M. pulled his own face off, as if it were a mask, and a gray, mottled alien face appeared, evil and terrifying. It walked toward her, towering. No way out except through the door.

Jess backed up until she could go no further, trembling in sheer terror as the gray monster drew closer, *closer.* She could see her own reflection in its large, pitch eyes now—no longer the face she'd known all her life, but gray-skinned and black-eyed—another alien.

She woke up screaming. She didn't know it, but her terror was so intense, it jolted Martin awake. He already knew all that had taken place between her and Dr. M., not through any conscious eavesdropping on his part. He sifted the information from the air as naturally as he breathed oxygen. Jessica's scream, however, not only jolted him awake, but transferred some of her own fear, leaving him trembling and terrified, unable to return to sleep.

***

It was difficult for Martin to hide from Aaron and the others what he knew about Jess and the doctor, but he did. His task was difficult enough already, just listening to Dr. M.

With the realization that there were mics in all the tables, there was nowhere the group could talk except the Atrium, and only two people at a time could go.

When Jess and Dr. M. first returned to the facility, Martin had been in the cafeteria eating breakfast. He simultaneously heard both their thoughts—so shocked by the shift in circumstances—he almost choked on his scrambled eggs.

He quickly left the cafeteria and returned to his room, attempting to recover himself. There, while focusing all his efforts on gleaning the details of what had occurred between Jess and the doctor, he realized that Dr. M. was deliberately relaying the information, thinking so hard, it made Martin's temples throb.

In the background, he could still hear Jess, her thoughts providing confirmation of Dr. M.'s unspoken message.

***

It never occurred to Jess that she could use Martin to communicate. In her mind, it wasn't communication if she couldn't gage a response. Not to mention, her mental capacities began deteriorating rapidly in isolation.

Jess could not possibly know, of course, about anything going on outside her own small room, but Dr. M. had informed Martin that the only safe place to talk now was the flower meadow in the Atrium. They never spoke in person of course. Their communications occurred through the medium of Martin's mind. Martin wished he could send thoughts back, but unfortunately, his gift was a one-way street.

***

In the afternoon of Jess's first day back, Martin found Aaron—after recovering enough from the sheer shock of what he'd learned about Jess and Dr. M.—and told Aaron to meet him in the Atrium meadow. He wanted desperately to talk to Hanley first, but he could not. Hanley was not allowed in the Atrium, only the courtyard. Dr. M. had not told him the courtyard was safe, and Martin wasn't going to take any chances.

Out in the meadow, Martin told Aaron everything about Dr. M., leaving out the details of he and Jess's new intimacy. Aaron listened to most of it in stunned silence, especially the revelation that he, also, had been the victim of intimidation and blackmail, including the seeing through of the threat on his father's life. Aaron listened intently, only interrupting when Martin informed him of Doctor. M.'s intentions to help them escape.

"*Why?*"

"He's not as bad of a guy as we thought." Martin shrugged.

"Dude, what happened to him sucks, but he still threatened to kill your *wife*. How can you say that? He still turned into a creepster-jerk of a monster. He's the one who put you in here. He's the reason you're a prisoner and haven't seen your own wife in how long now? And," he continued for good measure, "she doesn't know what happened to you, or even that you're alive. This guy isn't a saint, just because he had some bad stuff happen to him, once upon a time. He turned around and did the exact same thing to countless others."

"I understand," Martin said, ever the peacemaker. "I'm not defending all the bad things he's done, Aaron. But the point here, is that he's changed, that's all I can tell you. He's different now."

"*How?*" Aaron stared at Martin in utter disbelief. "What could possibly make him change that way?"

Martin held his tongue, knowing it would only complicate matters if he tried to explain to Aaron what he knew about the doctor and Jess. He simply shook his head.

"He just is, okay? Trust me."

"What if you're wrong?"

"Then we're all screwed. But he can't deceive me. I'd know. He really didn't know about the mics."

"Why would he want to come with us?"

"He's a scientist," Martin lied, shrugging. "They're aliens. Why else do you think he'd want to come?"

"You're telling me Dr. M. actually *believes* Hanley?"

Martin simply shrugged again.

"I don't believe in them. Jess doesn't believe in them. Why would he?" Aaron asked.

"He doesn't, as such, but he *hopes.* Can you imagine what it'd be like for a mind like his, having the opportunity to learn about an entirely alien species?"

Aaron shook his head, still not convinced, wanting to know how they could possibly trust a man who had deceived and bullied all of them for so long. Martin caught the query from his thoughts and answered.

"You'll just have to find a way, I guess. What choice do any of us have? I guess you'll have to try a little faith."

***

There was no way to tell Hanley. That was the worst of it for both Martin and Aaron. Martin took turns the very next day, separately telling Earl and Alma, neither of whom believed in the alien rescue, but both eventually acquiesced to the fact that they had no other choice now but to try and trust Dr. M. in aiding their escape. Aaron took Jesus out into the meadow two days later. Jesus took it much easier than anyone else, merely shrugging his compliance.

When Aaron asked him how he could so easily accept everything, Jesus smiled.

"I believe we will get out, no matter how it happens. Things will be however they're meant to be. I have faith."

Aaron walked away at that point, mumbling to himself.

"Everyone in this place is crazy."

***

Every time she heard Ben's voice on the intercom, Jessica *hoped*— that she'd see him, that there'd be news of something—anything. The means she'd employed thus far to occupy herself were beginning to fail, and her mind itself frayed along with them.

***

Almost every room in the facility was monitored, and every event and interaction relayed and recorded. A small army of technicians monitored the various feeds, immediately notifying the doctor of any anomalies or suspicious behavior. Few such instances had occurred for over a year now—not since Malcolm, Jenny, Alma and Rachel had attempted their escape. The only real exception had been when Jess blew up the cafeteria, and although Dr. M. hadn't known exactly when that might take place, it was far from unexpected.

Fortunately for the doctor, owing to the general lack of events within the facility, the technicians often paid little mind to the monitor's audio feeds, unless one of their subjects became particularly agitated. In those rare circumstances, they informed Dr. M. and turned the matter over to him.

The techs sometimes took breaks, others filling their seats while they were gone. Once a week, Dr. M. took the feed-room seat for two hours. He realized that this was greatly to his benefit now, as the days wound on, slowly watching Jess spiral down into despair and inevitable insanity.

It might have been comical watching her various attempts to stave off madness, were they not so dangerous, and if he didn't care for her as deeply as he did.

Jess took to watching soaps on her TV every day at noon, right after lunch. After only a week, she became so invested in the storylines, she began talking back at the screen whenever the characters did anything she didn't like.

"What? No... you can't choose *Paolo*," she'd tell the screen. "You're supposed to be with Rick, you ... so stupid..." Then she'd catch herself in a moment of realization.

"So stupid, *so stupid*."

***

By day thirteen, she took to walking on her hands and doing headstands against the walls for minutes on end. She'd twist her hair into odd, messy ponytails and spin around the room until she got so dizzy she fell to the floor.

On day fourteen, she got so sick of staring at the television, she threw the remote control at the wall and it shattered into pieces. Later, she clumsily tried to piece it back together, but to no avail. She took to sitting in the wooden chair in front of the TV, close enough to change the channel without getting up.

She braided her hair into rows then took long naps. She showered two and three times a day, for an hour at a time, filling the bathroom with so much hot steam, she could hardly breathe. It made her feel more alive.

By day fifteen, she began having imaginary conversations on her bed with the wall above her pillow. She'd pretend she talked to Hanley, or Martin, or Jesus.

When this happened, Ben got very worried. The cracks were getting larger. It wouldn't be very long before they broke wide open.

On day sixteen, the doctor became desperate. For the first time, he looked for a way to use his authority to help a member of The Society, instead of manipulating them.

***

On day eighteen, Jess heard Ben's voice again. She went to the orchard as instructed. Walking through the featureless hallways, she didn't entertain the slightest hope of seeing him, or anyone.

Once outside, she sighed shakily, walked to her usual spot, and stood staring out over the expanse of burnt, crumbled trees and charred earth.

She couldn't concentrate, couldn't *pulse*… Dropping to her knees on the blackened dirt, she sobbed, her entire body shuddering. She stayed this way for several minutes, then jolted at the sense of a hand on her shoulder. She looked up. *I'm dreaming, it's not real.*

Ben stood there, smiling down at her, his eyes filled with tears. She felt so overjoyed at seeing him, she jumped up and hugged him, throwing her arms wildly around his torso, clinging to him desperately.

What last shred of rational thought remained told her he would have to shove her away, if only to maintain his façade of indifference. Relief flooded her when he did not. Instead, he wrapped his arms around her tightly and rocked her in effort to soothe her sobs.

"Okay, Jess. It's okay."

He held her for several minutes while she cried. Eventually, she pulled away. He raised her chin up with his hand until her eyes met his.

"Whatever happened to my firecracker, huh?"

Her faculties suddenly flared, flooding her with forgotten awareness.

"They'll see. Oh, my God. They know, don't they? What did I do?!"

"The cameras have been turned off."

"How?"

"I'm in charge of the project, remember? It has its perks, in this case."

"You don't know that. They could be watching, and you don't know, just like with the mics!"

"No," he said, shaking his head. "They had a small panic over the plans you came up with. With you and Sarah in isolation, it's all but out of their minds. I just had to wait a few weeks for them to move on to something else. Now they're so focused on reading my reports and following my progress with Sarah, they couldn't care less about you, other than finding your next assignment."

"Is that why you're here? Am I going back out?"

"No, not yet," he said. "That's one small grace."

"But something's wrong, isn't it?"

"No, everything is going as planned, it's just—there *isn't* any concrete plan, Jess. Sarah's progressing, but it's slow. She's eleven, and scared. It's harder to threaten her, with her in isolation. She has no friends she cares about, and no family on the outside. Not to mention, it's decidedly more difficult for me, threatening people now. Especially a child.

"I know you've been going through a lot these last weeks, but I need you to know you're not alone. I'm going through it with you." He pulled her to him, hugging her tightly again. "I'm going through it with you," he repeated.

"How long?"

"I don't know."

She stayed quiet for a while, content in his arms. He held her for what felt like forever. When she spoke next, his heart pounded in his chest.

"If you can turn the cameras off here, can you do it in my room, too?"

"Maybe. Not right away. I wouldn't want to do it again, too soon."

"But you *could?*" she said, pulling away.

"I could… try to work out a way."

He faltered, blushing—the look in her eyes now and the tone of her voice were so forward—it caught him off-guard. He hadn't kissed a woman in five years. The last time he'd been intimate with one had been much longer. Now, all that he'd been missing for so many years—those lost connections—became a desperate ache in his core, like hunger, only more urgent.

"I'll try, okay?"

She nodded. "How long?"

"A week," he said, no longer blushing. "But I have to go now. It's been too long."

"Okay."

"You'll be okay, Jess. You have to be."

"I know."

"I'm with you, Jess, always remember that. I'm working with Sarah a lot, so it's not all the time, but I'm watching you. Not as much as before, but I do see you."

"How much did you watch me before?" She sounded more like her old self now, thank God.

"Well, not that much."

"Yeah? Because, you're sort of coming off as a stalker, you know? It's not a turn on."

"Good to know," he laughed.

He wanted to stay longer but knew he couldn't. He sighed desperately, and pulled her into his arms, kissing her passionately. Unlike any of the kisses that had occurred on their plane ride, this lasted much longer. The heat and intensity so overwhelming, Jess's stomach churned quickly from tickling butterflies to slightly painful pangs inside of her. She felt Ben's arms around her, and the passion coming off him in waves so consuming, she felt safer and better cared for, enveloped in his body, than she'd ever felt in her entire life. She kissed him back fervently, wishing and wanting to stay with Ben like this forever. The whole world fell away in those moments, for she and Ben, both.

It didn't last anywhere near long enough for either of them to be truly satisfied, but it was enough for Jess to return to her room willingly. That night, she had no bad dreams.

14

Ben's superiors read his updates and reports. There was a strict system to be followed—one he endeavored to maintain—following the assignment with Jess. He sent out a report and scheduled a video conference with General Levin to keep him informed. He did this at the end of every week, standard protocol.

This week, as he sat at his desk in the same room where Jess first drank the Luci—Ben patched into the video feed, pulling up General Levin on the monitor.

"Doctor."

"General," Ben saluted.

"I've read your latest report. Looks like things are moving along with Sarah Marchland. That's good news. I'm not too excited to hear about the degenerating state of Jessica Wembly, however. We've barely begun using her in the field. We can't risk her becoming non-viable, now can we?"

"No, General, we cannot."

"Mmm-hmm. Well, we certainly can't risk putting her back into The Society," he said, lifting the file which contained Ben's report. "But your suggestion that she be allowed a visitor to her room can certainly be granted. I've run it over with Doctor Stanlowe, and he thinks Aaron would be a good choice."

Ben tried to sound unaffected. "I'm not so sure that would be the wisest choice right now."

"Oh? Why not?"

"At the level of emotional strain she's reached at this point, I think any romantic interaction would only complicate matters. She would be better served if she could simply talk with a friend. I think Hanley should suffice."

The General looked at Dr. M. for a few moments, thinking. Then he nodded. Ben stood his ground the entire time, appearing completely professional.

"Very well, you know your subjects better than anyone, Dr. Milbron. I trust you."

"With all due respect, General, if you had trusted me, I would have been informed of the mics in the cafeteria."

"I'm not proud of that, Doctor, but it's how they wanted it done. You know Martin Keane can hear everything. If you'd known about the mics, so would he, and that little escape plan might have been missed."

"I understand that, General, but in the future, I'd like to be fully informed of *any* changes within this facility. After all, this is *my* project."

"Yes, it is, and you've done a wonderful job up to this point, Doctor," the General said. "I apologize if you've felt deceived in any way."

"No, of course not."

"Well, you know about the mics now, so you're fully apprised, all right?"

"Yes, Sir."

"And so long as Sarah is never allowed into The Society, I think we've got things well under control, isn't that correct?"

"Yes, Sir."

"Fine, then. That's all. Unless you have anything to add to this report?"

"No, Sir, it's all there. As always."

"That's what I like about you, Doctor. You're all business."

"Yes, Sir."

"How long after she begins to socialize do you think it will be for Wembly to get back out there?"

"I'd like to observe her for a few weeks, General. I'll get a friend in there today, if that's permitted?"

"Of course, of course. And you want to send in Hanley?"

"They've become good friends, General. It should more than suffice for brightening her spirits."

"No wagering, Doctor; it *has* to work. I can give you a few weeks, but we need her ready not too long after that. Understood?"

"Yes, Sir. Something big planned, Sir?"

"You'll receive that report once we're certain the girl is ready. And she *will* be ready, Doctor." The General did not pose this as a question. "I look forward to your next report, especially on the little girl."

"As do I, General."

"Good day, Doctor," the General said. He did not salute.

Once the screen went blank, Ben breathed a sigh of relief. He then went straight to the monitoring room to find out where Hanley was.

***

Hanley wasn't used to hearing Dr. M. calling him up on the intercom. Usually, it was a tech's voice that ordered him to the testing lab. It had also been a while since he'd even been tested, as preoccupied as Dr. M. had been with training Jess, and now the little girl. When the doctor's voice came over his intercom this mid-morning, it nearly startled Hanley out of his skin.

"Hanley."

"Jeezus!" Hanley exclaimed, dropping his book.

He looked over at the intercom, frowning. Then he threw a prolonged, annoyed glance at the camera in the corner across from his bed. In the control room, Ben smiled.

"Hanley," he repeated, trying not to laugh.

Hanley walked over to the intercom, pushing the red button.

"Dr. M.?"

"Yes, Hanley, it's Dr. M. How are you today?"

"Fine," Hanley said, growing nervous. *Since when does the Doc ask me how I'm doing?*

The only reason he could fathom the doctor calling into his room on this day, was if there was a big assignment—the type he'd come to dread. They didn't come up too often, which he was grateful for. Hanley sighed, pushing the red button again.

"What's the assignment, Doc?"

"How would you like to visit Jessica this afternoon? She could use a little company."

"Jess?"

"Yes, Hanley. Would you like to visit her in her room?"

"I thought she was in isolation?"

"She is, but she's not handling it too well. It's affecting her ability to perform. I trust that I can be up front with you about that."

"Huh," Hanley said. "Well, thanks."

"We think a little socializing will help relieve some of her anxiety, help her get back into shape. I thought you would be a nice choice."

"Well, honestly, I'd love to see Jess, but, I think Aaron would like to see her a little more."

"Well, that's not up to you, now is it?"

Hanley fell silent, excited at the thought of seeing Jess. He'd missed her greatly over the last few weeks, as much as any of them, including Aaron.

In truth, Hanley had grown annoyed with Aaron lately. He'd taken to moping around like a sullen child. It was sort of pathetic. Then again, up until Jess arrived, Aaron had shown not the slightest concern for any of them, especially Hanley. He couldn't deny a sense of puerile victory that he'd been the one chosen and not lover-boy.

"Hanley?" Ben said again.

"Yeah?"

"You'll visit Jessica this afternoon."

"Okay, just say the word."

"At three o'clock, go out into the hallway. Say, "Jess," then follow the arrows."

"Is that what it is? Aaron's been saying, '*Jess's room,*' over and over, but nothing happens."

"Even if he says, 'Jess,' nothing will happen. *I* decide who has access to the rooms around here, you know that."

"Yeah, I know, but that doesn't stop Aaron from trying, over and over and over and—"

"*Hanley.*"

"Sorry."

"Three o'clock. And don't be late."

"Are you kidding?" Hanley said. "Not on my life."

Hanley knew what the consequences were for not following the Doctor's orders to the letter. He had no way of knowing that circumstances had changed.

***

In the control room, Ben patched into Jess's intercom and called her up.

"Jessica." He had to sound normal, and it killed him to do so, but he spoke in as monotone a voice as he could muster.

She lay in her bed, staring up at the ceiling. She ran to the intercom, her heart fluttering.

"Yes?"

Since their meeting in the orchard, she'd been anxiously awaiting the time he might contact her next, replaying their passionate kiss in her mind again and again. She depressed the button, wondering if the time had come. She felt breathless.

"How would you like to have a visitor come to your room?"

"Um, yeah, of course." Her heart beat madly now.

"How does Hanley sound?"

"Hanley?" She frowned.

"I thought you could use some company, a friend to talk to."

"Oh…" she sighed, sounding disappointed.

"It would do you some good, I think."

Jess frowned. She could tell Ben was trying to tell her something, but she had no idea what. Was Hanley code for *him*? She didn't think so. And what could she even talk to Hanley about? Everything she said or did was monitored and recorded.

"Jessica," he said again, flatly.

"Yeah?"

"It really will be good for you to talk to a friend," he said, his voice softening a bit. "It will *really* help."

She realized he'd pulled some strings to loosen the rules of her isolation. Once past her initial disappointment at not being able to see Ben, she realized she eagerly hungered to converse with someone, *anyone,* face to face.

Not Aaron. Martin would have been okay, and Jesus would be even more welcoming. But Hanley would've been her first choice. Of course, Ben would know that, wouldn't he? How often had he expressed how well he knew her? She suddenly wished Ben were closer—in the room with her. He had kept his promise to get her through this as best he could. Hanley was his gift to her.

"I'd love to see Hanley," she said, genuinely meaning it.

"Yes, I thought so. He'll be knocking at your door a few minutes after three o'clock. It will unlock to let him in. Okay?"

"Yes. *Thank you.*"

He didn't respond. She sat back down on her bed, fidgeting her feet. She looked at the clock and sighed.

It was only ten in the morning.

***

The hours dragged by for Jess and Hanley. Ben worked all morning with Sarah, then went back to the control room at 2:55 p.m.

At three o'clock, when the tech left on break, Ben sat down at the controls. He watched on the screens as Hanley followed the arrows to Jess's room.

Ben pushed the button to unlock her door and watched Jess and Hanley's reunion, switching his view to the camera in Jess's room once Hanley was inside. The tech would be back at 3:15, and they didn't have very much time.

***

In her room, Jess eagerly paced the floor until she heard the knock. She flew to the door, tearing it open, almost shell-shocked at the sight of Hanley standing there, smiling at her. He looked so happy to see her, he could barely contain his excitement. They embraced each other fiercely, then let go, smiling at each other for several moments. Hanley had tears in his eyes.

"Can I come in?"

"*Yes*, of course!"

Hanley came in and closed the door, then sat down in the chair at the table, turning it around to face her. Jess sat down on the bed.

"How are you, kiddo?"

"I'm okay. A lot better now."

"Isolation can be tough," Hanley said. "Especially coming straight off your first assignment."

He turned to the camera when saying this, as if to chastise Dr. M. He turned back to Jess, looking deadly serious.

"What happened? Did you botch it up?"

"What?"

"Your assignment."

"No. I did everything I was supposed to."

"Then, why'd they lock you up in isolation as soon as you came back?"

"It's… hard to explain."

He doesn't know, she realized. *With the tables mic'd, how could he be told?*

They stared at each other for several moments, both jumping as the doctor's voice suddenly came over the intercom.

"Jess."

"Jeezus!" Hanley yelled. "That guy's gotta stop doing that today!"

Jess ignored Hanley, rushing to the intercom.

"Jess…"

"Ben," she sighed.

"You have ten minutes," he said. "Look at the camera. See the red light?"

"No."

"That's right. You have ten minutes to say anything you need to, understand?"

"Yes."

Meanwhile, Hanley sat in his chair, looking completely bewildered.

"Who's Ben? Did the doctor just call you Jess? Since when is he allowed to do that?"

"Okay, Hanley, just shut up and listen," she said, sitting back down on the edge of her bed. "I have ten minutes to tell you everything, and you're not going to believe me, or like it much, okay?"

"Okay…"

"Okay. First off, there are mics in the tables in the cafeteria, and I guess in your courtyard, too…Maybe."

"Wait, how—?"

"Just shut up and *listen to me*." She took a quick, shallow breath and went on.

"Martin knows everything, since he can hear both our thoughts. He must know everything, but he hasn't been able to tell you, because there's nowhere safe he can. The only safe place to talk now is the Atrium meadow, and you're not allowed out there, so you don't know."

"Know what?"

"He knows everything."

"Who?"

"Ben."

"Who's Ben?"

"Sorry, I meant Dr. M."

Saying that felt strange on her lips, and Jess smiled, blushing. Hanley squinted at her, growing suspicious, but said nothing.

"He knows about our plans to escape," she continued.

"How could there be mics in the tables without Martin knowing?" Hanley sounded skeptical.

"Because, Be—, I mean, Dr. M. didn't know about it. He was on leave for a few days, right? After Alma tried to escape with Rachel and the others?"

"Yeah?"

"That's when they put the mics in. They did it while Ben was gone, so he wouldn't know. And if he didn't know…"

"Then neither would Martin," Hanley finished. "*Shit!* So, our whole plan is ruined. No wonder Martin's been acting so funny. You know, he won't even talk to me anymore?"

"No, the plan's still on."

"What? *How?*"

"Because," she sighed. "Dr. M. is going to help us."

"*What?!*"

Hanley stared at Jess in complete disbelief. Then he saw that she was serious and grew agitated.

"Jeezus, Jess, did he tell you that? What a bastard!"

"No, he's genuine, Hanley. Martin knows. You've *got* to believe me."

"He *plays* people, Jess. You *know* that. Jeezus!" Hanley rubbed his temples.

"It's true, Hanley. He wants to help," she continued. "He's going to help us."

"Yeah, right. That's why you're in isolation," Hanley said, shaking his head and frowning. "Why is he calling you Jess? And why are you calling him *Ben*?"

"Well," she shrugged. "That's his name."

"No, Jess, it's not. He's Dr. M."

Jess blushed and looked down at the floor, unable to meet Hanley's eyes. He stared at her for several moments, then sat back in his chair, looking as if he were about to have a heart attack.

"Holy shit! Are you kidding me? *No*… this is not happening."

He stood and began pacing the room.

"Please... *please* don't tell Aaron."

Hanley shot her a look of anger and defiance. She looked back at him, pleading with her eyes.

"Jeezus and Jehoshaphat, Jess! What the hell happened to you? What did he *do?*"

"Nothing."

"Bull. What the hell happened on that assignment?"

Hanley sat back down, looking at Jess in complete shock, but she could see he was at least beginning to settle.

"Hanley... Remember when you told me I needed to go on faith?"

"Yeah...?"

"Well, now I need you to."

"That's a lot to ask, and you know it."

"I know, but I need you to *listen*, okay?"

"Okay, okay. Try me."

"He's changed," she said. "He found out about our plans, and he wants out, too, just as much as the rest of us. He wants to go *with* us."

"The Doc wants to go with us." Hanley repeated her words in robotic monotone.

"Martin must already know everything. I'm assuming he's told Aaron, and the others. At least, some of them. But there was no way to tell you."

"How'd Dr. M. find out about the mics, if he didn't know before?" Hanley asked.

"His superiors supplied him with the audio the day before I went with him on assignment."

"So now... the upper-*upper* brass knows?"

"Yeah. And Ben needs to look like he's diffusing the situation. So, I'm on lockdown, and so is Sarah."

"But now we're stuck relying on Dr. M. to help us pull it off."

Jess nodded.

"And you *trust* him?"

"Yeah, I do."

He stared at her for several moments, trying to take it all in.

"That's big... for *you.*"

Jess nodded, looking down at the floor.

"You're blushing." Hanley's voice came out thick and nauseated, yet oddly resigned.

"What? No, I'm not."

"Yeah, you are."

Hanley rubbed his temples again. "But... you also look *happy.*"

"I do? I've been in isolation for over two weeks, Hanley. I'm doing handstands in here."

"Yeah, well, that's further testimony, because you're practically glowing. I hate to say this, all things considered, but I *never* saw that look in your eyes when you were with Aaron. You certainly never *blushed.*"

Jess looked down at the floor again, picking at her fingernails. "I never meant for any of this to happen," she said. "I never meant to hurt Aaron."

"He's not hurt, not yet, anyway. But he will be."

"Well, we can't worry about that now. I'm sure we're out of time. Do you understand what's going on?"

"Yeah. And I sure hope we can trust the Doc, because, if we can't, we're all screwed."

"Hanley, if you only knew... I mean, *really* knew. He's lost people, too. They threatened people he loved, at the beginning, and just like you, he thought they were only bluffing." She leveled her eyes at him. "They weren't. He's lost family, Hanley. They've killed people he loves, to make him become what he has."

"Who?" Hanley frowned.

"His father."

Hanley stared at Jess. It was impossible for her to read his face, however.

"Hanley... I know he's hurt you in ways that are unforgivable, but do you believe people can change?"

"You're living proof." His voice came out as barely a whisper, and she realized he was choking up, near tears. Clearly, he was reluctantly beginning to understand the doctor a little better. It would take time, she knew, but the road to change had already begun. She sighed deeply.

"Then, we're okay?"

"What do you mean?"

"Are we still friends?"

Jess looked at Hanley nervously, but he smiled warmly, which she didn't expect.

"We'll *always* be friends, Jess."

She smiled, her eyes filling with tears. She jumped off the bed and threw her arms around Hanley in a bear hug. Hanley reciprocated eagerly. Just then, Ben's voice suddenly came over the intercom again.

"Time's up, Jess, I'm sorry."

Hanley walked over to the intercom, glancing up at the camera to see if the light was on. It wasn't.

"Oh, Doc?"

"Yes, Hanley."

"You got some *'splainin'* to do."

"In time, Hanley, in time. But time's up for private talk, okay?"

"Uh, sure... *Ben*."

"See the red light?" Ben said. "It's about to come on. After that, it's strictly regular chit-chat, got it?"

"Sure," Hanley replied, releasing the button.

He looked up, saw the red light on the camera illuminate, and sat back down. They resumed their normal visit.

He and Jess talked for over an hour, about how Jesus was, and Alma, and Martin. They pulled the table closer to the bed and played King's in a Corner with her deck of cards, while talking and laughing.

"Oh, man, I didn't tell you? Alma's in love with some new chick that arrived last week. She can *shock* people."

"Shock people?"

"Yeah, you know, like a Taser? Knock 'em right out."

"Is she dangerous?"

"Don't know," he shrugged. "She hasn't shocked any of us out yet."

"Huh," Jess smiled. "And what about Earl? Is he walking through walls, yet?"

"Pfff," Hanley rolled his eyes. "He keeps talking about it, but no one's seen him do it, yet."

"Training," Jess rolled her eyes.

"Tell me about it."

They sat playing in silence for a few more minutes, then Hanley sighed. Jess looked at him, rolling her eyes.

"What?"

"Um... it's kind of a delicate subject, but considering what *you* shoved onto me today, I guess I'm allowed."

"*What*, Hanley?"

"All right. I know about what you and Jesus talked about, regarding..." he trailed off.

"If Martin told you—" Jess began, growing agitated, but Hanley cut her off.

"Martin didn't tell me anything. Jesus told me. I need to know where everyone stands. You expect me to go on *faith*."

"Watch it," Jess warned. She shot her eyes up towards the camera.

"Look, I'm *crazy*. Why don't you let me entertain you with a story, huh?"

"What, about me?"

"About something a little rabbit told you... you know... about what's up?"

She frowned at him, not understanding. He rolled his eyes.

"Didn't you ever watch cartoons? 'What's up...'" He eyed her. Suddenly her eyes lit up with understanding.

"Oh... Yeah, I mean, I know that show, but..."

"And, you've made a huge assumption, Jess, a wrong one, about something you heard that *Wascally Wabbit* say."

"Uh, huh?" She smiled now, fully comprehending him. "And that is?"

"He told you, like everyone, that the special carrot he loves so much was put there, right? On purpose?"

"Right, so?"

She wasn't expecting this to be the subject. She was confused.

"So, why are you assuming the *cartoons* did it?" He didn't even try to come up with a sensible code for that one. She smirked. "You suck at this, Hanley."

"Crazy here, remember?" He threw his hands up.

"But, you told me they did."

"No, I didn't."

"Yes, you *did*. You said when the *cartoons* found the... rabbit hole, they found what they were looking for, and they put one of their own carrots in."

"That's not what I said—I told you that when the *cartoons* found the rabbit, they discovered something *unique*—and that they could alter the rabbit to give it different carrots. I never said the original carrot came from them. They just found out, like *Wascally* did. They basically just made the same discovery. I never told you *they* did it."

Jess gave up all pretenses of a code in her frustration. "Yes, you *did*, Hanley. You said, '*just one gene, in the right place, and whammo!*'"

Jess lowered her vocal register to mock Hanley's voice while making quotation marks with her hands, then slapped her hands together the same way Hanley had when he'd said it. He laughed, amused.

"And you say *I'm* bad at this? Anyway, it doesn't mean what you assumed it meant. 'Cause right after that, I also said it doesn't work on everyone. I said you have to have the right DNA sequence, remember?" He eyed her in chastisement. "Duh! I told you right there in that conversation that *Wascally* said someone put the extra carrot there, but also that the *cartoons* didn't put the carrot into us either. I guess I thought you knew that. I didn't know you thought the opposite. If I'd realized that back then, I'd have corrected you on the spot. It seems to have muddled everything in your mind."

"What do you mean?"

It was Hanley's turn now to give up on any kind of code. He leveled Jess with his eyes. It was the most serious look he'd ever given her, which was saying a lot. She immediately listened as if receiving instructions from a drill sergeant, Hanley's look commanded such authority.

"The Graylings didn't put one of their genes inside of us. It was already there when they found us. Then they discovered, just like *Wascally*, that they could activate it. Imagine their surprise when they realized what it did to us."

"So much for Looney Tunes code."

"Whatever," Hanley was clearly tired of playing games. "I'm crazy, you're crazy, we're all crazy for I don't give a flying f—"

"Wait! I'm confused. If they didn't put the gene there, then who did?"

"Who knows? Take any number of guesses. Just…"

"*What,* Hanley?"

"Just… it doesn't need to rule out your God, is all I'm saying."

"You think *God* did this?"

"I have no idea. I'm agnostic."

"What?"

"All I'm saying is, it leaves the door open for you to… you know… *believe.*"

"Are you making this up, just so I'll believe?"

"No. You can ask Martin, if you don't believe me. I'm telling you the truth, Jess. *Wascally* says we were built, that the gene doesn't come from Earth, and if it didn't come from the Graylings, well, then…"

"It came from *somewhere.*" She frowned. "I thought we were done with stupid codes? This whole conversation is just nuts. What's up with 'what's up'?"

"Heh… I enjoy calling a certain someone *Wascally*. It fits."

She sighed.

"Look, Jess—I'm not trying to make you believe anything, okay? Just… don't lose faith, like Jesus said, all right? No one has any real answers when it comes to any of this. Not really. We're all flying on faith, in the end."

And that was the end of the conversation. They went back to playing in silence. After another hour, Dr. M. spoke over the intercom and told Hanley it was time to leave.

"Everything's going to be okay," Jess told him.

"I hope so." Hanley waggled his fingers at her, smiling, and waved goodbye, but before he left, he turned back to her, smiling so big, she laughed.

"Those big hugs you gave me?"

"Yeah?"

"First hugs from a person that I've had in almost a decade," his eyes were wet. "Thanks, Jess."

She threw her arms around him then, and hugged him fiercely, yet again. He hugged her back so hard, it restricted her breathing, but he let go a second later, looking goofy and embarrassed. He shrugged and offered his signature waggly-fingered wave one last time. Then he closed the door, leaving her alone once again, but not half so much as before.

***

Hanley found Martin that night in the cafeteria.

"You're a good friend, Martin," was all he said.

Martin picked up on his thoughts immediately, and smiled, relieved beyond belief.

"Finally," Martin sighed. Then he winked and threw a lopsided grin Hanley's way. "Thanks."

15

Sarah was eleven-years-old and scared out of her mind. Pale, thin, and fragile-looking, yet extremely beautiful, her eyes were almond brown, matching her sleek, long hair. She'd gone through the shocking loss of both her parents and then found herself, only days after their deaths, inside the facility.

Upon arrival, she immediately met Dr. M. and was given Luci in a glass of water, just as Jess had been. Her ability was discovered when, the following day, she went running through the hallways, sans arrows, and a tech came towards her, brandishing his Taser.

She stood her ground, somehow instinctively knowing he couldn't hurt her. He approached, Taser raised, but when he still stood several yards away, he put his arm down at his side, simply gazing at the young girl. Dr. M. witnessed this, approaching Sarah in the hallway, and walked her back to her room.

He explained to her how the arrows worked and how to get to the cafeteria. She went there immediately, for she hadn't eaten in almost a day. He questioned her as they walked down the hall together about what she thought had happened to the man with the 'electric gun,' as Sarah called it.

Sarah told Dr. M. that she knew the man wouldn't hurt her. She knew he'd put the gun down and would not use it on her. By the time she entered the small cafeteria, both Dr. M. and Martin knew what she could do, as did Hanley.

***

Martin listened as Sarah grew stronger and stronger, slowly gaining control of her ability. Dr. M. wasn't using threats, for he truly had none. Also, with Sarah being so young, even Ben's team of Psych Advisors warned him that scaring Sarah would be counter-productive.

For the first time, Dr. M. found himself having to use very different tactics to gain Sarah's trust. At first, she looked at him with dark, mistrusting eyes. Slowly, painstakingly, she began to trust him, and finally, to feel fond of him.

***

Dr. M. had changed, and as he continued working inside the facility, pretending to be the same cold, uncaring man he'd been for so many years, he found he could not deceive those he'd been so cruel to. It was best for him not to see their faces. He had no contact with anyone, except Sarah, and the brief meeting with Jess in the orchard. Other than

148

that, he remained completely cut off.

Everyone waited, including Jess. She felt particularly anxious, for it had been over a week since she'd seen Ben in the orchard, and he'd told her he would try to see her.

***

Ben had told Jess he needed a week. It was now eight days since he'd said that, and three since Hanley had visited her. Jess still felt stir crazy but seeing Hanley had greatly relieved her anxiety.

She was ordered only once that week, by a tech on the intercom, to leave her room and perform her exercise. She did so immediately and pulsed without any problem.

On day nine, she got the call she'd been hoping for. Ben came on the intercom at ten in the evening and told Jess he would be coming to her room in five minutes. Her heart began to pound.

She'd had nine days to grow impatient, not to mention nervous, about seeing him again. She quickly looked at herself in the mirror then went to the bathroom. While in there, she looked at the white towel hanging over the shower curtain bar and smiled.

***

Ben felt equally unsettled, like Jess. He'd not only been anxiously anticipating their next meeting, he also had to find a way to orchestrate it. He finally decided that the best way was to assert his full authority with the night tech who manned the viewing station. He walked into the viewing room, addressed the tech by his military title, then re-addressed him by his first name, which surprised the young man.

He looked at Dr. M. and stared. Ben looked back at him and smiled, which unnerved the tech even more.

"Private Dowling. *Richard.*"

"Ye—... yes?"

"You've been working very hard for me."

"Yes, Sir."

"You're doing a wonderful job."

"Yes, Sir. Is there a problem, Sir?" the man said, sounding increasingly nervous.

"Not at all. But it's come to my attention that you haven't had any time off since coming to work for me here at this facility."

"Sir, I don't need a vacation, Sir."

"I'm not suggesting you do."

"No, Sir."

"However, as your superior, I reserve the right to give you leave, do I

149

not?"

"Sir, yes, Sir. But is there a problem, Sir?"

"First, you can start by calling me Doctor, not Sir. We both know my military rank is an honorary title only. Second, despite it being honorary, the title still gives me rank over you, and I am your superior, acknowledged?"

"Sir, yes, Si—… I mean, yes, Doctor."

"Good. Then if I order you to take leave of your shift tonight, you will follow those orders without question."

"Yes, Sir." Dowling sighed. "I mean, Doctor. Am I being fired?"

"No," Ben laughed. "I want you to take the night off."

"Sir?" The man cringed and sighed again. "I mean, Doctor."

"You're married," Ben motioned to the man's hand.

"Yes."

"I want you to go home and spend the night with your family, Private. Is that understood?"

"Yes, Doctor, but—"

"No *buts,* Private. That's an order. This is my project, and I reserve the right to grant leave to my employees, when I see fit. Now, don't feel this has any reflection whatsoever on your job performance, Private. Simply take your leave, be grateful for the time at home, and enjoy it."

Private Dowling stood, staring at the Doctor for several moments, unmoving. Ben smiled at him.

"You may take your leave now, Private Dowling."

"Yes, Sir." The man groaned. "I mean, yes, Doctor."

"I'll see you back here tomorrow evening, Private."

"Yes, Doctor."

Private Dowling breathed a sigh of relief at the reassurance he would be returning to his job the following evening.

"Oh, and Private?"

Private Dowling turned to Ben, looking nervous again.

"Yes?"

"Don't worry about the leave. Your paycheck will still appear as if you worked your shift, understood?"

"Yes, Doctor, *Sir.*" Private Dowling said, this time on purpose. A wide smile broke across his face, and he sounded so relieved, Ben laughed.

"I'm not always a hard-nosed bastard," Ben said.

"No, Sir, I never thought that, Sir."

"Well, if you did, I wouldn't blame you. Goodnight, Dowling. See you tomorrow night."

"Yes, Doctor."

Private Dowling saluted Ben, who looked at him in total surprise, before saluting back. Dowling left the room, and Ben sat down at the controls in front of the screens, sighing in relief.

"Well, what do you know?" he whispered. "Kindness *does* work."

***

In his room, Martin smiled. "Guy's comin' full-circle, finally."

***

With the tech gone for the night, Ben sighed nervously and patched into Jess's room. His hands shook. He told her he'd be there in five minutes.

Ben switched the camera in Jess's room off, then switched over to the outside cameras and waited until Private Dowling was off facility grounds before leaving the monitoring room. His heart beat so fast by the time he reached her door, he had to steady himself and take several deep breaths.

***

"Holy Jehoshaphat." Martin lowered his book, lying on his bed in his room, rolling his eyes at the featureless ceiling. He had never wished more than on this night that he didn't have to be mercilessly subjected to every thought floating around the facility. He grumbled to himself. "For a man who's acted so tough all these years, this is absolutely *ridiculous*."

***

Ben took several minutes to calm himself before knocking on Jess's door. Even then, he couldn't keep himself from shaking.

"Come in."

As he stepped inside, Ben's heart hammered more fiercely.

She smiled nervously at him, standing in the middle of her room, wearing only a towel. Ben looked down at the floor, his face flushing.

"I didn't have anything to wear, other than those stupid blue scrub things, and they're not so sexy."

"This is ridiculous," Ben laughed to himself, breathlessly. "Here I am, old enough to be your father... far too old to be feeling this clumsy."

He shook his head, laughing even harder. "Look at this, my hands are shaking," he said, speaking softly, not looking her in the eye. "Some tough guy I turned out to be, huh? King-scientist, master-genius, knocked off his throne by a girl in a towel."

She looked at him, her eyebrows raised, feigning insult.

"I mean, a beautiful *woman* in a towel," he paused, frowning, "An *extremely* beautiful woman wearing a towel. Wearing *only* a towel."

She laughed. He smiled. She walked up to him, looking him in the face, forcing him to meet her eyes.

"Hey. This is me, okay? This is what I want. I've had a lot of time to think about things."

"You don't think clearly when you're in isolation," he said, his voice gentle, yet slightly chiding.

"And here you are, and you haven't been in isolation."

"Haven't I?"

He bent down to kiss her, and she raised up on her toes to meet him. They kissed for several moments, timidly.

Jess pulled away and took his hand, leading him to the bed. He stopped short and she turned around.

"It's been a long time since I've done this," he said, although, now he no longer sounded nervous, only apologetic.

"Well, I haven't done it so much, myself."

"Neither have I."

"Great, then we're even."

"This is ridiculous," he said again, looking up, talking to the ceiling.

Jess stood in front of him and unbuttoned his shirt. She looked up at his face, finishing with his shirt, then moved to his belt and pants.

Her eyes burned with intensity, and suddenly, all Ben could think about was how all-encompassing his passion had been for her when they'd kissed in the orchard. His heart fell right back to that moment, simply from the yearning for him clearly shining in her eyes. As she reached her hand up to grab the back of his neck, pulling him greedily down to her, he relieved her of the effort, leaning down, meeting her halfway, in a sudden explosion of passionate heat-intensity. They kissed fervently, in a vigorous storm of desire, both utterly consumed, and it wasn't long before they fell into Jess's bed, in a fervent tangle of arms, legs, and repressed longing.

***

Martin groaned, dropping his book, and turned over onto his side to face the wall.

"Now, that's just… *disturbing*."

He bent his pillow tightly around his ears, attempting to blot out what he heard, to no avail. He groaned again.

"Someone, *please,* knock me out!"

***

They fell asleep facing one another and slept that way for over an hour. Ben woke, suddenly panicked, till he looked at the clock, and saw it was only midnight. He had until four to stay with Jess.

He watched her sleep and marveled over her curves beneath the sheet. This was all a revelation for him. He'd never felt this way before.

He brushed hair away from her face, studying her features. She looked like a heavenly creature, perfect in every way.

She opened her eyes and met his, blinking sleepily. Then she smiled and covered her mouth.

"What are you doing?" he laughed.

"Morning breath."

"It's only midnight."

She looked at the clock, then back at him, smiling again.

"Well, I think that term applies to anytime you fall asleep next to someone you don't want to disappear when you wake up."

"I'm not going anywhere, Jess."

"Ben," she whispered, smiling.

"Yes?"

She turned over onto her back, looking up at the ceiling.

"I was only saying it."

"Oh."

He lay on his back then, too.

"Jess."

She smiled. This was a different kind of happy than she had felt with Aaron, or any other man she'd dated or slept with. She felt certain she'd never been in love before. She frowned. Ben caught her expression.

"What is it?"

"Nothing," she said, quickly smiling again, but he could see that it was forced.

"What?"

He suddenly felt self-conscious. When she wouldn't answer, he grew insecure.

"Was it bad? Do you feel like you made a mistake?"

"What? No, of course not."

"You do."

"No," she said, turning to him.

"Then, what?"

"I don't want to say."

"It was bad, the worst you've had."

She laughed. He scowled, moving to get up, becoming upset.

"No!"

She sat up with him, pulling on his shoulder. He looked back at her, feeling embarrassed.

"It wasn't bad," she said. "It was really, *really* good, okay?"

"You don't have to say that, Jess."

"No, it's true. I mean, for someone who hasn't done it in a long time, I sure couldn't tell."

She eyed him warily.

"Well, I wasn't lying, if that's what you think."

"No, that's not what I meant," she said, raising her voice. Then she sighed, becoming flustered. "This is stupid. I don't believe this. We're actually having a fight?"

"Because, you're not being honest with me."

"And you're being insecure!"

"But you're being dishonest."

"No, I'm not! Maybe I just don't feel like sharing every single thought I have in my head with you the moment I have it."

"That's fine."

"Well, apparently not!"

"Fine," Ben sighed.

He closed his eyes, trying to stay calm, to keep his mind straight, but he had no idea what had happened between them, or how they'd come to be this way, so fast.

"I love you."

Her voice drifted to him, soft and trembling. Tears stood in her eyes. "I just didn't want you to know," she sighed, closing her eyes tight. "I was afraid."

"Are you kidding me?"

He cradled her face in his hands. "I love you back, Jess."

She shook her head violently and tried to pull away. He wouldn't let her.

"Why not?"

"I don't know."

"I love you," he said again.

She looked at him, eyes pleading. He felt utterly confused. Wasn't this supposed to be the part where they started making love again? He shook his head in consternation.

"I've never loved anyone before," she finally said, barely above a whisper.

"That's incredible, Jess."

"No, it's not!"

"Why?"

"Because, I'm afraid! Please tell me this isn't an act. That you're not going to let us all down. You're going to give us all up, aren't you?!"

He couldn't contain his horror at this.

"You don't trust me? You still don't trust me, after all of this?"

"I do. I want to."

"But you don't. You kiss me, you sleep with me, you say you believe in me. Then you accuse me of lying to you?!"

He stood to leave. She spoke so quietly, he barely heard her.

"Please don't yell at me like that."

"Why not?"

"'Because, when you do, you sound like Dr. M."

He turned to look at her, sitting dejectedly in her bed, holding the sheet up over her chest, and suddenly, he felt overwhelmed, utterly awash, bathed in shame.

He'd treated her with nothing but cruelty for the first several months she'd known him. He'd only treated her with kindness for a few weeks, and yet, she'd opened herself to him, told him she loved him.

"I…" he faltered. He came back and sat down on the edge of the bed.

"I know I've been awful, and I forget all the time how hard this must be for you to believe, but I'm a better man than… than..."

He paused, struggling for the right words.

"I treated you… *all* of you… so terribly."

His voice hitched and stopped.

He suddenly bent double and sobbed without warning. Jess sat frozen in horror, watching the emotions overcome him. Then, she reached out and gently placed her hand on his shoulder. Suddenly, she felt as if they were both back on that plane, when she had first glimpsed the real him.

He could not look at her. "I'm so sorry."

She got up on her knees and scooted closer to him. She tried to grab his face and turn it to hers. He wouldn't let her, so she kissed the side of his face. He still wouldn't turn to look at her. Her kisses never stopped.

He reluctantly relaxed to her advances as she continued kissing his cheek, finally turning to face her, so overcome with emotion, he pushed her back down on the bed, returning every kiss she'd given.

They made love violently, and when it was over, they did not fall asleep again. They lay in silence, gazing at one another. This time, Ben would not let her hide anything. He took the first turn.

"So, the deal is, that I love you, Jess. No way around it, no rationalizing it away. I love you. And whether you trust me or not, I'm still going to love you. And if you trust me one minute and not the next, I'll just have to accept that. Trust takes time. That's easy for me to forget. I guess with how I've behaved, it's one step forward, two steps back."

"No. No more steps back. That was the last one, I promise."

"You don't have to make that promise, Jess. I told you once—I won't hold you to anything that happens while we're here, and I meant that. Maybe once we're out—then I can begin to prove myself to you."

"You have me," she said. She looked at him, smiling, and he looked back, loving her. "You *have* me," she said again, and kissed him.

He kissed her back, and they made love again. When it was time for him to leave, he felt agonized.

She stood, still naked, now wrapped in the bed sheet, as he came out from the bathroom, buttoning his shirt. He smiled at her.

"I like that outfit," he said.

She smiled and laughed. He looked at her apologetically.

"I don't want to leave you, Jess. I don't want to leave you all alone."

"I know."

"When I'm gone, it will be so easy for your mind to start working again. Convincing yourself, in this tiny room, that I'm still Dr. M."

He looked at her, his face pleading, his voice full of emotions he would never be able to express to her in words.

"I'm not him anymore, Jess."

"I know." Her eyes filled with tears. "I know."

"Do you? I don't want to be impatient, Jess, but I *need* you to believe me. I need to know I can count on it."

"I do."

He smiled, relieved. He had her heart, and she had his. Somehow, in that moment, they both felt it. He turned, opening the door, sparing her a smile. Then he closed the door… gone.

***

Two weeks passed by and Jess didn't see or hear from Ben. Hanley was permitted to visit twice a week, for one hour, but never again were the cameras turned off. Hanley's visits were strictly for company. They couldn't talk about the escape, but Jess remained grateful for the company, nonetheless.

Every three days, she received orders, via tech over the intercom, to go to the orchard and pulse, and she did so without any difficulties. She had adjusted to life in isolation, albeit, with visits from Hanley, and fell into a simple routine, coping extremely well by this point.

***

Ben monitored Jess's progress and continued sending reports to General Levin every week. He grudgingly reported that Jessica Wembly was one hundred percent rehabilitated and ready for the field again. He did not want to send this report. He knew what it meant for her, but he had no choice.

***

Seventeen days after they made love, Ben received the order for their next assignment. As he read the itinerary, he closed his eyes and sighed, his heart sinking. Par for the course, he scheduled a video conference with General Levin, to discuss the assignment.

As he patched into the network, he sighed again, preparing himself for the conversation. Things were too close for him to give anything up now. He believed he was only a few months away from Sarah having her ability under control. But a few months would come far too late to spare Jess the torment he'd been so desperately hoping to protect her from.

"General Levin, Sir."

"Doctor. Good day. Good day, indeed."

"Yes, Sir."

"I've read your latest report, and now you've read mine."

"Yes, Sir."

"I'm very pleased you kept your promise, Doctor. I gave you two weeks to have Wembly up and running again, and you did just that."

"Yes, Sir."

"Those visits with Hanley really seem to have done the trick, Doctor. You truly do know your subjects best."

"Yes."

The General nodded.

"Good work. You have your itinerary for the next assignment. Any questions?"

"None, Sir."

"Good. I don't have to tell you that this is a big one—the biggest in a while. As for Wembly, would I be accurate in describing her as the most effective subject we've ever had?"

"Yes, Sir. She can do amazing things." Ben attempted to put on a play of professional pride, but inside his heart broke.

"We haven't done anything on this scale since Kandahar," the General said. "I'm still not pleased that we lost Harley on that one."

"Neither am I, Sir."

"And Wembly doesn't even wear a blindfold," the General sounded worried.

"No, Sir, not with her ability. It just wouldn't do."

"Well, can she do this?"

"Sir?"

"Can she perform, Doctor?"

"With all due respect, I thought you said you trusted me with my subjects."

The General looked at Ben for several moments, not speaking. Ben finally broke the silence.

"Sir, Kandahar was almost two years ago, and there've been no miscalculations since that time. Also, I was the one who called it right, sending Hanley in, instead of Aaron. That was my call, and you trusted me on it. Wembly *is* ready, as promised."

The General smiled, erupting in loud brays of laughter. Ben feigned a smile, his stomach turning in knots.

"Doctor, I like you. I like you *a lot.* You don't stand for any BS, do you?"

"Sir, not on this project, no, Sir. Not on your life."

"Not on *your* life, Doctor."

"No, Sir."

"It's not as if this is your first time going on an assignment of this magnitude, so I'm going to trust that everything will go smoothly."

"Absolutely, General."

"Again, good work, Doctor." The General saluted, signing off.

***

There were no more nightmares for Jess—only dreams of what she and Ben had enjoyed, from which she woke smiling in faint but sweet embarrassment. She missed him far more than she thought possible, emotional longing mingling with a physical want that ached more than any hunger she'd ever experienced.

As per every morning, a tech brought her breakfast, and she ate every bite, then went to the bathroom. After she'd showered and changed, she sat on her bed, smiling. Then her heart leapt in her chest. It was the first time she'd heard Ben's voice in eighteen days.

"Jessica?"

"Yes, Dr. M.," she smiled, proud of herself for remembering to play along.

"It's time for your next assignment."

Her smile faded.

"Go out into the hallway and follow the arrows."

She did as instructed, finding herself in the same white room she'd met the doctor in for her first assignment.

Her initial instinct was to rush to Ben, throw her arms around him, and shower him with kisses. However, she also saw the look on his face, and his quick glance upward, toward the camera in the corner. They were being watched.

"Hello, Jessica. How are you feeling today?"

"Fine."

"It's time for you to go back out into the field."

"What's the assignment?"

"Have a seat," he said, indicating for her to sit. She did.

It did not escape her how strange all of this was—the same chair, the same table between them—were the memories not so intense, she might have believed it all a dream, and they'd never moved beyond the status they'd established that very first day.

"I don't normally apprise transgens in this much detail about their assignments before we go out," he paused. "However, this assignment is a little different. I won't lie to you, Jessica…" he trailed off, looking her dead in the eye.

Although she doubted the camera picked up on it, she saw something in his eyes. A sadness, perhaps? No—an apology. She sighed, closing her eyes. Ben saw this, and his heart broke, but he kept speaking. He had no choice.

"This one's big. It's imperative that you follow my orders without any hesitation, or *doubt*." She smiled reluctant confirmation, reading the imperative in his voice. His heart broke all over again.

"Can you do this for me?"

He fought to keep his voice steady.

"Yes."

Her voice was flat. He loved her even more.

"Then we'll get on our way." He rose from his seat.

"We'll be flying again. I hope this won't prove too problematic for you?"

"No problem," she said.

"And this time, we'll have company," he said, turning towards her. "We won't be alone. This is a *big* assignment, Jessica."

He saw the disappointment on her face and fought from mirroring it.

She'd been imagining what they would spend the flight doing. Now, she felt disgusted with herself for being so single-minded. Still, she couldn't deny the frustration at having to itch and ache even longer, especially given that the means of scratching would be within ready reach throughout.

"Who's going with us?"

"Mr. Gees."

"Oh… good."

The relief was obvious in her voice, and Ben understood. At least it was someone she knew and liked. Mr. Gees had always been friendly with her.

Ben tapped on the back wall. The invisible door opened, and they entered the green brick corridor.

Mr. Gees stood by the car in the clearing outside, holding the passenger door open for her. She smiled at him as she got in and he smiled back. As before, Dr. M. disappeared into the citrus grove.

Everything went the same way it had on her first assignment—all except for the detail of the third party. Jess sat in the same aisle seat as before. Mr. Gees sat on the left side of the plane, in the window seat. He never spoke, idly leafing through a magazine before falling asleep. Ben drew down Jess's window shutter, and later in the flight, as before, he brought her food.

She ate her lunch ravenously, and Ben watched her, always amused. Once finished, he took her plate, like before, then brought a tall glass of root beer. As he handed it to her, he motioned for her to move over, just as he had on the first flight. She glanced over at Mr. Gees and saw that he still slept.

She felt immensely relieved when Ben sat next to her, so close, although, she doubted he would kiss her this time. His shoulder brushed against hers, and her stomach immediately flip-flopped, aflutter with butterflies, tickling and almost painful.

I've got it so bad, she smiled to herself. Ben looked at her. The longing in his eyes was unmistakable. He wanted her just as badly as she wanted him and knowing this somehow relieved some of her tension. She visibly relaxed, looking over at Mr. Gees again.

"He's asleep," Ben whispered. "But we have to follow protocol."

His voice sounded a clear warning.

"But you're sitting next to me."

"That's not against protocol, especially when the assignment is so big. It's just part of the briefing process. Besides, part of my ability to control my subjects is that they feel dependent on me outside the facility. It's normal for you to be clingy, remember?"

She nodded. "Stockholm."

"That's right."

"So, what is it?"

"Something bad. That's why I must tell you everything to expect up front. I would have anyway, even as Dr. M."

She looked away, her eyes cast down into her lap.

"I'm going to kill someone, aren't I?"

Ben felt as though he'd been stabbed in the chest. He nodded, then realized she hadn't seen. She still looked down.

"Yes, there will be casualties."

"How many?"

"I don't know, Jess. Honestly. But..." He couldn't continue.

Jess looked over at Mr. Gees again, saw that his eyes remained closed, and quickly took Ben's hand in hers, squeezing. Her hand felt ice-cold, but it comforted Ben all the same. She only held it for another few moments, then let go. It was all she could give him, but it was enough.

"I can't tell you where we're going, although, once we get there, you'll see that it's not in the U.S. We'll land and arrive at a hangar, then board a car. Mr. Gees will be in the passenger seat. I'll be in back with you, helping you prepare. We'll be driven to a town market area."

Jess's head snapped up and she looked at him in complete dread and disbelief. He looked back, his eyes empty now.

"We'll be dropped off there. You'll change into civilian dress on the plane before we land, as will I. We'll walk together to the designated area, then I'll leave you and walk to a safe distance. I'll point you in the right direction. You'll be instructed to count to one hundred after I leave your side. When you reach one hundred, you'll pulse. After you're done, I'll be there, right back at your side."

Her eyes welled up with tears. He loved her more than life itself. If he could spare her this pain, he would, but he couldn't. No one could.

"Roughly four minutes will have passed for you, in an instant, but I'll have spent those four minutes making my way through the chaos, back to you."

"Chaos?"

"Before you pulse, Jess, you'll be looking at a daytime scene of green grass and trees, people walking, people talking. You'll have to look at all those people, Jess, and you'll have to pulse."

"Ben..." her voice trembled. He closed his eyes.

"I know," he said, barely above a whisper. "It's the worst assignment I've even seen. The worst I've ever been on."

"What if I can't?"

"You have to." He took the risk of turning toward her and took both her hands in his.

"You have to, Jess, because if you don't, everything's ruined. If I don't appear to have control of this project, I'm gone. And if you fail to comply with my directions, I'll be forced to follow through on threats I've made to you in the past."

"Could you really do that?"

"No. But when I can't, they'll remove me, and they'll bring someone in who can."

She trembled all over.

"No matter what happens with me, if you don't follow orders, someone in the facility will die, or be completely destroyed. They'll either kill Aaron, or bring in Martin's wife, and make him watch her die. Those are the choices, Jess."

"Sarah," she choked.

"She's not ready. She's close, but it will be another few months. Only another few months, Jess. Remember that."

"A few months, living like this? That's a lifetime."

"I know."

There was a long pause as they sat in utter silence.

"I love you," Ben whispered into her ear, kissing the side of her head. "I love you, and I'm so sorry, Jess."

"I love you, too, Ben, but… what if I really just can't?"

"Then I'll never see you again, and no one will ever be free."

She closed her eyes, turning away from him, unable to look at him anymore. He got up and sat back down across from her, glancing over at Mr. Gees, who still slept soundly.

***

A half-hour passed. Ben grew increasingly nervous, watching her. She sat with her eyes closed, head bowed, chin against her chest. He saw a tear drop from one of her eyes, but only once. He worried about her mental state. He looked away, at Mr. Gees, still sleeping, and jumped when Jess spoke to him.

"Why?"

"Why, what?" Ben attempted to sound smooth, like Dr. M.

"Why would they do this? To what purpose?"

"They don't tell me that."

"Postulate."

He nodded. She needed to know.

"I can't say for certain, but I wouldn't be surprised if the news tonight reports about a large-scale bombing by a terrorist cell, on the civilian population of a certain country."

"So, it's all a set-up," Jess said, in disgust. "We're framing some terrorist cell, and it's really us who are the terrorists. *I'm* the terrorist."

"Actually, Jessica, you won't be a terrorist," Mr. Gees suddenly spoke. Both Jess and Ben jumped. Mr. Gees smiled.

Jess had never heard him speak like this before. His voice sounded oily and smooth, and belied a devilish arrogance his face had never shown. It frightened her.

"You'll actually be doing a very good thing. You'll be inspiring an entire army to action. You'll also be aiding our forces immensely. Because of you, a certain war," he said, eyes darting across to the doctor, "might end sooner than it would have. We never condone the loss of civilian lives, but in this case, those few lives will most likely save hundreds more down the line. Sometimes, to become passionate about the fight, there needs to be an incentive."

"But it's a lie! My God, were there *ever* any terrorists? Wait… was 9/11 a *transgen*?!"

"No," Ben said, immediately.

"No, it was not," Mr. Gees confirmed. "That was all *them*."

"It doesn't matter," Jess said. "How can you people do this?"

"The loss of a certain amount of lives is acceptable in times of war, as are certain tactics," Mr. Gees said. "End of story."

The warning in his voice rang clear. She saw him cast a stern, heavy look at Ben, and realized she was very close to ruining his cover.

"I'm sorry… you're right. None of it matters, for me anyhow."

Mr. Gees glared at Jess.

"I only take orders," she said. "But I'm still human, I'm not some trained soldier who can just walk into a crowd of people and shoot. Forgive me if the first time I commit *murder* might take a few minutes of adjustment."

"As your Doctor, Jessica, I can fully appreciate what you must be experiencing," Ben broke in, playing his role. "Mr. Gees is not a trained psychologist, nor does he understand your mental state nearly as well as I do. It would be best if he left any further preparations to *me*."

Ben shot a warning glance at Mr. Gees, who seemed to take the warning to heart, settling back in his seat, returning to his magazine.

Jess was grateful for that. She looked at Ben, her eyes cold, not wanting to give anything away. She only nodded her thanks, and he nodded back.

***

As they began their descent, Jess turned to Ben, who sat next to her, once again. She'd been excused to the bathroom earlier to change her clothes.

She now wore a dark blue burqa, and when they exited the plane, her face would be covered by a mesh panel. Ben wore a white cotton thawb down to his ankles with a sirwal underneath. He wore sandals, but even Jess's feet were covered.

She felt other-worldly in her disguise. It could have been a game, like playing dress-up as a child, or even a costume for Halloween.

She surprised Ben after coming back from dressing by asking for more food. She told him she felt hungry.

"I won't pulse as well if I'm hungry, right?"

He sympathized—she needed a distraction—anything to take her mind off what she had to do.

"Maybe the stress is using up more energy," she shrugged.

He got up and came back with a small ham and cheese sandwich, hastily prepared. She thanked him and ate it ravenously. *Her equilibrium is off. Good God.* He prayed it wouldn't affect the mission. When she had finished eating, he also brought another glass of root beer that she greedily drank down. He spoke to her gently, not caring if it made Mr. Gees suspicious in any way.

"Can you do this?" he asked.

She sat back in her seat and closed her eyes, breathing deeply. When she opened them, she refused to look at him.

"What choice do I have?"

16

The last thing they did before disembarking was place a microphone in Jess's ear, so she could hear Ben even after he reached a safe distance, and he could hear her. If she did have difficulty pulsing, he'd be able to help her trigger using tried and tested methods.

Ben was furious the General and his superiors would send her on an assignment this hefty on only her second time out. It was entirely possible she could lose her ability altogether from such a trauma. Even as Dr. M., he would have questioned the decision to put a transgen into a position like this so soon, with so little experience.

If Jess couldn't concentrate, she would not be able to perform, no matter what the consequences were. She already seemed distracted, showing signs of disequilibrium, and he felt afraid for her, not to mention himself, and the rest of The Society.

They disembarked, and Ben shepherded her into the back seat of a black Sedan, taking the seat next to her. Mr. Gees got into the front passenger seat, next to the anonymous driver. He did not speak, nor make eye contact with Jess or Ben the entire drive.

Apparently, the reigns had been turned over to Ben, for the moment. Mr. Gees wore a microphone in his ear, too, however. Ben would be told where to lead Jess and where to leave her.

She didn't know where she was, but there were foreign soldiers with guns every twenty yards or so. She could not read any of the street signs, let alone understand them. Then she saw a sign with one word on it.

"Khardush?"

Ben nodded but didn't speak.

A few minutes later, they turned and headed toward the heavily crowded market alleys. Jess looked at all the people in bewilderment. There was an incredible mix of dress styles—such an eclectic array of conflicting fashions and uniforms. She turned to Ben, suddenly panicked.

"We don't fit in!"

Mr. Gees glanced back at her, appearing amused.

"Yes, we do, Jess," Ben said.

"No, I saw a man in a *suit.*"

"There are a lot of styles that blend together in places like this," Ben said. "It's not uncommon to see the traditional Bedouin dress on one man, while another in a suit stands next to him, talking on a cell phone."

"Bedouin?"

"Never mind," Ben warned.

"But we'll stand out."

"No, we won't. See?"

He pointed out her window.

"Look there, and *there*. We won't stand out at all. This is perfectly normal."

Jess didn't relax, but she believed Ben and fell quiet again. He looked at her, genuinely concerned.

"Are you okay, Jessica?"

She nodded quickly, still extremely nervous. He looked at her hands, which she fidgeted with in her lap. Her fingers trembled. He wanted to take her hand and hold it but could not.

The car drove through the crowded market, and Jess wondered how they weren't running over people's feet. Then the car turned the corner, drove to a less crowded area, and stopped.

Her heart suddenly started beating wildly in her chest then. She felt dizzy. She breathed heavily and quickly, gasping for air. Ben turned to her, panicked, forgetting about any guise of putting on a show. He no longer cared about appearances.

"Jess, *look at me*. You're having an anxiety attack. It's perfectly normal. This is a very big thing for you, a very big thing they're asking of you."

He shot an angry, accusing glance at Mr. Gees, who turned around, facing forward again.

"Ben?"

"Don't worry about them, okay? Look at me, do you see my eyes?"

"Yes," she said, still gasping for air.

"Good. Look at my eyes, Jess. You can do this, all right? We just need to calm you down. We need to slow down your breathing."

She nodded, still hyperventilating.

"Okay. Breathe with me, all right? Exactly as I'm doing."

Ben took several long, deep breaths, holding them for several seconds each, then exhaled slowly. Jess did the same. This went on for several minutes, until she finally relaxed again. Mr. Gees looked at his watch and became impatient, finally speaking after about ten minutes.

"Isn't there something you can give her, Doctor? To help her relax?"

"No. No drugs. She must be able to concentrate. A drug to help her relax will ruin her ability to perform. That's why I have to have their complete trust."

"You do have control, don't you Doctor?" Mr. Gees said.

"Yes," he shot back over his shoulder, never taking his eyes off Jess.

She kept looking in Ben's eyes, for it was the only place she could look that calmed her down.

"Okay, Jess," he said. "We're going to get out of the car now, and I'll be with you every step of the way, all right?"

He nodded, prodding her, and she nodded back. He then gently affixed the mesh panel over her face, covering all but her eyes. He opened his door and got out, then came around and opened hers. She got out, keeping eye contact with him. As he took her hand to help her out of the car, it felt ice-cold, more so than before.

As soon as the door closed behind her, the car drove away. Ben walked with Jess, holding her hand. This would not be witnessed by Mr. Gees now.

They walked straight, passing the crowded market street on their left and continued down the road for a quarter-mile. Then, on the left, the road opened on a market square. As soon as Jess saw it, she froze. Ben's heart hammered. This was by far the worst thing he'd been an accessory to. How could he have ever been on board with this project?

Jess turned to him, pleading with her eyes. His own filled with tears.

"Please, Ben, *please...* there's got to be another way."

"No," he said, tears slipping down his cheeks. He removed his earbud. "There isn't."

She cried silently, and he sighed, still holding her hand, and walked them both into the town square.

Jessica's feet floated. None of it seemed real. Surely, this must all be a dream.

Ben walked with her, still holding her hand, to stand at the edge of the green grass in the large square. There were white, wooden benches on all four sides of the grass's outer edge. A path cut through the center, also lined with white benches. Jess scanned the area, noting the people she saw.

She looked at the shops that lined the streets around the square, and marveled as she watched an old, white-bearded man in an outfit like Ben's, walking along the asphalt with a goat on a twine rope.

As the man and goat walked past a dry-cleaning store, a businessman, obviously of Middle Eastern descent, walked out of the shop door in a very expensive-looking suit. Dry cleaning draped over his arm, he talked on his cell phone excitedly. She wondered who he was talking to, and what the conversation was about.

It was very busy in the square, the shops bustling with activity. Jess felt nauseated as she realized they were placing her here at the busiest time of day, when there would be the highest number of casualties.

"How can they do this, Ben? How can they expect me to even do this, when all I've ever done before now is blow out a power station?"

"You have no choice, Jess," Ben said. "I'm so, so sorry."

"Me, too."

"I have to leave you now, Jess. Do you remember what you're supposed to do?"

"Count to one hundred, and then…"

"That's right. Can you do this?"

"Yes."

"I'll be able to hear you, all right? At least until you pulse."

"Okay."

"I won't be with you, but I can hear you Jess, okay? I'm still with you. You're not alone."

"Yes," she said, breaking his heart. "I am."

He squeezed her hand, then let go and walked away, making Jess feel like the loneliest woman on the planet. As he walked away, he put his earbud back in place.

***

The only way Jess could function now was by insisting none of this was real, even though she knew that was a lie. She did not feel the light breeze against her clothing or on what little skin remained exposed on her face. She did not hear the people talking, nor the laughter of a couple that sat at a bench almost directly in front of her in the middle of the square. She did not allow herself to think about the fact that the couple, now kissing, surely did so for the last time. Nor did she let it in fully that every person she saw in the square was about to take their last breath.

She took a breath of her own and began counting, slowly, not even comprehending that with each number she reached, she grew closer and closer to mass murder. It was simply too much for her mind to take in.

"One, two, three, four, five, six."

She had the presence of mind to remind herself to go slowly, not so fast, so Ben would have time to reach a safe distance.

"Seven… eight… nine… ten… eleven… twelve… thirteen…"

She closed her eyes, not wanting to look as an elderly woman, also wearing a burqa and head scarf, walked through the square.

"Fourteen… fifteen… sixteen… seventeen…"

***

Ben's heart pounded away in his chest as he counted in his head along with Jess.

She reached twenty-five, and Ben now stood back at the spot where the car had stopped to let them out. Still, he kept walking.

"Twenty-six… twenty-seven…"

He counted with her, though she was not aware.

"Twenty-eight... twenty-nine..."

Suddenly, Ben froze, his feet inexplicably stuck, as if in hard cement. His heart faltered, for Jess had stopped counting. His mind reeled, his world suddenly spinning, sinking down into darkness at the silence in his ear.

***

At twenty-nine, Jess opened her eyes and saw something that took her breath away. A young woman, surely not much older than she, entered the square, pushing a stroller.

She watched hazily as the woman pushed the carriage to the bench opposite the kissing couple, and sat down, her back facing Jess. The woman sat forward, reached deep into the bassinet cavity, and released her baby from its protective straps.

She watched in horror as the woman lifted the small infant up and placed it on her shoulder, gently patting it on the back, rocking back and forth. Jess didn't realize she'd stopped counting.

She stood in the square, on the edge of the grass, unaware that Ben now ran back to her in a desperate attempt to find out what had gone wrong. He could not even hear her breathing.

It felt like an eternity before he finally passed the corner buildings on his left and the square bloomed into view. He ran to where she stood, limply staring.

As he reached Jess, standing on her left side, he took in the vacant look in her eyes, then followed her gaze. What he saw took his own breath away. He saw the woman, sitting on the bench, his gaze immediately falling on the infant's face. The baby smiled. He let out a breath, all the air leaving him, and closed his eyes.

Jess turned to Ben then, snapping out of it. She pulled the mesh panel off her face and stood looking up at him, visibly broken.

He looked in her eyes and a tear slipped down his cheek. He turned his body to face hers and reached out his hands to touch her. He bent his face down to hers until their foreheads met. There, they stood, frozen.

"I can't do it, Ben," she whispered.

"I know," he whispered back.

His microphone was still in place.

"I can't," she said, growing angry. "I can't, I can't, I can't."

"It's all right, Jess. I know you can't. It's okay," he cried.

"No, it's not... It's not okay. Nothing's okay!"

"Jess, I understand. You can't do this. I could never expect you to."

"It's not okay! It's not okay for them to try to make me do this!"

Jess cut him off and Ben froze in sheer panic.

She was losing control of her emotions. She was going to pulse.

"Jess, you've got to control it. Don't lose control, control it!"

He had her by both shoulders now, grasping so tight, there would be dark bruises later, but at the time, she didn't feel anything.

She was too angry to feel anything other than her own rage—the fire boiling her blood to ether. It was too late to stop her. There was no time, nowhere Ben could run or hide.

She had only moments. With what little faculties remained, she stepped forward onto the grass and took one step to her left, standing directly in front of Ben.

He realized, moments before it happened, what she was doing and closed his eyes, waiting. She lifted her arms up and bent her wrists, throwing her palms outward, towards the square.

***

In an instant, a compression wave flew out from Jess's body with an intensity of force that flattened everything within the square. It hit the buildings on the other side and cracked the walls with such impact, the structures buckled and collapsed.

On her left and right, the compression ringed outward, shattering every window, sending tiny shards of glass everywhere. These buildings also cracked and buckled but did not fall. The compression wave flattened cars parked on the sides of the nearest streets surrounding the square, hurling them against buildings.

Several seconds into the blast, clouds of smoke, dust, and debris flew upward in a small-scale mushroom cloud.

The EMP knocked out electricity to the entire city, which Jess could not possibly know contained over 70,000 residences, over a twenty-mile radius. Several minutes after the blast, the dust remained so thick, visibility was cut to mere feet in front of her.

There were no people inside the square anymore. Many who had been inside the closest buildings when the compression wave hit, were knocked unconscious, their eardrums shattered from the pressure. Many would never hear again.

Countless dozens were cut with deep lacerations, some blinded for life by the glass that ripped into their eyes. Others would be crippled, riddled with scars from the cuts and deep gashes received. Still others suffered immediate amputation of limbs, their injuries from the blast so great. These were the lucky ones, those not utterly obliterated in the blast.

The damage was immense, and more than Ben's supervisors could have ever hoped for, but he was not concerned with this. He'd closed his eyes, and when he opened them, he knew almost four minutes had passed.

Jess stood in her spot, not moving, arms now loose at her sides. Ben took in the scene of chaos and destruction around him briefly, then spun Jess around to face him. She moved as limply as a rag doll, and when he looked in her eyes, he saw nothing.

He spoke to her, his own voice sounding faint and far off.

He looked at her, then back at the square. The smoke still hovered so mercifully thick, whatever might remain of any bodies was blocked from view, shrouded in the clouds of debris.

"Jess," he said, then more loudly, "Jess, *Jess*!"

Nothing. For the time being, at least, she was gone. He pulled on her wrist, dragging her with him down the street. In his haste, he yanked so hard, he heard a bone snap in her wrist, but didn't care. He just wanted to get her out of there.

After only a few feet, she stumbled and fell. He bent to pick her up, and carried her, as he had done so many times before.

He passed several other men also carrying women in their arms and looked away as he walked past still other women who cradled children limply in their arms, wailing in utter grief. Everything appeared grey, dull, save for one color that blinded Ben's eyes. *Red*.

Jess's head lolled onto his shoulder, and he felt thankful she was being spared this scene. He'd been right when he told Jess that they would fit in. They were just another pair of survivors, hurt and traumatized, amid atrocity.

Ben did not even hear the voice of Mr. Gees in his ear as he was instructed where to find the car, yet, he somehow managed to follow the directions. Perhaps it was some subconscious, survivalist instinct kicking in.

He carried Jess to the car, and Mr. Gees opened the door, not looking concerned in the slightest. If anything, Ben thought, Mr. Gees looked smugly satisfied. He gently eased Jess inside the car and got in with her.

As they drove away, he hugged Jess to his chest and sobbed. Mr. Gees looked back, momentarily, still no emotion playing on his face.

At the airplane hangar, Ben carried Jess, still unresponsive, up the loading stairs and onto the plane. He carefully set her in the window seat, then sat next to her.

Mr. Gees closed the exit off and sealed it, then took his seat. The plane taxied out of the hangar and was in the air within five minutes.

Ben observed Jess, taking in her complexion. Her skin looked ashen. He brushed his fingers across her lips, which appeared pale, almost white. He turned to Mr. Gees, who didn't even look at them.

"Something's wrong."

Mr. Gees looked over, eyebrows raised.

"Something's wrong with her." Ben repeated.

"There's no medical on board, Doctor," Mr. Gees said, matter-of-factly. "It will have to wait until we get back to the facility."

"God dammit!" Ben yelled.

Mr. Gees's stare remained cold as ice.

"There shouldn't be a medical problem, should there? If she was physically ready for this assignment, as you reported she was?"

"She *was* ready," Ben said, exasperated, desperately worried. "I don't know what happened."

"She has a pulse, doesn't she?"

"Yes," he said, feeling her pulse with his fingers.

"Then she's fine. Whatever is wrong can wait till we reach the facility... *Ben.*"

Ben turned to look at Mr. Gees again, alarmed. Mr. Gees returned his stare, unwavering.

"What? That is your name, right? It's what *she* called you."

"You have a problem with that?"

"It seemed... overly intimate."

"Do not question my tactics, Mr. Gees, do you hear me? The girl panicked. I had to do something to pull her together. I know her better than anyone. I know what it takes to get the performance that your people demand of me. You asked me to get her to perform, and I did. You got exactly what you wanted, isn't that correct?"

"*More* than we had hoped for."

Mr. Gees sounded sickly pleased. It was the first genuine emotion he had displayed the entire trip, and it made Ben feel queasy.

"That's right, you got even better than you'd hoped for. So, I suggest that from now on, you don't question the tactics it takes to accomplish things, and don't ever question my authority again... EVER!"

Mr. Gees stiffened at these remarks but said nothing else to Ben for the remainder of the flight.

Jess did not awaken or even stir, despite Ben's repeated attempts to rouse her. When the plane finally landed several hours later, he immediately lifted her into his arms and carried her off the plane.

He loaded her into his car, in the passenger seat. He had changed back into his own clothes, but Jess still wore her burqa. He quickly got into the driver's seat and screeched away towards the facility. Mr. Gees stood staring after them.

17

Two hours passed, and although Ben felt utterly exhausted, he did not fall asleep. Finally, the nurse returned, smiling.

"Doctor Milbron?" Nurse Charles asked.

"Yes?"

"She's fine, about the same as the other times you've brought her in. She's being taken care of. Her wrist is broken, but that will heal in six to eight weeks."

"Why was she so weak? She's been eating the way she's supposed to, and even under that much stress," Ben shook his head. "She looked like she did the first time, when I almost killed her."

"Yes, she's in similar shape, Doctor. She's very weak and depleted. Are you certain she's been eating?"

"*Of course*, I'm certain."

"Well, all right then. I only wanted to make sure. You really should have brought her in sooner, considering her condition."

"I—I'm sorry, what condition?"

"You didn't know? Why, you're always so meticulous. You must have realized."

"Realized *what*, Nurse Charles?"

"Why, that she's pregnant, of course."

Ben stared at the nurse for several moments, grappling with the rising contradiction of emotions.

"Sh—... she's pregnant?"

"Well, yes, Doctor," Nurse Charles frowned, clearly exasperated. "You do follow the subjects' activities, don't you?"

"Yes, of *course*," he said and laughed, clapping his hands.

"Well, then you know she's been sexually active with another transgen."

He kept laughing and smiling crazily. He saw the look on Nurse Charles's face and this only made him laugh harder. She looked at him as if he were crazy.

"Well, I know it's a first, but it's not *that* amazing. It's only a baby, for God's sake."

"She's pregnant," Ben said to himself, still in shock, smiling so wide his cheeks hurt.

"Oh, really, Doctor," Nurse Charles scolded. "I know it's an exciting development for your project and all, but you act as if *you're* the father."

She turned and walked away, shaking her head.

"It's only a damn baby, not the Lost Ark," she said, to no one in particular, as she disappeared back into the next room.

"Nurse!" Ben yelled.

She poked her head back out, looking perturbed, then walked back up to him.

"What?"

"Can I see her?" Ben asked.

"Oh, yes, of course," she sighed. "Fine. She should be waking up soon. You're welcome to wait in her room."

"Thank you, Nurse Charles," Ben said, standing to tower over her, attempting to recover himself and reassert his authority.

She lowered her eyes, seeming to realize she'd spoken to him out of turn, and nodded her head. She opened the door and showed him in.

***

Ben sat watching Jess sleep for over an hour before she stirred. Her lips appeared pale pink now, instead of off-white. Her skin still waned porcelain, fearfully pale, but her cheeks had begun to color a light pink. Her left arm lay in a cast, hand, wrist, and forearm, all the way to her elbow.

Jess slowly opened her eyes. Ben could see her struggling to focus. When she saw his face, she crumbled. He moved his chair right up next to her bed and held her arm, above the cast. There were no cameras in this room.

"Hello."

She cried silently.

"Jess," he whispered. "You're going to be just fine."

"I don't care about me," she said, weakly.

He sat watching her, various emotions playing over her face—sadness, despair—but mostly horror at what she had done. His heart broke for her and he suddenly felt guilty for being so selfishly happy about the baby.

"Jess," he sighed.

"I'm a terrible person," she said, hitching. "I can never forgive myself."

"You lost control, Jess, it wasn't your fault."

"I wanted to walk away, but, I was so *angry*. How could I lose control like that?"

"It wasn't your fault, Jess. It was your hormones."

"My hormones? What are you talking about?"

"The reason you couldn't control your anger, it's because your hormones are raging right now."

"No." She shook her head. "No, my period isn't due for another few days. And it's never made me like this before. Even before the mission, I was..."

"What?"

"Nothing," she said, clearly embarrassed.

He felt disappointed—she still felt the need to hide things from him. She saw his look of disappointment and felt guilty.

"I was... horny, okay? It was bad, almost like... I felt completely helpless."

He smiled. She looked away.

"That was your hormones, too."

"Why, because I'm *in love*?" she said this with disgust.

"No," he said, although his own cheeks flooded with color and his heart rate sped up at hearing her say those words.

"I know they say when you're in love it changes the chemicals in your brain." She frowned. "Maybe even inside your body, too, but how could I be this out of control?"

"Jess, you're pregnant."

She looked at him, wide-eyed, for several moments, much the same as he'd done upon hearing the news.

"What?"

Her voice came out barely above a whisper. He smiled, teary-eyed.

"You're pregnant."

She continued staring at him, her mind visibly working behind those beautiful brown orbs of hers. He was lost. Her chin trembled, and she looked away from him. A tear slipped down her cheek, silently. He wiped it away, turning her face to look at him.

"No."

"*Yes.*"

"I... I killed a baby."

She broke down into sobs. He held her while she shook, her entire body racked with emotions coursing through her. He cried as well.

"I... I... k... kil... killed all those people!" she wailed.

"No, you didn't Jess. *They* did. They made you do it. You didn't have any choice."

"I was going to walk away," she cried, pulling away. "I said I couldn't do it, and you said you knew, that it was okay. You were going to let me walk away and I... I... I did it anyway."

"It's not your fault," he said, holding her tightly in his arms. Was it just his imagination, pushed into over-drive by stress, or could he *feel* her pain? Waves of bitter emotion washed through him, caustic and smothering.

She cried for what felt like forever. Finally, it seemed she simply could not cry any more. She had no tears left. He worried she had become dehydrated, but the IV drip connected to her hand ensured that wouldn't happen.

She sat not looking at him for so long, he grew worried she had slipped away again. He touched her face.

"Jess, please stay with me."

"I'm here," she said, softly, looking over at him, her eyes full of sadness. "Where else would I go?"

***

Jess spent a night alone in the infirmary—Ben having to leave her to fulfill 'Doctor M.'s' duties—before returning to the isolation of her room.

She sat in her room for long hours lying in bed, doing nothing. She'd lost the will to even attempt to entertain herself.

She slept for fifteen hours a day and went several days without showering. She still ate her meals when the tech brought them to her room. Despite her depression, her mental state seemed to have no effect on her appetite, for which she felt ashamed.

She ate the food they brought her, but never tasted it. She never left her room, not even to work in the orchard. The only saving grace was that they didn't ask her to pulse anymore.

***

Ben knew that General Levin would be receiving a report from Mr. Gees. Would it contain any observations the man might have made concerning his perceived intimacy of Ben with Jess? Ben made certain in his own report, to mention the agent's lack of cooperation.

He noted, particularly, Mr. Gees's inability to show any concern for the 'subject,' as Ben referred to Jess in his report, although it made him feel sick to do so. He also pointed out Mr. Gees's decided lack of interest in trying to preserve the 'asset.' Ben felt certain this would counteract anything negative Mr. Gees might have said in his own report. He also made certain to point out the resounding success of the mission, just as he had promised the General.

Another video conference was scheduled. Ben went into it with as much confidence as he could muster. He had too much at stake now to appear weak and submissive. He was tired of his own authority being usurped. Now that he knew Jess was pregnant, he needed to have utter control of the project more than ever.

The General appeared on-screen and Ben immediately, sharply saluted, his first attempt at establishing equality. The General saluted back, surprised.

"Dr. Milbron. I've read your report. First, allow me to congratulate you on the resounding success of your assignment."

"Yes, Sir. As Mr. Gees mentioned, it exceeded your expectations."

"Yes, regarding Mr. Gees. I'm sorry that you felt he was..." The General leafed through Ben's report to read his words back verbatim. "What was it?... Here we are: 'Distracting and unhelpful.' He 'questioned your tactics in front of the transgen, which could have greatly endangered your ability to maintain her trust.' Is that right?"

"Yes, General, that is exactly what I wrote."

"Yes, well, I've received a report from Mr. Gees as well. He seems to be a little surprised by some of your... *techniques.* But his overall assessment was very favorable."

"*Really?*"

"Yes. His only real concern was that you might be overly emotionally invested, but I'm paraphrasing that. I believe his exact words were—*slightly emotionally unstable.*"

Ben frowned, and the General smiled.

"That's exactly what I thought," the General said. "It's of no consequence to me, either way. The people I answer to merely expect results. You've given them to me. So long as you continue to do your job as specified, I don't give a rat's damn what you do with your transgens."

"Sir?" Ben frowned, confused.

"If it establishes a bond by allowing them to address you by your first name, it's fine by me. Hell, you can let them call you pick-a-ninny, or bunny muffin, or heck, I don't know, Rufus Sewell."

"Rufus Sewell?"

"Look, the point is, I don't care. Mr. Gees does, but I *don't.* And frankly, this isn't Mr. Gees's show, now is it?"

"No, Sir, it definitely is not."

"Exactly. And Mr. Gees answers to me, not the people I answer to. He wouldn't want to answer to them, trust me. Neither would you. So long as I can give them the results they want, and keep them off my tail, I don't give a flying fart what Mr. Gees says about first names, or even a little hand-holding—the girl trusts you—that's all that matters."

Ben let the General continue wagging his tongue, listening patiently, making what he hoped were the appropriate facial expressions at certain intervals. It proved a tricky exercise, considering the fury and disgust the General's words provoked.

"... and what kind of sick person would even imagine a twenty-four-year-old girl even entertaining a romantic attachment to a man as old as yourself?"

"General?"

Ben attempted to feign hurt feelings, but he didn't have to try very hard. In this case, art imitated life. The General laughed.

"Sorry, Ben, I didn't mean to offend you. Obviously, you're an intelligent, perhaps even good-looking male, I wouldn't really know. It's not about your looks, it's just that, well—a girl that age, and attractive as she is—you know what I'm trying to say, don't you?"

"Not really, Sir."

"Just that Mr. Gees has some sick thoughts going through his head. I sometimes question his observational skills. He's a pervert!"

Ben sighed and tried to ignore that remark altogether.

"Besides," General Levin said. "Mr. Gees doesn't know what I do. Our Wembly is pregnant?"

"Yes, Sir," Ben said, growing nervous. "I was very surprised to learn that."

"As was I. But you've stated the father is Aaron Tremaine, correct? That was her boyfriend before we locked her up in isolation. Well, looks like they got close enough before that happened, eh?"

"Yes, Sir. It's a big development for the project."

"Indeed. I wonder what kind of child we can expect from the mating of two transgens? Good work on getting those two together. I'm sure you had a hand to play in it, somehow. You're very good at what you do, Ben. We're all very pleased, excepting Mr. Gees, of course.

"By the way, he will not be accompanying you on any more assignments. I think his skills will be better served elsewhere from now on. He's being transferred to the East Coast, effective immediately. I'm sure you're very sorry to have missed the opportunity to say goodbye." The General winked.

Ben laughed. In his lap, his hands sweated profusely.

"We'll have to keep our eye on Wembly, hmm? See that she gets all the proper medical care. We would not have sent her on assignment, had we known about her condition. We do care about preserving her as an *asset*. Very well put. But, given that she almost died from performing while pregnant, I'm assuming she will be out of commission for the next nine months?"

"Yes, General. It would not be wise to risk her health, or the child's."

"Yes, because it's of the utmost importance now that we do preserve the life of that child. My superiors are curious, what with both parents having abilities. What do you think?"

"Sir, I think Wembly is an exceptional subject, and her offspring has a very good chance at being uniquely special."

"That's my assessment as well. Besides, she exceeded all our expectations, carrying out two missions in close succession. She deserves a break to become a mommy. She's earned it."

"Yes, Sir," Ben said, and fought to keep his voice steady.

"Then we're agreed. No more missions for Wembly, until after the baby's born. You can resume focusing on Sarah Marchland now, one hundred percent. She's the one we're looking at now to do our work for us."

"Yes, Sir."

"Then, that's all. Again, good work. Oh, and if Wembly's unable to pulse while expecting, she could, in theory, be removed from isolation, correct?"

"Ye—... yes, General," Ben faltered.

"Ben?"

"Sorry, I wasn't expecting that, General."

"It's true though, isn't it? She's no threat to any escape plan at this point, is she?"

"General, there is no escape plan. That problem is rectified by isolating Sarah."

"Yes, it is. And I doubt Wembly would even want to escape now. Her focus, presumably, will be on the upcoming birth. Isolation has been hard on her, and we can't risk her mental health during the pregnancy.

"Dr. Stanlowe thinks it would be healthy for Wembly to have access and emotional support from the father. It's of his opinion that keeping Wembly isolated now would be very harmful. This baby needs all the support it can get."

"Yes, Sir." Inside, Ben's heart burst with joy and pride. Outwardly, he appeared prideful of his job.

The General smiled and nodded. "You were the right man for this job ten years ago, Ben. I'm glad we picked you."

"Me, too, Sir."

"Good Evening, Doctor."

He saluted. The screen went dark before Ben even had time to salute back.

***

That evening, after his conference with the General, Ben gave Private Dowling the night off again.

It had been over three weeks since the last time he'd done this, and Dowling was more than happy to have another night off. This time, he went without pause, smiling and whistling.

Ben immediately located Hanley, in his room. He then turned the camera off in Hanley's room and went to see him.

***

"That made the best dressed list? Are they kidding?"

Hanley sat at his table, reading US Weekly, when a knock came at the door.

"Oh, ah... come in." The door opened. Dr. M. entered, closing the door behind him.

"Is this it... are we going?" Hanley stood up excitedly.

Dr. M. pointed anxiously up at the camera.

"Oh, shit."

Ben started laughing. Hanley frowned.

"I'm just kidding Hanley, the camera's off."

"Hah, hah, very funny, Doc. What's up?"

"A lot. You'd better sit down."

"Oh, geez. The last time anyone said that, I found out you and Jess were, like, a *thing*. What could possibly be worse than that?"

"Jess is pregnant."

Hanley's eyes bugged until Ben thought they might pop out onto his cheeks. He attempted to sit down on his bed, missed and hit the floor. Ben started laughing again, this time so hard, tears sprang up in his eyes.

"Holy fuck!" Hanley said.

"I prefer to call it making love, actually."

It took Hanley a moment to get the joke, and when he finally recovered himself, he laughed, looking at Ben in disbelief.

"Who are you?"

"I'm Ben."

He extended his hand, both to help Hanley up and for him to shake.

Hanley stopped smiling, his face growing serious. He eyed Ben's hand warily, refusing to shake it, and remained on the floor. He got up slowly and sat down on the bed.

"What the hell are you doing, Dr. M.?"

"Attempting to make amends."

"Did it ever occur to you that there are some things you can't make amends for? There are some wrongs you can never make right."

Ben immediately flushed, filled with guilt. Jess was not the first person he'd cruelly deceived, but Hanley was. Ben sighed deeply, the old shame rushing back. When he spoke, his voice shook, and it took great effort for him to even choke the words out.

"I'm sorry, Hanley. That's all I can say. I'm truly sorry."

Ben didn't say anything else, only stood with his head hung. Hanley sat looking at him, frowning. The two men remained in silence for several moments.

"Doc? Sorry won't make what you did go away," Hanley said, pausing for what felt like an eternity. "But I'm sure you already realize that. We all have things we're ashamed of, don't we? But I know we need you to get out of here. I've had a few weeks to think it over, too."

Hanley rubbed his temples, sighing. "And Jess is gonna have your baby." Hanley shook his head, still in shock. "So, I guess what I'm trying to say is—I won't forget the things you did to me, or Angelique. I can't forget."

Ben looked down at the floor, too ashamed to look Hanley in the eye. Hanley looked Ben up and down, this time with sympathy.

"I won't ever forget. But I think I might, *someday*, be able to forgive you."

This time, he couldn't hold back his emotions. Ben looked up at Hanley, tears welling up.

"Not tears," Hanley sighed. "What are you, a *girl*?"

"Thank you, Hanley."

"Shut up. And let's not talk about it anymore for now. Agreed?"

"Agreed. Can I sit down?"

"Yes, but only because you asked."

Ben sat down, staring at Hanley intently.

"They're letting Jess out of isolation."

"Really? Why?"

"They think she can't pulse while pregnant."

"Can she?"

"She already did, once. That's one of the things I need to talk to you about—we went on assignment, Hanley, and it was bad. The kind of bad you've experienced, only... this one was your worst nightmare times ten. She's real messed up."

"I tried to talk to her about it," Hanley said. "But there's no preparing for it."

"No."

"You were there?"

"Right by her side." The look on Ben's face told Hanley it was beyond bad.

"Is she... will she recover?"

"She has to. She's carrying our baby."

Hanley nodded.

"Anyway, she can pulse, at least she did, but it almost killed her. She's only a few weeks in. The further along the pregnancy goes... I just don't know how it will affect her ability. Even if she can still pulse, I'm not sure how it might affect the baby."

"So, what are you trying to say?"

"I'm saying that, when the time comes, we may need Jess's ability to get out of here."

"And?"

"And I'm not sure if she'll be able to help us."

"And if she does," Hanley finished, "she might lose the baby."

Ben nodded. Hanley rubbed his temples again, thinking.

"You getting all this, Martin?" Hanley spoke to the empty air. "He knows," Hanley said, tapping his temple.

Ben nodded.

"So, we wait," Hanley said. "We wait until after the baby is born."

"No."

"Why not?"

"Because Sarah will be ready in about ten weeks, give or take. And when she is, they're going to use her right away. She's only eleven. It will destroy her. I've seen what they did to Jess. I know what it's done to me. I can't imagine them putting an eleven-year-old girl at risk that way."

"She won't be at risk, though," Hanley said, looking Ben in the eye. "She's the one who makes them put *down* the guns, remember?"

"What if something goes wrong? What if she cracks? If she breaks before we can use her to get out, th—I—" Ben stuttered into silence.

"It's okay, I know what you mean. And I get what you're saying. She needs to use her powers for good. *Only* for good. So, the very first time she uses her powers, it has to be for getting us out."

Ben nodded. "Besides… I don't want my baby being born here. Jess shouldn't have to give birth to her child inside this prison."

"She may not give birth at all, even if we get out."

"Or, maybe she will," Ben said. "I just don't know what to do."

"We can't risk losing Sarah. If they break her, she's useless to us, and then we'll never get outta here, right? Then your child *will* be born in this prison. Are you willing to gamble on that?"

"No."

"Then, I guess you have your answer."

Ben nodded. Hanley shook his head.

"Jess is *pregnant*."

"I want you to talk to her, Hanley. I don't think I can help her. Not like you could."

"I'm sure she'd rather see you, *Ben*."

Ben stared at Hanley. Hanley stared back.

"You called me Ben."

"Yeah, let's not make too big a deal out of it, huh?"

Ben nodded.

"I'll talk to her, if you really think I'm the guy for the job," Hanley said.

"I do. Let her know she can come out of her room whenever she's ready."

"She doesn't know she's out of isolation?"

"I only found out just this afternoon, but, honestly? I still don't think she'll come out, even after she knows. She's fighting some bad demons, Hanley. On top of all that, she's hormonal."

"Oh, *now* I see why you're sending me in."

"I still don't think Aaron should know anything."

"Hell, I think he's gonna figure it out once he sees her." Hanley cupped his hands over his stomach.

"Hanley, she's less than one month along. No one needs to know she's pregnant for a while. She won't show until long after we're out of here, I hope."

"Oh, right."

"So, Aaron doesn't need to know. If he wonders why she's not with him anymore, just try and explain to him that she's messed up from her assignment. That won't be a lie. I doubt she's even interested in any romance right now, of any kind."

"She still loves you, Doc."

"How can you be so sure?"

"Because, I saw the look on her face when I first found out about you two."

Ben sighed. Hanley agreed to see Jess right then and there.

"I'll go, but before I do, I need to know what I'm dealing with. I need you to tell me everything about the assignment."

The horror and revulsion in the doctor's eyes were unmistakable. Hanley could see the mission had been every bit as disturbing for the doctor as it had for Jess.

Ben sat and told Hanley everything, including how Jess had lost control, because of the pregnancy. When he finished telling his story, Hanley was ready.

***

Jess was asleep. She heard a knock on the door and thought it was a tech bringing her supper, despite the fact she'd already eaten supper and the plate had been taken away over two hours ago. She heard the door open, her back towards whoever had come in. She lay staring at the wall.

"Hey, kiddo."

She didn't turn over to look at him. He sat in the chair, straddling it backwards.

"I got some good news and some bad news," he said. "The good news is, we're getting outta here in ten weeks and counting."

Jess rolled over, looking at Hanley intently. He saw the dark circles under her eyes, took in her greasy, unwashed hair and general appearance. His heart broke.

"What's the bad news?" she croaked.

"They're letting you out. No more isolation."

"Why?"

She sat up in bed, hugging her knees to her chest. Her eyes darted at him, then looked away again.

"Because, they're no longer worried you're an escape threat," Hanley said. "They think you can't pulse."

"They're right, I can't."

"Sure, you can, Jess."

"No," she said. "Never again."

Hanley remained quiet for a while before speaking again.

"I heard about the baby. Congratulations, Jess."

Her eyes darted to Hanley's face then away again, hot, bulbous tears springing up. They soon welled over and spilled down her cheeks.

"What's wrong, kiddo?"

"What you said."

"What, congratulations?"

"Before that."

"What, I… *Oh*," Hanley mentally kicked himself. He knew the whole story about the assignment, from Ben.

"Dammit, Jess. I'm sorry. I didn't mean it like that. I just meant—"

"I know what you meant. But it's all I can think about. I can't even be happy about *my* baby. Not after what I did."

"Jess, I'm sorry."

Hanley didn't know what else to say.

They both sat in silence for a long time. Then Hanley spoke again. Jess had to strain to hear him.

"You're down the rabbit hole."

She looked at him, her eyes haunted. He knew that look.

"Way worse than I ever was," he said.

"I didn't expect you to say that," she said, her voice trembling. "You watched Angelique."

"Yeah, I did. And I loved her. But what you're going through is even worse."

"Why?"

"Because you won't forgive yourself."

"How can I?"

He said nothing.

"Did you?"

"Not for a very long time," Hanley sighed. "And after it happened, I dreamed about it, every night. For weeks, months. Every minute of every day, it stayed with me. The first time I went a day without thinking about it, it all came back the next, only worse. I went a whole day without thinking about her, and I thought that made me a bad person.

"For a very long time, I wouldn't let myself get over it. There *is* no getting over it. But for a long time, I wouldn't allow myself to move on. I started *forcing* myself to remember, every day—punishing myself. I felt guilty for what I did to her, and I felt guilty when I didn't feel guilty. I felt guilty for making myself feel guilty then I felt bad when I pushed her out of my mind. This wouldn't make sense to a lot of people Jess, but I know you understand—guilt can be a real bitch."

She said nothing.

"You're down the rabbit hole now because you fell in, you didn't put yourself there. At some point, though, you'll have a chance to get out, and you won't take it. You'll force yourself to stay, because you don't think you deserve to get out."

"I *don't* deserve to get out."

"Sure, you do, but I can't convince you of that."

"*You* can get out, Hanley, because it wasn't your fault."

"Wasn't it?"

"No, you didn't kill Angelique. She killed herself. You didn't kill her sister. Dr. M…" Jess trailed off. Hanley quickly jumped in.

"He didn't kill her either, did he?"

He frowned, looking like he might be sick. Jess stared at him in disbelief.

"Ben came and talked to me—told me about what happened back then, with his dad. He also told me everything about *your* mission. I get that the project was new. I understand when he says a team of psychs were calling the shots. I don't like it, but I get it. I don't wanna get it, but I do. You see? Down the rabbit hole some more."

Hanley looked at Jess with such intensity now, she looked away. He commanded her to look back at him, and she did. Hanley had never commanded anything of her before.

"If you don't let yourself out now Jess, then *when*? A week, a month, a year from now? We *need* you. We're getting outta here in ten weeks, but only if you're on board. Everyone's counting on you, Jess. You get us out of here, then you can deal with your demons, okay?"

"I can't just put it all aside."

"Yes, you can."

"How?"

"By moving on."

"*How*?"

"You can start by getting out of that bed."

"What good will that do?" she moaned.

"It'll be a start. Everything else will follow. You're going to have a baby, Jess. And I know a certain guy who loves you and wants to share all this with you."

"How can he still love me, after what he watched me do?"

"Oh, Jess, you think Ben doesn't love you anymore? He's the father of your child. He loves you more than life itself. Don't you get that? He loves you so much, he came to talk to me, face-to-face. He was too chicken shit to ever do that till now. He did though, and you know why? Because he thought *you* wouldn't want to see *him*."

"Why would he think that?"

"He thinks *you* don't love *him* anymore."

"What?"

"Ain't love grand? It's a front row ticket to the show called *Doubt and Insecurities*. Really, it's just another rabbit hole, if you let it be. Don't. He loves you, and you love him. And now? The two of you are gonna have a baby. He doesn't want his child born inside a prison... Do you?"

Jess shook her head, thinking about it for the first time.

"See? That's how you get out, Jess," he said. "You think about the other people who're stuck in here with you. We all want out. Your baby's gonna want out, too. And you're not the only one who's dealing with demons. You're forgetting that Ben was there with you, right by your side. He carried you out of there in his arms. He's carried you more than once, hasn't he? Now it's *your* turn to carry *him*. While you've been here in your room all alone, he's been all alone, too, inside his own head."

"I never meant to leave him alone."

"No, just like I never meant to hurt Angelique, and Ben never really meant to hurt any of us, not really. That was Dr. M. The man who came to see me tonight? It wasn't Dr. M. Tonight, I met a guy named Ben, who's desperate for his freedom, and looking to make an act of contrition. And I realized that so long as I can't forgive him, I won't ever be able to forgive myself. So, I let go, Jess. Just tonight. I let go of it all. I'm ready to get out of here. Are you?"

She nodded, hot tears spilling down her cheeks again. He smiled.

Jess looked at Hanley then, her eyes grave. He frowned.

"What?"

"I'm ready to get out of here," she said. "But, where you say we're going, I…"

"Jess, I already told you… you *need* to believe it. You can't go into it blind."

She sighed, closing her eyes.

"We're their only hope," Hanley said.

"No," she whispered, "They're *our* only hope."

She shook her head. It was all just too much for her, no matter how much she tried to prize her mind open.

"Why can't they just beam us out of here, Hanley? If they're as smart as you say they are, why can't they just… I don't know, *materialize* us to wherever they want us to be? Or just melt the fence themselves?"

"You still don't get it, do you, Jess? You think they can melt fences like me or float like Malcolm? You think they can do what you can do? They don't have any powers. They're just as helpless as Dr. M. They don't have the gene, get it? Why would they have abilities?"

"I… I never thought about that, I guess. I just assumed."

"Exactly. They have no powers, Jess. And they don't have weapons."

"But they have technology," she said. "Why can't they just beam us aboard, all at the same time or something?"

"This isn't *Star Trek*… sorry. I didn't mean that to sound so…"

"Condescending?" she offered.

"Yeah, sorry. They have a ship, okay? And the knowledge and technology to manipulate matter and energy to travel through space. They can travel through wormholes, go from one side of the universe to the other. And I'm sure melting a fence would be a snap. What they can't do is hurt a living thing. They have no way of pacifying an army with guns trained on us. They'll pick us up, once we get out, and all of this will be over, like a bad dream."

Jess sat, stunned.

"And they want us to help them with that… Bailon race, right? How are we supposed to help them fight?"

"Don't know, kiddo," Hanley smiled. "But they seem to really think *you* can help out in that department."

"Me?" Jess frowned. "What could I possibly do?"

"Oh, I don't know… use that amazing power of yours to wipe out the Bailon's weapons, maybe?"

"That's ridiculous."

"Look, for now, all you have to do is *believe*. That, and be on board when the time comes. Can you do that?"

Jess nodded.

"Good. Because I know someone who would love to see you."

Hanley stood to leave the room. As he opened the door, he looked back and winked at Jess.

"I really missed you, kid."

His voice trembled. He was on the verge of tears.

"Hanley," she called him back.

As he turned around, she gave him a weak effort at a smile. It wasn't much, but it was appreciated. He smiled back and left the room, leaving the door standing open.

Ben appeared a few moments later, and Jess stood up quickly, a rush of emotions flooding her. She still loved him, and she suddenly realized just how much she'd missed him the last several days.

She crumpled, her face contorting into a grimace. He rushed forward to hold her. He did so for several minutes, then pulled away to look at her.

"How are you?"

"Better," she sniffled.

"How are you feeling?"

He placed his hand on her stomach.

"Fine. The same. I wouldn't even know."

"That's good."

Then he kissed her for the first time in so long, he'd forgotten how wonderful it felt to touch her that way. She kissed him back.

He did not want to push her, so he backed off. She let him. Eventually, they lay down in her bed, and he held her in his arms while she slept. He stayed with her for several hours, also falling asleep.

When he woke up and saw the clock, it was only ten minutes before the morning tech was due on shift. He didn't want to wake her, but he didn't want to leave without saying goodbye.

As he moved to get up, she woke.

"I didn't want to wake you."

"It's okay."

She looked at the clock. "Gotta go," she sighed.

"Yes."

"When can I see you again?"

He thought about it for a long while.

"I'd say in a month, because I don't want to give Dowling another night off any sooner than that, but, then I'll have missed a whole month of…" he trailed off, touching her stomach again. "I should be here for you, every day."

"But you can't. I know that."

"Soon, Jess. We're getting out of here. Ten weeks. Ten weeks and I can hold you in my arms every night."

"And watch me get fat," she said, looking down.

"And watch you carry my child into this world."

"Not into *this* world, according to Hanley."

He smiled. "There's just the tiniest hint of a firecracker in there."

She smiled back. "Maybe, but I'm not the same person you fell in love with. I'm not the same person I was when you first met me."

"Neither am I," he said.

She smiled at him again, grateful. He hugged her.

"I'll try and figure something out. I might be able to meet you in the Atrium, if I can turn the cameras off. Give me a week. I'll send word through Martin. Okay?"

"Yeah," she said.

He kissed her once, then got up and left before leaving became impossible. She watched him go, a small but undeniable ember of hope kindling inside her.

18

The time had come for Ben to test Sarah's ability with other people. He had waited this long because he wanted to make certain she was ready.

Her training was simple. He could afford it to be—for the very first time, he was dealing with an ability that posed no threat to him. If Sarah lost control, the worst that could happen was that he'd be overcome by a sense of profound peace and contentment. This was Sarah's gift.

They began by using flashcards—the traditional first exercise for all transgens. The images were of her home, her old room, some of her most beloved toys—all designed to provoke stirring emotion. In extremis, he had images of her dead parents, too, but did not use them.

In Sarah's case, sadness proved an impotent motivator, but he still had to try, and it made him feel awful.

After several weeks, once Sarah was through the worst of her grief, these images began to make her smile, even with her tears. Once she began to accept that her parents were truly gone, as well as her old life, the images evoked fond memories, as well as sadness. In time, Ben knew, Sarah would only remember the good things.

This was why her training had to take so long. There simply was no way to rush a person through grief. Ben had to remain patient with her. She seemed to acknowledge this herself, somehow empathizing with his position.

They finally reached a point where Sarah only smiled at the images, instead of sobbing (which she did at first) or silently crying. The first time this happened, Ben felt an incredible surge of hope. The next step in her training, however, would need to be done very carefully, so as not to set them back several weeks.

Sarah could call up her ability at will now, for he could feel it whenever he was in the room with her. He simply gave her the command to use it, and she did, trusting him completely. But could she summon her ability when under *threat*? The only way to test her ability under those circumstances was to expose Sarah to them and hope she could still concentrate sufficiently to summon her power.

So, the day came when Ben went to Sarah's room, and told her that today's training exercise would be… *different*.

***

Sarah was incredibly intuitive for a girl her age. Ben had become aware of this over the weeks of getting to know her. She seemed to be incredibly sympathetic to Ben's emotions. On more than one occasion, he wondered if this was not also part of her gift.

A few weeks before the scheduled shift in drill took place, during a standard exercise in which he held up a poster image of her old bedroom, she stared at him in a manner that made him feel as though his skull were as transparent as a fish bowl—the thoughts swimming behind as clear to her as angel fish in their aquarium. He looked back at her, growing concerned. When she spoke, he nearly fell from his seat, overcome by the sudden wave of warm feeling that washed over him.

"You're different," she said.

"How so?"

"When I first met you, you were nice to me, but it seemed... *forced*. Now you do it because you want to. You're nicer now."

He looked at her for several moments, and she stared back, smiling.

"Well, of course I want to be nice to you." He giggled, euphoria washing over him as Sarah's ability heightened.

"I know, but before it was because you wanted something from me. You still want me to help you, but, I know that if I can't, you'll still be nice to me. Because you just are nice, now."

"And before?"

"You were nice to me because you had to be, to get me to do what you want. Now you're nice to me even if I can't do anything at all."

"You can see all that?" Ben asked.

Sarah nodded, still smiling. He set the image down on the table.

"Sarah, do you know what I want from you?"

She glanced up at the camera in the corner, nervous and unsure, then back at Ben, nodding.

"Can you read my thoughts?"

She shook her head, looking confused. "I can feel what you feel," she said. "It's how I know to use my gift. I can feel when people want to hurt me."

"But you've been using it with me, I've felt it."

"Because I feel that you want me to."

"So, you know I don't want to hurt you."

She nodded. Ben relaxed, tension seeping from him.

"Sarah, what you can do is very important. You know that, don't you?"

She nodded.

"But at some point, we'll need to discover exactly how powerful your ability is. Do you understand what I mean by that?"

She shook her head.

"When I'm in this room with you, I can *feel* your gift. It makes me happy. I couldn't harm a fly, even if I wanted to. But this is a very small room. If I was, say, on the other end of a football field, do you think I'd still feel it?"

"I don't know."

"Exactly. And neither do I. That man with the electric gun... Remember him?"

She nodded, looking scared.

"He couldn't shoot you with it until he got at least a little bit close to you—close enough that your gift stopped him before he could shoot, but..."

Ben sighed, stopping. He knew he had to be very careful about what he said next, to avoid frightening Sarah too much.

"Let's say he had a regular gun, okay? A gun he could shoot from far away. The bullet could reach you in a second, it travels that fast. That's why guns are so dangerous, Sarah. People can shoot other people, even from very far away. Your gift is so amazing, and it can help keep you safe. It can even help keep other people safe. It could keep people from shooting each other, even."

"Like in a war?"

"Yes, Sarah, like in a war. But, only if your power can reach all those men with guns, even when they're far away. That's what we need to find out, Sarah—how far your gift can reach. Do you understand?"

"Yes," she said, her eyes those of a woman twice her age. "If the men with guns know what I can do, and they are far enough away, they can still get me."

"That's right, Sarah. Then, even the men who are close to you, who put their guns down, won't do you any good."

"Because of the hiding men."

Ben looked at her, frowning. She looked back, unblinking.

"There are bad men," she explained. "Sometimes they hide, where you can't see them. They want to get you. They can even see you up close, with their gun."

"Are you talking about snipers?"

"Is that what you call them?"

"I think that's what you mean, Sarah, but," he looked at her, wondering. "Sarah, can you see these men?"

She nodded, slowly.

"Sarah," he said, lowering his voice. "You can't read minds, but you can feel people's hearts, their intentions. Do you also know things?"

"Like what?" Her tone implied she might already have a good idea of what Ben asked.

"Do you feel like you know something's going to happen even before it does?"

She nodded slowly, then more emphatically.

"And you've seen men with guns, who hide?"

She nodded again.

"Then, you're probably seeing the exercises we'll be doing very soon." Not the whole truth, not a complete lie. It was too early to place so much concern on her shoulders, but even so, Ben couldn't suppress a contradictory sense of hope and foreboding. What she saw, what she felt... was it just the training exercise, or part of their impending escape?

***

The day arrived. Ben came to Sarah and told her it was time. She nodded, already standing. He took her out into the fields surrounding the facility and walked her through the trees, into a clearing. It was not the Atrium, nor the orchard where Jess had trained, but another outlying area surrounding the facility.

Standing on the other side of the grassy clearing, Sarah could see a soldier in fatigues. She froze and looked up at Ben, her eyes filled with fear. He didn't want to ruin all their hard work, and quickly reassured her.

"He won't shoot you, Sarah. It's only an exercise."

She nodded, her eyes filling with tears. She looked over at the man and sighed.

"Can you sense him, Sarah?"

She nodded, and he felt relieved.

"Okay, Sarah. I'm going to give him an order to raise his gun. Not to shoot, never that. Only to raise it. I want you to concentrate very hard, and make it so he can't do that, okay? If he can't raise his gun, he can't shoot you. He can't hurt you, Sarah. Do you understand what you need to do?"

She nodded. Ben felt extremely proud of her, but also nervous, for the outcome of this exercise could spell the loss of any hope for their plans.

Sarah smiled and suddenly Ben knew everything was going to be okay. A warm feeling of happiness and hope filled him, waxing to the point of euphoria. She was already using her gift.

"Don't be nervous, Uncle M."

He looked down at her in surprise, for it was the first time she'd called him that. "I won't fail."

In that moment, her voice was that of a grown woman.

"Mark," he spoke into his earpiece, squinting in the direction of the soldier. Ben's heart beat anxiously inside his chest.

The seconds passed, and the soldier remained standing, unmoved. After what felt like an eternity, Ben sighed, for he'd been holding his breath the entire exercise.

"Ensign?"

"Sir?" The man sounded confused, his voice light and tinny in Ben's ear.

"Why didn't you do as I commanded?"

"Sir, I don't know, Sir," he said, sounding completely bewildered.

"What do you mean, you don't *know*?"

"Sir, I'm sorry... I just... couldn't."

Sarah looked up at Ben, smiling brightly. Ben looked back at her, his eyes wide and unbelieving. Then he smiled at her, feeling nothing but love.

***

The exercises became more and more complex over the next several weeks. Ben organized a series of tests, each more and more taxing, demanding more and more of Sarah's energy and concentration. With each test, he thought surely this would be the day Sarah failed, but she never did.

He set marksmen a hundred yards away, then two hundred, three hundred and so on. When soldiers placed outside the boundaries of the facility, over a mile away, could not raise their weapons to put Sarah in their scopes, Ben knew she was ready.

***

He surrounded the facility with over fifty armed marksmen, at various intervals. None of them could raise their weapons. He drew the exercises out to a few minutes at a time, then ten minutes, then twenty. When Sarah could hold over fifty armed soldiers at bay, nonstop, for over an hour, Ben knew it was time.

On the day of her final exercise, he smiled at her, and she smiled back, hugging him fiercely. He knew then that he loved her. She loved him as well.

"Just think of it as practice," she said to him.

"What do you mean?"

"For when you become a daddy."

He looked at her in shock and surprise, pulling his earpiece out so no one could hear what they talked about next. He stooped down, so that they could see one another eye to eye.

"You know about that?"

She nodded. "She's your little Angel."

His eyes filled with tears and he smiled, his chin quivering. She wiped his tears away.

"Don't cry, Uncle M. Everything's going to be okay. She'll be just fine."

"She?"

"Angel."

"But, Jess, the pulse," he choked.

"She's special, too," Sarah whispered.

"Jess?"

"No."

"Who?"

"Are you not following me, Uncle M.?"

"I'm afraid I'm not, Sarah."

"The baby," she said. "She has her own power."

He sat, blinking at Sarah for several moments. Then he shook his head.

"No, it doesn't work that way. With two transgens, yes, because the non-coding DNA's been activated, but with only one transgen, the gene can't carry on. The sequence marker that carries the pseudogene can't replicate unless both parents carry it. It's complicated, Sarah, but, trust me—there's no way the baby could have an ability."

Sarah smiled as he explained all this. When he had finished, she giggled. "You're funny."

He looked at her, completely exasperated. She smiled, still whispering.

"You're very smart, Uncle M. But you don't know so much."

The old Dr. M. would have taken great offense at this remark, but Ben only continued looking at Sarah with wonder and bewilderment.

"Okay, Sarah, suppose I believe you. Let's suppose, even though it's impossible, the baby has a power, with only Jess's gene somehow carrying on. Let's also suppose the baby, while still in utero, somehow has an ability, without Luci. How do you know?"

"I just do. She's gonna put you back together."

"Huh?" He stared at her.

"Doesn't matter, Uncle M. All you have to do is *believe*. Can you do that?"

He looked at her again, thinking very hard. He thought about Jess, his heart fluttering. He thought about the baby, and how he did not want it being born here, inside these walls.

He nodded at Sarah, standing up and putting his hand out for her to take. She took it and they walked back inside the facility. Ben quickly fumbled with his ear mic, putting it back in place.

"Dismissed, gentlemen. Good work."

***

After Hanley visited Jess in her room, she still wasn't ready to see anyone quite yet. It was four in the morning when Ben left her, and she simply went back to sleep.

She woke up in the morning feeling ravenous, as usual, and squinted at the clock. It was eight a.m. and no tech had brought her breakfast. She sighed, realizing that if she was no longer in isolation, her meals wouldn't be brought to her anymore.

"Dammit," she grumbled, getting out of bed.

She quickly jumped into the shower and washed her hair, which she hadn't done in almost a week. She changed into clean underwear and clothing, quickly towel-dried her hair and reluctantly opened her door.

She stood out in the hallway for several moments, feeling nervous. Then her stomach growled, and she rolled her eyes.

"Cafeteria."

When the arrows stopped, so did she, staring at the white door with trepidation. Behind it was a very large, bright room that was guaranteed to contain at least a few people. One of them, most likely, would be Aaron.

Jess didn't know how her meeting with him would go. She didn't want to treat him coldly, but if he rushed up to her and threw his arms around her, what should she do?

What if he rushed up to her and started kissing her? She imagined a humiliating scene where she had to push Aaron away, in front of several on-lookers—the embarrassment and hurt that would play across his face—the betrayal she would surely see in his eyes.

Jess sighed again, finally pushing herself to open the door, for her hunger was simply too great to ignore. After all, she was now eating for two, and it wasn't her baby's fault if she was too cowardly for the confrontation she knew had to be.

She'd have to talk to Aaron at some point. Might as well get it over with sooner rather than later. Besides, she was excited to see some of her other friends, whom she missed terribly.

She took a deep breath and opened the cafeteria door. She stepped inside timidly and looked around. To her great relief, she saw that Aaron wasn't there. Martin was, however, and he smiled at her warmly. He sat at the table directly in front of her. She realized he must have known she was coming, had heard every thought she'd had while still standing on the other side of the door, and she smiled back, walking over to him.

"Still snooping?" She smiled at him, her eyes misting over.

"Can't help it, you really should know that by now," he smiled back. "By the way, you might want to thank me."

"Why?" She looked at him with curiosity.

"Because, I realized you were heading here around the time you finally decided to take a shower. I told Aaron if he hurried up and finished eating, I'd meet him in the rec room for a game of pool."

"You got rid of him for me?"

"Thought it'd be easier your first time back if you didn't have to deal with that."

"Thanks, Martin."

"Yeah, well, like you already know, you can't put it off forever, now can you? In fact," Martin paused, scrunching up his nose. "He's thinking about coming back right now, wondering what's taking me so long."

"Oh."

"Better go," he sighed.

Jess watched Martin stand, but as he walked past her, she grabbed his arm. He looked down at her in surprise.

"Just let him come looking. I should get it over with. But I'll feel better if you're with me."

"He might not make a scene if I'm here," Martin nodded. "I really don't know. Can't read that thought. He's not having it yet. The few scenarios I've picked up from him all involve seeing you again for the first time when the two of you are alone," Martin shrugged. "Spur-of-the-moment thoughts tend to catch me off-guard."

"Aren't all thoughts spur-of-the-moment?"

"You'd be surprised just how predictable some people can be."

"Well, I'm sure you must have been surprised by some thoughts you've heard lately." Jess led, eyeing Martin and thinking about Ben.

"Yeah. It's a real circus around here sometimes, you know? I hear *all* the thoughts. Even the *X-rated* ones."

She nodded, blushing.

"But, I can hear all the thoughts, Jess. Including the 'I'm-so-in-love-with-you-I-can't-live-without-you-would-die-for-you-you're-my-everything' thoughts… And those are just *his*."

Martin eyed Jess shrewdly, still smiling mischievously.

"Surprisingly, *you're* the perverted one."

She stared at Martin, blushing even more.

"But that's okay. I guess you can't help it, being all hormonal and all."

Martin then tapped on the table, to remind Jess that in here, they were being listened to.

"Right, well, now that I'm, you know. I just don't feel that way about Aaron anymore. I guess it was just lust. He doesn't know, does he?"

"No, but he'll find out at some point," Martin said. "And he still loves you, or at least thinks he does."

Jess sighed, closing her eyes. Martin sat back down and took her hand in his, but this time, there was no spark between them. Jess's heart did not flutter.

"It's not your fault, you know. You never promised Aaron anything. He'll have a hard time understanding, but he'll get over it, in time."

"Until he finds out about the baby," she said. "What about then?"

"Let's not worry about that until we have to, hmm?"

"Right."

"Well, get ready, because there's about to be a show. You got about thirty seconds, kid."

Jess stiffened, her heart suddenly beating harder in sheer nervousness.

"Hey, it's too late now," Martin shrugged.

About ten seconds later, Aaron walked back into the cafeteria, eyeing Martin, looking annoyed. It took him a second to register the person sitting with him, her back turned.

He stood staring at Jess for several moments, an expression of surprise frozen on his face. Then he broke into a huge, goofy grin, and ran up, hugging her from behind, practically strangling her.

"Easy there, Aaron. Don't strangle the poor thing. Let her turn around!" Martin said.

"Jess! Oh-my-God! Oh-my-God!"

Aaron walked around to her left side, kneeling, and attempted to grab her hand, but it was still in a cast. He frowned at it.

"Oh, no, what happened? What have they been doing to you?"

He looked at her with a silly frown, his brow furrowed, almost like he was talking to a baby, or a small child.

"Did they do this to you?"

"No, it's fine, it'll heal."

Aaron smiled at her. Then he stood and took the seat next to her, on the other side, ignoring Martin completely.

"Was isolation bad? Why did they do that to you, huh? What happened? You had a bad mission?"

Jess turned away from Aaron then, for he had forced her to suddenly think about the assignment and everything that had happened. In an instant, she saw the baby, smiling over its mother's shoulder, and her eyes filled with tears. Martin heard her thoughts and grew visibly upset, for he could hear the torment that raged inside her mind. He'd been able to the entire time.

"Hey, Aaron," Martin snapped.

Aaron looked over at Martin, who gave him a look of warning so severe, he immediately shut up. Martin drew his finger across his neck forcefully, his face coloring with emotion, his eyes delivering a death stare. Aaron felt like the biggest idiot in the world.

"Jess, I'm sorry, that was stupid of me, I wasn't thinking. I'm just so happy to see you, you know?"

She nodded. He felt awful as he watched the tears spill down her cheeks. He reached to wipe her face and she jerked her head away, turning from him.

"I'm sorry, Jess," Aaron said, looking disturbed.

"Aaron, I think she could use a break, you know? It's her first day back. Just back off and give her some space, huh?"

"Yeah, okay."

"I'll be in the rec room in a few minutes, all right?"

"Yeah, sure."

He seemed to get the hint just fine and stood to leave.

"I'll see you later, Jess?"

She sat with her back to him and did not respond. Aaron walked out of the cafeteria, his shoulders slumped.

After he left, she continued crying silently for several minutes. Martin sat, looking away, but he could hear every anguished thought she had. Even he began to cry.

They both sat silently, Martin sharing Jess's pain. Then he audibly heard her stomach grumble, no ability needed.

"Hey, kiddo, you need to eat, huh?"

She nodded and stood, not looking at him, and went to get some food. A few minutes later, as she sat down, Hanley came into the room. He wasn't smiling.

"Hey," he said, sitting down.

Martin nodded. He'd known Hanley was coming.

"Aaron," Hanley said, and Martin nodded again.

"Opened his big, fat mouth, huh?"

Martin nodded a third time, and then got up to leave. He couldn't get away from Jess's thoughts but putting a little distance between them would hopefully obscure the most horrific.

"Gotta go play pool," he sighed. "I keep my promises."

Hanley waved him off, looking at Jess with sympathy. She simply ate, ignoring him.

"Stupid Aaron. I told you, he doesn't understand. He's never had to deal with what we do. No one sends him out on assignments to change flowers and color the pretty plants."

"It's not his fault," Jess said.

"Yeah, but still. The guy's gotta get a clue some time, right?"

"No," she said. "If he can't understand, he can't understand."

"Well, there's your reason to break up right there. Aaron should understand that at the very least. He can't expect to meet your needs if he can't understand you."

Jess nodded. She kept eating, still not looking at Hanley. He pursed his lips.

"You want me to go?"

She shook her head and he relaxed.

Hanley understood that even if they didn't speak, his being there comforted her. So long as he was there, she wasn't alone.

He kept her company the whole time she ate and never said a single word. She eventually calmed down and regained control of herself, her energy returning. She got up a second time to get more food. Hanley just waited till she was ready to talk. The signal came when she set her fork down, pushed her plate away, and looked Hanley directly in the face. She glinted a quick attempt at a smile—all she could muster.

"Better?" he asked.

"Better," she said, still quiet. "So, Aaron's pretty upset?"

"He'll get over it. Honestly, no matter what he thinks he's feeling, it ain't love. More like ownership or something, you know? Like, 'hey, look what I got'. It makes me sick. Always did."

"Hanley," Jess said, chiding him. "If you think you're in love, it doesn't matter. It still hurts. I'm still going to hurt him."

"Yeah, but at this point, it shouldn't come as that big of a surprise, should it? The kid's a moron, no offense. He only sees what he wants to see. He was always too young for you, even before. You're way older than him now."

"I'm only two years older, Hanley."

"You're older than that now, and you know it. Pain ages you, in more ways than one. That's another thing Aaron won't ever get about you. He still thinks you're the same girl now that you were last time he saw you. Even after seeing you just now. He probably thinks you just need a little time, that you'll *'come around.'*"

Hanley made quotation marks with his fingers, shaking his head.

"Look, if you want to get the whole thing over with, I suggest you just do it. And be direct, because that guy's not gonna get a clue unless you spell it out for him. The longer you wait, the longer he'll keep hoping. That's not good for him, or you."

"I thought you didn't care about Aaron's feelings, Hanley?"

"I don't, particularly, but still... he's one of us."

"Yeah," she sighed.

She looked over at Malcolm and Jenny at their own table. They both glanced over at her and smiled. She frowned, thinking.

"I hardly even know those two."

"They keep to themselves. I mean, they *really* keep to themselves, but Martin says they're on the up and up. They're not stuck up or anything. They've seen how things work around here, and they don't want to get played."

"They aren't training to go out?"

"Nope," Hanley said. "That all stopped after you came. Doc changed his focus. Jenny was the only one of the two who was useful anyhow. And you proved to be more useful. Now, it's Sarah. So, in a way, they should be grateful. You took the focus off Jenny for a while."

"Huh," Jess said. "They haven't ever bothered to say hi."

"Don't worry about it, huh? You're forgetting that the last time they made friends, it was with Alma, who talked them into trying to escape. Bad idea, and now, they figure it's just best to keep to themselves. You can't blame them for it, can you?"

"No."

She stood up to leave. Hanley followed her.

"You going back to your room?"

"No, I'm going to end things with Aaron."

"Good girl," Hanley said, smiling.

"Yeah, try not to sound so excited about that, huh? I'm about to break a guy's heart."

"Sorry," Hanley said, still smiling, but trying to hide it. "Mind if I tag along?"

Jess turned to stare at him and he balked.

"Not for that, I mean, just to the rec room."

She nodded her consent.

***

When they entered the rec room, Aaron and Martin played pool, and Alma sat watching TV with an attractive-looking strawberry-blonde. Jess looked at the two of them, her face questioning.

"Oh, yeah, that's Kate. The new girl. Remember, I told you about her? She's the one who can shock people?"

"Oh, right," she said. "Huh."

Aaron saw Jess and immediately stopped playing. Martin shrugged. Hanley came over and took the pool stick out of Aaron's hand.

"I got it from here," he said.

He turned, eyeing the table for several moments, sizing things up. "Six ball in the corner pocket," he said, and made the shot, sinking it.

"Shit," Martin said.

Aaron walked over to Jess, looking wary. She returned his look, giving him a tiny smile.

"Hey," he said.

"Hi. Can we talk?"

"Yeah, sure," he said. "Atrium?"

She nodded, and they walked silently. At one point, he tried to take her hand. She pulled it away. When they finally reached the meadow, he turned to her, visibly broken, his chin quivering.

"It's over. Isn't it?"

"Aaron," she said, unable to look him in the eye.

"No, it is. I can see it all over your face. You can't even look me in the eye, Jess."

Aaron stared at her intently, then looked away.

"They did this to you—to us. I hate them. I hate Dr. M."

"He didn't do this to me," she said. "It just happened."

"It was that assignment, huh?"

She nodded.

"Talk to me, Jess. If you just tell me what happened, we can get through this. It doesn't have to be this way."

"Yes, it does… I can't talk about it, Aaron, okay?"

"But, Martin knows, I mean, he must."

"Well, there's no choice in that. I didn't tell him. I can't."

"If you keep it all inside, it'll eat you up. You need to just get it all out."

"Don't tell me what I need," she snapped. "You have no idea what I need, Aaron. You don't know me at all."

"Yes, I *do*, Jess."

"Aaron, I'm sorry. This just isn't going to work."

"*Why?*" He looked like he was about to cry.

"Because you have to ask me that. I shouldn't have to explain things to you. I'm sorry, but I just—I can't be with you, not like before. I'm not the same."

"You'll get better."

"*No.*"

She was beginning to understand why Hanley couldn't respect him.

"I won't get *better,* Aaron. I'll deal with it more easily as time goes by, maybe, but I'll never be over it."

"Please, Jess."

"No. I can't deal with this. It's not helping things. It's not helping me. If you can't understand that, then that's exactly why I can't be here with you."

"But…"

"I'm sorry, Aaron. You're my friend… but that's all."

He looked away at the meadow then, smiling sadly.

"All the flowers died," he said. "Change of seasons."

She looked at the empty field realizing he was right. He looked back at her, his face resigned.

"They'll be back next spring," he said.

She nodded. "But we won't. We're getting out of here, remember?"

"Yeah," he laughed.

"What is it?"

"Just… I wish I could have known it was our last day, here, with the flowers all blooming. I could have known to remember it better. Does that make any sense?"

She nodded, her heart breaking at his pain. She truly felt bad for hurting him. He saw her pain and lifted her chin with his hand.

"Hey," he said. "It's okay, Jess. I'll be okay."

"Yeah?"

"Yeah… Eventually."

She sighed and suddenly hugged him. It only lasted a few moments, but he closed his eyes.

"You're still coming with us, aren't you?"

"Of course. Someone's got to make sure you're safe. I don't trust Dr. M. like everyone else does. And I know you don't, either."

Jess looked away. Aaron continued.

"I don't care what Martin says is in that jerk's head… look at what he did to you. Look at your hand. He ruined *us*."

"He didn't do anything, Aaron. He was only taking orders."

Aaron looked at Jess in disbelief. Fire jumped into his eyes.

"I don't believe this! Not you, too, Jess. It's *Dr. M.* Wake up!"

"Look, you're just going to have to trust everyone on this, we can't escape without him, Aaron."

"I know, and I'm just going to have to fly on faith—that's what everyone keeps telling me. Well, sorry if I don't immediately trust a guy who's tortured everyone for years."

"Aaron, let's not talk about this anymore, okay? If you're with us, you're with us, end of story."

"Fine."

"Friends?"

"Yeah," he said, attempting to brush a loose hair away from her face.

She flinched, and he stepped back, looking down.

"Friends."

They walked back into the facility and Jess said goodbye to him, heading back to her room. Once there, she got back into bed and sighed. That, at least, was over.

***

Things got easier from that point on. Jess was eventually able to walk around more comfortably, not feeling any more anxiety before entering the cafeteria or rec room.

Alma said hello to her on her second day in the cafeteria and introduced her to Kate. Kate seemed very quiet and Jess thought she was probably the most beautiful girl she'd ever seen. Flaming bright auburn hair, porcelain skin with a peppering of near-matching light auburn freckles speckling her nose and cheeks, and lucid blue eyes that held a kindness in them Jess rarely saw. Five-foot-five and thin, with dimples that popped when she smiled. No wonder Alma had dropped for this girl, who looked to Jess like Strawberry Shortcake in human form. She smiled at her and Alma. They looked happy.

19

Over the last ten weeks it took to train Sarah, Ben met with Jess once a week. He simply turned the camera system in the Atrium off when it was his turn to watch the monitors, same as he turned the cameras off in both Hanley and Jess's rooms when he needed to talk to them in private. The two-person only rule still applied to the door, however, since that program was implemented from a separate system in a different building, not at the facility.

He had taken to manning a regular shift for two hours every Wednesday, right before Dowling took over in the afternoons, under the guise of wanting to monitor all the members of The Society in a more hands-on manner, not just leave all the observation up to the monitoring staff, while waiting for any reports to come to him. He simply ordered Dowling to come into work on Wednesdays two hours later, but reassured him that everything was fine, and that he'd still get paid for the missing hours. With his rank over Dowling, the Private never questioned his superior, and he seemed more than happy to receive two extra hours off each week, while still getting paid.

He could have chosen to simply spend that time with Jess in her room every week, but after all the hours she'd spent there in isolation, he figured the beauty of the outdoors, combined with the fresh air and sunlight might be good for everyone, including the developing baby. He was also simply sick and tired of the inside of the facility, and the claustrophobic feel of the long white hallways and rooms, most of which had no windows to view the outside.

***

On the first Wednesday, five days out of isolation, Martin came up to Jess while she and Hanley ate lunch together. Aaron sat at a different table, alone.

Since their conversation back on day one, he'd kept mostly to himself, always eating alone when he was in the cafeteria at the same time as Jess. A lot of times, he wasn't there when she was. She knew that Aaron was purposely changing his routine to avoid her. It was childish and annoying, but on the other hand, she *understood*. Aaron was simply dealing with things the only way he knew how.

Martin walked up and sat down. Jess smiled at him. He smiled back.

"You wanna go for a walk with me out in the Atrium?"

"Sure."

She finished eating, and the two of them left the cafeteria together. Aaron watched the duo go, eyeing them the whole way out. After they left, he looked down at the table, shaking his head. A few moments later, he stood up looking angry, his chair scraping noisily across the floor. Hanley watched all this, rolling his eyes, and shook his head.

"Big baby," he whispered to himself, as Aaron stormed out of the cafeteria.

***

In the corridor, Jess walked with Martin, feeling a little uncomfortable. He kept smiling at her crazily and nodding. She finally laughed.

"I can't read your mind, Martin."

"I know," he grinned from ear-to-ear.

As they drew to a halt before the Atrium door, he suddenly turned back, walking away.

"What are you doing? Where are you going?"

She asked this at the same moment she began turning the knob on the door. She frowned when it wouldn't open.

"Why won't this open?"

"Guess I'm not far enough away yet," Martin called. He was about fifty feet down the hallway. "I can't go into the Atrium with you."

"What? Why? What's going on?"

"Only two people allowed in the Atrium at a time, remember?" he called, turning and smiling at her. "Let me skedaddle far enough away, and you should be able to go through. I guess *somebody's* already out there."

He smiled at her again, nodding. Her cheeks flushed, her eyes filling with light as comprehension dawned. Martin laughed and walked around the corner, out of sight.

"Don't do anything I wouldn't do," his voice drifted playfully to her from around the corner.

She waited another few seconds, then tried the door again. This time, the knob turned immediately, and she ran excitedly down the dirt path, through the trees and out into the open meadow. She stopped up short at the sight of Ben, who stood in the middle of the clearing, waiting for her. As she got closer, she saw he had a picnic blanket spread over the brown grass. A basket sat at one corner.

"I already ate," she said, teasing him.

"Worth a try," Ben shrugged.

"Of course."

She walked up to him and threw herself into his arms, kissing him eagerly. He kissed her back with equal fervor. They quickly fell to the ground, on top of the blanket, and made love for the first time since their original coupling.

When they were done, he lay with her, eyes closed. Foreheads together, they continued kissing for several more minutes, still in a tangle. Then they finally fell apart, onto their backs, gazing up at the sky, but he couldn't bear to not touch her. She smiled, breathing deeply as his hand made contact, hooking his pinkie finger around hers.

"Pinkie-swear?" she asked.

"Sure," he laughed. "What am I swearing about?"

She turned, gazing into his eyes.

"You're swearing," she thought about it momentarily, "that you'll still love me when I'm gigantic." She laughed. "Also, when I'm craving something weird, like, pickles and peanut butter."

"Ew," he said, crinkling his nose.

"No, you're not allowed to say that." She playfully slapped his shoulder. "Now be quiet. This is *serious*."

"Oh, right." God, he loved her.

"You have to swear you're not gonna hold me to the way I look now." She motioned to herself. "Because, there's no way I'm gonna look the same after pushing a baby out of my, well…"

"Done." He covered her mouth with his hand. She brushed it away.

"I'm being serious."

"I know."

"No, I mean I'm being *serious*-serious. Do you have any idea how big I'm going to get by the end of this whole thing? What am I going to wear? Do you even have scrub pants that big?"

"I don't know… Jess, I don't know what we'll have. We'll be on board an alien ship."

She looked down at the blanket beneath them, suddenly lost in its patterns.

"Jess, you have to accept that it's *real*."

"I know… *I have*, it's just—" She sighed.

"What?"

"I don't know. It's just scary to me, that's all. I'm scared every time I think about *seeing* them. They'll look so… *different*."

She thought back to her nightmares—how menacing the alien in her dreams had looked.

"I'm sure we look very foreign to them, too, Jess."

"How do you know they don't want to get us on their ship to… I don't know, eat us or something?"

"What?" Ben laughed.

"Don't laugh, it's not funny."

"Jess, this is our only way out, you know that."

"I know, but…"

"What?"

Ben was gentle with his inquiries, never demanding or annoyed by her insecurities. She loved him for that, among so many other things.

"How do you know when we leave here, and get on board with them, that we won't just be walking into another prison?"

"I don't. But I *believe,* Jess. I believe that whatever's in store for us up there," he pointed to the sky, "It must be better for us than staying here. Better for *everyone.*"

He placed his hand on her stomach, so gently, Jess felt like taking him into her arms and loving him all over again. Ben told her about Sarah.

He told her about his discovery that Sarah had precognitive abilities and seemed to have wisdom well beyond her chronological age. He told her that when he was with Sarah, he simply felt that everything was going to work out.

"It could just be her powers. She puts you at ease, but, at any rate, none of that matters. We simply must take the chance. We need to get away from here, and almost anything else is better than this place. Our baby cannot be born here. End of story. This is a project, Jess. Everyone in here is a *subject,* and that includes your baby. *Our* baby. Don't think that once it's born, you'll be free to raise it. They'll take it from you."

"You think they would do that?"

"Jess, they brought an eleven-year-old girl into this place. Who says they won't mess with our kid, once it's old enough, or even before that? They think it's all some big experiment. To them, it's not a baby, and it certainly isn't human. To them, it's a lab rat, to test and poke and prod. To find out what it can do."

"What it can do?"

"They think Aaron's the father, Jess. They think this baby is the product of two transgens. There's no telling, in their minds, what kind of powers it might develop. You're nothing but a walking, talking, breathing incubator to them now."

"That's disgusting." She felt sick.

"You're not free in here, Jess. Your baby won't be free either. I'd much rather gamble on going with Hanley and his friends than stay here. This is my baby, too."

"I know that," she said, kissing him, but he pulled back.

"No more doubts about where we're going, okay?"

"No," she said. "But I'll still be afraid."

"It's normal to be afraid of the unknown, Jess. I understand. I'm frightened too, actually, out of my mind."

"You are?"

"Of course, but Sarah... if you could meet her, Jess. I wish you could."

"I will," she said. "Soon enough."

"Everyone will meet her on the day we leave." He told her he thought that day was now approximately ten weeks away. Her heart sped up, thinking about it.

"It's not true, is it?"

"What?"

"Our baby," she said. "It won't have... *abilities*, will it?"

"No, because I'm the father, not a transgen."

He proceeded to explain to her why it was impossible, scientifically.

"It seems to be random, anyhow," he said. "Every transgen inside this facility... None of your parents had the gene. It's not passed on genetically, at least not at first. You and everyone else in The Society received the gene somehow. It was built into you. You're all the first generation, basically. After that, it'd be up to random chance. Two unknowing transgens would have to get together and reproduce. Even then, the child would still need a dose of Luci to activate the gene sequence. Remember, with this particular pseudogene, the coding sequence is inactive—*dormant*."

He grew quiet, thinking. Jess didn't say anything.

"Did you even understand any of what I said?" he asked.

"Not in the least," she laughed, and he kissed her.

"Except... If all the transgens in here received the gene randomly, and you don't know for certain who, or how... if it's that random, then how do you know it won't happen with our baby? I mean, it could, couldn't it? What about Malcolm and Jenny? They both have the gene."

"Malcolm and Jenny aren't actually related. Jenny is adopted."

"She is?"

Ben nodded. "Another long shot. Do you know what the chances are of someone with the pseudogene just happening to adopt a baby that also has it?"

She shook her head. "Then our baby could have the gene," she said, suddenly afraid.

"Technically it could, but the odds of that are *astounding*."

"How astounding?"

"Well, you're one in one-hundred-thousand. And I'm an absolute zero. The chances of the offspring of only one transgen parent, and someone like me, also randomly developing the gene, from whatever source it comes from... I'd guess that to be somewhere in the region of a one-in-a-billion chance. Understand?"

She nodded, but still looked uncertain.

"Besides, even if our baby was randomly born with the gene, like you were, however it happened with all of you in here, it wouldn't develop any powers unless we gave it Luci, remember that. There is no way at all that our baby could ever have an ability. It's impossible. Not a billion-to-one, or even a zillion-to-one. *Impossible*. Okay?"

She nodded, smiling. He kissed her again. They spent the rest of their time that afternoon making love. They met the same way for nine more weeks.

***

On their fourth week of meeting, Ben told Jess that Sarah was now ready to begin using her powers against soldiers with guns.

"Are you scared?" she asked.

"Terrified," he sighed. She kissed him.

"Jesus says, everything happens for a reason."

"Does he?"

She nodded. She'd spoken with him in the meadow just two days before. For some reason, she had felt comfortable with him that day, and told him everything that'd happened during her last assignment.

It was the first time she'd told anyone or spoken of it out loud. She thought Jesus would somehow understand. He surprised her by telling her something she'd not even considered. She recounted his words to Ben now.

"Jesus said if I wasn't pregnant, I wouldn't have lost control of my emotions, and I wouldn't have pulsed. I would have walked away."

"He's right."

"So," she said, taking a deep breath. "What would have happened if I'd walked away?"

"You know the answer to that." He didn't even want to think about it, let alone say it out loud. She said it for him.

"You would have been removed from the project, and Aaron would have been killed, or Martin's wife."

"You already knew all this," he said, confused. "How did Jesus help?"

"He said if it weren't for the baby, everything would have been ruined. Even though it caused me to pulse. Even though I killed all those people, and that baby."

"Jess… are you blaming our baby for what happened?"

"No! No, that's not it. Jesus said that's the reason the baby happened—because it was meant to be."

"I don't know, Jess."

"No, Ben, think about it. If I hadn't become pregnant, everything would be different now, right?"

"Yes, it would, but—"

"Then this was all meant to happen."

He smiled at her. This was the first time she'd been able or willing to talk about what had happened that day in Khardush, and she did so without crumbling to tears, reduced to a non-functioning, hot mess. Whatever Jesus had said to get Jess to this point emotionally, Ben felt eternally grateful.

"What else did Jesus say?"

***

Jess remembered that day, in the meadow, sitting with Jesus, listening to his philosophy.

"Look at it this way," he said. "There's a race of people out there who need our help. They need it so much, they traveled all over the universe to find us. They hand-picked us to be their saviors. What's not to like about that?

"If we stay here, there is no life for us. If we leave and it turns out we're on our own, maybe we die, but we die free. If we stay here, we do bad things. I don't want to kill anyone. But if we leave here, and Hanley is right, we save a whole species. We can either stay here and become weapons that kill, or we can leave, and become heroes that save lives."

"But if *all* of Hanley's story is true, it's a war, Jesus, don't forget that. If what Hanley says is true, we'll be leaving here to fight an entire war. You think that won't involve taking lives?"

***

"So, you've made peace with what happened?" Ben asked.

"No," she said, frowning. "I can't, but if it's all part of a plan, then how can I question it? Jesus says we'll make it, no matter what obstacles get in our way. He says he believes everything will work out, because we're simply meant to go. He believes we can't fail."

"Jess, I don't know if that's a healthy way to look at things."

"Why? I want to believe this is going to work, Ben."

"As do I, but I still recognize the chance that we could fail."

"You don't believe the baby happened to help us get out of here?"

"I... I don't know, Jess. Yes, if you weren't pregnant, you probably wouldn't have pulsed, and we probably wouldn't be here right now. And no one would be planning any escape, but..."

"What?"

"I don't know, Jess. It could just be a lucky coincidence."

211

She scoffed at him. He glanced at his watch and suddenly realized they'd been so deep into this topic of discussion, the time had slipped away, unnoticed.

"Shoot, Jess," he quickly stood up and then took both her hands to help her up. "Dowling will be back in only ten minutes. We have to go."

They quickly folded up the blanket and headed back towards the facility. Jess, however, wasn't done debating him.

"Ben, all of this can't just be a coincidence, can it? It must all be for a reason. And if this baby happened so our plan to escape could go forward, then it *must* mean that we're meant to go with the Graylings. Just like Jesus says. Why, do you think that's too, religious or something?"

"You're not religious, Jess. You're spiritual," Ben said, smiling at her. "But if you believe you're meant to go with the Graylings, why are you so afraid of them?"

The Atrium door now stood in sight. As they neared it, she stopped momentarily to get one more point in before they hurried inside.

"Because... they're not us. No, that's not it. I don't know... I'm afraid to leave everything I've ever known behind. *Everything*, Ben. Do you realize that? No more mountains or streams, or holidays. I mean, no more shopping, or Christmas decorations, or Fourth of July. It's not like we're moving to another city."

"It'll be hard to leave," Ben said, stroking her face. "I'm sure we'll all suffer from the worst kind of home-sickness anyone ever could. But, if you ascribe to Jesus's theory, and embrace all of Hanley's doctrine... you're meant to do something incredible, Jess. Don't forget that."

"Then, so are you."

He opened the door, and they both entered the facility together, Ben carrying the blanket, and Jess carrying the picnic basket looped through her arm. Normally, he would have brought everything in by himself, several minutes earlier than this, and Jess would have waited to come back inside for at least ten minutes after he left her in the meadow. This was the first time they'd entered from the Atrium together.

He quickly glanced at his watch and saw that he had only five minutes left before Dowling's shift began, but he needed to say these last few things to her. There was still time enough for that. Just one more minute.

"Not me. I love you, and I'll go with you anywhere. I'll follow you to the end of the universe. But I can't help the Graylings. It has nothing to do with me."

"That's not true," she said, dropping the basket and cradling his face in her hands. "I can't do this without you. You make me strong. I need you by my side, Ben. That's why we're together. You're just as much a part of helping the Graylings as anyone. If my ability, or anyone else's in here helps to save them, it all originates with *you*, Ben. I wouldn't have my ability without you. None of us would."

"I love you, Jess." Ben kissed her. "And I never thought I would feel this way about anyone. You think I don't know this is all happening for a reason? I know. What's happened, up until now, is already impossible."

"Nothing's impossible," she breathed, pulling him down to kiss her again, then putting her forehead against his. "Nothing."

"Jess?" It was Aaron's voice.

***

Jess looked up. Aaron stared back at her. Her heart stopped.

"What the...?"

But he couldn't say anything more. He simply looked from Jess to Ben and back again, his face contorting.

Ben closed his eyes and sighed. How could they be so careless and oblivious? And of all the people to happen upon them... *Idiot... idiot!*

"This is impossible," Aaron whispered. Tears filled his eyes, cold rage flushing his features. "What have you *done*?" His eyes were on Ben, no longer cold, but burning. "What have you done to her?!"

Too loud.

Aaron's voice shook uncontrollably, and all Jess could do was look at him, her heart icy-cold with dread.

"Aaron," she whispered.

"How could you do this? *With him!*"

"Aaron," Jess shook her head. "I'm sorry."

"No!" Aaron yelled. "You don't get to be sorry for this. This is just... sick!"

"Aaron," Ben said, breaking in. "I can explain."

"You can *explain*?" Aaron scoffed, laughing in a way that made Jess feel nauseated.

"Aaron," Jess said. "I never meant to hurt you. This just... happened."

"It just happened?! This is what happened on your mission, huh?!"

"No, Aaron. It's not like that," Jess said. "I love him."

"You *love* him? *Him*? Jess... Look at who you're talking about! After what he's done to you?"

"He's getting us out of here, Aaron."

"Oh, Jess. He's the one that put you in here!" Aaron screamed. Tears of hurt and rage stood in his eyes.

"If I could take it all back, Aaron, I would," Ben said.

"Shut up, just shut up! You can't fool me, like you can her."

"He didn't fool me, Aaron. He didn't do anything. This was my choice."

"That's *sick*. You make me sick!" Aaron spat in her face.

Jess gasped, then stood in silence, stunned at the insult, but Ben was infuriated. He rushed at Aaron, punching him in the face so hard, he flew back, sprawled on the hallway floor, laid out flat. He looked up at Ben in pain and anger, but also in fear. Ben towered over him, moving in to hurt him again.

"Stop!" Martin yelled.

He'd been playing pool with Hanley when he suddenly heard Aaron's thoughts. By the time Martin realized where he was headed, along with the fact that the secret couple were late coming in, and entering *together*, it was too late. The perfect storm had brewed up and blown in. Martin couldn't catch up to Aaron in time to stop him.

He helped Aaron back up onto his feet, the look he flashed Jess all apology. He was supposed to be listening up to help them avoid anything like this, but he'd become too complacent after multiple weeks of non-incident. That and the fact that Aaron had decided to change course from his room to the Atrium at the very last second.

"I heard his thoughts too late," he shrugged. "Spur-of-the-moment, remember?"

Jess nodded, looking at Aaron with sadness. He looked at her, then at Martin, awareness dawning.

"You knew about this, didn't you? Of course, you did." Aaron looked at Martin in disbelief and disgust. "You hear everything, isn't that right? Did you listen to them when they screwed, huh? What did that sound like, I wonder? Was it nice and dirty? Did she beg for it? Did she call him *Daddy*? Was it nice and dirty? I bet it was." He turned to Jess, radiating contempt.

She returned it in kind. She never thought Aaron could say anything like that about her. Aaron's eyes looked to Ben.

"I wonder what your bosses would say, if they knew you were diddling their special prize, hmm?"

"Shut up," Jess said. "Don't you ever talk about me like that… EVER!"

Jess's hands curled into fists.

"Oh, did he diddle you, Jess?" Aaron said, taking no notice of her growing anger. "He did, didn't he?"

"Aaron, you are now fighting for your life," Martin said, barely above a whisper.

"What?"

He turned to look at Martin, then back around to Jess and the doctor. Ben looked at Jess intently, whispering in her ear, trying to calm her down. He knew she lacked the control she would normally have. She continued curling and uncurling her fists, desperately fighting to remain calm, but she fought what seemed like a losing battle.

"Jess, please don't lose control, *please.*"

"What, you're gonna hurt *me*?" Aaron looked at Jess in disbelief. "You won't hurt me, you *can't.*"

"Yes, she can," Martin rasped from behind Aaron.

"*Please,* she's trained. Our little pervert of a doctor has her on a nice, short leash. I just didn't know how short. You disgust me, Jess. You're nothing but a sick... filthy... **SLUT.**"

Ben closed his eyes. It was a lost hope now for Jess to be able to control anything. He'd already lost control and punched Aaron in the face once, and now he felt the overwhelming urge to do it again. He opened his eyes and looked at the boy with resignation.

"Run, Aaron."

Even as Ben said this, Martin pulled on his shoulder. Aaron saw the look on Ben's face, realization dawning far too late. Martin forcibly turned him, half dragging him away.

They made it almost to the hallway corner, before Martin looked back, stopping in his tracks. He listened to Jess's thoughts, the look on his face scaring Aaron badly. He turned to look in the same direction. Something very bad was happening just fifty feet away.

***

Ben did not watch the two men run—there was only Jess, whose face he took in his hands.

"Jess, you don't have to do this. You need to stop. *You have to.*"

He kissed her. He didn't know what else to do. He kissed her hard, and he focused every ounce of love he had inside of him into that kiss, hoping it would somehow bring her back around.

Her skin raged. He could feel the heat coming off her in waves—an odd sensation crawling over his skin, almost like a static charge building. The energy still inside her, welling up.

"It's not too late Jess, do you hear me? It's not too late. You cannot pulse here. If you do, it will destroy this building. It will knock out the power and trip the escape protocol, do you understand me? I won't be able to hide it. They'll lock you up. They'll take you away from me. They can't know you can still pulse. Do you understand me? They can't know!"

"Ben," she whispered, her voice shaking wildly. "It's too much. I can't keep it in. *I can't.*"

"Yes, you can, Jess. You must. If you pulse now, it will give everything away. And I don't know what might happen to the baby."

She thought of the life growing inside her, and a tear fell from one eye. A small release, but it seemed enough.

She smiled weakly. Ben felt all the hairs on his body stand on end, electricity running through him in a low, humming stream. It only lasted a second, then it was gone, but as soon as the feeling passed, heavy waves of heat began emanating from her, so hot, he had no choice but to back away, and even then, he received several burns to his arms, as he lifted his hands to shield his face. His palms immediately blistered, and he cried out in pain.

Suddenly, a large arc of heat flew out from Jess in all directions. Ben was thrown backwards several yards, where he landed with a heavy thud.

It was all over. Jess stood in the middle of the hallway, blank and exhausted. She had not pulsed, but Ben couldn't tell the difference. She stood, looking just as shell-shocked and worn out as she had the last time she used her ability to its fullest. Her face, pale and shiny, her skin moist with perspiration. All around her feet, the white hallway floor was singed black for several feet in a rounding arc. Ben walked back towards her, forgetting his own pain. He grabbed her face in his hands, crying tears of joy.

"You did it, Jess. You *controlled* it."

He hugged her to him, alarmed at how loose she felt, like a rag doll, as before. He heard plodding footsteps from behind. Martin and Aaron had returned.

"Jess?" Ben shook her by the shoulders. "Jess, can you hear me?"

"She's in shock," Martin said. "I heard her, while it was still inside her."

"What?" Aaron said, confused.

"So much energy. It had nowhere to go. She's never had to keep it inside before."

"Jess." Ben cradled her face in his hands. "Jess... *look* at me. You have to come back, you hear me!"

"She's gone," Martin said, miffed. "Wherever she went, I just can't hear her anymore. She's not *here*."

"This is how she was before, on our mission, after she pulsed. She was catatonic for hours after that! She almost died!"

"I'm sorry, Ben," Martin said. "I just can't hear her. It's like she's literally not there."

"What?" Aaron's tone was one of perturbed annoyance. "What the hell are you guys playing at?"

He turned to leave.

"You did this to her!"

Ben launched himself at Aaron, choking him. Martin tried to pull him away, but Ben was too enraged. Aaron was much smaller than Ben to begin with. Ben fell to the floor, on top of him, hands around his throat.

"If she loses it, I'll kill you," Ben whispered, spitting the words in Aaron's face. His entire body shook with emotion. His eyes streamed tears of rage.

"Ben, let him go. He doesn't know." Martin said, but Ben paid no attention.

"Ben," Jess said, from behind him. Her voice so quiet, he didn't hear her. "Ben." Louder this time, her voice weak and shaky.

Ben let go of Aaron and crawled off him, turning and running to rejoin Jess.

Her eyes were exhausted and ringed with darkness. She was still bathed in a heavy sheen of sweat, hair damp to the touch. Her whole body shook, but she smiled weakly. It was all she could manage.

"I heard..." she whispered. "I heard... us."

"Jess," Ben had never been so afraid for Jess as he was then. "What are saying...?" A tear slipped down his cheek.

"I heard *me*," she smiled. Then she croaked out a laugh, her voice cracking. She sounded mad. "*I heard the later me.*"

Then her legs buckled beneath her. Ben caught her in his arms, cradling her gently to the floor. *Please don't let her mind be broken.*

"Ben," she whispered. "I felt it. So much energy. It rushed through me, through the baby, too."

"Jess, don't ever do that again, do you hear me? EVER!" Ben cried. "I thought I'd lost you. I thought I'd lost you."

Aaron sat on the floor, only feet away, stunned. He stared, wide-eyed at the unbelievable scene of Ben holding Jess so lovingly. He shook his head, upon hearing Ben's words of love for her, and he *cried*. He eventually snapped out of his shocked daze. Turning to Martin, he stood, his face full of shame.

"She'll be okay, right? *Right?*"

"You have no idea what you've done." Ben spoke with seething rage, looking up at Aaron with hate in his eyes. "She's pregnant! She's pregnant with my child. What have you made her do?"

Martin stepped up, speaking in Aaron's ear.

"She can't control her emotions anymore, because she's going to have a baby."

"And if she loses this child, *I will kill you*," Ben said through clenched teeth, his voice holding such conviction, Aaron knew that he meant what he said.

Ben turned back to Jess, pressing his face against hers, cradling her body tight. He wept over her, hugging her to him. She lay limp and unresponsive, but her eyes were aware.

"I didn't know," Aaron said, his own tears now falling. "How could I know?"

He looked on as Ben continued holding Jess in his arms, weeping uncontrollably. No one said a word.

Minutes later, Aaron turned and limped away. Martin watched him go, hearing his unspoken lamentations of a heart that'd been torn out and shattered. Only time would heal his hurt. For now, Martin was at least satisfied that there'd be no more drama from him today.

Martin approached Ben, kneeling next to him.

"Hey, maybe we should get her to medical, huh?"

"No," Jess said, her tone absolute, for all its lack of strength. "No. I don't want them to know I even came close to pulsing. It might mess everything up."

"It might, Jess, but, if they can help the baby…" Ben said.

"*No.* Remember what I told you, Ben. If we're meant to have this baby, then we will. If we're meant to leave here, we will. I *believe*," she breathed. "I finally, fully *believe*."

"What happened to you, Jess? Where did you go?" Martin said, looking at her in wonder.

"I don't know. I don't remember. All I know is—I'm not afraid anymore. I know everything's going to be okay."

"Jess, you were speaking nonsense," Ben whispered. "What did you mean when you said, '*I heard me*'? You said…" he frowned, trying to remember. "You said, '*I heard the* later *me*'… Do you remember?"

She shook her head, dazed. Then she smiled at Ben and touched his face. He was still crying. She pulled his face to hers and kissed him, weakly.

"Everything is just as it should be."

"She's telling the truth," Martin said. "She's not afraid at all." He smiled at her in wonder, again, along with deepening awe.

"I just need to sleep, get some rest, and I'll be okay. But I don't think I can walk."

Ben said nothing, simply picked her up and carried her in his arms.

He walked past cameras that he knew captured them on tape and didn't care. He brought Jess to her room and gently laid her down in bed. She smiled up at him, feebly, then closed her eyes and slept.

20

When Ben walked into the monitoring station, he found Private Dowling sitting at the controls, unmoving, his shoulders stiff. Ben closed his eyes and sighed. He'd come back to his post far too late. Dowling had come on shift for his 4 p.m.-4 a.m. slot and had seen everything—at least he'd been witness to Ben carrying Jess through the hallways, back to her room, and he didn't know how much more he'd witnessed before that.

He looked at the far-left monitor and saw that the Atrium cameras were back online, which meant Dowling knew they'd been purposely shut off. He looked at the clock and saw he was ten minutes late. He didn't know how much ten minutes had given Dowling to witness, but it didn't matter. There was no way for Ben to explain things away.

"Private Dowling—I can't explain to you what you just saw."

Dowling turned to Ben. There were *tears* in his eyes.

"I've worked for you for three years, Dr. Milbron. Up until two months ago, I thought you were the meanest, most heartless, cold son-of-a-bitch I'd ever met. A man with no heart. When you started being nice to me, I couldn't figure out why. Now I know."

"Dowling," Ben frowned. "I never meant to be heartless."

"I know," Dowling said. "No one ever does, not really. But you got lucky, Ben."

Ben felt a chill in his heart when Dowling addressed him by his first name. He'd given him permission to do so, but Dowling had never taken the liberty before.

"The only thing that can change a man's heart is love," Dowling said. "I thought it was all just an act, before. I didn't know why you were being different, I just figured it wouldn't last, because people don't change. But you did. Now I know it. You found love, didn't you?"

Ben looked down at the floor, nodding. "I know you have to turn me in, Dowling."

"For what, falling in love?" Dowling said. "The world's an ugly place, Doctor. Even here… Ha, *especially* here. So, why would I go and destroy the one thing I've seen in these last three years that's good? Would I be helping anyone if I told? Or would I only be making the world an even uglier place?"

"You're not going to report me?" Ben looked at Dowling in complete shock and disbelief. The Private smiled.

"You must think *I'm* a heartless son-of-a-bitch. But you know what, Ben? There's already been enough of that to go around."

Dowling held Ben's gaze for only a moment, then his smile suddenly faded, and he turned back around to face the monitors.

"I do have to report a slight malfunction though, Sir. I must have hit a wrong switch there, because for a couple of minutes, none of the cameras would record anything. I wound the tape back, to check, even. There's nothing there. I'm sorry about that, I just have no idea what went wrong. I hope you're not gonna write *me* up, Sir?"

"No, Private Dowling," Ben said, drained, yet relieved. "Of course, not. Everyone makes small errors, now and then. What say we just forget about the whole thing?"

"Sir, I was hoping you'd say that."

Ben looked at Dowling's back for a few moments, then turned to leave.

"Good afternoon, Dowling."

"Same to you, Doctor."

***

Ben walked through the hallways in a complete daze. He found himself, inexplicably, at the library. There, he found Jesus, sitting on a couch, reading. He sat down next to him, and looked up at the camera, knowing Dowling was watching. Then, he watched as the red light on the camera suddenly disappeared, and Ben's heart became so filled with hope, he could hardly contain himself.

"Jesus."

Jesus simply looked up at him, seemingly unfazed by the fact that Ben sat next to him in the library—an event that had never happened before.

"I need to ask you about your beliefs, what you told Jess... about how we'll succeed." He frowned.

"We *will* succeed," Jesus said. "I don't know how, but I know we will."

"What makes you so certain?"

"I just am," Jesus shrugged. "If we are meant to get out of here, we will. It doesn't matter how. A way will just *be*. If there is an obstacle, there will be a way around it. If we can't take one path, another will open. If not now, then later. Whenever the time is right, will be right. Then we will go."

Ben looked at Jesus in complete wonderment, blinking several times. He looked up at the camera again. Still no light.

"What do *you* think, Dr. M.?"

He turned, still stunned, blinking several times more, trying to take everything in. Then he sighed, shrugging.

"I think from now on I'd prefer it if you call me Ben."

"Ben?"

"Yes."

"Okay, but you didn't answer my question, *Ben*—What do *you* think? It doesn't matter what I think. I'm good with me. Are you good with you?"

"Yes, Jesus, I think I am."

"Then everything's good," Jesus shrugged, and went back to reading his book.

***

The following week floated by for Ben as if he were constantly dreaming. Jess took several days to recover, sleeping an alarming number of hours the first few days after her non-pulse, but by day three, she was up and about as if nothing had happened. She also didn't seem to remember any of the incident, or the strange words she had uttered. The ordeal, however, had convinced Ben that they simply could not risk using Jess's abilities as part of their means of escaping the facility. He didn't know how to put the baby's life at risk yet another time.

This left him no choice but to think outside the box on how to get everyone out of the facility, without using Jess's powers. Once that option was removed, however, and after witnessing the innocent simplicity with which Jesus reasoned and believed, Ben realized instantaneously, like a lightning bolt striking, just how basic and easy their escape plan could be.

He was needlessly over-complicating everything, he realized—adding more steps than were needed, mixing too many components together, creating more drama than necessary. *I've seen too many action films*, he laughed to himself.

In the end, there would be no need for explosions, chaos or confusion, or, as his mother used to say, any need for 'fuss and muss'. Once again, Ben found that his 'genius' intellect was getting in the way. Their escape, once he gained clear sight of it, was so obvious, he couldn't believe it took him so long to finally see it.

***

The following Wednesday, when it was his turn to man the monitoring station again, he turned *all* the cameras off, then made his way to Jess's room. He'd had enough of the Atrium and had made certain to send the message along via Martin, that he wanted to meet her this week in her room. She stood waiting for him.

The moment the door closed, she was on him, showering kisses, eagerly groping him all over. It was extremely tempting to simply give in, let go, and dissolve with her into a frenzy of desire and bliss, but he reined in his passion for the time being. He needed to talk to her.

"Jess," he said, gently, stepping back. "We have to talk."

She saw the serious look on his face, and immediately grew concerned, leading him over to the chair at her table to sit. She sat on the edge of her bed and waited, ready to listen. He sighed, closing his eyes. Then he smiled at her, tearing up.

"We're leaving here tomorrow night."

He stared at her, and she stared back, uncomprehending. The silence in the room was unbearable.

"Did you just hear what I sai—"

"Yes," she said, looking dazed. "But… how?"

He shook his head and shrugged. "Because it's time. And Sarah is ready. She passed her final test this morning."

"But, how? What about my pulse? What about everyone else, and what is everyone supposed to do, and—"

"Jess, you don't have to do anything, except walk out of here with me," he smiled at her. "None of us has to do anything but walk right out of here. All we need is Sarah." He was close to tears now, choking them back. "Well, that and Hanley needs to melt the perimeter fence. But that's it. Two people with powers, and a basic plan. And we're free."

She frowned. "But…"

"I know, Jess," he sighed. "Believe me, I know. I've been thinking about how to do this for months. But it's not difficult at all. It's so easy, it's ridiculous. All I need for you to do is simply tell everyone to wait to go to dinner tomorrow night until 9:30. And then tell them that at 10 p.m., we're all walking out of here. On the way out, we'll be picking up Rachel in her room. That should make Hanley happy enough to melt a thousand fences. Oh, and speaking of Hanley, you might want to give everyone a head's up about his intergalactic taxi service, so they won't be caught completely off-guard."

"Hanley's already told everyone about the Graylings a gajillion times." She rolled her eyes. "They've all heard it. I just don't know who all believes."

Ben nodded. "You need to explain to everyone about Sarah, and what she can do. You need to convey to them that even if we get surrounded by an entire army of soldiers, which I think will be the case, none of us will be in any danger. They also need to know what Sarah's ability feels like. There will be a huge wave of happiness and euphoria that washes over everyone. It can be a bit overwhelming, but it's not a bad feeling. In fact, it's quite the opposite.

"Oh, and I don't expect you to have to do this alone. I've sent all this along to Martin. He's already begun telling people, by now. I told him to start with Hanley, since he's the one, after all, that needs to order our taxi."

She nodded her understanding. "So, go to dinner tomorrow at 9:30. And at ten, then what?"

"I'll get Sarah out of isolation in her room at exactly ten o'clock and bring her to meet you all in the cafeteria," he shrugged. "She'll begin using her powers before we even leave her room."

"Why?" Jess frowned.

"Because the moment I take her out of isolation, the tech manning the monitoring station will see. He may trip the alarm immediately, which will scramble the escape protocol into place. I don't know if he can do that, if Sarah is using her powers or not. I'm hoping not, but... he still might. Tripping an alarm isn't the same as lifting a rifle. But even if the alarm isn't set off by me getting Sarah, or all of us marching down the hallway together, no matter what, Hanley will need to melt the perimeter fence, and *that* will trip the alarm for certain, if it isn't already. It only takes three minutes for over a hundred soldiers and snipers, even floodlights, to be moved into place."

"Floodlights?"

"Yes. You need to tell everyone to expect that, too. Most likely, we'll be walking out into the night, blinded by lights, and surrounded by an army of armed soldiers."

"Are you sure we'll be safe, Ben?"

"No," his voice shook slightly. "I'm betting all of our lives, including our unborn child's, on an eleven-year-old girl, who only just hours ago performed to the level she needs to, for us to succeed. She's done it once. And I'm going on faith, that she will do it again tomorrow night, and that by this time two days from now, you and me, and everyone else in The Society will be free."

He looked deep into her eyes, dragged in a prolonged breath, and sighed all his anxiety out. Jess found herself doing the same thing. She smiled at him.

"Are you scared?"

"Yes," he said, his voice cracking. "But it's time, Jess. Sarah's training is complete. My next report to General Levin is set for Friday. He'll begin making plans to put her out in the field as soon as he can. We can't risk that. We take Sarah, and we all leave here before I ever even send that report. If she's ready, why wait? Why even take the chance? Tomorrow night, Jess. We go to our freedom tomorrow night."

***

Ben went to finish his work, which was plenty. Before he left, however, he let Jess know that there was still over an hour left before Dowling returned. A little over an hour, with all the cameras off, to try and tell everyone. He told her to pick one person to go to immediately, to make certain they heard it directly from her. He suggested Aaron, which surprised her.

"He needs to know, Jess, and it can't come from me. And I think things should be smoothed over between you two before we walk out of here. Whether that's possible or not, I don't know, but I think you should try."

She nodded. "Thank you for trusting me."

He looked at her with so much love, she wished they had more time alone together. He saw her look and understood. Then he left, quickly kissing her, and went to finish his own tasks, and Jess headed to Aaron's room, where she was certain he'd be.

***

Hanley told Martin, going directly to his room. He and Martin next told Alma and Kate, who sat together in the rec room. Hanley immediately explained to everyone that a transport ship would pick them up and take them to a much larger ship out in space. Nearly every single person whom Hanley told simply stared at him, saying nothing. After the rec room, Hanley and Martin went to find Jesus in the library. Alma went with him, to his surprise. Kate followed Alma, trailing behind them in the hallway.

"Hanley, after we get on this transport ship, what about my sister?" Alma asked.

"That's right, I forgot. We'll stop by and get her, okay? Her and Martin's wife." Hanley said.

"Just stop by, like, we're picking them up?"

"Sure, why not?"

"I don't know. I guess… Okay." She shrugged.

"It's not so simple as it sounds," Hanley said. "Your sister hasn't seen you in almost two years, Alma. You're gonna show up on her doorstep in the dead of night to take her onboard an alien ship where she'll have to leave Earth and everything she's ever known behind, forever."

Alma's eyes filled with fear. She looked at Kate, to see if she felt the same thing. Kate simply shrugged, wide-eyed.

"Hanley, it's all real, isn't it?" Alma asked.

Hanley sighed, rubbing his temples. "Man, where do you think we're gonna go when we walk out into those hills, the Riviera?"

"No, I just... wanted to double check."

She followed Hanley to the library. Jesus looked up from his book, smiling welcome as they all approached.

"Is it time?"

"Yep," Hanley said, telling him the instructions. Jesus didn't need to be convinced of anything.

All four of them went to Earl's room, and he just stared at them for several moments, his eyes growing wide. He looked from one face to the next, shaking his head.

"Man, this place is a real loony bin, you know that?"

Everyone looked at him, saying nothing. Finally, Earl sighed.

"But if there's a way outta here, I'm takin' it," he laughed. "Aliens or no."

Hanley sighed again, not even attempting to convince Earl of what was about to happen. Everyone would see for themselves in just a few hours, regardless.

Long before the final hour was up, everyone had been told in some manner or another. Everyone except Aaron.

***

Jess knocked gently on Aaron's door.

"Come in."

She found him sitting up in bed, writing in a small book.

"What are you doing?"

"Keeping a journal," Aaron said, closing it.

"I didn't know you did that."

"You don't know everything about me, Jess."

He'd been avoiding her like the plague since the Atrium incident. Jess had recovered just fine, but still, he couldn't shake the conviction that he'd almost caused her to miscarry.

"Aaron." She sat down in the chair at his table. "We're leaving tomorrow."

He didn't say anything, just fidgeted with the journal in his hands. Finally, he spoke.

"So, it's time?"

"Yeah." She told him the whole plan. "So, are you ready?"

"I have to be," he said.

"You still don't believe in the aliens, do you?"

"What makes you think that?"

"Well, you were always a hold-out on that one."

"Not anymore." He saw her look and shrugged, hardly able to look her in the eye.

"I saw him, Jess—Dr. M.—that day in the hallway. The way he held you and cried like that? When he thought you might lose the ba—…You know?"

She nodded.

"The way he looked at you, the way he touched you, the way he spoke. I know he loves you. I don't like it, Jess. I never will. But I still saw it, and I can't *un-see* it. You know?"

She shook her head.

"I never loved you like that," he said. "I loved you, Jess, don't get me wrong, it's just… not like that. He'd die for you."

"You said you'd rather die than be without me," she frowned.

"I know."

"You lied?"

"No, I meant it Jess, but, I wouldn't die *for* you, there's a difference."

"There is?" She frowned again.

"I'm sorry, Jess."

"You're apologizing to me? I broke *your* heart, and you're apologizing to *me*?"

"I thought I loved you enough," he said. "But I didn't. And I never thought Dr. M…." Aaron shook his head.

"His name is Ben," she said.

"I never thought I'd see him that way, and with you," he continued, shaking his head again. "If he can change like that, then, anything is possible. So, yeah, I believe. *Now*."

She smiled at him. "Thanks, Aaron." And although he could not read her mind as Martin could, he knew she meant it. He nodded, smiling.

They fell into a comfortable silence, both lost in their own thoughts, until Aaron finally spoke again.

"We're getting out of here," he said, almost as if only truly realizing it at that moment. His smile grew wider. "We're really getting out of here, aren't we?"

She smiled, nodding.

"And you're gonna have a baby… on an alien ship!"

She laughed at this, and he laughed even harder. They both laughed until they cried.

Eventually, they got themselves back under control, and Jess excused herself. She told Aaron she needed to spend the rest of the afternoon alone. He understood.

***

After Ben left Jess, he went straight to see Sarah. She was expecting him. Two hours had passed since her last exercise. He got down on both knees, to look straight into her face.

"It's time, Sarah."

"I know."

"I'll come and get you tomorrow night at exactly 10 p.m. As soon as we leave this room, you'll begin using your power."

Sarah nodded. Ben looked at her in wonder. She smiled.

"I can't wait to meet Aunt Jess."

Ben sighed. "Something tells me, I don't need to explain to you where we're going… but if you have questions, I'm here. You know it's okay to be scared, right?"

She shot forward, clasping Ben's neck. He hugged her back just as tight. "Sarah, I know you'll be scared, but everyone will be with you. You won't be alone. You have a lot of friends who are very anxious to meet you."

Ben felt so proud of her, of how *strong* she was. He hugged her once more before leaving, making certain she would be okay. Then he left to carry out the rest of his plans.

21

Ben came to the door of Rachel Harley's room, and removed a key from his pocket. Her door was not under the influence of electricity. Even with the power out, she couldn't escape. He knocked, then unlocked the door and opened it.

He hadn't visited Rachel in over four months. She sat on her bed, staring into nothingness—her long blonde hair stringy and unwashed. She smelled. Her skin looked greasy. He sat down in her chair, turning it around, pulling it up closer to her.

He wasn't worried that she'd do him harm. she was incapable of even the slightest hurt after the trauma she'd suffered. Rachel had a conscience simply too pure, and the things he'd made her do on assignment had broken her mind.

"Rachel," he said, leaning forward and taking her hands in his. "I need you to listen to me, can you do that?"

She looked at him, making eye contact—still all too easily influenced. He hated taking advantage of that now, but he had no other choice.

"Rachel, I'm taking you out of here tomorrow night." She smiled, looking dazed.

"Rachel? Everyone's leaving here tomorrow, and we want you to come with us. Hanley will be there, too. Do you understand?"

She nodded but showed no real awareness.

"I need you to pay attention to the time on your clock tomorrow night, okay?"

Not the slightest sign of comprehension.

"At ten p.m., I need you to be ready to go. I'll be along shortly after that, to get you."

He gave her all the instructions and information she needed. He told her about Sarah, and what she could do.

"I'm coming to get you last. Everyone else will be with me. We won't leave you behind, Rachel. You're one of us. We want you to come. Understand?

"Hanley will take care of the fence, then we'll all walk past men with guns. They won't shoot us, Rachel. I can't explain it to you, not really. I can only tell you that Sarah, the little girl I told you about? She has a very special gift. She makes people feel *happy*. She makes it so they don't want to hurt anyone. So, no matter how scary it might seem, you must believe me when I tell you that they won't do anything to hurt us. Okay?"

Rachel surprised him at that moment by nodding again. It was small, but enough. Her expression slipped back into emptiness immediately after. Ben had no idea how to explain the next part.

"You… remember all that stuff Hanley used to talk about? Aliens, *the Graylings?*"

No reaction from Rachel this time. Ben continued explaining anyhow.

"They're coming for us, Rachel," he said, feeling foolish.

Rachel gave him no further acknowledgment. Did she understand? Had she even heard a single word? It didn't matter at this point. He had no other choice than to believe that everything would be okay.

***

Ben made his way back to the monitoring station just minutes before Private Dowling arrived at his post. Ben stood and saluted him when he arrived, and relaxed when Dowling smiled.

"Good evening, Doctor."

"Good evening, Private Dowling."

The Private sat down at his post but called over his shoulder just as the doctor turned to leave the room.

"Good shift, Ben?"

Ben thought he detected a note of playfulness in Dowling's voice.

"Same as always," he said, attempting to sound normal.

"That's too bad," Dowling turned around in his seat to look at him. "Must have been pretty boring."

Ben frowned at Dowling, not getting his meaning. Dowling had an odd shine in his eyes. What kind of snooping had he been up to? He turned back around, sighing.

"I can tell it was a real boring shift. Tomorrow night will probably be even more of a snore-fest."

He knows? How could he know?

"Yep. Figures, too. I'm taking my wife on vacation next week, so I traded my Saturday shift with tomorrow night's tech. Just worked it out, right before I came here. So, *I'll* be here tomorrow night… For the *snore-fest.*"

"Private Dowling?"

"Yeah?" The Private didn't turn to face him, his attention fixed on the monitor array.

"I just want to let you know it has been a pleasure working with you the last three years."

Dowling swiveled his chair around again and stood to salute Ben. "Doctor."

"Private." Ben saluted.

"Sir, it has been a pleasure for me as well. Especially working in the secret audio department, Sir. Reviewing the mic feeds."

"The secret audio department?"

"Sir, yes, Sir. The one with the mics put in place along with the table mics in the cafeteria a year ago."

"What mics?" Ben's heart sank.

"Sir, the microphones put into the lapels of everyone's scrub shirts, Sir."

The world swam.

"Mics in place on transgen's clothing means that everything... everything—"

"Sir, yes, Sir. Including your *missions*, Sir," Dowling said, his voice thick and nauseated. "But I have found, while reviewing the hours and hours of tapes assigned to me, that the transgens don't talk much."

Ben stared at Private Dowling in complete shock.

"Sir, this can be a real bitch of a boring job. But not lately."

Dowling saw Ben's confused look of bewilderment and smiled.

"Sir, the kind of job that wouldn't be missed."

"*You* will be missed, Dowling." Ben nodded.

"Sir, so will you. *All* of you."

He knew. He knew they were leaving.

"And might I add, Doctor, Sir, I think you'll be an excellent father."

Ben felt completely overcome, blinking back tears. Dowling turned away yet again, sitting down, facing the monitors.

"Private Dowling," Ben said, collecting himself, quickly clearing his throat. Keeping his back to Ben, Private Dowling cut him off, however, before he could say anything more.

"Goodbye, Doctor Milbron. And God Speed."

"Goodbye, Dowling," Ben frowned, in wonder. "And the same to you."

***

Ben left the room, walking down the hall as if in a dream. He would have been furious over the fact that General Levin had continued deceiving him, but he felt too elated to care.

He began to wonder more and more about Jesus's statements that if they were meant to succeed, a way would be paved for them, and any obstacles that might come up, they would find a way to navigate around. *We really can do this*, Ben thought. *We can pull this off. We're going to be free.*

***

Jess left her room for the last time at 9:30 p.m., following the arrows to the cafeteria. When she walked through the door, she saw that everyone else had already arrived, sitting together at the same three tables—Hanley, Martin, Alma and Kate at one, Aaron, Jesus and Earl at another. Malcolm and Jenny sat at the third table by themselves.

Jess felt starved. She went and fixed herself a huge plate and sat down between Hanley and Martin. They'd kept the seat between them open for her. She ate while everyone watched.

"How can you eat like that?" Hanley scowled.

"You didn't eat?" Jess said with her mouth full.

"A little but, you know," he trailed off. She nodded.

"Food's good. Keeps your energy up."

Everyone nodded. No one talked for several minutes, as Jess continued eating. The room fell eerily quiet. Finally, Martin spoke, for Jess sent him a thought, telling him it might seem odd if everyone sat around the tables in silence. Of course, none of them knew that didn't really matter, since they were all unaware of Private Dowling's assistance, or even his existence, save for Jess.

"So, Hanley, what are your plans for the rest of the evening?" He didn't know what else to say, shrugging. He felt too nervous.

"Ah, the usual. I like my routines, you know that."

"I do. I do know you like your routines," Martin said.

After that, silence pervaded again.

Over at the next table, Aaron sat quietly, holding his journal. Jess realized he'd brought it with him, to take. She hadn't brought anything with her.

It didn't look to her as if anyone else had brought anything with them, either. Not that anyone had any real personal items, anyhow. Still, the realization struck her as sad. They were about to leave their home planet, taking nothing with them but the clothes they wore, and those weren't even their own. Martin heard her thoughts. He looked at her and smiled, reaching under the table, taking her hand. She'd finished eating. He wanted to tell her that she *was* bringing something with her... the baby inside of her... but didn't say anything.

"Anyone wanna play Kings in a Corner?" Hanley asked.

He produced a deck of cards from his pocket, and Jess sighed in relief. Several people spoke at once, agreeing to play.

"Easy, easy," Hanley said, pulling a second deck from his pocket. "Two can play, two can play." He threw one of the decks to Aaron, who caught it on the fly.

"Everyone know how to play? Four to a game, the rest can watch."

He deftly dealt the cards into four equal piles in front of the players at his table, in under thirty seconds.

"Hanley," Jess laughed. "You should have worked in a casino."

"What makes you think I didn't?" He winked at her.

She frowned, realizing she didn't know anything about his life before he came to live in The Society. She didn't know much about anyone's life from before, except that Martin had a wife, and Alma had a sister she felt extremely close to. That and the few details about Aaron that she'd gleaned.

Jess had no idea what jobs everyone had held before coming there. For that matter, no one had ever asked her what she'd done, either. It was as if, from the moment each of them arrived, their lives had started from scratch. Or perhaps it was simply too painful, remembering what they'd lost. It was easier not to think about it, and not to ask, she figured.

Jess looked over at Aaron, just eighteen-years-old when he'd arrived. She knew he'd been an orphan, bounced around foster homes until he came of age, but still—she wondered at the lack of mental development in a now twenty-two-year-old man who'd never really been out in the world. Aaron had never paid rent or held a job. And now, he never would.

So much to think about. As they played their card game, she couldn't help but talk to everyone about her feelings. Although she didn't know about Private Dowling being at the controls, she wasn't worried about the mics in the tables. She reasoned that whoever might be listening would simply assume they all reminisced about their lives before the facility, instead of fondly recalling and saying goodbye to their home planet. She talked in code.

"You know what I miss most, being in here?" She looked around at everyone, breaking the silence. "I miss shopping." She shrugged. "I used to work in a mall."

"I miss fast food joints," Hanley said. "I *loved* Big Macs, man."

"It's bad for your health, Hanley," Martin said, taking his turn.

"Oh, well, I still miss it. And I'll never have it again."

"I miss traveling," Alma said. After a few seconds, several people laughed, then the rest joined in. It took a few more moments for Alma to realize the irony of her statement. Then she laughed the hardest. "No, I mean, to places that I love. I miss San Fran. *A lot.*"

"I miss going to the beach," Aaron said over at the next table.

"I miss Christmas decorations," Jenny said, looking over at everyone. "And Halloween, and costumes, and all the holidays where you decorate."

"Yeah," Kate said, smiling. "This place is a real bitch."

"Well, I'm right there with you, Hanley," Earl threw in. "But for me, it's Popeye's beans 'n rice. Mmm. That stuff's *good.*"

Everyone laughed, some people so hard they cried.

"If you could get out of here for just one day," Jess said to everyone, "And choose one last thing to do, what would it be?"

"Watch the sunrise on the beach," Aaron answered quickest, smiling. "That's a no-brainer."

"I'd go get a Big Mac," Hanley said.

"Oh, Hanley, seriously?" Martin said. "You can do *anything* and that's what you'd choose to do?"

"Okay, fine... I'd go to the movies. I used to love going to the movie theater. I'd get a huge tub of that movie theater popcorn and put tons of that nasty, oily butter stuff on it, the kind that's supposed to give you a heart attack. I'd go see a comedy... or two, or three. A triple feature, with Steve Martin, and whoever else is funny."

"I'd spend the day with my sister," Alma said, holding Kate's hand.

"I'd visit my mom's grave," Kate said, quietly. "I'd write her a long note and leave it there for all the days I couldn't visit her."

Kate began to cry, and Alma hugged her tight.

"I'd take my wife to a really fancy, expensive dinner, at a restaurant where a nice steak costs at least thirty bucks," Martin said.

"Oh, yeah, because *steak's* healthy," Hanley quipped.

"Then we'd go for a walk in the moonlight, or maybe take a horse carriage ride."

"They don't have carriages in California," Hanley said.

"I'd take her on a date in New York City," Martin said. "We'd walk through Central Park."

"And get mugged."

Everyone chided Hanley, but they all laughed at him as well.

"I'd go shopping," Jess said. "Just window shopping though. Look at all the stuff I'll never have. I'd pick out my own baby crib and clothes and toys, though. I'd buy those."

"I'd take Jenny on a day cruise to Catalina," Malcolm said. "To Avalon Bay."

"Yeah, that sounds nice," Jenny said, smiling at her dad. "I'd like to smell the ocean again. I *love* that salty-sea smell."

Everyone nodded. Then it got quiet again except for when Hanley said, "Thanks, Jess," and smiled at her.

***

They all silently played cards, or watched the others play, when ten o'clock hit, unnoticed. Suddenly, the quiet room grew raucous. It started with light giggling that grew into loud laughter and exclamations. Sarah had turned on her power, but no one realized this. The only thing they all knew was that suddenly they felt giddy, euphoric, even tipsy—all of them exhilarated.

"Whoo!" Hanley whooped, throwing his fist in the air. Then he slapped a King down on top of his card pile.

"That's a king in the corner, folks. See it and weep."

Next table over, at the same time, Earl slapped his own final King card down. "Now *that's* what I'm talkin' 'bout." Aaron tossed his remaining cards up into the air lightheartedly and laughed as they rained back down. Malcolm snorted, watching the scene from the next table. He and Jenny leaned together, lost in gales of laughter. The world swam on a sea of happiness and giddy jubilation for everyone.

Ben walked in the door holding Sarah's hand. No one noticed at first. He just stared at the members of The Society, as drunk as the rest of them on the peaceful and joyous intoxication of Sarah's gift. He sighed deeply, feeling exalted.

Martin first picked up on the little girl who caused the entire scene of absurdity to unfold. Through his laughter and tear-filled eyes, he turned his head to gaze over at the cafeteria door, where she and the doctor stood. He gestured drunkenly towards them. One by one, everyone noticed, as others slowly turned their heads, following one another's gaze. When everyone had turned to stare at Ben and Sarah, he gently walked her over to the three tables where the inebriated bunch sat.

Sarah stepped forward, eyes shining. Ben put his hands on her shoulders, proudly presenting her to the group.

"Everyone, this is Sarah. Sarah, this is everyone."

Everyone said hi at the same time, then multiple bursts of laughter broke out.

"Hi, everyone," Sarah said, smiling brightly.

This made everyone laugh again.

"Okay, it's time we got going. Okay, everyone?" Ben asked.

Various phrases of consent blurted out, with more laughter and giggling. Ben looked down at Sarah. He got the distinct impression she'd lent a hand at helping him think straight, feeling grateful.

"Sarah, I'll lead you. We have to get Rachel, then head outside, but once we go through that door, you'll go in front, okay?"

She nodded. Everyone looked at her reverently now. Jess sighed in contentment. Sarah turned to her, smiling wide.

"Hi, Aunt Jess!" She rushed up, hugging her. Jess laughed.

Ben took hold of Jess's hand in his left, holding Sarah's in the other. The three of them turned and started off. Everyone left the cafeteria, following the three of them.

**

They all marched in a group, Ben in front, holding Sarah and Jess's hands, and went directly to Rachel's room. He took the key to her door out of his pocket, hands shaking. When he opened her door, he felt relieved to see Rachel standing, waiting for him. She giggled lightly. She'd even washed her hair.

"Rachel? Are you ready to see all of your old friends, plus a few new ones?" Ben practically sang to her.

Rachel nodded. He motioned her forward, and she stood in her doorway, peering out, staring at the group of people, most of whom she already knew.

"Sarah, this is Rachel. Rachel, this is Sarah. Our very special helper for this evening," Ben said, giggling like a child. In the back of his mind, he realized Sarah had her abilities turned on high, for he'd never felt quite this goofy and happy before.

"We're going to head on out now, everybody, okay?" He turned, facing forward again, and headed down the hallway.

"Man, I feel *great*." Ben practically skipped.

In the farthest back reaches of his mind, he felt panic. In his euphoric state, he didn't have a good handle on time. Everything felt slow and drawn-out, as if hours had passed, like the effect of a drug. He stopped, looking down curiously, as he felt Sarah tug on his shirt.

"Yes, Sarah, my sweet?"

"It's only been five minutes… and I don't feel any bad men yet."

Ben breathed a sigh of relief. "Thank you, darling."

Rachel watched all the other members of The Society pass by her, down the hallway. Most just smiled lazily, a few nodded to her. Aaron gave her a dizzy thumbs-up. Then suddenly, a very familiar face appeared. Hanley stopped up short, staring at Rachel, whom he hadn't seen in over a year.

"Rachel!" He threw his arms around her, hugging her tight. She hugged him back.

Earl passed them, shaking his head.

"Gonna miss the bus, y'all."

"Come on," Hanley said, taking Rachel's hand.

The group of thirteen walked down the hallways, following Ben, Sarah and Jess, until they abruptly stopped. Ben spun around to explain.

"The Atrium door won't open if there's more than two people within one hundred feet. The sensors are just around the next corner. I'll take Sarah, and she and I will open the door." Suddenly, Ben began laughing hysterically. Tears squirted from his eyes. He looked directly at Jess, barely able to squeak out the further explanation.

"It's all so simple. You don't have to blow anything up or cut the power for us to get the door open. It won't open for more than two people, and so far, everyone that goes through just lets the stupid door close behind them," he giggled again, almost losing his cool. "But once the door is open, all I need to do is stand there and hold it, instead of letting it close…" more giggling, "and we can all just walk right through the damn door." At this point, Ben completely lost it, doubling over, clutching his stomach with cramps from laughing so hard. He barely wheezed out, "What a bunch of stupid, incompetent, security-planning *idiots*!"

"But, how did they know to not open the door for Hanley?" Jess chirped up, placing her hand on Ben's shoulder in attempt to comfort him in his chaotic chortling. "Do the sensors… *sense* him?" She giggled.

"*No*," Ben's voice sounded as high as Sarah's now. "When the tech here in this facility notices that Hanley is getting close to the Atrium door, he has to call the other tech at the second station," he wheezed out. "I told you it was too complicated, I didn't even see it… I was gonna have you blow up half the building to cut the power!"

"You're *stupid!*" Alma laughed from behind Jess. This made everyone in the group crack up.

"I know!" Ben exclaimed, laughing and pointing at Alma.

Sarah gently tugged on Ben's shirt again, patiently. When he didn't immediately respond, she tugged harder. Finally, Ben got himself under control. He wondered if she'd dialed her power down a bit again, to help. He turned to her, getting down on his knees, fairly recovered to calm now, save for a bit of silly giddiness, as if moderately tipsy. She put her hands on his shoulders, and he smiled.

"You're going in front. Okay?" he said.

She nodded. Ben looked around, searching for Hanley, standing back up on his feet.

"Hanley!" he drunkenly barked.

Hanley quickly stepped forward, sidling between everyone, and stood in front of Ben, messily saluting.

"Yeah?"

"You ready to melt a fence, tough guy?"

"I was born ready, Doc."

"Great. Everyone else ready to walk by a bunch of guys with guns?" Ben smiled.

They nodded in unison, swept up and soaring on the warm waves of

Sarah's gift.

***

Ben opened the door and Sarah crossed the threshold, sending her love out in even more powerful arcs than ever before. Hanley went next, followed by Jess, then the rest of them. When everyone was through the door, Ben let it close, and ran to catch up to Jess and Sarah, again taking both their hands.

They all gasped at the incredible feelings of love and exhilaration that flooded over them. They felt as if they floated, their feet not touching the ground.

Outside, it was pitch black as they walked down an unfamiliar dirt path through the citrus trees. They soon entered a clearing, and walked across, able to see a little further now, for the moon was almost full. They crossed the clearing and walked through another thick stand of citrus trees on the other side, then came to another clearing.

Several yards past the other side of this, they came to the fence, and everyone stopped. Ben snapped his fingers in the murky moonlight, and Hanley stepped forward, motioning for everyone to move back, pushing his hands through the air. When people still weren't far enough away for his liking, he gestured more dramatically, smiling crazily the entire time.

Hanley looked back at Sarah, who smiled at him encouragingly. Then, he turned around and stood with his back to everyone.

They watched in amazement as the cross-hatching metal of the electrified fence began to shine, much like a glow stick, emitting a bright orange-yellow light.

As the metal super-heated, sparks showered out in arcs, the fence continuing to scorch. The metal turned a yellow-white, then simply fell away in liquefied puddles and large globular drops.

Ben walked up to Sarah and looked down at her. She looked up at him, her face serious now. She no longer smiled.

He knew that the moment the fence had started glowing, their escape was known. Despite his giddy state, he felt well-aware there were now dozens upon dozens of armed soldiers, snipers, trained killers, all massing together, forming a perimeter around the area of fence that would have been indicated on the monitoring screens of the external base outside the facility. And with Sarah's uncanny intuition, he knew she must be aware of this fact, to some degree or other, as well.

"Are you okay, Sarah?"

"Yes, Uncle M."

She stepped through the opening in the fence, and everyone followed behind.

***

It was slow-going in the dark. Ben mentally kicked himself for not thinking about bringing a few flashlights along. It took them several minutes to travel across the terrain, even a basic football field's length. No one knew how far they'd need to go before their galactic taxi would show up. About 140 yards beyond the fence, they were all suddenly bathed in such bright light they stopped and covered their faces with hands and arms. All looked away, or at the ground, attempting to shield themselves.

A ripple of panic ran through the group, and then another wave of reassuring comfort washed over them. As their eyes adjusted to the floodlights, the group saw that they were surrounded by soldiers in fatigues. Dozens of trained killers arrayed throughout the trees, along both sides, and more positioned across the hillside before them. Still, others ran to close the perimeter behind, penning them in a large, elliptical trap. They were surrounded, yet, none of them felt afraid.

Sarah stood in front, looking into the faces of the soldiers closest to her. Another powerful arc of overwhelming emotion washed over everyone present. More than most could take, grown men in uniform began to weep. They looked at her in wonderment. Some of the men who lay on the ground in position, now suddenly stood, and many who'd hung back amongst the trees stepped forward.

They held their weapons limply at their sides. Others laid their weapons down on the ground in front of them, as if in offering. The group watched all of this unfold, only dimly aware, the whole thing like a dream to most. They looked around at the soldiers, taking in their reactions as the men gazed at the little girl.

Slowly, Sarah walked by the men. They turned to watch her go, their eyes never leaving her. The Society followed.

First behind Sarah, were Ben and Jess, side by side, holding each other's hand. Behind Ben and Jess, Hanley and Rachel walked, also holding hands. Martin followed them, alone. Next came Aaron, Earl, and Jesus. Alma and Kate followed behind, clinging to each other. Malcolm and Jenny were the last.

The soldiers watched them pass, unmoving, unblinking. As the group continued walking, the men and the floodlights quickly faded, falling further and further behind. Still, they kept walking, the elemental love washing over and through them, proof against any fatigue.

Sarah stopped walking after another hundred yards or so, turning back to face the group. Ben turned to search out Hanley.

Hanley stepped forward, his eyes unfocused, as if listening to a voice far off in the distance that no one else could hear. Martin peered at Hanley closely. He could not hear the Graylings, only Hanley's side of the conversation, but this time he listened in awe and wonder, truly believing for the first time, utterly without doubt, that there *was* someone listening and responding on the other end. He still had no real proof, and yet, Martin, who had been the most accepting of the beautiful notion of it all, finally believed fully at that moment. Eventually, Hanley spoke.

"They're coming," was all he said.

***

The moon had fallen behind a heavy scud of clouds, a light, chill breeze herding them in ragged streamers across the sky. Then the lights appeared.

Jess looked up, still holding Ben's hand. She felt calm, but her heart beat fast in her chest all the same. She watched as the dull-gray ship descended. Shaped like a giant lemon drop, the transport hovered just a few feet above the ground before them, making no sound. Even when a metal hatch slid open and down into a ramp, revealing a tunnel-like opening, no one moved. The ship was as large as a goodly sized house. A bright light emanated from inside the tunnel opening.

Hanley stepped forward then, turning with an expression of such childlike joy, Jess couldn't bear to look him full in the face.

"If you're coming, *come*." Then he vanished, disappearing up the ship's boarding ramp, into the light.

Sarah watched him go, then turned back to Ben and Jess. Ben turned to face Jess, and she smiled at him, taking a deep breath. She nodded. He clasped hard to Jess and Sarah's hands, and together, the three of them boarded the ship.

The rest followed, by and by. No one refused. Everyone in The Society boarded the ship. Within moments of their boarding, the entrance ramp slid up and folded closed, and the vessel silently disappeared into the night, taking with it an unknown salvation.

Book Two:
TRANSCRIPTION

1

The rounded tunnel turned sharply downward, opening into a large circular cavity evocative of a plane's interior cabin. Everything colored various shades of gray, glinted dully under lights lining the sides in a vague way suggesting newness.

As Sarah, Ben and Jess entered the rounded cabin, that's exactly what Jess thought. She felt as though she walked into a brand-new car. Even the smell of the cabin suggested newness to her mind, the odor different from a car's interior—a scent unlike anything she'd smelled before—reminiscent of a combination of baby powder and bitter metal. It made her smile.

Everyone smiled crazily as they entered the ship, because Sarah still used her powers. She would not stop until she knew the ship was high into the air. Now, everyone stood, looking at one another, still in a dazed fog of euphoria.

From a doorway at the fore of the cabin, an arched opening slid sideways, and everyone stared at a man, who stood smiling hazily, also affected by Sarah's powers—drunk on happiness. He wasn't very tall, Jess noticed. Ben towered over him, but then again, he tended to tower over most people. The man appeared extremely amicable, however. His hazel eyes shone with bright elation, head covered in short, light auburn hair, with a thin scruff of red beard covering his face. Sarah blinked, dropping both Ben and Jess's hands, and walked up to the man, hugging him. Hanley walked over and shook his hand.

"Everyone, this is Rafferty. He'll be our pilot for the evening."

Rafferty's smile widened, and everyone simply nodded, still in a fog. He quickly disappeared back into what Jess assumed to be the cockpit of the ship. She briefly saw a screen before the door closed, and witnessed Rafferty sit down, working away at a control panel of some kind. Then the door closed, cutting off her view.

"We should all sit down," Hanley said, motioning around him to the gray chairs that lined the walls in a circle all around them. The chairs were attached, or rather, seemed to grow out of the walls— sixteen in all—eight on either side of the ship's round interior. The only break in their circular form was for the tunnel entryway they had all just entered from, and the cockpit door.

Everyone chose a seat. Sarah, Jess and Ben sat on the right side, along with Jesus, Martin, Hanley and Rachel. On the left side, Alma and Kate sat with Malcolm, Jenny, Aaron and Earl.

"Looks like we got almost a full house," Hanley said, still smiling. "Better put on your seatbelts, folks."

Hanley reached over his shoulder and pulled a harness of some kind out of the wall, across his upper body, attaching it to a hook on the chair's metal frame, just below the soft cushion. Everyone else did the same, still completely calm.

"Seatbelts?" Jess giggled.

"It's more for your own state of mind, than any actual use," Hanley said. "So you'll feel more secure at take-off."

"Why, is it bad?" Jess still giggled. Ben played with her hand, which he had never let go of, also smiling lazily.

"You'll see," Hanley said, leaning his head back to rest against the cushioned headrest. Everyone else copied him.

"No one panic," he added loudly, eyes still closed. "It'll only last a second, then everything's smooth sailing again."

"What...?" Jess said, then quickly shut up, head snapping from Hanley, on her left, straight forward. Her heart plummeted along with her stomach.

At that moment, everyone felt a sudden dip, their stomachs somersaulting in each of their abdomens. It felt as if they rode in a car speeding very fast, then suddenly dropped off a cliff. All felt a lost, floating sensation, as if the bottom of the ship had simply dropped out from under their feet. It reminded Jess of those free fall rides at theme parks that strap riders in, hoist them up several hundred feet, then just drop. In a split-second of complete free fall, everyone's heart suddenly lurched into overtime.

At that moment, Sarah finally let go, her powers shutting off like a light switch. Suddenly, there was no warm blanket of love and comfort covering everyone's emotions. They were each left emotionally naked, to muddle through their fears, doubts and panic. Everyone looked around as if woken from a long, strange dream. Looks of dread, dismay, even disbelief washed over them.

There were several moments of silence, as the events that had just unfolded sunk in on each person. Martin frowned, then looked horrified, as he recalled walking past all the soldiers with guns. Malcolm and Jenny sat, frozen in horror. Kate and Alma cried lightly while holding onto one another. Aaron sat, staring straight ahead, as if in complete shock. Jesus was the only calm one. He sat smiling, eyes closed, as if taking a nap. Earl physically trembled and shook.

Ben looked over at Jess, saw her ashen face, all the color drained from her cheeks. He realized the hand he held felt ice-cold. Hanley shook his head but smiled slightly. Ben looked across Jess to Sarah, growing alarmed. Her head lolled to the left, chin hanging down. She appeared to have lost consciousness. He worried about Jess's mental state, but much more about Sarah.

"Holy Shit!" Hanley cried out, as the events they'd all been through replayed in his mind and sank in. Everyone jumped.

"Hanley," Ben said, sounding panicked. "Is it okay for me to get out of my seat?"

"Sure, I guess so, but wh…?" he trailed off, watching Ben.

As soon as Hanley said the word 'sure' Ben was on the move. He quickly unlatched his harness, jumped out of his seat, and spun around, coming to rest directly in front of Sarah. Jess watched him, still dazed.

Ben lifted Sarah's head, her face cradled in his large hands. He pushed her head up, to rest against the back of the chair, and forced her eyelids open, checking for the dilation of pupils. He checked her pulse as well, then breathed a heavy sigh of relief. Jesus had come awake and looked at Ben with concern.

"Is she okay, Doc?"

"Yeah, she seems to be sleeping," Ben said.

"She must be exhausted," Jesus mused, his voice full of emotion— overflowing with love. He gazed at Sarah for several moments, then looked around at everyone else as they watched in silence.

"What she did," Jesus continued, his voice cracking. "I can't believe what she did."

"She saved all of our lives," Jenny said, looking up at her father.

"She got us on the ship," Hanley said. "We wouldn't be here without her. We never could have left the facility without her. It's why the Graylings had to wait so long."

"Who's that Rafferty guy?" Jess said.

"He's our pilot," Hanley shrugged matter-of-factly.

"But," Jess said, "he's human?"

"Yeah, but he's a transgen, just like the rest of us."

"There are other transgens?" Malcolm asked.

"Yeah, but the Grayling's don't call them that. They simply call them hybrids, because of the special gene," Hanley said.

"How many are there?" Aaron wanted to know.

"Not many," Hanley said. "The Grayling's don't take people who have families."

Hanley looked at Ben while saying this, accusation in his voice. Ben colored and looked down at the floor, still kneeling in front of Sarah. Jess moved into Ben's empty seat, so he could sit with Sarah, his arm around her while she slept against him.

"Rafferty was a bum, wandering the streets," Hanley said. "Suffered from schizophrenia. He also had a special gene, so the Graylings picked him up. Nothing aggressive in that."

"So, a *schizophrenic hybrid* is driving an *alien ship* with all our lives on board right now, is that straight?" Aaron looked at Hanley with fear and annoyance.

"He's not schizophrenic *now*, you *moron*," Hanley said. "The Grayling's fixed him."

"They can fix that?" Martin said.

"They can fix a lot of things," Hanley said. "Rafferty's just a normal guy now, his mind's as clean as a whistle."

Jess frowned. She wasn't sure how a whistle was 'clean', she'd never understood that saying. She looked at Hanley in curiosity.

"How do you know all this?"

"I'm en comunicación with our old Rafferty as we speak," Hanley said.

"Wait, you mean, you can hear his thoughts? I thought you could only do that with the Graylings?" Jess said.

"Well, Rafferty has an ability, too. And it seems to be enabling him to talk to me, and me to him. Two-way radio, lucky us," Hanley shrugged again, looking around at everyone. "Look, there's a lot to learn, okay? You're not gonna get everything all at once, all right?"

Everyone just stared at Hanley. Hanley sighed, rolling his eyes. He looked at Martin, who also stared. Martin couldn't communicate with Rafferty.

"Okay, fine," Hanley sighed. "I'll try and explain it in a nutshell, but *don't*," he looked at everyone, his eyebrows raised in emphasis, "ask me any questions, okay? Just listen."

Everyone sat and quietly listened. Hanley spoke quickly, clearly annoyed.

"The Graylings have collected a small number of hybrids just like us, and they have abilities, just like us. There aren't that many, only half a dozen. Almost all of them were homeless, or mentally disabled in some way. They were on their own, no family. The Grayling's wouldn't take them otherwise. One of the hybrids can alter minds. He can open a channel, so the human in question can talk to the Graylings, sort of... get linked up, if you know what I mean? I have that ability on my own, along with my 'metal magic'. But others? They can now communicate with the Graylings as well, thanks to Ezra."

"Ezra?" Earl said.

"Yeah, that's his name, according to Rafferty. The Graylings can't speak. They no longer have vocal cords, okay? Their species evolved a long time ago, due to their telepathic abilities, so they all think to each

245

other. They're all linked to one another already. But without Ezra's ability, they would never be able to communicate with us. Our minds just aren't designed to receive thoughts. Now, our dear Martin has some of that ability, in the form that he can receive our thoughts. But he can't send them out. It's a one-way street. And he can only hear us. I can hear the Graylings, and apparently, now Rafferty, because a channel was opened in his mind to hear the aliens when his ability was activated. Maybe because I have that channel open already, too, with the Graylings… I don't know. That's just how it is, I don't have all the answers. I can hear Rafferty, and he can hear me. End of story. And later, once we're aboard the main ship, anyone who's interested, can visit Ezra, and get linked up."

"Wait, you mean, linked up to the Graylings?" Jess looked at Hanley in fear.

"Yeah," Hanley said, sounding surprisingly gentle. "But only if you want to be."

"So, you mean, if we choose to, we could talk to the aliens, too?" Jesus sounded intrigued.

"Yeah, Ezra will hook you up," Hanley said. "But you don't need to worry about any of this right now. We just traveled at thousands of miles an hour, straight up. We're already up in space, you do realize? We passed up and out of the Earth's atmosphere several minutes ago. We're now sitting in space, waiting."

"For what?" Aaron asked.

"For everyone to realize what's happening, deal with the panic, then come to terms with everything," Hanley said.

Everyone stared at him, stunned or frowning. He looked back at everyone with sympathy.

"You were all so focused on the escape," Hanley sighed. "Some of you didn't even know about that, even, until less than a day ago. What you might have to deal with after, was just that… an afterthought. I get that, and I knew this is how it would be. But we've escaped, we're out of the facility, and now… no more hiding. You're all gonna need to face the music. We're on board an alien transport ship, and before too long, we'll be on board the main ship, where we'll be living."

"Jeezus," Earl said, looking like he might puke.

"Look," Hanley said, still sounding gentle and sympathetic. "You all knew this was coming, you just didn't want to deal with it. Not until you had to. Now you *need* to," he said. "If it's too much, then, you have a few choices, really. We let you go, and you're on Earth, hiding and on the run. Your two choices then, are, continue to hide, and risk being hunted down, possibly killed. Or, turn yourself in, and go back to the facility. If they hunt you down and don't kill you, you're going back into the facility, and there won't be any escaping next time. Those are your choices."

"How long?" Earl said.

"How long, what?" Hanley asked.

"He wants to know how long we'll be living on the ship," Martin said, sounding sad.

"Oh," Hanley said. "Well, even with their stellar technology, and their ability to bend time and space, they've come a long way. They've plotted the most direct course back to their side of the Universe, but even then, it'll take ten years to get to their home planet."

"Ten years?!" Jess looked at Hanley in shock and surprise.

"Yeah, how long did you think it was gonna take?"

"I don't know," Jess frowned. "Maybe… a few weeks?"

"A few weeks?! Do you have any idea how vast the Universe is, Jess? How far they had to come, before they even stumbled upon our Solar System? They've traveled for hundreds of years, Jess."

"Hanley, we get it," Ben sighed, putting his free arm around Jess to comfort her. She had her face in her hands. "You don't have to yell."

"Sorry."

"You know, we haven't been talking to the *Graylings*," Aaron said, sounding bitter and sarcastic, "for the last ten years like you have. You're just throwing all this stuff at us, out of nowhere."

"No, Aaron," Hanley said, growing agitated. "I'm not. You knew this was coming, you simply chose not to believe. You couldn't face it."

"Hey, I'm facing it now, aren't I?!" Aaron yelled.

"Okay, okay, that's enough!"

Malcolm yelled, surprising everyone. No one had ever heard Malcolm raise his voice before. Even Jenny tensed up at his side.

"It's a lot to take in," Malcolm said, lowering his voice. "Hanley's had time to process it. Let's all just try and remain calm," he said, even as he roughly, nervously rubbed Jenny's shoulder.

"Okay," Earl said, sounding resigned. "So, we travel for ten years. Then what?"

"We fight a war, at least, some of us do," Hanley said. "The ones who've been chosen for the job."

"Which is who?" Earl asked, sounding fearful.

"Not you," Hanley said, looking at Earl and smiling gently. "Possibly me, maybe. Jess for sure. Rachel, probably? And Sarah."

"That's it?" Aaron asked. "Four people, to fight an entire war?"

"That's all I can guess, for now," Hanley said. "The Graylings know all our powers. I'm sure they can figure out what to do with us. We're just the chess pieces, they'll move us around. I'm only *guessing* at who they'll use, mostly, but, if the Graylings ultimately say four people can win their war, they know what they're doing. You're just gonna have to trust them, okay?"

"Trust aliens I've never met," Aaron said. "With *Jess's* life. *My* life. *Your* life?"

"Yeah," Hanley said, then fell silent.

"And we're just supposed to fight their war for them, when it has nothing to do with any of us," Aaron continued, as if trying to rally the troops to his side. "Jess, you want to risk your life for them? People you've never even met?"

"Technically, they're not people," Martin said.

"Whatever," Aaron said, waving off Martin's quip. "Jess, why would you even care?" Then Aaron redirected his gaze to Hanley. "Why would *we* even care?"

"Because they just rescued your ass," Hanley said, sighing.

"No, they didn't, Sarah did!" Aaron yelled. "Sarah got us out of there."

"And after that, where did you think we were gonna go, Aaron, huh? Did you think we were just gonna run off into the hills?! They rescued us, we're safe up here. Sarah's ability can only cover us all for so long. I mean, look at her. She's completely spent."

Everyone looked at Sarah, still fast asleep against Ben. She slept through everything, including the raised voices, and all the fighting.

"Look, I don't really care," Earl said. "I'm outta that shitty hell hole. And personally, the life I was living before the facility? I wouldn't care to go back to that."

"You wouldn't be able to, anyhow," Hanley said. "So long as any of us is on Earth, they'll hunt us all until they recapture us, or kill us."

Earl nodded, beginning to accept things. Malcolm and Jenny seemed to be working through the same process. Aaron obviously resisted. Jess simply felt numb. Ben had accepted his fate almost immediately, and had chosen to come, generally understanding what was coming. He knew Jess would struggle, but she would get there, eventually, at least, he hoped she would. He looked over at Rachel, who'd had almost no time to process any of it.

"Rachel, you okay?" Ben asked.

"Jeezus," Hanley breathed, suddenly realizing.

"Hey, Rach, you okay, hon?" he spoke to her gently, taking her hand. She'd been sitting next to him the whole time.

She nodded at him, speaking for the first time. Jess looked at her in wonder. Rachel was beautiful, with long, full hair the color of the sun.

She looked about ten years older than Jess, she guessed. She appeared to be in her mid-thirties.

"I don't care where I'm going. I'm just glad to be out of isolation. And I have no interest in running around on Earth, hiding, and living in fear. I feel safe here, now. And I trust you, Hanley," she said, squeezing his hand. He smiled at her. Whether he or anyone else consciously thought it, it was obvious he was in love.

"Honestly, I'm just glad to be here with all of you. My friends," she said, beginning to cry.

Everyone nodded. They all looked around at each other. What they had just been through—living at the facility, sharing in that experience, escaping, and now on board an alien ship—the entire ordeal had been such an emotional roller coaster, it bonded them all. They'd been through something fantastic—a series of unbelievable events—and they all suddenly realized how close it had brought them. Even Aaron, who didn't get along with certain people very well, felt fond of everyone. He certainly still felt protective of Jess.

"We're a group," Jesus said, nodding at Rachel, as if in thanks. "We go together, or not at all. I don't know what's in store for us, but it sure beats any plans I ever had for my own life. So, I say, let's go. Let's go save a planet."

"What about after?" Jenny asked, looking at Hanley.

"After what," Hanley said, still holding Rachel's hand.

"We live on board a ship, we travel for ten years, some of us prepare to fight some sort of war, and I guess, assuming, that we win... What then?"

"We come back to Earth?" Aaron said, looking at Hanley with hope.

"No," Hanley said, in consternation. "We can never come back. If they ever find out we're back, they'll still hunt us down. And besides, if it takes ten years to get there, it will take ten years to get back."

"So, great," Aaron said. "After twenty years, they won't be looking anymore."

"And you wanna just be dropped off, with no money, no real way to integrate back into society?" Hanley looked at Aaron in reproach.

"Sure, why not?"

"After twenty years, let's just see if you still feel that way, okay?" Hanley said, talking to Aaron as if he were a child.

"Fine," Aaron shrugged.

"The rest of you," Hanley said, "need to realize, this is a one-way ticket. We leave Earth tonight and that's it. There's no coming back. I'm assuming we'll live out the rest of our lives on Hesperia, once it's been cleaned out of the Bailon."

"Hesperia?" Jenny said.

"Bailon?" Malcolm and Kate echoed.

Hanley sighed, rubbing his temple with his free hand. Rachel squeezed his other hand, as if to remind him to be patient with everyone. Jess saw this action, and Hanley's reaction (for he looked at Rachel and his expression softened), and immediately, Jess loved Rachel; she was good for Hanley.

"The Bailon are the crappy aliens that slaughtered the Graylings and took over their home," Hanley said. "They're the ones we have to... exterminate. Hesperia is the name of the Grayling's planet. Well, not really, but in their language, it wouldn't even translate, so they gave it a name we could understand. To them it's called something I can't even begin to translate. To us, it's Hesperia."

"Like the city?" Aaron said, frowning.

"Like the Greek myth, with Hesperides in their Garden," Jesus said, smiling and nodding. "Cool. Did you pick that, Hanley?"

"You like it?" Hanley smiled back. "I knew you'd get it, you book worm."

"Wait, you got to name a planet?" Aaron sounded jealous.

Several people broke out in giggles and laughter at this, smiling, their eyes shining with tears. Amazingly, almost everyone by this point had begun to relax. It was as if their minds had been under so much pressure, they simply gave, and full acceptance of the situation came flooding into everyone, almost simultaneously. Hanley smiled and breathed out deeply, releasing considerable tension he'd been holding.

2

By his side, Ben heard Jess sigh deeply and looked at her in concern. He leaned over and whispered in her ear, to which she nodded at him and smiled. Aaron saw this and a twinge of jealously played at him. He looked down and away from the scene.

"We escaped," Jesus said, sounding incredulous. He looked around at everyone, smiling. "We're free."

Everyone nodded. Martin looked troubled, however. At that moment, the cockpit door opened, and Rafferty stepped forward, looked around at everyone, and nodded at Hanley.

"Hello, everyone," he said, looking nervous. "I'm Rafferty."

"I already explained," Hanley said. Rafferty nodded, still looking uncomfortable.

"Well, it's nice to meet you all, finally," Rafferty said. "Everyone's excited to meet you."

"Who?" Jenny asked.

"Uh," Rafferty said, looking at Hanley, who only shrugged. "The rest of us on board the ship? There's me, obviously, and Grace, and Ezra."

"The mind-meld guy," Hanley said. "Ezra."

"Wait, it's a mind-meld?" Aaron said, his face crinkling in disgust.

"No, not really," Hanley said, sounding annoyed again. "I was just trying to use a term you might understand."

"Well… yeah… anyway… Um…." Rafferty said, fidgeting. "We sort of have to… get the rest of you now, so… are we ready?"

"The rest of us?" Malcolm said.

"My sister," Alma said, growing visibly excited. "Right?"

Rafferty nodded. Then he looked over at Martin, who appeared to be on the verge of tears.

"And your wife, right?" Rafferty spoke softly. Jess trusted him immediately, he seemed so nice. Then Rafferty looked back to Alma.

"Lucia," Alma said, her voice shaking.

"We'll go to her first," Rafferty said. "She's the closest stop, in Palo Alto?"

Alma nodded. Rafferty came over and knelt in front of her, looking over his shoulder at Martin, nodding his head for him to come over. Once Martin knelt next to Rafferty, he spoke very softly. Jess stood and walked over to listen, as well as Jesus. Ben stayed with Sarah, still asleep against his body.

Everyone around Alma leaned in closer to listen as Rafferty spoke. He talked to her as if he'd known her for years, and Alma felt completely comfortable.

"Alma, it's very important that when you speak with Lucia, you explain everything. I know it will be a lot for her to take in. You've been missing for almost two years, and you're going to show up at her door, in the middle of the night. Have you thought about what you're going to say?"

Alma shook her head, crying. Rafferty nodded, taking a deep breath.

"You must explain to her about the Graylings. I know it's a lot to ask, but... Under no circumstances can you get her on board without telling her. It simply wouldn't be fair. It's very important to the Graylings that everyone comes on board of their own free will."

Alma nodded. Aaron frowned, shaking his head. Rafferty looked at him with concern, for he knew Aaron did not understand. He knew none of them fully did, except for Hanley. Rafferty looked around at all the faces, his eyes sad and pained.

"You may not know the Graylings, but they know you. You can't hear them, but they can hear you. They've been with you all along. Every thought, every emotion. Every horrible thing you've endured—your missions."

Rafferty specifically looked at Jess, then over his shoulder to Rachel. He smiled, tears in his eyes.

"They've felt everything you've felt. And mental anguish is something that greatly distresses them. They would never want to cause this in any of you, in anyone. If anyone comes on board and starts to panic, it will cause them great distress. They'll hear your pain like nails in their heads. They're very sensitive. Causing pain or emotional harm to any living thing is very upsetting to them."

"Oh, yeah, sure," Aaron said, scoffing. "But they're willing to bring us to *Hesperia*," he sneered, looking at Hanley, "and *terminate* all the Bailon. Yeah, they're real peaceful."

"Yes, they are," Rafferty said, remaining completely calm. "But if you had seen what I've seen, what they've shown me, of the memories they share of their own extermination, then you would understand. They *are* peaceful. That's why they need you. It brings them great anguish, knowing they will cause so many deaths, but they have no choice. They simply cannot live on board a ship forever, now can they? They've managed to do that for over two hundred years, but time is running out. The longer they're away from their planet, the quicker they die. Their lifespans are cut in half away from their home. Two thousand of them escaped, two hundred years ago. Now, only a few hundred are left."

"They've lived for two hundred years?" Alma said, sounding reverent. Rafferty nodded.

"But their lifespans on Hesperia are considerably longer. Thrice that, and more. Out here? They age much quicker and are weaker. And on top of that, with humanity, they must deal with great mental anguish, in all our emotions and thoughts. They simply cannot help it. To bring others on board, they must know ahead of time what they are coming into," Rafferty nodded at Alma again.

"How you are going to explain all of this to your sister after being missing for two years is up to you. You know her best. But you must explain. If she gets upset, you'll get upset, and all of us on board who are activated will end up relaying the drama to the Graylings, who'll be subjected to all of it. I would like to spare them any more pain than is necessary. Free will is very important to them. They only want people on board who choose so."

"They sound like regular saints," Aaron said, scowling.

"I wouldn't expect you to understand, Aaron," Hanley spoke up. "Or any human, really," Hanley sighed. "I told you," he said, to no one in particular. "They couldn't harm a fly."

"I can talk to her," Alma said. "But, how much time do I have? Cuz, like, five minutes ain't enough for her to decide, you know?"

Rafferty shook his head adamantly.

"Of course, you have more than five minutes. We have several hours before sunrise. The ship can only land in the dark, while everyone is sleeping. We'll find someplace nearby, like a park. You'll walk off the ship and see your sister. If it takes an hour, we'll wait an hour."

"We're just gonna sit, waiting for her?" Malcolm said.

"Sure, why not?" Hanley said.

"I don't know, it just seems so… strange, after what we just went through. We're just going to park and pick people up?" Malcolm said.

"Yep," Hanley said. "The hard part is over, people. We just escaped from a high-tech facility that they never thought we would ever be able to pull off. We're in the clear."

Everyone collectively breathed a sigh of relief. Alma sat up then, for she'd been leaning forward, her elbows on her knees, while speaking with Rafferty.

"Well, time's wasting, right? Let's go!"

"I'll need the address for your sister," Rafferty said.

"What, like, you can do that? You got, like, a GPS, or something?"

"Something like that," Rafferty smiled. "We've been here a while, you know. The Graylings have been ready to get your friends for a long time. Long enough to map every street in the state. Download the maps from databases. There's a lot to learn, we can explain everything later. The address?"

"Oh, right. 543 Springfield Street. It's an apartment complex. Oh, God, unless she moved?!"

"We'll worry about crossing that bridge if it comes, okay?" Rafferty said.

Alma nodded, but she did not relax. Rafferty looked at her with concern. "Right now, I need you to be thinking about what you're going to say, remember?"

Alma nodded again, still looking tense and nervous. Rafferty nodded back, then stood and went into the cockpit, the door closing behind him again.

"Seatbelts," Hanley said, sighing, and everyone quickly went back to their seats, at least, those that had been kneeling with Rafferty. Everyone fastened their harnesses, and a moment later, they all felt that same stomach-dropping sensation, then nothing.

Everyone sat in silence for several minutes. Many people glanced around nervously at each other's faces. Some smiled and nodded, others looked down at the floor. Fifteen minutes passed this way. Then there was another stomach-dropping lurch, and a moment later, Rafferty emerged from the control room of the ship, looking nervous.

"Okay, everyone, we're here. I found a large park, about two blocks from the complex. Alma, I don't know if she's there, but if she is, then this is it. You're about to see your sister for the first time in two years. Say your hello's, do your hugging and crying. Then, once she's recovered, you'll have to explain in whatever way you're going to. We'll simply be here waiting, for when you come back. You can take your time, but not too much, okay? Martin still needs time to talk to his wife, as well. Understand?"

Alma nodded. She smiled at Kate, then let go of her hand.

"Wait, so, she's just gonna go, and we're all gonna sit here, waiting?" Earl said.

"Yeah, so?" Hanley said.

"Nothing, it's just, nerve-racking."

"If you want to wait at the entrance, to see when Alma's heading back, you can," Rafferty said. "In fact, you may want to. This will be your last chance to see Earth, albeit, in the dark. You all might want to say your last goodbyes."

Everyone looked at each other. Alma stood and looked at Rafferty, questioning. "Is the door open?"

Rafferty nodded.

"Is that safe?" Earl said. "Won't people see the spaceship and freak out?"

"We're parked in the dark," Rafferty said. "It's two in the morning. Everyone's sleeping."

Earl sighed, shaking his head. No one stood to follow Alma, except for Martin. Everyone else remained seated. As Alma passed Jesus, he reached out and grabbed her hand, squeezing it gently.

"Good luck, Alma," he smiled at her. She smiled back, already crying. Then she disappeared down the short tunnel and out of sight, Martin following.

Jess turned her attention to Ben, with Sarah sleeping against him. He looked at her, worried.

"Is she okay?" Jess asked.

"She seems to be. Her pulse is strong, her pupils are reacting," Ben said. "But she's out cold. I don't think I could wake her, even if I tried."

"She wore herself out," Jesus said, looking at Sarah in awe. Ben nodded.

"She definitely gave it all she had. More than in any of her training exercises. I suspect we barely made it out of there, before she became completely drained. For all we know, another five minutes, and she simply wouldn't have been able to keep it up."

"She will wake up, though, right?" Earl said, looking worried.

"She should. She just needs a lot of rest," Ben said. "She's sleeping very heavily. It's not a coma, but... Probably as close as you can get to one. She's breathing, her vital signs are good. She's just exhausted, is all."

Ben stroked Sarah's hair, looking at Jess, smiling.

"She called you Aunt Jess," he said.

"She called you Uncle M.," Jess gave back. They both smiled at each other. Then Ben put his hand on Jess's stomach, gently.

"You feeling okay?"

"I'm fine," Jess said, nodding to Sarah. "She made it okay, no stress. I think she saved the baby, too. I felt so calm."

"Everything is as it should be," Jesus said, quietly. Everyone looked at him, in awe. His state of complete calm, simply unbelievable to most. He nodded at the faces that turned to look at him.

After several more minutes passed, Jess got up, sighing tensely. She began pacing, playing nervously with her hands.

"This waiting is driving me crazy," she said.

Malcolm stood, taking Jenny's hand.

"Let's go look, okay?" Malcolm said to his daughter.

Jenny nodded and followed her father. After they disappeared around the corner, Jess paced another few moments, then followed them, shooting a glance at Ben.

"Okay?"

Ben nodded, still stroking Sarah's hair. Jess smiled at him.

"Don't you want to see? One last time?"

"No," Ben said. "I've already said my goodbyes. Besides, everything I care about is here, on this ship."

"I think I need to, Ben."

"I know," he said. "I understand. And besides, you heard what Rafferty said. You need to board the ship calm. No anguish."

"I think that's more for us, than them, though, right, Hanley?" Jess asked.

"Yeah," Hanley said, nodding. "They don't want us upset. They care."

Aaron snorted, shaking his head. Jess ignored him, quickly turning, walking down the tunnel.

***

It wasn't much of a view. At the entrance to the ship, she found Malcolm and Jenny looking out at the dark trees lining the park. Martin sat, near the bottom of the ramp, chin in hands. Jess sat down next to him, breathing in the cool night air, and then huddled up, hugging her knees.

"It's so quiet," she said, after several minutes.

Martin didn't look at her. "Not for me," he said, still looking out at the night.

Jess frowned at him. "What do you mean?"

"I never had my abilities outside the facility," he said. "The Society is small, barely over a dozen people. And mostly, I slept around the same time as everyone else was awake, save for meals in the cafeteria, or the need for companionship, like playing pool with Hanley. So, what few thoughts I heard, were just that… thoughts of a *few* people who were awake, and a vivid dream here or there. Plus, every now and again, a loud nightmare. But still, it was only a dozen people or so. Now? There are a hundred voices, all going at once."

"But," her frown deepened. "Aren't they all asleep?"

"Not everyone's asleep. But, most of them, yeah," Martin said. "Still, that doesn't mean I can't hear their thoughts. Their dreams. There are a lot more voices to listen to out here than I'm used to. It's overwhelming."

"So, go back inside," Jess said, growing concerned.

"That won't help," Martin said. "Besides, I don't mind. It's sort of fascinating. Once I single one thought out from the next. There's a lot of overlap."

256

"So, what do you hear?"

"You really wanna know?" Martin looked at Jess in wonder.

"Yeah," she said, curious.

"Okay, let's see. Hmmm… Ew… Someone's having quite an exciting dream. Very X-rated."

"Really? Give me some details. What exactly is he dreaming about?"

"Trust me, you don't want to know," Martin said. "And who said it was a *man*?"

Jess looked at Martin, amused. She laughed, shaking her head.

"Okay, what else?"

"What else, let's see," Martin sighed, smiling. He closed his eyes and concentrated.

"Huh. Some lady is dreaming that she's a bumblebee, swimming underwater."

"You can hear that?" Jess said, disbelieving.

Martin gave her a look, and she shrugged. Then she looked at him in wonder.

"I wouldn't want to do what you can do. I mean, it must be completely unnerving. All those thoughts, just streaming in. And you can't control it?"

"No," Martin sighed. "The voices are always there. It was overwhelming at first, but, you get used to it. No choice, really."

"We're going back in," Malcolm said. He and Jenny turned to go back down the tunnel.

"Are you sure? It's your last look," Jess said.

"Yeah," Jenny said. "I just wanted to, smell it, you know?"

"Yeah," Jess said, nodding. She did know. She understood all too well.

She watched as Malcolm and Jenny disappeared. She and Martin were alone.

"Martin," Jess said. "What's your wife's name? I never even asked."

"Eileen," Martin said, his voice full of love and adoration.

Jess smiled. She sat for a moment, then laughed and sang a few quick lines from the song she knew.

"Come on, Eileen, I swear on my… something," she said, frowning. Martin laughed, picking it up.

"I swear, well he means… At this moment, you mean everything. You in that dress… my thoughts, I confess, verge on dirty… Oh come on, Eileen."

"Really," Jess said, laughing. "That's what he's saying?"

"Yep," Martin said. "She hated it when I sang that, practically forbade me from doing so."

"Yeah, well, I don't blame her," Jess said. "Your singing voice is… not so great."

"What?" Martin said, feigning hurt. He purposely sang even more off-key. "What are you talking about, wait, listen again… Come on, Eileen… Oh… come on, Eileen, Oh, come on, let's… take off everything… that pretty dress… Eileen, tell him yes, oh, come on, let's, oh, come on, Eileen."

"No, now you're ruining the song for me," Jess said, shaking her head, but still laughing. Martin smiled now, laughing too.

"I thought that song was more romantic. Now you're just making it sound dirty."

"It *is* dirty, you didn't know that?" Martin said.

"Well, I thought it was about this guy who was in love with a woman named Eileen."

"Well, maybe he is in love with her," Martin said. "And he wants to take her dress off."

"No, see, that's not romantic," Jess said. Martin laughed again, looking out into the night. Jess giggled, then grew quiet. She stared along with him, out into the night, impatience prickling slowly to concern.

"It's been a while. What do you think is happening? Can you hear Alma?"

Just then, Jesus came out and sat down next to Jess. She smiled at him and he smiled back. Martin listened.

"They're still talking. That's why I came out, originally, to listen to them. See how it went," Martin said. "I stopped listening during their reunion. It didn't… feel *right*, snooping on that," he said, and Jess nodded.

"But, you can hear them now? Are they talking about all of this?" She motioned around her, and to the ship's entrance behind. Martin closed his eyes concentrating.

"It's hard, listening, like I said," he further explained. "There are a lot of other voices I'm not used to. I've gotten used to listening to all of *you*," he looked at Jess. She looked away, thinking about what thoughts he must have heard between she and Ben, especially during certain activities. Martin sighed.

"Yeah, I did," he said, and she knew he answered her unvoiced pondering about whether he'd heard she and Ben having sex. She blushed, her heart rate speeding up, embarrassed. Jesus said nothing. He had no idea what they were talking about.

"Sorry, but you asked," Martin said.

"No, I didn't," Jess said back. Then she shot him a thought. He looked at her, a bit shocked.

"No, I hadn't thought about that," he said.

For Jess asked him if he had thought about the fact that when he saw Eileen, he'd be able to hear her thoughts, and it might be odd, hearing her inner voice, that he'd never heard before. Almost like getting to know a new side of her that he'd never met. She immediately felt bad for telling him that, even though it was true.

"I'm sorry," she said, then quickly changed the subject. "Can you hear them now? Alma and…" she couldn't remember the sister's name.

"Lucia," Jesus said, speaking for the first time.

"Right," Jess said. "Can you hear them?"

"Yeah," Martin said, sounding relieved. "They're coming, actually. They're coming back."

Jess realized that Martin was excited because this brought him closer to seeing Eileen. She scanned the darkness of the park, looking for any sign of the two women, but didn't see anything.

All three of them stood, looking intently into the night. Martin stepped forward, an odd look on his face.

"Do you hear them?" Jess said, and quickly shut up.

Martin threw his hand up to silence her, tilting his head, listening to something she could not hear, worrying her. She looked at Jesus, who only shrugged.

"Martin?" she said, but he waved his hand at her, silencing her again.

"I hear something… *weird*," Martin whispered. "Light and whispery… calculating."

"Someone's dream?" Jess asked.

At that moment, Jess saw the shadows of two people enter the park from across the street, quickly passing in and out of the street lamps on that side. It was Alma and her sister. Jess smiled, relieved, but Martin still stood, listening, his body rigid, his head cocked to one side, concentrating.

"What?" Jess said, lightly, looking at Jesus again for an answer.

Jesus stared at Martin in concern. Jess looked back out into the park, a deep feeling of dread coming over her. Something was wrong, she felt certain of that now. Suddenly, Martin exclaimed, causing Jess's heart to freeze.

"Jeezus, it's a sniper! Alma, Lucia, run!"

"What?!" Jess screamed, in frantic panic.

She stood, frozen, but Jesus was already gone. He ran towards Alma and Lucia, both also sprinting, their shadows barely visible in the dark, bobbing up and down.

"Get down on the ground!" Martin screamed, his voice cracking in desperation.

At that moment, a shot rang out. It was not loud, rather, dull and weak, but in the dead silence of the night, Jess heard it anyhow. It was a sickening sound, for she heard the bullet hit home, sinking into flesh. In the darkness in front of her, she heard a woman let out a slight gasp, and saw a figure go down, pulling another with it. Then another shot reached her ears, dully. She saw a third figure, that of Jesus, still running towards the two women, also go down.

"No!" Jess screamed, even as she instinctively dropped to her stomach.

***

Inside the ship, the screaming voices of Martin, then Jess, reached the others, who still sat, waiting. Everyone looked around in confusion. They had no idea what was happening. Rachel, however, stood suddenly, and ran down the tunnel. Hanley quickly followed. Ben moved Sarah off his shoulder, gently, but swiftly, securing her back in her own seat, then ran down the tunnel in a dazed panic. No one else moved, frozen in fear.

At the entrance, another shot rang out, but missed, glinting off the metal siding of the ship, causing a bright spark to flare up in the pitch darkness. It was the only light they had, but in an instant, Martin pointed out into the trees, to where the brief flash had been spied by his eye, from the sniper's weapon.

Inside the cabin, no one heard the first two shots, but they heard the third bullet as it twanged loudly off the outside of the ship. Earl looked at the few people who remained sitting in the cabin, unable to move.

"Was that a gunshot?"

At that moment, Rachel appeared at the entrance ramp, just as the bullet sparked off the ship's side. Her eyes immediately darted to where Martin pointed. Her face held no fear. Quickly, swiftly, she walked down the ramp, past everyone, towards the sniper.

Martin ran out to where the three figures lay prone on the ground. Alma screamed and cried. Kate appeared at the entrance and ran to her. Martin picked something up, and Jess realized with a sick, sinking feeling, as he headed back to the ship, that he carried a body.

Ben appeared next, rushing to Jess's side. As he dropped down to where she lay, another bullet twanged loudly, directly behind where his head had just been, glinting brightly against the metal of the ship, then ricocheted off into the darkness. He screamed at her, breaking her shocked state of paralysis. She followed his order to go back inside the ship, simply turning to walk, not run, dazedly back down the tunnel and into the cabin, where everyone stared at her, their faces questioning. She simply stood there for several prolonged moments, staring off into space, shell-shocked. Then she numbly sat down next to Sarah, and pulled the girl's head onto her shoulder, more to comfort herself than for Sarah's sake, for the little girl was still out cold.

Back at the entrance, only eight seconds had passed since the first shot rang out. Everything happened so fast, no one had time to fully process anything taking place. Out in the park, yards away, everyone heard a man start screaming, his voice ringing out in blood-curdling wails.

Martin came back into view, his body falling into the dull light from the ship's tunnel, now illuminated at half-power. He carried the body of a woman. Kate and Alma followed close behind. Kate steadied Alma, who sobbed. Ben ran out to find Jesus, for he realized when he saw Rachel walk off, and heard the screams, that she was taking care of business. He was not afraid for his own safety. He briskly walked out onto the grass, several yards away from the ship, and stooped down laboring to lift Jesus up into his arms. He managed to do so, and turned, stumbling, back to the ship's ramp. Hanley was only vaguely aware of Ben brushing past him, carrying Jesus—too busy squinting out into the darkness, waiting for Rachel to return. The wailing of the sniper had now ceased.

After what felt like an eternity to Hanley, yet less than half a minute, Rachel returned to the ship, silently walking up the ramp, past him. He was the only one still standing there. Rafferty appeared, pulling Hanley in, as the ramp pulled up, shutting everyone inside.

Hanley walked back down the tunnel and came upon a grizzly scene of blood and gore. Ben had fallen onto the floor in the middle of the cabin, no longer able to support the weight of Jesus's body. He laid Jesus down and backed away, sitting next to Jess in complete shock, staring down at the scene that lay before his eyes.

Rafferty walked past everyone, and everything, and locked himself into the cockpit. He did not even warn anyone to harness themselves in, nor did Hanley. No one noticed the lurching sensation as they took off again, straight up into the night. As the ship hurtled through the air at hundreds of miles a minute, engulfed in bright fire, no one was even aware of the ship in motion.

3

On the floor, next to Jesus, lay the body of Lucia. Alma sat on the floor, cradling her sister in her arms, sobbing, covered in blood, as was Kate, for she'd been bloodied just hugging Alma. Martin, who had carried Lucia in his arms, sat soaked in blood as well. Ben, who had carried the body of Jesus, was also drenched. Jess looked at him, taking in the blood all over his front, then turned back to stare at the floor, still in utter shock.

As the ship continued moving at a mind-boggling rate, everyone sat in their seats, save for Alma and Kate on the floor. Everyone cried or looked away. Aaron stared in complete shock. Malcolm cradled Jenny in his arms, looking away, shielding her against his chest. He cried silently. Hanley sat down with Rachel, quietly taking in the whole scene. Rachel looked forward, a pinched look of pain on her face, staring into nothingness.

Ben sat and cried, silently, leaving Jess still cradling Sarah's head on her shoulder. He buried his face in his hands, his body bent in half. Jess vaguely saw, out of the corner of her eye, Ben's body shaking, racked with sobs.

Earl looked down at the bodies, then around at everyone, as if he simply could not believe what had just happened. Kate held Alma, and Alma held Lucia, whose arms flopped lifelessly, sticking out from her sister's embrace. She would not stop screaming and sobbing, and Aaron closed his eyes, covering his ears with his hands. Earl looked away then, crying as well.

Jess stared down at Jesus, whose body lay in the middle of the floor. She watched, dully, as a thin trail of blood appeared at his head, then traveled slowly toward the direction of the tunnel. The ship flew at a slight angle, but Jess did not know that. She simply watched the blood streak appear and elongate, as the last of the life in Jesus escaped. Already dead, his body continued bleeding out for several minutes.

Everything moved in slow motion, for Jess, at least. She could not know it, but it was the same for everyone else. Time had slowed, and they all remained in the cabin with the lifeless bodies of their friends for what felt like an eternity. Everything felt like a dream. No one believed anything to be real.

***

Rafferty came into the cabin, looking away from the scene on the floor. He turned to Hanley, looking for help, clearly flustered. He did not know how to deal with the situation that had unfolded, visibly shaking. He knelt in front of Hanley, and took his face in his hands, trying to focus his eyes.

"Hanley... *look* at me," Rafferty said, and Hanley did.

"We have to remove the bodies. Do you understand?"

Hanley nodded. He looked around at everyone, then locked onto the doctor.

"Ben, I need you. Can you pull things together with me?"

Ben nodded, still dazed and looked at Hanley, then at Rafferty, who nodded.

"It's not how I wanted to do things, but, it can't be helped at this point. We're going to enter the ship, through the cargo bay. We need to get everyone off, away from this... the blood."

"The Graylings," Hanley said.

"They feel your pain, they know how awful this is. They're greatly distressed, believe me," Rafferty said. He looked to be on the verge of a breakdown, his eyes welled up with tears.

"I know," Hanley cried. "I can feel it."

"They're in pain for *you*," Rafferty said, tears silently falling down his cheeks.

He stood and went back into the control room, the door once again shutting him off from everyone. Several more minutes passed, then he came back out, nodding at Hanley and Ben.

Both men stood, and Rafferty asked them if they could each carry a body. Hanley and Ben nodded. In the end, Rafferty had to help Ben carry Jesus, each carrying one end. Ben lifted Jesus by the shoulders, under his lifeless arms, and Rafferty lifted his feet, and they stumbled down the tunnel awkwardly, while everyone looked away.

Alma screamed again, as Hanley attempted to pry Lucia from her arms. He closed his eyes, trying to remain calm.

"No, no!!" Alma cried, and Kate pulled her away, into her arms, nodding to Hanley to quickly take the body. Alma collapsed against Kate, and Hanley lifted Lucia into his arms, crying the entire time. He disappeared down the tunnel, after Ben and Rafferty. Everyone sat, waiting, stunned, shell-shocked.

***

Ben and Hanley were the first to see the inside of the ship, albeit the cargo bay. Once down the ramp, they found three people waiting. The first, a black woman in her late forties, attractive. A man who looked to be in his mid-thirties, shorter than Rafferty, even—all of about five foot five—with pale skin, dark hair and eyes, and a closely cropped, dark beard. Lastly, stood a much taller man, in his late thirties, with blond, receding hair, and a pale, doughy face. The three of them looked at Rafferty, their eyes growing wide and full of sadness. They looked at the two bodies, covered in blood, and at the three men who carried them, crying, and quickly turned. The blond guy darted in, however, and took Jesus's legs, which greatly relieved Rafferty.

Ben, Hanley, and the stranger followed everyone out of the cargo bay, through a door, and into a hallway. Rafferty followed last. Everything appeared brightly lit from the bottom and top, glinting gray, just as the inside of the transport ship. Down the hallway, they turned right, and stopped at a door. The woman touched a panel to the right, and the door opened. They went into a mid-sized room containing several long metal tables.

The blond man helped Ben place Jesus's body on a table, then backed away, looking down at his gray shirt, now streaked with blood. He examined his hands, somehow also bloodied, and trembling. He looked like he was going to be sick. He left the room without saying a word.

Hanley placed Lucia's body on the next table over. Then everyone went back to the cargo bay.

Once there, the woman turned to Hanley and Ben, looking grave. She extended her hand for them to shake and they each did so.

"This is not how I wanted to meet you," she said, sounding close to tears. "My name is Grace. This is Ezra. The man who ran out of the room, was Arnold."

Ezra shook the two men's hands, saying nothing, chin trembling. Grace looked at Rafferty, her eyes troubled.

"Surely you're not going to attempt another pickup? Not after this?"

Rafferty looked at Ben and Hanley, shrugging. Ben looked at Hanley, who shook his head.

"Martin's heart will be broken. I don't know if he can come with us. He won't leave her behind, Ben. He simply won't."

Ben silently nodded, thinking hard. Then he looked at Rafferty, Grace and Ezra.

"I have to discuss this with the others. We need to decide what to do together."

The three of them nodded, and Ben quickly turned with Hanley to get back on the transport. Rafferty followed. Grace and Ezra simply watched them go.

***

Ben and Hanley re-entered the transport. Everyone turned to look, except Alma and Kate, who remained on the floor, holding each other.

Ben looked at Jess, and she returned his gaze, offering a supportive smile, weak as it was. He felt grateful. The eye contact was all he needed to know she was still okay, holding on, despite recent events.

"Martin," Ben said, gently, looking at him. Martin looked down at the floor, but he spoke with conviction.

"I don't care," was all he said. "One way or the other, we're going after Eileen." He lifted his head, looking Ben straight in the eyes. "I'm not leaving here without her."

Hanley nodded.

Ben looked around. He spoke softly, but with conviction, his voice strong.

"All right, then. We have a rescue mission on our hands."

"A rescue mission?" Aaron looked confused.

"That's right," Ben said, looking grave. "I made a terrible mistake. I assumed once we left the facility that we'd be safe. There were no other protocols to plan for, beyond escaping the facility. At least, none that I was ever made aware of," he said, looking sickened. "But it's clear to me now that there were protocols in place I never considered. If they had time to put one sniper in place, just minutes after our escape, in a city that's a five-hour-drive away, then, by now, they will have had plenty of time to put considerably more men in place around Martin's wife. I should have known," he said, voice faltering.

Jess stood and went to him, taking his hand. Sarah still slept, blissfully unaware of any of the horrific events that had unfolded. It was a small blessing for her, Jess thought. Ben took her hand, and, feeling its warmth, spoke again.

"I should have realized they might assume some of you, who had family, might go there. I never could have realized, however, that they would act this fast. Martin," Ben said, looking at him in sadness. "If we don't go after Eileen, they'll take her. They'll wait, for now, hoping to set a trap, but if it becomes clear you aren't immediately going after her, they'll move her to a secure location, away from her residence. I would imagine they'll do so by dawn. We need to move fast, and we need to come up with a plan to get her out and on this ship without anyone else getting hurt and without anyone getting caught. We're not leaving anyone else behind."

"Sarah," Earl said. "Let's just wake up Sarah. She can make anyone surrounding us put down their weapons. We can just walk in, and walk right out again, like we did before."

Ben shook his head, looking at the sleeping young girl. He sighed, his heart breaking. It would be perfect, if he thought she might be in any shape to use her powers again so soon. But she slept so heavily, he doubted he could wake her, and he told everyone so.

"Even if I could wake her, I doubt she has enough energy left to use her ability so soon, and on another large scale like it would take. There could be only half-a-dozen men surrounding Martin's house, or there could be over fifty. I have no way of knowing how mobilized they are by this point. In retrospect, we got lucky in the park. If there had been more than one sniper, more of us would be dead right now."

"More of us would be dead anyway, if it hadn't been for Rachel," Hanley said, from behind Ben, stepping forward.

He walked over to Rachel and knelt before her, taking her hands. "Rachel, you saved all of our lives," he said. "Understand? You did a good thing."

She nodded, a single tear slipping down her cheek. It was the first life she'd taken in over a year, and the second time she had done so without orders. Hanley was amazed and relieved that her mental state seemed as strong as it did. He wasn't certain what to expect from her, but she continued to surprise him.

"You need me to help, now?"

"What? No," Hanley said, trying to soothe her, for her voice shook. "No, honey, that's not what I meant. I only wanted to make sure you were okay with what just happened."

"Well, now, wait a minute," Earl said. "That's not a bad idea. Is it? I mean, if we can't do things peaceably, with Sarah's help, what other choices do we have? I can walk through walls, but I ain't bulletproof, and neither is Martin's wife," Earl said, looking at Martin in apology. He nodded back, understanding.

"Hanley's power can't help, either, unless you can melt the guns—can you?" Earl continued.

"I can only focus on one object at a time," Hanley said. "I couldn't possibly take out all their weapons at once, no."

"Okay, so you're out. Martin can't help, no offense," Earl shot over to him, then kept going. "Malcolm's not bulletproof, his floating won't help either, and Jenny can't blow people up, so they're no help."

Hanley sighed, taking Earl's meaning, as he continued.

"What's left? Aaron…" he only trailed off there, "and the Doc can't do anything. That leaves Jess. But even if she could take out all the soldiers, she'd take out the wife with 'em, right?"

Jess nodded, slowly, thinking it over. Everyone looked at Earl, who looked at Rachel.

"Can you control who you… you know… hurt? And who you don't?"

Hanley took Earl's full meaning then, and stood in front of Rachel, reeling to face him. He looked furious.

"What's wrong with you?" he screamed. "You're talking about asking her to commit mass murder. You can't expect her to do that!"

"Why not," Rachel said, from behind Hanley, standing, causing everyone to back away in surprise, and partly in fear. Her eyes had a fierceness to them that frightened everyone.

"It's not like they're giving us any choice, really," she said, her voice deep and bitter. "It's kill or be killed, the way I see it."

"Jeezus, Doc, what did you create?" Hanley whispered, and Ben closed his eyes, stabbed in the heart by Hanley's comment.

"It's not his fault," Rachel said, her voice softening a bit. "I loved Jesus," she said. "And Alma. And I know how much she loved her sister. I sat here, with the rest of you, and looked at their bodies. *They* did this, not me. Not us. But I'll be damned if we're leaving Martin's wife behind. He only came because he thought he was going to be with her again, isn't that right?"

Martin nodded, looking at the floor—looking at the blood—desperate.

"They did this, not us," Rachel repeated. "And if it's a war they want, then it's a war they'll get. Yes, Earl, I can choose who I hurt and who I don't. I never had to before," she shot her eyes at Ben, and he looked away, ashamed.

"I just burned everyone... but when I killed that tech, there were others there. None of you even felt the heat, did you?"

Malcolm and Jenny looked at each other, and then shook their heads, looking down. Alma did not respond in Kate's arms.

"I'm pretty sure I can do it," she said. "I'll need Martin's help, though. I'll need you to tell me exactly where Eileen is at. And I'll need you to listen, for all the voices, and tell me how many men there are, and where, if you can do that. Can you, Martin?"

Rachel looked at Martin with cold, calculating eyes, and waited for his answer. He looked at Ben, who only nodded, sending Martin his thoughts. Ben told Martin that Eileen would surely be lost if they did not go after her *now*, and if they did not follow Rachel's plan. It was the only way, he reasoned. He knew Rachel was right. He knew that Earl was right. This was the only way, with Sarah unable to perform, without her powers available to them.

***

The decision was made. Ben gave everyone the chance to exit the transport, for no one really needed to go, except Martin and Rachel, but everyone decided to stay, except for Alma and Kate. They left the ship, where they were greeted by Grace and Ezra.

Rafferty asked for Martin's address, and then immediately exited the cabin, disappearing into the cockpit. He flew the ship out of the cargo bay and headed back toward Earth. Everyone sat quietly and waited.

During the flight, Ben gently shook Sarah, attempting to wake her. When she would not budge, he shook her more forcefully, feeling bad about it, but he had to try, he told everyone.

"If there's any other way," he explained. Rachel watched, intently, with hope in her eyes.

"Of course, Ben," Earl said, nodding.

He shook Sarah violently then, and her eyes fluttered open, briefly. She looked at him, attempting a smile.

"Uncle M.," she sighed, then fell back to sleep.

Ben hugged her, crying silently. He had tried. There was no other way. Rachel sighed, then closed her eyes, mentally preparing herself for what she had to do.

The ship landed shortly after. Rafferty came back into the cabin looking clearly afraid. He nodded to Martin. "We're in the hills, behind your home," Rafferty said. Martin nodded. His house was lined by hills for several miles. Their cul-de-sac backed up to nothing but nature.

"Good ole Redding," he whispered. He nodded at Rachel and she stood with him, and together, they walked to the entrance. The ramp was still closed. Rafferty went with them, as did Ben. No one else went, for Ben told everyone to remain seated. He didn't want Martin to be distracted by too many people standing around. He also instructed everyone to try and clear their minds, so their voices, at least, wouldn't interfere with Martin's listening.

At the tunnel entrance, Martin stood with his hand against the metal frame, caressing it. He didn't even seem aware that he did so. He listened intently, standing that way for several minutes, making Ben extremely nervous. Rachel watched, her eyes set and calm.

Finally, Martin exhaled loudly, lightly smiling. He opened his eyes and looked at Rachel. She looked back expectantly.

"There are only eight of them," he said.

"Are you sure?" Ben looked at Martin intently.

"I'm sure," he said. "They're all around the back, lining the ravine, except for two out front, behind the bushes in my yard. Eileen's asleep, in bed, upstairs."

Rachel nodded, still looking intently at Martin. He looked back, his eyes grave.

"Their orders are shoot to kill, on sight," he said. "After what happened to the last sniper. Before that, the orders were to allow us to take who we came for, like they let Alma walk away with Lucia. They were supposed to follow them, to find the rest. But the plans were changed after our stop in Palo Alto. Now their orders are to wait until they're certain whoever is coming to the house, is there, then shoot whoever it is."

"But then, everyone else will just leave in the ship," Jess said. Everyone turned to look at her. Ben walked over, taking her face in his hands. Martin answered her, for he heard the rest of her thoughts.

"They don't care anymore," he said. "They only want to pick off as many of us as they can. They have no interest in recovering us alive."

"I thought I told you to stay in the cabin, huh?" Ben said, cradling Jess's face. He looked at her with such intensity and love, she smiled. He hugged her tightly.

"If anything happened to you, I would die," Ben said. "Please, Jess, go sit back down."

"Ben, if anything happens to *you*," she said, beginning to cry. He hugged her again.

"Nothing's going to happen to me. I'm not leaving the ship."

"But what if they're out there, right now, and as soon as the door is open—"

"No, they're not there, Jess. They're at Martin's house. We're parked on the other side of the hills. They don't even know we're here, right Martin?"

Martin nodded, smiling at Jess. Then he turned his attention back to Rachel.

"We can do this," he said.

Ben looked at the two of them, and nodded at Rafferty, who left, returning to the controls, to open the door. Jess followed behind him, into the cabin, to sit with Sarah.

"We'll be waiting," Ben said, nodding to Martin, who nodded back, as the ramp slowly lowered down.

4

Martin and Rachel walked into the night, over the hills, then dropped down into the ravine, on the far side. Martin led the way, and Rachel simply trusted him. He could hear the thoughts of all the snipers. She could hear nothing but crickets. They walked very slowly, carefully setting their feet down gingerly, to keep their footfalls silent. The going was slow and slightly maddening as it took several minutes in this fashion to travel only a few feet.

The six men in the ravine all faced towards the house, their eyes trained on the backyard, waiting for any sign inside the house. This is what Martin whispered into Rachel's ear, for he could hear her trepidation, the constant stream of worries filtering through her head. He listened intently to the men, for any indication they heard he or Rachel sneaking up. He also listened for any sign of stirring or waking from Eileen. The snipers listened intently to their earbuds, to the two men who waited in the front yard. These two men looked out into the circle.

It simply didn't dawn on any of them that someone might come up from behind, from over the hills. These men had been scrambled for a mission, but they knew nothing of aliens, or spacecraft, nor of humans with abilities that didn't involve manmade weapons. They knew no details other than shoot to kill anyone who attempted to enter the residence. They were not even expecting an air drop from a helicopter, let alone a silent drop from an alien vessel. And so, the secondary escape protocol plan that had been put together by General Levin contained a key flaw, in the General's attempt to keep the left hand from knowing what the right hand was doing.

They crept up quietly, as far as Martin dared go. Then he very quietly whispered into Rachel's ear. She listened, nodding in the darkness. Although Martin could not see her nod, he heard her thoughts, and knew she understood.

"This is as close as I dare get us. There are six men about one hundred yards to our left, all of them facing their backs to us. They will shoot to kill, the moment they hear us. Do you understand what I'm telling you?" he whispered directly into her ear, so the snipers would not be able to hear.

Rachel nodded. She would need to kill those six men, with their backs to her, before they ever even knew she was there. It was the only way. She closed her eyes, and the bodies of Jesus and Lucia—the former of whom she never even got to meet—flashed through her mind, along with all the blood. She let the pain flood into her, and the sadness as well. She allowed the unpleasant emotions to take over, channeling her anger. She had been preparing for the possibility of something like this for the last year, although, no one knew it, except for Martin. He heard it now, heard it as soon as Rachel asked Hanley if he needed help. She was prepared to kill, and he felt grateful.

Martin stood, breathless, waiting. He did not know what he waited for until the screams began. He fell to the ground, covering his ears, but this did not keep the screaming out. It continued inside his head, the shrieking so loud, he thought his head might burst. He panicked as the upstairs bedroom light came on inside his house—sudden brightness in the dark.

The screaming only lasted about twenty seconds, but Martin could hear the two men from the front scrambling, their thoughts panicked and jumbled. They headed around the sides of the house, towards him and Rachel.

He grabbed her by the hand, as he spoke, and they ran further into the ravine, right up to the iron-railed fence of Martin's backyard. He briefly tripped over something, and realized it was the body of one of the snipers. He quickly pushed all thoughts out of his head, other than Eileen.

"Rachel, two more men are coming at us, right now, from both sides of the house."

He heard that Rachel understood. He looked up at his own bedroom window to see Eileen peeking out from behind the curtains.

"Please, Eileen is at the window," Martin whispered.

"I won't hurt her," Rachel said.

More loud screaming came, as the two men from either side of the house rounded the corner and were immediately set to their blood boiling. They stopped dead in their tracks, dropping their weapons, enveloped in sheer and utter pain. The screaming was brief, shorter than before, even, only lasting about fifteen seconds, but it felt like an eternity. Martin felt as if he could not move. He shook all over. Lights started coming on in the houses on either side of them. Martin saw people looking out their blinds and curtains.

A man in the house next door, on their left, opened his window and bellowed out into the darkness.

"God damned kids! I'm calling the cops, you bastards!"

"Is that everyone?" Rachel said, sounding desperate and panicked.

Martin closed his eyes and concentrated, listening for any other voices, of anyone waiting to shoot them. He sat several moments, and Rachel grew restless and worried, her heart skipping and jumping in her chest. Finally, after two whole minutes, Martin sighed his relief.

"No, we're alone."

"Then go get your wife," she said. "I'll stay here. But you won't have the time to explain."

"I know," he said.

He left Rachel and briskly walked around the side of the house, lifting the latch on the iron gate, and entered his own backyard for the first time in two years. The lights had gone back off in the houses surrounding them. Apparently, everyone had decided not to bother calling the cops. They only wanted to go back to sleep. None of them realized that eight men lay dead around the ravine. The neighbor on the right side thought the screams were coyotes attacking raccoons or rabbits. The screaming had been so high-pitched and odd-sounding, it didn't strike anyone as the sound of grown men screaming for their lives.

Martin knew this, heard the thoughts, even as he entered his own backyard, and his stomach flip-flopped. He wretched and vomited into the grass, turning his head away, to his left. Then he staggered away, quickly feeling around in the grass for the tiniest pebbles or rocks to throw at Eileen's window. He did not want to call out her name or cause any more noise to re-awaken the neighbors.

He found a rock and threw it at the window. It missed and bounced off the stucco siding of the house. Martin sighed, fumbling on the ground for another rock, found one after several seconds, and threw it even harder than the last. He winced as it made contact against the glass and cracked it. The light in the room quickly came on again, and Eileen peeked timidly out the window.

"Eileen!" Martin risked yelling now. He wanted her to hear that it was his voice, for he could hear that she thought a teenager might be outside, or even a burglar, lurking around. She was very frightened.

"Eileen, it's Martin!"

He waited, his heart pounding away in his chest. The curtains suddenly and forcefully raked open, and he saw Eileen in full view, lit up by the light behind her. She clawed at the window, failing to open it, then beat at the glass wildly, panicked and desperate. She heard his voice. She was crying. He could hear her thoughts, and they made his heart break. He heard that she'd never given up hope that he would come back home to her, someday. She never allowed herself to believe he was dead or gone forever. Martin loved her so much in that moment, he fell to the ground, sobbing aloud.

"Eileen!"

"Martin!" she screamed, scratching at the window. Then she turned, running from the room, and he knew she was coming to him. He heard her mind cry out, as she ran down the stairs, into the living room, and unlatched the patio door, yanking it open. Then, suddenly, and unbelievably, she lay in his arms, sobbing, and he held her, sobbing back. She hugged him so fiercely, he could hardly breathe, but he didn't care. He hugged her back just as tight.

"Martin," she sobbed. "Oh, my God." She couldn't speak anymore. Whatever words she might have said became inaudible, lost in her sobs. He heard her words, anyhow, in her thoughts.

Love you so much. Oh, my God. I love you... knew you'd come home... you're okay... knew you weren't dead.

"Eileen, I never meant to leave you," Martin choked. "They took me away. They took me away," he sobbed.

I know, I know, she thought, although he knew she didn't truly know, couldn't possibly comprehend. She simply believed he'd been taken, by somebody, or that something had forced him away, and that he would never willingly leave her, and she was right.

"Martin," Rachel hissed. She'd come all the way up to the fence. "What if more soldiers come?"

"Who is that?" Eileen pulled her head up and tried to peer out into the darkness.

"Eileen, listen to me," Martin said, pulling her face into his hands, looking into her eyes.

"We have to leave right now, okay? I can't explain, except to tell you that there are very bad men coming to get me, and *you*."

"Bad men?" Eileen repeated, dazed. She hugged him again. "Oh, Martin, I love you. I missed you so much."

"I know, baby, but we have to leave. We have to leave now, and I want you to come with me, okay?"

"Anywhere," she cried. "Anywhere."

She looked at him, trying to see his face more clearly in the darkness, with only the light from the upstairs bedroom to see by.

"Can I bring anything?"

He shook his head at her, and she seemed to understand. She hugged him again for a few short seconds, then let go, standing. He took her hand, feeling overwhelmed, his whole body shaking. They walked, hand in hand, out of the yard and down into the ravine, neither of them ever once looking back. Rachel followed, several feet behind.

As they stumbled in the dark, Martin spoke, knowing how crazy he must sound, but feeling he had no other choice. Eileen said nothing, and neither did Rachel. Eileen never even asked about the woman following behind them. To her, Martin's words became incoherent babbling beyond sentence one.

"Two years ago, I was kidnapped by the government, and put into a secret facility. We escaped from the facility tonight, thirteen of us... only now there are only eleven, no wait. Lucia would have made fourteen, two are dead, so now there's twelve, and you make thirteen... I think."

"Someone died?" Eileen said.

"Martin," Rachel said, warning him with her mind to stay on track. He heard her. He also heard the confusion in Eileen's mind, and sighed, beginning again.

"I know this is going to sound crazy, honey, but... we're going on a spaceship."

"A spaceship?" Eileen repeated after Martin, still dazed.

"Yeah, there's no subtle way to put it," he said, whisking her along. She kept pace, but when they crested the hill, and she caught sight of the transport vessel, she froze, her eyes bugging wide. She looked at Martin, then her eyes went back to the ship, then back to Martin's face. He smiled, giving her time to take it all in. He could hear all around him, and there was still no sign of any new soldiers or snipers moving in. They were alone.

"Is that..." Eileen trailed off.

"Yes," Martin said, trying to be gentle. He was very anxious, however, to get back on the ship, where he knew, for certain, they would be safe.

He pulled gently on Eileen's hand, beckoning her forward, while shooting a glance back at Rachel, who returned his look, appearing slightly amused. How quickly they had all accepted the situation, she suddenly realized. Now their job was to pass the news on to another, and get them on board, so to speak.

When they reached the ship's ramp, Ben stood waiting, looking immensely relieved. He took one look at the expression on Eileen's face, and couldn't help but burst out laughing. Martin smiled. Eileen turned to him, opening her mouth to speak. Martin answered her question before she had time to ask.

"That's my friend, Ben," he said.

In the back of Ben's mind, he felt warmth fill him up at hearing Martin call him both Ben, and his friend. Rachel walked past the couple, and Ben, and quickly returned to the ship's cabin. She sat in her seat. Everyone looked at her, but she looked down into her lap. Hanley scrutinized her, searching her profile for any clue that the woman had cracked, but could not read her. She closed her eyes, leaning her head back against the seat. After a few moments, she sighed, never opening her eyes.

"I'm all right, Hanley, just give me some time," she breathed. "I'll be okay."

Hanley breathed his own sigh of relief, and turned his attention back to the tunnel, waiting anxiously for Ben to return, with Martin and Eileen.

Back at the entrance, Ben put his hand out to help Eileen up the ramp. Martin trailed after, supporting her back. Eileen felt very shaky at this point. Hearing her thoughts (which she also had no clue about), he winced. She told herself, again and again, that it was all a fantasy. He didn't blame her at all. He felt awful, for he knew she did not climb on board one-hundred-percent of her own free will, not if she believed it all to be a dream, but he simply could not help the situation.

Everyone turned to look as Ben appeared inside the cabin, along with Martin and Eileen, who looked around, briefly, at all the unknown faces staring back. She shyly glanced at the floor, then frowned, looking at Martin in horror.

"Is that blood?"

Martin nodded, taking Eileen up into his arms, finally letting go, sobbing. She hugged him back tight, and the two of them quickly sat down, always holding each other, never letting go for the entire flight. Eileen did not even notice the sinking feeling as the transport ship lifted off the ground and accelerated at an astronomical speed, up, away, into the night.

No one realized, nor would they have cared at that point, that as the ship left the Earth's atmosphere, they all left home for the final time. They flew away from the Earth without lament, for none of them thought about their lost home, their hearts in mourning only for their lost friends.

5

The Society arrived in the cargo bay, faces shiny and tear-stained, many soiled in now-dried blood. All of them sweaty, dirty, shell-shocked, and generally dazed.

When the transport ship docked in the cargo bay for the second time, Grace and Ezra once again waited to greet everyone. Arnold remained absent, still too shook up after carrying Jesus's body and being covered in blood. Everyone took turns shaking hands, one by one, and Jess asked about Alma and Kate.

"They were shown to their rooms, and Kate elected to stay with Alma. We gave Alma a light sedative, to help her sleep," Grace explained. "She should remain asleep for at least a few more hours."

Ten people followed Grace as she took them out of the cargo bay. Ben carried the eleventh, Sarah, in his arms, for she still slept soundly. Everyone shuffled along in a daze, completely exhausted from the evening's events. They had been awake all night, endured through so much, emotionally, every single one of them felt utterly drained. Ben's soaked shirt, now covered in dried blood, was thankfully hidden by Sarah's body as he carried her.

They went out into the long hallway that Ben and Hanley had already been down, but this time, they turned left, walked down a different hallway, then turned right. They walked this hallway for several yards, where it opened into a large, circular room, carpeted in the middle, with doors lining the walls all along the sides, on the outer edge. There were nineteen rooms, altogether, and Grace explained that this would be where everyone slept. Each spacious room consisted of a small living room, bathroom, and sleeping quarters on either side of these.

"You can choose to group yourselves any way you wish. You can bed alone or have a roommate. It's entirely up to you. These first four rooms are already taken, the fifth one has been claimed by Kate and Alma. The doors are numbered," Grace said.

Everyone looked to see that Grace was correct. Each door had a number etched into the gray metal. It was difficult to see at first, but when they looked, the numbers easily jumped out to them, reflected in the light. The ceilings were high, over twenty feet tall. Grace walked them past room five, motioning.

"Kate and Alma are in there," Hanley reminded everyone.

"We know, Hanley," Aaron said, sounding annoyed.

Aaron immediately stood in front of room six and looked around, confused. There were no door handles. Grace smiled, coming over.

"Just put your hand here." She motioned to the gray panel next to the door. "Flat," she said, still smiling.

Aaron placed his flattened hand, palm up on the panel, and the door disappeared into the ceiling. Aaron looked around, amused.

"How do you knock?"

"Once you claim a room as yours, if anyone else puts their hand on the panel, it won't open, but it will notify the person inside that someone is at their door," Grace said.

"Oh," Aaron said. "Cool. What does it sound like?"

"What?" Grace looked at him, perplexed.

"The noise, to notify someone there's someone at their door. Is it, like, a bell?"

"Why don't you try it and see?" Grace nodded.

"Wait, so, this is my room, now? I've claimed it?"

"If you want it, yes."

Everyone stared at Aaron, and he looked back. Then he went into the room and turned to watch the door slide closed behind him, silently. Grace put her hand to the panel and waited.

"Oh, I hope he realizes he has to put his hand on the panel to open the door for me," Grace said, sounding worried.

A few moments later, the door opened, and Aaron stood, with his hand on the inside panel, a look of relief spread over his face. Everyone laughed.

"You have to put your hand on the panel, to open it," he said, pointing at the panel.

"So," Earl said. "What sound did it make?"

"A clicking noise," Aaron said. "Like snapping, or clucking with your tongue, sort of? Not too loud, or anything."

Everyone nodded. Aaron came back out and the door closed behind him. He looked amazed.

"Does everyone want to choose their rooms now? They all look the same. Their completely identical," Grace said.

Everyone broke into groups and wandered around the large circle. Ben still carried Sarah. He and Jess went to room eight, because Hanley stopped at room seven, along with Rachel, who followed, holding his hand. Ben looked at Jess, and his eyes darted to Hanley and Rachel. Jess smiled, put her hand on his shoulder and turned him toward the door.

"How do we program the door to open for more than one person?" Jess turned to find Grace. She came over.

"That's easy, simply put each hand on the panel, before going in. Once the door closes, no new hands will be recognized."

Grace nodded, as Jess put her hand on the panel, and the door slid up and open. Then Ben put his hand on the panel, and last, he put Sarah's hand on. Then all three went into the room, and the door closed behind.

Hanley and Rachel watched this, then each imprinted their hands on their door's panel and went inside. As Grace helped these couples, Ezra explained similar aspects to Earl, and Martin and Eileen. Earl decided to room alone, as did Aaron. Malcolm and Jenny shared quarters. The group of thirteen people ended up occupying a total of seven rooms.

***

Every single person had the same reaction upon entering their separate compartments. They shuffled in, found the bedrooms, and more importantly, the beds, and nearly everyone, simultaneously, lay down to sleep.

Aaron was out before anyone, in his room. Next to him, Hanley and Rachel curled up together in the same bed, without saying a word, and both were asleep within moments. So was Earl.

Ben carried Sarah to the bedroom on the left and gently placed her under the gray covers that Jess pulled down for him. He tucked the blanket around Sarah's chin, then he and Jess gazed down at her, their faces full of love.

After a few moments, they silently left, and much as Rachel and Hanley did, they curled up in their own bed together, spooning, and quickly fell asleep.

The only ones to stay awake for any amount of time were Martin and Eileen. They lay in bed together, simply staring at one another. Martin caressed his wife's face, and she silently cried. He wiped her tears away. She eyed his shirt, covered in blood. She had only just then noticed, with the excitement and confusion of everything that had happened.

"I'm sorry, baby," he said.

"For what?"

"That you didn't have time to choose this. To leave home, Earth. There's so much I didn't have time to tell you," he said, looking sad.

"So, tell me now." She kissed him.

"Everything? Aren't you tired?"

She shook her head. "You've been gone for two years, Martin. I just got you back. I can't possibly sleep."

"I can read minds," he blurted, searching her face for a reaction. She didn't say anything, but he heard her anyhow.

Can you hear my thoughts right now? He nodded.

What animal am I thinking of?

"A giraffe," Martin said, and Eileen's eyes grew wide. He smiled.
"Did the government do that to you?"

"Sort of," Martin said, and launched into the arduous tale of everything he knew, everything Ben had originally told him about his genetics, the pseudogene, the aliens, the war—everything. It took over an hour, including painfully going over his life while living inside the facility and briefly touching on all his friends, and a few details about their lives. Eileen simply listened, very few thoughts going through her head, not wanting to distract him. He loved her for that.

When he had finished talking, he looked at her, waiting. She looked back, not thinking or speaking, and he grew concerned, afraid she'd gone off, mentally cracked, but then she firmly kissed him, sending out her thoughts, finally. They made love for the first time in two years, and afterwards, just as the other couples had, they fell asleep in each other's arms.

6

"Uncle M.," Sarah whispered. Ben opened his eyes, fighting to focus, and saw Sarah looking down at him. He immediately sat up, peering at her intently.

"How are you feeling?" He instinctively reached out and took her pulse, putting his fingers to her wrist. She smiled.

"I'm hungry."

Jess woke up at this, sat up in bed, behind Ben, and smiled at Sarah.

"Hi, Aunt Jess," Sarah beamed.

"Hey, kiddo," Jess said, rubbing the sleep from her eyes. "Ben?" she said, concerned.

"She's hungry," he chuckled, looking at her over his shoulder.

***

The three of them stood in front of the door for several moments, before Ben remembered that one of them needed to place a hand on the panel. He shook his head, sighed, and did so, and the door immediately opened. The three of them stepped out into the round, common room, and saw a man standing a few feet away, waiting for them. It was the blond guy, Arnold, from the night before, Ben realized.

"Hello?" Ben said, looking nervously over at Jess to see if she looked anxious. She smiled, reassuring him. Sarah held onto his hand and swung it from side to side. She, at least, seemed fully relaxed.

The man looked worried and relieved at the same time. He walked over to the three of them, smiled, and extended his hand for each of them to shake.

"I'm Arnold." His smile and gentle tone seemed so friendly, Jess immediately liked him. He looked to be in his late thirties, average height, maybe five-eleven or so, (still several inches shorter than Ben) with slightly receding, blond hair, blue eyes, and pale skin.

"Are there any *un*friendly people in here?" Jess looked at Arnold with bemusement. He looked perplexed. Then he frowned, looking down at Sarah.

"You're hungry?"

She nodded, as did he.

"Follow me." He turned and walked away. The three of them quickly followed, down a hallway on the left of the large circle. As they walked, Jess spoke to him, and he eyed her warily.

"So, you can read minds?"

"No," he sighed. "I have really good hearing."

He looked at her, waiting for a reaction. She had none, only looking back at him, expressionless.

"I heard her stomach growl," Arnold said, nodding towards Sarah. "I also heard the three of you getting up, and Sarah told Ben she was hungry."

"You heard us in our room?"

"Yeah," he said, eyeing her again. "It tends to put people off."

"Well, it's the same for Martin," Jess said, trying to reassure him. "Only, he can hear everyone's thoughts."

"Yeah, I heard about that," Arnold said, smiling. It took a moment for Jess to get the joke, then she smiled back.

They walked a short distance, then the hallway opened again, this time, onto a large rectangular room, to their right, containing several metal tables and chairs, each table seating four. The far wall contained a counter with two large basins, and to the left of this, metal cups, and some sort of spigot coming from the wall.

"Follow me," Arnold gestured.

He walked over to the spigot, took a metal cup, and touched the faucet. A thick, pinkish-orange liquid flowed, filling the cup, until he touched the spigot again to stop it. It reminded Jess of a fruit smoothie, and when Arnold handed her the drink, that's exactly what it tasted like. It was the most delicious drink she'd ever tasted, in fact.

"Mmm," she said, handing the cup to Ben.

He took a sip and raised his eyebrows, then gave the cup to Sarah. She sipped the coral liquid gingerly at first, then drank greedily, emptying the cup. She handed it back to Arnold, and he smiled, filling it again.

"It's good, isn't it?"

"What is it?" Jess asked.

"Amino acids, mineral compounds, vitamins, protein, fiber."

"It's a smoothie," Jess said.

"It's *the* smoothie. Most of us just have this every morning. If you don't feel like going into the kitchen to wrangle up breakfast, this is our preferred morning pick-me-up. Which is why it's out here, in the dining area."

"Huh," she nodded. "So, there's no coffee?"

"No," he eyed her with trepidation. "You know, that's one thing we don't grow on this ship—coffee beans." He frowned. "And there's no milk, since there are no livestock, that would be too messy, too hard to keep after," he continued. "We do have a greenhouse, though, if you want to call it that. And a park, mostly for aesthetic purposes. It's nice to take a walk, amongst the trees and flowers. Jemma and Roslyn are our botanists, they tend the gardens… and I'm babbling." He blushed.

"It's fine," Ben laughed. "Who're Jemma and Roslyn?"

"Oh, they're here on the ship, with me, and Grace, and Ezra. Oh, and Rafferty, who you've already met. That's right, you haven't even met them yet. Jemma's… good with plants? I guess that's the best way to put it. She helps them grow, keeps them healthy."

"Like Aaron," Jess said.

"Sort of," Arnold nodded. "Only she doesn't affect the chlorophyll, just expedites photosynthesis."

"Huh," Jess said, looking at Ben, who only shrugged.

She didn't even bother asking Arnold how he knew what Aaron's ability was. It seemed clear that Arnold knew a lot about them, already. Jess still felt too dazed from the events of the last twenty-four hours to give it too much thought.

"So, there's you," she said, indicating to Arnold, who nodded. "And you can hear things," she said. "And Rafferty can…" she trailed off.

"Rafferty can communicate with the Graylings, even before Ezra came along."

"Right, like Hanley," Jess said. Arnold nodded, smiling.

"Grace, who you have already met, can purify water," Arnold said.

"Purify water?" Jess frowned.

"Right," Arnold said, frowning as Jess's face clouded over. He looked at her intently, with concern. After several moments, he spoke softly.

"I can't read your mind, Jess, not even if you think really loud."

"It's nothing, it's just that, our friend, Jesus… he had a gift with water, too."

"I'm so sorry about your friend," Arnold said. "We all are. That should never have happened."

Ben sighed and teared up. Jess turned to him, beginning to cry.

"It wasn't your fault, Ben," she said. He nodded, a tear falling.

Arnold filled another cup. It seemed he wanted to change the subject. He handed the cup to Jess.

"You need to eat as well," he said, gently. He quickly turned and filled a third cup, handing it to Ben.

"So, who else is there?" Ben asked, clearing his throat, and Arnold looked grateful.

"Well, you've also met Ezra. Short little dude with the beard? He can connect people with the Graylings. Jemma and Roslyn tend the garden, and they're roommates. Roslyn can… keep people calm? I guess that's the best way to put it."

"Like Sarah?" Jess asked.

"No, no. Nothing like Sarah," he said, looking at the young girl with reverence. "Roslyn can't take people's aggression away. No, it's more like… if you're feeling sad, or troubled, she can make you feel better. But only temporarily, minutes at a time."

"Was she the one who tended to Alma last night?" Ben asked.

"Yes," Arnold said, looking sad. "And Grace gave her a light sedative to help her sleep. When she wakes up today, however, she'll be on her own. If it gets truly bad, Roslyn can tend to her, but at some point, Alma will need to deal with her grief. Roslyn can't be by her side every moment of every day, nor would that benefit Alma, in the long run."

Jess nodded. She understood what Arnold meant.

"So, that's everyone," he counted on his fingers. "Grace… water. Ezra… mind hook-up. Rafferty… natural telephone, and apparently, he and Hanley share a link as well, their own personal party line," Arnold shook his head, smiling. "Me… hearing," he pointed at his ear. "Jemma… plants. And Roslyn… natural Xanax."

"Well, okay, then," Ben said, smiling at Jess.

"And we already know what all of you can do," Arnold said. "And you've met everyone now, except Jemma and Roslyn."

"And, this is the only food?" Jess said, frowning.

Arnold laughed. "Uh… *no*. Come with me."

He led them out of the dining area, further down the hall, which curved gently to the right. He stopped several yards down from the dining area. Here there stood two saloon-style, double-sized doors that freely swung open. As they followed Arnold inside, Jess gasped at the sight of the largest kitchen she'd ever seen, almost as big as the entire larger cafeteria back at the facility.

"Good gracious!"

Ben laughed. He'd never heard Jess exclaim that phrase before. Even he had to admit, however, the kitchen looked impressive. One entire wall contained several large ovens, from the look of things, and a long row of stove burners ran along one side of a counter island in the middle. The other side of the island looked to be for counter space and food preparation. The far-left wall had another long counter with cabinets underneath and above, and what looked to be large refrigerators. The back wall held another long counter, covered with various appliances.

"Is this a kitchen, or a factory?" Ben said.

"Heh," Arnold huffed, nodding. "Well, we make everything here ourselves. And I mean, *everything*. We malt our vinegar, dry our own raisins, press our grapes into juice, and ferment our own wine. Press our own olive oil for cooking, make our own margarine. Peanut butter. Roast assorted nuts. We grind barley and wheat into flour—"

"You grow barley and wheat on the ship?" Ben frowned.

"Oh, yeah," Arnold shrugged. "We even grow our own rice."

"Holy moly," Jess delivered, surprising Ben again. "I used to bake cookies at the mall, with pre-prepped buckets of dough. And the cooking area was practically a closet."

"How do you grow all of this?" Ben frowned again.

"Oh, dude, you haven't seen anything yet," Arnold smiled.

They followed him down the hallway again, to another door, this time on the left, much farther down. The first room Arnold showed them, he called the 'greenhouse'. It was a vast hall, that seemed to go on forever, easily five football fields in length, and another five wide containing forty-foot ceilings with bright light emitting down, and slightly weaker light shining along the sides, halfway down the walls. The air inside felt warm and humid. Half the expansive area was filled with large, white circular columns, several feet in diameter, in parallel rows, roughly ten feet apart, each. Many of these columns were covered in leafy greens, vines, flowers, and visible fruits and vegetables. Ben whistled, clearly impressed.

"Hydroponics?"

"Better," Arnold said. "*Fog*ponics. Each of these columns is hollow inside, and they're infused once every hour for ten minutes with a highly-concentrated vapor that contains the perfect mix of nutrients, minerals—and fertilizer when needed—to grow anything and everything you could ever want," he paused, frowning. "Except for coffee beans. I can't believe we overlooked that. Caffeine's not really needed here."

"This is amazing," Jess marveled. "Look, tomatoes!"

"Are you kidding?" Arnold laughed. "Name almost any edible plant that you might ever want, and we've probably got it, including watermelon and cantaloupe... I can't believe we forgot coffee plants..." Arnold was clearly disturbed by this fact. He shook his head. "Unbelievable."

"So, anyway," Ben chuckled. "What about the wheat and barley? And you said you grow rice?"

"Yeah, I'll show you those, they're fog tables." Arnold waved them down one of the long rows of what he called 'fog pillars'. "Any one pillar grows as much of that food as we would ever need or want. Each column is large enough in diameter, and we grow so far up, a single vertical pillar is equivalent to a quarter-acre of flat farmland."

Ben whistled again, looking around. "How many—"

"Over two hundred."

In the further back reaches of the immense hall, Arnold showed them lines of thick white tables in multiple rows that covered the entire back expanse. He explained that the tables were also hollow, like the columns, but many were almost constantly filled with the same nutrient-rich, nitrogen-infused vapor.

"These are our equivalent of rice paddies, wheat and barley fields, we've got our corn sections in the far-left corner, potatoes, and…" He ushered them along the back end, over to the right side of the room, where the growing tables and columns stopped, replaced by over a dozen large tanks, each equivalent of half- and full-sized Olympic swimming pools.

"These are our hatcheries and freshwater marine habitats. The fish droppings are recycled into fertilizer that basically ends up in the vapor mix. We've got insect larvae composts, which some of the fish eat, and other fish simply live off the algae that naturally grows in their tanks. Everything is self-sustaining, and closely monitored. I spend a good deal of time in here, overseeing things.

"But, yeah, anything freshwater that you can eat, we got it. We've got our warm water tanks, for Largemouth bass and catfish, our cold-water tanks with brook and rainbow trout, Atlantic salmon. We have pike, and walleye, and yellow perch. There's crayfish and blue crab. But we also have a whole row of saltwater tanks as well, for Chinook salmon, halibut, let's see, what else… Oh, we've got giant tiger prawn and scallops. *So* good."

"But no coffee beans," Jess reminded, winking at him to tease.

"I'm gonna remember you said that," he joked back. "You aren't impressed, huh? Come with me, mwahahahah…" Arnold delivered a devious grin while twiddling his fingers together like a prankster.

Next, he led the three of them to the 'park', every bit as large as the fogponics room had been, but twice as tall. Acre upon acre of fruit, nut and conifer trees grew, along with beautiful flowers, and berry and nut bushes.

"And if you mention the lack of coffee bushes, I'll feed you to the turkeys."

"Turkeys?" Sarah said, speaking for the first time. She'd been touring everything in silence, seemingly overwhelmed. Ben wondered if she simply wasn't growing tired again, perhaps needing more rest.

"Right this way, milady," Arnold gestured.

As they walked, she heard bird calls, and looked at Arnold in excitement.

"There's birds?"

"Oh, no," he said. "That's just the sound system. There are insects though. They help pollinate the trees. Which reminds me, we also do quarterly releases of ladybugs in the fogponics room, in case you were wondering how those plants get pollinated. Oh, and don't be surprised if, from time to time, you see a butterfly flitting down the hallway, or even a bumblebee here or there. Every now and then, one escapes. The doors close immediately, once someone enters, but, it doesn't always keep everything in."

Arnold walked them down the pathways, through the almost jungle-like atmosphere. He pointed out the watering lines hanging from the ceiling. In the far-left corner, furthest from the door, he pointed out some large roosts of butterflies in a stand of sumac trees, which did indeed flit by from time to time. There were beautiful yellow and black Monarchs, and smaller butterflies with brown and brilliant blue. Arnold saw Jess eyeing one of these and smiled, reciting detailed facts.

"A skipper butterfly of the family Hesperiidae. They are named after their quick, darting flight habits. There are more than 3,500 recognized species of skippers in the Hesperia genus, and they occur worldwide, but with the greatest diversity in the Neotropical regions of Central and South America. When Hanley chose that name for the translation of the Graylings planet, Jemma insisted on them—thought it was *funny*. It's a nice touch, really. But netting the poor things, a few years back, was a real pain in the behind parts, let me tell you."

Jess laughed, looking at Ben in amusement. He shook his head, looking down at Sarah. She appeared completely enraptured now, seemingly adjusted to her new life aboard the ship so far, brilliantly. She seemed happy.

In the far back of the park, chicken coups and turkey pens stood, and in the far-right corner sat several artificial bee hives.

"We use honey as our sweetener of choice. It works just as well as granulated sugar, but I think it makes everything taste much smoother and better, in fact. Mix in some raspberry or blueberry juices, and you get flavored syrups." He raised his eyebrows. "There's plenty of corn and leftover veggies for our poultry, and then we have meat and eggs."

Jess laughed. "You're really proud of all this, aren't you?"

"Hey, before I came on board this ship, my idea of growing anything involved old leftover Chinese food in little cardboard boxes, with green furry stuff." He waited but got no reaction. "That would be known as mold, folks. I was successful, at times, in growing mold."

"Yuck," Sarah crinkled her nose.

"No kidding." He nodded. "And, yes, I'm quite proud. Except for the whole coffee thing... that and, we don't have larger livestock, like cattle, so nothing like bacon, well... unless we want to try making turkey bacon... and no hamburgers. Which means, no Big Macs around here. Which I've heard will be greatly upsetting for Hanley."

Ben and Jess laughed.

Arnold informed them the tour was far from over. Next, he walked them down the hallway, which seemed to go on forever, in a ridiculously large elliptical circuit that he informed them was over three miles. They walked a few hundred yards and came to yet another door.

"Next is the library."

Inside here, they beheld a mid-sized, round room, with seats lining the walls, that contained clear-glass rectangles the size of large monitors about every three feet, connected to the wall by metal bars. Below each screen was a touch pad, with normal keyboard symbols, along a rounded counter. Arnold sat at a monitor and instructed everyone else to do the same.

"There's another one of these stations in each person's room, as well, but we thought it would be nice to have a sort of 'internet café', and a public library so people hopefully won't just hideout in their rooms all the time. That's also why there's that large common room in the middle of the apartment section, with all the couches and various chairs," he shrugged. "I mean, we're human beings, we thrive on social interaction, whether we think we enjoy it or not."

Ben nodded, remembering the very early days back at the facility, when people were only kept in their own private rooms. It became evident very quickly that this did not foster good mental health, and that was when he had discovered the need for imprisoned transgens to form themselves into a society. He quickly pushed these thoughts out of his mind, feeling ashamed, and focused on what Arnold did.

He touched the glass, and the screen lit up. Everyone followed his cue, each taking a seat at a separate station. A search bar came up, and Arnold looked over at Ben.

"Would you like to learn everything there is to know about the Hesperia Genus of butterfly? Just type it in and hit enter."

Everyone did so, and their screens suddenly filled with page after page of information on butterflies, with brilliant images and illustrations to match.

"Or, let's say you want to read Shakespeare's 'A Midsummer Night's Dream'," Arnold said, typing in the words. On his screen, the play appeared at Act 1, ready to read.

"Or perhaps you want to know everything about your baby's development," Arnold said, winking at Jess. He typed in the word 'pregnancy, human' and the screen filled with information about everything involving human gestation.

"You know about my baby?" Jess said, walking over to Arnold's screen. Ben got up and put his arm around her, gently rubbing her shoulder.

"Of course," Arnold said, smiling. "The Graylings are very happy for you." He quickly continued. "The entire library of the Earth is in the ship's databases. The Graylings have downloaded everything, from every mainframe computer, even the entire database of Wikipedia, up-to-date. Of course, now that we've left Earth, there won't be anything new, so you'll never know what happens next on 'House', 'The O.C.', or 'Lost', I'm afraid."

Jess looked at Ben, a feeling of loss suddenly hitting. He rubbed her shoulder again, harder.

"What's 'Lost'?" Sarah asked, and Ben laughed.

"Nothing, honey, it was just a TV show," he said, smiling at her.

"Is there TV?" Sarah asked.

"Yes," Arnold said. "That's been downloaded as well, up-to-date. You can watch every episode of Friends, or Seinfeld. Or SpongeBob," he said, winking at Sarah. "And almost any movie you can think of, that was digitally uploaded or streamed. What else? What am I forgetting?"

He stood up from the monitor. "Oh, there's an exercise room. With a real track."

They left the library, following Arnold as he walked briskly. He stopped at the next door down, several yards again on their right. Inside housed a large room, with walls containing floor-to-ceiling screens displaying forests, flower-filled meadows, and a bluff overlooking the ocean, on separate walls. The sounds of birds and ocean waves gently met their ears. A spongy, four-lane track ran the perimeter of the room. Along the inside of the track was a metal sidewalk and parked in the middle of the room were several ten speeds. Sarah ran over to a girl's bike, complete with pink streamers shooting out from the handlebars. Arnold smiled. Jess looked at a small red tricycle, her eyes filling with tears.

"We... got a few things for the children," Arnold said. "It wasn't stealing, necessarily. We just... didn't have any money."

"What about a crib, for when the baby comes?" Jess said.

"We have one," Arnold said, brightening. "It's in storage. We also have a bassinet, pacifiers, little mini nail clippers..."

Jess blushed. Arnold didn't even lose a beat.

"We don't have diapers, but there is this amazingly absorbent cloth the Graylings have. It's self-adhesive. It can be incinerated, and remanufactured, using synthetic fibers. It should be terrific, and way better than Pampers, if you ask me. Don't worry, Jessica, everything is going to be fine. We'll make sure you have everything you need to feel comfortable, okay?"

She nodded. Ben hugged her from behind. Arnold looked at them, smiling.

"It will be an adjustment, living on a ship, away from your home. It takes a while. Trust me, I know. I came aboard two years ago. I was one of the last, other than Jemma. I'm still adjusting myself, honestly. I miss movie theaters, parks, grocery stores. I miss snacks during the Super Bowl. Of course, I've still been watching it, up till now. So, like the rest of you, those of us who've already been living aboard the ship are also leaving Earth behind at the same time as you, even if we haven't actually been living on it for some time now."

"Shouldn't we be floating, or something?" Jess asked.

"No, there's manufactured gravity. The Graylings are very good at making sure we're comfortable. They wouldn't have enjoyed floating around everywhere for the last two hundred years, either."

Sarah happily rode her bike around the track, smiling and waving at them. Each time she rode by, she rang a small bell on the handlebars and giggled.

"There's one more stop. Two, actually," Arnold said. "Are you tired? Overwhelmed? Because we can always finish another time."

Jess shook her head. She wanted to see everything and get it all over with. She'd been unable to imagine what living on board an alien ship might be like, and she felt immensely relieved by what she'd seen so far. It was nothing like she'd expected. It didn't even feel like a spaceship, really, although, she had asked herself many times what that was even supposed to feel or look like, but this felt more like a five-star hotel, like The Ritz, or maybe an exotic cruise ship.

"Sarah? Are you ready to go?" Jess asked.

"We have all the time in the world," Arnold said. They all stood and watched Sarah ride for another ten minutes before she was ready to leave.

"You can come back any time you want, Sarah," Arnold said. "It's really just down the hallway... a few miles," he laughed. "You can take your bike and keep it in your room, that way you can bike your way back here, if you want, not always have to walk."

"I can ride my bike outside the room?" Sarah's face lit up brighter than ever.

"Are you kidding?" He winked at her. "I ride in the hallways all the time. And don't worry about knowing your way around, either. It's just a long, elliptical orbit. You can't get lost in here."

Arnold walked them down the hallway, and it curved right again. He brought them to a door with a star symbol on it, smiling.

"This is my favorite room," he said, opening the door.

Inside, Jess gasped, her heart faltering. She felt filled with a sudden, deep fear, and trembled. Ben put his hands on her shoulders. Arnold came over, apologetic.

"I'm sorry. I forget how scary this must look when you're not expecting or used to it. I'm so sorry."

Jess stared, wide-eyed, at nothingness. They stood in a large circular room, a view of space filling everything—floor, wall and ceiling. Tracks of light in rows along the bottom sides provided the only source of light, seemingly set on dim. Otherwise, pitch blackness filled the space. It reminded her of a large IMAX screen, only Jess knew she beheld the view outside the ship. She had a fear of heights, and this was way worse than that.

Ben took Sarah's hand, walking over to the farthest edge. Jess elected to stay behind. Arnold walked over with the other two, smiling.

"Is there glass?" Sarah said, sounding worried.

"It's a projection screen. There are, in fact, several dozen feet of metal between us and the outside of the ship. You can't fall. I know it feels that way, but it's just solid wall and floor, see?"

Arnold stomped his foot lightly, then touched the wall, the image unaffected beneath his hand.

"Where are all the stars?" Sarah whispered.

"Well, we're moving so fast, you can't see them," Arnold explained. "And every now and again, we go through a wormhole as well."

"What does *that* look like," Jess said, coming over and taking Ben's hand. He felt proud of her for being brave.

"Like… light all around you. Just… *white*," Arnold said, in wonder. "It only lasts for a moment, but afterwards, we're an indescribable distance from where we started. We've only experienced it twice, recently. The Graylings wanted to test-run things, it'd been a while since they'd done a jump. When we knew you were coming on board soon, they started readying everything for our true departure."

"Have we gone through one yet?" Jess asked.

"No," Arnold said. "The Graylings always tell us, beforehand, so we can come and look. Afterwards, we remain stopped for a while, to view the Universe.

"And you can talk to the Graylings?" Jess clearly looked scared now. Arnold nodded.

"They are very adventurous, the Graylings. They've tried to make the most out of being stuck in space, off their planet. They've made incredible discoveries. After all, they found Earth, didn't they? While waiting for you, they catalogued every life form, also from the databases, and learned everything there is to know about Earth and its many forms of life. They enjoy learning, observing. And they value knowledge, beyond anything.

"They've made certain that we, as humans, continue having opportunities to grow and learn, also. When Grace first came on board, she was a meth addict. Now, she's a doctor. Rafferty spoke to people who weren't there. Now he can fly and fix the most complicated spaceships and machines known to man. He's quite the mechanic, if I do say so. Jemma and Roslyn had a few addiction problems as well, and they were both homeless off and on before being found by the Graylings, but now they can grow just about anything. They're very anxious, once we reach Hesperia, to discover the varied alien plant life on the Graylings' home planet. It will be interesting to see if our own plant life can integrate."

"What about you?" Jess asked. "How did the Graylings find you?"

"Well…" Arnold sighed. "I was a manic depressive, prone to falling for crackpot conspiracy theories. I made myself homeless on purpose, ironically enough, chasing after flying saucers and little green men, out in the Nevada desert, near a tiny town called Rachel. Area 51 is nearby. I was practically starving to death, and fixing to run the posted military signs, which probably would have landed me in prison for at least a short while, and more likely a mental institution. Next thing I know, I'm living here, I can think straight for the first time in years and learning more than I ever thought I'd be capable of. They changed my whole life for the better." Arnold choked up, his eyes welling with tears. "Actually, that's putting it quite mildly. The Graylings *saved* my life." After that, Arnold couldn't finish, too overcome with emotion.

Sarah tugged on Ben's shirt. He looked at her, concerned. "I have to go to the bathroom," she said, looking embarrassed.

"Of course," Arnold said, clapping his hands together once, quickly.

They left the observation deck, as Arnold called it, and they walked down the hallway, which quickly opened back onto the rounded common room they'd started out in, but on the opposite side. Arnold issued them to their door. None of them had even looked in the bathroom yet, Jess realized. Arnold stood outside and allowed the door to close behind them. After a few moments, the door opened, and Jess motioned for him to enter.

Sarah came out of the bathroom a few minutes later, smiling.

"It flushes like a regular toilet!"

"Yes," Arnold laughed. "It does. The shower and bathtub are normal, just like you're used to. You can drink water from the tap. Oh, and Jemma always leaves large bowls of fruit in the dining hall as well, so there's that along with the smoothies. People always grab that stuff for quick midnight snacks, since it's so close, and you can bring that back to your rooms, too."

He paused momentarily, looking nervous again, suddenly. "There's just one more stop… at least for Jess, when she's ready. In the infirmary."

"The infirmary?" Ben asked.

"Yes, that was going to be the last stop. It's next to the… where you and Hanley first came before…" he trailed off, taking a deep breath. "That was the morgue. The Graylings, from time to time, have had need to attend to their own fatalities, over the years.

"But next to that is the infirmary, where Grace studies and learns. She's dealt with human cadavers a few times, but usually practices on holographic simulations, mainly. She's an expert in anatomy, and with the Graylings medical knowledge applied to the human body, I would say she's the best doctor you could ever ask for. She'll help you deliver your baby, Jess. She just wants to do a basic, initial exam, but whenever you're ready. There's no hurry at all. Just, you know… before you go into labor."

Jess looked scared at that remark. She wasn't even showing at all yet. She was just ending her first trimester. She looked down at her clothes, suddenly, then up at Arnold. She'd barely noticed that he simply wore gray sweatpants and a gray sweater and had been walking around in gray socks.

"What about clothes? Will I get new ones? Will they look like yours? And will they fit me when I get bigger?"

He smiled, shrugging.

"Not very fashionable looking, perhaps, but very comfortable. The Graylings can manufacture clothing. They can piece together molecules however they want."

"With their minds?" she asked.

"No," Arnold laughed heartily. "With machines they've built, to manipulate matter. Grace can scan your body and put in the numbers. We'll make you some clothes. You can simply get new ones, when the old ones get too small. Okay?"

"What about laundry?" Ben asked, looking down at his bloody shirt front, which had long since dried while he slept, the bright red blood now appearing more like a giant, dark brownish-black mud stain.

"Oh, geez, I barely noticed... I was so nervous about meeting you, excited to show you around... worried about Sarah's hunger, and Jess's baby, you know, she needs to eat, too..." Arnold babbled, clearly flustered. "I guess I'd even, somehow, gotten used to it, it doesn't look like... you know, it's not red anymore, and none of you have showered, so you look like messy hell..." he suddenly hitched and shuddered, then quickly recovered himself, sighing heavily.

Meanwhile, Jess simply stared at Arnold. Ben smile-frowned in slight amusement. Sarah seemed oblivious to everything, staring around the common room dreamily. A slight smile hung on her lips, and she appeared utterly peaceful. Arnold finally spoke again, his composure intact once more.

"Let me take you to Grace right now, hmm? We'll get you some new clothes right away."

7

Ben left with Arnold to see Grace. He made a cursory inspection of the infirmary, immediately impressed. The large room was filled with equipment he did not recognize. Grace pointed out the functions of everything, quickly. There were cabinets full of various vials and syringes, everything labeled in symbols he did not recognize, etched into the glass of each bottle.

Grace smiled as she watched Ben investigate. She quickly took his measurements by standing him in a doorway arch then pushed a few buttons on a nearby panel. She also swabbed his forehead with a cotton ball, or what looked like one, anyhow, and dropped it into a receptacle. She then went to a monitor and began typing.

"You'll have to explain all of this to me," Ben said, in sheer curiosity.

"Of course," Grace said. "We're very excited to have a scientist on board. Of course, we're also very excited to see what your ability will be."

Ben stared at Grace, not comprehending. She blinked back.

"Your ability, Ben? I understand you not wanting to activate it while running the project. It wouldn't do to be locked up with the very people you were working with, now would it?"

"What are you talking about? What ability?"

"Why, your ability, Ben. I assumed once you came on board, you'd be ready for your dose of Luci. I've got it right here." Grace walked over to a cabinet, motioning.

"Luci won't do anything to me," Ben said. "I'm not a transgen."

"I've got a Genus scan here that says different," Grace said, motioning to the screen in front of her, to her left.

"You're mistaken," Ben said, getting flustered.

"No, Ben, there's no mistake. I thought you knew? You didn't know?"

She looked at him in shock and surprise, frowning as she read the look on his face. She shook her head.

"I assumed you entered your own DNA in the Genome project. You didn't?"

Ben shook his head. His heart beat suddenly elevated, making him feel woozy. He recalled a story he'd listened to time and time again, as a young boy, where his mother talked about how she'd gone into…

"…labor early," Ben whispered. Why hadn't he ever remembered that before now? How could he not have made the connection? He shook his head.

"No, that can't be. What are the chances?"

Grace laughed. She looked around her.

"I was a meth addict before I came here," she said. Ben nodded.

"Arnold told you that, did he? Well, that's all right. Before I got here, and the Graylings alleviated my addiction? I had no control. Now? I'm a doctor, and every day, I'm surrounded by meds, and I never feel the urge to use them. Not unless I'm saving a life. So, you tell me, Ben. What are the chances? Of anything? Of any of this?"

Ben shook his head, looking for somewhere to sit down. Grace quickly came to his aid, leading him to an examination table, instructing him to sit. He did so without complaint.

"I'm a transgen?" He looked dazed.

"Yes, you are. But you're currently not activated. Would you like to be?" Grace looked at him kindly. She smiled. "You don't have to decide now. I thought you knew. You don't have to do it, Ben, if you don't want to. It's your choice."

"But, if I'm a transgen, and Jess is activated, then, our baby..." he trailed off.

"Yes, your baby will have an ability," Grace said, her voice soft.

"Sarah knew," Ben whispered. "I told her it was impossible, but she insisted. She *knew*."

"It's part of her gift. The Graylings have it, too," Grace said. "They may not have a pseudogene, but they seem to possess a foreknowledge for certain things, that is absolutely unnerving. It's no accident that you're here, Ben. Any of you. Or me, even."

"Did they know that Jesus and Lucia would be killed?" Ben looked at Grace with dawning horror.

"No," Grace said, quickly. "They didn't know that. I would have heard it in their thoughts. They don't know specifics. It's more like, they know the general outcome of things. And they believe—they feel, or sense—that everyone who's here now? Was meant to be here. And that everything will succeed. Everything is just as it should be," Grace said, smiling at Ben.

"That's what Jesus said," Ben said, his face falling.

"I'm sorry, Ben," Grace said. "I truly am sorry for the loss of your friend. No one knew that was going to happen. The Graylings would never put your people through that, if they had known to avoid it."

"I have to tell Jess," Ben said, rubbing his face. "I have to tell her that the baby she's carrying is... will have an ability. And that..." he looked at Grace, sudden comprehension spreading.

"It won't need Luci," he said, and Grace shook her head.

"The Pseudogene should have already coded, the moment of conception" She nodded. "Your baby will be born an active hybrid, but we don't know if that means being born with an ability, simply… an active gene code. I doubt your child will manifest any ability for many years, although, I can't be sure. This will be the first transgenic baby born from an active transgen. Possibly, the ability will remain dormant until puberty, is my best guess. But I could be wrong. There's simply no way of knowing."

"I promised her," Ben said, looking sad. "I promised her we'd have a normal child."

"Ben," Grace said, taking his hand. "You and Jess are going to love this baby, no matter whether it's 'normal' or not. What does that word even mean, anyway? Jess has an ability. Do you love her any less for it?"

Ben shook his head.

"Of course, not," Grace said. "So, what does it matter, whether your baby has an ability, or not?"

"It doesn't," Ben sighed. "I guess. I just promised her, is all."

"Well, you probably should have run your darn genome first, before promising her anything," Grace said, laughing to try and lighten the mood. Ben looked at Grace for several moments then began laughing himself. He nodded, in consternation.

"Yeah, I guess I should have, huh?" He shook his head.

***

Grace told Ben she would have new clothes for him in about one hour. He wanted to take a shower, so she told him she would leave the clothes outside his door.

Ben quickly found his way back to the common room, and saw Arnold starting Martin and Eileen on their tour. Arnold saw Ben and smiled, before turning away to continue along with the couple. Ben turned to see Ezra standing askance, looking at him awkwardly. He looked like a deer caught in headlights.

"I'm just waiting for whoever else might come out, to show them around," he said nervously.

"Oh, right," Ben said. "No one else is awake?"

"Alma and Kate are in their room," Ezra said, looking sad. "Roslyn's in with them. Trying to help. Rafferty took Earl and Aaron on a tour, but they're not back yet. Hanley and Rachel are still sleeping, I guess? I'm waiting for them. Malcolm and Jenny should be coming out soon, according to Arnold. He can, uh," Ezra pointed to his ear.

"Yeah, I know," Ben said.

"So, I'm just waiting," Ezra said, swinging his arms nervously. Ben could tell people made Ezra uncomfortable. He smiled.

"Well, good luck," he said. This only seemed to make Ezra more anxious, and Ben couldn't help but chuckle to himself as he went back into his room.

**

Once back inside, he saw Jess sitting on the gray couch that sat in the small living room, looking morose. He sat down next to her and she looked at him, her chin trembling.

"Grace is going to leave my new clothes outside the door. I think you should go to her next to get scanned. We could all use a change of clothing."

"Some more than others," she said, looking away from his shirt.

"Jess," Ben said, taking her hand. "I'm so sorry about Jesus."

"I know," she said, barely above a whisper. "I've barely even thought about it, with everything," she motioned around. "But he should be here," she said, her voice growing angry. "It's not right. He *believed.*" Her eyes welled and brimmed over.

"I know," Ben sighed. He decided now was not the time to tell her about the baby. He frowned, looking around.

"Where's Sarah?"

"She went to ride her bike," Jess smiled weakly, chin quivering, swiping at the tears on her cheeks.

**

Ben walked Jess to the infirmary and Grace scanned her measurements. She also did a brief check-up, then entered the data into her console. Ben held Jess's hand as Grace ran an instrument over her abdomen, and the entire far wall bloomed alive, with a giant view of her womb. Grace pointed out the arms and legs and head. The image looked so clear, Jess could hardly believe it.

"Ho—how big is it?" she asked.

"Not nearly as big as the wall makes it look," Grace laughed. "Your baby is a little smaller than your fist, roughly."

"But that's so small," Jess said.

"Yes, but your pregnancy should progress a bit faster now. You're entering your second trimester this week," Grace explained. "In the next few weeks, you should see your abdomen getting noticeably rounder. It won't be much at first. You should still look almost normal, under your clothes. But within roughly a month, perhaps a bit longer, you'll be a little walking, talking, pregnant lady. No hiding it, then. Not that you'd want to."

"No, of course not," Jess said. "Can you… tell what it is yet?"

"You mean the sex?" Grace asked.

Jess nodded. Ben looked at her, concerned.

"I don't want to know," he quickly said.

"Really?" Jess looked surprised.

Ben thought back to the day of Sarah's last exercise. She'd clearly told Ben the baby was going to be a 'she' and had called 'her' his little angel. He hadn't even told Jess that even, let alone that the baby was going to be born with an ability that would manifest at an unknown time, or that he, himself, was a dormant transgen.

"I'd rather be surprised," he said. "Wouldn't you?"

"No," she said. "Too many surprises lately."

"Why don't the two of you think about it for a few days, and discuss it a little more, before deciding, okay?" Grace nodded, smiling her support.

Jess nodded, looking at Ben to see if he was okay with that. He nodded, smiling, and kissed her.

They returned to their room, and Ben took a long shower. At some point, while Jess sat on the couch, spacing out, she heard a light clicking noise and went to open the door. On the ground lay a pile of neatly folded clothing. She smiled and brought them inside. She left a full outfit outside the bathroom door for Ben, then took the rest of the clothes and put them away in compartments built into the walls of their bedroom. These had small knobs that she could pull to open. She looked at the men's and women's underwear that were with the shirts and pants, and then marveled at the bra included in her clothes, everything made of stretchy gray material that felt soft, like angora. She smelled it and smiled. The material had that same hint of baby powder, mixed with a cottony-fabric odor. She couldn't wait to put the clothes on.

Ben eventually came out, and found Jess in the bedroom, lying on the bed. She smiled when she saw him, sitting up, taking him in with her eyes.

"That outfit actually doesn't look so bad on you. It fits," she said.

"It's very comfy," he said, coming over and bending down to kiss her. She pulled him into the bed with her, and they made love. Afterwards, Jess took a shower.

***

She discovered containers of white liquid in the bathroom shower, on a small shelf farthest from the showerhead. She unscrewed the lids, smelling them and smiled at the sweetly fruity scent. One seemed syrupy, yet slightly watery, more so than the other, and she could only assume this to be the shampoo, the thicker concoction, the conditioner. A gray metal razor sat in a soap dish, next to a sweet-smelling, thick bar of soap. After her shower, she noticed a toothbrush sitting on the counter, and another in a cup, and Jess felt it with her fingers. It was moist. Ben had used his. A jar with a lid sat next to the cup, and Jess opened it, sniffing. It smelled minty, but subtle. She put some on her toothbrush by dipping the bristles in, and quickly brushed her teeth.

Jess opened a cabinet on the right wall, next to the mirror, and marveled at the tiny gray metal tubes inside. She pulled one out and twisted it open, then laughed, discovering it to be mascara. Another tube of base and concealer lay next to the first tube. She found a compact with pressed powder—everything gray, with a distinctly generic feel—homemade. Everything had that new, baby powder smell that made her feel so warm. She finished exploring the bathroom with its various homemade products, then came back out to find Ben sitting on the couch, looking grave. She sat down, feeling nervous.

"Does this place remind you at all of the facility?" She frowned.

"Not in the slightest," he said, taking her hand in his.

"You're scaring me," she said.

"I'm sorry," he said. "I have to tell you some things. Not because I want to upset you, but because I need to. Some of these things I only found out an hour ago. One thing, I learned two weeks ago."

She sighed and looked at him, open and ready to hear what he had to say. He told her everything he knew. He started with the day of Sarah's first exercise, and told Jess what she had told him, and how he'd argued with her. Jess grew agitated but said nothing. Next, Ben told Jess what Grace had told him, about his own genetics. She began to cry. He tried to soothe her as best he could.

"It doesn't matter, Jess," he said. "We're not in the facility. There won't be any experiments. Our child will be free to be… whatever she's meant to be."

"What if she's meant to fight in the war?" Jess's eyes filled with tears.

"No, Jess, of course she won't. She'll be barely nine years old when we reach Hesperia. She may not even have any abilities at that point. She may not have any abilities until puberty. And that won't happen at age nine."

"How do you know?"

"What?"

"How do you know she won't have her abilities by then? You don't know. You can't. There's never been a baby like this before, has there?"

"Babies are born every day, Jess," Ben said, his voice lacking any real conviction.

"But not like this. Not with an active gene. For that matter, you don't even know, for certain, that this baby will develop normally, do you? For all you know, it could reach puberty at age six, and that would be normal for it."

"Stop calling it an 'it' Jess, *please*," Ben said, feeling agitated.

"You don't know anything, Ben. This baby could be a monster!" Jess yelled.

"Stop it, Jess! Just stop! It's a *baby*, okay? A normal, *human*, baby."

"No, it's not!" Jess yelled even louder.

"Jessica Wembly!" Ben shouted, and she immediately grew quiet. "This is *our* baby! Do you hear me?! *My* baby," Ben breathed, attempting to calm down. "It is not a monster. Grace did your check-up, and you saw it, right on the screen, remember? If there had been anything unusual, we would have seen it," Ben said. "It's just a baby, Jess. *Our* baby. The one we made because we fell in love and couldn't stand to be without each other. Remember?"

Jess nodded her head, crying softly. She hugged Ben and apologized. He also cried, pulling her out of his arms, taking her face in his hands.

"I love you, Jess. And I love our baby," he said, his voice barely above a whisper. "Our little girl. And look at us, here—*free*. Waking up in the same bed. No facility, no having to pretend we're not in love. We're together, Jess, and we're fighting?"

"I know, I'm sorry," she hitched. "I'm sorry, Ben."

He hugged her tightly as she cried. They held each other for over an hour, eventually falling asleep in each other's arms, right there on the couch.

***

Hanley and Rachel woke up nearly simultaneously. They faced each other and came awake gazing into the other's eyes. He had missed her. He knew he had. Ever since she'd been put into isolation. He had missed her, and he'd worried about her. When he saw her again for the first time in over a year, he'd been heavily under the influence of Sarah's power, his heart filled with an overwhelming sense of love, hope, and euphoria. When the feelings were suddenly gone, once Sarah lost consciousness, he still felt an overwhelming love for Rachel.

She was different, after isolation—stronger. He realized that as soon as she went after the sniper. She'd handled taking the man's life so coolly, it scared him, but even so, he felt immensely relieved that this was her reaction to murdering someone, as opposed to becoming catatonic again.

Hanley knew he was in love with Rachel the moment she told everyone she trusted him. His heart simply went out, becoming hers. He felt this and didn't mind one bit. He didn't need it, he figured.

He hadn't loved anyone, not since Angelique. He was fifty-three, Rachel, thirty-seven, and he didn't care. She was beautiful. He looked at her now and wondered if she felt the same way about him.

"You okay, Rach?"

"Yes, are you?"

"Sure," he said, still looking at her. "But I wasn't the one who spent a year in isolation, only to be rescued by aliens, and then turn around and commit murder, to get us all free."

"You think I'm falling apart?"

"No, I don't," Hanley said, looking concerned. "I think you're handling it too well, actually. It scares me."

He couldn't help being totally honest with her.

"I'm sorry if I scare you," she said, turning away.

"Hey, you don't scare me, Rach," Hanley said. "Okay?"

He turned her chin with his hand, to look at him.

"Your reactions scare me, that's all. A year ago, you killed one man and went crazy. Yesterday you killed several, and you slept like a baby. What's that all about?"

"You think I went crazy because I killed that tech? That's not why. And I didn't go crazy, Hanley. I just—needed to be inside my own head. I needed to be alone."

"Down the rabbit hole," Hanley sighed, turning on his back, looking up at the ceiling.

"No," Rachel said. "I just needed to deal with what I had done. It was those children," she said, choking up. "Not the tech. I went inside my own head, to deal with the difference. I can't expect you to understand. I'm not sure I understand it myself. I just needed to go away. And there was nowhere to go, stuck inside the facility. The only place I could go was inside my own mind. So, I went, to deal with things. Because... Hanley, when I killed that tech, I realized I had way more control of my ability than I ever knew. When Earl asked me if I could choose who I hurt and who I don't... I'd already figured that out. I needed to be alone, because I *knew*—I understood—if I ever wanted to escape again, I could probably do it. I'd just have to be ready the next time. More so than before."

"Ready for what?"

"To kill all those men. And if Sarah hadn't come along, right when she did, I was getting ready to. You don't know how close I came, Hanley. All that time, in isolation. I was just getting myself ready. To kill *everyone*. I was days away from it, when Dr. M. came to tell me we were all getting out of there and how. When he told me what Sarah could do, and I found out we could all walk out of there, and I wouldn't have to kill anyone? Yeah, I was okay. She saved me, Hanley."

"But you had to kill, anyway," Hanley said, sounding bitter.

"I'd already built myself up for that, Hanley," Rachel said. "Remember? And it wasn't nearly as awful as I'd been imagining, when I thought it would be fifty soldiers, facing me. Not nearly so bad, in the dark. I couldn't even see the blood. The screaming was bad, but at least I didn't have to see any blood this time."

"Rachel," Hanley said, turning to touch her face. She pulled away.

"I know what you must think of me," she whispered. "That I'm a terrible person, for being able to kill those men, in the dark, with their backs to me."

"I didn't know that," he said, closing his eyes. "But even learning it right now, I don't think that."

"Yes, you do," she said. "'*What did you create, Doc?'* That's what you said." She looked at him, her eyes pained.

"Rach, I didn't mean it—"

"Yes, you did," she said. "But I did it to help. To save people."

"I know," he said.

"Do you? Because you're the one who thinks it's okay for me, if I go and kill a whole race of beings, to save your friends. So how come I'm a monster for killing a few men?"

"I'm sorry, Rachel. I should never have said that. I was just surprised. I was expecting a basket case when you came out of isolation. I wasn't prepared for this."

"What?"

"*You*," he said. "You're stronger than I remember. Before, you could be convinced of anything. Now? You're making your *own* choices. No one's ever gonna sway you again, are they?"

"No," she said, shaking her head. "But that doesn't make me a monster."

"No, just different. And I only needed a little time to get to know the new you."

"And?" She looked at him, her eyes hopeful.

"And…"

He dared to lean in, kissing her softly on the lips. He wasn't sure what her reaction would be, but she surprised him once again, and returned the sentiment, eagerly.

To Hanley's great surprise, he found himself making love to a woman for the first time in well over ten years. It felt passionate, warm, vigorous, and wonderful.

8

Arnold returned from his tour with Martin and Eileen and sat down on the couch in the middle of the common room, next to Ezra, who still waited for Malcolm and Jenny to come out, as well as Hanley and Rachel. Arnold smiled and waved as Martin and Eileen went back into their room. Then he sighed, looking at Ezra.

"Whatcha doin'?"

"Waiting," Ezra said, fidgeting.

"For what?"

"People to come out."

"Who?"

"Malcolm and Jenny."

"Still sleeping," Arnold said, after listening momentarily to something Ezra could not hear.

"Well, then, Hanley and Rachel."

"Yeah, um… they won't be out anytime soon, from what I'm listening to."

"Why, what are they doing?"

"You really don't want to know that, do you?"

Ezra looked at Arnold for a moment, saw the look on his face, and looked away.

"Gross."

"Heh, well then, you probably don't want me to tell you what I'm hearing in those two rooms, either."

"Which rooms? Who?" Ezra looked at Arnold, in disgust.

"Well, there's Ben and Jess… again," Arnold said, blinking and smiling. "And Martin and Eileen are just getting started… again."

"What the hell is wrong with all these people?" Ezra got up and stalked off.

"You're such a prude!" Arnold yelled.

As Ezra stomped away, a pretty woman in her late twenties, with short, dark hair tucked behind her ears, passed him. It was Jemma. Average height, she stood five foot five at equal eye level to Ezra. She spoke with a British accent.

"Hey, Ez!"

Ezra just grumbled, ignoring her. Jemma flopped down next to Arnold on the couch.

"What's his problem?"

"Nothing," Arnold said, sounding playful. "He's upset because people are having sex."

"Ooh, who's having sex?" Jemma pulled her knees up and leaned in closer to get the scoop from Arnold. He feigned as if listening carefully, then smiled at her.

"Um, pretty much everyone," he said. "Except for Malcolm and Jenny, since he's her father, and that would just be gross."

"Huh," Jemma mused. "Who did we bring on board our ship?"

"A bunch of horny bastards," Arnold sighed, laying his head back on the couch. He sighed again, more heavily. "Man, I wish I was having sex right now." He turned and looked at Jemma wishfully. She returned his stare, looking playfully icy.

"No."

"Darn, thought I'd try."

"Well, maybe you'll hook up with one of the newbies?"

"Doubt it, they're all taken, except for the daughter."

"Not your type?"

"Don't know," Arnold frowned. "Haven't met her yet, actually."

"Well, maybe you'll get lucky then," Jemma mused. "'Course, you'll have to deal with the dad, after you use her and break her heart."

"What makes you think I would do that?" Arnold sounded hurt.

"Oh, what, you wanna fall in love, Arnie?" Jemma teased.

"Yeah, actually, I do," he said, looking more hurt than ever.

"Really?"

"Is that so hard to believe?"

"I guess not," she said, looking at him in disbelief. "You just never said anything about it before."

"Yeah, well, you never asked."

"We're friends, Arnie. I just don't…"

"Don't feel that way about me, I know. I've heard it many times."

"I'm sorry."

"I know." Then he frowned. "Why are you so cheerful?"

"I just met Sarah in the exercise room."

"Isn't she a sweetheart?" Arnold said. "She's so tiny, and then you realize, she could bring all the Bailon down on their knees. Scary."

"Wonderful," Jemma said. Arnold nodded.

"I'm sorry you're lonely."

"You're not?"

"No," Jemma said. "I have Roslyn, and Grace, and you."

"Yeah, but those are friends," Arnold said. "Don't you, you know, want something else? Something more?"

"Maybe, someday," Jemma shrugged. "If Rafferty…" she sighed.

"Oh, God, when are you going to get over that?" Arnold groaned.

"I can't help it."

"Why don't you just tell him already, huh?"

"Because," Jemma sighed again. "If he turned me down, I'd lose my only chance at love."

"You're living without it already." He looked at her with sympathy.

"You're a good friend, you know that, Arnie?"

"Yeah," he sighed. "So are the rest of them."

"What do you mean?"

"I mean, they're a real tight-knit group, from what I've been hearing," Arnold said. "I feel like an outsider, despite that we were here first."

"They probably feel the same way about us. Like we're our own little click."

"We are."

"Time to mix the old with the new, Arnie."

"I know. But how do you get close with people who are close with each other because they've shared something amazing? Something we didn't share with them?"

"I don't know," she said. "But Sarah's open to making friends. She asked about you."

"Really?" He brightened.

"Arnie, you're so lonely!"

"Nah," he said.

***

But Jemma was right. Arnold had been living on board the ship for two years with only five people. In the end, he got up and found Sarah, and to her great excitement, he rode his bike around with her for over an hour, laughing and enjoying her company.

They got so carried away, they both rode their bikes out of the exercise room, through the hallways, and Arnold almost knocked Jenny down, when he rounded the corner of the common room. Jemma had long since gone off somewhere. Ezra hadn't returned after stalking off, and when Malcolm and Jenny finally came out of their quarters, they were left standing in the common room for several minutes, not knowing where to go or what to do.

Arnold skidded to a halt, turning sideways, missing Jenny by bare inches, and crashed into the wall, bruising his arm. He winced, and Jenny ran over to him.

"Are you okay?"

Arnold stared at the pretty brunette in wonder for several moments. She stared back at him, worried.

"Uh, yeah. I'm okay," he laughed, feeling stupid.

"Arnie, are you okay?" Sarah rode her bike up to him.

"Hey, Sarah. What are you guys doing?" Jenny smiled.

"Riding bikes, wanna join? There's more bikes for grown-ups."

"Um, maybe later. Right now, Daddy and I are trying to figure out what to do about food."

"Oh, gosh. No one's here to give you your tour. Ezra left after he, I mean. He was supposed to wait for you guys to get up. I'm sorry. Here, let me just," he got off his bike and propped it against the wall.

"Sarah, do you mind if I give this pretty lady a tour, and we can ride some more after?"

"Sure," she said, and rode off. He smiled after her.

***

Arnold didn't know it, since he could not hear her thoughts, but Jenny was already very taken by him. He gave her and Malcolm the same tour he'd given Jess, Ben and Sarah, and she was greatly impressed by his manners. He was ten years older than her, but she thought he was the sweetest guy she'd ever met.

***

At some point in the late afternoon, word spread that everyone should meet in the dining area for dinner at six. To everyone's surprise, when they first entered their rooms, they'd found that there were digital clocks on the walls in the bedrooms.

Everyone showed up in the dining area at about the same time, and the old boarders attempted, poorly, to mix with the new, sitting at the various tables. Rachel and Hanley sat with Jess and Ben. Earl and Aaron, who seemed thick as thieves by this point, sat at their own table. Jemma sat across from Rafferty. Ezra sat with Grace.

Everyone turned to watch as Alma entered the dining hall. No one had seen her since Lucia was shot. She looked sickly pale, her eyes sunken. Kate looked not much better. Roslyn sat with Alma, who had been doing so poorly since boarding the ship, she found that she could not leave her side. She felt greatly worried by this. Roslyn had been drained of her energy by this point. She wasn't used to using her ability for prolonged periods.

Everyone looked at Roslyn with curiosity, seeing her for the first time. Petite, Asian, five foot three, olive-skinned and beautiful, in her mid-twenties, with long, dark hair, tied back with a satin string. She looked like a China Doll.

Arnold and Sarah sat with Jenny and Malcolm, and Arnold purposely sat directly across from the young woman. He couldn't keep from glancing at her intermittently, taken by her immediately. She kept looking at him, as well.

Malcolm observed this, rolling his eyes. His daughter was a fully-grown woman, he reasoned, and he couldn't care less who she dated, so long as they treated her well. From what he could tell so far, Arnold seemed like a stand-up guy. Malcolm frowned, however, watching them shyly regard one another. He did the basic math in his head, and realized while sitting at the table, that with the Earth now far behind them, this small group of people would be the only choice for Jenny, if she ever wanted to find a mate.

Martin heard these thoughts and almost choked on his smoothie. He couldn't believe he'd heard Malcolm use the term 'mate'. Eileen looked at him in concern, and he shook his head. She was still adjusting to the fact that her husband could read people's minds.

It got quiet for several moments when Alma, Kate and Roslyn entered the room. It remained quiet until they sat down. Then chatter slowly picked up again, until things were loud. Hanley and Rachel gazed at each other, completely enraptured, deeply in love. Martin turned around to look at them, smiling, in surprise. He'd been busy making love to Eileen while Hanley and Rachel were having their 'talk' and had not learned a thing about them until now, as he heard their puppy-love thoughts drifting to him. He shook his head, and again, had to shake off Eileen's questions.

He looked over at Arnold, still smiling shyly at Jenny, who smiled shyly back, and picked up on their thoughts, and sat back in his chair, overwhelmed. Then he looked over at Jemma, pining silently over Rafferty, and he couldn't take it anymore.

"Man, it's like a soap opera going on in here," he sighed.

"What?" Eileen said.

"It's a freak show in here," he said, shaking his head.

At that moment, Hanley stood, looking nervous, and beat his cup on the table to get everyone's attention. Everyone turned to look at him, the room growing quiet again.

"Uh, hey, everyone," Hanley said, looking around. "Uh, I just wanted to make an announcement. In case anyone was speculating, or there might be some gossip going around," Hanley shot a glance at Martin, who just shook his head.

"No? Oh, okay, well. Anyway, too late now. Uh, Rachel and I, are sort of, well," he trailed off for several moments, shrugging, and blushing.

Jess smiled wide, for she could tell what was happening. Pretty much everyone could, and The Society all knew as soon as Hanley and Rachel decided to share a room, but the new couple didn't realize that.

Rachel stood nervously, spluttering out, "We did it. Today, this morning," and then quickly sat back down.

Hanley was left mortified, still standing.

"Uh, yeah. I was just going to say that we're together now. As a couple. And that... we're in love," he said, gazing down at her as he said this. She looked up at him, beaming.

He quickly sat down, kissing her, forgetting about the rest of the room. Everyone ooh'd and aah'd, except Ezra, who looked angry. Martin shook his head some more.

Arnold stood up then, looking more nervous than Hanley had. He didn't bang a cup on the table. He just waited for everyone to notice him and get quiet. It didn't take very long.

"Hey, everyone. I'm Arnold. You've all met me, by now. Uh, I'm in room two, with Rafferty, so if anyone ever has a question, or needs anything, feel free to just knock. Okay?"

He motioned to Grace and quickly sat down, shooting a glance and a smile at Jenny, who smiled back. Grace stood then, looking serious.

"Hello, everyone. I'm Grace. Most of you, by now, have been by the infirmary for your measurements. If you didn't get your fresh garments yet, they're probably outside your doors by now. I'll make sure everyone gets them before bedtime. Um, I'd like to request that we meet here, for dinner, every night. I think it would be good for everyone to spend time together. We need to get to know one another.

"Now, I understand that this is still a very big adjustment, but we do need to understand that there is a purpose to all of this. We are going someplace to do something. Something very important. And we simply can't accomplish our goals unless we all know each other very well. We need to be a tight-knit group. I think if we dine together every night, it will help to aid in our bonding faster."

"We have ten years, right?" Aaron said.

"Yes, and of course, there's no hurry," Grace said, nodding at Aaron. "However, I think if we get in the habit of pulling away, which could happen if we're never all together, it might be a hard habit to break. I'm not saying it's mandatory, even, only that, well... those of us who have already been here a while will be here, every night at six. A few others along with myself always prepare dinner, but anyone is free to start lending a hand there. As for dinner, anyone who wants to join us should feel free to do so. I'm in room one, and as Arnold said, the same goes for me. If I'm not in my room, you can always come by the infirmary."

"How come we have clocks in our rooms?" Earl asked. "I mean, there's no sun anymore, right? Isn't time, not really time anymore?"

"We count time on this ship the same as we did on Earth," Grace said. "Because we, as humans, still age the same as we did on Earth. Our circadian rhythms have evolved over thousands of years, based on the time as it passed on Earth. If we didn't continue to keep that time, it would throw all of us off, possibly even cause psychosis. So, here on this ship, a day is still twenty-four hours. Seven days are still a week. Today is October 12th. And I will be turning 49 in eight days. And even though we can't see the sun rise, five a.m. is still five a.m. and I never get up before seven."

Everyone laughed. Grace continued. "The other reason I wanted to talk to you all tonight is because we need to plan some funerals."

Everyone fell silent at this. Alma cried softly, and Roslyn looked on in sympathy. She was so drained, she couldn't use her powers any longer. Alma was flying solo, less than twenty-four hours after having Lucia gunned down by her side.

"I know there's a lot of pain. And I'm sorry for that. We are all so very sorry for your losses," Grace said, choking up. "But we need to remember our loved ones. It's customary, on Earth, to hold a funeral, and a memorial. I think we need to do that."

"I'd like to do that," Jess said, quietly. Ben took her hand.

Grace nodded.

"It's up to all of you, what you want to do, as these were your friends. We can hold a funeral, and you can choose a burial in space, or we can store the bodies here, in our mausoleum."

"You have a mausoleum?" Earl said, looking disturbed.

"Yes," Grace said, looking solemn. "The Graylings have lost many of their own. But they never lost hope that they would return to their home, one day. Many have elected to wait and bury their loved ones back home, on Hesperia."

"I don't want to send Jesus out into space," Jess said, sounding panicked. "I don't want to leave him behind, all alone like that." She started to cry.

Aaron cried silently at his table, as did Earl. Hanley and Rachel cried as well. Martin sat with his head down.

"I want Lucia with me," Alma said, barely above a whisper. Tears streamed down her face. "I want her where I can visit her. And when we get to Hesperia, I'm going to bury her, where I can put flowers on her grave, every day," she said, and sobbed.

Anyone who hadn't been crying at that point, began, including the old-boarders, even Ezra. Grace sat down quickly to try and recover herself. After a few minutes, she stood again, wiping the tears away.

"We'll keep our friends with us," Grace said, nodding. "We can hold a funeral service, and anyone who wishes to, can always visit them, in the mausoleum. You can bring flowers, from the garden."

Alma nodded, then buried her face in her hands, silently crying. Kate comforted her, and Roslyn felt monumentally helpless.

"We can do it whenever everyone feels ready," Grace said.

"Tomorrow," Aaron said. "Jesus shouldn't have to wait. He deserved better than that."

"Is everyone all right with holding a service tomorrow?" Grace asked.

Several people nodded through their tears. No one disagreed. It was decided, and they all planned on attending the service at one in the afternoon.

Everyone finished their dinner in silence after that, as Jemma and Grace eventually brought in platters of roasted chicken and potatoes, steamed squash, and pitchers of juice and water. Some people ate, others did not. Near the end of the evening, Jess stood and went over to Alma's table. Everyone watched her go.

She knelt next to Alma in her chair and whispered in her ear. Alma kept her eyes closed, but she squeezed them even tighter at Jess's words, and turned to hug her, crying louder again. Ben came over, and he hugged Alma as well. After Jess and Ben went back to their seats, everyone began, one at a time, or in groups, coming to Alma, giving her their condolences. By the time everyone finished, Alma's crying had tapered off, and Roslyn looked relieved, for it seemed as if Alma might be through the worst of the hurricane-crisis of emotions storming through her.

***

Everyone went to bed that night holding each other. Those who had no one to hold spent time with a close friend. Ezra went to see Grace, for she was his closest friend. She could tell something was wrong, but she waited for him to say something. Finally, he did.

"No one likes me," he said, and she smiled. He continued. "Jemma loves Rafferty. Arnold even likes one of the newbies."

"I said you guys shouldn't call them that," she said, sounding gentle.

"And all the newbe—... new arrivals, are already with each other."

"That doesn't mean you can't be their friend, Ezra," Grace said. "You need to get to know them. None of them will be willing to connect with the Graylings if they don't trust you, you know that."

"I know," he said, frowning. "I'm just not... *good* with people. I don't know what to say."

"Just be yourself, Ezra. They're *hurting*. You can help. You may not be good with people in social situations, but clinically? You rock."

"I rock?" He looked at her, mocking her tone.

"You know what I mean, Ezra."

"So... Earl's not with anyone," Ezra said, quickly changing the subject.

"So?"

"So, I just thought, that maybe, you and he... maybe."

"Why, because we're both black?" She smiled, amused.

"No," Ezra said, sounding defensive. "It's just that, everyone seems to be pairing up, is all."

"Not everyone," Grace said. "But it's not so surprising, is it?"

Ezra shrugged.

"It's the human condition, Ezra. People *need* each other. They fall in love. They even satisfy purely physical needs. There's no shame in it."

"I didn't say there was," he said, not looking at her.

"You didn't have to. The bottom line is, it makes you angry, because you don't have it."

He looked at her, his face hurt. Then he softened a bit, shrugging.

"If something is meant to be, it will happen, Ezra. You can't force it. Be happy for those around you who've found love. And be patient. If love is meant to find you, it will, when the time is right. For now, do what you're good at. Don't second-guess yourself. Just be yourself, without any expectations. Okay?"

He nodded. Soon after, he left Grace's apartment, but Martin sat in the common room, on a couch. He nodded to Ezra as he came out of Grace's room, beckoning him over. Ezra immediately felt awkward. Then, he sighed, exhausted, and sat down in resignation.

"You're catching a lucky break with me, kid," Martin said, and Ezra stared at him, not comprehending. Martin tapped his temple.

"I can hear your thoughts," he sighed. "So, I know you mean well. And I can hear what you're wanting. All of you. You're all walking around on a completely different page from the rest of us, except for Hanley. Shoot, you're all walking around in awe and reverence. It's practically a form of being in love, in some odd fashion."

"What are you talking about?"

"I'm talking about the Graylings," Martin said. "They're here, right?"

"Yes," Ezra said. No one had bothered asking about them.

"On another level of the ship, above us," Martin said, stating it. "And at some point, you need to convince people to allow you into their heads, so you can connect us. Correct?"

"Yeah," Ezra said, sounding surprised.

"Well, I can help you do that," Martin said.

"Why would you want to help me?"

"Because I know your intentions are good," Martin said. "I can hear every thought you have, Ezra. And I know we're all on board this ship to carry out an unbelievable task, and I happen to believe in that mission. Jesus believed in it, too. He's probably the only one who could have convinced her," he said, his voice cracking.

"Who?"

"Jess," Martin said. "You need her, if I'm not mistaken, to even have a hope of saving the Graylings planet, am I right?"

"Yeah," Ezra said, sounding stunned. He was not accustomed to Martin's gift. Martin smiled and tapped his temple again.

"Man, and I thought Arnold was annoying."

"Oh, I'm way worse than Arnold. People can hold their tongues, but they can't stop their minds from turning. No matter how hard they try."

"Crap."

"Yep."

"So, how are you going to help me?"

"Well, you were right about what you said to Grace. You suck with people. It's just a fact, so don't feel bad," Martin said, stopping Ezra from responding.

"There's no way you're going to convince anyone to let you inside their heads, not by yourself. But I can help with that. Especially if I go first," he said, leveling his eyes on Ezra.

Ezra stared back at Martin in complete shock. He swallowed.

"You want to go first?"

Martin nodded.

"Just like that?"

Martin nodded again. "My best friend can talk to the Graylings. Told me for years he was doing it, and I took it on faith that he was telling the truth. It could have been voices in his own head, but I chose to believe he wasn't crazy. Now, here I am, aboard an alien ship. *I* want to *hear* them. I want to hear the voices of the ones who've been leading Hanley all this time. They told him about Sarah, helped us organize our entire escape. They saved all our lives, and I can't even say *thank you*.

313

And I'd like to, Ezra. I'd like to say thank you. And I'd like to know who it is I'm supposed to be helping."

"Okay," Ezra said, sounding relieved.

"And once I do it, and tell everyone, I'd like to think it will help get the ball rolling. No one really gets it yet, Ez. You know that, don't you? We're not talking to them, like the rest of you are. We have no idea."

Ezra nodded, swallowing hard. He looked at Martin, thinking his next question.

"Not tonight," Martin said. "I need to say goodbye to my other good friend, the one I lost last night." Martin's voice wavered, on the verge of tears. "Everyone needs to get past the funerals, first, before we can even begin dealing with everything else."

Ezra nodded. He began to relax and let things in, hearing what Martin communicated. Martin was the bridge Ezra needed, to reach all the others.

"What about Jess? Why did you say that about her?"

"Because it's true," Martin said, sighing. "Jess has always resisted this whole idea of the Graylings, the war, fighting their fight for them. Hell, it's a miracle she made it this far. She'll be the last person to agree to let you into her head, scramble her brain, put the Graylings inside her thoughts. She's too afraid of losing herself. And Jesus was probably the only person who could have convinced her to give them a chance."

"You're right, though, Martin. We need her ability. According to the Graylings, she's more important than any of you. Even more than Sarah."

Martin nodded, tapping his temple again. Ezra shrugged.

"I don't know why, I only know it's what they say," he added, and Martin nodded emphatically.

"If Jesus was the only one who could convince her, what can I do?"

"Leave it up to me," Martin said. "I have a plan. I said Jesus was *probably* the only person. There's one other hope."

"Who?"

"Ben."

"Her boyfriend?"

"Don't call him that," Martin said, sounding cold. "Don't ever call him that. He's her life, end of story. If you could hear what I hear, when they're together? I never would have thought it. If you'd told me six months ago, that they were going to be flippin' Romeo & Juliet, I would have laughed. But those two are the real deal. He'd die for her, in a heartbeat. There's a lot of that kind of thing going on around here. It's overwhelming. What you're seeing as 'hook-ups' and 'pairing-off's'?"

Martin shook his head. "You have *no idea* what's happening on board this ship, do you, Ezra?"

Ezra stared at Martin, lost. He looked back at Ez and felt sorry for him.

"Forget it. You wouldn't understand, not unless you heard what these people feel for one another. Not unless *you felt it*. Let's just say, if I can get Ben on board, he may be the only person alive on this ship who can convince Jess to meet the Graylings."

"Okay," Ezra said, accepting Martin at his word. "So, tomorrow, we deal with the funerals. You're right, no one can move on until they deal through their grief. It's a total roadblock till then."

Martin nodded, gaining a small modicum of respect for Ezra, for he heard the longing, deep inside his mind, where he knew Ezra was not even aware it resided. He sighed. "Are you aware, at all, that Roslyn has a thing for you?" he said, annoyed, yet smiling. Playing matchmaker wasn't his top choice.

"What?" Ezra snapped his head up to look at Martin.

"And Grace thinks you rock clinically? I sure hope that's true. Yikes," he said, standing to walk away.

"Wait, why do you think that?"

Martin turned, tapped his temple one last time, shook his head, and went back into his room, to his wife.

Ezra sat on the couch for several minutes. He thought about everything Martin had said, including Roslyn. Mostly, he thought about Roslyn.

9

Arnold and Grace had the unfortunate job of preparing the bodies. Grace pulled Rafferty into the morgue, along with Arnold, early in the morning, to discuss things with them. She did not show them the bodies, merely explained that Lucia, who'd been shot in the head, would not be suitable for an open casket. Jesus had been a clean shot to the heart, his face still intact.

Grace asked Arnold to bring Jemma, for she was best suited to prepare the body with makeup. None of them had any training in mortuary science, however. They'd never needed to know anything about it, until now. Grace could preserve the bodies well enough, but she needed Jemma to prepare Jesus's face.

Jemma came into the morgue, looking nervous. She brought some supplies. There was no real makeup on board the ship. The Graylings had created tubes of mascara, base and compact powder, or at least, something similar. She used these products now, to try and fix the coloring of Jesus's face. Even with the base she used, and the powder, his face looked pale, his lips were white. His body had been greatly exsanguinated by the fatal shot through his heart. She did the best she could, but she cried when she finished.

Grace came over and hugged her. She looked at Jesus's face, and told Jemma she did a good job, for it was the truth. Jemma applied a light coating of pink lip gloss, and Jesus's lips were no longer white, at least.

The next task the four of them faced was dressing the bodies. Grace took their measurements, with a handheld instrument, while the bodies lay on the tables. The clothing was made and delivered to the morgue. Jemma brought it. She helped Grace remove the old, torn and bloody clothing from the body, and then proceeded in helping Grace redress them, in the same soft gray clothing that everyone on board the ship wore. Grace and Jemma dressed Lucia's body, while Rafferty and Arnold dressed Jesus.

It was decided that Lucia's body would be put on display, but a gray cloth would be placed, securely, to cover her head. Rafferty and Arnold wheeled the bodies on two long metal tables, out into the cargo bay, where there would be enough room for everyone to attend. The tables were covered in gray blankets, and Jemma slowly brought chairs from the dining hall and lined them up, several feet away from the bodies. Once the bodies were in place, Rafferty and Arnold helped Jemma with the rest of the chairs.

***

Roslyn decided to gather bouquets of flowers to leave at everyone's door, so they would have something to place on the bodies. She was in the park garden, when Ezra came in. He walked back to her, where the wildflowers grew in great profusion. She looked at him in surprise, her arms full of blooms.

"I thought you might need some help," he said, shrugging.

She nodded, and handed her armload of flowers to him, so she could gather more. After she gathered another large armful, they sat down together on the dirt path. Roslyn had satin-like string, shiny and translucent. She showed Ezra how she wanted each bouquet arranged, and how to tie the flowers together with the thread, into a bow. He watched her, thinking about what Martin had told him just the night before.

In the four years he'd known Roslyn on board the ship, she had never given any indication that she liked him. She was very pretty, he always thought, but she never seemed to want anything other than his friendship.

Jemma and Roslyn were best friends and it was no secret, at least to Ezra, that Jemma had a thing for Rafferty. Ezra also knew that Arnold had held a slight thing for Jemma, off and on, over the last few years. Now, however, he had taken a liking to Jenny, which was obvious to everyone on the ship. Ezra thought about all these things in silence, while putting together the bouquets. Roslyn went to gather more flowers and came back.

"What are you thinking about, Ezra?"

Ezra's heart sped up. He took a deep breath. "I'm thinking about all the pairings on the ship, lately."

"Like who?"

"Ben and Jess."

"The pregnant one?"

Ezra nodded. "I talked to Martin last night. The one who can read minds? He called them Romeo & Juliet."

"Wow," Roslyn said. "Who else?"

"Martin and Eileen. Then there's Rachel and Hanley, and, well. You were there for that announcement."

She nodded, looking at Ezra with stars in her eyes, watching him tie a bow. He did not see her look, had missed it for months, in fact. He kept right on talking.

"And now Arnold is falling for Jenny, Malcolm's daughter."

"Yeah," Roslyn laughed. "I think she likes him back. That's good. Better than Jemma."

"He should have known better with Jemma. Everyone knows about her thing for Rafferty," Ezra trailed off. Then, together, they said, "Except Rafferty," and laughed.

He looked up at her then, and saw her eyes, and felt that what Martin had said was true. She blushed and looked down at her work.

"Who else?"

"Kate and Alma," Ezra said, sounding uncomfortable.

"They love each other, Ezra."

He nodded.

"You think it's wrong?"

"It doesn't concern me," he said. "I guess, so long as they're happy. Whatever."

"I think it's okay," she said, looking at him, trying to read his face, looking to see if he disapproved. He only looked at her, shrugging.

"If they truly love each other, I think any two people should be together," she said, and he wondered, *is she dropping a hint? Only one way to find out.*

"There's one other couple I've been thinking about." Ezra took a deep breath, looking down at his work. He tied his bow into a knot, then had to start again.

"Oh, yeah? Who?"

"You and me," he said, setting his flowers down and closing his eyes, for he'd said it and it was now too late to take it back. He opened them, and dared look at her, to see the expression on her face.

She looked down at the flowers in her lap, blushing madly. Ezra felt as if he floated, like he had become a completely different person, out-of-body, as if dreaming. He dared to do something unthinkable. He pushed his flowers aside and walked, on his knees, until he sat directly in front of her. Then he raised her chin with his hand, gently, and looked in her eyes.

"Why didn't you tell me?"

She shrugged, a tear tracking down her cheek. "You're not so easy to talk to."

"Grace says I rock, clinically."

"Clinically is not what I needed."

"I know," he said, gently caressing her cheek. She looked up and into his eyes then, and he fell in love, then and there. He saw it in her eyes, too. *Martin was right.*

"Must be something in the water," he mused.

"What?"

"Nothing," he said, and gently kissed her. He'd never kissed a girl before. He'd wanted to, but never dared. He was always too shy, and she was always only a friend.

He kissed her very briefly, awkwardly, then pulled away, feeling like his old self again, nervous and uncomfortable. She looked so happy, however. This time, she kissed him, to his surprise. It caught him so off-guard, he pulled back a little, but she would have none of it, grabbing his head, holding him in place, and he suddenly felt a brief, fluttering of hope explode into a raging inferno in moments.

After all, in the end, he was a man, and biology quickly took over. He kissed her back, and soon, he could no longer think about anything but the feel of her lips, the energy of her body beneath his hands, the heat between them. They kissed themselves into a frenzy, then she pulled away, panting heavily, blushing and flushed.

"Did I do something wrong?"

"No," she said. "But, the flowers. The funeral," she gasped.

"Right," he said, and set back to work on the remaining bouquets. There were only a few left to assemble. Once they finished, Ezra and Roslyn carried the fragrant bundles and placed them, two at a time, before every occupied room. They made forty bouquets in all, very small, but respectful and pretty, each containing half a dozen multi-colored flowers.

Arnold walked by carrying two chairs and stopped in mid-step, as he witnessed the new couple walk away from the final door, and Ezra took hold of Roslyn's hand. They walked past him, smiling crazily, and he turned to look after them, feeling like he'd lost his mind. He frowned, then resumed bringing the chairs, mumbling to himself and shaking his head.

"Gotta be something in the water."

***

Slowly, one at a time, they each came out of their rooms. Arnold stood waiting for them. He smiled, his eyes grave and sad. None of them were connected to the Graylings, except for Hanley. Arnold, however, could feel the Graylings' sorrow, along with all the other connected old boarders, and he knew he felt what these seeming strangers did, by proxy. He felt so overwhelmed by these emotions, he began to cry as he led everyone down the long hallway, turned left, and ushered them into the cargo bay.

Everyone chose their seats, taking their first glances at the bodies lying on the tables, then looking away. Jess, Ben and Sarah walked down the aisle, and as Jess caught sight of Jesus's prone body, so still, her breath caught in her throat. Her eyes welled up with tears, and Ben had to lead her by the shoulders, to her seat. Sarah sat on her left, Ben on her right, in the front row. Sarah held Jess's left hand, Ben held her right.

Martin and Eileen came next, sitting on Ben's right. On the left side of the aisle, Kate sat with Alma. Hanley and Rachel sat next, leaving the last chair on that side empty. Aaron and Earl sat on the left in the next row, followed by Malcolm and Jenny. Arnold sat next to Jenny, on her left. In the second row, on the right, Ezra sat with Roslyn. Further in, Jemma followed Rafferty and sat down. The last seat remained empty, as Grace elected to sit in the front row, on the left, filling in the empty seat next to Rachel.

Everyone sat in silence for several moments, their heads hanging down, or turned into someone's shoulder. Grace finally stood and went to the middle of the aisle, in front of the two bodies. She also cried, softly. She looked at Alma and nodded, then looked slowly around at everyone, recognizing each face. Everyone met Grace's eyes, at one point or another, and saw the pain inside. Everyone knew—somehow, on some level—that she felt their pain. Eventually, Grace spoke.

"This is the first time we've ever needed to bury our own. To remember our own people. I'm sorry. I wasn't prepared for this. None of us were."

Grace looked at the second row, to the four old-boarders on the left, then over at Arnold on her right. She took a deep breath then continued.

"I'm not a minister. I don't know what I'm supposed to say in this situation. I'm not even sure what everyone's personal beliefs are. So, I'll leave it up to each of you to handle this whatever way feels right for you. If anyone wants to speak, feel free to stand. And take your time. Say whatever is on your heart. Alma?" Grace spoke gently, with a look of incredible love on her face. "You knew Lucia best. None of us ever got the chance to know her. Would you like to speak?"

Alma nodded. She looked back at Roslyn, pleading with her eyes. Roslyn nodded, getting up to go to her side. She'd had a chance to rest overnight, and felt she had enough energy to help Alma through at least the next hour.

Alma stood up front, with Roslyn holding her hand. She still looked pained, but her crying tapered off. Jess wondered at Roslyn's gift. She looked at Sarah, then at Ben. Ben smiled at her, squeezing her hand.

"My sister was a beautiful person," Alma said. "She was all I had. And then, I left her all alone, and she didn't even know why. She didn't know what had happened to me. She thought I might be dead."

Ben hung his head. He felt a deep stab of pain and regret at Alma's words. This time, it was Jess's turn to squeeze his hand. He closed his eyes, grateful for the support.

"You should have seen the look on her face, when she opened the door, and saw me again," Alma faltered, and Roslyn took a deep breath, seeming to prop Alma up. Everyone could see her gift at work. Alma's eyes shone with tears, but they could all see she remembered Lucia fondly, without the pain.

"She loved me so much," Alma said, smiling. "And I loved her. We talked for a while. I told her about the facility. But mostly, I told her about all of you. I told her about my friends. That I wasn't alone, all this time. You were all with me. This made her so happy. I can't even explain. She wanted to come with me, and she was so excited to meet all of you."

Alma turned to Roslyn then, and pulled her hand away. Roslyn looked at her with great concern. Alma nodded, speaking lowly.

"I need to do this. I can't explain without it," she said. Roslyn nodded, heading back to her seat.

"I guess it must seem strange, choosing to feel the pain," Alma said. "But it doesn't feel right, somehow, covering it up. Lucia deserved better than that," Alma said, taking a very deep breath, tears streaming down her face.

"This is so hard," she cried, and everyone cried with her. "Because… I will never forgive myself. I could have left with all of you, and my sister would still be alive."

Alma buried her face in her hands, shoulders shaking. Grace covered her mouth to stifle a sob. Everyone waited. After several moments, Alma finally stopped crying, and continued speaking.

"But then, she would have lived her whole life, never knowing I was okay. Never knowing I was even alive. Her eyes were so sad when she first opened the door. And when she realized who I was, you should have just seen the joy. It's the only thing getting me through this. I have to believe that the hour of joy she had while she was with me, was so much better than a whole lifetime of not knowing."

She began to cry again. Jess stood and went to hug her. She couldn't help herself. She whispered in her ear, and Alma nodded, hugging her back. Then Jess sat back down.

"Thank you," Alma whispered, nodding. She looked around at everyone. "Martin," she said, looking directly at him. He looked back, fearfully.

"You must already know what I'm going to say," she said, smiling. "If I hadn't gone to get Lucia, our first stop would have been to get

Eileen. And we wouldn't have known to be so careful. And I don't know how that would have turned out."

Everyone sat in silence, for none of them had thought of this. Everyone looked at Martin and Eileen. They both cried, Eileen in Martin's arms.

"I'm not saying this is your fault, you know that, right?" Alma said, and Martin nodded. "All I'm saying is, maybe my sister dying and even Jesus, maybe it saved a lot of other people from getting killed. I don't know. Jesus always said, 'everything is as it should be'. It always drove me crazy. But, I don't know if, maybe he's right. You have no idea how hard it is for me to say this." She cried again, softly.

"I don't want to think my sister had to die for this. But it's nice to think that maybe there is a reason for it. And if that reason is good, I need to believe that everything is okay. That everything is as it should be, like Jesus said. That's how I'm getting through this. I just needed to explain. I can't fall apart," she cried. "Because then Lucia dying would be for nothing. And it can't be for nothing."

She sobbed then, quickly sitting down. Kate put an arm around her, as Alma's shoulders shook. Jess sat for several moments, then took a deep breath and stood, occupying the same spot Alma had vacated.

"I'm just going to say something that Jesus would understand. It was something we talked about. Something he and I shared. It was how I first really got to know him, his heart. Maybe it will make sense to you, maybe not. I won't explain. It's just, what I need to say."

She looked over at Ben, and he smiled, tears in his eyes. She closed her eyes, for she'd memorized the whole thing just that morning, in the library.

"If I speak in the tongues, of men and of angels, but have not love, I am only a resounding gong or a clanging cymbal. If I have the gift of prophecy and can fathom all mysteries and all knowledge, and if I have a faith that can move mountains, but have not love, I am nothing. If I give all I possess to the poor and surrender my body to the flames, but have not love, I gain nothing.

"Love is patient, love is kind. It does not envy, it does not boast, it is not proud. It is not rude, it is not self-seeking, it is not easily angered, it keeps no record of wrongs. Love does not delight in evil but rejoices with the truth. It always protects, always trusts, always hopes, always perseveres.

"Love never fails. But where there are prophecies, they will cease; where there are tongues, they will be stilled; where there is knowledge, it will pass away. For we know in part and we prophesy in part, but when perfection comes, the imperfect disappears.

"When I was a child, I talked like a child, I thought like a child, I reasoned like a child. When I became grown, I put childish ways behind me. Now we see but a poor reflection as in a mirror; then we shall see face to face. Now I know in part; then I shall know fully, even as I am fully known.

"And so, these three things remain: faith, hope and love. But the greatest of these is love."

Jess quickly sat back down, tears streaming. She knew what the words meant for her. She could only hope they would affect and comfort everyone else.

No one spoke for a very long time. Finally, Hanley stood, his own tears still drying on his face. He smiled at Jess, and silently mouthed a 'thank you', his chin trembling.

"Jesus was my friend," he began, then had to stop. He cleared his throat. "The best friend I ever had. And that includes before the facility," he said, nodding towards Ben, who smiled, weakly.

"I don't know about what was meant to be. I don't know if there's any such thing as fate, or destiny. Or preordainment. I'm agnostic," he shrugged.

"All I know is, however it ended, however he was taken away from me, I'm better from having known him. I'm better because of his friendship. His faith, his beliefs; even if I didn't share all of them. He inspired me. He kept me strong. Sometimes his unshakable hope was the only thing that carried me through.

"And even though he's not here anymore, no longer with us. He's still here, in me. In my heart. He changed me. I'm not sure how, exactly, I just know he did. I hear his voice in my head, when I need it, telling me, 'everything's going to be okay', and 'it'll all work out'. 'Everything is as it should be'." Hanley broke down then, crying hard. He turned and placed the bouquet he'd been holding on Jesus's chest.

"I love you, man," he sobbed and quickly sat back down, burying his face in Rachel's shoulder.

Everyone silently cried then. The entire room. For several minutes, everyone simply let the pain take over, and cover them. At some point, everyone looked up to see Arnold standing in front of them, his eyes puffy and red. Their hearts went out to him, as they saw his own pain. Everyone was bonding, whether they realized it or not. It was what Arnold had pondered to be impossible only hours before. Even he did not realize that all of them were now sharing something incredible.

He stood in front, shaking his head, crying again. He looked at everyone, smiling, even as the tears stood heavily in his eyes.

"I wish I had known Jesus. Seeing how much you all loved him. And Lucia, I wish I could have known her, too," he smiled at Alma. She nodded back.

"I just want to say, I'm happy to have everyone on board. You have no idea what it was like, knowing you all existed, and waiting to meet you. We heard so much about you, for months, *years*. And even though you didn't know about us until a day ago… For the last several years, we've known you would be coming on board, eventually. And we thought of you as part of us, part of our family, for so long. I may not know you yet, personally. But I feel like I've known you all, forever. I know how crazy that must sound, but, it's true."

Several people nodded, for they understood in some strange way. Everyone felt caught up in their sorrow, and yet a strange joy also began to bloom in many people's hearts, at realizing they had gained new friends in the last day—realizing there were new hearts to love—to replace the one's they'd lost.

"I hope everyone knows that we're all here for you, if you need us. We are a family. And my friendship is open and available to you all, always."

Arnold nodded and sat back down, his hands shaking. Jenny saw this, and quickly took his hand in hers, smiling at him. Malcolm saw this and simply felt joy for his daughter. He was convinced, despite that there could have been an entire world of men for his daughter to choose from back on Earth, that Arnold was the best choice there ever could have been. He briefly wondered over the adage everyone kept bantering around, that Jesus had left them all with.

'*Everything is as it should be*'.

Malcolm stood, walked to the two bodies, and left his bouquet on Jesus. He turned and grabbed another bouquet from a pile on a small table to the left of the bodies, gently placing it on top of Lucia. He stood, eyes closed, thinking his thoughts. Martin, of course, heard them, but no one else did.

When Malcolm sat down, everyone else slowly, one by one, paid their respects to the two bodies. Everyone elected to place a bouquet on Lucia, as well as Jesus, and Roslyn felt extremely relieved that she'd decided to make so many extras. In the end, only one bouquet remained on the small table.

The funerals ended. After everyone placed their flowers and paid their respects, they filed out, slowly, when ready, returning to their rooms.

The old-boarders were left alone. They silently stood and cleaned everything up, saying nothing. Arnold and Rafferty wheeled the bodies back to the morgue. They helped Grace lift them each into their cryo-chambers, where they would remain preserved until burial on Hesperia. Grace programmed a gadget, then scanned it over the first mausoleum door, etching the name 'Jesus' into the metal. Grace did the same for Lucia's interment.

Small, pull-out shelves extended beneath each compartment, and the flowers everyone had placed were put there. Later that evening, at dinner, Grace let everyone know this had been done, and that from then on, anyone could visit their friends, anytime they wanted to.

The chairs were returned to the dining hall, and the old-boarders then returned to their rooms. Everyone remained there until six o'clock, when they all gathered for dinner. Grace was pleased that everyone came. No one was absent.

The tables were pulled together, surprisingly, by Aaron, Earl, and Rafferty, into two longer tables, of twenty chairs, ten on each side. Only one chair remained empty, for there were nineteen people total now on board the alien ship. The integration had truly begun, and now there were nineteen human beings, all friends with one another. They had been displaced from their home planet, and now hurtled through space, together, on an amazing adventure, with an unknown outcome.

10

The days carried on, and Martin went forward with his plans. He met with Ezra, the day after the funerals, and they talked about what to expect. The process was simple, Ezra explained. He had the ability to alter minds. It only took moments, really, for him to make the connection. He told Martin that there would be a slight feeling of vertigo.

"Almost like you're falling," he said, gently, so as not to frighten him.

Ezra explained all this in Martin's room, and Eileen listened intently, standing next to the couch where Martin and Ezra sat. She had agreed to go along, for Martin's sake, but he knew she felt terrified. She could not hear the sincerity inside Ezra's head.

Martin could hear everything, and he knew that the old-boarders, as everyone now referred to them, were all sincere in their desire to connect the 'newbies' with the Graylings. Martin understood Eileen's fears all too well, however. She kept throwing words out, and he caught them, sighing heavily. Words like, *brainwashed, body-snatcher,* and, *lose you,* kept coming at him, even as he tried to concentrate on hearing Ezra, attempting to understand the experience about to befall him.

Martin looked up at Eileen, standing to hold her hands. Ezra watched them in awe and wonder. He no longer felt angry or jealous, however, for he and Roslyn were now very much in love.

"Eileen," Martin said. "I'll still be me, okay? Ezra's not trying to kidnap my mind. He's sincere. You just have to trust me on this, okay?"

She nodded, tears falling. Ezra had never seen so much crying as in the last two days. It overwhelmed him. None of them had been prepared for so much highly-charged and conflicting emotion. Everyone walked around mentally and physically exhausted the last twenty-four hours. It felt like some strange, torturous initiation ritual into a very select club, he mused. Martin heard this, and looked over his shoulder at Ezra, amused. He was begrudgingly beginning to like the strange kid.

"Are you ready for me to do this?" Martin looked at Eileen with concern. She nodded, saying nothing. She backed away, and Martin turned to look down at Ezra, who offered a sympathetic smile.

"It won't hurt," he said, gently. "It'll just feel disorientating for a few moments, and then… You'll be able to hear them. They know what we're about to do. They're waiting. And they know how frightening and overwhelming it is. Only a few will talk to you. The ones elected to do so," Ezra explained.

"Their leaders?" Martin asked.

"The two eldest," Ezra nodded. "There are only a handful left who were alive when… they left Hesperia. They're the ones you need to speak to first. They're the ones who can show you, first-hand, what they went through," Ezra said, looking sad.

"They can show Martin their memories?" Eileen looked on in wonder.

"Yes," Ezra said. "It's sort of like watching a movie playing inside your head. Only, you get all the emotions along with it. You feel what they felt. And I warn you, it can be very overwhelming. You'll feel their emotions, Martin. And they are highly sensitive. Whatever sadness you, as a human being, have felt? You have no idea. I won't lie to you. You will be different."

Ezra looked at Eileen with tenderness and trepidation.

"Martin will be different, because he'll know things he didn't before. He'll literally experience all the emotions of the Graylings' extermination. The loss of their families, their culture, their home. Their displacement, and the loneliness of wandering through space, in the darkness, lost."

Eileen looked at Ezra, sadness filling her eyes. She looked at Martin with sympathy, asking him with her mind, whether he truly felt ready to go through the process Ezra described. He only nodded to her, giving his answer.

"It's what we're here for, Eileen. Jesus believed that. It's what we were all made for. He believed that, and so do I."

Ezra nodded, holding Martin in great reverence. He motioned for Martin to sit down, facing him.

"I'm going to place my hands at your temples," Ezra said, nodding to Martin. Martin nodded back. "Just close your eyes and I'll do the rest, okay?"

Martin nodded again, immediately closing his eyes.

Ezra took a deep breath, preparing to use his ability. The last time he'd connected someone had been three years ago, when he opened a channel for Arnold, and before that, Roslyn. He briefly wondered, suddenly, if that was not, perhaps, the moment her feelings for him had begun. Martin sighed.

"Pull it together, kid, okay? This is my mind we're dealing with here."

"Sorry," Ezra said, smiling and blushing.

"A flipping soap opera," Martin sighed, never opening his eyes.

Ezra frowned at Martin, amused, then quickly re-gathered himself to do his job. He placed his hands over Martin's temples, closing his own eyes. He felt the energy extending from the tips of his fingers, in tiny, invisible tendrils. He always thought of the process in these terms. He quickly, effortlessly found the center of Martin's mind. It appeared like a bright grain of glowing sand, in the middle of darkness. The tendrils led him to it, every time. He touched this small, nearly invisible place inside Martin's head, and everything came alive in an instant.

Just as Ezra described, Martin felt as if he were falling. A slight euphoria accompanied the free-fall effect, and then he merely floated on air. Suddenly, he became aware of nothing but an incredible feeling of love and well-being, covering his entire body.

He also sensed someone else inside his head. Thoughts simply arrived, suddenly there, and he fully engaged in a conversation with a Grayling. Everything he heard came in English, Martin marveled. The conversations happened so fast, thoughts came and went out instantaneously. He did not wonder about intentions or worry about deceit. The thoughts that arrived in Martin's head felt so pure, undiluted, he never doubted the sincerity. There were no jumbled thoughts, like he heard flitting around inside the minds of human beings. There were no insecurities, or ulterior motives. No manipulations, nor ill intentions. He simply received pure, unaltered thought. Martin felt utterly overwhelmed by this experience, for it truly was 'alien' to him, and he smiled at the irony of his own revelations. He suddenly knew how far his own race still had to go, to even hope of evolving into what the Graylings had become. He knew how flawed human beings were, as a race. He saw his own weaknesses, for it seemed like comparing a soiled garment to fresh white silk.

In the end, Martin knew of no way he could even put into words, to himself, let alone anyone else, exactly what he came to know in an instant. For most of the wisdom he received arrived in the form of intense feelings, and deep emotions, none of which had any name. He knew none of his friends could understand. They simply would not 'get it' until they each felt it for themselves. He realized how this lent to Eileen's idea of 'brain washing' but nothing could be done about that, he realized, sadly. For Ezra could only connect transgens. Eileen had no pseudogene. She would never be able to communicate with the Graylings.

The conversation between Martin and an alien race took only seconds to complete. Two Graylings introduced themselves. They gave human names, and Martin understood this to be for his benefit, for their own language was so complex, there were no English translations for their true names, and certainly no pronounceable equivalent.

My name is Harold, the eldest one said.

I'm Ramona, the other said. They were 'joined'. Martin immediately understood this to be the closest equivalent to the human term 'married'.

He knew there were many families on board. He also knew many had been lost, and still others were born on board the ship. There were even children, and new arrivals expected. Martin cried as he felt their pain. He felt every loss that had taken place over the last two hundred years. They grieved the same as anyone. He searched their minds for answers but found none. Their God, they conveyed to him simply as 'The Creator'. They were spiritual beings, who believed in a 'soul' and a life beyond physical death. They, like humankind, had attempted to find proof of the soul but failed. Martin heard and felt that these beings also held faith in their hearts, so pure and unshakable, lacking the doubts that men held. He knew all of this.

We are sorry we cannot give you proof, they both said, together. *We reached the conclusion, hundreds of years ago, that the condition of eternity must lie in the belief alone. It is a journey every living being must take. Faith is what the Universe is provided with. It is a mathematical certainty, as is infinity. It is the one thing, by definition, that must remain unproved. There is no way to quantify emotion. We have concluded that the soul lives in the same place that our emotions originate from. This is all we can give you.*

Martin understood. He *felt*. They asked if he was ready to see what had happened to them, and he consented. In an instant, his senses became flooded with terror, dread, pain, sorrow, and torture in the form of immense grief, so heavy, he thought he might die. He saw the Graylings, what they looked like. But he saw them through *their* eyes, and they did not look alien to him, rather, they felt as familiar as his own human form. He became one of them. He saw their planet, in all its beauty and glory. He saw the sky, in a familiar hue of light green, the periwinkle oceans, and the dark pod-like ships descend to the ground. He saw the first glimpses of the Bailon. He felt the Graylings great fear, as the attacks began. He saw incredible bloodshed, so gruesome, he thought his mind might break. He saw the Graylings as they fled, most obliterated. Flight being all they knew, lacking the instinct or ability to fight. They could not defend themselves. The overwhelming drive to survive took over. Their vast ships, designed and used for exploration and discovery, in a moment of panic, became their escape.

Their vessels of curiosity and knowledge became their drifting homes. But only one ship had escaped. Martin felt the overwhelming pall of grief fall over him, as he experienced what the Graylings had.

Most of their fallen loved ones were not with them. Their bodies had been left behind, on their lost planet.

He felt their loneliness and despair, as Ezra had warned. Everything so much more intense than any emotion Martin had ever felt, utterly pure and concentrated. This defined the Graylings' peaceful way. In moments, Martin *knew* the Graylings. He knew everything he needed to know about them. They were his friends. He felt how much they loved him, and how they now also knew *him*. They saw the darkness inside of him, and they also saw the good. Their faith told them the ugliness inside of him—in the form of anger and violence—resided there, in their belief, for the purpose of fighting the Bailon.

He thought, briefly, that the Graylings seemed very similar, in their assessment of the situation, to Jesus. They believed everything happened for a reason, and Martin sensed their overwhelming feeling of certainty for the successful outcome of events. It lacked a sense precognition, in any detailed knowledge, which he received, but rather, a *feeling* of unshakable certainty that something led them all. The Graylings seemed much more adept, in their mental state of purity, to follow the *feelings*. It had directed them to Earth, Martin sensed. It brought them, in their natural curiosity of all life, to discover the existence of the pseudogene, and in their vast knowledge and understanding of biology, they found the key to the existence of the gene. They found the purpose hidden inside humanity.

Martin learned all these things in mere seconds. Eileen watched, full of fear, as he wept, smiled, laughed, and wept again. Ezra pulled his hands away, leaving Martin to his revelations, watching him cry. He understood Martin's journey and experience—he'd been through it himself, several years before.

Martin opened his eyes feeling as if hours had passed, with no idea that mere minutes had gone by, for he felt as if decades—an entire lifetime of events—had flooded his head. He felt he'd lived the lives of others, and he did not see his world the same. He had changed. It happened in an instant. He was not the same man he had been. Martin sat, now convinced beyond any doubt, that all of them were there for a reason more important than any living being could possibly fathom, not even the Graylings. Their minds could accept this belief, however, with unfaltering faith.

Martin struggled with it, his human emotions flooding back. But he could now hear the Graylings speaking to him. He reached out, and instantly received reassurance. They understood his base emotions, if not the aggression, anger, or any of the negative feelings. Most importantly, they understood his pain and sadness, for these emotions were universal between them.

He looked at Ezra, tears spilling down his cheeks, suddenly reaching out to hug him fiercely. He now felt a deep connection to Ezra as well, on a completely new level. Ezra clapped him on the back, laughing.

"I'm sorry," Martin said. "I didn't understand the gap between us."

"It's okay," Ezra said. "You couldn't have."

Martin nodded. He looked over at Eileen, who cried. He stood and embraced her.

"It's okay," he said. "Everything is okay."

She pulled away and looked at him, searching his eyes, more afraid than ever. He could still hear her thoughts.

"I'm still me," he said. "But," he looked back at Ezra. Ezra nodded, encouraging him. "Eileen," Martin said, "I've changed. I know everything the Graylings have been through. They're my friends."

"Just like that?" She looked so frightened, Martin felt bad for her, but he knew he could never make her understand.

"Just like that," he said, and kissed her. "But it doesn't change *us*. It doesn't change my love for *you*."

He kissed her again, and Ezra looked away, smiling. He stood to leave.

"Ezra," Martin said, turning to look at him. "I'll work on the others."

Martin nodded. Ezra nodded back, then left the couple to be alone. Once he had gone, Martin lay down in bed with Eileen, stroking her face. She looked at him, face full of hope.

"I love you," he said.

"I know," she said, frowning. "I just wish I could go where you're going."

"You can," he said. "You just have to believe, Eileen. It's all the same, whether you can hear the Graylings or not. Whether you can see what I've seen, or not. You must take it on faith, by seeing how I've changed. It's the only thing I can offer."

She nodded then laughed, bitterly.

"I'm jealous," she said, looking ashamed. "You love something I don't understand."

"I still love you, Eileen. As much as ever. I'm still yours."

She nodded, taking it all in. He kissed her, and she kissed him back, desperately. She needed to be with him, he heard it in her thoughts. He needed it, too. They made love, then fell asleep in each other's arms.

***

Before and during the events with Ezra in Martin and Eileen's room, Arnold came out of his room, and went to call on Jenny. She answered her door, and when she saw him, her face broke out in joy and relief. He could tell she'd been crying—so had he—everyone had.

"I thought you might feel like going for a walk," he said, sounding nervous. "I thought it would be nice." He sighed.

She said nothing, only surprised him by immediately leaving with him.

"Daddy, I'm going for a walk!" she called over her shoulder.

"Sure," Arnold heard Malcolm say, although the door had already closed.

Jenny immediately linked her arm through Arnold's and his heart fluttered. He felt secure that they liked each other. They walked through the park garden, then later, down the hallway, and took in the expansive view of darkness on the observation deck.

"It will look much more interesting, after our first jump," he said. "Then we'll actually be able to see something."

"You've already been through a worm hole?" Jenny asked.

Arnold nodded. He looked at Jenny with incredible fondness. He told her the same thing he'd told Jess when she asked him about the wormholes during she and Ben's tour their first day onboard the ship.

"They needed to test things out. It's been a while since they've traveled that way. Been parked near Earth for over a decade. Plus, they wanted to teach Rafferty. He knows everything there is to know about this ship. He's a genius, really."

"What about you?" she asked. "You seem to know a lot."

"Me? Nah, I'm not so good with math or science. Grace learned medicine. Jemma has a green thumb. Roslyn comforts people. Ezra can connect people to the Graylings. Me? It turns out I'm... not good at anything, really," he frowned. "Except snooping. That can't be helped."

"Oh," Jenny said, growing concerned. "Well, if you can hear so good, even from far away, then, isn't my voice right next to you, like a bullhorn?"

Jenny instinctively lowered her voice, worried the volume might be hurting Arnold's ears. He looked at her with amusement and endearment.

"No," he chuckled. "I don't hear things any louder than anyone else. I can just hear things others can't."

Jenny frowned. Arnold smiled.

"My hearing is no different from yours, save for one, main thing. Deep inside, past the ear canal, past the Tempanic Membrane, or eardrum, there's a nerve. It's called the Eighth Nerve. It transmits messages from the inner ear to the brain. My Eighth Nerve is different. Special. Instead of thousands of nerve endings, it contains millions.

"Grace explained it all to me, a while back. Neurons in the brain's auditory cortex interpret incoming sound signals and send them to the rest of the nervous system, in the brain and spinal cord. A normal person receives thousands of neuronal signals, and their brains interpret them.

"Because of my special Eighth Nerve, my brain's auditory cortex receives millions of signals, instead of thousands. My auditory cortex is different as well, so it's able to interpret those millions of neuronal signals.

"My brain is simply able to receive and translate more sounds. I can hear *more*, not louder. Which is good for me, because otherwise, I'd be in pain a lot. I wouldn't be able to be around people, or listen to normal, everyday sounds, or room voices, now would I?"

"No, I guess not... Strange," she said, although she looked at Arnold in sheer fascination. He missed her look, however, for he now looked down at the floor.

"Yeah, I guess I am strange," Arnold said, sounding sad.

"No, I didn't mean that *you're* strange," Jenny said, feeling embarrassed. Then she laughed.

"What?" Arnold frowned.

"Nothing, it's just, you said you weren't good at anything. Science or math. But you seem to understand a lot more than I think you give yourself credit for."

He looked at her, feeling warm and complimented. "I only know what I just told you because of Grace," he said, looking away, feeling modest.

"So? I'm sure you're good at a lot of other things," Jenny reassured him. "You've made everyone feel comfortable. You're very good with people."

"I am?"

"Yeah," Jenny said. "I mean, that Ezra guy? Not good with people. Jemma and Roslyn? They're nice, but... And so is Rafferty, but still."

"What?" Arnold looked at Jenny with great intensity now.

"You just have this way of... making people feel like you're their best friend. Like we can trust you, immediately. It's hard to explain. You make people like you. You just seem so genuinely nice. It makes people love you."

"Love me?" Arnold felt surprised by this comment, his heart began pounding away, uncontrollably. "Are you speaking of everyone, or someone in particular?"

"Well, I-I sort of just assumed everyone had the same response to you as I did," Jenny said, faltering, realizing what she'd just implied. She frowned, for she only then became fully aware of exactly how strong her feelings for Arnold were. She suddenly turned away, quickly walking out of the observation room.

Arnold followed, not wanting to push her. He never intended to embarrass or make her feel uncomfortable. He wasn't expecting any of this. He trailed her down the hallway, head reeling.

When they reached her door, she turned to look up at him, glancing shyly. He smiled, heart warmed—loving her. He knew it then.

"Thanks for the walk," she said.

Arnold shocked her then. He leaned down quickly and kissed her. He wasn't shy like Ezra. The moment he realized he loved Jenny, he became brazen.

He kissed her for several moments, then pulled away, searching her face for a reaction, half-expecting anger, perhaps even a slap to the face. He had experienced nothing but rejection, with Jemma, over the last two years. Right now, however, Jemma was the last thing on his mind. He realized, somewhere in the back of his thoughts, that Jemma had been merely a crush. What he felt now was decidedly different. If he thought she wouldn't be scared off by his intensity, he would have proposed to her then and there.

Jenny only stared at Arnold, looking stunned. He immediately felt horrible for being so aggressive. He looked down and away, about to turn and leave, but she reached up and kissed him forcefully on the mouth, with so much eagerness, his eyes flew open in surprise. Then they simply melted together, kissing wildly for several moments, before Jenny finally, reluctantly, pulled away from him, breathing heavily. He leaned in towards her, trying to restrain himself. Trying to show her respect.

"I should go inside," she breathed. "I mean, we have time."

He nodded, also breathing hard. He wasn't sure who he tried to convince, himself, or Jenny. He closed his eyes, sighing. Her point held perfect validity. They did have plenty of time.

"I'm sorry," he breathed, opening his eyes to look at her.

"For what?"

"Rushing you," he said, closing his eyes again. Had he just ruined everything, before anything even began?

She quickly put her hand on the panel, opening the door. Then she kissed him once more, quickly, his eyes still closed.

"Thanks for the walk," she sighed.

Then she was gone, the door closed, cutting off his view of her, but not before he saw the smile on her face. He stood staring at her closed door for several moments, then turned and sat on the couch in the middle of the room, dazed. He had a goofy grin on his face.

He watched foggily, as Martin's door opened, then Ezra walked out, beaming. He came over and sat down next to Arnold. He turned and looked at him, smiling bigger than ever. Arnold smiled back, laughing.

"What's with you, Ez?"

"Like you don't know."

"Know what?"

Ezra looked at Arnold in disbelief.

"You mean, you weren't just snooping out here, listening?"

"No," Arnold said, sounding hurt.

"How long have you been out here?" Ezra said, suspicious.

"I just sat down," Arnold defended.

"Oh," Ezra said. Then he looked at Arnold, smiling wider than ever. "I connected Martin."

"For real?" Arnold said, sounding wondrous. "Then it's happening."

"What?"

"The beginning of them changing. To truly understanding us," Arnold said, and Ezra nodded. Arnold looked close to tears.

"This is really happening, finally, isn't it? We're going to help them, Ez. We're really going to save them."

Ezra smiled, his own eyes filling with tears. He nodded his head. Arnold sat back, thinking. He looked around the common room, at all the doors.

"This place looks so different now," he mused.

"What are you talking about?" Ezra frowned. "It looks the same as it always has."

"No, it doesn't," Arnold said. Then he made an odd noise, and Ezra looked at him, saw his eyes, and laughed.

"What the hell's wrong with you, Arnie?"

"Nothing. It's just funny. We knew they were coming on board for so many years. And we knew when they came here, that we would change them. It never dawned on me, though, that they would change us."

Ezra sat, stunned by Arnold's statement. Mostly because he realized it was true. They'd been a group of six people for over three years now, and in just two days' time, with the arrival of the newbies, their lives had all changed. Ezra sighed.

"Yeah, if it wasn't for Martin, Roslyn and I might never have..." he trailed off, musing.

"What, might never have what," Arnold said, looking at Ezra in amusement and curiosity.

"Nothing," Ezra said, blushing.

"Hah!" Arnold's face grew excited, his mouth falling open in disbelief. "Did you two get it on?!"

"What? No!" But Ezra's blush deepened.

"You did, you dog," Arnold said. "I didn't think you had it in you. Or maybe I should say, in her, actually."

"You're disgusting."

"I'm kidding," he laughed. "Sort of. But, you guys are... together now?"

"I guess so."

"You guess so? You either are or you aren't."

"We are," Ezra said. "But, we're taking things slow."

"Huh," Arnold nodded. "Yeah, I get that one."

"Really?" He looked at Arnold, who now blushed slightly.

"Wait a minute. You and that Jenny girl—"

"I don't kiss and tell."

"I think you just did."

Arnold looked at Ezra, a stern warning on his face. "This isn't like Jemma, okay?"

"Sure," Ezra shrugged.

"Jenny is..." Arnold sighed.

"Oh, God," Ezra said. "Now you, too? What is with everyone?"

"What's with *you*, Ezra? Apparently, you're not immune."

"No, but, it's weird, isn't it? They come on board, and suddenly, everyone's pairing up?"

"Not everyone," Arnold said. "Jemma's still pining after Rafferty."

"And Grace doesn't have anyone," Ezra said, sounding sad.

"Maybe she doesn't want anyone." Arnold sat back, thinking hard. He looked intrigued. "Do you think the Graylings knew this was going to happen?"

"What?"

"This. All of us. The coupling off?"

"I've never heard about any of this in their thoughts," Ezra said.

"Neither have I, but maybe this is what they mean, when they tell us, 'everything is going to work out'? I mean, think about it, Ez. We're going to another planet, right? There are nineteen of us. There should be twenty-one, but," he sighed. "How many couples would it take, to successfully rebuild humanity?"

He looked at Ezra with interest. Ezra stared back, Arnold's theory suddenly registering.

"You think they want us to repopulate?"

"Well, what else is supposed to happen when we get there? The Graylings love us, right? It's not as if they're going to use us, then throw us away. They have too much respect for our lives. But there are only a handful of us they truly need, to beat the Bailon. Hell, I'm not even one of them. Neither is Jenny, I don't think. Technically, there was no reason for the Graylings to bring all of us, or the newbies, let alone any of their family."

"They did this for us, so we would be happy," Ezra said. "So, we wouldn't be sad."

"I know," Arnold said. "And we're not, are we? We're all finding love."

"So, what, they're matchmakers?"

"No, they just want what's best for us," Arnold said. "Ten women, nine men. Jesus would have made ten."

"But, Lucia would have made eleven women, ten men," Ezra countered.

"Wrong. Jesus would have made ten men, Lucia, nine women."

"How do you figure that?" Ezra frowned.

"Kate and Alma don't count," Arnold said, smiling.

"Oh," Ezra said. "It's still not perfect. The numbers aren't perfect."

"Yeah, but close. And the way I fell for Jenny. How did they know?"

"They couldn't have. And your theory is still flawed. Not everyone is paired up."

"Not yet," Arnold said. "Maybe not even until we reach Hesperia, for some. But maybe… at some point. Who knows?"

"I still say it's something in the water."

"Grace would never do that," Arnold joked. Ezra laughed.

"So, you're in love?" Ezra asked.

"Yeah," Arnold smiled, sighing. "Are you?"

"Yeah, I think I am," Ezra said, sounding perplexed.

"Well, then, you can't fight it, buddy-boy. Time to admit you're human."

"What does that mean?"

"It means, time to do what humans in love do. Do I need to explain the birds and bees to you, Ez?"

"Why do you always tease me about this stuff?"

"Because, it's so easy to do, Ezra," Arnold laughed, shaking his head. "Look, there's nothing to be afraid of. Why are you so nervous? It's not like you haven't ever done it before, right?"

Ezra looked down at his hands, fidgeting.

"Holy shit, you've never done it before?!"

"Shhhh! Keep your voice down," Ezra said, blushing wildly.

"You're like, thirty-five, dude," Arnold said, in disbelief.

"So, it's not like you've done it lately."

"Yeah, but I have done it before in my lifetime."

"Well, I was never in love before. And even if I had been," he looked at Arnold, embarrassed.

"What?"

"I don't want to do it until after I'm married," Ezra said.

"Oh," Arnold said. "Does Roslyn know that?"

"We just kissed for the first time yesterday," Ezra said, growing annoyed.

"Okay, okay," Arnold said, thinking. "Well, I guess you'll have to tell her that, at some point, and then, hope for the best."

"Hope for the best?"

"Yeah," Arnold said. "Like, hope she says yes, when you ask her to marry you."

Arnold looked at Ezra matter-of-factly.

"Otherwise, you ain't never gettin' laid, boy," he said, winking and chuckling. He got up and went into his room, leaving Ezra alone to ponder everything Arnold had said.

11

Ben had been thinking about marriage. Jess didn't know it, but he'd been thinking about asking her to marry him ever since he found out she was pregnant. It had never been a question of whether he felt certain she was the one, or whether he was ready to be with her for the rest of his life. The moment he fell in love with Jess, his heart belonged to her. She felt the same way, he believed. But even before they left the facility, he knew he wanted to marry her. As soon as they arrived on the ship, Ben started pondering how to ask Jess, and when.

Her spirits were so low, however, after the funeral, Ben did not dare to ask. He waited several more days, until she seemed to brighten up a bit. Exactly one week after they arrived on the ship, while lying in bed together after dinner, Ben finally decided it was time to bring it up. There could be no elaborate way of doing so, for he had no ring. And he realized it wouldn't be legal, for they were no longer on Earth, and there was no legal system.

He lay next to her, frowning. She saw this and sighed.

"You're frowning," she said. "That's never a good thing."

"I was just realizing, now that we're not on Earth, we have no legal rights."

"Legal rights?" She laughed. "What are you talking about?"

"Well, I mean, what if we break up? There are no lawyers here. What if you decide you want full custody of the kid?"

"Are you serious," she said, turning to him, smiling.

"And I can't even put my name down on the birth certificate, saying I'm the father. See? No legal rights," Ben said.

"This isn't Earth," she said, kissing him. "And I'm glad, actually. Out here, things are just... different. We don't need lawyers. Everything's better."

"What do you mean?"

"I don't know, don't you just feel it?"

"Feel what?"

"I don't know," she said, frowning, looking up at the ceiling. "It's almost like, as soon as we left Earth, I felt... so much more... *free.*"

"We are free, Jess."

"I know, but what I mean is, I just feel like, maybe, if we'd tried to make things work on Earth, with the way everything is, it just would have been a lot harder, you know? And out here, we're free to just, be together."

"But I can't marry you," Ben said, his heart beating faster.

"Marry me?"

He rolled over to look at her.

"I want to marry you, Jess."

"Okay," she said, but he couldn't tell if it was an answer or not.

"Was that a yes?"

"Did you actually ask?"

He sighed, feeling like an idiot. He looked her in the eyes, smiling.

"Jessica Wembly, will you marry me?"

"I thought you said we couldn't get married?" she whispered, her eyes welling up with tears.

"Shut up and answer the question, silly," he whispered back.

"Yes," she said, the tears now falling. He kissed her.

"But how?"

"Well, the way I see it, we're on our own," Ben said. "Our lives are in our own hands. I mean, Martin and Eileen are married, right?"

Jess nodded.

"So, prove it," he said. She frowned.

"Anything that might have legally proven their marriage, was left behind, on Earth," Ben sighed.

"So, what are you saying?"

"I'm saying, the only reason they're married now, is because they say they are."

"They have rings."

"I'm sure we could get rings," Ben said. "How hard could that be for the Graylings to make? Or even Rafferty, with a blow torch."

Jess laughed.

"All we need is a small ceremony, and witnesses."

"Who?"

"Everyone," Ben said. "I want everyone to see."

"I don't like public speaking," Jess said, looking nervous.

"The Society is now comprised of nineteen people, Jess. I want to marry you, and I want every human being on this ship to see it. It's what I want, okay?"

"Okay," she said. "But there's no minister."

"I was thinking, I would ask Hanley to officiate."

"He's not a minister."

"Do we need one?"

"I guess not," she frowned.

"Like I said, we're on our own up here, Jess. But if I stand up in front of all our friends and say I marry you, then to me, that means we're married. Do you agree?"

"Sure. But, if that's how easy it is, then we could just say 'I Do,' right here and now."

"You think it's easy?"

"Well, no, that's not what I meant," she said, growing agitated. "Wait, you think we'll get divorced, and that I'll take our daughter away?"

"No," Ben said, caressing her face. "I don't. I think if you say you're with me for life, then you're with me for life. Right?"

She nodded, kissing him. He loved her so much.

"Marriage is what we say it is now, Jess. We say it's official, and it is. Okay?"

"Yeah," she sighed, her eyes full of love.

"And I want to do it soon."

"How soon?"

"Two days."

"Two days?"

"Okay, a week," he said.

"Why so fast?"

"Do you have doubts?"

"Of course not," she said.

He sighed. "I want to do it long before the baby comes, okay?"

She nodded. "I love you."

"I love you back," he said, and she smiled.

***

Ben went to Hanley the next day, as soon as he woke up. Hanley was in his room with Rachel. They both sat down on the couch, smiling. Ben looked at them for a minute before rolling his eyes.

"Damn that Martin."

Hanley laughed, slapping his knee. "I'm honored you want me to do it, though."

"So, you agree?"

"Hell, yeah," Hanley said. "Let's make that little baby official, huh?"

"Hanley," Rachel chided.

"What? I'm only joking."

Ben watched the couple and smiled. They shared a quick kiss, then Hanley sighed, turning to Ben, and leveled him with a serious look. He wasn't smiling.

"I need to talk to you about something, Ben."

"Okay," he said, sitting down, for Rachel stood up and offered him her seat. She disappeared into the bedroom.

"What's up, Hanley?"

"Several days ago, Martin let Ezra open a channel into his head," Hanley said. Ben stared, waiting for the rest.

"He talked with the Graylings, just like I've been doing all along. Got the whole scoop, directly from them."

"Okay," Ben said, again, sudden dread tingling. "And?"

"He's a believer now," Hanley shrugged. "And we need to get everyone else on the same page, at some point."

"And you want me to convince Jess," Ben sighed, rubbing his temples.

"Not now, but at some point, yes. She'll have to, Ben. There's no way she can possibly fight for them, if she doesn't know what she's fighting for."

"Okay, but, we have ten years, right?"

"Right, I'm not saying it needs to be anytime soon, Ben, just... It needs to happen. So, I'm telling you now."

"Is anyone else thinking about channeling in?"

"Rachel's going tomorrow. She wants to know what I know. And she sees how Martin has changed. You didn't notice?"

"I've been preoccupied," Ben sighed.

"I bet. Getting married, having a baby, living on an alien ship," Hanley shook his head.

"Anyone else?"

"No, not yet. But Alma and Kate are probably the next we'll try to tackle. I think Alma might be willing. For Lucia and Jesus."

Ben nodded, sighing deeply, and looked at Hanley with resignation, his face gravely serious. "And you think Jess will do it for me, once I've done it."

"Huh?" Hanley stared at Ben in complete confusion.

"You're telling me all this, because you want me to channel in to the Graylings," Ben said, matter-of-factly.

"You can't, Ben. You know that," Hanley said, frowning. "Ezra can only connect transgens. You gotta have the gene."

"But, don't you know? I thought you were telling me all this because you know."

"Know what?" Hanley's frown deepened.

"What Grace told me."

"No."

"Martin didn't say anything?"

"About what?"

"I'm a transgen."

"What?" Hanley stared at Ben in disbelief. "What?!"

Ben nodded. Somehow, Martin had missed it, he guessed. It was no wonder. He hadn't thought about it since he found out. He'd purposefully been avoiding allowing it into his own head.

"Martin, how did you miss this one?" Hanley said, out loud to the room. "You're a transgen?"

Ben nodded again.

"Since when?"

"Since they scanned my genome when I came on board, I guess. I never ran my own sequence. It simply never occurred to me. I even knew I was a preemie, and still, I never realized, never put it together."

"What are the chances?" Hanley said.

"Astronomical," Ben answered.

"And you still don't have faith?"

Ben shook his head, looking down at the floor, sighing. "I came on board, didn't I?"

"You came to be with Jess," Hanley said. "If you're a transgen, Ezra can channel you in."

Ben nodded. "Theoretically."

"What do you mean?"

"I'm not active," Ben shrugged. "I need a dose of Luci."

"So, what are you waiting for?"

"I'm not sure I want an ability, Hanley. I like things the way they are."

"But, if you're channeled in with the Graylings, Jess has gotta come on board, right?"

"I'm not going to use her trust in me to do that, Hanley," Ben said, growing angry.

"I didn't mean it like that."

"No?"

"No," Hanley said, trying to sound gentle. "I only meant, if you understand what we're dealing with, then Jess will see, she'll have to. She'll want to be where you are. She'll want to know. It changes you, Ben. It changes everything."

"That's what I'm afraid of," he said. "And I know it's why Jess is scared."

"It's not a bad change," Hanley said. "Loving something. Look how far it's already taken you, from who you used to be."

Ben looked at Hanley, surprised by his statement. Then he nodded, letting it all in.

"I have to activate the gene, to channel in," Ben sighed.

Hanley nodded. "You're the Doc. You'd know."

"I know."

"Is Jess okay with you activating?"

"I don't know, we haven't talked about it. I came here to ask you to marry us, Hanley."

"Okay, let's do that first, then," he said, smiling at Ben.

Ben shook his head. "Now, I need to tell her, *before* I marry her. She should know."

"Are you sure that's a wise choice right now?"

Ben shrugged. "No, but I can't marry her, then spring it on her after, now can I?"

Suddenly, a clicking noise sounded off in the room. Hanley got up to open the door. Martin stood there. He came in, beaming.

"Sorry, Hanley, I've been a little distracted lately."

"Yeah, I know. Getting to know the Graylings is pretty huge."

Martin nodded then smiled at Ben in wonder.

"So, you're one of us, hot damn." Martin shook his head, smiling huge, and infectious. Ben couldn't help but laugh, and Hanley joined in. Ben left soon after to talk with Jess.

***

Jess paced back and forth in their room. When Ben came in, she rushed up to him and placed his hand on her stomach, looking at him, expectantly. He didn't feel anything, then after a moment, he felt the tiniest tap against his palm. His eyes grew wide.

"Did you feel it?" She looked at him, scared and anxious.

"Yes, I did." He smiled and hugged her.

She pulled away, restless. "Yeah, well, look at this," she said, pulling her shirt tight across her stomach. It was noticeably rounder. "Overnight," she said. "Overnight!"

"Okay," he said, "Okay, Grace said it might seem sudden. You're pregnant, Jess. You have to start showing sometime."

"Ben, there's an actual person in there," she said, pointing to her stomach. "Living in there."

"Yeah, that's how these things work, Jess," he said, trying to sound understanding, but he also struggled not to smile or laugh.

"No, but..." she trailed off. "I can't give birth, Ben."

"Of course, you can," he said.

"No, I can't. It's gonna get big, before it comes out, you know? Like, really, *really* big. There's no way I can get this thing out of me!"

"Jess, your hormones are all over the place, okay? You just popped out overnight, which means, you're definitely having a hormone spike today, okay?"

"What are you saying?" She sounded angry.

Oh, shit. He tried to repair things. "All I'm saying is that your emotions are heightened. The fear you're feeling right now isn't you. It's your hormones. Okay? Everything's going to be okay."

"No, it's not!" She screamed, and stormed from their quarters, out into the common room. Several people sat out there, including Arnold and Jenny. Two more couches had been brought in, and the common room had become a popular place to hang out. Ezra and Roslyn sat on another couch, and Hanley and Rachel, on a third. Martin and Eileen came out right then also, for Martin could hear the fight going on in his head but wanted to watch it unfold.

"You're not listening to me, Ben!"

"Jess, please try and stay calm," Ben sighed, self-conscious of their audience, which she seemed completely oblivious to.

"Don't talk to me like I'm crazy. Just because my hormones are a little out of whack, doesn't make me crazy."

"I didn't say you were crazy, Jess. I never said that. All I said was that everything was going to be okay."

"Ooh. I guess he told her," Hanley said, looking over his shoulder at Martin. Martin shook his head at Hanley, violently, trying to tell him to shut up. Then he closed his eyes, as Jess turned to stare at Hanley, frowning. Ben also closed his eyes.

"Told me what?" She stared at Hanley, then looked at Martin, and saw the look on his face. She turned back to Ben, her face pink and shiny with anger.

"Told me what?"

Arnold just watched the entire scene with interest, for he and the other old-boarders had no idea what was going on. He was no longer in the habit of actively snooping on people. He could tune it out, when not thinking about it, and had been doing so lately, while with Jenny. Things between them had become very serious, incredibly fast. Jenny now roomed with Arnold, for Rafferty had moved out, and gone to live with Malcolm.

Everyone stared at the scene now unfolding. Jemma came walking down the hallway just then, for she'd been in the dining hall, and heard Jess yelling. She entered the common room to see what was happening.

Jess and Ben now had a large audience. Jemma, Ezra, Roslyn, Arnold, Jenny, Hanley, Rachel, Martin and Eileen now all watched the couple fight. Rafferty came out of his room, for he heard Hanley's thoughts, and grew interested. Malcolm, his new roommate, followed Rafferty out, and soon, almost everyone on board the ship watched the scene unfold. It was the most excitement anyone had seen in a while. The only people missing were Grace, Earl, Aaron, Alma, and Kate, for

Sarah also came riding her bike into the common room, just then, and skidded to a halt.

"Tell me what, Ben?" Her voice was so angry, it almost cracked.

"Jess, now's not the time," Ben attempted to sound calm.

"What's Hanley talking about, tell me what?"

Ben closed his eyes. "Jess, *please*."

"Tell me!"

Ben sighed. "I've decided to take the Luci."

"What? You decided," she snapped. "Without even telling me? Without even asking me how I feel about it?"

"I was going to tell you, Jess—"

"When, Ben, huh? When were you going to tell me? After we were married?"

"They're getting married?" Jenny gasped, looking excited.

"Heh, maybe not," Hanley quipped, under his breath.

"Hanley," Rachel hissed, stabbing his ribs with her elbow to shut him up.

"Ow."

"I was trying to tell you just now, Jess, but the baby—"

"Oh, so it's the baby's fault now? It's the baby's fault that you're too chicken shit to tell me you want to become a freak?"

"You're not a freak, Jess."

"Why? Ben, why would you want to do this? You don't need an ability."

"I have the gene, Jess. I'm one of you."

"Wait, Ben has the gene?" Jenny looked confused now.

Arnold looked at Ben with interest. "You're a hybrid? How come I didn't know?"

"Because it's Ben's business," Grace said, coming out of her room next, joining the group. "And it's his choice."

"No," Jess said, shaking her head, still angry. "Ben, this is huge. How could you not talk to me about this? How could you just decide, without even telling me?"

"I wanted to, Jess."

"But you didn't!" she yelled. She began curling her fists. "Were you going to marry me, without telling me?!"

"No, Jess, I would never do that."

"Why, why would you do this? It's bad enough our baby's gonna be, God knows what?! Now you wanna change too?"

"What's wrong with the baby?" Jenny whispered, too loud.

Jess heard. Ben closed his eyes.

"Look at me, Ben! How can you say this baby is normal? I started showing overnight! It's moving around inside me!"

"Jess, that's completely normal," Grace said, using her most gentle voice.

"No, you're only saying that to try and cover it all up," Jess said, turning on Grace, a look of hatred in her eyes. "This baby cannot be normal. You don't know. You've never seen what happens when two transgens reproduce, have you? Have you?!"

"No, but the baby is normal," Grace said. "You saw the ultrasound, Jess. You saw the baby."

"No, that could have been a trick."

"Dude, she is wiggin'," Arnold blurted.

"Jess, you're not making any sense," Ben said.

"I'm not crazy," Jess said, rounding on Ben. "Stop talking to me like I'm crazy!"

"Jess, please," Ben said, tears in his eyes. His heart was breaking.

"Ben," Martin said.

Something in the quality of Martin's voice stopped Ben's blood. He looked at Martin, who looked at Jess with growing dread. Ben knew that look. He looked at Jess again, saw the look in her eyes, and his heart stopped.

She was losing control. Her fists balled up tight, her face taught and pale now, her eyes empty.

"Jess, please, listen to me," he said, moving towards her, but she backed away, looking at him with fury.

"Stay away from me," she whispered.

"Jess, you can't pulse in here. You'll kill everyone."

"Wait, what?" Arnold said, his expression suddenly stunned serious. Jenny stood, pulling him away.

"Everyone leave the room, *now*," Martin warned.

Everyone quickly stood to run, but at that moment, something astounding happened. Jess threw her hands out in front of her and simply disappeared.

Everyone turned and looked at the empty space where Jess had been standing only moments before, stunned.

"Jess?" Ben said, panicked.

"She can't pulse in here, Ben," Grace said, sounding relieved. "Right, Rafferty?"

Rafferty nodded, slowly, thinking. Ben also thought hard. He thought out loud. Everyone just watched him.

"She needs mass, gravitational mass to manipulate, to twist, and store energy inside of."

"The ship's gravity is pulsed, it isn't constant," Rafferty said, looking at Ben.

"Right, and it's based on residual energy conversion, correct?"

"Yeah," Rafferty said, sounding impressed. Ben nodded.

"She can only pulse on a planet," he said, sounding wondrous. "She can't pulse in space."

"So, where did she go?" Jenny said.

"Part of her ability has nothing to do with gravitational fields. She can also bend time and space, jumping forward. I guess, even without the compression wave, or the EMP, that part of her ability still works," Ben said.

"So, she'll just reappear, like she always does," Hanley said. "That's so cool, you guys, wait until you see this."

"Hanley, shut up," Ben said, still thinking. He looked at Rafferty, who frowned back at him, confused.

"She bends time and space, and comes back to a fixed point," Ben said, looking at Rafferty with sudden panic. Rafferty stared at Ben, translating his science speak, working it through his own head. Suddenly, dawning horror spread over his face.

"Are you saying what I think you're saying?" Rafferty went pale.

"I don't know, I don't know!" he said, looking frantic.

"What the hell is going on, Doc?" Hanley said, but Martin looked like he might puke, hearing Ben's sudden revelation, along with Rafferty's.

"Stop the ship!" Ben suddenly screamed. "You have to tell them to stop the ship, and reverse course! We have to go back to exactly where we were the moment she disappeared."

"What?" Rachel looked scared. "What's he talking about?"

"It's just a theory," Martin said, sounding sad.

"Not one I'm willing to gamble on," Ben said. "You have to tell them to take the ship back," he said, his voice full of desperation.

"We already have," Grace said. "Rafferty, me, Arnold, Jemma, Roslyn, Ezra, Hanley, and Martin," Grace said. "We all told them. They heard us. They know."

Ben looked at Hanley and Martin, dismayed. They both nodded. "But I don't feel anything."

"The ship is designed that way," Rafferty said. "There's an energy field all around. The field moves, we basically float inside. No sensations of acceleration, or deceleration," he explained. "No inertia." All the newbies nodded.

"We have to go back to exactly where we were," Ben repeated.

"They know," Rafferty said. "We're already there."

"Are you sure?" Ben said, his voice shaking.

"Yes, Ben, they're sure," Rafferty said, very gently. "It's the Graylings. Their calculations are perfect."

"Ben, what the hell is going on," Hanley said. Everyone looked at him, wondering. He closed his eyes, taking a deep breath.

"When Jess travels through time, she returns to a fixed point in space. The spot she's occupying when she pulses. I don't know if that spot is tied to her physically, meaning wherever her feet are touching, her immediate surroundings, or simply a fixed point. Normally it wouldn't matter. If we were on a planet, there'd be no problem. The difference in the placement of the earth, after only a few minutes, would barely register on the eye. I never even thought to measure it."

"I don't get it," Jenny said, looking completely confused.

"It doesn't matter on Earth, because although the planet is rotating, the difference in her position would be centimeters at most. Completely negligible. Not enough to do any harm. But we're in space, on a ship that's moving at thousands of miles an hour."

"Are you telling me, that when Jess reappears, it could be outside of this ship? In space?!" Hanley said.

"Yes," Ben answered. "Quite possibly, she will return to that specific spot in physical space, which at the time she moved, was right here, in this room. Four minutes later? We would have left that point in space and be hundreds of miles away."

"But maybe not, right?" Jenny said.

"Maybe not," Ben said. "I hope not. If she's tied physically to this actual space," he motioned to where Jess had been standing. "And this space has moved with us."

"It's been almost four minutes, hasn't it?" Hanley asked.

Everyone looked at the spot where Jess disappeared from, then looked at Ben.

"Are they certain we are exactly where we were when she went?" Ben asked Rafferty. He nodded, emphatically.

"Because if we are even a few feet off," he said. "Or even a few inches." He looked at the couches.

"What?" Rafferty said.

"She could end up occupying the same space as a wall, or the furniture," Martin said, thickly.

"Everyone move the couches away! There, towards the far wall," Ben instructed.

Everyone rushed to grab a couch end, and noisily dragged them over to the far-right wall, several yards away from where Jess had been standing.

Ben looked at Sarah, her face scared, silently crying. She didn't seem to possess any precognitive powers now. She looked terrified. He looked at her in apology.

"It's going to be okay, Sarah," he said, surprising himself. "Everything is going to be okay, okay?" He nodded, and she nodded back, a tear slipping down her cheek.

At that moment, Jess suddenly, simply reappeared, looking as angry as ever. Everyone was stunned. Some people screamed out in surprise.

"Jess!" Ben rushed forward and hugged her so hard, she exclaimed in pain.

"Ow, Ben! You're hurting me! Let go!" She pushed him away, still enraged. Ben had long forgotten what they'd ever been fighting about.

"You don't get to do that," she said. "You don't get to try and make everything okay, by hugging me. You've upset me!"

Ben broke down, crying now, and everyone simply watched the scene unfold, their mouths hanging open.

"Did she move?" Hanley said. "It looked to me like she appeared right in the same spot."

"I think she did," Arnold said. "I couldn't tell any difference."

"Me neither," Jenny said.

"Jess," Martin cried, "you're okay!"

Hanley and Martin both rushed up to Jess and hugged her at the same time. Jess looked around at everyone, confused, frowning. She looked at Ben, crying uncontrollably now, and her face softened. Grace came over and put her arm around him.

"It's okay, Ben, just let it out," she soothed.

"What's going on?" Jess said, her voice now shaking. She looked around. "Why is everyone standing around looking at me so strange? And why are all the couches gone?"

Ben fell onto his knees, still sobbing. Jess went to him, forgetting her anger.

"Ben, what's wrong?" She looked around at everyone in a panic. "What's wrong with him?!"

"You almost died, Jess," Hanley said, looking angry. "You almost killed yourself, you idiot!"

"What?!"

Jess didn't even know she'd used her powers. She wasn't drained like usual.

"Jess," Ben sobbed.

"Ben, you're scaring me."

"You gave us quite a scare, Jess," Grace said, kneeling on the floor next to Ben, looking up at Jess sternly.

Grace proceeded to explain exactly what had just taken place. As Jess listened, her eyes grew wide and her mouth drew down in a sickly grimace, as she slowly realized what she'd put Ben through, and what might have almost happened to her. Then it dawned on her that she'd used at least some of her powers, and she became scared, gently caressing her abdomen. She was afraid her disappearing act had hurt the baby. She asked Grace about this.

"Would you like me to check? We can do an ultrasound right now." She smiled gently, and Jess nodded.

Grace, Jess, and Ben stood and headed for the infirmary. Over her shoulder, Grace instructed Rafferty to help everyone put the common room back in order. Sarah ran after Jess and Ben.

"I wanna come!"

Ben knelt and lovingly caressed her face. "I know, honey. But right now, I need to be alone with Jess, okay?"

Arnold came over, Jenny following close behind. "Sarah, would you like to come with me and Jenny? I could use a nice bike ride."

Sarah looked at Arnold and smiled. She knew what he was trying to do. She nodded and grabbed his hand. He smiled at Ben and Jess, then quickly turned and left.

12

In the infirmary, Grace used her handheld scanner to look over Jess. She swabbed her face with a cotton ball and dropped it into a machine. She then ran another small gadget over Jess's abdomen, and the far wall burst into full view, showing Jess her baby, for the second time.

"Is she okay?" Ben held Jess's hand. He looked at Grace, concerned.

She frowned at her hand-held device. She looked up at Ben, smiling, but he could tell something troubled her.

"Which 'she' are you referring to, Ben? Your daughter is just fine," she said, and Ben sighed in relief, closing his eyes. "And Jess?"

"She's fine, too," she said, sounding hesitant. "But, her hormone levels are off the charts."

"What does that mean," Jess asked, looking worried.

"I'm not sure," Grace said. "Jess, I won't lie to you, and seeing as how you've already pointed out the obvious, you're right. There's no way to truly know what's normal with your pregnancy. We simply have no way of knowing what the normal developmental patterns are of a baby born from two transgens."

"What's wrong with my hormones?"

"They're very elevated. Now, this could be a side effect from you using your powers, or your hormones may have been elevated already, which led you to lose control of your emotions. I suspect the latter, but the two, generally, go hand in hand. Since I didn't get a reading on your hormone levels before you used your ability, I simply can't tell why they're elevated now."

"But, will it hurt the baby?"

"No," Grace said, her voice reassuring. "What it does mean, is that you're highly emotional. And that is very dangerous, Jess. For everyone."

"I know," Jess said. "I'm sorry. I don't know what's wrong with me."

"It's not your fault, Jess. You can't be expected to control your emotions with your hormones at these levels," Grace said.

"Can you lower them, do something?"

"I wouldn't want to try," Grace said. "Your hormones may be at the levels they are, because it's helping aid your baby's development somehow. I have to trust that whatever you're experiencing, it's normal for your pregnancy."

Jess started to protest, but Grace continued, adamant.

"Your baby is just fine. Her heart rate is normal, her growth is right on track. The amniotic fluid is clear. All your daughter's organs are growing where they should be. Brain development looks good, there's healthy blood flow through the heart and brain. Everything is as it should be."

"Except I'm psychotic!"

"You lost your temper," Grace said, attempting to soothe her. "It happens with all pregnancies. Tomorrow, you might feel sad, or even a bit depressed. Don't be surprised if you break into crying spells for seemingly no reason. Or, even laugh at something that's not that funny. These are normal mood swings when you're having a baby. All your hormones will return to normal once your daughter is born."

"But, what if I lose my temper again, and I try to pulse, and I—"

"Jess, it won't happen again," Ben jumped in.

"How do you know that?"

"Well, I'm not going to do anything else to make you mad."

"I'm sorry, Ben, that I freaked out like that. I just wish you had told me about the Luci."

"You've decided to take Luci?" Grace said, raising her eyebrows. He nodded at her.

"But, I won't do it, Jess. Not if it's this upsetting to you."

"Ben, I don't want to be that kind of wife," Jess said. "I don't want to cut your balls off. If it's important to you, I guess I can try to understand."

"Jess, nothing is so important to me, I would risk my happiness with you. I would never want to do anything that hurts or upsets you. It has nothing to do with my balls." Ben laughed, shaking his head.

"You know what I mean," Jess said, sounding annoyed, but she also laughed. Then she looked at Ben in all seriousness. "You once told me you could only wish you had an ability like mine. That you weren't special. I almost forgot you said that. You said you wished you could do what I can do."

"I was stupid when I said that, Jess. I was a different person then."

"But you were right. Back then you could only wish. Now, by some strange twist of fate, you can have what you wanted."

"I want you, Jess."

"You have me," she said. "And I know you're special, Ben. But I need you to know it, too. I want you to know how wonderful you are. You said there were other scientists, other geniuses even. That you were nothing special. And now, you're on board a ship, built by an alien race that knows more than you could probably ever hope to understand, am I right?"

Ben nodded, reluctantly.

"This is your chance, Ben. This is your chance to be able to do something that no one else can do. You deserve that chance."

"Jess," Ben shook his head.

"No, it's okay, Ben. I want you to find out what's inside you. What amazing thing you can do. I think you need it, maybe, and don't even know it."

Ben looked at Jess and felt so much love, he knew he needed nothing else but her. He wanted to tell her so, and he opened his mouth to say it, but she shut him up with her hand over his mouth.

"Shut up, Ben." She slowly lowered her hand. He finally spoke, softly.

"I can't believe you're now the one actually attempting to talk me into doing this," he said, smiling at her. "What if this decision you're making is your hormones talking, huh?"

"Do you want to be in trouble again?"

"No," he said, and quickly shut up.

"Ben?" Grace called from the meds cabinet. She held a cup of what looked to be water. He could only assume she'd already laced the liquid with a dose of Luci. She looked at him, questioning.

He looked at Jess, and she breathed out deeply, nodding. He squeezed her hand and walked over to Grace, taking the cup.

"You should already know what to expect, symptom-wise," Grace said, and Ben nodded. He took the cup. She smiled at him, looking supportive. He nodded again, then walked back to Jess laying on the table. She sat up. He stood in front of her, holding the cup. He looked at her, questioning. She nodded at him again and smiled. He leaned his forehead against hers, shutting his eyes tight.

"I love you, Jess."

She said nothing. She was too emotional to speak. She nodded at him one last time. Ben looked Jess in the eyes and smiled. Then he quickly swallowed the entire contents of the cup in one large gulp, breathing out in anxious relief.

"I think you two should go back to your room, now," Grace said. "Lie down, get some rest. Ben, if you need to see me for any reason, I'll be here, or in my room. The same goes for you, Jess. But remember, everything looks perfectly fine right now."

Ben and Jess headed back to their quarters. As they entered the common room, everyone looked up, wondering.

"I'm going to tell them, okay?" Jess looked at Ben, and he nodded. He went in the room to lie down.

Jess walked up to everyone, looking at the floor. She felt embarrassed and ashamed.

"I'm sorry, for scaring everyone. I just… I'm having trouble right now, controlling my emotions. It's no excuse, but Grace said my hormone levels are off the charts."

"Hey, kiddo, it's okay," Hanley said. "Is the baby okay?"

Jess nodded. "But Ben took Luci, just now. I'm going to go be with him. Make sure he's okay. I'm sorry," she breathed again, then quickly turned and went into her room.

***

Ben lay in bed, and Jess came over and laid with him, hugging him tightly, her head on his chest. He put his arms around her.

"How do you feel?"

"Fine," he said. "It's only been a few minutes. I shouldn't feel anything for a bit longer. Maybe as much as another half-hour."

"Are you hungry? I can get you a smoothie."

"No, I'm fine," he said. Then he blinked and looked at her.

"I just realized, we haven't been keeping track of your calories, and we've been here for over two weeks."

"I'm fine, Ben. I'm not pulsing, so I don't need more calories, remember?"

"But, I should have at least thought about it."

"Not with everything that happened the first few days after we got here. Dealing with Jesus, and Lucia, and the funerals. I'm okay, Ben."

"I'm going to take better care of you from here on out," he said, looking at her, sadness in his eyes. "I shouldn't have done this. I should be focusing all my attention on you, on the baby. Instead, you're asking me if I'm okay."

"We take care of each other, Ben. Okay? That's how marriage works."

"Are you still going to marry me? I thought we might be on the rocks, earlier tonight."

"I'm about to have your baby," Jess chided. "We'd better not be on the rocks. You're stuck with me, you know."

"I know, and you have no idea how happy that makes me."

He kissed her passionately. She kissed him back, then looked at him suspiciously.

"Are you sure you're feeling okay?"

"Yeah, fine," he said, sounding a bit dazed. "Good."

"Are you dizzy?" She frowned.

He thought about it. Then nodded. Then he huffed, a giddy little laugh, and Jess laughed with him.

"You're drunk!"

He laughed harder.

"You are so out of it," she said, suddenly looking sad. "It's starting."

He looked at her, growing nervous. He kissed her again, and she could tell what he was trying to do.

"You wanna make out right now?" she asked, incredulous.

"Why, do you?" he asked, sounding hopeful.

"Uh, I guess so," she said. And they did. Then they fell asleep, and when Ben woke up in the morning, he found he had a whole new outlook on everything.

***

Ben didn't need to find a trigger for his ability. It simply manifested itself, immediately, the moment he opened his eyes. Jess lay sleeping quietly by his side. At first, it didn't register on him that something unusual had happened. He felt so groggy from his slumber, he sat up, blinking for several moments. Then he looked around, blinking repeatedly, taking in what he saw.

Their bedroom was small, the walls gray metal, with lights implanted in the floors and high ceiling, emanating a dull, comforting light. Like the panels on the doors, there were panels on the walls to control the lights. They'd left them on when they fell asleep after making love the night before, Ben realized, for as he sat up, he could see everything, he realized—everything and *more*. He looked at the lights in wonder, for they emitted an incandescent glow that appeared every color in the spectrum. Wave after wave of rainbow-colored light floated from the lights in little waves that spread, as if floating on the surface of water. It was the most beautiful thing Ben had ever seen.

He looked at the doorknob of their bedroom, for it moved, and Ben could see tiny silver lines spreading from it, in small arcs. He frowned. Then the handle turned, and Sarah came bounding in. Ben marveled at her steps, for the same, tiny silver lines arced all around her feet. He looked at Sarah's face, beaming bright and wide.

"Hey, kiddo." He smiled, then laughed as he saw watery lines emanating from his own mouth.

"Uncle M.," Sarah breathed. "I knew you were awake."

The same silvery threads issued from her mouth, but even more so, from her throat, floating off her skin, drifting away.

"Huh," Ben said, looking at Sarah in wonder.

"What's wrong Uncle M.?" Sarah frowned, and Ben immediately decided to tell her the truth.

"Remember when I gave you Luci to drink, and then you developed your powers?" He looked at her, and she nodded.

"Well, last night, I took Luci."

"And now you have a power?" Sarah looked excited.

"Yes, I think I do," Ben said, sounding amused.

He stood up, walking around, marveling at the sound waves emanating from his own footfalls. Jess sat up, rubbing her eyes, and watched Ben walk around in circles, slowly. She looked at Sarah, and they both shrugged, watching Ben continue circling. He laughed.

"Ben?" Jess frowned.

He looked at her, eyes shining. He smiled a goofy, dreamy grin. Then he walked out of the room, and Jess quickly got out of bed to follow.

Ben walked into the common room, Jess and Sarah following behind, hanging back several feet, holding hands. Martin came out with Eileen, and they both followed Jess and Sarah.

Ben walked down the hallway, looking at everything. He seemed very taken by the lights. He entered the dining area and went over to the smoothie faucet, filling a cup and laughing. He turned and looked at Ezra and Roslyn, who sat at a table. He smiled at them. Then his face grew wide with excitement. He quickly left the dining area, and Ezra and Roslyn followed as well. No one said a word.

He entered the library next, and everyone crowded around the door's entrance, for everyone instinctively gave Ben plenty of space. Jess and Sarah looked at each other again.

Out in the hallway, Arnold and Jenny came around the corner and saw the crowd gathered in the library doorway. He looked at Jenny, shrugging. "What now?" They went to the crowd, standing on their tiptoes, trying to see inside.

"What's going on?" Arnold said, craning his neck to see.

"Don't know," Ezra said. "Ben's being weird."

"Oh, yeah. Like that's anything new," Arnold snorted. Jenny slapped his arm.

"What? After what happened yesterday? Am I wrong?"

"I can see it," Ben said, pointing to the monitor he'd turned on. "I can see it!"

"See what, Ben?" Jess asked.

"You see?" Arnold teased. "Total weirdo."

Ben rushed up to everyone, silently beckoning them to move out of his way. Everyone parted, and Ben walked through. A large crowd now following him. He went back into the common room, looking around. Then he looked at Jess, his eyes narrowing.

"I wonder...?" he said, quickly going back into their room. This time, only Jess and Sarah followed.

Inside, Ben went into the bedroom, and closed the door, after Jess and Sarah entered. He went to the panel on the wall and touched it. The light dimmed. He touched it again, plunging the three of them into total darkness. Ben laughed heartily.

"Ben," Jess said, sounding concerned, afraid he might be cracking.

"Jess, I can see you."

"What?"

"I can see you. Plain as day."

"It's pitch-black in here, Ben. How could you possibly see anything?"

The room flooded with light again, as Ben touched the panel. He looked at Jess, smiling. He rushed over and hugged her.

"Ben, what is it?"

"Something wonderful," he said, pulling away. He looked down at Sarah, who smiled.

"See?" she said. "It's not something bad."

"Huh?" Jess frowned.

"She's right," Ben nodded. "I was worried, when my ability manifested itself, it would be something destructive. Something hurtful."

"Like my ability," Jess said, sounding hurt.

"No, Jess, that's not what I meant. I only meant, your ability is important. We need it, according to Martin and Hanley, and the Graylings."

Jess frowned.

"What you can do is amazing, Jess. It's just, we don't need another force that strong. I was afraid I might wake up today, blowing things up."

"And?"

"It's beautiful," he said. "I can see everything."

"What do you mean?"

"I don't know, I'm guessing. My ability seems to allow me to see everything, as far as I can tell. I think I'm seeing the entire electromagnetic spectrum. Things that are normally invisible to the naked eye."

"Like what?"

"Like sounds, sound waves," Ben said. "I can even see the ultraviolet rays emitted by the lights. It's fantastic."

"So, what does that mean? I'm confused."

"If I can see the entire electromagnetic spectrum, I should be able to see *everything*," Ben said. "Various ranges of energy; radio waves, radar, infrared, visible light, ultraviolet, power waves, x-rays, gamma rays; even cosmic rays. Anything that travels using energy, including sound."

"So, you can see energy?" Jess said, trying to understand.

"Yeah, basically. Yes. That seems to be what I'm experiencing right now."

"But, you're not upset?"

"No, I'm ecstatic!"

"You're not using a trigger. I thought it took a trigger?"

"Your power needed a trigger, Jess. It initially took incredible amounts of anger, for you to begin storing the energy it takes for you to manipulate gravitational force fields. Your ability is all about anger. Mine, it's peaceful. Like Arnold. Like Martin. Martin never needed a trigger. His ability was simply, just, there. He can't turn it off. He always hears people's thoughts. Just like Arnold can't help but always hear everything. They can try and train themselves to turn it off, or maybe, tune it out, but they're stuck with it."

"Wait, are you saying that you're stuck just seeing things? You can't choose to stop?"

"I don't know," Ben said, looking at Jess in concern. "Why?"

"So, everything just looks different to you? Like, everything around you?"

"It's beautiful, Jess. I don't mind," Ben said, sounding gentle.

"But," she said, looking at him in fear. "Do I look different?"

"No," Ben said, suddenly understanding her fear. "You look the same."

"Really?"

"Yes," he said. He looked down at Sarah, smiling.

"And you, too," he said. Sarah smiled, nodding.

"Except in the dark. In the dark, you glow. I can see the heat energy emitting from your body. Then you look... like an ember. Again, it's simply beautiful. The only difference with people in regular light is that I can see your words. The sound waves of energy, issuing from your mouths and vibrating off your vocal cords."

"Wait, you can see things coming out of my mouth?"

"Honey," Ben said, taking her face in his hands. "Sound waves. It's wonderful."

"What does it look like?" She still looked fearful.

"Like," Ben thought hard, trying to find the words to describe it. "Like little wisps of silver, shining through the air. Thin bits of translucent thread, like the outer edges of water, ringed by silver light, spreading out in circles, drifting on currents of space. It makes me think of a song."

"What song?"

"Silver Bells," Ben said, laughing. "Like little silver bells of sound. Only the sound, I can see it. Like wave after wave of energy, falling from your lips."

"That's what you see?" Jess had tears in her eyes. He nodded, looking at her lovingly.

"I see beauty," he said. "It's wonderful, Jess."

"It's good," Sarah said, looking up at them.

"Jess, you knew this was going to happen. We both did. You knew I would develop an ability."

"I know," she said, breathing out slowly. "I just didn't know it would change how you *see*... everything."

"Not everything," Ben said. "It only enhances what I see, it doesn't change *me*. It doesn't change how I *feel*."

She nodded, looking deep into his eyes. "And you're happy? You're okay with your power?"

"Thrilled," he said. "Are you?"

She nodded, smiling, and hugged him. Sarah left the room, allowing them to be alone. She went out into the common room, where everyone stood waiting.

"Well?" Arnold said. "What's going on?"

"Nothing," Sarah said. "Uncle M. just got his ability, that's all."

"I know that," he said, smiling at her. "What is it?"

Sarah looked at Martin, and everyone's eyes went to him.

"What is it, Martin?" Arnold asked.

"It's not my place to say, really."

"Like that ever stopped you before," Hanley said, coming out of his room. "What's going on?"

"Ben got his ability," everyone said.

"Ooh, what is it?" Hanley said.

Everyone looked at Martin again. He sighed.

"Fine," he said. He looked at Sarah, who nodded her consent.

"He can see energy. Like... all energy."

"Could you... clarify that?" Arnold said, looking confused.

"Anything that gives off energy, he can see. Sound waves, microwaves, electromagnetic waves, ultraviolet light, heat. Everything."

"Dang it!" Arnold yelled. Everyone looked at him, a few people jumped. He blushed. "I got the sucky ability. His might actually be useful."

"Your ability isn't useless, Arnie," Jenny said, rubbing his back.

"Yeah, well, it can't exactly help save the Graylings, now can it," he said, standing and turning to walk away. Jenny smiled, looking apologetic, and quickly went after Arnold.

"Cool," Hanley said, smiling. "The saga continues."

13

Two weeks earlier, Jenny had gone back into her room after her walk with Arnold, the evening after the funerals, and sat down on the couch, looking dazed and happy, much the same as Arnold had done, in the common room. While he and Ezra were having their heart-to-heart talk about Roslyn and Jenny, she and Malcolm were doing the same. Malcolm came out of his room when he heard Jenny return from her walk. He knew she'd been out with Arnold. He could also tell, had known since before the funerals, that Jenny and Arnold would end up together. He felt happy for her.

He sat down next to her on the couch, took in her goofy, glassy-eyed stare, and laughed. She looked at him, dazed.

"That is exactly how I felt, the day I met your mother," he said.

Jenny looked sad then. Her mother had died of cancer, five years earlier. She felt bad for her father.

"What do you think mom would have thought about all this?" Jenny asked. "Would she have come with us?"

"In a heartbeat," Malcolm said.

"She would have gone with *you*. I'm not blood."

"How many times do we need to go over this, Jen?" Malcolm said, sounding gentle, but firm. "Blood doesn't guarantee love. That has nothing to do with it. Your mother loved you just as much as she ever could have. You were her daughter, Jenny. She loved you more than life itself. Why do you always fixate on biology?"

"I don't know. It's stupid, I guess."

"I love you, honey, you know that?"

She nodded. He gazed at her endearingly. "Besides, you and I share a gene that Ben says is so rare, the chances of adopting a child who has it should be *astronomical*, as he described it."

"So?"

"So," Malcolm said. "Maybe it wasn't an accident, that your mom and I got you."

"You believe in fate?"

"I believe… there are no coincidences," Malcolm said. "Including the fact that we came on board an alien ship with only six people, three of them male, and one of them, you now happen to be madly in love with."

He looked at her, his eyebrows raised. She looked at him, embarrassed.

"Daddy!"

"Am I wrong?"

She shook her head slowly, thinking about it. "You think it's meant to be?"

"I think your mom and I were meant to be," Malcolm said, sounding thoughtful. "And I had a whole city to choose from. You don't have that."

"So, you think I'm just taking whatever I can get?"

"No, let me finish. I think it doesn't matter whether you have an entire planet of choices, or one. You can't make love happen, just because there's only one person in front of you. You either love someone, or you don't. You can't fake it, and you can't mistake it. So... Are you in love?"

She looked at him, frowning. "Hopelessly."

He nodded. "And since I don't believe in coincidences... Maybe, just maybe, this is exactly where we were meant to be."

"I love you, Daddy."

"I know. But you're all grown up now, sweetheart. And at some point, you can't live here with me."

"Then where am I supposed to live?"

He looked at her, delivering an 'as-if-you-didn't-already-know' look, his eyebrows raised.

"Daddy, I only kissed him for the first time tonight!"

"My mother and father got married after only one week," Malcolm said. "They were happily married for over forty years."

"You want me to *marry* Arnold?"

"I want you to do whatever makes you happy, sweetie."

"Arnold makes me happy," she breathed.

"Then simply follow your heart."

"But, I don't want to move things too fast."

"Why?"

"I-I don't know." She frowned.

"If you both feel the same way, how can anything be too fast?"

"I'm not sure."

"You think he's just playing around?"

"No." She frowned again. "I think he feels the same way I do."

"How do you know?"

"I don't know, I just do," she said, shrugging.

"So, what's too fast?"

She looked at him, her face coloring, her eyebrows raised in her own 'as-if-you-didn't-already-know' look. He suddenly got it, looking away.

"Oh," he said. "Well, the more reason for us not to live together."

"When?" She looked at him, sadness in her eyes.

"When you're ready. And I suspect you already are, and just don't know it yet."

"I don't want to lose you, Daddy," Jenny said, crying.

"Honey, at best, I'll only be a few doors down. And I have to let you grow up. You're twenty-seven-years old. It's time I let you go."

"I'll always love you, Daddy."

"I know," he said, looking at her with great love. "You see? Nothing to do with biology."

She gave him the largest bear hug ever. He squeezed back, closing his eyes tight. She pulled away and looked at him.

"So, this was our '*Pretty in Pink*' talk?"

"Our what?" he laughed, smiling at her.

"Nothing, Daddy. Goodnight."

***

The next day, Jenny set out to find Arnold. She no longer felt afraid. She knew how she felt, and she was not shy, like Roslyn. She found Arnold quickly, in the library, after breakfast. He sat at a monitor, chin in his hands, reading about the Korean War. She smiled, knowing Arnold liked to learn. He had told her he was bad at math and science, but his voracious appetite for knowledge was one of the things she'd loved about him immediately.

She sat down in the chair next to him, and he looked over at her shyly. She could tell he felt nervous about upsetting her. She felt bad, remembering how he'd looked the night before, when she pulled away. She had seen longing in his face—an incredible intensity—and it overwhelmed her. He was aggressive in his feelings for her, and she knew the moment she let go, gave in to her own feelings, their relationship would be unstoppable. Already, she could tell (and had imagined) that he would make an energetic lover. She'd never been with a man before, but the thought no longer frightened her. She felt excited by it. She suddenly realized she could hardly wait.

She looked at him, feeling nothing but love, but underneath that, an incredible fire burned. She felt surprised by it, hadn't really explored that part of herself, but she knew she wanted to explore it with Arnold. Him, and no one else. She surprised herself by what she blurted out.

"I want to make love with you," she said, her eyes suddenly going wide. *Did I really just say that?*

Arnold stared at her, in complete shock. His heart rate doubled in sheer moments. He took in a sudden, shallow breath, then frowned.

"I'm sorry," she said, standing to leave.

Arnold's feet moved, even if his brain still sat at the monitor. He gently grabbed her shoulders, quickly stepped in front of her body, to stop her movements. He took her face in his hands and kissed her passionately, and she fell into his arms.

Luckily, no one came into the library while they were occupied with their activities, because the two of them were so overcome by their desires, they never left the room, but fell to the floor and made love immediately.

Afterwards, Arnold held Jenny in his arms, stroking her hair, as they lay on the floor. He looked completely mystified. He felt more in love than he could have ever hoped to be. He smiled.

"What," she said, looking at him, for he let out a sigh.

"The Graylings."

"What about them?"

"Nothing. Just that, I don't think it's an accident that you and I ended up on this ship together, is all."

She looked at him, considering. "No one can make love happen," she said, repeating her father's words.

"No, but they have a way of knowing things. They know where to put pieces, place things in the right order."

"I don't get it." She frowned.

He looked at her in complete seriousness. "Would you like to?"

"What do you mean?"

"Would you like to meet them, Jenny?"

"You love them, don't you?" She searched his eyes, deep in thought.

"Yes," he said, "I do."

"Then, yes," she said, not faltering.

"Don't you want to think about it a bit?"

"No," she said, standing and putting her hand out to help him up.

The two of them walked, hand in hand, smiling crazily, down the hall. They went straight to Ezra's room. He answered his door, frowning at the two of them. He stared for several moments, then rolled his eyes, stepping aside to allow them in.

"Ez, you in the mood to hook someone up?"

Ezra stared at Arnold for a moment, his eyes slowly moving to Jenny. She nodded. He smiled then, looking incredibly happy, for using his ability did this. It was, after all, his purpose, and he never questioned it.

He sat Jenny down on his couch and explained everything to her, much the same as he had for Martin. The only difference was that Jenny's partner had already channeled into the Graylings and was completely supportive. She looked up at Arnold, and he smiled at her, tears in his eyes. She looked at Ezra and nodded when he asked if she was ready.

He channeled her in, and suddenly, Jenny *knew* the Graylings. Arnold looked on, crying. He understood what she went through. It was what he had gone through, two years before. When everything was over, Jenny stood and walked over to Arnold, embracing him tightly. She now understood him in a way she simply couldn't have before.

They moved in together that afternoon. Rafferty moved out, for he'd been rooming with Arnold, and he simply exchanged places with Jenny, moving in with Malcolm.

That was simply how Arnold and Jenny became a couple. No one questioned it, for they were clearly in love. They went everywhere together from that day forward, always holding hands.

This was also how Malcolm and Rafferty became roommates. Although, Malcolm would soon learn, same as Arnold had, that Rafferty didn't really live in the quarters in the common room at all—mostly, he slept in the cargo bay—where he spent most of his time working on machines and gadgets. No one really saw Rafferty much, save for at mealtimes, mostly dinner. Otherwise, Rafferty was a ghost.

***

The wedding of Ben and Jess was simply beautiful. They got married in the garden, and everyone watched. Hanley officiated. Ben asked Rafferty if he could make rings, and he brought the most exquisite-looking, titanium rings to the room the very next day.

They were married exactly one week after Ben discovered he could see energy. He adjusted to his new ability quickly. It simply became second nature to him. To Jess's great relief, it didn't seem to change Ben at all. Within twenty-four hours of gaining his ability, the only thing they talked about was planning their wedding.

They did not wear anything special, merely the same gray clothing as always, but Jess wore a ring of colored flowers on her head, which Roslyn strung together.

Everyone stood, no chairs were brought in. Jess felt nervous about having to 'perform,' and told Ben the last thing she wanted was a long, drawn-out scene with she and Ben centerstage. He reminded her that this was the whole point of a wedding, and she sighed.

She wanted a short ceremony. He agreed, because he loved her. All he wanted was for everyone to witness it. Whether they said long vows, or short, did not matter to him. He just wanted to profess his love, and his intentions to spend the rest of his life with her, in front of all his friends. The Society was Ben's family, and he had grown to love all of them as if they were his brothers and sisters. Even the old-boarders, whom he had known for a much shorter time, were held in the fondest of his thoughts.

In the end, Hanley asked Jess if she loved Ben. She said yes. He asked Ben if he loved Jess, and Ben, of course, said yes.

"Do you want to spend the rest of your life with him?" Hanley asked Jess.

"Yes," she breathed, smiling up at Ben.

"Ben, do you want to spend the rest of your life with Jess?"

"Yes," he said, "I do."

"Then," Hanley said, shrugging. "By the power invested in me, whatever that means, I now pronounce you man and wife."

"What about the rings?" Earl said.

"Shit! I forgot."

"You can't say 'shit,' at a wedding, Hanley," Aaron scoffed.

"Sorry," Hanley said, sighing. "Who's got the rings?"

Martin stepped forward, taking a ring from his pocket, and Alma came forward also. Jess had asked her to hold her ring, and Alma agreed, eagerly. She looked better now, Jess found, much to her relief. She asked Alma to hold her ring, in hopes it would be a welcome distraction from her grief, and it seemed to be working.

Martin gave his ring to Ben, and he placed it on Jess's wedding finger. Jess took the ring from Alma, who smiled with tears in her eyes.

Jess put her ring on Ben's finger, and the two of them held each other's hands, smiling crazily. All Jess's stage fright had dissipated now, and she only had eyes for Ben.

"Okay... *Now* I pronounce you man and wife. You may kiss the bride."

Ben bent down and gently kissed Jess. Everyone in the audience sighed, even most of the men. Arnold and Jenny held hands, as did Ezra and Roslyn.

There was a grand feast in the dining hall, as the wedding took place less than an hour before the normally appointed dinner time of six o'clock. Everyone shuffled out of the garden and into the dining hall, where Jemma had outdone herself with two large, roasted turkeys, stuffing, roasted and mashed potatoes, steamed veggies, garlic brown rice, roasted ears of corn, flatbread and wheat dinner rolls, wine and grape juice.

She sat next to Rafferty during the meal, as she did every night, and as usual, he didn't take much notice, their conversation kept to a bare minimum, he quickly disappearing back into the cargo bay upon completion of his plate.

Martin heard poor Jemma's thoughts, however. She'd gone all out on the wedding feast, imagining that the meal following her *own* wedding (to Rafferty, of course) would be just as glorious.

***

Over the next two weeks, there were two more weddings, as Arnold and Jenny followed suit, then Ezra and Roslyn. A month after Jess and Ben were married, Rachel and Hanley also wed. So, everyone was together, except a small handful of people.

Kate and Alma never got married, but there was no question that they were together. Aaron and Earl were not dating anyone. Earl had looked at Grace, concluding there was nothing between them. Grace seemed nice enough, but she was fourteen years older than him, and he simply wasn't interested in her that way, nor she, in him. So, that was that. The couples were together, and those who were with no one, seemed not to mind at all, except for Jemma. She was still in love with Rafferty, and hopelessly helpless to do anything about it.

Martin grew tired of listening to it, and talked to Arnold about it, since they had roomed together for two years. Arnold laughed.

"Dude, you've probably talked more to Rafferty than I ever have." He eyed Martin. "I heard he actually gave whole speeches on that transport ship." He shook his head. "Y'all witnessed a minor miracle that night, you just don't know."

Martin laughed. Still, he implored Arnold to do something to tip Rafferty off, because, as he informed Arnold from listening to his thoughts, "Rafferty is completely oblivious. Worse than Ezra, which I didn't think was even possible, but... Rafferty has machines on the brain, 24-7. He even dreams about them."

He eyed Arnold, nodding, looking serious. Arnold sighed, shaking his head.

"Look, man. He'll probably be most receptive to hearing it from you. And, seriously, whether he knows it or not, he needs this thing with Jemma just as badly as she wants it with him. He needs to come out of that cargo bay. He ain't all there."

Martin swirled his finger around his head. "He's got Grayling on the brain, and he thinks he can handle it, but he needs some human contact."

"What?"

"Nothing," Martin said quickly. "Just... trust me on this one, okay? Go talk to Rafferty. I can't take much more of Jemma's pining thoughts. It's driving me nuts."

***

Arnold followed Martin's advice, taking matters into his own hands a month after he married Jenny. He went to see Rafferty one afternoon, in the cargo bay. This was where Rafferty spent most of his time, working on various gadgets and machinery, including the transport ship. Not to mention, he also spent a fair amount of time on the upper decks, studying the propulsion systems of the ship with the Graylings' engineers.

Rafferty was in the cargo bay, not upstairs, however, on the afternoon Arnold went to see him. He couldn't be certain, but it looked as if Rafferty scanned some sort of motor on a table with a hand-held device. He looked up at Arnold as he approached, nodding.

"Whatcha doin'?" Arnold asked, friendly enough.

"Solving a problem for Grace," Rafferty said.

"What problem?"

"I'm modifying the ultrasonic frequencies on her console to provide enhanced resolution of DNA samples for her imaging system."

"Okay, then," Arnold said.

"What do you need?"

"Well," Arnold sighed, feeling nervous. He suddenly had no idea what to say.

Rafferty looked at Arnold, clearly annoyed. "Is something broken?"

Rafferty liked to fix things, utterly consumed by this need, in fact. Jemma tended the garden, growing plants and liked to cook. Rafferty built machines. The two simply lived in different worlds. Arnold wasn't certain exactly what it was about Rafferty that Jemma liked so much. He thought it might be the simple fact that Rafferty was so aloof, which made him most alluring to her.

Rafferty was okay with people, when he had to be. He needed to be while flying the transport ship on the night of rescuing The Society. But in that case, he was the only human on board who understood the Graylings' machinery well enough to pilot the ship. Partly, the reason he'd been so good with everyone that night was because Rafferty needed to be sympathetic with everyone, for the sake of the Graylings.

Other than that night, Rafferty didn't socialize with people all that much. He could communicate with Hanley, and the two conversed, but not often, and always about the Graylings.

Arnold stared at Rafferty now, no idea how to proceed. He suddenly realized why Jemma struggled so poorly with how to approach the gearhead. Arnold wasn't even emotionally invested in the subject, yet, here he stood, struggling, suddenly extremely nervous and fidgety, sweating lightly. He laughed.

"My, how things look different when you step into someone else's shoes." He laughed even harder, for he no longer felt annoyed with Jemma, only sympathetic.

"Is something broken," Rafferty repeated, sounding more annoyed.

"Um, gosh." Arnold shook his head. "And I told Ezra he was bad with people. Now he's married!" Arnold bellowed nervous laughter, crossing his arms over his chest, nodding at Rafferty.

"So... nothing's broken," Rafferty concluded, turning his attention back to his gadgets.

"Actually," Arnold said, getting an idea. "Something is."

"What?" Rafferty now looked concerned.

"Jemma."

"Jemma?"

"Jemma's broken." Arnold nodded.

"How can Jemma be broken?" Rafferty squinted at Arnold. Then his eyes grew wide and concerned.

"Is she hurt?! Is she in the infirmary?" Rafferty immediately headed around the table, towards the door, but Arnold jumped in front, stopping him.

"She's not in the infirmary." Arnold sighed. "But, there is something wrong with her. *Definitely...* something wrong with her," he mumbled, backing up, eyeing Rafferty up and down.

"What? What's wrong?"

"Do you care?" Arnold eyed him, getting excited.

"What? Of course, I care, why wouldn't I?"

"Would you care as much if it were me? Or Roslyn? Or Grace?"

"What are you talking about, are they hurt, too?"

"No, just Jemma."

"Well, what? What's wrong with her?"

"She has a broken heart."

"A broken heart?" Rafferty looked confused all over again.

"Yeah. This guy, he hurt her really bad."

"Who?" Rafferty squinted, looking angry now. "What guy."

"This guy on the ship."

"Well, obviously. Who is it? Aaron? Did Aaron do something to her?"

"I—I don't," Arnold stammered, trying to figure out what to say next. "If you could do something to fix it, would you?"

"Sure, I'll kick his ass," Rafferty said, starting around Arnold, who jumped in his path again.

"Stop, okay? Just stop, Rafferty. Kicking someone's ass won't help Jemma, now will it?"

Rafferty stared at Arnold, not comprehending.

"Jemma's heart will still be broken, whether you kick Aaron's ass or not. And besides, it's not Aaron."

"It's not?"

"No."

"Then, who?"

"You."

"Me?" Rafferty looked at Arnold, completely confused. "I didn't do anything to Jemma."

"Exactly. And she's been hoping you would, for a very long time. Trust me."

"What…" Rafferty trailed off, thinking. Then he looked at Arnold in disbelief. "But—"

"No but's. She's been waiting for you to notice her for years."

"Years?" Rafferty's expression still looked completely confused. He shook his head. "No."

"Yes."

"How do you know?"

"Because it's all she talks about it. Trust me, dude. I couldn't make this junk up, even if I tried."

"But, years?" Rafferty looked completely miffed.

"Yep," Arnold sighed. "And now I know why. You are *impossible* to talk to."

"No, I'm not."

"Yeah, you are," Arnold sighed again. "Look, the bottom line here is, Jemma is hopelessly in love with you, okay?"

"Hopelessly in love?" Rafferty repeated.

"Yeah."

"In love?!" Rafferty yelled.

"Yeah," Arnold sighed yet again. "And I'm sick of seeing her walk around here, sighing, looking sad. And Martin's tired of hearing it inside his head. And everyone else is tired of watching her sit next to you at breakfast, lunch, and dinner, hoping you'll give her the slightest little hint. The tiniest glance her way, and you just sit there… doing nothing. The woman's a goddess, okay? I know. I pined away after her for years, and I never even stood a chance. Know why?"

Rafferty shook his head.

"Idiot!" Arnold yelled.

"But, you and Jenny…"

"Yeah, I got real lucky there," Arnold said. "Turns out I never really loved Jemma. She's beautiful, don't get me wrong, but Jenny? She's my *Queen*—the most beautiful woman I've ever seen. So, I'm happy. But

Jemma's still my friend. And Jemma is suffering. I'm happy, and I want her to be happy, too. And the only thing that will make her happy? Is you."

"Me?" Rafferty squeaked, his voice now high with shock and surprise.

"Yeah. She's *broken* Rafferty. If I can explain things in terms you might understand. She's a broken machine. And you're the missing part that will make her work again. Get it?"

Rafferty thought about this, and after several moments, dawning comprehension spread across his face.

"Good for you," Arnold said, relieved.

"Are you sure?"

"I'm positive."

Rafferty brushed past Arnold, quickly heading for Jemma's room. Arnold opened his mouth to cheer him on, but Rafferty had already exited the cargo bay.

"Okay," Arnold said. "Guess that went well. My work is done."

***

Rafferty went to Jemma's room and knocked, waiting for several minutes, fidgeting. Then, he quickly left and headed straight for the garden. Those who sat in the common room at the time merely looked on momentarily, before going back to their conversations. A table now stood in the middle of the room, and it was commonplace for Hanley to be out there with several decks of cards, ready to start a game with anyone interested. He contained a plethora of knowledge on various card games, looking up and learning several new ones in the library.

Rafferty wandered quickly through the garden, treading the dirt path on its twisting, elliptical trail, until he found Jemma. He came upon her suddenly, tending to some delicate fronds in the middle of the left side of the garden. Her back faced him, she did not hear him approach. He simply stood, looking at her, growing nervous. He quietly watched her work in wonder.

Jemma reached her hand out, lightly touching a fern with only the very tips of her fingers. Rafferty watched in awe as the delicate, lace-like ends of the fern turned from dark green to a lighter, more vibrant shade. The color slowly traveled from the tips of the thin nettles, down to the stem, spreading to the stalk, then slowly spidered outward to the rest of the canopied leaves, until the entire plant transformed to a bright, healthy green—thriving. Jemma had brought its health back up, Rafferty saw; keeping it alive. He had no idea how she did it, he only knew it was her ability, her gift, and he felt amazed. He had never seen her use her ability before. He felt ashamed. He had always been so caught up in his own work, he never bothered truly looking around, at anyone. He certainly never looked at, or truly saw Jemma until that very moment, despite sharing thousands of meals with her, and his heart ached with a deep longing that took him by surprise. He knew he loved her.

Jemma worked for several minutes, never knowing Rafferty stood behind her. Then she stood up, backing away from her fronds, as Rafferty watched, unmoving, gazing in awe. She backed into him, quickly turning, startled, and stared at Rafferty, who gazed back, smiling.

"Oh," was all she said.

He frowned next, not knowing what to say. She looked up at him, blushing, as she always did, but this time, he saw. Her cheeks bloomed with color, and he knew what Arnold told him was the truth. He had no idea what to do. He continued frowning at her, and she looked disappointed, thinking he wouldn't do or say anything, as normal. She, herself, did not have the courage to do anything. Despite her feelings, she was, in fact, the shyest female on the ship, at least, when it came to Rafferty. She could talk to Arnold for hours, about almost anything, and Ezra as well. When it came to Rafferty, however, even Jemma's smile felt awkward and painful to her.

What she didn't know, as Rafferty continued staring at her, frowning, was that he simply worked things through in his head. He looked at her for the very first time, attempting to translate her facial expressions into something he could understand. He watched as her slight smile faded, and the light that shone in her eyes became dull. He saw her face fall, and the high color in her cheeks fade, as her disappointment sank in. Simply, in his eyes, he watched as her machinery began to falter. He saw her breaking, and that is exactly what he thought of, watching her expression go from joy to sadness. He saw her face break and knew her heart did the same. Finally, he spoke, and it was Jemma's turn to frown.

"I'm sorry I broke you. I didn't mean to."

She looked at him, completely lost. He never spoke this way, addressing her straight to her face. Now he looked right at her, inches away. They were never alone like this. Her hopes had spiked so high, then fallen so low, and when he said his words, she felt completely and utterly baffled.

Rafferty didn't know what else to say. For several moments, he stared, again translating her expression. He saw that she was confused. He blurted out his words, feeling awkward and uncomfortable.

"I don't know how to fix you. Wh—what do I do?"

"Fix me?"

"Arnold said you have a broken heart," Rafferty said, looking at Jemma with intensity now.

"Oh," Jemma said, her heart flitting lightly. She looked down.

"I want… I want to fix you."

Jemma looked at him, tears in her eyes. "I'm not a machine, Rafferty."

He frowned, looking at the ground. Then he walked away, brushing past her.

"Wait!" Her voice cracked, and he heard it as broken cogs and springs. He spun around again, walking back up to her, desperate to fix things. He grabbed her face in his hands and kissed her, aggressively. She kissed him back.

At first, it felt awkward and jumbled, as their bodies attempted to move together, in different rhythms, out of sync. Rafferty innately picked up on the discrepancies, and quickly adjusted his movements to match Jemma's. The way his mind worked—calculating, reading, putting all the pieces together to create singularly smooth, running machines—was similar, he found, to the act of making love. He read her body's movements, interpreted them, and continued adjusting his own actions to complement hers. Even as he did so, on some level, everything happened so quickly, his actions ran on auto-pilot most of the time.

Jemma fell into Rafferty's world, going along with his movements, reeling at how expertly he seemed to move exactly where she wanted him to. She didn't know he simply read the intricately small messages her body gave off. She only knew that when she wanted him to run his hands down her back, he did, never realizing she made the tiniest adjustments in her own body, that led him to do exactly what she hoped.

Rafferty, it turned out, was an expert lover. Able to turn the entire act of lovemaking into a finely oiled, expertly tuned machine. When they had completed the act, Jemma felt hopelessly lost in love and passion, completely swallowed up. Rafferty was also in love, for he knew he had fixed Jemma, but recognized on some basic level that he needed to remain with her, to keep her from immediately breaking again. He now simply thought of her as *his* and felt overwhelmingly protective of her. She instantly became his most precious machine. It was simply the way he saw the world. It was different than how most others saw things, but it didn't change his emotions. He felt genuine love for Jemma, even if his waking mind continued thinking in terms of cogs and springs, nuts and bolts.

Jemma and Rafferty were together from that day forward. They were married just three days later, and Jemma got her magnificent feast, without having to cook it herself. In the end, however, the meal wasn't important. She only cared that Rafferty was finally *hers*.

14

Roslyn had moved out of Jemma's room as soon as she married Ezra, and Jemma had been living in her room alone for the last month. Rafferty moved in with Malcolm after Jenny took his place in the room he shared with Arnold, and he moved in with Malcolm. Now, Rafferty moved out on Malcolm, and moved in with Jemma. This left poor Malcolm alone again, but happy to see yet another coupling.

Just as all the couplings had taken place, so had something else. Martin was the first of the 'newbies,' to be channeled in with the Graylings. He instantly changed—different—his eyes opened to the incredible task that lay ahead for them all. The moment any of them became connected to the Graylings, they opened to a whole new outlook on things. It simply could not be helped. In an instant, they each plunged into the minds and emotions of an alien race, the beings no longer foreign. Channeling in allowed them direct access to the emotions, experiences, and memories of the Graylings. Every human being that channeled in suddenly found themselves intrinsically linked, with an instant understanding of an entire race, greater than any connection they could have had with their own kind.

For each person, thinking did not occur in terms of *their kind*, and, *our kind*, but rather, as a simple understanding that the Graylings were a race of beings innately peaceful and pacifistic, with hearts full of positivity and honor. The Graylings were incredibly empathic and well-meaning. Anyone that channeled in became instantly aware of their kind nature, and immediately loved them—trust, fondness, awareness, and ambition—all automatically born with a combined drive to help, for the Graylings were powerless to claim their planet back for themselves.

As each new person gained full comprehension, so did they also learn that the Graylings were dying, their bodies linked to the circadian rhythms of their own home planet, and evolved in such a way that now, after over two hundred years away from home, they had become drained of their energy. Their lifespans, Hanley had already explained to most, were significantly shorter, cut easily in half. The few eldest that remained on the ship, alive during the extermination, were now frail and ancient.

Martin had been the first to channel in. Rachel went next. Then Jenny, after she and Arnold were coupled. Hanley tackled Alma and Kate, a month after they came on board, amidst the joy of the new couplings and weddings. Jenny talked to her father, after she channeled in, and Malcolm consented.

By the time Rafferty and Jemma were wed, over half the original members of The Society had channeled in. All six old-boarders already had been, for the last few years and more. Less than two months on board the ship, only five people remained who were not connected: Aaron, Earl, Jess, Ben and Sarah.

Ben knew of all these events, for he, Martin, and Hanley talked about it often. He was apprised of each new person who channeled in, always amazed at how instantly they changed. They became focused on the mission at hand, talking about Hesperia, and the War. They were instantly concerned about the Graylings, and desperately filled with the desire to help save them.

Ben watched all this with growing dread. Not because he felt afraid of channeling into the Graylings himself, but because he knew the challenge still lay ahead, in convincing Jess.

He wanted to wait, he told everyone, until after the baby arrived. He and Jess needed to focus on that, and everyone agreed and understood. It was also decided that Sarah would not channel in. Everyone agreed that eleven years old was too young, and the gruesome visions of the extermination, helplessly streaming into her consciousness would be too much of a burden for Sarah to bear, and that she would need to wait till she turned eighteen. It seemed a random age to choose, they concluded, yet grounded on the lingering culture from their section of Earth, generally interpreted as when adulthood commenced.

***

The Society had been on board the ship for nine weeks, a little over two months. In that space of time, four new couples had formed: Hanley and Rachel; Arnold and Jenny; Ezra and Roslyn; and lastly, Jemma and Rafferty. In the same space of nine weeks, there were also five weddings: Jess and Ben; Rachel and Hanley; Ezra and Roslyn; Arnold and Jenny; and lastly, Jemma and Rafferty.

Jess entered week twenty-three of her pregnancy, with only twelve weeks left to go—now in her third trimester. She'd grown considerably over the last two months, since she first started showing, the day of her disappearing act. Thankfully, she never had another episode. Her emotions spiked, here and there, but she never lost her temper again.

Life on board the ship, for all intents and purposes, went on as usual. The newly formed couples reveled in their feelings for one another. Most of The Society walked around holding hands, hazily staring into each other's eyes. The only people immune to this behavior were the few not coupled with anyone.

No one realized, most so caught up in new relationships, that they'd made incredible adjustments—living on an alien spacecraft. Love carried everyone through, shielding them. Even those not in romantic relationships, became caught up in new friendships, still buoyed through the thickest tangle of emotions and adjustments, always, with the strength of love.

***

Grace observed all the couples, feeling grateful, for she realized how the couplings aided in making the transition from Earth to space travel that much easier. She continued working in the infirmary, furthering her medical knowledge, and occasionally worked with the hybrids, discussing their abilities.

Like Jess, Malcolm could not use his ability while on board the ship. His ability to float relied on a constant, large gravitational mass to manipulate. The manufactured gravity of the ship, and the energy fluctuations emitted made it impossible for Malcolm to float. He did not mind, however, for he had never really used it all that much to begin with, nor had Jenny used her own power too often, and always under duress back in the facility. She still had the ability to blow things up, albeit, objects containing less than ten percent water. Malcolm and Jenny didn't use their abilities on the ship at all. Neither did Hanley, for he had no further reason to melt anything. Rachel never needed to boil anything, so many of the people on board stopped using their abilities the moment they left Earth.

Grace used her ability to purify water. No one realized it was she who provided the ship, and all its inhabitants with usable, drinkable water, except Ben. He spent time in the infirmary with Grace, learning about all the equipment, and he asked about her ability one day, as she looked Ben over, attempting to understand his new ability of enhanced sight. Scanning his eyes with her monitor, he said nothing at first. When he finally asked, she sighed lightheartedly, then launched into explanation.

"The water on board the ship is comprised of compressed hydrogen and oxygen molecules, collapsed into storage containers the size of a car's glove box."

Grace looked at Ben, who simply nodded, saw that he understood, what with his extensive scientific background, so continued.

"I manufacture the chemicals into water molecules, and lastly, I purify the water, in large tanks below us. The rest is simple, Ben. The water travels through a series of pipes, like any building's plumbing infrastructure. The only difference is that the water is one hundred percent pure, no minerals, nor trace amounts of extract, or calcium buildup. No chemicals of any kind, nor organic matter, no dangerous bacteria or microorganisms. The pipes will never rust, and our bodies are never exposed to anything so harmful as a single particulate.

"Everyone on board is in the best health of their entire lives. It's one of the reasons the smoothies taste so good. You'd be surprised what a difference truly clean water makes, Ben. Even your showers get you cleaner than you've ever been in your life. Think about it. Have you used deodorant since coming on board?"

"You're amazing, Grace," he said, smiling at her. "How much water can the tanks hold?"

"At any given time? Over a billion gallons. Or about three-point-eight billion liters."

"You can purify that much water at a time?"

"That's not so much," she said, shrugging. "I could keep clean water running daily, perhaps, for a population of about fifty thousand people."

"That's all?" he joked.

She shook it off, tilting his head back, peering into his eyes for the dozenth time with her retinoscope.

"Amazing," Grace said. "Your pupils dilate differently now, to let in more light. Normally it would blind a person, but with you? It seems to aid your ability to see things."

"Well, I'm just grateful my eyes look the same."

"Why? What do you mean?"

"Are you kidding me?" Ben shook his head. "Suppose my ability had actually changed my eyes. Given me a tapetum lucidum, for example."

Grace laughed. "Now, *that* would be interesting."

"Yeah, and it would have freaked Jess out permanently."

"Well, the biggest change in you, seems to be on a neurological level. While your initial ability lies in the lengthened exposure of light through your crystalline lens, your retina is operating in a fascinating new way. Your retina, Ben, is responsible for capturing all of the light rays, processing them into light impulses through millions of tiny nerve endings, then sending these light impulses through over a million nerve fibers to the optic cord."

"Thank you for that illuminating overview of optic function, doctor," Ben said, sounding sarcastically amused.

"I know, smarty pants," Grace said. "You already know all of this, *Genius* that you are. I also know that you are aware that the optic nerve operates like an extension cord connecting to the brain. It's a bundled cord of more than a million nerve fibers. The light impulses travel through this nerve fiber to the brain, where they are interpreted."

"Yes, I'm aware of all of this," Ben sighed, looking at Grace, waiting for her to finish explaining.

"Well. Your retina seems to be firing at over one hundred times the speed of a normal human eye."

"Okay?" Ben said, looking at Grace, waiting for more.

"Well, first off, as I said, your retina is firing at more than one hundred times the speed of a normal human eye, Ben. Which means, light is traveling from your retina, to your optic nerve, faster than the speed of light."

"How is that even possible? How can light travel faster than light?"

Grace shrugged. "There comes a time, Ben, when even science, or at least, our knowledge of it, fails to explain anything."

"I can't accept that," Ben said, matter-of-factly.

"Well, I'm afraid you're just going to have to," Grace laughed. "You really don't have any other choice in the matter, now, do you?"

Ben shrugged again. "You said first off, so, what's second?"

"The light impulses are traveling faster than possible," Grace sighed. "They are then hitting what now appear to be not just millions of nerve endings on your optic cord, but *billions*. You've grown billions of new nerve endings, Ben."

"Huh." He frowned, shaking his head. *All from a tiny dose of Luci.*

"But none of that would mean anything if the neurons in your brain weren't able to interpret the newly arriving information. The retina is part of the brain that is isolated to serve as a transducer for the conversion of patterns of light into neuronal signals. The lens of the eye focuses light on the photoreceptive cells of the retina, which detect the photons of light and respond by producing neural impulses. These signals are processed in a hierarchical fashion by different parts of the brain, from the retina to the lateral geniculate nucleus, to the primary and secondary visual cortex of the brain. Signals from the retina can also travel directly to the Superior Colliculus. And this, Ben, is where you've changed the most. You've also grown new receptors, and synapses, to capture firing impulses inside the Superior Colliculus. Your brain has changed. It's *grown*. By miniscule amounts, in physical terms. Your brain isn't any larger, but, it is decidedly different. Would you like to look at your neuroscan?"

"Absolutely."

Ben learned to understand his ability, at least, what could be understood, and struggled to let go of what could not be comprehended. In the end, however, he simply resigned himself to the parts he could not understand, by merely feeling grateful he had an ability at all and reveled in constant awe that it contained properties of mystery beyond even his genius intellect.

***

Earl worked with Grace at perfecting his ability, for he hadn't gotten close to completing any kind of training back at the facility on Earth, only able to walk through walls twice in captivity, immediately after taking Luci, but never again after. Grace and Earl, together, worked at finding a trigger. It turned out, anger did not work for Earl. Extreme states of relaxation, however, did. Grace took to inducing this state synthetically, with enzyme injections into his cerebral cortex. Earl started walking through walls all around the ship, generally scaring the heck out of everyone on board. He found it highly amusing, sneaking up on people.

Grace told Earl that if he didn't stop startling everyone, she wouldn't supply him with the ability to relax anymore, and this behavior quickly stopped. At some point, Earl got a handle on his ability without the use of injections, by spending periods of time practicing relaxation methods with Grace instead. They spent long hours in meditation, sitting on mats in the garden. Arnold and Jenny did research on transcendental meditation using the ship's database, and soon took to joining Grace and Earl in the garden. It wasn't long before Ezra and Roslyn, plus Hanley and Rachel, also joined them, and soon enough, a large group took to meditating most mornings, after breakfast. Jess came to watch one day, looking at Ben with cynicism. He laughed, putting his arm around her.

Earl quickly mastered calling up his ability at will, but only used it to walk in and out of his own room without opening the door. However, he also inspired daily meditation with large groups of people on the ship. He even got Aaron to try, but, like Jess, it simply felt too weird for him. He attended one session, feeling stupid and highly uncomfortable, later telling Earl the whole thing was, "too out there," for him, and Earl shrugged, letting it go.

Alma and Kate eventually became regulars at the morning sessions, and Malcolm joined after seeing how much it relaxed everyone else. Ben went almost every morning, even though he knew Jess didn't understand.

In general, however, the members of The Society continued bonding, growing exceptionally close to one another. They had become one large, happy family.

***

They still observed an Earth calendar. They celebrated the passing of birthdays and acknowledged holidays. When Halloween came around, they could not trick-or-treat, but they reminisced about their memories of the event, dimming all the lights in the dining hall that evening at dinner, and Jemma made spooky-themed foods, like blood soup (really, just tomato), and bread rolls in the shapes of ghosts, bats, and witch's hats.

Several people had also carved various gourds from the fogponics room into Jack-o-Lanterns earlier in the afternoon. Rafferty made little lithium cell lights to insert inside and illuminate the faces, and the lantern's glowing features caused shadows to dance eerily around the dining hall all evening, the gourds lining the back counter next to the smoothie spigot.

Aaron surprised everyone with small bouquets of black roses in tall vases on each table, and Hanley proved to be quite the storyteller, providing several decently creepy campfire-style tales during a special dessert (again, care of Jemma) of eyeballs (peeled grapes) in blood sauce (honey flavored and colored with raspberry and blackberry juice).

The evening proved every bit as spooky as any of their most cherished and nostalgic childhood Halloween memories, and this became the new yearly tradition for the holiday from that first year forward.

When Thanksgiving rolled around, everyone crowded into the kitchen to make their own favorite dish for the feast. They ate leftovers for days.

The daily smoothies (the preferred breakfast for most) were sweet and delicious and had properties to them that satiated appetites for hours at a time, not to mention, improving their diets with the best nutrition any of them had ever had. They all felt energized and invigorated. Besides the meditation, people ran on the track in the gym, rode bikes, or simply went for walks in large laps through the long elliptical hallway of their deck.

***

Christmas arrived, and Jenny, lover of decorations she was, worked with Roslyn, Jemma, and Aaron, to make red and green wreaths, comprised of carnations and leaves. Rafferty provided magnets affixed to the garland circlets, so everyone woke on the morning of Noel with Yuletide chaplets on their doors. Once again, on Christmas evening, an extravagant dinner was laid upon the dining hall tables. Separately and individually, each couple also made something small to give one another.

Ben went to Grace and put an order in for some baby clothing. Grace had to simulate a model of a baby on her computer console, which Rafferty was more than happy to help with. Proportional measurements were estimated, and Grace put the order in. Less than an hour later, Ben had several stretchy, gray onesies for the baby. He also tasked Roslyn and Jemma with gathering the darker colored flowers from the garden, along with deep-colored berries (he'd received the idea at Halloween when Jemma made 'blood sauce'), and the result became varying shades of pink, purple, red and blue, used to dye the onesies, which he surprised Jess with on Christmas morning. It wasn't long after this that people opted (though not all, some of the men didn't seem to care) to dye their gray clothing different colors, and suddenly, gray gave way to a plethora of hues in the outfits people wore.

A few other couples received surprise gifts on Christmas morning as well. Grace was flooded, around weeks ten through twelve on board the ship, with females who had missed their period. They had all initially been provided with feminine materials for their menstrual cycles, much like the material Arnold described to Jess, for the baby diapers. Highly absorbent, and flat, the napkins had an adhesive quality that attached to their underwear.

However, by the end of the third month on board, only Alma and Kate still needed such materials. Grace no longer had her period, at age forty-nine, but Alma and Kate were not prone to the same pregnancy worries with any lack of birth control use.

The first to come in was Jenny, followed by Rachel, then Roslyn, then Jemma. Eileen came in last, several weeks later, after Christmas.

Shortly after Thanksgiving, Jenny, Rachel, Roslyn, and Jemma, all learned they were pregnant. Each elected to wait to tell their husbands until Christmas morning, although, none of them discussed this with each other, unaware of the coincidence.

Later, when Eileen found out she was pregnant, she was the only one who couldn't choose to keep it a secret, with Martin for a husband. He knew she was expecting the moment her period was late. It was his idea to send her to Grace, and he went with her. Grace did a simple chemical test, by swabbing Eileen's face, feeding it into a machine, and within less than a minute, she confirmed the couple's suspicions. Martin heard it in Grace's thoughts, the moment she read the screening results, and hugged Eileen, appearing miffed, looking over Martin's shoulder at Grace, who simply smiled and nodded.

***

The rest of the women went to Grace alone, for they wanted it to be a surprise. And so, on Christmas morning, there were presents, or rather, surprises for several people.

On Christmas morning, Arnold awoke to find Jenny staring at him, smiling. He smiled back.

"Are you watching me sleep again?"

"Why not? You do it to me all the time."

"Yes, but I'm certain that you look much prettier while sleeping than I do," he teased.

"You're cute when you sleep," she said. "You snore."

"I snore?"

"Yeah."

"And you think it's cute?"

She nodded, beaming. He kissed her lightly on the lips, then apologized, citing morning breath. She giggled, quickly kissing him back. He gazed at her in complete rapture.

"How did I get so lucky?"

Jenny took a deep breath, looking troubled, and he frowned.

"What's up?"

"It's Christmas."

He didn't understand why this would upset her. "So?"

"I… have a present for you," she said, looking at him tentatively.

"What? Well, that's not fair," Arnold said. "I didn't get you anything. Three years on board, we sort of got out of the habit."

"It's okay, Arnie. You did get me something."

"I did?"

She nodded, looking scared and nervous. "The present is for both of us," she said, sounding shy.

"What? How can it be for both of… us—" He looked at her now with dawning understanding. "No," he said, breaking into a huge grin, causing Jenny to visibly relax. She nodded.

"Really?" Arnold beamed.

She nodded again. He saw how nervous she felt, and kissed her passionately, then pulled away, looking at her in concern.

"Are you okay? Do you feel sick?"

She shook her head.

"When did you find out?"

"Two weeks ago."

"Two weeks? And you've been walking around keeping it to yourself?"

"I thought it would be a nice surprise, for Christmas."

He looked at her with intense love and longing, kissing her again, even more passionately. It wasn't long before they began doing exactly what it took to create the baby in the first place. Several other couples went through a similar morning as Jenny and Arnold.

Martin listened to everything going on around him, while lying in bed, reporting to Eileen. She came to enjoy his updates. It was something they did almost every night and early every morning. She could not hear thoughts the way Martin did, but they still found a way for Eileen to partake in Martin's ability, in a way that helped her feel connected to everyone. It was exactly how Martin used to update Hanley, back in the facility (which he also still did, most mid-mornings in the common room, after mornings in bed with Eileen), so Hanley felt as much in-the-know as ever (and naturally, in turn from Hanley, Rachel), if not slightly delayed. For these two couples, most secrets were generally known within hours of the thoughts received by Martin.

Martin relayed to Eileen the news of all the pregnancies revealed on Christmas morning to the various husbands, and the inevitable activities that ensued. At the time, Eileen didn't know her period would soon be late. She would not learn this for another two weeks. As she and Martin listened to the news the other couples shared, neither realized they had conceived a baby only the night before.

15

Jess was nervous about the impending birth of her daughter. In fact, she felt terrified. She was young, after all. She celebrated a birthday, however, and had now turned twenty-five. The baby was due in less than two months, and Jess grew exceedingly anxious. Mostly, she worried about the pain, but underneath that, she still held onto a nagging feeling that the baby might not be normal.

She had crazy dreams the last several weeks before the baby arrived; some of them bizarre. In one, she could see the full outline of her baby's head, sticking out from under the skin of her stomach, and she conversed with it, as if it were a fully aware adult. She woke from this dream feeling decidedly strange. The reverie stuck with her for several minutes, even after she got up, took a shower, dressed, and left her room to have breakfast. She walked around in a fog all morning, feeling creeped out.

Some dreams were downright nightmares. In one, she gave birth to a baby alligator, and woke up screaming. In another, she gave birth to a miniature 'grayling,' that looked like a micro version of the grown-up alien from her nightmares inside the facility.

Ben knew Jess was having bad dreams, simply because he slept right next to her every night, but Martin knew as well. When Jess refused to talk about it, Ben wasn't proud of himself, but he went to Martin, asking what the dreams were about. Martin reluctantly told him a few details, but not too many, for he felt awful about going behind Jess's back.

Ben learned just enough to understand the gist of Jess's nightmares, and the base root of her fears. She still worried that the baby wouldn't be normal, and perhaps, not even look fully human. He tried to comfort her as best he could, but her anxiety continued.

She met with Grace, who attempted to coach her through some breathing techniques, but Jess was cynical about the effectiveness of what she called, "simply panting," and soon quit. She asked Grace if there would be drugs to dull the pain and was told yes. Grace did have meds to help relieve the pain of childbirth, among other things. There were a varied number of medications on board, many with no names in terms of conventional medicines on Earth. They were made by the Graylings, in their vast understanding of human biology, and much more effective than conventional medicine. The medical knowledge Grace had was equivalent to where humanity on Earth could only hope to be, in perhaps a few hundred years' time, she figured.

Ailments on the ship were few and far between, however. The members of The Society were so healthy, due to their diet and exercise regimens, and their intake of truly clean water, no one ever fell ill. There were no communicable diseases to be spread among anyone, nor any viruses. The worst anyone might suffer was the occasional headache, or for the women, light menstrual cramps, and even these were minimal, also due to their overall, improved health aboard the ship.

Jess opted for pain meds, and felt she needed no further preparation for the impending birth. In truth, she simply didn't want to partake in any activity that caused her to think about the labor. She had two more ultrasounds done, and each time, the baby appeared normal—one hundred percent human—in every way. Jess's nightmares continued, however, until exactly one week before she went into labor. At that point, the dreams simply stopped, and Jess was grateful.

***

The day of Jess's given due date arrived, and quietly passed. Everyone knew she was due March 21st and noted that it would be on the Spring Equinox, in Earth terms. The equinox came and went, however, and she did not go into labor, nor the next day, or the next.

On the morning of March 24th, Jess woke feeling a tightness in her abdomen. She frowned, sitting up. The baby wasn't kicking, which was unusual; she usually did her most active gymnastics in the mornings. Today, Jess couldn't detect even the slightest hint of a bump, thump, or tap.

She stood, feeling her stomach—hard as a rock. She took in a deep breath, holding it. Then, as she still stood there, her muscles relaxed a bit, slowly, and she breathed a sigh of relief. It felt natural. She padded out of the bedroom and into the bathroom, to brush her teeth. She paused while applying the toothpaste to her toothbrush, setting it down, as her stomach hardened again, and once more, she felt her abdomen with her hands, and again, it felt hard as a rock. She felt incredible tightness all around her middle, taking in another deep breath, holding it for several seconds, then slowly let it out again, as her stomach once again loosened.

Jess picked up her toothbrush to resume, but stopped mid-brush, as she heard an audible popping noise, and felt warm liquid begin trickling down her leg, wetting her pants. She frowned. The tightness began again, this time much more intense, and Jess held her breath, for it felt slightly painful. She closed her eyes, exhaling deeply, for she now recognized that she was in labor.

She grabbed a sanitary napkin and placed it in her underwear, for she continued leaking, consistently. Then, she walked back into the bedroom and quickly changed her pants. Ben still slept. Jess gently patted him on the shoulder and he stirred feebly. She patted him again, more forcefully.

"Ben," she hissed, trying to keep her voice down, although she had no idea why.

"Huh?" He groggily turned over, looking at her through squinted eyes.

He quickly sat up. Jess thought it was because of the look on her face that told him she was in labor. However, Ben took one look at her, surprised to see wave after wave of silvery-threaded energy emitting from her midsection. He immediately knew what was happening.

"It's time," she said, looking nervous.

"I know," he said, throwing the covers off, jumping out of bed. "Are you in pain?" He looked at her face with such concern, she smiled, loving him.

"No, I'm okay. But I have a weird feeling, Ben."

"What do you mean?"

"Well, I read that the first labor can take a really long time. Over a day even, but, I just know I don't have that long."

He looked at her, frowning. She smiled, reassuring him, and the irony was not lost on him, for he had just spent the last several weeks trying to comfort and reassure Jess, yet, here she was, switching roles with him in the face of her imminent delivery.

"I'm not sure what you mean," he said, trying to remain calm. His heart beat far too fast.

"I mean, we'd better get to the infirmary quick. I feel like I don't have much time at all."

"But, you're not in any pain?"

She shook her head. Ben looked at the clock. It was only six in the morning. Grace wasn't awake yet, much less already in the infirmary. Ben quickly went into Sarah's room and woke her. She turned over, still sleepy.

"Shhh... Hey, Sarah. Everything's okay. Okay?" Ben said. "But I need to take Aunt Jess to the infirmary now, okay?"

"Is it time?" Sarah sat up, growing excited, immediately awake.

"Yes. But you need to stay here. We might be in there for a while."

"No, you won't. You'll be done before seven."

Ben frowned, looking at Sarah closely. He had a strange feeling now, combining Sarah's comments with what Jess had said.

"How do you know that?"

Sarah shrugged.

"Well, even if we are done in just one hour, I need to be with Jess alone. Her and the doctor only, okay?"

Sarah nodded, getting out of bed. Ben watched her walk out of the room, frowning.

"Aunt Jess," Sarah said, entering the living room with a smile.

"Hey, kiddo." Jess panted, holding her stomach.

"I know I can't come with you. But I wanna wait in the common room, okay?"

"Sure. But you'll get bored. No one's out there yet."

"Martin is. He already knows."

"Oh," Jess sighed. "Right, of course. Martin." Jess rolled her eyes but smiled.

Ben came out of Sarah's room and looked at Jess with concern.

"Still no pain?"

"No, just tightness. It's more uncomfortable than painful. But we really need to get going, especially if we need to wake up Grace. Ben, we don't have much time."

He didn't argue with her, nor did he ask her again how she knew these things. Between Jess and Sarah, he was willing to take their word for it. He quickly took Jess's hand, helping her up, and all three of them left the room. Stepping out, they all saw Martin sitting on the couch facing them, smiling wide. Eileen sat by his side, looking sleepy.

"Morning, Martin," Jess said, smiling.

"Morning, Jess. Ben," Martin nodded. "Congratulations, you two."

"You snoop. Don't you dare go telling the name to anyone. I want to tell everyone. Especially Hanley."

Ben frowned at Jess. They hadn't even spoken about names. She hadn't been willing to talk about anything to do with the baby, her trepidation so great, till now.

"Since when did you pick out a name?"

"I didn't, I was just thinking about it. I was going to run it by you, after the baby comes."

"Okay, good to know."

"Well, I only came up with the idea a few days ago."

"Okay," Ben said again.

He quickly left Jess standing with Sarah and knocked on Grace's door. When she didn't answer, he knocked again. Finally, after what felt to Ben like an eternity, Grace stood in front of him, looking grouchy.

"This better be good," she said, looking past Ben at Jess, who now panted while holding her stomach.

"How far apart are the contractions, Jess?"

"Um," Jess thought about it. "I don't know, a minute?"

"A minute! Why didn't you get me sooner?"

Grace immediately left her room and ushered Ben and Jess to the infirmary. Halfway there, Jess had to stop walking and lean against the hallway wall. She cried out in pain, and Ben's heart began to pound.

"Jess?" He held her hand.

Jess now panted uncontrollably. It felt natural to her and she did it without even thinking. After about a minute, she could walk again, but had to stop for another contraction just outside the infirmary door.

"It's been less than thirty seconds since your last contraction, Jess," Grace said, her voice strained, her face taut with concern. She shot an angry glance at Ben.

"You really should have woken me sooner, Ben."

"I woke you as soon as I knew."

"It's not his fault," Jess said, still panting.

They walked into the infirmary and Grace motioned for Jess to lay down on the examination table.

"I only woke up fifteen minutes ago. My water broke while I was brushing my teeth," Jess explained.

"How many minutes ago did your water break?" Grace called over her shoulder, as she gathered the things she needed from a nearby cabinet.

"Um, maybe about, five minutes?" Jess said, lying down on the table.

"And your contractions are already this close together?"

Jess nodded. Ben looked worried. Grace hurriedly washed her hands in a sizable sink, and put a large, white, apron-like smock on. Ben watched in wonder as he witnessed Grace stick her hand into a deep bowl of water, up to her elbow for several moments. Then she pulled her hand and arm back out. He realized she had purified the water in the bowl.

She quickly came over, setting the bowl down behind her on a table, and instructed Jess to take off her pants and underwear, even as she draped a gray sheet over her lower body. She wheeled a light stand over and trained it down, to illuminate Jess's lower body, then quickly pulled white gloves on.

"Let's see how dilated you are," Grace said, feeling under the sheet.

Ben held Jess's hand, and she looked up at him, smiling. He smiled back, weakly, very worried. Jess started panting again, heavily, and he could see from her expression that the contractions had grown much more painful. Jess cried out and squeezed Ben's hand.

"I'm here, Jess," Ben said, bending down to look in her eyes. He stroked the hair away from her forehead lovingly.

"My God, you're already fully dilated. Jess, I can see the baby's head crowning. You're having your baby now!"

"See," she panted to Ben, "I told you."

"Okay, Jess," Grace said. "Your contraction is over. The next one should be coming in about thirty seconds. When you feel the next contraction, I want you to take a deep breath, and hold it, then push as hard as you can. Okay?"

"Okay," Jess said, suddenly sounding nervous.

"You can do this, Jess," Ben said, stroking her face. She nodded at him. She sweated slightly, her face shining. She looked radiantly beautiful. She didn't know it, but Ben could see shimmering waves of heat energy floating off Jess in all directions. It was the most beautiful thing he'd ever seen. She looked as if she floated in silvery-translucent water.

Her face tensed as the next contraction began. She pulled in a deep breath and held it, sitting up slightly, and pushed. Ben squeezed her hand, unaware of doing so. Jess closed her eyes, and Ben did the same, placing his forehead against the side of her head, silently praying that everything would be okay.

She made no sound while pushing, but after about thirty seconds, Jess exhaled, groaning.

"You're doing wonderful, Jess," Grace said. "The baby is crowning. A few more pushes, and I think she'll be here."

Jess nodded, looking up at Ben, worried. He smiled.

"You're doing great, Jess," he said, his eyes moist. "This is it. We're having a baby."

She smiled at him, nodding. He squeezed her hand again and knelt next to her, sighing as he saw her face pulling into another grimace of pain.

Jess drew in another deep breath and pushed, again in silence. Ben closed his eyes. Nothing but silence filled the room for what felt like an eternity. Then Jess exhaled again, crying out loudly. Ben looked at her face and saw the energy dissipating, floating away, and her appearance returned to normal; no more energy waves coming off. He looked at her, worried, for her face had gone blank with exhaustion, and he didn't know what was happening. Several moments went by as he stared down at her, completely dazed. Grace continued working, behind Ben's back, but he remained oblivious.

Then Ben heard the most beautiful sound in his entire life. His daughter cried out for the first time from behind him and he turned to see Grace holding her. She had already been cleaned off and wrapped up in a small, gray blanket, and Grace carried her over to Ben.

"She's…" Ben could not finish his sentence.

Grace handed Ben's baby to him, and he took her into his arms, like the tiniest doll he'd ever seen. She felt like she weighed nothing. He peered down at her tiny face and cried. She looked perfect, truly angelic and beautiful.

"Jess," Ben spluttered, tears in his eyes. She looked up at him and smiled.

"She's perfect," Ben said, kneeling to show Jess the baby. Jess attempted to sit up, and Grace rushed over to adjust the table-back into place to support her. Jess gazed at her baby in complete awe. Ben placed the baby into her mother's arms, and Jess looked at her face with such shock and wonder, Ben laughed. Jess looked up at Ben in surprise.

"She's totally normal."

"Of course, she is," Grace said. "She's absolutely perfect, Jess. A perfect little angel."

Ben's heart sped up at hearing her statement.

"Why did you call her that?" Jess looked at Grace in amazement.

"I don't know," Grace said. "I guess, because it's true. She looks like a little angel, doesn't she? Absolutely perfect."

"But, that's the name I decided on," Jess said, looking at Ben. "I decided to name her Angelique. I thought Hanley would like that."

Ben nodded, tears in his eyes. He heard Sarah's voice ringing in his head, saying, *"She's your little angel,"* and he finally understood what Sarah had really meant.

"Ben?" Jess looked at him, worry on her face. "Is that okay? Do you like that name?"

"Angelique?"

Jess nodded. "I thought we'd call her Angel, for short. But only if you like it, too."

He nodded consent, tears slipping down his cheeks. He gazed down at the tiny bundle in Jess's arms, in reverence.

"Angel," he said, hearing it for the first time as the name of his daughter.

"Angel," Jess whispered, also looking down at her beautiful daughter.

Ben remembered another thing Sarah had said on the day of her final training exercise. She'd told Ben everything was going to be fine. She told him the baby would be okay.

"She's going to put you back together again."

Ben thought of those remarks now, while looking at Jess, and knew Sarah was right. She no longer felt afraid of the birth, for that now lay behind her. Jess no longer seemed worried about the baby being normal or not, for she could clearly see that Angel was a perfectly healthy, human child. All the tension between he and Jess suddenly felt as if it had flown away, in a matter of minutes. There no longer stood a divide between them. They had simply become a happy family of three. Sarah had been right about Ben's little 'angel,' all along. She did put them back together again. She put all of them back together again. Angel made Ben's family complete. He leaned over and kissed Jess. She smiled at him, looking radiant.

"I love you, Jess," he breathed.

"I love you back," she sighed. "Everything is just as it should be."

Ben felt so relieved to hear her say that, he let out a tiny sob, both laughing and crying at once. He suddenly felt immense joy come over him. He asked Jess if she minded if he went and told everyone in the common room. She nodded.

"Well, wait," Grace said. "They'll want details. Is it all right if I take Angel for just a few minutes?"

"Okay, but what for?" Jess asked, looking worried.

"Only to weigh and measure her. I can do it right here, while you watch. Angel will never leave your sight. Okay?"

Jess nodded and handed Angel to Grace, who unwrapped the baby and laid her on a small table.

"Seven pounds, two ounces," she said, smiling at Jess. "Perfectly normal."

She then placed Angel on a different table and gently pushed her head to the top, stretching her feet out, very gently, with her hand.

"Twenty inches, exactly," Grace said. "Again, perfect."

Grace quickly wrapped Angel back up and handed her to Ben, who took her back over to Jess, placing her into her mother's arms.

"Okay?" he asked. Jess nodded.

In the common room, Ben appeared. It wasn't even seven in the morning yet, but now Martin and Eileen sat on the couch, as well as Sarah, Aaron, Earl, Arnold, Jenny, Hanley and Rachel. Everyone else still slept. Those awake all looked at him expectantly.

"It's a girl," he said, with a sigh of relief. "She's perfectly healthy. Seven pounds, two ounces, twenty inches long." Ben paused, looking directly at Hanley. "We've decided to name her Angelique."

Hanley stared at Ben for several long moments, saying nothing. Then he wiped at his eyes, looking at Rachel. He smiled, embarrassed.

"We're going to call her Angel, for short," Ben continued, looking at everyone.

"Doc," Hanley choked out, clearing his throat. "I mean, Ben... *Thank you.*"

Ben nodded at Hanley, smiling. The name was perfect. He looked at Sarah, who beamed, and nodded to her as well. She ran up, hugging him tightly.

"Do you want to come and see Aunt Jess?"

Sarah nodded, immediately jumping up to go with Ben. He looked at the group one last time, still smiling wide, then turned to take Sarah to meet Angel.

16

Over the next several weeks, Jess and Ben adjusted to life as new parents. Sarah adored Angel, and loved her as a sister, and whenever Jess needed a break, she was right there to watch the baby, so Jess could take a nap, or a shower. Jess and Ben took turns getting up in the middle of the night, rocking Angel, soothing her when she cried. Angel, however, didn't cry very often. Jess didn't know the difference, but Grace remarked one day that Angel was, "the calmest baby I've ever seen."

Ben and Jess could only take Grace's word for it. Neither had ever spent any time with a baby before Angel came along. Jess, however, fell into the role of motherhood like a pro. She loved Angel immediately, and Ben felt greatly relieved. Her anxiety about the baby, which had plagued them both throughout the pregnancy, was immediately forgotten, like a bad dream. Jess simply fell in love with Angel, the moment she arrived.

All the expectant mothers looked to Jess, catching a glimpse of what might be in store for each of them. All the men looked to Ben, to take a cue on the paternity front. Ben was an amazingly loving father. It became common for people to see him, walking through the halls, carrying Angel wherever he went. He looked so happy, everyone could tell that Ben had fallen in love all over again.

***

As Sarah celebrated her 12th birthday, on June 11th, all the other expectant mothers looked on, as Jess set Angel down in the common room, and she struggled up onto her knees, and sat, rocking back and forth. She was just shy of three months, and already preparing to crawl.

The closest due date after Angel's birth, would be Jenny, but her due date still hung back, nearly two months away, in August. Eileen wasn't due till November. Not only did she not become pregnant until a full month after any of the other women, but her pregnancy would last a month longer also.

Alma surprised Grace one day, by coming into the infirmary and asking if she could hang out. Grace simply looked at her, curious.

"Hang out?"

"Yeah, you know, maybe I could like, intern, or something?"

Alma looked at Grace, her face eager and expectant. She had been on board the ship for over half a year, and had grown restless, looking for something to occupy her time. She and Kate were not expecting a baby and were not nearly as preoccupied as the other couples. In short, Alma had become bored. She discovered her interest in medicine while perusing the ship's database, trying to understand Kate's ability to shock people.

Kate, like so many others, had no use for her ability on board the ship. Nothing needed to be shocked. She spent her time reading, exercising, and playing cards with Hanley and many of the others. These activities were enough for Kate, but she saw how Alma wasn't satisfied. Kate was the one who brought up medicine, initially, after Alma grilled her about her ability one night, asking question after question. Eventually, Alma decided to see Grace, and give things a try.

"You want to study medicine?" Grace said, looking surprised.

"Well, why not? What did you do before you came on board?"

"Meth," Grace said, looking solemn. "You?"

"Nothing," Alma shrugged. "I took care of Lucia, then she graduated from high school and we both worked stupid little office jobs. Then I got taken away to the facility. I didn't do anything there, except plan my escape. I guess it's time now, for me to finally do something." She shrugged, and Grace smiled, chuckling.

"After all… We got, like, nine-and-a-half-years left on this boat, right? I don't want to play cards for a decade, you know?"

"Yeah, I do," Grace said.

"And I ain't having no baby, so, you know?"

Grace smiled. She liked Alma. She also understood her. She recovered from her surprise quickly, and from that day on, Alma studied medicine. Grace found it gave her something new to do as well, and she welcomed the new preoccupation of teaching another. It made her feel fulfilled in a new and surprisingly happy way.

***

Jenny was the first to have her baby, after Jess. On August 9th, she went into labor, oddly enough on her due date. Like Jess, Jenny's labor was short, lasting only two hours. Also, like Jess (who was apprised of the fact afterward, for she didn't realize it), Jenny used no pain meds of any kind. Both women had completely natural births.

Jenny and Arnold ended up with a son, whom they named Malcolm, after Jenny's father. They called him Mal for short. They, like Jess and Ben, fell in love with parenthood.

Arnold and Jenny's baby, Mal, was extremely calm, just the same as Angel. All the transgenic babies, it would turn out, were extremely placid, and relatively easy to take care of. Grace noted the tranquil, relaxed behavior of the first two babies, one day, frowning. Ben went to see her in the infirmary, to talk about things. Eileen still had not given birth.

Grace looked over medical scans with Alma, of all people, when Ben came in. He wasn't aware that Alma had begun studying with her, although, she'd been doing so for almost two months.

"Hi, Ben," Grace said. "Is something wrong?"

"No, everything's fine," he said, nodding to Alma. "Hi, Alma."

"Hey, Ben." She barely looked up from a scan she perused.

"Alma's interested in learning about medicine," Grace explained.

"Oh… Sure."

"Well," Alma said. "Ten years on a ship in space. You have to do something to stay occupied, right?"

"Right," Ben said, smiling at Alma, impressed. "How's it going?"

"Good," Alma said, smiling radiantly.

"Better than good," Grace said. "It turns out, our little Alma, has a knack for understanding human anatomy. She's learning even faster than I did."

"Oh," Alma said, looking embarrassed. "I don't know about that."

"Well, that's great," Ben said, and he meant it.

"So, what can I do for you, Ben?" Grace asked.

"Actually, I wanted to talk to you about the babies."

"The babies?" Grace frowned. "Is something wrong with Angel?"

"No," Ben said, frowning.

"Is Mal okay?"

"Yeah," Ben said. "It's just that, when Angel was born, and she was so quiet, you said it was unusual. Now Mal's here, and everyone keeps saying how good he is, and the rest of the babies…" he shrugged, trailing off.

"You think it's strange," Grace said, nodding. She understood his feelings all too well, finishing his thoughts for him.

"And Mal is also a baby born with the pseudogene already coded, just like all the other babies," Grace continued.

Ben nodded.

"But, Ben, there are worse things than having well-behaved babies on board."

"I know, and I'm not complaining, it's just that," Ben looked at Alma. "Alma, you won't say anything to any of the other moms, will you?"

"No," Alma said. "I don't even know what you're talking about."

Ben nodded, walking over to the two of them. He looked at Grace, curious.

"You've scanned the genomes of the babies, right?"

Grace nodded.

"And you've compared them to the rest of our genomes?"

Grace nodded again.

"And?"

Grace sighed, nodding a third time, looking resigned. She knew Ben would figure things out. She took him over to her console, pulling up the genome readings.

"It's a slight difference, in the alleles of gene A401, subtext 9." She looked at Ben to see if he understood. He nodded. Grace narrated for Alma, who frowned.

"It's a set of genes that we know to affect behavior. Specifically, personalities, and emotions such as anger and aggression."

"So, the babies don't have the gene?" Alma asked.

"They do," Grace explained. "But the sequence is different than the rest of us. And I suspect the difference lies in the levels of aggression we'll see in the children as they continue to grow and mature."

"Are there any other differences?" Ben looked worried. He knew this would freak Jess out.

"No," Grace said, and her voice reassured Ben that she told the complete truth. "And like I said, there are much worse things than having well-behaved children."

"I don't get it," Alma said. Grace looked at her, intrigued, for she could see Alma's mind working, wanting to know. She smiled.

"The reason the Graylings chose us to help them, partly, is because we have something they simply don't. We contain within us the incredible urge to fight. We get angry, we lash out. We go to war. We use our intellect to create weapons. Much like the Bailon, we are an aggressive race, although, not nearly to the same extent. We're more like… Bailon-lite, if you will."

Alma smiled at this comparison. She nodded.

"Well, it's not pretty, but in this case, it's immensely helpful for the Graylings, as they simply can't fight for their home, to reclaim it. By nature, physically, they are pacifists, in every way. Genetically, they simply don't have tempers. They don't yell, or fight, or get into physical confrontations."

"So, what does that have to do with the babies?" Alma looked at Ben.

"Well, it appears that, genetically, our babies are more like the Graylings," Ben said. "They're human, of course, but, they seem to lack the genetic makeup that defines human beings as… fighters."

"Human beings are fighters?"

"You don't believe that," Grace said, sounding cynical. "Try putting two three-year-old's in a room, with one toy. See what happens."

Alma looked at Grace, thinking about the scenario she outlined, then nodded, looking sad.

"Right, so, human beings are naturally... they argue."

"They are naturally aggressive," Ben said, nodding. "Our first instinct is to hit. Fight. Talking things over isn't going to happen with a young child."

"So, with the babies..." Alma looked at Ben, wondering.

"So far, it looks like, with the babies that are being born with two transgens for parents, the genes governing aggression aren't present. A different sequence is coded in place, which makes them naturally calm. They cry less, they don't get upset. And, I suspect, as they get older, and begin walking, talking, and interacting with one another, they won't resort to kicking, biting, pushing, or hitting."

Grace nodded.

"Wait, so, they won't fight? Like, at all?"

"I'm not sure," Ben said. "I'm not sure how involved the gene differences really are. They may still fight, but perhaps, less?"

"They'll be pacifists, like the Graylings?" Alma sounded hopeful.

"Not like that," Ben said. "Not to the extreme the Graylings are, just, less likely to lose control, or resort to violence."

"So, what's so bad about that?"

"Nothing at all," Grace said. "But it does mark a definitive change in the human genome."

"And all the babies will be born that way," Ben said. Then he sighed, thinking hard. "Except for Martin and Eileen. She's not a transgen."

"Which might be helpful," Grace said. "Their baby will be a control for the behavior of the others. We can directly compare the differences in behavior and reaction, from the moment he's born."

Ben nodded. Alma looked dismayed. "What, like they're little lab rats, or something?"

"No, of course not," Ben said. "But having a baby born without the new sequence will allow us to directly observe the differences in behavior as the children grow."

"But they're still human," Alma said.

"Yes, they simply have a slightly altered gene sequence," Grace answered.

"Like having red hair, instead of blonde," Ben explained. "Except, the difference lies in their behavioral choices."

"It's a good thing," Grace said. "If all humans were born with this sequence, quite likely, there would be no wars."

"Wait, so, it's like, a step forward, for people. That's what you're saying, right?"

Ben and Grace thought about it, then both nodded, looking at Alma in awe. She smiled, all radiant innocence.

"Theoretically, as more and more transgens are born, it becomes more and more likely that some of them, eventually, by chance, will reproduce with other transgens. At some point, several generations down the line, there would end up being more humans born with the new sequence than there is without," Ben said.

"Right, and eventually, it would make humanity more peaceful," Grace said. "But, as Ben says, it would take quite a while."

"So, it's evolution," Alma said. "For humanity to lose its aggressive ways and become more capable of getting along."

"Yeah," Ben said. "But here on this ship, with the population consisting solely of transgens, save for Eileen, we're ending up with an entire generation of the new and improved human, all at once."

"You think the Graylings knew this would happen?" Alma said. "You think the Graylings wanted us to be this way?"

Ben shrugged, looking at Grace. She nodded back.

"If we're going to live with the Graylings, and continue multiplying, it would only make sense that the future generations of humans would need to be peaceful, to co-exist with them on the same planet." Grace concluded.

"So, it's not to help us, back on Earth?"

"It seems to be a two-fold solution," Grace continued. "One so scary in its implications, I can't even wrap my head around it."

"What do you mean?" Alma frowned.

"She means," Ben said. "Whatever is in control of this pseudogene, however it ended up being inside all of us, it wasn't a mistake. It seems to be designed specifically to help us, as a race back on Earth, yet also aid in this entire situation with the Graylings, here on the other side of the Universe."

"But, the Graylings didn't give us the gene," Alma said. "So, who's in charge?"

Ben and Grace looked at Alma, shrugging. Her eyes got huge and wide. She shook her head.

"This is too much," she whispered. "We can't be that important."

"It's too much for any of us to wrap our heads around, fully," Grace agreed. "Even the Graylings feel overwhelmed by it, at times."

Ben nodded. He looked at Grace.

"I have to channel in, don't I?"

Grace nodded. She smiled at Ben, trying to soothe his fears.

"This is *big*, Ben. Bigger than all of us. And I do mean, *all of us*, the Graylings included. Now, I don't know about you, but I feel like I've been invited to attend the most important party ever thrown. I'm honored. It's the best that I can do, that I know how to be. To simply accept that I've been chosen to take part in something so important, that two species have found one another, and we're traveling, together, across space and time, to do something so monumentally great.

"Now, as to *why*? I don't know. But there are simply too many coincidences going on around me, to question it any longer. Each of us needs to arrive at that conclusion, at some point. Including you, Ben. And Jess." Grace looked at him with trepidation.

Ben nodded, closing his eyes. He knew it was time to deal with this subject between he and Jess. He talked with Grace for a bit longer, Alma listening intently. Then, he left the infirmary to walk the halls and think.

***

Ben went to see Hanley. Martin was there, already waiting for him in Hanley's room, and the three of them went into Martin's room, for he didn't want to talk about anything to do with Eileen or the baby behind her back. She deserved to know. He'd help her deal with it, he told them.

In Martin's room, Eileen looked as big as a house. She was due in less than two weeks. Her pregnancy was progressing more slowly than the other women. She wasn't expected to go into labor until week forty, as opposed to week 35 for the others.

Eileen listened to the men talk. She had come to terms with everything that was happening. The only difference for her was that she simply stood on the outside of everything. When Ben mentioned Grace's metaphor of being invited to 'the most important party ever thrown,' it resounded with Eileen, for it summed up exactly how she felt—as if a huge party was being thrown—and she simply wasn't invited. As she listened to Ben talk about the babies, she felt even more left out. She realized her baby would be different from the others. Martin heard all her thoughts, and got up to hug her, looking over her shoulder at Ben, mouthing for him to stop talking.

"I'm sorry, Eileen," Ben said. "I'm not saying your child will be less special-I…" he faltered.

"But aren't you?" Eileen said, her voice raising slightly. She pulled away from Martin, looking angry.

"I'm the only one on board this ship who's only human. Cro-Magnon human, from the way you're describing things. I'm a Neanderthal, and my kid will be a cave baby!"

"That's not what he means," Martin said.

"Martin, I'm sorry," Ben said, and he truly was. Martin nodded.

"No one's saying you're worth less than the rest of us," Hanley spoke up. "Or that your baby will be less important. If anything, you and your baby will be *more* important, because you'll be the last link to what we once were. We've left Earth and everything we know behind. We've lost everything. Our culture, our ways. Once we get to Hesperia, I'll bet we even lose our calendar, at some point. There will be new days there, with different hours. Our clocks, with our time, won't mean anything. I don't know about you, but I feel like I'm losing everything that made me feel human. And it scares me, more than anyone will ever know. Even you Martin. Because even if you can hear my thoughts, you still can't *feel* what I'm feeling."

Hanley looked at Martin, who nodded. Eileen looked at Hanley with sympathy. He gazed at her in reverence.

"I've changed. I have abilities. I'm already set apart from the rest of humanity. Hell, the government could see that. That's why they were rounding us all up, locking us away. Hiding us from the world. We were already one step ahead of everyone else. But one step ahead, is still one step *away*, Eileen. One step apart. Separate. And we're the minority, if you consider all of humanity that we left behind. Now, all our children are a step apart from us, even. Having you here…" Hanley faltered. He looked at Eileen with such respect, his eyes filled with tears, making Eileen's heart swell.

"Having you here and knowing your baby will be part of the original human race, the one I was born into. In some strange way, it makes all this craziness easier to handle. It's comforting. It's something to hold onto."

Hanley's tears spilled over and he quickly wiped them away. He smiled, embarrassed.

"Eileen," he sniffled, smiling. "You and your baby are the only culture we were able to take away from Earth, other than the databases stored in the ship's computers. You're the only real, living, breathing thing we have, of all that we left behind. We're never going back to Earth. You're the only thing we have left, to remember where we came from. Don't sit there thinking you're less important than the rest of us, because you aren't. That couldn't be further from the truth, babe."

Eileen laughed, and wiped her own tears away. Martin hugged her tightly. He nodded his thanks to Hanley. Ben hung his head in shame, for he didn't mean to start any of this, or cause any ill feelings.

Hanley quickly turned the subject back to the reason Ben came to him in the first place. Ben was grateful.

"So, you've decided it's time to channel in?" He looked at Ben, asking with his eyes. Ben nodded.

"But I'll need to tell Jess, first. I guess I just… needed some support. She was resistant of me taking Luci, of manifesting an ability, even. She's afraid of change." Ben sighed, rubbing his temples.

"We're all afraid of change," Eileen said. "But I'd channel in, if I could. I *wish* I could. Martin's different, but it's not a bad thing. I could tell her that, if you want me to? I know what it's like to be afraid of it. Martin is different, but, he's still the same, too, if that makes any sense? I could tell Jess all of this."

"No," Ben said. "It wouldn't help. She's not afraid of herself changing. Her greatest fear, I think, is that *I'll* change, when I do it. She's afraid it will change my feelings for her."

Martin nodded. Ben was right. He knew Jess so well, Martin marveled, for even without being able to read Jess's thoughts, he had nailed it.

"So, what are you going to say to her?" Hanley asked.

"I don't know. I could try to assure her that I won't change, but her argument for that will simply be that I have no way of knowing that for certain. And she'll be right."

"Ben, tell her to look at Martin. At me, at Rachel, Jenny; all the old-boarders. None of them love each other any less," Hanley said.

"It won't matter to Jess," Ben sighed in frustration. "The only thing that matters to her is me, *us*. No one else is us, and she'll be afraid of losing us."

"Then tell her that caring about the Graylings won't take away your ability to love her. That won't change. She should know that by now," Hanley said.

"She does," Ben said. "She just… has doubts. You can't blame her. That's also a part of our human nature," he said, and everyone nodded.

"She could be the last one left who hasn't channeled in and she'll still resist it, I know," Ben said. "Even after she sees that my feelings for her haven't changed."

"Why?" Eileen asked.

"Because… For her to channel in, she'll have to accept that *she's* meant to help the Graylings. She's heard you talk. You all keep saying *she* is going to help them, *her* power can save them. You have no idea how much it's taken for her to even come *this* far. There's still a gap between her and full acceptance. She's still fighting it. She takes a step forward, then two steps back, always landing behind her fears again, as a stumbling block. She can't accept that this is all part of some larger plan, or understand how *she* fits in. It just... doesn't fit into her belief system. I don't think you all realize how much you're asking of Jess. The amount of faith it will take, for her to believe that all of us are somehow going to save an entire race from extinction, and that *she*, somehow, is needed most of all. Hell, *I* don't even know how that's possible."

"Neither do the Graylings," Hanley said, and Martin nodded. "They only know it *is* possible. They *feel* it. It's led them this far, to all of us."

"I don't understand that," Ben said, shaking his head. "And if *they* don't even know why, themselves—if the very beings that we're supposed to save, are flying on faith—then, you're just asking too much of Jess. She's one person, a human being, and that's expecting too much for one mind to take."

"I know," Hanley said. "But it must happen, one way or another. The Graylings need all of us, Ben. That includes Jess."

"If your theory is right," Eileen said, "If all of this is some sort of cosmic plan, then at some point, she will come to terms with it, somehow, right?"

"You mean, if everything is preordained," Hanley sighed.

"Well, that's what we're talking about here, isn't it?" Eileen said, matter-of-factly.

"This transcendentalist BS is getting too tiring for me," Hanley said. "I'm agnostic, remember?"

"What does that matter?" Eileen said. "I never named anything specific, did I? I just said, if it's a cosmic plan, then everything will fall into place."

"Well, now you're getting into the argument of whether we even have free will," Hanley stated.

"No, I'm not. I had a choice, whether to come with Martin or not. I chose to come, because I love him. And all of you chose to plan an escape, right? Because you wanted to be free?"

"Yes," Ben said. "And I wanted to be with Jess. I wanted to be free to love her. But, yes, Eileen, it was a choice. And Jess is completely free to choose to channel into the Graylings or not. It's her choice, whether she decides to help them or not. She could simply choose not to help."

"Right. So... My whole point simply is, if helping them is the right thing to do, and in the cosmic plan, good prevails, she'll make the right choice. It's like, fate or destiny, only, by choice. If that makes any sense at all?"

"Crap," Hanley said. "In some weird way, it does. It's like Jesus always said. *'One way or another, the correct outcome will come about.'* Somehow or another, everything will be as it should be."

"So, perhaps we're not here to try and help Ben figure out how to convince Jess to have faith, or choose the right path," Eileen continued. "We're here to convince *ourselves* to have faith. To believe that, at some point, whether we *know* how it will come about or not, Jess will make a choice. And we must assume that she'll eventually choose to help the Graylings, since that's what all of us are on the ship for. We're on our way to Hesperia. We still have nine years to go. At some point in the next nine years, something will happen that helps Jess decide."

Everyone stared at Eileen, stunned by her revelation. She was right, they all realized. Hanley looked at Martin in wonder, then stared Eileen in the face.

"And you think you weren't meant to be here?" he said, smiling at her. She blushed and smiled back, looking proud.

So, Ben decided, there, in that room, that he would tell Jess he had chosen to channel in. But the subject of whether Jess should channel in would not be brought up, at least not by any of them. Ben would put no pressure on Jess to decide. If she was meant to choose, then one way or another, she would.

17

That night, while lying in bed together, Ben brought the subject up. Angel slept in her crib, close to the bed. They could hear her tiny, quick breaths, in the silence of the room. She was now five months old.

"I love listening to her sleep," Jess whispered.

"I know," Ben said, turning over to look at Jess's face. "I love you so much, Jess."

"I know. I love you back so much."

"Jess," Ben sighed, preparing himself. "You know that several people have channeled into the Graylings." He said it, not as a question, but a statement. She sighed, for she knew what was coming next.

"I messed up, by not telling you about my decision with the Luci. I tried to, but—"

"I know, it's not your fault," Jess cut him off. "Besides, I was kind of hoping that event wouldn't come up, like, ever."

"Sorry," Ben sighed, laughing. "Gone and forgotten, okay?"

She nodded, smiling.

"Jess, I'm going to channel in," Ben said. He decided the best thing would be to simply say it, no beating around the bush. Jess nodded, and Ben looked at her in surprise. He expected more of a reaction.

"You're not upset?"

She shook her head.

"Why are you not upset?"

"Do you want me to be?" she scoffed.

"No, of course not, but…" he trailed off. "Why aren't you?"

"Because," she looked him right in the eye. "I know you love me, but you also love The Society. You feel responsible for them, because none of us would even be here if it weren't for you. I know you feel bad about hurting everyone. Now, you have this, I don't know, Father Complex, or something. You act as if you need to take care of everyone, to make up for everything you did before. But you don't have to do that, Ben. I'm sure everyone has forgiven you, at this point. Everyone's happy. No one even cares about anything that happened at the facility anymore. That was a lifetime ago."

She turned away then, onto her side, placing her back to him. He sighed.

"You are mad," he said, and placed his hand on her shoulder.

"I'm not mad. I just knew that you would want to channel in. I knew as soon as the first few people started going. I knew you would, eventually, so you won't feel like you're leaving everyone alone. You'll go with everyone, wherever they go. You'll keep taking care of everyone."

"Jess, the only people I need to take care of now, are you and Angel and Sarah."

She turned back to Ben, looking in his eyes, intently. "That's not true, Ben. Look me in the eye and tell me you don't still feel responsible for the original members of The Society."

He looked at her, and thought about it, hard. He realized she was right. He wanted to channel in, so he could know what everyone else was experiencing. He wanted to do it, to make sure everyone else who had, was okay. He needed to know what they were going through. He needed to understand them, for he felt if he could no longer understand them, he could never fully help any of them, ever again.

"You see? A Father Complex."

"I'm sorry, Jess. I didn't realize."

"Yeah, well. I know you better than you know yourself," she said, sighing.

"Then you understand that this is something I need to do."

She nodded.

"Jess, you must know by now that no matter what happens, I'll still love you the same as I always have. You know that, right?"

Jess nodded, looking at him intently. "And you must know that just because you do it, doesn't mean I will."

He nodded. "It was never my intention to talk you into it, Jess. What you do or don't do is up to you. You're too much of a firecracker to operate any other way, remember?"

She nodded and laughed, kissing him. "I'm just glad that you remember."

"I always remember, Jess. I remember everything when it comes to you," he sighed, touching her face. "Every moment, since I met you, is seared into my mind. If you only knew. If you only, truly knew, it would probably scare you away."

"Never," she said, kissing him passionately. She began touching him in a familiar way. It was how she always touched him when she wanted to make love.

"You know," he said, pulling away slightly, stopping her advance. She sighed in frustration. "If we keep going on like this, we're going to have another baby on our hands."

"Well… Grace said as long I'm breast feeding, I'm not ovulating. It's like, nature's way of spacing pregnancies out, remember?"

"Yes, but at some point, we'll have to decide what we want to do."

"You don't want to have any other kids?"

"No, I do, but, what if it happens again, right away?"

"I don't care. I love Angel. And I don't get why everyone says that having kids is so hard. I mean, she's so perfect. I feel like I could have, I don't know, ten more, just like her."

"Ten?!"

"Shhh, you'll wake her up," she giggled. "Okay, maybe not ten, but, I wouldn't be upset if we had another one." She looked at Ben with concern.

"And you're worried I don't feel the same way?"

She nodded. He kissed her passionately, then pulled away, caressing her face.

"What happened to you knowing me better than I know myself?"

She shrugged. He kissed her again.

"So?"

"So," Ben said, looking at her with intense affection. "If we're going to have another one, we'd better get crackin'."

Jess laughed. "Crackin'?' You did not just actually say 'crackin'." She continued laughing.

"I did," Ben said, kissing her neck, his hands roaming over her body. She reciprocated, her own hands roaming freely.

"Crackin'," Ben whispered in her ear, and she laughed even harder. They both laughed, even as they began making love.

***

Midway through fall, all the pregnant women had given birth, except Eileen, now due any day. The Society had traveled through space for one year, and in that time, five new lives had begun. A sixth life would come into existence any day. Just as with Jess, and Jenny, all the proceeding births were relatively easy, and quick, with very little pain involved.

Hanley and Rachel welcomed a son, named Robert, after Hanley. This was the first time anyone ever learned that Hanley was 'Robert Hanley'.

He simply shrugged. "My name's Hanley, okay? My son is Robert," he said, beaming at Rachel, holding the tiny bundle. Robert was born two weeks after Jenny and Arnold welcomed Mal.

Next came a daughter for Ezra and Roslyn, three weeks after Robert came into existence. The happy couple named their little girl Vera. Two weeks after Vera was born, Jemma gave birth to a little girl, and she and Rafferty decided to name her Mara.

Then, Eileen finally gave birth. She and Martin received a healthy baby boy, whom they named Eric. Eileen's labor was decidedly more difficult than all the other women. It took over twenty-four hours for her labor to fully commence, before Eric was born, and Grace had to use medication for the pain, for the first time. Alma stood back, watching, as she was still new to apprenticing. She watched and learned, taking everything in.

In the following months, as all the babies grew, it became apparent that the phenomenon of calm behavior in the first two births, in fact, was not a phenomenon at all, but the normal inclination of the new generation of transgenic babies. Clearly, they were a generation of passive, peaceful human beings, and Ben watched all the babies grow in total fascination. Everyone did. Except Eileen. She knew her baby would not be the same as everyone else. Not only would her child not have an ability, its behavior would be decidedly, and noticeably different.

The months passed, and all the babies started crawling. They seemed to reach their milestones earlier than a normal Earth baby. They all began crawling between three to four months of age, and stood up, cruising around on furniture by six to seven months. By the time Angel had turned nine months old, all the babies, other than Eric, were cruising, and Angel could walk, albeit, clumsily, all by herself.

***

The day arrived when Rafferty told everyone they would be making their first jump. He announced it at dinner, the night before. He stood, and everyone stared, for he never spoke aloud to the group.

Everyone grew quiet and waited expectantly. Arnold smiled, shaking Jenny's hand excitedly in his, for he already knew what Rafferty was going to tell everyone, feeling infinitely excited.

"Hello," Rafferty said, looking down at the table. All the women held their babies, except for Angel. She happily cruised around all the table legs.

"Uh, tomorrow we'll be making our first jump," he said, and quickly sat down.

Everyone started talking at once, and Rafferty quickly stood up again, as Jemma urged him on. Everyone asked questions at the same time, and Rafferty put his hand up, clearly overwhelmed.

"Look, I'm not going to explain it in detail, okay? I'll be on the upper deck, with the Graylings, watching them operate."

Everyone looked at him in awe. None of the newly channeled members had met the Graylings in person, even though they could now converse with them anytime they wanted. Everyone felt extremely close to all of them. They also felt particularly close to the two Elders, Harold and Ramona.

Rafferty, however, interacted with the Graylings much more than anyone else, including the old-boarders. He was the only one who seemed completely comfortable around them. Perhaps even more so than around his own species.

"Once we make the jump, I'll come down to the observation deck, to be with all of you," he said, smiling down at Jemma. "We've made a jump before, at least, the six of us who were here before we left Earth. So, we know what to expect. Basically, it goes like this. You won't feel any acceleration. You won't feel any real change at all, but…"

"But there *is* an odd sensation," Arnold said, standing and nodding at Rafferty. Rafferty nodded and sat back down, grateful for someone else taking over.

"It's really hard to describe," Arnold continued. "But don't be nervous. It's nothing so weird. We decided, after the first time we all did it, that everyone should be on the observation deck. To see it. That way, you know what's happening, and exactly when."

"What he means is," Roslyn now stood, taking the reins. "There will be a bright flash of white light. It only lasts for a moment, but in that time, the ship, and all of us, will literally cross over millions of years of distance, in an instant. It doesn't feel like anything physically, but somehow…" she faltered, searching for the right words. "Somehow, deep inside somewhere, it's almost as if your mind is aware of what's happened. I guess that's the best way to put it. It feels like jet lag, a bit. It takes your mind a moment or two to catch up, deal with what's happened. It's so hard to describe. It feels like you're floating, almost. Or like you're dreaming, but only for a moment. Or like you're falling. Like it felt when you first channeled into the Graylings."

Several people nodded. Jess looked around at everyone, not comprehending. She looked at Ben, who only shrugged, for he hadn't channeled in yet. They had just talked about it a few nights before.

Roslyn sat down, and Arnold remained standing. He nodded at Roslyn, to thank her.

"Yeah, that's pretty accurate. But, as I've told most of you, after the jump, we'll be standing still for a while. And then, everyone will get their first real look at what's around us. The observation deck will be black, like always. There will be a bright, quick flash. Then, you'll be able to see… everything. Once you re-establish yourself, get over the sensations that Roslyn described, you'll be seeing the most beautiful view you've ever seen in your entire life."

Arnold quickly sat down again, taking Jenny's hand once more, obviously very excited. Everyone felt the same enthusiasm, including Jess. It dawned on her then, that they were doing something incredible. She realized that all of them would be the first human beings to ever see space this way—the first of her race—to ever travel this far and be in this part of the Universe. She also wondered if they would be the only ones. She wondered if anyone they left behind on Earth would ever travel this far. She suddenly felt terrifyingly alone, and it frightened her. She quickly stood, chair scraping the floor, and left the dining hall.

Ben scooped up Angel and quickly followed. Everyone watched them go in silence, then resumed their meals and conversations about the jump that would take place the following day.

***

"Jess," Ben called, carrying Angel, who cooed over his shoulder. "Jess," Ben repeated, catching up to her. "Everything's going to be okay."

"I know."

"Then what's wrong? Are you worried about the jump?"

"No."

"You're worried about the side effects? They'll only last a few moments."

"I know, it's not that."

"Then, what?"

"I don't know," she said, frowning, trying to put her feelings into words. He waited for her to gather her thoughts, remaining ever patient.

"I just... I'm afraid of what we'll see after," she said, sighing heavily.

"What do you mean? Arnold said it will be beautiful. I can only imagine. Maybe we'll see giant gas nebulas, up close, or stars that are still only just forming. It will be a galaxy full of stars, whose light is so far from Earth, they haven't seen them yet."

"I know, and *that's* what scares me. We're already so far away, we're completely off the map, Ben. There's no way to even explain to any human being where we are, because we're so far, already, we're in places that no human being has ever seen. We're flying through stars with no names, unknown, and..." she trailed off, looking down at the floor. "I just feel so alone."

"Jess—"

"I know I'm not alone, Ben," Jess rolled her eyes. "But we're on a ship, and all I can picture, is us, on this tiny piece of machinery, in this huge, black, nothingness. I know we're not lost, but it feels that way.

411

Like we're floating in this huge, vast, nothingness. I just feel, physically, like we could all start falling, and falling, and never stop. I don't know how to describe it."

"It's scary," Ben nodded. "I know."

"We were not meant to be here," she said, her eyes full of fear. "We could never be here on our own. And I just know—I don't know how, but I *know*—that even as far as we've already come, no other people will ever be here. We'll never leave Earth and come this far. People, they won't. We're all there is out here. There will never be any other human beings that come this far. I feel it, Ben."

"Well, I'm sure the Pilgrims felt that way, when they came to America on their ships."

"This is not that, Ben," Jess said, looking incredulous. "This is so much bigger than that, and you know it," she frowned. "The Pilgrims? Colonizing? Compared to this?! It's like, comparing a grain of sand to a mountain, Ben. This is huge. I can't even," she shook her head. She couldn't finish, just turned to walk away.

"It's a lot," Ben stopped her. "I know that, Jess."

"How do you keep from losing your *mind*," Jess turned back to him, angry and desperate.

"I stay sane because I have *you*," Ben said, standing in front of her, close. He looked at her face with so much love, Jess immediately loosened visibly.

"And this little thing I'm holding," he said, juggling Angel, who cooed and giggled. Jess smiled.

"The two of you are all I focus on. That's all I can handle right now. It's enough. It's small, but it's my world. Anything else outside that? Is simply too big."

Jess nodded. She motioned for Angel, and Ben handed her over. Jess placed Angel over her shoulder, hugging her tight. She looked up at Ben and smiled. He took a deep breath, closing his eyes.

"Jess, I think I should see Ezra and channel in tonight."

She closed her eyes, feeling Angel's heartbeat against her shoulder. She nodded. She knew he would say that, from the moment Roslyn compared the jump feeling to channeling in and saw so many heads nod in understanding. Ben needed to understand things. It was part of the reason he became a scientist. He needed to know how things worked. She opened her eyes, still nodding. He saw that she understood and sighed. She really did know him far too well.

***

That night, in Ezra's room, Ben channeled in. Everything changed for him in an instant, just as it had for all the others. The Graylings were no longer a fable, or some distant beings that he only thought about in some vague, obscure way. He could no longer push them aside, or even deny that they were there on board with everyone else. He met them, *knew* them, felt what they felt. Just as everyone else did. In an instant, he contained every memory and feeling the Elders experienced. He felt awed, moved, horrified, saddened, and elated, all at once. And just as everyone else experienced, the phenomenon remained uniquely humbling for him, as he struggled in the aftermath of such a revelation—working it into his own mental constructs and views of the world.

What Ben learned—but what none of the others truly understood—was how absolutely amazing it was that everyone who channeled in could handle things so well. It escaped their knowledge that the average human being would simply break under so much strain—with such a demand of change, of reordering one's personal views of life, love, the world around them—their Universe.

The Society would never realize just how special they were—how uniquely shaped (and each, singularly different) yet, they made the change, the transfer of thoughts with relative ease—although nothing could be further from the truth. The change was inherently, indescribably difficult, all the same. But none of them broke, or lost sanity, and they all assumed this would be so of any human that channeled in, but it wasn't. None of them knew how remarkably rare they were. None of them even came close to grasping how inherently perfect it was, that they—together, and as individuals—were the perfect assortment of humans for the task that lay ahead. Yet, this revelation landed on Ben when he channeled in.

Ben changed. His eyes were opened to the monumental task that lay ahead, on Hesperia. He loved the Graylings and knew how amazing they were as a species. He knew they needed to survive, to live, to gain their planet back, to thrive again. They were a species so inherently pure in their view of the Universe, it would not be the same if they died out, he realized. They needed to exist. Everything that was good in life was contained inside the Graylings. They were a perfect species, with a pure balance of intellect, lack of aggression, and ability to learn, to progress, without destroying or hurting the world or the Universe around them. They were not human beings. They did not tear down or break apart. They built, and learned, and loved. They saw what the reality of their Universe was, and they simply co-existed with it, in perfect harmony.

The Bailon took everything away from them, and in some strange way, Ben now realized, it threw the Universe off balance. It set in motion a string of events that would someday affect even humanity. Ben *knew* somehow, that eventually, the Bailon would inevitably find humanity, and Earth, even if it took another thousand years. He knew in an instant that it wasn't only the Graylings they needed to save, but also themselves, and ultimately, perhaps many other races and planets in between.

These were all the revelations that landed in Ben's waking consciousness. Everyone who channeled in learned something mysterious, and it was simply too much knowledge for each separate person to fully realize consciously—all that came to be inside their minds—they each took away something special that helped them incorporate their new wisdom. Each person found that they landed on certain aspects, and each mind focused on whatever they needed, to make sense of it all. The emotions were the same, inherently across the board. Whatever waking knowledge each person walked away with inside their mind, they all experienced the same awe, love and hope for the Graylings.

Ben needed to come to terms with the knowledge in the wake of his own unique encounter. He immediately knew that they would all be saving Earth from some far-distant, horrible fate. It was true, that humanity was just at the beginning of a monumental shift in design— only just beginning to touch upon the ability to live in peace—yet, the change had begun. When they did reach this amazing achievement in evolutionary development, however, it would be just the right timing for the Bailon to move on from Hesperia, to another world, and at some point, find Earth.

Ben somehow knew *all* of this, even as he met the Graylings for the first time. Humanity would progress towards peace, but in doing so, be unable to defend themselves against a species inherently outside the laws of nature, utterly bent on destroying and simply taking things that did not belong to them.

The Bailon were the worst of what lay inside the still infant human id—the lowest form of human aggression—combined with the sad fact that they contained the intellect to travel so far, and reach other life, but without the constraint to honor what they found. The Bailon were much as Grace tried to describe human beings to Alma—like immature toddlers, who had come upon the Graylings and their home, and saw it as a toy they wanted. They did not know how to share, only take and hurt. They were a childish race, whose intellect charged far ahead of emotion, barren of constraint, control, or even basic courtesy.

Ben could sense, however, that the potential to develop civility was simply lacking in the Bailon. It was not a matter of time, before they grew as a race. They had grown all they ever would, and their destructive behaviors would continue, unabated, polluting the Universe.

Humanity would eventually evolve, far from the end of the spectrum that the Bailon inhabited, and more toward the ways of the Graylings. Ben knew this, could see humanity was well on its way, with the introduction of the first transgenics into the world back on Earth. They would make it. But not if the Bailon found them first, the way they found the Graylings.

The way Ben logically thought, it seemed as if Humanity had been selected to make this jump, to survive and elevate to the next tier of existence and understanding, just as the Graylings had. The Bailon were not, and they had to be stopped. The night before their first jump, Ben learned the same knowledge everyone else who channeled in did, although, no one openly spoke of these things. Some did not speak of it because they were not fully, consciously aware of the knowledge inside of them. Others were simply too overwhelmed—many still couldn't fathom how it was even possible—nor could any of them understand how they would ever succeed in such a task.

It felt like being born all over again—into a new world of beauty and purpose—and overwhelming love, security, and hope. Ben went back to Jess a changed man, but his love for her did not lessen, in fact, it grew. He entered their room, and she sat, waiting, sitting on the couch, looking infinitely worried. Angel was fast asleep, as well as Sarah. It was late, after ten o'clock at night.

Jess stood, looking at Ben expectantly, nervously wringing her hands. He rushed up and hugged her so fiercely, she melted against him, no longer a firecracker, but a lost and scared human being who only wanted someone to take care of her and tell her everything would be okay. And that is exactly what Ben did.

"Everything is going to be okay, Jess," he breathed in her ear, and her heart slowed—instantly calm—for she could hear that he was still Ben, no matter what had happened to him. She felt the way he held her, felt his heart beating against her face, and she knew he still loved her the same. She felt it. She also felt that whatever had happened to him, it made him infinitely happy. She pulled away, reaching up, taking his face in her hands, tears in her eyes. She looked at him, her heart full of love.

"Everything is love, Jess," Ben said. "That's simply all. Everything is for love."

She cried, hot tears slipping down her cheeks in stinging tracks. She kissed him, her heart breaking for joy. She loved him so much. He kissed her back, and they went into their room and made love. It was the only way, the only thing to do, whenever they felt overwhelmed by each other. It seemed as if they were overwhelmed by their love for one another almost endlessly.

That night, as Jess lay in bed, listening to Ben and Angel breathe, she felt a revelation inside her heart. She loved Ben too much not to be in the same place where his heart resided—to know what he knew and feel what he felt—she couldn't be left alone, on the outside of something clearly so big, it made Ben's heart burst with happiness. She wasn't jealous of his newfound love of the Graylings, she merely wanted to share it with him. There now lay a gap between them, and Jess knew she needed to close it.

18

The following day, everyone gathered on the observation deck at ten in the morning. Everyone was very excited. Most were now connected to the Graylings. Only four people weren't: Aaron, Earl, Sarah and Jess.

Everyone gathered, except Rafferty, who would come down once the jump was complete, to see the view with everyone else. Each person stood, looking around, their faces excited, nervous, anxious, and even a bit fearful, some more than others.

Jess stood in front of Ben, leaning against his chest, feeling his heart beat against her shoulder. He wrapped his arms around her, leaning his face against the top of her head, lost in love. Sarah held onto Jess's hand, standing to her left. Hanley and Rachel stood side by side, holding hands. Arnold cradled Jenny in much the same fashion as Ben. Ezra and Roslyn stood side by side, also holding hands, and Jemma stood on Roslyn's right side. Martin stood with his arm around Eileen, their heads leaning together. Eric slept quietly in Eileen's arms, a small blessing, his head on her shoulder. Despite his behavior being more difficult than the other babies, Eileen still loved her son more than life itself.

Aaron stood next to Earl, and they looked out at the vast blackness in both trepidation and awe. Malcolm stood with Grace on his left. On her left, stood Jenny and Arnold. Jenny smiled, her eyes glistening. Kate and Alma stood on the end, on the far-left side of the wall of black, holding one another.

Everyone knew the jump was coming, but Ben had the presence of mind to narrate for the few who couldn't hear the Graylings.

"It's about to happen," Ben said, intrigued. "We're about to do something no other human being has done."

Everyone looked out at the vast expanse of black, their hearts beating in overtime. Arnold heard it as one steady hum in his ears. It comforted him, hearing the collective heartbeats of the entire group. He hugged Jenny tighter.

"One small step," he said.

"Not so small at all," Jenny retorted, and Arnold giggled. He was nervous, despite the fact the six old-boarders had made the jump before. It was only practice then, and this was the real deal. This jump would take them infinitely further than they had ever gone and bring them one step closer to the purpose they had all been brought together for. Arnold realized this and kissed the top of Jenny's head.

Everyone had set their babies down on the floor behind them in the center of the room when they first entered. The babies all sat quietly, calmly, or crawled around. Angel cruised busily around, taking no notice of what went on around her.

"Ben," Jess said, sounding scared, "When?"

"Right now," he whispered in her ear, holding her hand tight. She looked straight ahead, nodding.

It was so quiet in the room when Ben whispered his answer into her ear, everyone heard. Arnold, of course, heard it, as well as Martin, but so did the rest of The Society. They all turned their attention to the vast, twenty-foot high, floor-to-ceiling view of blackness in front of them, and held their breath, waiting. Three seconds passed with no change, but it felt like an eternity.

Then, suddenly, everything was white. Not just the vast expanse of view in front of them on the rounded wall—everything—the flash so intense, the entire room bathed in white light, but only for a fraction of a second. It felt so shocking, however, it played tricks on everyone's mind. They felt the brightness lasted for several seconds, their eyes trying to readjust to the normal lighting around them. The flash was so short, it didn't have time to hurt their eyes. It was like having a camera go off in their faces, however, and everything held an afterglow for several moments. Everyone felt as if they floated; euphoric and giddy. Then everything felt normal again. Everyone's feet touched the floor once more.

They all blinked, attempting to adjust their eyes. Several of the women looked anxiously around at their babies, to see if they were okay. The babies didn't seem fazed. They kept crawling, or cruising around, as if nothing had happened, although, they now all appeared as if they walked on stars, the floor covering the entire expanse of the room also projecting the view of space around them, as well as the ceiling. As eyes refocused, gasps and sighs sounded off, in domino fashion, as one-by-one, they took in the view that filled the room.

Many people cried, the view so beautiful, tears were their natural reaction. Jess stared in awe and wonder. She thought she would be terrified, but instead, she stood, as if time had stopped, and looked at the Universe around her in complete humility.

They all saw colors—dazzling, bright lights—shimmering in darkness. Stars stood suspended, many still thousands of light years away, but still more radiant than anyone had ever seen. The brilliant hues came to their eyes in such vivid arrays of yellow, orange, blue, red, violet, and green, they all felt as if they had never truly seen a star before that moment, and it seemed the same of the very colors and shades they beheld.

To the right, in the far corner of vision, a large nebula shaped in a lazy circle, ringed in brilliant lapis lazuli and filled with bright yellow, red and white, amazed their eyes. It was the most beautiful thing any of them had ever seen.

"It's so close," Jenny said.

"No," Arnold said. "It's actually still over three hundred thousand light years away. It's just that big."

Rafferty silently came in and joined Jemma, standing proudly at her side, taking her hand. His eyes filled with tears as he took in the view with everyone else.

Ben saw the same colors as the rest of The Society, but he also saw halos of floating, dissipating energy ringing everything, traveling, swimming to his eyes in rainbow colors of vividness that made him feel as if he had never seen colors before that moment. Everything glowed, shimmered, and danced in front of him. He cried, tears streaming down his face. He could see the energy the Universe contained, and it awed and humbled him. Cosmic rays radiated out from dark places, arriving to his eyes from unknown destinations far-off in the vast expanse of space. These rays traveled on bright, rippling golden arcs that reminded Ben of sunlight reflecting off water. Where everyone else saw large patches of pitch, between the light, Ben witnessed complex luminosities of energy radiating from everywhere. There was no darkness in his view, only varied wavelengths of energy, in diverse shades, swirling in subduction, moving through other colors of energy, everything overlapping. The beauty was overwhelming.

Jess let out a large sigh, tears standing in her eyes. She walked up to the wall and caressed the sights beneath her fingertips, smiling and crying at once. Martin cried, for he could hear Jess's thoughts, as well as Ben's, and could hear their progression. He knew what was coming, and his heart filled with such joy, he spoke aloud.

"Jesus," he said, remembering his old friend.

No one took any notice of these events, each caught up in their own experience at seeing the Universe so close, in front of their faces. They all floated, enveloped inside of it, and instead of feeling lost or alone, they felt protected, safe, and warm. They all felt love—even the ones who weren't channeled in—for, no one was connected to Jess, but they all felt they understood her in that moment, and they all understood what she felt when she spoke.

"I'm touching God," she whispered, crying tears of joy. "I'm touching everything."

There were no words, ultimately, to describe what any of them felt. Jess felt unbelievably small, yet so infinitely special in that moment.

She knew she was alive for a reason. She suddenly *knew* she was not alone, and that nothing she looked upon was an accident.

"I'm part of everything," she breathed. "We're the first."

It made no sense, and yet, everyone felt they understood, including Aaron and Earl, even agnostic Hanley. Sarah smiled, holding Ben's hand.

Jess turned to Ben with a look of urgency. He frowned, worried the view had rocked her world too much, that she might be on the verge of a breakdown. It was a wonder, he thought quickly, that none of them had broken yet, even as special as he knew them all to be.

"I want to channel in," Jess said, searching Ben's face.

"Are—are you sure?" He frowned at her. She nodded emphatically.

"I need to *know*," she said, and Ben nodded.

He wasn't going to argue with her. In the back of his mind, he worried that Jess might only be making this choice while caught up in the euphoria of the jump, the decision not being made with a clear mind. He thought this, but then, he was afraid to hesitate, for fear she might change her mind.

He knew that even if her decision was being made rashly, once she channeled in, it wouldn't matter. Once Jess channeled in, she would know, *understand*, and it would change everything. She would not regret even a hastily-made decision, once she felt the love, and learned everything.

He looked at Martin, saw him nod, and did not hesitate a moment longer, but quickly searched out Ezra, already stepping forward, now beaming.

Everyone parted for Ezra, as he walked quickly up to Jess, taking her hand in his, and turned to lead her into the center of the room.

"You're going to do it here?" Jenny said, sounding shocked.

Ezra shot her a look that closed her mouth. He, like Ben, worried that at any moment, Jess would change her mind, and he knew it was of the utmost importance that Jess do this. If now was the time, so be it. He didn't want to lose this chance. It might not come around again for years, if ever.

Once it happened, everything would change. They all felt it. Even the ones who weren't channeled in sensed this. Jenny had simply spoken without thought, and she immediately fell silent.

***

Jess and Ezra sat on the floor, Indian-style, while everyone gathered around to watch. Aaron and Earl looked on with interest. Everyone else simply smiled, for they were about to see Jess change. Angel cruised over, touching Jess's shoulder, and she turned, smiling, but she looked nervous. Ben quickly scooped Angel up, and Jess turned her attention back to Ezra. He took both her hands, letting out a huge breath.

"Okay, it's really simple. You'll feel a moment of dizziness, and then you'll be connected."

Jess impatiently nodded, and Ezra told her to close her eyes. He placed his hands over Jess's temples and began feeling his way in, the tendrils of energy once again threading into the darkness of the mind. He quickly found the shining grain of sand, glowing bright and golden, and smiled. He always smiled at this part but had no idea. Everyone looked on in anticipation and utter silence. Even the babies made very little noise, still crawling around.

Ezra saw the glowing center of Jess's mind. In an instant, he enveloped it inside his energy, and it burst alive, infinitely bright, like a star's birth. Jess connected, suddenly falling. Then, as quickly as it began, she landed, surrounded by warmth, comfort, and love. She smiled, already crying tears of overwhelming joy.

She met the Elders, and was not afraid, for she knew everything about them instantly. She saw the Graylings, and they looked nothing like the monsters of her nightmares. She saw them through their own eyes and knew them as herself. She was them, they were her, and it made complete sense to both races. They asked if she wanted to see what had happened to them, and warned her it would be greatly upsetting, disturbing, and painful. She consented, for she knew they would be right there with her, to comfort her all the while.

Then she *saw*—all the horror that had come upon them—what they had endured. She learned everything the rest of The Society had seen and already knew. She cried, in agony and sadness this time, tears slipping down her cheeks, even while her eyes remained shut tight. All the while, Ezra still held both her hands, and cried with her. Many of them cried. They were all channeled in with her, reliving their own knowledge, along with Jess. She could sense them all around her, and she knew she was not alone. It was the only comfort that got her through the horrors playing inside her mind and emotions. She lived someone else's experiences as if they were her own. She lived through an entire lifetime of memories of the Graylings inside her own mind, and suddenly, she simply was one of them.

When it was all over, she opened her eyes, and just as the rest of them did, she saw the world differently. She looked up at Ben, and smiled, and he felt such immense relief, he fell on his knees next to her, still holding Angel in his arms. Jess cried, looking at Ben's face, deep into his eyes.

"Ben," she whispered, barely able to speak. "Ben…" she couldn't finish.

"I know," he said, crying tears of relief and utter joy, for he truly did understand. She saw it in his eyes.

That was the first of six jumps, as they hurtled through space, traveling to the other side of the Universe and beyond. Headed directly for Hesperia as quickly as they possibly could.

***

Earl and Aaron channeled in shortly after Jess. Aaron was the last to go, as he was even more resistant, it turned out, than Jess. Watching her do it, however, and how happy it made her—how peaceful—in the end, even Aaron gave in. Partly because he was the only one who hadn't, other than Sarah. Though, also partly because he simply didn't like feeling left out or alone.

***

Shortly after Aaron channeled in, he came to see Jess. He came to her door and asked if she would walk with him. Jess looked over her shoulder at Ben, who played with Angel on the floor, searching his face with her eyes, to see if he minded. He smiled and nodded. She smiled back, giving her thanks, then left with Aaron.

They walked the hallway, passing the common room quickly. Hanley was there, playing cards with Rachel, Jenny and Arnold, Earl, Malcolm, Martin and Eileen. It was later in the evening, and most of the babies were already asleep. Martin smiled at Jess and Aaron and couldn't help but think back to their days inside the facility.

Hanley also thought of this, and sent an odd thought to Martin, as the sight of Jess and Aaron walking together flooded his mind with old memories.

It's funny, Hanley thought. *When I think back to my days in the facility, I don't remember anything bad. All I remember now, is all of you—my friends.*

Martin nodded, and a few people saw this. He spoke aloud, still smiling fondly.

"Yeah, I know. That's all I remember, too."

Arnold and Jenny looked at Martin and Hanley. Jenny smiled, for she suddenly caught on to what they were talking about. It was odd, but they all knew each other so well by this point, they could practically read one another's minds, even without possessing Martin's ability. Jenny turned and explained to Arnold.

"Seeing Jess and Aaron walking together like that reminded some of us of our time inside the facility," she said. Arnold nodded.

Jenny had told Arnold everything about her time in the facility, of course. Once they were together, living in the same quarters and married, they spent long hours every evening talking. They told each other everything about themselves. They discussed their childhoods. Arnold talked about his homeless days on the street as a manic-depressive, living in various shelters, including his odd foray into the desert, to Area 51, before being found by the Graylings and having his gene activated. Jenny talked of her mother, the cancer, and losing her so painfully. Arnold knew about every experience, every moment Jenny lived inside the facility, because she told him. When she told him how seeing Jess and Aaron brought memories back, he nodded, for she had told him about all the relationships that developed inside the facility, including the brief courtship and romance between Jess and Aaron.

"That time doesn't even seem real to me anymore," Earl said, picking up the topic along with a card, and everyone nodded. "It feels like that was another lifetime, a decade ago. Even though it's been little more than a year since we escaped. Can anyone believe that?"

Everyone shook their heads. Arnold stroked Jenny's hand. He could not believe that only one year ago, he didn't know she existed, at least, not as anything more than a simple name and an ability. A year ago, he had never been in love, and now, he would gladly die for Jenny, or little Mal, if he had to.

***

Jess and Aaron walked in silence for a short while, then Aaron shot a sideways glance, looking shy. She looked back, feeling awkward. They had not interacted much in the last year. This was the first time they were alone like this since the day they had escaped from the facility, when Jess went to see Aaron in his room.

"This feels weird," Aaron said. "But it feels strangely familiar, doesn't it? It brings back memories."

Jess nodded.

"I thought we could walk in the garden."

"Okay."

They entered the garden, and once on the winding dirt path, Aaron sighed, and began. Jess was patient.

"I channeled in."

"I know," she said. "You were the last... except for Sarah."

"Yeah," Aaron said, and stopped walking, looking at Jess.

"I can't believe I once stood in front of you, trying to convince you that Hanley was crazy."

"You didn't try to convince me, Aaron," Jess defended. "I was the one who didn't believe the Graylings existed."

"Neither did I. And I told you the only reason I would leave the facility, was for you."

Aaron looked down at the ground. Jess didn't know what to say, suddenly worried that Aaron might not be over her, after all this time. She couldn't read his mind and didn't feel connected to him as well as she did to everyone else. She frowned. Aaron saw this, and immediately reassured her.

"Don't worry, Jess. This isn't about you and me. That ended a long time ago, way before we even came here."

Jess nodded. She still felt bad for hurting him.

"You and Ben," Aaron sighed. "I told you once that I never loved you as much as he did. I meant that, Jess. It was hard, letting you go, but, I knew it was the right thing for me to do."

She nodded.

"You're still my friend," he said, and watched a tear slip down her cheek. He wiped it away.

"But now that I'm connected with the Graylings, everything's changed," he said gently.

She nodded again.

"Jess, I can *see* now how everything that happened between you and Ben was meant to be. And I'm sorry I ever tried to get in the way of that. I'm sorry for the terrible things I said."

"Aaron, that was a lifetime ago. It doesn't matter."

"It does to me. Because I see how much the two of you love each other. I also see how much you guys love Angel. She's beautiful, Jess."

"Thank you," Jess whispered, still heavily emotional.

"And I almost caused you to lose her," Aaron said, his voice shaking.

"But I didn't lose her, Aaron," she said, looking him in the eyes. "Don't you know by now, after everything we've all been through, that everything is okay?"

"Yeah, I do. Everything's changed, Jess."

"So?"

Aaron sighed. "I was a different person back in the facility and on the transport. I talked down to Hanley, even after we were on board the transport ship, Jess. Even after we docked in the cargo bay, here on the Graylings' ship. I was the last to channel in, even after I saw everyone around me changing. And I only channeled in, Jess, because of you."

"Why are you telling me this?" She searched Aaron's face, looking confused.

"Because I hurt you, Jess. I think part of the reason you resisted channeling in for so long... was because of me. I supported you in your disbelief. I was right there with you."

"It doesn't matter, Aaron. It's all forgiven. We're here. Right where we're meant to be. I never blamed you for anything. You must know that by now."

Aaron nodded, frowning. He looked at Jess, searching her face.

"What, Aaron? What's wrong?"

"Everyone that channels into the Grayling changes. Everyone sees something different, takes something different away. I mean, it's all there, but, everyone gets something separate, too."

Jess nodded, for she understood what Aaron meant. Each person's connection to the Graylings and their vast knowledge was universally moving and emotional, yet extremely unique and personal for every individual in question. Just as they all had the pseudogene, but each manifested a different ability. Yet, they were all intrinsically linked by a common force and bond.

"Jess. You have to *believe*."

"What do you mean?"

"You have to accept whatever the Graylings tell you."

"What are you talking about, Aaron? I *do* believe. How can I not?"

"You have to meet them."

Jess looked at him in shock, and instinctively recoiled in fear. "No one has met them, yet, except Rafferty."

Aaron nodded. "But you *need* to, Jess. Everyone else can if they want to. Most of us just don't feel the need. We're already connected mentally and emotionally. We can talk to them whenever we want. Ask our questions. Be reassured."

"So?"

"So, I don't feel like I need to be in the same room with them."

"And you think I do?"

"I *know* you do, Jess."

"Why? How?"

"I don't know," Aaron said, smiling weakly, looking sad. "I only know that when I channeled in, it's one of the things I took away. And that I needed to tell you. Everyone takes something of their own. If they decide to share it with the others, they do. When the time is right, or if they feel ready. Now's the right time for me... to tell *you*. What I took away from channeling in, Jess. I know I was wrong, about everything. Nothing is a coincidence, Jess. Even me. I'm not useless."

"You were never useless, Aaron," Jess said, sounding sad and hurt. She still cared about him.

He began walking again and smiled at her. He took her hand, and she knew he didn't mean it in any other way than as a friend. He led her to the wildflowers and pulled her in, until they stood surrounded among them. They were not nearly as tall as the sunflowers in the old meadow at the facility. Most of the flowers only grew up to their thighs, some a bit taller, most even shorter, at knee-length. Aaron reached down and picked a white daisy. He touched the petals one by one, turning each a different shade, until the flower held every hue of the rainbow. He handed it to Jess.

"It may not help the Graylings, but it can make you smile," he said, looking at her face.

"It's beautiful. But you were never useless, Aaron."

"Maybe, maybe not. But I'm not the same whiny kid that you met inside the facility, Jess. I've changed. I believe now. I believe everything. And I know you still don't."

"But, I do," she argued.

"No," Aaron shook his head. "If you did, you'd be training already—preparing, asking more questions—doing something. I'm sorry, Jess, I'm not saying any of this to upset you or piss you off. It's just the truth. You don't fully believe. And any part I ever played in that is over. I'm here to tell you that you need to believe. I used to say that Jesus was crazy. He believed. He had faith. It drove me nuts. But he was right, Jess. Jesus was right. Everything happens for a reason. We each have a part to play. And it's not my place to decide or know how big a part I'll play, or how small. I'll go wherever the Graylings tell me to go. I'll do whatever they tell me to do."

"And you think I won't?"

"I'm not sure," Aaron said, searching her eyes, looking scared. "Jess, you need to meet them. I know you're scared, but, you *need* to. I can't even explain how I know. I just do."

"Because suddenly you have faith, out of nowhere?" Jess sounded bitter.

"Yes," Aaron said.

"How dare you question my loyalty to the Graylings, Aaron. You don't know me. You think you do, but you don't. I've come here, haven't I?"

"Yes, you have, but coming here is not the only step, it's only the first."

"No, but I connected to the Graylings. I've done everything I'm supposed to do," Jess's voice sounded high and reedy. Her breathing came in short bursts.

"No, you haven't," Aaron said, his voice remaining low and calm. "You still have doubts. You're still questioning your purpose. Look me in the eyes and tell me that's not true."

Jess did not look Aaron in the eyes. She looked down at the ground, shaking her head. She looked at the daisy, twisting it in her fingers.

"After denying all this for so long, you're actually standing here? You, of all people, Aaron, telling me to have faith?"

"I know," Aaron laughed, sounding bitter. The irony was not lost on him. "I'm living proof of how much a person can change, Jess. So is Ben."

Jess looked at Aaron, surprised. He smiled, nodding, tears in his eyes.

"I may not love you as much as Ben, but I do still love you, Jess. You're my friend. You always will be. Please know that. I'm telling you what I'm telling you right now, because I love you. You're still struggling. The Graylings can help. But even they can't take your doubts away. Even if you meet with them, they can't give you faith."

"And you think you can?" She looked at him, incredulous.

"No," Aaron said, sounding infinitely sad. "No one can. But after everything I did to you in the past, I need to at least try. It's the least I can do. The rest will be up to you. It will all depend on how much love you allow into your heart."

"I love the Graylings, Aaron."

"I know. But you need to realize that everyone else loves them, too, just as much as you. Everyone else has faith, Jess. If your love for the Graylings isn't enough to hold onto, then maybe…"

"What, Aaron? Then maybe what?"

"Maybe you're love for The Society will be," he finished. "Promise me you'll go and see them. I know Rafferty will take you."

"I don't know if I can right now."

"Why?"

"I'm pregnant," Jess said, her voice low.

"Jess," Aaron smiled, his voice so gentle, it broke her heart. "Congratulations. That's wonderful. Does Ben know?"

Jess shook her head. "I was going to tell him tonight, after Angel goes to sleep. I only found out this afternoon." She smiled, another tear slipping down her cheek. "I don't think it would be a good idea to put myself through that stress, with the baby."

"No, of course not," Aaron said, for he knew going to see the Graylings would be extremely frightening for her. "It can wait. But, Jess. Promise me after your baby is born, you'll go to Rafferty and ask him to take you to meet them. Will you promise me that?"

Jess looked at Aaron, thinking hard, considering his request. She saw the desperate longing on his face, and she knew he had changed into a better man. She nodded her promise to him, and he smiled, looking amazed and relieved.

"Thank you, Jess," he breathed.

They left the garden soon after. Jess walked back to her room alone. That night, she told Ben she was pregnant with their second child. He was thrilled. She also told Ben about Aaron's request that she go see the Graylings, after the baby was born. Ben shrugged. He knew everyone took something different away with them when they channeled in. He didn't know how to question it, if Aaron took away the pressing need to tell Jess she needed to meet the Graylings. He tried to be gentle with her, for she had already come further than he ever thought she would. He did not want to push her. He played the only card he knew to use, and still felt bad for it, for he knew all her weak spots. But it was also the truth, and it was right.

"You promised him?"

She nodded. He nodded back.

"If you promised him, Jess, you have to honor it. For, what are we, if we cannot keep the promises we make?"

Ben lifted his hand and held it in front of her face. He twisted his wedding ring around on his finger, and Jess understood his point perfectly.

19

Eight months later, Jess and Ben welcomed a son, whom they named Alexander. They called him Alex for short. He was born exactly a year-and-a-half after Angel. After that, they elected to use birth control, for Jess felt she needed to focus her attention on raising the two children they had, and channel the rest of her concentration into their impending arrival on Hesperia, and the task that lay ahead for them all.

All the other couples elected to use birth control after their first child, except for Jemma and Rafferty, who did not stop until after the birth of their fifth child. Everyone wanted to focus on preparing for the War.

***

It wasn't until after Alex turned two, that Jess decided she finally felt ready to meet the Graylings. A few others would also go, slowly, one at a time, but only half a dozen met them in total, including Rafferty. One was Sarah, although, she would not do so for several more years after Jess. Another was Hanley, for he'd wanted to meet them in person, after being in contact with them for so long. Martin met with them as well, and Arnold. That was all.

Other than Rafferty, however, everyone opted to meet the Graylings only once, because the experience was singularly humbling, and greatly distressing. Jess could not understand this until she met them for the first and only time. Ben did not feel the need to meet them, and this made it more difficult for Jess to honor her oath to Aaron. The only reason she went was because of her promise. She greatly regretted making it, as the thought of meeting the Graylings frightened her more and more.

Rafferty brought her, leading Jess down the far hallway, to the right of the cargo bay, and they entered a small elevator she never even knew was there. He explained that they were going up three decks, to where the Elders, Harold and Ramona, lived, and that these two were always the ones who met with the humans, each time one elected to do so. Rafferty was the only one who worked with anyone else besides, for he spent a large amount of time with the engineers.

"When the doors open, we'll get off, walk down a long hallway, and go into a large room. Harold and Ramona will be there, but only those two."

"Are you sure I'll only meet two of them?"

Rafferty nodded, looking sad.

The elevator doors opened, and they went down a long hallway, then stopped at a door. Rafferty put his hand on the door's panel and thought about warning Jess one last time but decided not to. She would soon know for herself.

The door slid open, and Rafferty led Jess into a large, rounded, gray metal room. There were chairs, but they were much larger than the seats on her deck. They were rounded, with long, slender armrests. The ceilings on this deck, in the hallways and in the room, were taller than on her deck, by at least another nine feet. On the far wall, on the other side, another door slid open, and Jess's heart began to race, deep in fear.

Being connected to the Graylings, and meeting them in person, were two very different things. Although she'd lived their lives and experiences, had seen their images through their own eyes, she found that once the initial connection ended, her mind could not clearly recall their faces, or bodies. Instead, she mentally reverted to classic alien images as stereotyped from Earth culture.

The human psyche could take learning all the Graylings memories, but, as it turned out, had trouble reconciling the visual experience of seeing something so infinitely alien, the mind rejected it almost immediately. Jess felt like she was dreaming. She felt fear and wanted to run. But she also heard Harold's voice inside her head, like that of an old, dear friend, and she looked on in wonder, as he walked toward her.

In detail, her mind knew what she saw: A tall, slender being, with pale gray skin, and large, dark eyes. They were not at all shaped like the classic alien orbs her mind had adopted from Earth. The conceptions of little green men, Martians, and the heart-shaped alien head that she'd subconsciously come to expect, seemed laughable in the face of the being she now looked upon.

His eyes were dark, almost black, and almond shaped, the thinner end pointed upward, toward his forehead. His eyes were also extremely large, filling nearly a third of the upper half of his face. He had no mouth that Jess could discern, and yet, she got the distinct impression of a line, near the bottom of his face, just above the chin, which came to a rounded point, but his face appeared more oval-shaped. Centered just beneath the eyes were two small holes on either side of a raised ridge; his nose and nostrils. His cheek bones were visible under the skin, giving his face a chiseled look. Despite Harold being, indeed, alien in form, still, somehow, he seemed handsome. Jess received the distinct feeling of incredible esteem when looking upon him, as if his very physical stature screamed Elder authority and wisdom. She felt instantly awed and humbled in his presence. He was beautiful.

Immediately, he seemed familiar to her, for she'd witnessed the world through his eyes, and had seen the Graylings in the familiarity of her own species. She'd lived a lifetime as Harold, but now she stood in front of him, outside of his race, saw him as a separate being, and she felt overwhelmingly afraid.

Harold felt this fear, and tried to comfort her, and this helped, for she could sense his own trepidation and concern for her well-being. She felt how much he cared about her, and her emotional state. Her fear quickly dissipated, as she continued to look upon him, in awe and wonder. She suddenly felt ashamed.

Harold asked why she was ashamed, for he could feel it as his own emotion. She thought quickly back to him.

I'm sorry I'm afraid of you. I don't know how to stop it.

It is only reasonable to be afraid of something that looks so different from yourself. It is the normal, natural reaction of every human being that sees us, Harold told her.

Are you afraid of us?

Yes, Harold thought. Jess frowned.

You are very alien to us as well, as we struggle in subjection to your emotions, for many of them are feelings we do not experience, save through you.

So, we force you to feel pain? Again, Jess felt ashamed.

Yet, through those feelings, we have come to know how truly helpless you are, as a race, to deal with your own uncontrollable emotions. It is what you, as a species, must deal with, even as you grow out of this phase, and into the next.

I'm still sorry, she thought, crying, a single tear slipping down her cheek.

Suddenly, Jess frowned, for she felt exhausted. She looked at Harold in confusion and realized one of the reasons he seemed so alien, wasn't his physical appearance, but the feeling he gave off.

She felt wave after wave of subtle energy floating off Harold, reaching her in small whispers, making her feel drained and weak. She didn't think she could be around him for too much longer, it was utterly debilitating.

And now you know why we don't live among you, Harold sent. *To be so close to us, you are connected to our minds without interruption. Your minds, although channeled in, are not designed to connect constantly. To do so for prolonged time, would exhaust you, and possibly take you beyond recovery. Your mind could snap, you risk losing sanity. We could not bear that, Jess. It would break our hearts. We know you like a daughter.*

Jess nodded, crying harder now, for she felt his love for her. She loved him back. She could not understand, however, the fatigue coming from him. He answered her thoughts with sadness, and she realized he was afraid to cause *her* any mental anguish. He didn't want to make *her* sad.

It is my energy, slowly leaving me, Harold explained. *The longer we are away from our home, the more quickly we… leak.*

Is everyone this way?

Yes. But Ramona and I are in a much more accelerated process of the phenomenon.

Where is Ramona? Jess felt sudden fear jolt through her.

She is too weak to stand, Harold said. *She is too weary today to even connect, and for that, she is infinitely saddened. She very much wanted to meet you, Jess. She wanted to meet the one who is so special.*

"But I'm not," Jess said out loud, raising her voice without meaning to, without even knowing she had. Rafferty winced.

You are, Harold said, sending out wave after wave of comfort and understanding. *Even we do not understand fully why, we simply know this to be the truth. When we reach Hesperia, you will defeat the Bailon.*

But, how?

We do not know, Harold sent.

"Then how can you be so certain I'll be able to help? What can I possibly do that will defeat them all?" Again, she spoke out loud.

Harold said nothing, and Rafferty looked at the floor, confused. Jess cried, unaware she did so.

"I can't do anything so big. All I can do is knock out the power for a mile, maybe two. That can't possibly defeat the Bailon. How could it?"

Again, Harold said nothing.

"How do you know these things?" Jess needed to know, and Harold sensed it.

All I can tell you is that we sense everything will work out. We will return to Hesperia, and somehow, you will shine bright. We see you, in brightness, and we sense the Bailon nowhere. It is a brief glimpse of what we can only guess is the outcome of the War. Our ability to see and know things is greatly limited to feelings. We are very rarely granted even the slightest visions of the future, Jess. And yet, we've seen you, in light, and we've sensed that the Bailon are not among you. You have defeated them all.

"And all the others? What of their abilities? If we're all meant to be here, what about everyone else? None of this makes any sense! If I'm the only one to defeat the Bailon, why is everyone else even here?!"

We do not know, Jess, Harold said, remaining ever-patient with her. *We only know that each one of you aboard this ship was meant to be here for one purpose or another. We can only assume that some of those purposes will never be fully revealed to us, but we hold to the belief that even if we know not how or why each of you is here, it was meant to be as it is. Everything is as it was meant to be, just as the stars have formed in each their own fashion, to shine when they were meant to. Everything is as it should be, and everything will be as it was meant to be.*

"But then, you're saying the Bailon were meant to kill everyone? That was supposed to happen?"

The Bailon chose to kill us. But every imbalance from conscious choice in the laws of life will be balanced by the Universe. It simply is. It will be.

"How?! The Universe can't *think*, it's not *alive*! How do you know?!" Jess yelled, completely exasperated. "What if the Bailon win, and we all die?!"

Everything dies, Jess, Harold said. *It is also part of the Balance.*

"What?!" Jess yelled, and Rafferty pulled her away, for she looked pale, her eyes sunken—beginning to show the physical effects of the toll Harold's energy took.

She quickly calmed then, for she saw the energy coming off Harold, and suddenly realized that he *glowed.* She had not seen it before, or if she had, she'd tried to tell herself she hallucinated. This entire encounter felt like a dream from the moment she laid eyes on Harold. The experience held the quality of a mirage or reverie.

"You're glowing," Jess whispered.

"He's *dying*," Rafferty said, and Jess looked first at the mechanic's face, then back at Harold, who now sat in a chair, looking deflated. His gray clothing, the same material as hers, loose on his frame. He appeared emaciated, as if wasting away. Her lip trembled.

"It's not a hallucination," she whispered. "I can see your energy leaving you."

Harold nodded, and she saw. It was such a human action, in her mind. She laughed.

Your mind cannot take much more, Jess, Harold thought to her. *You must leave me now, for your own sake.*

"But, you're so tired," Jess started to cry again. "And I've only upset you."

It cannot be helped, Harold soothed. *We are subjected to your human emotions, in such proximity, just as you are subjected to the effects of being near us. Now you fully comprehend the reason for our separation from you. It is not by choice, but out of necessity. For, you do understand how we feel about you?*

"Yes," Jess wept, tears now streaming down her cheeks. "I don't want you to die."

Again, Harold nodded. Jess watched him deflate further, and she felt panicked.

Rafferty started to pull her away again, but Jess suddenly ran to Harold, no longer afraid of his alien form. He stood well over nine feet tall, and even in his chair, sitting collapsed, he towered over her, as she, appearing infinitely small, stood directly in front of him. Her body belied that she no longer feared him. She felt so filled with love for him, he appeared to expand slightly, reinvigorated for a few moments.

They regarded one another silently, even in thought. Seeing Harold this close, Jess could only feel, not think in words. He was simply another being, one full of pure kindness, she felt soiled in his presence. She dared to question him, when his knowledge came from someplace so ancient and primordial, sage and unknown, she could never even dream of understanding it. The vision of his people was hard for her to imagine, but in that moment of regard, looking deep into Harold's face, his eyes, she gave up trying, and resigned herself to its truth, simply accepting.

She suddenly darted forward and hugged him. It was something no human being had ever done before. None had ever dared, their fear of his physical form always overtaking them if he attempted to stand closer than several feet away. None had ever dared approach him, paralyzed by terror, yet, as Jess stood in front of him, her legs nearly touching his knees, she rushed up to him feeling nothing but love. Harold sensed it, for the undiluted emotion flooded into him. He knew she was going to hug him, even before she leaned in to do so, and he instinctively moved to embrace her, reciprocating.

It was the first and only time a Grayling and a human would touch one another on board the ship, but every Grayling present in the vessel lived the experience as if they were Harold, in that room, holding Jess. They all felt her emotions, both happiness and hope. They also felt her love. The humans on board, three decks down, all stopped what they were doing, feeling what happened as well.

Jess felt Harold's arms around her, and her heart broke. She knew he would die before they reached Hesperia. She also knew it was inevitable that whatever would be, simply would be. She knew she would fight, somehow, and knew not what her actions would be, only that when the correct time came, she would act. Harold's mind carried her, giving her strength, even faith. She *felt* his belief, his certainty that she would succeed, and it became her own belief, if only in that moment.

Jess would never believe with as much conviction again. But Harold had given her a gift, in that one moment of certainty they felt together. She felt it through him, as her own certainty. Even if it faded, and she could never get it back so strongly, she held it in that moment, in Harold's embrace. She would recall and rely heavily upon that feeling of faded memory, and she held onto it for the next seven years. It guided her through, without her even knowing.

She slowly let go of Harold and sent him her thoughts.

I won't fail you. I don't know how I'll do it, but I will fight, and I will win. I'll do it for you. All of you. And if I fail, I'll still try. I'll die trying. I promise.

You will not die, Jess, you will succeed. You will prevail, Harold sent back to her, while simultaneously thanking her for the gift she'd given him. She did not understand this part but accepted the sentiment without argument.

She left Harold alone then, only looking back once to smile. He waved, and she turned away, exiting the room with Rafferty. She never saw Harold again.

20

Jess had come so far from the person she started out as when she first came to the facility back on Earth. Her life there, and back then, felt like another existence, many decades ago. She'd grown so much. They all had. The years went by, and they all aged, and grew, and changed. Their babies began to walk and talk, and before anyone knew it, they were faced with the task of teaching their young ones how to read and write, and deciding what, exactly, to teach them of Earth; a world that never was, nor ever would be, their home.

When Martin and Eileen first welcomed a baby boy named Eric, the differences were apparent almost immediately. Eric cried a lot and suffered from melancholy. Poor Eileen walked the hallways looking haggard, for it was obvious she was getting very little sleep. Many people lent her a hand, taking the baby, rocking him, playing with him, attempting to pacify his tears. This was normal while rearing a baby, but none of the new mothers realized. Their only experiences raising a child, were with the new generation of passive babies, so Eric seemed to be a nightmare.

As Ben and Grace had anticipated, Eric was noticeably more aggressive and rambunctious than any of the other children. Since none of the couples had raised a child before, they'd become accustomed to the calm behavior of their children. As compared to Eric, all the other children were literally angels, and Eric seemed a terror. He was not any different than any of them had been as children, nor the average child born on Earth, but the standards of judgment had greatly tilted, unnoticed. An entire generation of children with a decidedly more passive nature grew up on the ship—the first generation of a new breed of human—whose main drive in life was to learn and explore, not take or claim.

Eileen struggled with the differences in behavior of Eric compared to the others. She worked tirelessly at teaching him wrong from right and how to control his emotions. She told him again and again that physically acting out was not okay.

It was not uncommon for the children to play together, and one would begin crying, for Eric had kicked or pushed someone, or even bitten them, and they could not understand his actions. If he wanted a toy, or said something rude, and the children did not act in accordance, then, as any human child would, Eric reacted physically, in frustration. His anger was not unusual at all, except for in the face of such passive peers. This resulted in an endless cycle of frustration for Eric, and as he grew older and more mentally aware of the alienation he felt, he began to pull away from the others. He became a loner, for this seemed the only solution he could come up with.

Angel was the only one who still interacted with Eric, as all the children grew into walking, talking, tiny people. A little over seven years into their journey through space, Angel was now six-and-a-half. It had been three years since Jess met with Harold. As things tend to do, life went on steadily for quite a while, then several things seemed to happen all at once.

***

Sarah grew into adolescence, and suddenly, her 18th birthday arrived. Jess and Ben marveled at how quickly time had passed. Jess would soon be turning thirty-one. They all kept the calendar, but the holidays eventually began to lose much of their meaning. Around year four or so, they began merely acknowledging the special days with a basic mention, although Aaron, of all people, got into the holiday spirit the most.

Everything that defined them as human beings, as tied to Earth, slowly began falling away. They were each stripped to the bare essence, all subconsciously eager to arrive at Hesperia, to discover whatever they would become under the influence of an alien world.

The Pilgrims had changed greatly, upon landing at Plymouth Rock, Jess reasoned aloud one night at dinner. It was only natural that they should do the same. They were a work in progress, put on hold, until they reached their new home, she mused, and everyone agreed and understood that they were partaking in the greatest adventure ever known.

And so, Sarah's 18th birthday arrived, by the date on their now nearly defunct calendar, and the only thing different that day was that Sarah informed Ezra she was ready to channel in. She did not tell Jess and Ben. They had begun treating her as an adult, capable of making her own decisions, several years before. She grew, over the years, into a beautiful young woman, with dark hair and eyes, and everyone was in awe of her. She still held a wisdom in her eyes that confounded them. At any given age, she seemed twice that. So, by age sixteen, she came and went, as an adult, although, still living in the same quarters with Jess and Ben, and she honored the original assessment that she wouldn't channel into the Graylings until she turned eighteen.

Angel shared a room with Sarah (Alex eventually inhabited a bed in the living room), and Jess and Ben often remarked that some of Sarah's timeless wisdom had rubbed off on their daughter. There were times when Jess looked in Angel's eyes and felt as if she held the thoughts of a grown woman. For Angel also held the same sage look of wisdom that Sarah possessed. It frightened Jess at times. She couldn't help thinking back to when she was pregnant and recalled her base fears that her child would be unusual, perhaps, not even fully human.

None of them were even sure anymore, just what it meant to be human, however. Everything was constantly being redefined. No one even bothered questioning it any longer. They simply couldn't, without feeling their minds begin to slip. They only held onto each other, for 'The Society' was the one definition they could not lose. They were a family, albeit, a growing one, with many new additions and changes.

Sarah channeled in and met Harold. Ramona had died two years before. Everyone felt her go, except the children. But they all saw how it affected their parents, and growing up in that environment, the idea of an alien race living on the ship's upper decks was not strange to any of them. The children lived with the notion their whole lives, even if they never met the Graylings.

***

Sarah was not any different after meeting the Graylings. She did, however, come to Jess, the day after she turned thirty-one, and cried. Jess hugged her.

"Harold is going to die," she said. Jess looked at Sarah in horror. "When?"

"Soon," Sarah said, and began to weep.

Jess immediately sent her thoughts out to Harold. He didn't answer. Others did, however—the next elected in line after the Elders passed away—from the first generation born after the Graylings' exile. A new couple had been chosen. Their names were Albert and Paula.

Jess spoke with the new Elders, immediately knowing them, and loving them. Then, she finally, vaguely sensed Harold. Sarah was right. He was dying. With all her concentration, Jess reached out, and she knew he was going, even as she mentally connected. She sensed his happiness upon hearing her. She didn't send thoughts. She knew how to communicate with Harold, and she needed no words.

She sent him an image and a feeling. She sent him her memory of the day they met, when she'd hugged him. He sent it back, giving her thanks. As he took his final breath, in his mind, Harold died in Jess's embrace.

She felt him go, as if in the moment, living inside the memory. Harold died in Jess's arms. It was the first time, since the day it happened, that she remembered the full certainty of faith that she would succeed. Then Harold was gone, and the feeling of certainty quickly faded, dying with him. Jess was left alone with not only her grief, but the incredible fears and doubts that continued to surface time and time again, plaguing her, that she might fail in her quest to help save the Graylings.

***

Aaron spent much of his time in the garden. Because of his ability with plants, it was only natural that he would gravitate to spending his days there, much as Jemma did. The two did not work well together, however.

Aaron's ability was to alter the chemical balance in the chlorophyll of plants. While it was a nice trick, and made for pretty-looking, rainbow-colored flowers, it didn't help the overall health of the plants. The flowers that Aaron touched tended to thrive poorly if he failed to change them back within a day or so. They simply couldn't photosynthesize the same way, or nearly as effectively. It wasn't uncommon for Jemma to come into the garden, after Aaron had left, and walk around sighing, attempting to fix the damage he'd done.

On several occasions, Jemma could be seen storming into the dining hall, or common room, yelling at Aaron to come and fix the mess he'd made, and Aaron would hang his head in shame, following her to clean things up.

Once again, he was reminded of the fact that his ability was useless. It was only a form of entertainment for others, one that quickly wore off. He elicited occasional smiles from people, by leaving red and green flowers at everyone's doors on Christmas morning. It was the only gift he could think of to give.

He left green roses scattered around on St. Patrick's Day, and black carnations and roses for Halloween. So, in this way, the holidays were still acknowledged. His ability was one of the few things that kept The Society's holiday culture alive as anything more than a passing date on the calendar. People were grateful, but Aaron never realized this, and still felt generally useless.

***

Seven years had passed since boarding the ship. Sarah was now a grown woman, no longer the scared, eleven-year-old girl who had helped them all walk through a horde of soldiers with guns. She had grown several inches, into a fully-figured woman. She was also radiantly beautiful.

Aaron was also much more grown. He was now a man, no longer resembling the clingy, needy young boy he'd ultimately been at age twenty-two, when he'd thought he was in love with Jess.

He was no longer a sullen, bitter young man, either. He'd grown physically and emotionally into a twenty-nine-year-old, quiet gardener, who spent most of his time either changing flowers (then changing them back) or reading. He had adopted Jesus's love for books, and Arnold's passion for learning. Earl was his best friend, but he played cards with everyone in the common room on nights when he didn't have his nose buried in a book, but even then, he was mindful not to isolate himself too much to his room, but rather, read quietly in a chair in the company of others.

Sarah had been noticing Aaron more and more the last few weeks, the last several months, in fact. She was still so young, her physical awakening into womanhood still new to her, along with all the feelings, desires, and longings it brought. Aaron was always so quiet, she noted. It made her look at him, wondering what he was thinking about.

More and more lately, she found herself, in the common room, or in the dining hall, gazing at him, trying to see into his mind, into his thoughts. He was often reading a book, or even writing in his journal. She thought she was invisible to him.

Yet, Aaron had noticed Sarah as well. She was quiet, like him, and always seemed deep in thought. He found himself wondering what she was thinking about, but he never quite knew how to start a conversation with her. But sometimes, in the evenings, in the common room, or at dinner, he'd look over to catch her looking at him, and she'd quickly glance away. He wasn't certain, but at times, she seemed to blush. It was only because she so quickly turned her gaze away, that she missed how Aaron's cheeks flushed in response to her scrutiny, and she could not possibly know that along with this came a warm feeling of hope and euphoria in the pit of his stomach and his chest.

Unbeknownst to each, they had both lain in bed, more than one or two nights, and imagined what it would feel like to linger in an embrace or share an innocent kiss. Innocent fantasies soon gave way to deeper desires, and more aggressive scenarios, and poor Martin was the only audience member with an unwanted ticket to these shows.

***

Everyone felt it, when Harold died. The Society walked around in a pall of grief for several days. They had not felt this sad since the day of Jesus and Lucia's funerals.

Sarah walked around in a daze. She was greatly affected and saddened by the death of Harold, for her connection to him when channeling in was still new, only months old, so the feelings of kinship were especially fresh. The day after he died, she entered the garden. She walked through the plants, on the winding trail of dirt, and found herself crying inconsolably.

Aaron was in the garden, as Sarah came around a turn in the path. He walked amongst the wildflowers, weeping silently. He, like all the others, had felt Harold's passing, and was greatly saddened.

He looked up, tears standing in his eyes, to see Sarah come around the bend. She stopped, startled, then simply looked at him, her own tears falling. This only made him cry harder, and Sarah began to sob. Several yards apart from one another, they both cried together. The shared experience was so strong, so connecting, they didn't need words to know they both felt the same heartbreak.

Aaron slowly walked up to Sarah, the tears beginning to taper off. He smiled at her through his tears. She smiled back. And without thought, for all he wanted at that moment was to comfort her, he gently lifted her chin with his hand and lightly kissed her. It was over in a moment.

He stepped back, embarrassed, afraid he'd overstepped his bounds. His mind flashed back to old movies from Earth, and he half-expected her to produce a drink to throw in his face, or simply square up to him and slap him.

"I'm sorry," he faltered, "I didn't mean to—"

"You didn't mean it?" She looked hurt. He stared at her, stunned. And suddenly, he fully understood all her looks, and knew it wasn't his imagination, or only his hopes. His heart raced, and a fire began to build inside his chest. He stepped forward again, only inches from her, newly emboldened.

"Can't you tell how I feel?"

He leaned down and gently kissed her again, still for only a lingering moment, slightly longer than the first. He didn't want to scare her off, for he realized this was the first time anyone had ever kissed her. She stood, feeling his lips against hers, her mind reeling. She reveled in the emotions she experienced, taking everything in—his soft lips, his warm breath, the tingling sensation in the pit of her stomach—and how it seemed to tickle. She looked up into his eyes, saw how tenderly he looked down at her, and she knew she was in love. She smiled, overcome by the euphoria of her emotions, and Aaron smiled back, greatly relieved. He kissed her again, lingering this time for several moments, and Sarah eagerly kissed him back. Within moments, they were breathless, carried away in a quickly building inferno.

They pulled away, simultaneously, and Aaron looked at Sarah with such intensity, she felt like he was a magnet, pulling her closer. She felt as if she couldn't possibly ever get close enough.

"Will you marry me?" he asked, and she couldn't breathe.

***

Things on board the ship were simply done differently. Without the Earth pulling them down, like a huge weight, the people on board the ship simply floated freely, without any of the societal fears that had come to burden them on their home planet. There were still fears and doubts, but not when it came to items like love, or even forever. Everything simply evolved unencumbered, more naturally in the ship's environment. People fell in love, got married, became parents, in such short succession, perhaps it should have frightened them, but it didn't.

***

Aaron's question did not frighten Sarah or seem rash.

"Yes," she breathed.

They were married two days later, and Sarah moved out of Jess and Ben's room, to live with Aaron. Angel now roomed alone for the first time in her young life.

21

Many things changed over the years. Alma became a doctor. She studied for seven years under the tutelage of Grace, and the student eventually exceeded her teacher. Grace looked on in absolute awe, after only the first two years, as Alma began teaching *her* new things. It was Alma who delivered Jemma and Rafferty's final three children.

Alma studied models and read every medical journal on hand in the databases. She became an expert in anatomy. She knew how to run every piece of medical equipment in the infirmary, and Rafferty made models and simulations for Alma to practice any and every medical procedure she could possibly think of.

Then, one day, four years into her training, Alma discovered a use for her ability. Jess came into the infirmary, after Alex was finally weaned completely from breast milk, and asked Grace for birth control.

In this case, for all the women, they performed a simple procedure that tied the fallopian tubes, using a special thread. This was done in such a way as to not scar the tissue. However, it was still surgery, and a small incision was made, through the belly button, to insert the thread.

On the day Jess came in, Alma had been thinking hard the last few weeks about something she'd not yet dared to try. She simply didn't know if it would work. But as Jess lay on the table, and Grace stood over her, poised with her scalpel to make the tiny incision, Alma told her to stop, without even knowing what she was going to do next. She had never even performed the procedure herself, only watched Grace, but she worked quickly now, and Grace stood back in amazement.

Alma inserted the thread, with a small surgical needle, into Jess's belly button, but made no incision. Then she poised her hands over Jess's abdomen and quickly buried them inside, using her ability. She'd never had a use for it up till now, but her hands quickly, simply dissolved, disappearing into Jess's body, up to Alma's wrists. She worked now, inside, where she could see the procedure taking place on the monitor, and used the image to guide her own, invisible hands.

Grace looked on in wonder, at the monitor, as she saw the thread moved into place and tied by an invisible force. Alma wasn't even sure exactly how she did it, only that she could manipulate her own molecules enough to work, even while inside Jess's body. There was no need for any incision, and the procedure was done in mere minutes.

Jess sat up, looking mystified. She had been given an anesthetic to numb her abdominal area and had no idea the procedure didn't go as planned. She remained on the table for several minutes, waiting as the numbness slowly wore off. Then she walked out of the infirmary, sterile for as long as she chose, with no recovery needed. She thanked Alma, and left smiling.

Alma found a use for her hands, if for nothing other than the painless, quick sterilization of the women aboard the ship. From then on, she used her hands, whenever any procedure was necessary, which was rarely. But it did give her a new purpose and use for her previously, seemingly useless power, and that made her happy.

***

Sarah finally used her ability again, seven years into their stay on the ship. She was now happily married to Aaron and living with him in his quarters. Angel came to her one day and asked if Sarah would spend time with Eric. Angel wanted Eric to be able to play with the other children, but inevitably, he always grew frustrated and ended up lashing out physically, or was simply forced to leave the group, before he became violent. In time, Eric would outgrow this behavior, as he came into manhood, but for now, it was greatly distressing to Angel, watching Eric suffer, and be socially cut off from all the other children.

It came to be that for a few hours every afternoon, Sarah would sit with the children, in the common room, or on the observation deck, or wherever the children happened to be playing, and use her ability. It not only relaxed Eric so he could play with everyone peacefully, it also made the rest of the children giddy and euphoric. They all ended up the equivalent of a dozen-or-so children who were *high* for two hours every day. Eric made friends with everyone again, and they all knew their newfound, daily enjoyment was brought on, in part, thanks to him. So, in a way, Eric became a celebrity, and more popular than ever among them.

He and Angel were now best friends, for she was the one who cared enough about him to try and find a way to help integrate him back into the younger society of children aboard the ship. Angel's need to fix things had begun to blossom in her personality, even so young.

***

One night at dinner, Jemma carried a glass bowl of fruit into the dining hall, and stumbled, dropping it. The bowl shattered into dozens of small shards, and Jemma cut herself attempting to extract the fruit from the broken glass. While Alma was busy taking Jemma to the infirmary to stitch up the gash on her palm, Angel got down from her chair and walked over to the broken glass on the floor.

"Honey, don't touch that, you'll cut yourself, too," Jess said, walking over. She stopped short, staring at Angel in complete shock.

Angel sat hunkered on the floor in front of the glass, staring. The broken shards glinted, reflecting light from the ceiling, the pieces slowly moving and vibrating. Jess could see this as she got closer. She frowned, looking around, confused.

"Ben?"

Ben walked over and stopped short, also staring. Everyone slowly got up from their chairs and formed a circle around Angel, looking on in wonder as the pieces of glass vibrated more quickly, emitting a strange, high-pitched humming sound.

"My God," Hanley said, stunned, his voice cracking.

"What? What is it?" Jess looked at Hanley, panicked.

Martin also looked on in wonder, for he heard Hanley's thoughts. Hanley had seen this ability before and recognized it for what it was. Martin looked down at Angel in reverence. Ben also realized, from years ago as Dr. M.—a time he'd long since forgotten for a reason— what his daughter was doing. A tear slipped down his cheek.

The pieces of glass continued emitting a high-pitched, ringing tone. Then suddenly, each shard impossibly stood on end, defying gravity, balanced in air, barely touching the floor, suspended for several moments. Then, in a fraction of a second, all the pieces rushed together, and the bowl sat on the floor, wholly reformed. Not a single line or crack, nor any other evidence remained that the bowl had ever been shattered.

Jess stared at Angel for several moments, tears in her eyes, then looked over to Hanley. Her eyes searched out Ben next.

"It's the same ability, isn't it? It's what Angelique could do, right?"

Hanley nodded, tears slipping down his cheeks now. Angelique was the one thing from the facility that Hanley never let go of. He never forgot her face, or how she looked the day she came apart piece by piece. He looked at Jess now, crying, and nodded again.

"What made you choose her name for your daughter, Jess?" he said, looking resigned.

"I don't know," Jess said. Her heart felt gripped in ice. "It just felt right."

"It's the same force that's guiding everyone, Jess," Hanley said. "The same thing that led the Graylings to finding you, and all the rest of us."

"No," Jess said, shaking her head. Her old doubts suddenly blooming very much alive inside her head. "No, it's just a coincidence."

Everyone stared in wonderment at her blindness. Even Ben marveled at Jess's vehement denial of what every other person aboard the ship saw not as a coincidence, but a sign.

"Jess," Ben said, trying to sound gentle, so as not to upset her. "What are the chances that you would decide to name our child after Angelique, and now Angel happens to have the very same ability that Angelique had?"

"I… I don't know," she stammered. "But it has to be a coincidence. That's all."

"Mommy, are you mad at me?"

Angel started to cry, for she thought she had done something wrong. It was the first manifestation of her ability. She thought the raised voices, her mother's agitation, and everyone standing around her meant that she'd been bad.

"Honey, no," Jess said, bending down and hugging Angel to her. "I'm not mad, I love you, you know that."

"Is it okay that I put it back together again?" Angel whispered, looking over Jess's shoulder, up into her father's eyes.

Ben stared down at Angel and felt a chill. He looked over at Sarah, who smiled, nodding. He remembered what she had said so many years ago.

"*She's going to put you back together again.*"

Ben smiled down at Angel and nodded, bending down to look her in the eyes.

"It's wonderful," he said. "It's your ability, and you were meant to use it. Don't ever be afraid to use it, okay?" He felt an urgency to get this message across to her for some reason, one he could not fully understand.

"Okay?" Ben said again, and Angel nodded, pulling herself out of Jess's arms and rushing to hug her father. Jess looked at the two of them and felt ashamed of her doubts. She simply couldn't help herself. She stood, quickly leaving the room.

***

Martin and Hanley went after her, for Martin told Ben to stay. Ben trusted Martin, and agreed, still holding Angel in his arms. Everyone else went back to dining.

In the common room, Hanley and Martin caught up with Jess, just as she reached her room. Hanley needed to talk to Jess for his own reasons. He didn't know what Martin's reasons were. They both started talking at the same time.

"Jess, I know what you're thinking," Hanley said, looking at Martin in confused annoyance.

"Jess, it's not what you're thinking," Martin overlapped.

Hanley sighed, for obviously between the two of them, Martin's statement was much more accurate. He nodded at Martin to continue.

"Jess," Martin said, looking her dead in the eye. "You're wrong. You know that. Angel has nothing to do with this."

"How do you know that?"

"Because. Harold told you that *you* are going to defeat the Bailon. Not Angel. The Graylings saw *you* defeat them."

"What?!" Hanley looked at Jess in complete shock. "Wait, the Graylings told you *that?*"

Jess nodded. She looked at Hanley with tears in her eyes.

"You remember what you told me about Angelique?"

Hanley looked at Jess, confused. Jess sighed in frustration.

"You told me once, if a plate broke, she could put it back together again. But you also told me she could take a person apart, piece by piece. I never forgot that, Hanley. Because it sounded so horrific."

"And you think Angel is going to be able to do that." Martin finished, looking at Hanley, who looked aghast.

"Jess," Hanley said, completely overwhelmed. "Why didn't you tell me the Graylings told you that you were going to defeat the Bailon?"

"Hanley, *you* tried to tell me that, too, even before we left the facility," she argued. "You said the Graylings needed *me.*"

"I said they needed all of us, Jess. Not just you. Or if I ever said anything that implied that, it's not how I meant it. Holy Jehoshaphat, Jess. I would never put something that huge on you... *especially* back then."

She shook her head, grinding her teeth.

"But everyone who channels in learns about what we have to do. And, surely, when I spoke to Harold, you all heard. You must have. I mean... Doesn't everyone know?" Jess frowned.

"No," Rafferty said, from behind all three of them. He had left the dining hall shortly after the others. He knew it was time to finally talk to Jess. "No one knows except Martin, of course... and me. Not even Ben, who knows a lot, even has a clue."

Hanley and Martin stared at Rafferty. He walked up to them, looking grave.

"I was with her, when Harold told her. I heard everything. But Harold's message was for Jess only. Everyone that channels in gets it all, and they get what part they'll play, or at least, the general feeling. We all serve a purpose, one way or another. But, Jess... They told her it will be *her*, and *her alone*, who wins the War."

"And you've just been carrying this around, all this time?" Hanley looked at Jess with great deference. She looked away, not meeting anyone's eyes.

"Jeezus, Jess. You shouldn't have been carrying this around, all by yourself. It's too much."

"Too much for any human mind to take," she said, her voice trembling, barely above a whisper. "And he was wrong, Hanley, he had to be."

"No," Rafferty said. "He wasn't. He couldn't be. They've *all* seen the vision."

"What vision?" Martin and Hanley said, together. Martin didn't know about this, even with his ability. He hadn't seen what the Graylings had. He knew Jess was special, they all did, but none of them knew why. If the Graylings didn't know, none of them could.

"Harold told Jess he saw a vision. It's very rare to glimpse anything so vividly. He told her she was surrounded by a bright light, and all the Bailon were gone. Defeated... By her," Rafferty looked at Jess in pride and awe.

"What do you mean, gone?" Hanley scoffed.

Rafferty leveled him with an icy stare. Hanley shook his head.

"And you think Angel has something to do with it?" Hanley asked.

"She's my daughter," Jess said. "She's seven-years-old, and she's already manifesting. You told me Angelique could take a person apart, Hanley, right?"

"Right?" Hanley said, confused.

"So, what can *I* do? Knock out power? How would that defeat all of the Bailon?"

"Harold didn't say you'd defeat them," Rafferty said, looking sympathetic. "He said they were all *gone*."

"I can't possibly kill an entire race of people!" Jess yelled, her tone taking on an odd ring in everyone's ears.

"Can't, or won't?" Rafferty said, challenging her.

"Now wait a minute," Martin said. "You have no right to just assume to know what Harold's vision meant."

"You're not listening to me!" Jess yelled louder, ignoring Martin's statement, looking at Rafferty with such intensity, he became scared.

"Even if I could do something that horrendous, my ability simply isn't strong enough to do something like that! Even Rachel couldn't possibly wipe out an entire species with her ability! But Angel?! I think maybe she could! If Angelique could take things apart..." she trailed off.

"Jess, you don't actually think a child could just disassemble a whole species, do you? Is that what you saw back in that dining hall?!" Hanley asked, looking shocked.

"Her ability is far more likely to win the War than mine," Jess said. "I can't be the one, I simply can't! Maybe the Graylings got confused? Maybe they thought they saw me, and they were really seeing Angel instead?!"

"No, Jess," Ben said, and everyone turned to look at him. He held Angel in his arms, but he set her down and told her to take her brother and go inside their room. She immediately did as told, without argument. Alex, now five years old, trailed behind them. He took his sister's hand and followed her into their room.

Jess looked at Ben, tears in her eyes. He looked back at her in sadness.

"Why didn't you tell me?"

"Because," Jess choked out. "I don't believe it, Ben. I don't *believe*. And I know you do, all of you. I know what I felt, I know what Harold and all the other Graylings believe, but, I still don't see it. I don't see *how*. How can I defeat the Bailon? My God, Ben, I can't even pulse out here! I'm just supposed to go there, and pulse, what, for the first time in ten years? And then hope I even remember how, and somehow, it wipes them all out? I love the Graylings, Ben. I do, but still. How could I kill a whole race, no matter what they've done?"

"Because if you don't, they leave Hesperia someday... and find Earth," Ben said.

Everyone stood gaping at Ben in shock. No one had let it in yet. The information was inside all of them, but no one had ever truly allowed themselves to think about it. Everyone stood, stunned by Ben's blatant revelation. He continued unabated.

"You know I'm right, all of you!" he said, raising his voice.

One by one, everyone who remained in the dining hall came streaming in, joining the conversation in progress, sending their children back to their rooms. Within moments, the adults were alone. Everyone was there, all of The Society.

"The Bailon will never grow or change from what they are now. What they did to the Graylings, they did to other races, before coming to Hesperia. And they will leave Hesperia one day. It's only a matter of time before they find Earth. If the Graylings found our planet in less than two hundred years, and they weren't even looking to find a planet full of life, how long do you think it will take the Bailon to find Earth? Another two hundred years? We'll have grown into a peaceful race by then. Humanity on Earth, within the next two hundred years, will be comprised of more transgens, not less. They won't be a minority."

"No, but we'll still have weapons, Ben," Hanley said. "We can fight them off."

"No," Ben said, sounding sad. "We won't."

"Why?" Arnold looked inquisitive, but he thought he already knew the answer to Ben's question.

"For the same reason that none of our children ever hit back when Eric attacks them," Ben said, sending an apology out to Martin with his thoughts, even as he said it. "I'm sorry, Eileen," he said, and she nodded. He continued.

"Humanity is changing. We're evolving towards peace. True peace cannot happen in the presence of such emotions as anger, hate, violent tendencies. Our children are the first generation of transgens born with an active code. It also renders them completely pacifistic. It must— imagine a child with the ability to blow something up, and the tendency toward aggression. As we develop these abilities, we must lose what makes us violent. Humanity will be just as helpless to defend themselves from the Bailon, as the Graylings are, in just a few generations' time.

"Don't you understand? We are the gap between an old race and a new. We have abilities, and the anger to use them to defend ourselves, or cause a lot of hurt and pain to others. We're the only ones able to do so. We will be the only ones who are *ever* able to do so. We were meant to be brought here, to fight. For everyone, not just Hesperia. We're here to fight for Earth as well. For any planet with peaceful life."

"That's huge, Ben," Hanley said. "That's too huge."

"I know," Ben said, looking at Jess. "It's too big for an entire race to handle, or the whole of The Society, let alone one person."

Everyone looked at Jess. She looked down at the floor. After several long moments, she looked up at everyone, tears in her eyes.

"You're all looking to me? You think I can destroy the Bailon? I killed an infant once," Jess said, turning to Ben.

"I took a life, many lives that day, and it almost destroyed me. I can't do it, even if I was physically capable, which my ability does not make me. I can't take that many lives. What would possibly make me do such a thing?"

"No one ever thought you would channel in," Eileen said. "But we all had faith that when the time was right, something would make you change your mind."

Everyone looked at Eileen.

"Something did happen, to make you change your mind, right?" Eileen looked at Jess, intently.

Jess nodded.

"Then I must assume," Eileen said, speaking slowly, picking her words carefully, "that when the time is right, something *will* happen… that will move you to fight. Something will push you into action, and then you will be able to do what needs to be done."

"There was never any question of what we came here to do," Martin said, looking at Jess in sympathy, but with determination. "Did you think we were just going to send Sarah down there, to force all the Bailon into passivity? And then what? Walk them onto their ships and send them on their way?"

"I don't know," Jess said, her voice low and weak.

"Did you think we were just going to ask them nicely, to please leave?" Martin continued.

"I don't know," Jess said, her voice shaking.

"We all knew we were coming here to exterminate the Bailon," Martin said, looking around at everyone. "To fight them, because the Graylings can't fight for themselves. Was there ever any doubt, in anyone else's mind, that our mission was to wipe the Bailon out of existence?"

No one said anything. A few people, however, shook their heads. Deep down inside, everyone knew that was their job.

"We keep using words like War, defeat, exterminate," Martin said. "Wars cause deaths. The Bailon tried to wipe out all the Graylings. They exterminated them. They took their planet. And, according to Ben, they'll do it again, to Earth, the first chance they get."

"Now, wait a minute," Ben said, sounding angry. "You *all* know this. Don't put it all on me, Martin!"

"Fine, we all know you're right. We feel it deep inside. Just, no one wants to say it. Well it's time to start talking about it now. Jess," Martin said, looking her straight in the eye. "None of us is the same anymore. We've all changed—so have you. After all this time, you still don't believe?"

"I believe I could get angry enough to want to hurt the Bailon," Jess said. "I do. I believe I could do it, emotionally, to save the Graylings. I promised Harold I would save them all," her voice cracked, and she hitched in a breath. "But what you're asking me to do," she said, shaking her head. "Even if I wanted to, no one is listening to me! I can't! My ability simply cannot be enough to wipe out an entire race of people! My ability is *not strong enough* to do that!"

Jess looked at everyone, her face set. No one said anything.

"Do you *hear* what I'm saying to you all?! My ability cannot kill an entire race!"

***

"Yes, it can." Rafferty spoke gently but firmly. Everyone looked at him.

Jess stared, then shook her head. "No," she whispered.

"Yes," Rafferty said, stepping forward, his jaw set.

"How," Ben asked, looking at Rafferty with intensity. Already, the scientist in him began calculating, trying to understand. He squinted his eyes, scrutinizing Rafferty. There was something behind the mechanic's eyes that told Ben he knew much more than he was willing to let on.

"I can't explain it, not here. It's not for everyone to know, anyhow," Rafferty said, sounding annoyed.

Everyone in the group let out a collective sigh of discontented disappointment. Hanley exclaimed, "What?!" Arnold said, "What the hell, dude?" Even Ezra piped up with, "Are you kidding me?" While still others, including Earl and Aaron, snorted their disapproval.

"Look, I'm sorry," Rafferty said. "I will explain it to Ben and Jess, but the rest of you are just going to have to trust me on this. You need to have a little faith."

"That's my mantra," Hanley said.

"It was Jesus's mantra, too," Alma said. "He believed we were meant to be here. He believed that whatever happened was supposed to happen. I never thought I'd be able to use my ability for anything. I certainly never thought I'd be a doctor. Now, I can fix people without ever cutting them open. I can use my hands to heal. Literally. If that's not some kind of miracle, I don't know what is.

"If Rafferty says Jess can do this, I believe him. If he says he doesn't want to explain it, he shouldn't have to. I'm going to trust him. I'm going to trust everyone," Alma said. "Whatever part I have to play in all this, I'm just going to play it. That's all."

"I know who has to play," Sarah said, suddenly sounding eleven again, for one moment.

Everyone parted for her, as she stepped forward, to stand in the middle of the group. The room grew deadly quiet. Everyone looked at Sarah. Her eyes held that same, familiar look they had all come to know. Sarah knew things. Even she didn't understand how.

"I know who will go to Hesperia, and who will stay on board the ship," she said.

"You do?" Aaron looked at Sarah with expectant eyes.

"Not you, Aaron," Sarah said, her tone apologetic. "You won't be part of the fight."

He looked down at the floor, nodding.

"Who?" Earl asked.

"I only know who's going. I don't know why, or what it is you'll need to do. I can't see that. I only know who needs to go on the ship."

"Tell us who, Sarah," Hanley gently urged.

"Rafferty," Sarah began, taking a deep breath.

"Well, duh, he's the only one who can fly the transport," Alma said.

"Be quite and let her finish," Arnold said.

"Jess," Sarah said. "Ben, Arnold."

"Me?" Arnold looked incredulous.

Sarah nodded. "Because you won't let Jenny go alone."

"I'm going?" Jenny said.

"I only know you're supposed to be there," Sarah said. "And I see Arnold with you."

"Just be quiet and let her finish," Hanley said.

Martin looked down at the floor. He already knew the rest of the people Sarah was going to name. He knew Eileen would be upset, and he put his arm around her shoulders, to comfort her. She closed her eyes, for she knew what her husband's actions meant, even before Sarah ever said his name.

"Alma," Sarah said.

Alma gasped.

"Kate," Sarah said. She took a deep breath, then continued.

"Martin... Me," Sarah continued. "And... Angel and Mara."

Everyone gasped and stared at Sarah, and Jess shook her head.

"No," she whispered. "Angel is only a child."

"But I see her there," Sarah said.

Jemma quietly cried and took hold of Rafferty's hand. Rafferty looked shell-shocked. Neither parent said anything, as Jess continued to argue.

"But it's *me* who defeats the Bailon," Jess said. "I was wrong to think what I did. Angel could never hurt anyone. She's too pure. Ben is right, she's not capable of hurting anything with her ability, none of our children are capable of that kind of violence, like Ben said. So, if she can't fight against the Bailon, why would I bring my daughter into a War Zone?"

Jess turned to Ben, her eyes filling with tears. Ben rushed up, hugging her.

"I don't know, Aunt Jess," Sarah said, her eyes filling with tears as well. "I only know what I see. I only know what I *feel*. All the people I've named need to be there. I don't know why."

"Why Jenny?" Arnold said, holding his wife tight.

"I don't know," Sarah repeated.

"If Sarah says I need to be there, Arnie, I'm going," Jenny said, turning and facing Arnold, looking in his eyes.

"And there's no way I'm sending you off this ship, on a transport, to land on Hesperia alone," he said, looking in her eyes. He nodded at Sarah, reverent, then looked around at everyone, in awe.

"Sarah's right, if Jenny goes, I'm going with her. Sarah is right, when she says she sees me there. I wouldn't send my wife down there alone. Never."

"That's why I'll go, too," Kate said, turning to look at Alma. "I'm not letting you go alone, Al," Kate said, crying.

"Eleven people," Earl said, counting it out on his hand. "According to Sarah, eleven people will go to Hesperia, to fight the Bailon, one way or another."

"And according to Rafferty, Jess will somehow wipe all the Bailon out," Hanley said, nodding. Then his tone turned uncharacteristically bitter. "Do you wanna revise your statements, Raff? Considering you just learned your own daughter is supposed to go down there?"

Rafferty lunged at Hanley, who backed instinctively away. Several people moved to restrain Rafferty. It was Jemma who calmed him down, however.

"Raff…" She took his face in her hands and gazed at him so lovingly, people turned away to give them privacy. "You've done more to plan this fight for the Graylings than anyone. You've put yourself through so much pain," she cried. "And you did it all out of love… and faith.

"I know you love Mara as much as I do. I know that, Raff. But if she has a part to play in this fight, we must accept that. You can't lose faith now. Raffie, you're the glue to this whole plan."

At this, she turned to everyone, her face full of pride and admiration for her husband. "You all have no idea what Raff has sacrificed for this mission. And if both of us are willing to let our own daughter go down there… If Raff is going to fly the ship which carries my baby girl down there, I don't want to ever hear any of you question his loyalty, his commitment, or his certainty ever again."

Hanley hung his head in shame at Jemma's remarks. She turned to Jess and Ben.

"Jess," she said, gently. "I'm a mother, just like you. And I love my child," she choked up, then cleared her throat to continue. "But I am going to trust the Graylings, and my husband, and Sarah, too… and choose to believe that everything will be okay. If my daughter is needed in this fight, I have no place holding her back from that. That is *her* part to play. I have to let her go, as young as she is. I have to let her do whatever work down there it is that she's meant to do. That's all."

Jemma finished speaking then, and backed up, taking Rafferty's hand. She leaned her head on his shoulder, crying lightly.

Everyone stood quietly then, looking at one another in complete silence. No one spoke for several, long minutes. People just cried, and hugged one another, as the true realization began to sink in with each one of them. They all slowly let it in, who would be playing a part, and who would not. Even Jess merely stood, in Ben's arms, taking it all in.

***

Endless minutes passed, before Jess finally turned to look at Rafferty, searching his eyes. He returned her gaze stoically, and she saw the certainty she looked for. Next, she sought out Aaron, and found his face, with Sarah. He held her in his arms now, but he met Jess's eyes, over his wife's shoulder, and smiled. He nodded at her, and this action from him told her to have faith.

He had asked her once, if she would not fight for the Graylings, if she'd be willing to fight for The Society, instead. He reminded her of how much love she held for all the people on board the ship. She looked in Aaron's eyes now and remembered.

She closed her eyes, concentrating, pulling up the memory of her embrace with Harold. She felt his love all around her, in that moment, even while she simultaneously felt the love of all the people surrounding her, in the present, in that very room. She felt the love of all the Graylings. She felt the love of everyone in The Society. She glimpsed that certainty again for one moment, briefly, as she had the day Harold told her about the vision of her surrounded in light. She caught hold of his faith, and for one shining moment, she held it, attempting to place it inside her heart.

But it flitted away, and she lost it. The conviction, however, was not lost on her. She promised Harold she would fight. She told him she might die trying, but she made him a promise that day. She made all the Graylings a promise that day. She told them she would fight, and now, she realized, she must honor that promise.

***

Jess did not know why Angel, or any other child would need to go to Hesperia. She knew she could not possibly have the strength to go without Ben by her side. Just as Alma would not go without Kate, nor Arnold let Jenny go without him. She knew she needed Ben. Why Angel would go, she didn't understand, but time was running out for doubts. They were now less than three years away from Hesperia, and it was time for Jess to face the truth.

She would be fighting for the Graylings, and apparently also for Earth. She somehow contained within her, in her gift, the ability to defeat the Bailon. She would just have to trust Rafferty on it. Rafferty and Sarah, too. She would have to trust everyone in the room with her, for all of them, together—including Harold and the rest of the Graylings—all were a part of The Society. She needed to trust it all.

***

Jess broke free of Ben's arms then and came to stand in the middle of the group. She looked at everyone, smiling through her tears. She nodded at Rafferty, and he smiled. Ben closed his eyes and breathed a sigh of relief. He loved Jess in that moment so much, his heart could have simply stopped beating.

"I don't understand any of this," Jess said, but she smiled at everyone, nodding. "But I love you all, so much. You have no idea."

"Yeah, we do," Martin said, gently.

Jess smiled again, even laughing briefly. She nodded.

"If everyone else is going to fight, I'll be damned if I'm letting you go alone," she said, her voice growing in strength and volume.

Several people broke out in huge smiles. Others breathed sighs of relief, or simply closed their eyes, crying tears of release. Jess turned to Rafferty and Ben.

"I want to know everything you know, Rafferty," Jess said, nodding to him. "And Ben, you're the one who first taught me to control and use my ability. So, I'll need you to help me train, and get me back up into running order." She nodded to Ben and he nodded back.

"Fine, then." She looked around at everyone in solidarity, utter devotion shining in her eyes. "Let's begin."

Book Three:
REGENERATION

1

Rafferty took Ben and Jess into the cargo bay. It was nine in the morning. He walked them back, behind the transport ship, parked in the far corner, and led them through a door, into a large, rectangular room that looked like a tactical army facility. Large monitors lined all four walls, with a keypad under one. Various machines that looked like giant CPU's lined the far wall, near the door. A long table sat in the middle of the room, lined with several chairs on both sides.

Rafferty motioned for Ben and Jess to sit down, not speaking. Ben took hold of Jess's hand. It felt cold. Rafferty sat down at the monitor with the keypad, his back facing them. He quickly typed, and all four screens in the room bloomed to life, displaying schematics, blueprints and illustrations.

Rafferty turned to look at Ben and Jess, his eyes serious. Ben looked at the screens, fascinated. He stood and walked up to one of the monitors, touching it. He looked at the images that flashed in front of his eyes, taking them in.

"Are these what I think they are?" Ben turned to Rafferty, surprised.

Rafferty nodded. Ben turned back to look at the images again.

"Do you have schematics of their ships, too?"

Rafferty turned back around and typed something new on the console. The picture on Ben's monitor dimmed, then flared to life again, displaying a large, pod-like craft. Jess gasped, for she recognized what she saw.

"Isn't that..." she trailed off, unable to finish. Rafferty nodded, yet again.

"I recognize it," Jess said. "But, how?"

"I spend a lot of time with the Graylings," Rafferty said. "I specifically met with Harold and Ramona, several times a week, for short amounts of time," he said, looking at Jess gravely. She nodded, understanding.

"No more than two or three minutes, each time," he sighed. "But it was enough. Enough to see their memories, and push past the emotions, to look, to *see*—take it all apart."

"I don't understand," Jess said.

"He took the Graylings memories and used them to extract replicas of the Bailon weaponry, their machinery," Ben said. "You made schematics of everything you saw?"

Rafferty nodded. Then he shrugged. "It's what I do. I make machines. I also take them apart, see how they work. Put them back together again. You'd be surprised how much you can tell about machines, just by looking at them."

Ben nodded. "It never occurred to me, to use my memories this way, Rafferty. It should have, but it didn't."

Rafferty nodded again, always silent in his agreement.

"So, you know what weapons they have?" Ben asked, but already, his voice belied respect, clearly impressed.

"Yes," Rafferty said. "But I know a lot more than that. I have them, too. The Bailon. I have a full diagram schematic of their bodies. I pieced it together, from several of the Grayling's memories."

He went back to his monitor and typed again. Ben's screen changed, displaying a frontal view of the ugliest creature Jess ever saw. She gasped again, for this, she recognized far too well.

"That's them," she said, her voice fearful. Her heart beat faster. Seeing an image of a Bailon brought up all the horrific memories that remained locked inside, from her connection to the Graylings. She looked away from the screen, nauseated.

Even Ben appeared shaky on his feet. He sat down next to Jess, mouth pressed in a downward grimace, as if fighting off his own bout of queasiness. Rafferty spoke gently.

"Yes. That's a Bailon. I simply took what I saw, inside the Graylings' memories, and made a detailed illustration."

"That must have been very emotional," Ben said, his voice cold and stoic. He fought off panic, collecting himself. Seeing a Bailon in front of his face, albeit an illustration, brought up fears inside that Ben hadn't been aware of, that dwelt in his subconscious, hidden till now.

He looked back at the drawing, in fine, graphic detail, of his worst nightmare, and his physical reaction to the image felt out of his hands. He sweated, his heart beating fast, adrenaline coursing through his veins—an autonomic response that he and Jess both had no control over.

They had lived lifespans, inside their minds and emotions, as if they were the Graylings. Everything in real time, instantaneous, just as their first moments of channeling in had allowed them to experience. They didn't see a vague creature from a mythological text—something far removed from themselves—a second-hand rendering of a tale. What they saw, instead, was an image of the very creature that had exterminated *them*, and their own kind. The Graylings' experience was their own, and so were their fears. Neither Jess, nor Ben, could stand to look at the image any longer. Both turned their eyes away from the screen. Ben took Jess's hand in his own to comfort her, but his own hands shook badly.

"How did you do this, Rafferty," Jess whispered. "How did you put all this together, without losing your mind in fear?"

"Very carefully," he said, eyes full of sadness. "And very slowly. I've been working on these schematics for years, even before The Society ever came on board. But it took a very long time… and it made it difficult to be around anyone."

Rafferty looked down at the table, on the verge of tears. He quickly recovered, visibly forcing through the pain, and continued explaining.

"Especially when so many of you weren't channeled in. When most of you did not understand the old-boarders. When there was a gap between us," Rafferty said, looking up at Jess and Ben. A tear slipped down his cheek.

"Rafferty," Jess said. "You shouldn't have had to be alone with this."

"He's not alone now," Ben said, recovering from his initial shock, regaining strength in his voice. "You're not alone, now, Rafferty."

Rafferty nodded, quickly swiping the tear away. A small, bitter smile played at the corners of his lips.

"I can't understand their biology," he said. "That's not my area of expertise. I can break their weapons down for you, how they work, their destructive capabilities. I can even tell you, based on what I've interpreted in the attacks, what I think their most likely behaviors are, because as far as I can tell, the Bailon operate, they think, like machines. But I can't tell you anything about their bodies."

"Can we bring in Grace?" Ben sounded hopeful.

"It's too upsetting." Rafferty shook his head. "I don't want to upset anyone who doesn't need to see this. If they don't need to know, they don't need to go through this."

"Yes, but Grace is an expert in anatomy and physiognomy. She studies biological organisms. It's what she's good at. Alma as well."

"Why do we need to know about the Bailon's biology?" Jess asked.

"Because," Ben sighed. "The more we know about our enemy, the better prepared we can be to truly fight and defend ourselves against them. This is a war, Jess. You must know your enemy. Did you think we were just going to go into the fight with the Bailon blind?"

"No," Jess frowned. "But everyone just keeps beating me over the head, insisting that I need to have faith. Well, if I'm flying on faith, I don't need to know about the Bailon. All I need to know, is that I get down there, and somehow, I kill them all."

"I'm not sending you to face the Bailon without knowing everything I possibly can about them," Ben said, holding her hand tight. "And Rafferty, luckily, has had the presence of mind to think tactically.

Unlike me," Ben said, sighing. "So much for my intellect. I stopped being a scientist the moment we came on board."

"You were busy with other things," Rafferty said, gently.

"You mean, me," Jess said, looking hurt. "I distracted you. Marrying me, having Angel and Alex. Having a family to look after, being a father, a husband."

"Jess." Ben turned her face to his, for she looked away in shame. "My entire existence, I studied, learned, discovered. But I wasn't connected to people. I was dead inside. When I met you—when I fell in love with you—I realized everything I'd been missing in life. Nothing is more important than love, Jess. I was more than happy to focus on you and the kids. I don't care about anything else. Don't you know that? Don't you understand that by now?"

"Then why do you sound so disappointed?" Jess cried.

"Because, my job is to take care of *you*. And if I can use my intellect to help better prepare you for what you need to do, then that becomes my focus. It just didn't occur to me. I'm not disappointed in you, I'm upset with myself. I've let you down. I haven't been taking care of you."

"Yes, you have. I couldn't be doing any of this without you. You've done enough, Ben. You've done more than enough."

"Look, it doesn't matter," Rafferty interrupted, sitting with them. "The time just wasn't right before now, to focus on these things. Now it is. Whatever is meant to happen, will happen, all in good time. You were focused on each other before. On your family. That's a good thing. Now, you're ready to focus on the task at hand."

He sighed, shaking his head. "The Graylings are right, we're far too emotional as a race. It's too distracting. Our thoughts are so jumbled, it's a wonder we function at all."

Jess and Ben looked at Rafferty for several moments, taking in what he'd said, along with his disapproving head shake, his disdainful expression. Then they looked at each other, and both broke out in hysterical giggles.

Rafferty looked at them, his face serious for several moments, then he, too, joined them in reluctant laughter, covering his mouth in attempt to smother it, to no avail. "What so funny?" he said, through his laughter, voice high and reedy. Tears stood in his eyes.

"I don't know," Jess squeaked out, and everyone laughed harder.

"I think it's the stress, overwhelming us," Ben laughed, tears squirting from his eyes.

They all laughed for a while longer, then finally settled down, recovering themselves. They felt spent, exhausted, yet, somehow, strangely replenished. Ben looked at Rafferty, his eyes full of caution.

"I'd like to bring Grace in to look at the diagram of the Bailon. Possibly Alma, too. Two different minds, two different perspectives, couldn't hurt."

Rafferty sighed, then nodded his consent.

"Rafferty, this is a team effort. Everyone wants to be involved," Ben said.

"You heard Sarah, there are only eleven of us going. Why would everyone else need to know anything about all this?" Rafferty waved around the room, indicating at the monitors. "They don't need to feel all of this or go through it. You felt how much it shook you up, Ben. And you're more stable than some others."

Ben frowned, for he did not see how this was the case. He didn't consider himself any stronger than anyone else. Jess nodded, however. He looked at her, curious.

"He's right, Ben. You know how to compartmentalize. Define the emotions you're going through. It helps. I mean, Kate? I think she would just fall apart. She can't come in here. Alma, maybe, but not Kate. She's just going to have to understand that. Jenny, too, I think. And Sarah."

Ben sighed. He thought about what Jess said, letting it sink in. He slowly nodded, for he knew Jess was right. Not everyone could handle seeing an image of the Bailon, nor detailed images of the weapons they had watched rip the Graylings apart. A flash of gruesome images suddenly played across Ben's mind, and he flinched, feeling his stomach flop. Rafferty picked up on the image, for his ability was working, with Ben, in such proximity, and with everyone so highly emotionally charged.

"Jess is right," Rafferty repeated. "Not everyone can handle seeing everything again. Having the images forced back into your head. While you're awake, while you're completely, consciously aware."

Ben nodded, looking down at the floor. It occurred to him that the mental connections between he and all the members of The Society, and the Graylings, was so complicated and complex, ever attempting to explain it to an outsider would be an impossibility. He wondered how they would ever explain it to future generations, who would not be exposed to the Graylings memories. He knew he would not be able to explain it, even to his own children. The Society, and they alone, would be the only ones to ever fully understand this experience. There were no words to describe their emotions, the scenes inside their heads.

"I just hate leaving some of us in the dark," Ben sighed. "I understand that it's for their own good, but still. We're a group, all of us. We're all we have. And sometimes I think the reason why is because I personally couldn't do any of this without every single one of you by my side. The Society, it makes me stronger, if that makes any sense? I feel like if I'm not sharing this experience with everyone, I'm not as strong."

"We *are* all sharing this with each other, Ben," Rafferty said. "It's not like we're lying to anyone. We all play a certain part, but we still operate and work as one unit. Even if various parts serve differing functions. Look," he said, standing up.

He sat down at his console and typed. An animated blueprint image came up, of several cogs, all intertwined, turning, moving each other in concentric circles clockwise and counterclockwise, all in motion. Rafferty pointed at a cog on the far-left.

"See this one? See how it's turning? And look here," he pointed at a cog on the far bottom right. "This one is moving in a completely different direction, the opposite of the first, right? But it wouldn't even be moving at all without the first one. None of the cogs would be moving without all the others. But this cog here, that's not touching this one, doesn't even know what that cog is doing. And yet, its movement is affected by the other, regardless. The machine operates as one, within each cog's separate movements. You take one cog out, and the whole thing stops running.

"Ben, we're all doing our part, whether we know what the other knows or not. We're still a team. We always have been, even before we met each other. It's the very definition of The Society. We were meant to meet each other, to be here together on this ship. You're not leaving anyone out, Ben. You simply can't. It's an impossibility."

"Rafferty," Jess said, looking at him in awe and affection. "You're a philosopher, a poet."

"I'm a mechanic," Rafferty smiled. Jess laughed. Ben nodded, smiling.

Once again, he marveled at how everything Rafferty said made perfect sense and yet, to an outsider, it would probably sound crazy. At the very least, it was what Hanley liked to call, 'transcendentalist BS.' But even so, Ben mused, he could live with it, and he also knew he could never live without it.

**

Ben waited two days, before approaching Grace and Alma. He needed that time to recover from the shock of seeing a Bailon in front of his own eyes. Then he went to see Grace in her room. He thought she would handle the news better than Alma. Besides that, he reasoned that by this point, Grace knew Alma better than anyone, other than Kate, maybe. He reasoned that Grace should be the one to approach Alma.

"What's wrong, Ben," Grace said, her eyes shining. She knew it was something serious from the grave look on Ben's face. They sat side by side on Grace's couch, facing one another.

"Rafferty, it turns out, has some fairly interesting schematics," Ben said.

"All right. Schematics of what?"

"The Bailon."

Grace frowned. "The Bailon? How?"

"Rafferty went back into the Graylings' memories, dozens of times, and carefully, methodically sketched through everything he saw."

"Are you serious?"

Ben nodded, sighing.

"How can I help?"

"Grace, I have to warn you, seeing an illustration of a Bailon, it's—" Ben didn't know how to describe it.

"It's bad," Grace finished, nodding. Ben looked at her, apology written all over his face.

"It makes you feel like you're staring death in the face. It brings all the horrific memories of the extermination into your head. It forces the images to play inside your mind. It's… terrifying," Ben admitted.

"I can only imagine. Like looking at a mug shot of your attacker, and reliving the entire attack," Grace mused.

Ben nodded. "Only worse, because you relive it with all the vivid emotions, as if it's literally happening, again. And you feel it with the Grayling's emotions, Grace."

"Which are pure and more concentrated than our own," Grace finished for him, again nodding. She understood.

"If I could spare you this, I would."

"But you need me to tell you about the Bailon's physiognomy," Grace concluded. "So, you can understand what you're dealing with, right?"

"It can't hurt," Ben sighed, grateful that Grace so seamlessly grasped the gravity of the situation. "It can only, possibly, help."

"When do I go?"

"When you feel ready. I had no warning about what I was going to see. At least you do."

"Let's go," she said.

"When?"

"Now."

***

So, they went. Grace reacted to seeing the Bailon by raking in a large breath, backing away, stumbling, then clumsily searching for a chair to sit down. She closed her eyes, desperately waiting for the panic to subside. Images played through her head, uncontrolled. She saw the carnage, the ripped flesh, the spurting blood. It was far worse than when she first saw it with the Graylings, for back then, she'd also been emotionally connected. They had blanketed her in their comfort and love. Grace did not have that comfort with her now. All she had was the fear—uncontaminated and pure—undiluted and overwhelming terror. Sheer panic; she felt as if she ran for her very life, inside her mind. She began to hyperventilate, suffering a panic attack.

Grace was quickly removed from the tactical room, as they now referred to it, back into the cargo bay. Roslyn was called in, and she immediately came and held Grace's hand, calming her down considerably.

"What are you guys doing in there?" Roslyn said, looking at Grace with great concern.

"I'll be okay," Grace said, looking at Roslyn in appreciation. "Thank you, Roslyn."

She nodded, smiling gently at Grace.

"Roslyn," Ben said. "Please don't speak of this to anyone else, okay?"

"Sure," Roslyn said. She seemed to understand that whatever had upset Grace, it was not for her to know about.

After several more minutes, Grace let go of Roslyn's hand, and nodded to Ben and Rafferty. Roslyn quickly left the cargo bay without saying anything more. As the three of them headed back inside the tactical room, Rafferty tried to comfort Grace.

"It gets better. Eventually, you can look at the schematics without the emotions getting in the way. Then you'll be able to focus and study. It takes a few tries to get there."

Grace nodded, smiling weakly. Back inside the room, she sat in a chair and slowly looked up at the illustration with trepidation. She sighed deeply, taking the image in. Then she looked away, hanging her head. Ben worried that Grace couldn't handle it. Then she looked up at the image again and gazed. Her eyes squinted, then she closed them, lost in thought. Then she sighed deeply again, slowly standing up, and walked over to the image on the large screen. She stood in front of it for several minutes, while Ben and Rafferty looked on, waiting.

"This is an anterior view. Do you have lateral and posterior views as well?"

Grace turned and eyed Rafferty. He stared at her in confusion. Grace remained calm, speaking slowly, with purpose.

"Do you have views from the sides and back as well?"

"Oh, yes," Rafferty said, understanding.

He went to his console and typed. New images appeared on two more screens, three in total now holding a view. One was a view of the front, another the side, the third, the back of the Bailon.

"I need dextro and sinistral lateral views, please," Grace said.

Again, Rafferty stared at Grace, not comprehending. Ben smiled, for he understood.

"She needs views of the body from both the left and right sides, in profile," he said.

"Oh," Rafferty said, going back to his console. On a fourth screen, a second view of the Bailon, from the opposite side, appeared.

"Thank you," Grace said. "I need Alma."

Ben looked at Rafferty, then stared at Grace's back. She turned, eyeing them both. "Alma will see things I don't. And I need someone I can bounce ideas off. She's the best one for that. You'd be surprised how much you can tell about an organism, just by looking at it."

Rafferty and Ben looked at each other momentarily, then Ben nodded, immediately leaving the room. He went to find Alma. He tried to explain everything as best he could, including what to expect emotionally. He also called Roslyn to come back with him this time, right off the bat.

Ben returned to the tactical room with Alma and Roslyn. He prepared Alma to go in.

"I'd like to know what I'm dealing with," Roslyn said then, looking at Ben with such determination, Ben nodded in resignation.

"Can you comfort yourself?" he asked.

"Yes, but," she frowned. "I've never really needed to."

"You will now," he said, opening the door and taking both women inside.

The screens were dark, initially. Then Rafferty pulled up the 'anterior view,' as Grace referred to it, and both Alma and Roslyn gasped, entering the same emotional journey they all went through upon seeing their first waking, physical view of a Bailon in front of their eyes. Some handled it much better, more smoothly, than others.

Alma cried, burying her face in her hands. Grace sat next to her and placed her hand on Alma's back, trying to comfort her.

"It gets better, Alma, I promise," Grace said.

Roslyn stared, wide-eyed at the diagram, looking shell-shocked and nearly catatonic. After she stood this way, unblinking for several moments, Ben whispered to Rafferty, and he turned the monitors off, ripping the view away from Roslyn's eyes. She blinked repeatedly, then looked like she might vomit. Rafferty literally ran to place a trash basket at her side.

"I thought you said you could comfort yourself," Ben said, sounding panicked.

"Oh," Roslyn said. "I forgot."

She closed her eyes and breathed deeply, then slowly exhaled. She did this for over a minute, then opened her eyes and seemed perfectly fine again. As if nothing had happened to upset her.

"Can you help Alma, now?" Ben asked. Roslyn nodded and took Alma's hand, who seemed to relax immediately. After a few minutes, Roslyn let go, and Alma nodded.

"Okay," Ben said. "I think you should take a few days to adjust. Maybe then you can come back, take another look. See what there is to see."

Alma nodded, as well as Grace. Roslyn left with the two women, and Ben and Rafferty soon followed.

***

At dinner that night, the dining hall was quiet. Everyone knew something was going on. A few people knew, like Martin, who could hear everyone's thoughts. Arnold had snooped, with his super-hearing, so he knew. He told Jenny. Martin shared his knowledge with Eileen, and Hanley.

None of these people knew what the experience was like, however, to see a Bailon up close, albeit, a diagram. They could only imagine, from hearing about the experiences, and seeing the reactions of the people who had.

Roslyn told Ezra, and he tried to comfort her that night in their quarters. After Vera was tucked in bed and asleep, Ezra held Roslyn in his arms. All the children born the first year on board the ship were nearly ready to celebrate their eighth birthdays. Angel had already turned eight, and the rest of the children's birthdays followed in succession after her, in the weeks that lay ahead. Ezra tried to take Roslyn's mind off things by bringing this up.

"Vera's turning eight in one month. Can you believe it?"

"No," Roslyn said, looking in Ezra's face. "I can't."

"Was it so bad?"

"Yes. Like staring into the face of your own death."

He kissed her. A tear slipped down her cheek.

"Now I know why Rafferty said not everyone can know. I wish I didn't."

"He shouldn't have brought you in there," Ezra said, sounding angry.

"I asked him to."

"You didn't know what you were getting yourself into," he argued.

"But I needed to know, so I could help the others who looked."

"But, you're so upset."

"I can deal with it. Because, at least I know that diagram is all I'll ever have to see. I don't have to go to Hesperia to fight. And I've never been so glad in my whole life, Ezra. All these people who wish they could go? They have no idea what they're talking about. They want to fight, to help, to feel useful. All I want to do is hide, not deal with any of it. I'm glad I'm not one of the ones who has to go."

"Good. So, stay here with me, and be happy."

"I am. I just feel bad for the ones who have to go. They have no choice. I don't know how they can be so brave."

"I love you. And you're playing your part. You are being brave. You're keeping everyone strong, Ros. You're helping them deal with things."

"I know. It's a small part to play, but I'm happy to do it."

"No part in this is small. Everyone is needed."

"I need *you*, Ezra," she said, pulling him closer.

He kissed her passionately, and they made love, then fell asleep in each other's arms.

***

In a different room, Kate held Alma in her arms. Alma was quiet.

"Do you want to talk about it?"

"No."

Kate did not push her on the subject any further. Instead, she brought up a different topic.

"I've been thinking about us having a baby."

"What?" Alma turned over to look at Kate. "Are you serious?"

"Yes. We could ask one of the men to donate sperm. Be the biological father. I was thinking, maybe, Malcolm."

"Malcolm? He's so old, now."

"But he can still make sperm."

"I don't think I can focus on a baby right now," Alma said. "Besides, I don't know how supportive everyone would be of that. It's presumptuous enough that any of the men would be willing to donate to something like that."

"Everyone knows we love each other. Do you really think they would oppress us that way? When they love us as much as they do?"

"I know everyone loves everyone else. But people still have hang-ups. Even away from Earth. Ezra doesn't understand us."

"Well, maybe the new generations will be different than you think. Less judgmental."

"Kate... It's not even that I'm really worried about what people will think or finding a man who's willing to help. It's this war. It's a lot to deal with. I don't think I can focus on anything else. Especially the intricacies of how two women can have a baby together."

"If only we could do it on our own," Kate sighed. "Just get pregnant like everyone else. It would have happened on its own by now, naturally. Like everyone else. It's not fair. If love can happen between us so naturally, why can't that?"

Alma gasped, then went rigid in Kate's arms. She stopped breathing. Kate immediately became alarmed.

"Al, what is it?"

Alma didn't answer. She lay in bed, face blank, eyes gone off somewhere, deep in thought. Kate knew this look, had seen it before, over the years, as Alma tried to learn, understand the difficult subjects she studied.

Suddenly, Alma sat up in bed, a huge smile spread over her face. She quickly kissed Kate on the mouth, then stood, running from the room.

"Thanks, Katie!" she threw, over her shoulder.

"Did I do something?!" Kate called after her.

"Yes, and I love you for it!" Alma yelled, as she left their bedroom, and their quarters. Kate lay down in the bed, smiling.

***

Alma went straight to Grace's room and knocked, placing her hand on the panel next to her door. Grace appeared, looking moody. When she saw the smile on Alma's face, combined with her obvious look of excitement, Grace broke out in her own giant grin, the shadows across her face quickly dissipating.

"You saw something, didn't you? You've figured something out?"

Alma nodded. Both women immediately went to Jess and Ben's room, to call on Ben, who went with them, and Jess followed. The four of them called on Rafferty, who came out of his room and led them down the hall, into the cargo bay, and back into the tactical room. It was nearly midnight.

"Rafferty, can you pull up all the diagrams of the Bailon for me, please?" Alma asked.

Rafferty immediately did so. Ben and Jess sat, looking at Alma and Grace. Grace gazed at Alma expectantly.

"Remember how you started me out dissecting frogs, on the monitor?" Alma asked. Grace nodded.

"Remember what I asked you then, about their reproductive processes?"

"Yes," Grace said.

Alma looked at the diagrams now, up close, studying them. Grace looked, too. Both women scanned the diagrams for several minutes. Then Grace shot a look at Rafferty, her eyes shining.

"Rafferty. Is this a composite diagram?"

"Composite?" Rafferty frowned.

"Did you compile what you saw of several Bailon into one diagram?"

"What do you mean?"

"Do you have any other diagrams, of other Bailon, that look different from this one?" Grace asked, remaining patient.

"Can't look different. That *is* the Bailon. I scanned my memories for hours, going over these," Rafferty said, looking haunted. "As far as I can tell, every Bailon looks exactly like that one."

"I'll be damned," Ben said, looking at the diagram.

"You see it?" Alma said, turning and looking at Grace, then Ben, hope in her eyes.

"Yes," Grace said. "I should have noticed it sooner. I *knew* you would see things I wouldn't, Al."

"You would have seen it sooner or later," she said, humbled.

"Seen what?" Jess asked.

"The Bailon are asexual," Grace said. "There are no visible, discernable sex organs. And from what Rafferty says, they all look the same."

"So? What does asexual mean?"

"Asexual reproduction involves only one parent without the formation of gametes: the parent's cells divide by mitosis to produce new cells with the same number and kind of chromosomes as its own. Thus, offspring produced asexually are clones of the parent and there is no variation. That's why all the Bailon look alike," Alma said, answering Jess's question.

"Are you certain of this Rafferty? They all look exactly alike?" Grace shot an inquisitive look at Rafferty. He nodded, not needing to think about it, and Grace recognized his certainty.

"They're asexual, and if they all look exactly like this..." Grace trailed off, letting Alma pick up where she purposely left off.

"Then they can only reproduce by means of clonal fragmentation, through mitosis of a eukaryotic cell. And look," Alma said, pointing to the fingers on one of the Bailon's hands.

"You can even see where. See the autotomy mark, on the distal-sinistral appendage?"

Grace nodded. She looked at Alma, proud, then over at Ben, nodding.

"What else do you see, Alma?"

"Only a million things that back up our theory," Alma said. "Look at the symmetrical distance on both lateral sides. See how it's longer in proportion to the medial line?"

"Yes," Grace said, nodding emphatically.

"And look at the bilateral symmetry as well," Alma said, sounding wondrous. "And the caudal formation of the anteroposterior axis. The medial line is rigid. You can see the bone underneath," Alma sounded very excited now.

"That's right, what does that tell you?" Grace smiled.

"That there's no way they can carry offspring inside of them," Alma said.

"And if they contain eukaryotic cells for reproduction, and we know the rate at which eukaryotic cells split, and the phases of mitosis..." Grace trailed off again, waiting for Alma to pick up her cue.

"It's open mitosis, not closed," Alma said, and Grace nodded, smiling.

"That's right, because it's an animal," Grace said. "And with open mitosis, the nuclear envelope breaks down before the chromosomes separate. Walk it through, Alma. Remember your studies, remember what you read."

Alma closed her eyes, as if reciting from memory, directly from the text. This had been a topic of interest and fascination for Alma, years ago, and Grace did not refute this as mere coincidence.

"The process of mitosis is complex and highly regulated. The sequence of events is divided into phases, corresponding to the completion of one set of activities and the start of the next," Alma remembered. "The stages are prophase, prometaphase, metaphase, anaphase and telophase. During the process of mitosis, the pairs of chromosomes condense and attach to fibers that pull the sister chromatids to opposite sides of the cell. The cell then divides in cytokinesis, to produce two identical daughter cells."

"That's right, Alma," Grace said, sounding both proud and impressed.

"What the hell are you guys talking about?" Jess said, looking infinitely confused. Ben merely nodded emphatically along with everything Grace and Alma said. Jess felt completely in the dark. She looked to Rafferty for support. He only shrugged, sheepishly looking down at the floor.

"The Bailon reproduce with a vestigial appendage... here," Alma said, pointing to a 'finger,' on the Bailon's hand. There were four such digits on either hand, but on the left, there was a fifth, extra appendage.

"So?" Jess said.

"So, what that means is, essentially, the Bailon don't reproduce. They replicate. They clone themselves. That's why all of them look exactly alike. They all would have originated from a common ancestor."

"Okay, so what does knowing all of this tell us about the Bailon?"

"A lot," Grace said, sitting down to look at Jess. "First, organisms that use clonal fragmentation to reproduce are highly limited in how quickly they can do so. Secondly, the split appendage can only grow so fast, and we can guess at the total developmental time, from the start of prophase, to completion of telophase, when cytokinesis kicks in. This is when the final separation of the one, initial cell is complete, creating what is known as a sister chromatid. Once this process is complete, the two, twin cells begin to repeat the process, over and over, producing daughter cells. Each daughter cell has a complete copy of the genome of its parent cell. The end of cytokinesis marks the end of the M-phase."

"But what does that *tell* us?" Jess felt exasperated. Ben took her hand but did not speak. He could have jumped in at any time to continue explaining things, but he didn't want to steal the spotlight from Alma or Grace.

"With all types of asexual reproduction, there are costs. There is low genetic diversity within a regenerative species, and therefore susceptibility to adverse mutations that might occur. They generally have much shorter lifespans than species that reproduce sexually. They tend to suffer from mutations and diseases more often. Many offspring don't develop properly and fail to thrive. They can only reproduce as quickly as their vestigial appendage can regrow. It's generally relative to the size of the organism. For example, the smaller the organism, the faster it can grow a new vestigial appendage. Frogs do so several times a month. But frogs have a relatively simple DNA code. With the intellect and size of the Bailon—" Grace shrugged.

"Rafferty, what's the scale of this diagram?" Alma asked.

Rafferty sat back down at the console and typed in a few lines. A measurement scale appeared next to the anterior diagram of the Bailon on the monitor. Grace walked up to it, reading the numbers.

"Two-hundred-point-six-six centimeters," Alma announced.

"The Bailon are exactly six feet, seven inches tall. Shorter than the Graylings. Taller than us," Grace said. "However, in an organism that large, I would guess, in exponential terms, compared to smaller organisms, like a frog, that the Bailon can't reproduce more than about once every five years, or quite possibly longer, but certainly not less.

"And with asexual reproduction, a much larger portion of the offspring would be nonviable. On average, around thirty percent. Not to mention, the time it takes for the resulting anaphase organism to reach full maturity, at which time it is also capable of reproducing. Generally, the duration is roughly two-point-eight times the fragmentation process. In other words, the new resulting cloned organism is not capable of cloning itself until it reaches roughly fourteen years of age.

"Rafferty, exactly how many details were you able to extract from your memories? Do you remember how many Bailon were aboard each ship that landed? Or how many ships there were, in total?"

"Yes," Rafferty said, sounding surprised.

"You're kidding me," Jess said, sitting back. "This is crazy!" For she had begun catching on to what Grace implied.

"How many?" Grace and Ben both said at once.

"Each pod they landed in, held fifty Bailon," Rafferty said, growing excited. "There was a total of roughly two hundred pods."

"What about a mother ship?" Ben asked.

"No. Each pod was self-contained. No mothership. If there were, the Graylings would never have been able to escape in their vessel. A mother ship would have been waiting, to destroy them. It was always meant to be a ground extermination. They landed all their forces at once. Why not?" Rafferty sounded disgusted. "They knew the Graylings were no threat to any of them. They simply landed in their pods, en masse, and slaughtered them."

"So," Jess said. "What are we learning here?"

"Two hundred pods, containing fifty Bailon each," Grace said. "That makes a race of ten thousand Bailon, that landed on Hesperia, two hundred years ago, by human standards, of course."

"Ten thousand? That's all?" Jess said. "How many Graylings were there?"

"Over two million," Rafferty said, his eyes filling with tears.

"Two million? But, how could only ten thousand Bailon kill two million Graylings? They were so outnumbered."

"Because they can't fight, Jess, remember?" Ben said, gently. "They were sitting ducks."

"It was a slaughter," Rafferty said. Grace started crying.

"How could they do that?" Jess said. "How could anything ever do something like that? How do you just kill millions of people like that? For no reason?!"

Rafferty got up and typed on his console, quickly bringing up a blueprint image of a weapon. He turned around to address everyone.

"They did it with this. This was all they needed. No bombs, no grenades, nothing even so high tech, really. Just this."

"What is it?" Ben said, his voice thick.

"It looks like a gun," Alma whispered. Grace hugged her, crying.

"It is," Rafferty said, walking up to the diagram and directing his gaze to Alma, then back to Ben again. "It's a combination solid state laser. A CO_2 ruby photon, with neodymium-Yag, to boot."

Ben closed his eyes. He thought he might be sick. His stomach lurched. He could see the massacre playing inside his mind now, with an entirely new perspective to what he saw.

Rafferty pointed to a gray metal tube on the bottom of the gun. "This is the casing of the flash tube, which contains the ruby rod and two mirrors, one half-silvered. See how the trigger connects to the flash tube, and pumps it?"

Rafferty looked at Ben, who nodded. Rafferty knew his weapons all right. He knew machines front and back.

"I don't understand," Jess said, her voice thick with emotion. "What is a, Yag, dymium, whatever. What is it?"

"The weapon is two separate, high powered lasers, combined into one concentrated beam," Rafferty said. "High powered lasers are very dangerous. We use ruby lasers to cut and weld metal. At least, that's what they're used for on Earth. The reason CO_2 lasers are so dangerous is because they emit laser light in the infrared and microwave region of the spectrum. Infrared radiation is heat, so the laser basically melts through whatever it hits."

"So," Jess whispered, clearing her throat shakily. "What you're saying, is that ten thousand Bailon, with laser *knives*, just walked around cutting the Graylings into little pieces, shredding them into ribbons, by the millions. That's what you're telling me? They just landed, walked right off their ships, and started shooting their ugly laser guns at them, ripping them apart, knowing the Graylings wouldn't fight them? Knowing they couldn't do anything to stop them?"

"Gives you a whole new perspective on the memories they shared, doesn't it," Rafferty said, looking sick and angry at once.

"And you say I can kill them all?" Jess said, a fire growing in her eyes. "How many?" Jess looked at Grace intently. "Grace? If ten thousand of them landed two hundred years ago, can you figure out how many there are now?"

"Yes," Grace said, a fire beginning to glow in her own eyes. "Yes, I think I can. With thirty-percent non-viability per year, The Bailon, initially, can't possibly have increased by more than seven thousand a year. The exponential growth would increase beginning in year fourteen," Grace used her finger to draw on the table, doing the math. She shook her head, growing visibly flustered. Ben looked equally upset. Grace talked to herself by this point.

"So, without exponential values, we're already looking at millions, roughly. But we still don't know what their lifespan is, or how many years of that time they can reproduce. Even without all that, I'm well into the tens of millions," Grace whispered.

Alma cried out in consternation, throwing her hands up in despair. Jess turned to look at Rafferty, the fire slowing fading from her eyes, as doubt played across her face, once more.

"Rafferty," Jess shook her head. "Explain to me how it is that you're so certain I can wipe out *tens of millions* of Bailon?"

2

"It won't necessarily be tens of millions," Arnold said.

Everyone turned to look at him, for he stood in the doorway. No one heard him come in.

"Arnold, what the hell?" Rafferty said.

Rafferty walked toward Arnold, livid, his face full of color and rage. Arnold skirted inside the room, quickly darting around the other side of the table, away from him.

"Is this CPU hooked into the main database?" Arnold pointed at Rafferty's console, curious.

"Yeah," Rafferty said, still fuming. "How did you get in here?"

"Um, the door wasn't locked," Arnold said, busy typing away at the console. He pulled up a page of information. "This is a model for exponential population growth."

Everyone looked at the screen above Arnold's head. A table graph showed a red line that continued moving upward on the graph the further to the right side they looked.

"Unless the death rate of a species is the same number as the birth rate, any species will continue to increase in number, until infinity," he said. "Except that's not possible, is it?"

Arnold typed in another line and pulled up a different page. He turned and looked at everyone, his face dead serious.

"Nothing can continue to grow forever. Numbers are great, and calculations are fine and dandy, but species simply don't grow within a vacuum. There are dozens of outside influences that can affect the growth patterns and numbers of any given breed. Every species has limiting factors to their growth, not least of which," Arnold said, turning back around and typing on the console yet again, "includes their surrounding environment. Carrying capacity is the maximum population size that a given habitat can support. So, if you want to know how many Bailon are currently on Hesperia, you need to account for the environment on the planet, as well as understand the reproductive biology of the species in question," Arnold said, turning back around to look at everyone.

"So, what you're saying is, we need to study Hesperia now, too, right?" Alma said.

"Mmm, no," Arnold said. "I mean, yes, we could study and learn from what the Graylings remember of Hesperia, from before they left, but… What about the last two hundred years, since they haven't been there?"

"So, then, what are you trying to say?" Alma sounded utterly exasperated.

"What I'm trying to say is there are any number of factors that could affect the total population of Bailon we'll find on Hesperia when we get there. There could very well be billions of them, or less than ten thousand. The bottom line here is, the only logical conclusion we can possibly reach, is that we simply can't know. There is no way to know, until we get there."

"He's right," Ben said. "With all our intellect, all our differentiated knowledge, our specialties, our calculations, none of it will help in the long run."

"This is all too confusing for me," Jess said. "I don't understand any of this. I don't understand growth models, or mathematical formulas, vestigial appendages, dicadmium laser things, or even these stupid graphs."

"It's neodymium," Rafferty said, clearly frustrated.

"Whatever," Jess said, sighing. "I never thought I'd ever say this, but I'll take faith over all this confusing mumbo-jumbo any day."

"It's not mumbo-jumbo," Martin said, and everyone turned to see him now standing in the doorway. He looked right at Rafferty when he spoke.

"Rafferty, what you've done is amazing," Martin said. "And I'm sure Jess wasn't talking about all your hard work, when she referred to all this 'mumbo-jumbo,'" Martin shot a glance at Jess, and she hung her head.

"All these diagrams, the Bailon's physiognomy, their ships, their weapons, all the time you've spent pouring over everything, the *years* it took, and the *sacrifice*... It helps, Rafferty. Okay?" Martin tapped his temple. "So, don't go thinking it doesn't."

"Rafferty," Jess said, standing and walking over to him. "That's not what I meant. I know how hard all this has been for you over the years. It's not all your work I was talking about. What you did, what you put yourself through..." Jess took a deep breath, searching for the words to thank him. Finally, she took another deep breath, let it out and simply said it.

"Thank you."

"Yeah," Alma said. "If it wasn't for you, and your diagrams, I wouldn't have ever seen the Bailon. I was so scared at first, but now, look at me! I'm looking right at it, and I'm not scared at all. If anything, I just feel angry. You're helping us prepare to fight. Even if it isn't the way you thought it would be."

"Alma, I'm sure knowing the things we do about the Bailon's bodies will help, too," Jess said.

"Maybe," Alma shrugged. "But I still feel I got something out of looking. I'm really not afraid of them. They don't fall in love. I know that now. How can they, if they don't ever touch each other? I mean, think about it. They reproduce by copying themselves, by tearing their little pinky off? *Gross.* No wonder they're so aggressive. They must hate everything. I mean, how would *you all* feel, if instead of having sex with the person you love, you just, felt nothing, and ripped your finger off? How disgusting is that?"

Everyone stared at Alma for several moments. Then people began snickering, a few laughed out loud. The laughter began to spread, slowly, until everyone giggled, burying their faces in their hands, or even cried, they laughed so hard.

***

One of the models Arnold left up on the screen was of a large, animated, light-purple planet, spinning and rotating on its axis. It took several minutes before everyone calmed down and stopped laughing long enough to notice that Rafferty now stood in front of the monitor.

There were seven people in the room now, including Arnold and Martin, who sat at the long table with Alma, Grace, Jess and Ben. Rafferty didn't bother asking them to leave. He knew they could hear everything that was said or thought, even if he did kick them out. Besides, Rafferty realized, Ben was right. He stated that more minds brought in couldn't hurt, but only help to brainstorm.

"I'm sorry I tried to limit the people who worked with me on this," Rafferty said. "I was wrong. I only did it to spare everyone the distress of seeing the Bailon, especially those who don't need to."

"It's okay," Arnold said. "I'm sorry I snooped. And barged in."

"Arnold, if you hadn't barged in, I would probably still be trying to calculate numbers," Grace said.

"And I would still be looking at the Bailon, trying to figure out more about them," Alma said. "But I've learned enough about these nasties."

"I'm sorry I barged in, too," Martin said, snickering at Alma's latest comment. "But I could hear everyone's thoughts, and I knew Rafferty was getting upset. And we need him. Because, if I'm not mistaken, he still has something important to explain to Jess."

Everyone looked expectantly to Rafferty, who nodded. That was all that needed to be done, for everyone to know that all apologies were issued out and accepted. Jess looked up at Rafferty, her face calm now. He nodded back, then looked at Ben.

"Ben, I need you to try, in fairly simple terms, to explain to everyone Jess's ability. What it is, physically, that she does when she pulses. Can you?"

"Of course," Ben said. "I'll try and put it as simply as I can. Jess, you already know this."

"A review can't hurt," Jess said, smiling weakly, for she'd forgotten most of what Ben had told her about that, back in the facility. Almost nine years had passed since then.

"Right," Ben nodded. He took a deep breath. "Basically, what Jess does, at least when she pulses, is twist the Earth's magnetic field, and in doing so, she stores energy from electrons knocked out of atoms in the upper atmosphere around her."

"I'm already lost," Alma said.

Ben smiled. "The electrons travel in a generally downward direction at relativistic speed, which is more than ninety percent of the speed of light. This essentially produces a large pulse of electrical current, vertically. The electrical current is then acted upon by the Earth's magnetic field to produce a very large but brief electromagnetic pulse. It's like a lightning strike, only larger, and flat. Essentially, Jess is heaving the Earth's magnetic field out of the way, followed by a restoration of the magnetic field to its natural state. In her case, however, the stored electrons then fly outward, away from her, back to equilibrium with the atoms in the atmosphere. When they do this, it releases a lot of energy, which superheats the air, creating a compression wave."

"So, how come Jess can't pulse here on the ship?" Aaron said, entering the room and sitting down. He smiled at Jess, then looked at Rafferty.

"Mind if I sit down?"

"The more the merrier," Rafferty said, throwing his arms up in dismay.

"Why can't she pulse in space?" Alma said, nodding at Aaron.

"Because," Ben said, taking another deep breath. "She needs a constant magnetic field to manipulate, to pulse, and there isn't one on this ship."

"Ben, can you explain the Earth's magnetic field to everyone?" Rafferty said.

"Sure," Ben said, frowning. "Uh, the Earth's magnetic field is mostly caused by electrical currents in the liquid outer core of the planet as it flows in motion with the Earth's rotation. As it flows, the molten metals create an electrical current. Once set in motion, it stays in motion, so the

Earth has a constant magnetic field, until the Earth no longer rotates, or simply cools too much for there to be liquid in the core."

"Okay," Alma shrugged. "So? Why do you have Earth up on the screen, Rafferty? To show us the core?"

"This isn't a model of Earth," Rafferty said. "It's a scale model of Hesperia."

Everyone looked in wonder at the animation. It spun counter-clockwise, but simply looked like a large, periwinkle circle, with lines running laterally and perpendicularly across. Ben looked at it in curiosity.

"Rafferty, what is the scale of Hesperia, compared to Earth?" Ben's voice sounded strange—high and excited—he fidgeted in his chair.

Rafferty grinned, and the smile spread until his face hurt. He turned around and typed. A much smaller blueprint of a planet came up onto the screen, next to Hesperia. Everyone gasped. Arnold whistled. Aaron uttered an expletive. The difference in size was like putting a pea next to a basketball.

"That tiny thing is supposed to be Earth?" Alma said. Rafferty nodded.

Ben stood up and walked over to the screen, putting his face up so close, his nose almost touched. He closed his eyes, thinking, calculating. Nearly a minute went by in utter silence. Then Ben sighed, opening his eyes. He turned to Rafferty, his eyes grateful and full of tears.

"You figured this out, all by yourself, Raff?" Ben stood before Rafferty, humbled.

"Like I said, you've been busy," he said, gently.

"Yeah," Ben laughed, "I have. I spent my whole life learning, then was horrified to discover the best I could do with my intellect, was hurt people." He turned and looked at everyone with apology written all over his face. "I was ashamed. As soon as I left the facility, I wanted nothing else, really, to do with science, save a few things with Grace," he nodded to her. "I pushed it all out of my head. I had everything I needed. I still do."

Ben looked at Jess, his face and eyes full of love. "Jess, I'm sorry, for again, I've let you down." He looked at her, his eyes full of sadness.

"Stop saying that." Jess stood and walked over to him, burying herself in his chest and arms. He enveloped her, holding on tight. Everyone looked on in wonder, smiling. Ben looked backwards, over his shoulder, to Rafferty, and nodded. He kissed her head and whispered in Jess's ear, "You need to hear this."

"The strength of the blast that Jess creates is dependent not only on having a magnetic field to manipulate, but also how strong that magnetic field is," Rafferty said, nodding at Ben. "The strength of any planet's magnetic field depends on its size, speed of rotation, and the molten core it contains. For example, the Earth's surface ranges from less than thirty microteslas of energy, to over sixty. Hesperia's surface ranges from between 3000 to 4000 microteslas. The Earth spins once every 23.93 hours, which is fast, and has a liquid conducting core made of iron-nickel. Hesperia is roughly seventeen times the size of Earth, with a swiftly moving molten dual-liquid core, comprised on one level of silver and copper, and rotating in conjunction with that, is another level of plasma. These two, separate currents create what is known as the dynamo effect. It creates an immense electrical current, that is constantly traveling around the core of Hesperia, as it rotates. Hesperia rotates once every 18.3 hours. Faster than Earth. With a much more highly conductive molten core."

Ben hugged Jess very hard now. She pulled away, wincing.

"I'm sorry, Ben, I can't breathe," she sighed.

"Sorry."

"What does all this *mean*," Aaron asked, growing impatient.

"It means," Ben sighed. "On Earth, the best Jess could do, was generate a half kiloton blast. And that destroyed several buildings and leveled a park. It also fried every piece of electronic equipment and knocked out the power grid for seventy square miles."

Ben looked at Jess with tender eyes, trying to deliver this news gently, as he knew it would bring up painful memories. Jess nodded, for she understood he did not want to hurt her, but merely explain things.

"On Hesperia, she'll be able to generate a blast and compression wave, that—" Ben stopped speaking, shaking his head.

"It'll be like dropping the Atom bomb," Arnold marveled, for he'd been putting the pieces together in his head, trying to calculate, while looking at the models of Hesperia and Earth.

"No, it won't," Rafferty said, his voice soft, but firm. "The Hiroshima blast was equivalent to 12,500 tons of TNT. And that killed almost half a million people and leveled a city of 76,000 buildings. The blast Ben is talking about, is fifteen times stronger than that."

"Fifteen times stronger than the Atom bomb?" Alma looked at Rafferty in shock and disbelief. Rafferty nodded.

"Jeezus," Aaron said, covering his mouth, looking at Jess, worried.

"So, Jess is, like, a nuclear bomb?" Alma said.

"No," Ben said. "What she does is not nuclear. All the components of her pulse are generated outside her body, in the atmosphere around her. It just so happens that the atmosphere around her on Hesperia will aid in making her ability much more powerful than she ever could have been on Earth."

"The power from her pulse will be equivalent to fifteen times the Atom bomb dropped on Hiroshima," Rafferty confirmed. "Almost two hundred thousand tons of TNT. And it will all go off in a split second, and level anything in front of her, for over sixty miles."

"So, enough to level one of their cities, and wipe out a vast number of them," Aaron nodded, his eyes narrowed down into slits.

"It's almost like, Jess's power was tailor-made to be used on Hesperia," Grace mused. "Isn't it?"

Rafferty nodded. He turned back around, typing on the console. A blueprint came up of a city, surrounded on one side by a purple ocean, and a mountain range on the other.

"This is the Graylings' city, where they were living when the attack happened. Hesperia only has one continent. It's… large, to put it mildly, but much of it is mountainous. The low-lying lands were used for agriculture. The Graylings don't eat meat. There was one large freshwater table, far inland, that they used for irrigation, and all their drinking water.

"They lived in conjunction with nature. I mean, this *is* the Graylings we're talking about. They built where they had to, but their entire population resided in one large city, here on the eastern shore. It's one of the reasons the Bailon wiped so many of them out so quickly. They didn't have to go from city to city. All the Graylings were in one spot.

"But, I've studied all of this for years. Even if the Graylings couldn't fight back, why didn't the Bailon simply drop a bomb on them, level their city, take them all out in one step? Why slaughter them one by one, with their laser weapons? And I think I know the answer. They wanted to keep the Graylings' city intact. They didn't want to level all the buildings, because that would mean having to build new ones. I think the Bailon attacked the way they did to preserve the buildings, so they could simply move right in."

"That's so sick," Alma said.

"And lazy," Aaron said.

"But it makes sense," Grace said. "They arrived in small pods that only held fifty Bailon each, right? Where were all the others? Why were there only ten thousand Bailon total, that arrived on Hesperia?"

"They were the only ones who were able to leave," Sarah said.

Everyone turned to look as she lithely entered the room. She stood, looking solemn, her hand across her large stomach, for she was pregnant, and due in just a few short weeks. She and Aaron had been married for over a year. Aaron immediately got up and went to her.

"I really need to put a lock on that door," Rafferty mumbled.

"Sarah, what are you doing here?" Aaron hugged her. "Can we take that image off there, please?" Aaron said, sounding urgent. He motioned to the diagram of the Bailon still up on the far screen. He spun Sarah around in his arms, holding her tight, placing her back to the image, looking intensely, lovingly, into her eyes.

Rafferty quickly typed into his console and the screen went dark. Sarah had seen it, however, and looked shell-shocked. Aaron took her face in his hands, gently.

"Sarah? Are you okay?"

She nodded, smiling weakly. Aaron led her to a chair, pulling it out for her. She sat quietly for several moments, then began to speak. No one interrupted. Everyone sat quietly and listened.

"The pods are not even theirs. Or the weapons. They had a home planet, and another race found them. A peaceful race, who only wanted to make contact, learn about them, befriend them. They didn't know the Bailon were aggressive. They taught them, and when the Bailon grew to understand their technologies, they killed off the race who gave them everything. They took their space crafts for their own use.

"But their planet was dying. They'd used everything up. So, the ones who knew how, took all the pods and simply left everyone else there, to die. They fought amongst each other, even on the ships. Each pod erupted into war. Some died on the pods, out in space. Eventually, they found another planet, and they lived there. There was no intelligent life to kill. But again, they multiplied, and there were too many of them. They used up everything on that planet and had to go again. And again, they left everyone behind to die, and the only ones who escaped were the ones that made it to the pods in time.

"They just keep moving, from place to place. Fighting, killing, taking things over. They never build their own homes, they just take what's already there. And if there is any intelligent life, they kill it. They don't negotiate. They only find planets that don't have intelligent life, or life that can't fight, like the Graylings. And Earth. Because the children are changing, like ours. And when the Bailon finally leave Hesperia, we will be like the Graylings. Our weapons will be dismantled. We'll live in peace. And if the Bailon come to our home, we'll be slaughtered, and our homes taken over. They'll destroy Earth, like they're destroying Hesperia. Just as they've destroyed every place they've ever gone."

"How do you know this, Sarah?" Grace asked.

Sarah cried, and buried her face in her hands. Aaron tried to comfort her.

"So, what I'm hearing is this," Jess said, her voice surprisingly strong and steady. It sounded loud in the dead quiet of the room. She looked around at everyone, a fire growing in her eyes once again.

"I'm hearing that all the Bailon are in one place," she said. "Just as the Graylings were when the Bailon attacked them. They all live in one large city, there." She pointed at the blueprint on the screen. "In the Graylings city, the one they built. The Bailon, if you're all correct, are lazy, and won't have bothered building new structures, or moved anywhere else. And, according to Rafferty and Ben, I can level that city with one large pulse."

Everyone stared at Jess, taking her statements in. They all thought about it, processing, letting it in.

"Do I have that all about right?" She looked around at everyone. Her jaw set, her cheeks colored high with passion and anger.

"Yes," Rafferty said, his voice stoic.

"Yeah," Aaron said, nodding while still holding Sarah, his voice wondrous, full of hope and relief.

"Yes," Ben said, emphatic. He took hold of Jess's hand to comfort her.

"Fine, then," Jess said. "I'm in. Who's in with me?"

There were nine people in the room now, with the addition of Sarah. Jess raised her hand, waiting. It took less than five seconds for every person to raise their hand. Sarah turned her face out of Aaron's shoulder, to look at everyone, raising her hand even higher than her husband. She smiled at Jess, nodding, a solemn look of wisdom ringed inside her almond eyes.

3

Everyone either stood along the carpeted edge of the common room, or sat on the four couches, which were moved to line the outer edges. All the adults were present, save for Jemma, who had younger children that needed watching. The rest of the children, all now eight years old, save for Alex, who was five, had been instructed to play in the park, including Angel. Jess stood on a large taped X. To her right, three feet away, another large X was taped to the floor. Rafferty stood in the hallway, to Jess's right, his arms crossed over his chest, biting his thumbnail.

Ben stood in front of Jess, his forehead against hers. He talked to her lowly; only Arnold and Martin could hear. They both narrated to the people around them. There were no more secrets among the members of The Society; not at this point in their mission.

"Jess is afraid she won't be able to pulse," Martin whispered to Eileen. Earl nodded, standing next to them.

"She says she hasn't pulsed in over eight years," Arnold said. "And we all remember that one."

Everyone nodded. Some of them smiled, remembering the scattered way they had moved the couches. The ship had stopped, however. They no longer moved through space at thousands of miles an hour. They sat at a dead standstill.

Everyone took advantage of this, early in the morning, by going to the observation deck to look at the view. The only other time they got to do so was right after each of their jumps. They had been through five already, with one more to go. Thanks to Jess, today, however, everyone got an extra view.

"Ben, I can't do this," Jess breathed. She looked up into his face, her eyes pained and desperate. "I'm too out of practice. It's just been too long."

She had already tried to pulse twice, and failed, everyone looking on, holding their breath. When it became apparent, both times, that Jess was not going to do her disappearing trick, everyone let out a collective sigh of disappointment.

"Jess, remember your training," Ben said, sounding gentle. "Remember those feelings. Try and pull up the anger. If you need to trigger, remember the early days, when you didn't have control. Feel those emotions, Jess. You gained control once. You can do it again. You pulsed without even breaking a sweat, or your heart rate increasing. I know you can get back there, Jess. I know it."

"Ben, it's like I'm back to day one," she exclaimed, near tears. "After I pulsed before Angel was born, I promised myself I wouldn't do it again. I could have lost her, Ben. And when I was carrying Alex, I learned to push down the anger, no matter how high my hormones spiked."

"I know."

"No, you don't. You told me I almost died. I could have reappeared floating in space. Do you have any idea how much that scared me? I've spent the last eight years teaching myself not to pulse on this ship."

"I know, Jess, but nothing bad is going to happen. You won't pulse, you'll simply vanish."

Jess sighed, her heart rate increasing in fear. Ben held her face in his hands.

"The ship is stopped, Jess. You know it is. You saw the observation deck."

"But, you're going to move it."

"Three feet. That's all. And you may not even move."

Jess glanced over at the other X on the floor, in trepidation. Her eyes traveled further right, to the hallway wall.

"Jess, that won't happen," Ben said, reading her thoughts. "The Graylings calculations are perfect."

Ben looked at Rafferty, who still bit his nail. Rafferty nodded, quickly removing his thumb from his mouth. He smiled at Jess.

"I'm just too scared and nervous, Ben. I can't get angry. I just can't get mad enough to do this. I've already tried." She cried in consternation.

Ben sighed and pulled away from Jess, looking at the watching crowd, searching out the faces. He found Alma's round eyes and gave her a desperate nod.

"Alma? Come here a minute."

Alma walked over, slowly, looking extremely nervous. "Yes?"

Ben shrugged, looking at her in apology. "Give Jess a push."

"A push?"

"Yeah," Ben said, stepping away. He backed up, until he hit the far wall, giving Alma and Jess plenty of room. "And maybe, you can call her a few names?"

"But," Alma said, looking at Ben, hurt written all over her face. "I, I can't. I mean, she's my friend."

"I know," Ben said, hanging his head low. Memories of all the horrible tactics he'd employed over the years, back at the facility, suddenly came flooding back. He was ashamed to use any of them now, but he also felt desperate.

"It's okay, Alma," Jess said, smiling at her and nodding. "It's okay, Ben."

He met Jess's eyes, and saw the warmth, the understanding, the constant forgiveness. His heart fluttered. In nine years of knowing Jess, he never spent a moment out of love. He smiled at her, mouthing the words, 'thank you.'

"Yuck," Arnold breathed. "Those two make me sick." He put his arms around Jenny, however, and smiled down at her lovingly, kissing the top of her head.

"I told you," Martin said. "Romeo and Juliet."

All the couples held onto each other, hugging tightly, embracing, as they continued watching the scene unfold before them.

"Oh, brother," Earl said, for he had no one to hold onto.

"Mmm, hmm," Grace said, in agreement.

Alma looked at Jess for another moment, then stepped up into her face and shoved with both hands. Jess stepped back, her face filling with sudden surprise. Everyone in the crowd looked on, wincing, yet riveted, unable to take their eyes away.

"Dude, this is better than any TV show I've ever seen," Arnold said, excited.

"Shut up," several people breathed, still looking straight ahead, at the melodrama playing out several yards away. Alma shoved Jess again, this time so hard, Jess took several steps back, off her mark.

"Okay, Alma, okay," Jess said, laughing nervously.

"Alma, she needs to remain on the X," Ben called over, sounding nervous.

Alma sighed, as Jess stepped back onto her mark.

"I hate this, Jess, you know that?" Alma said.

Jess nodded.

"And I just want you to know, I don't mean anything I'm about to say, okay?"

"Okay," Jess frowned. "That kind of undoes the whole point, though, doesn't it?"

"Just pretend, all right?" Alma rolled her eyes, leaving Jess, walking over to Ben. Jess watched them, frowning deeper, already feeling a slight tinge of jealousy.

Alma leaned into Ben, speaking very low. She placed her hand on his left lower arm, demurely. Ben leaned in, to listen, for Alma spoke so low, he could barely hear her.

"Just play along," she said, touching his arm. "Don't look away from my eyes."

Ben looked in Alma's eyes, never breaking contact. He leaned in closer, until he and Alma's foreheads touched. Alma ran her hand up Ben's arm, caressing.

"Put your hand on my back," Alma whispered.

"Uh, oh," Arnold said, looking over at Kate in concern.

"What?" Earl said.

"Alma is one sneaky bitch," Arnold said. "But she might just be a genius, too."

"Kate, she doesn't mean any of it," Martin said. "She's scared out of her mind right now. Trust me, I can hear it."

"Thanks, Martin," Kate said, nodding and looking on.

"When she gets mad," Alma said, "I'm going to walk back up to her, and slap her face, and tell her she's fat and ugly, and—"

"That's really mean, Alma," he breathed.

"I know," she said, and he saw the pain in her eyes. "But we need her to pulse, and she can't unless she's really pissed off, right?"

Ben nodded, closing his eyes. He ran his right hand up Alma's back, while she continued playing with his other arm. Inside, his heart broke.

Jess looked at the scene that played out in front of her in complete disbelief. Never once, for a single moment since she and Ben became romantically involved, did she ever doubt his love for her. She never worried he would stray, or leave her, or mess around. The thoughts just never entered her mind. She told herself that what she saw was simply an attempt on Alma's part to upset her. She knew it was all an act, and yet, her mind instantly flared with jealousy. It was an automatic response to seeing another woman touch Ben in such a way. As she watched Ben run his hand up Alma's back, she told herself that Alma couldn't possibly be enjoying it, since Ben was a man, and yet, she looked on, in denial, as Alma pushed in closer, she and Ben now almost grinding together. Heat began to build in the pit of her stomach.

"Hey!" she yelled, her voice high and panicked. She stepped forward, and Rafferty pointed at her, in panic.

"No, stay on the X!"

"But," she said, motioning to Ben and Alma. She stepped back, and watched as Alma turned, a smug smile on her face, color high in her cheeks. Alma blushing, for some reason, inflamed Jess's anger even more. She did not know that Alma was flushed in embarrassment. To Jess, Alma looked extremely aroused. Her jealousy took over now, completely.

Alma walked up to Jess, and squarely slapped her in the face, the audible whap so loud, everyone watching winced, grimaced, or looked away.

"Oh, crap, look out," Hanley said. "This can't possibly be good. Are we certain she can't pulse out here?"

"Yes," several people said in unison.

"Good," Martin said. "Because, she is *pissed*."

Jess's head rocked back with the force of Alma's slap. Ben stepped forward, his face full of concern. Jess, however, did not look at Ben. Her face slowly came back around, the hair covering her cheek, falling away. She dropped her gaze steadily on Alma, nothing but hate inside her eyes. A slow, hot fire began to build. Alma was frightened and ashamed all at once, but she continued stoking the fire, not wanting to lose the momentum already built.

"That's right, bitch. I touched your man, so what are you gonna do about it, huh?"

"Alma, please," Jess breathed through clenched teeth.

"No, if you can't please him, maybe somebody else should. Someone who isn't fat from pushing two babies outta their hoochie. I ain't fat, I ain't had no baby. I look *good*. And Ben knows it, too. His hands felt *real* good running all over me. Felt like he enjoyed having a skinny chick back in his arms."

"Shut the fuck up!" Jess strangled out, the color in her face now high and bright.

"No!" Alma screamed. "I think I'll just go back over there, and FUCK... YOUR... MAN!"

"That's it!" Jess screamed, shoving Alma away. She had the presence of mind, briefly glancing down, to make sure she still stood on the X. Alma quickly stepped back as she saw Jess's face go blank, her eyes emotionless and dead.

Jess put her hands out in front of her, palms thrown up, in the familiar stance. Ben looked on, smiling, welling up with pride. He loved Jess so much. He was always in awe of her power.

Jess suddenly vanished. Everyone blinked, their minds trying to adjust to the fact that Jess simply wasn't there anymore. It was always a jarring sight. Ben looked over at Rafferty, nodding. Rafferty nodded back, starting up the stopwatch he held.

"Rafferty is telling the pilots to move the ship. They're moving it now, exactly three feet forward," Martin said.

Alma walked back, rejoining the group. Kate stepped forward, hugging her tightly.

Alma began to sob. "I love you, honey," she cried into Kate's shoulder.

"I know," Kate cried back.

Alma pulled away, cradling Kate's face in her hands, tears streaming down both women's faces. "I didn't mean any of that just now, you know that, right?"

"I know," Kate cried, her voice high and reedy.

"Oh, for Heaven's sake, get a room," Earl said, rolling his eyes.

Everyone else just ignored the scene. Ezra looked down and away. Ben looked at Rafferty in concern. Rafferty nodded.

"Did we move?" Jenny asked.

"Yep," Arnold said. "Now we wait and see what happens."

Hanley walked over to Ben, clapping him on the back.

"She'll be okay, Ben," he said. "The worst that can happen, is she moves three feet."

Ben nodded, pulling away from Hanley and began pacing nervously. Hanley went back to the group.

"My bet is on the second X," Arnold said. "Who's with me?"

"No," Martin said. "I'm guessing she appears right where she left."

"I'm with Martin," Aaron said.

"I'm going with Arnold on this one," Earl said.

"I don't believe this," Grace said. "You guys are actually betting on this?"

"They can't bet," Jenny said, giving Arnold a disapproving look. "It's not like money means anything, nor does anyone have any. What are you people betting for, anyhow?"

Everyone fell quiet for several moments, thinking about this. Then everyone shrugged and looked on, watching and waiting.

"Jeezus!" Hanley cried out, after three minutes passed. "This is so nerve-racking!"

"Shut up, Hanley!" Alma yelled.

Ben now stood still, a few feet in front of the first X that Jess had stood on when she disappeared. Hanley left the group again and walked up to Ben, eyes softening, his face taking on a look of sympathy.

"You think she won't move?"

"I don't know," Ben sighed.

"If she does, what will that mean?"

"It will mean we can't have her train without stopping the ship," Ben shrugged.

"Well, how often does she need to train?"

"Often," Ben shrugged again. "You saw how hard it was to get her to do it. She's far too out of practice. If we want her to be able to pulse, on Hesperia, on the edge of the Bailon city, she'll need to focus with incredible control. She needs to pulse several times a week, over the next two years. She must be able to get back to where she was on Earth.

She needs to be able to pulse without help from anyone else. We can't expect Alma to slap her on Hesperia, nor would it be likely to work, under those conditions." He babbled nervously.

"Well, Sarah said Alma was one of the people that needs to go," Hanley said. "Maybe that's why. Maybe it's to piss Jess off, get her to pulse?"

Ben shook his head in annoyance, looking at Rafferty. Rafferty stepped forward, looking at his stopwatch. Then he looked up, nodding to Ben.

"It's time," Ben said, out of breath.

Everyone looked on, gazing at the first X. Suddenly, Jess reappeared. She stood, hands still up, on the second X. Everyone gasped or exclaimed out in surprise at seeing Jess appear from thin air. Hanley sighed, hanging his head.

"Hah!" Arnold said. "I win."

Everyone ignored Arnold, looking at Hanley as he walked back.

"Hanley what's wrong?" Kate asked.

"She moved," Martin said, explaining Hanley's thoughts.

"So?" Kate said.

"So, when Jess pulsed eight years ago, if we hadn't moved the ship back to where we were, she would have reappeared in the middle of space," Martin said, sounding sad.

"She really did almost die, back then," Hanley mused, shaking his head.

Back at the X, Ben quickly turned to Jess, three feet to his left, walking over to stand in front of her. His eyes looked sad, yet relieved at the same time. Jess blinked looking at Ben as he stepped in front of her and looked around to find herself standing three feet further to her right, in a split second, from her point of view. She looked to her left, at the X she had been standing on, in her mind, only a second before. Then she looked back at Ben, tears welling in her eyes.

"I moved?" she said. Ben nodded, taking her into his arms.

Rafferty looked on, shocked and saddened.

"I love you, Jess. I can't believe I almost lost you."

"And you expect me to be able to do this, knowing what it really means?" she cried into his shoulder.

"That won't ever happen," Rafferty said, walking up to the two of them. "The ship will simply stop, every time you train. And from now on, we won't even move a single inch. Jess, your life will never be in danger."

"You have to understand, still," she said, looking at Rafferty, "how scary the notion of pulsing is to me now, here on this ship. In space. My feet are not on the ground."

"But the ship won't move," Rafferty repeated, his voice not wavering. He nodded at Jess, not even blinking. "And if you can't do it under these conditions of stress, how will you ever be ready to do it for real, on Hesperia?"

"Jess," Ben said, ignoring Rafferty's remarks. "You *did it*. You pulsed. You didn't even think you could again, but you did."

"Ben," Jess said. "You touched Alma."

Jess looked at him, her face infinitely hurt. He looked back, feeling equally destroyed.

"I know… I'm sorry," he whispered, touching his forehead to hers. "You know I didn't mean that, right?"

Jess nodded, as Ben took her face into his hands and kissed her passionately. Everyone looked away, until they were done, which took several minutes.

"Damn, Alma," Hanley said. "You are one hell of an actress."

"Thanks, Hanley," Alma said, but she looked ashamed.

"Okay," Rafferty said, when Jess and Ben finally pulled away from one another. "Let's figure this out, shall we?"

Jess, Ben, and Rafferty went to sit on one of the couches. Everyone else either stood, silently listening, or sat on the other couches, looking on.

"How many times a week do you need Jess to pulse, to keep her practice up?" Rafferty asked.

"Well, before, three times a week sufficed," Ben said, looking at Jess. Jess nodded, agreeing.

"Okay, so we'll stop the ship, let's just say, every other day," Rafferty said. "We'll set a time, say ten a.m.?"

"Yeah," Ben agreed, again looking at Jess, who nodded her consent.

"Great. Every other morning, at ten a.m., the ship will be stopped, for however long you need. Jess will pulse, she'll get better and better at it, and by the time we reach Hesperia, in two years, give or take a few weeks, she should be up to speed."

"What do you mean, give or take a few weeks?" Earl said. "I thought the Graylings calculations were perfect? Shouldn't we know exactly how much time we have left?"

"No," Rafferty said. "Not if we don't know how much time we'll lose on Jess's training."

"What do you mean?" Kate asked.

"He means," Martin said, "It will take another two years to reach Hesperia if we don't stop moving. But since Jess can't train while we're in motion, we must stop, literally every other day, for her to train. And we don't know how long each training session will take, so…"

"So, it will take us longer to get there," Jess said, looking sad. "Because of me."

"Jess, you're going to wipe out all the Bailon in one fail swoop," Aaron said. "I think a few extra weeks to get there is more than worth the wait."

Everyone nodded. Jess smiled at Aaron, thankful. Ben took her hand, comforting her.

"The first time's the hardest," he said. "I think once you pulse a few more times, it will get much easier. Hopefully we won't have to resort to such ugly tactics ever again."

"Hey, who you callin' ugly?" Alma said, but her voice held an amused tone. She stepped forward, looking at Jess with trepidation. She knelt in front of her, taking Jess's hand. Alma's eyes welled up with tears.

"Jess," she said, her voice trembling. "You know I didn't mean what I said, right?"

Jess nodded, her own eyes welling up with tears.

"You're my friend, and I love you. I never want to hurt you, ever," Alma choked out.

"Alma, it worked, you got her to pulse," Aaron said.

"Yeah," Arnold said. "And that's helping to save the Graylings. You did a good thing."

"I know," Alma said, never taking her eyes away from Jess's face. "But it still sucks. Jess, I would never mess around with Ben. He loves you. He would never do that to you, you know?"

"I know," Jess whispered, smiling through tears.

"Besides," Alma said, her voice growing stronger. "I really don't swing that way, you know?"

"We know," a few different people said, together.

"And even if I did," Alma said, going back over to Kate, taking her hand, "No offense, Ben, you wouldn't be my type. You're way too old for me."

Everyone laughed, including Ben, who hung his head, shaking it. Jess also laughed, smiling at Ben next to her on the couch. Soon after, the ship began to move again, and everyone went on with the rest of their day.

4

That night, in bed, Jess and Ben made love. Afterwards, he held her in his arms, her head on his chest. He was concerned.

"Jess?"

"Hmm?"

"Does it ever bother you?"

"What?"

He paused for several moments, afraid to ask the question. The room was deadly quiet.

"My age," he said.

"What?" Jess looked up at Ben, worried. "Ben, you know it doesn't."

"I'm not a young man anymore. I was already too old for you, back at the facility. Now, eight years have gone by, and, I can't even imagine what things will be like for you, in another eight years. Jess, in eight more years, I'll be almost sixty."

"Ben, it's not like you've aged alone. I'm thirty-two, now. In eight years, I'll be forty," she frowned, suddenly realizing this fact.

"And I'll still be almost twenty years older than that. I'll be fifty-nine. You'll be married to an old man."

"Ben, I don't care. I love you," she said, kissing him. "Besides," she said, giving him a lusty look. "You don't look like you're fifty-one. You don't look a day over forty. *And*," she paused, looking at him demurely, "you certainly don't make love like you're any more than thirty. So, we're pretty much matched up."

Ben laughed, hugging her. He kissed her, then pulled away again.

"Well, what happens when my body begins to lose its stamina, huh?"

"Well, we can worry about that *if* it happens. I'm not with you for the sex, Ben." She paused for several moments, dramatically. "Although, it's pretty darn good, I have to admit."

He kissed her again, more passionately. He whispered to her.

"It's good, huh?"

"Mmm-hmm," she breathed. "And I have no idea how your body still looks so good, either."

"My body," he said, his voice teasing.

"Yeah, you know… The first time I saw you naked, I was like, 'damn, he's actually *really hot*.' That first time, when you came to my room, back at the facility? You remember that?" She looked up at him.

"Yes, I remember," he said. He pulled the memory up, even as she said it, reliving all those emotions. He had been so nervous and unsure, not believing that Jess could ever possibly feel the same way as he did. He laughed.

"You came out wearing nothing but a white towel." He laughed again. Jess laughed with him.

"You said *'all I have are those blue scrubs. Those aren't so sexy.'*" He laughed even harder. Jess laughed harder with him.

"Oh, God, I remember," she said, blushing. "I was so nervous. I was so scared. I was completely, totally in love with you, and I didn't know if you felt the same way."

"I did," he whispered.

"I know that now. I didn't know that then. We had a fight, remember?"

"Yes," he said, remembering it, sighing.

"Because I laid there in bed, next to you, and I realized I loved you. I realized I loved you so much," Jess said. A tear slipped down her cheek. "And I thought there was no way you could possibly love me back that much."

"Hey," Ben said, wiping her cheek. "I love you, Jess."

"I know. And as much as I loved you then, I didn't think there could ever be anymore. But the way I love you now, you have no idea. In nine years, Ben, I haven't loved you any less. Only more. And I always will. No matter how old you get. It doesn't make any sense, but I just know you could age overnight, and it wouldn't matter to me. I could wake up next to you tomorrow, with you looking old, frail, wrinkled, with, like, two wisps of white hair left, and I would still love you just as much as the first day you kissed me."

"I'm not going to age overnight, Jess."

"I know, I'm just trying to make my point. I'm trying to make you understand. It doesn't make sense for me to love the Graylings, does it? They're not even human, but I love them as much as you, or Angel, or Alex. Or any human being, for that matter. I love them as if they're *my* species, or as if I was *them*."

"I know that, Jess. I feel the same way. I think we all do."

"Well, I love you that way, too. No matter what, okay?"

"Okay," he said.

"And you still have a nice body," she threw in. "You did at the facility, and you still do now. Maybe better, even."

He laughed, hugging her tight again. "It's all those laps around the track, and the pure water and smoothies."

She laughed, kissing his chest. "But, if at some point, you do get too old to be so energetic," she said, her hands beginning to roam, "We might as well enjoy it now, while the getting is still good."

"Oh, the getting is good, Jess," he said, running his hands all over her body now, passion overtaking him again. It always happened this way.

"It's still very, *very* good," he said, rolling on top of her, fervidly kissing her neck.

***

Angel manifested her ability when she was seven-years-old. Everyone was shocked. After the dust settled, however, all the parents looked to their own children, watching and waiting. But as the children's eighth birthdays came along, in succession, it was clear that none of the other children, besides Angel, were going to manifest.

The first to turn eight, after Angel, was Mal. Arnold and Jenny did not do anything special, as none of the parents did, really. As the ship now stopped every other day, however, they did take Mal, on his birthday, to see the view from the observation deck. There, they hugged him and told him he was now eight-years-old. They wished him a happy birthday, and Jenny even cried a bit, lamenting how quickly Mal was growing up. Arnold hugged her, and looked down at Mal, winking.

"Happy birthday, buddy," he smiled.

Mal reached up and touched his mother's hand with his index finger. Jenny gasped, her eyes growing wide, her body rigid. Arnold looked at her in concern. He had not seen Mal touch her. She was a statue, frozen, and her eyes had a far-away look.

"Jenny? Jen?" Arnold gently shook her. He began to panic when she didn't respond. He snapped his fingers in her face and she didn't blink. Mal had long since removed his finger from his mother's hand and simply stared at the scene unfolding. He had no idea he'd done anything.

Suddenly, Jenny snapped back, and began to cry. She blinked and looked down at Mal, in sorrow, happiness, wonder, and awe. She knelt to bring her face directly in front of her son.

"Thank you, sweetie," she cried, and hugged him tight.

"Jen, what the hell just happened?"

"It was amazing," Jenny breathed. She stood to look her husband in the face. She was flushed and excited. She looked five years younger.

"Mal touched me, and I... I... I just *saw* everything. Everything that's happened over the last eight years, from the moment I came on board the ship. Every memory I had, just flashed before my eyes, like I was reliving everything, in a single moment. It was, like, having it all back again, and remembering every feeling I ever had. It was *wonderful*." She started crying again.

Arnold hugged her to him, tightly, and looked down at Mal, who looked at his parents, his face innocent and calm. Arnold let go of Jenny after several moments and looked back down at his son.

"Mal? Could you do to me what you did to your mom?" Arnold's face looked infinitely hopeful and scared at once.

Mal nodded, and slowly reached his finger out to touch his father's hand. In an instant, Arnold relived ten years of his life. The memories that flashed before his eyes went even further back than Jenny. He relived his lonely years on the ship, with only a handful of friends to keep him company. He relived the day he channeled into the Graylings. He relived the night The Society escaped, and he felt Jesus's heavy body in his arms, as he carried him to the morgue.

Arnold saw, and more importantly *felt*, the first moment he saw Jenny, and later, the funeral, where he held her hand. He felt the moment Jenny told him he made people love him, and the hope that leapt in his chest, at the thought that Jenny might love him. He even relived the day she came to him in the library and told him she wanted him to make love to her, and everything that followed. He blushed, his heartrate increasing. He experienced, all over again, the day Mal was born and he became a father. Everything that had happened to him over the last ten years flowed back into his waking, conscious mind, filling Arnold with overwhelming emotion.

He looked down at his son, crying. Jenny cried along with him, for she understood what he experienced. She understood why he cried.

"I'd forgotten, so many things," Arnold said. "Thank you, Mal."

Arnold hugged Jenny tight again, then pulled away, recalling the memories of every time they'd made love. He looked down at Mal, embarrassed.

"Hey, buddy? You can't see what we see, can you?"

Mal shook his head, frowning. He didn't fully understand what he'd done, still.

"Do you know what you just did to your mother and me?" Arnold asked.

"Yes, sort of." Mal nodded, slowly. "I brought everything back, so you'd remember."

"Why?" Jenny said.

"Because you were sad, Mommy," Mal said, "And..." he paused, thinking. "I just felt like I was supposed to touch you, and I knew if I did, you'd remember. So, it wouldn't be like you lost everything."

"Lost everything?" Arnold frowned.

"Mommy said I was growing up too fast," Mal said, starting to cry. "So, I gave her all her time back, so she could see."

"See what?"

"That it's all still in there," Mal whispered. "So, she wouldn't be sad anymore. Are you still sad, Mommy?"

"No," Jenny said, shaking her head, wiping her tears away. "I feel wonderful. Don't you, Arnie?"

"Yes," Arnold said. "I do. But I still don't see how you knew to do that, buddy?"

Mal shrugged. Jenny looked at Arnold, her eyes filled with love.

"It's his ability. He's manifesting, Arnie."

Arnold looked down at Mal, instantly beaming proudly. He bent down and hugged him tight, yet again. Then he stood and hugged Jenny again.

**

Arnold and Jenny went to see Ben later that afternoon. Mal was busy studying in the library. They knocked and were welcomed inside.

"What's up, Arnold?" Ben said.

"Well," Arnold sighed. "Mal manifested his ability today."

Ben and Jess both looked at each other, then back at Arnold, excited.

"What is it?" Jess asked.

"It's kind of hard to explain," Jenny said. She looked at Arnie and he smiled and nodded, encouraging her to go on.

"He touched me, and Arnie too, and we both…" she paused. "We relived every memory we had, from the last several years."

"It was like, every feeling either of us ever had, we lived it all again, in a matter of seconds," Arnold said. "And it made us both feel like…" he paused, frowning.

"It made *me* feel like I got to live it all over again," Jenny said. "Even the bad things, it still helped. I'd forgotten so many things, even though I thought I remembered everything so clearly."

"It's like getting your memories downloaded back into you, but you're living them in real time," Arnold said, clearly excited. "It's amazing. It helps you remember what's most important."

"Huh," Ben said, looking at Jess.

"I relived channeling in for the first time," Arnold said. "And Ramona's death, and Harold's."

"Oh, Arnie, so did I," Jenny said, hugging him.

"I'm sorry, Arnold," Jess said, remembering how sad everyone had been when the Elders died.

"No, it's okay. Because it made me feel more energized, ready to push forward, face the task at hand. Also," he turned and kissed Jenny on the forehead. "It made me remember how I felt, the first day I met you."

"You forgot that?" she chided him.

"No, of course not. But I relived that day, eight years ago, as if it happened today. It was wonderful."

Jess took in a sudden breath, feeling an incredible longing. She looked at Ben, for it was only a few weeks ago, that they'd recalled their days inside the facility, and the first time they'd made love, as well as their first fight. Everything had been such a whirlwind back then, and Jess was caught up in so much emotion, confusion, and euphoria.

"Ben, we were just talking about this, remember? When I asked you if you remembered that day in the facility, and our fight?"

"Yes." Ben nodded.

"Wouldn't it be wonderful, if we could really remember it?" Jess said, feeling urgent.

"No, no, no, no, no… It's not just remembering things," Arnold broke in. "It's like *reliving* it all over again, in your head. It's like you're really doing all those things, all over again. It's," Arnold shook his head. "It's the most amazing thing I've experienced, since channeling into the Graylings."

"And for me, the most wonderful feeling, other than that, too," Jenny said. "That and the feelings I had when we escaped, and Sarah used her powers."

"Do you think Mal could do this for us?" Jess asked, looking nervously at Jenny and Arnold, from where she sat on the couch.

"Jess, Mal is an eight-year-old child," Ben said, sounding embarrassed.

"He did it for me, when I asked," Arnold said. "It's what I wanted to talk to you about, Ben. When Angel manifested, it was because Jemma dropped a bowl. And Angel seemed, simply, to know what to do. There was no need for her to train or find a trigger. I mean, look at all the work Jess has been putting into things, trying to get her ability up and running again. With the children, first Angel, and now Mal, it seems to be effortless. When the time comes, and they see the need, they just seem to know what to do."

"Interesting," Ben said, thinking. "So, your theory suggests all the children have their abilities already."

"Maybe," Arnold said, nodding. "And they simply don't know how to use them, until they're *needed*. Once Angel fixed that bowl, she was aware of her ability, in an instant. Mal seemed to know immediately what to do, as soon as he saw how sad Jenny was. He just touched her and made her happy again."

"Yes, but it still could be tied to the ages the children are at," Ben said. "They're just now beginning to develop the ability, cognitively, to empathize with other's feelings. To look outside of themselves, and truly observe the world around them."

"Or, it could simply be chance, that it took this long for Angel or Mal to see a need, and then know how to fix it. If they don't know to use their ability, until a need arises directly in front of them, some of the children may not manifest for several more years."

"Or, theoretically, they could manifest at an even earlier age," Jess mused, looking at Ben.

"I don't know," Ben said. "I'd say, since today is Mal's birthday, that his ability was meant to manifest at this age, except that Angel was seven. So, I'd have to lean more towards what Arnold is saying. It could very well be that the children will only manifest their ability when the need is directly in front of them. That's their trigger."

"It makes sense, Ben," Jess shrugged. "I only pulsed when I got really angry, but I felt threatened, so technically, I was defending myself. I was protecting myself. What if I never got that angry? What if no one who needed a trigger ever reached the emotional point where their power came forward?"

Ben nodded. She was right. All the powers that manifested were drawn out, either through a loss of emotional control, or when the need to use their power arose.

"Sarah first manifested to protect herself from a technician with a Taser," Ben said, more to himself than to anyone else. He thought hard. "Except for the ones whose abilities are constant. They don't have a trigger. They're useful for the person possessing them, from the very start. Martin simply had his ability, once the Luci set in. As did Arnold, correct?"

"Yeah," Arnold nodded.

"And me," Ben said. "I just had my ability. Nothing drew it out of me."

"So, it all depends on whether it helps someone else, or is needed, specifically at the time," Jenny said.

"Well, by that definition, each of the children will manifest their ability when the time is right," Jess said. "There will be a need, and someone will step forward. Someone will step up to help."

Everyone nodded. Jess stood to look Ben in the face.

"That means Alex has an ability just waiting to be needed."

"He's six-years-old, Jess," Ben breathed. "Whatever he can do, it can wait. It has so far."

"I know, but I wish I knew what it was."

"No one's going to address the elephant in the room?" Arnold asked.

Everyone stared at him, confused. He shrugged. "We know what Angel can do. That ability has manifested. And, we have no idea why or how she'll be needed on the mission." He eyed Jess gently, afraid to upset her. She nodded for him to continue. "But we don't even know what Mara's ability is yet." He looked around at everyone. "Yet, Sarah says she's needed for the trip. So…"

"But Sarah doesn't know why, either," Jess and Ben both spoke together.

"Because maybe Mara literally won't manifest until her ability is needed… *during* the mission."

The room was quiet for several moments, as everyone thought. Arnold finally broke the silence, and the discomfort, by switching topics back to his son.

"Would you like me to have Mal touch you?" Arnold said.

"Arnie!" Jenny looked at her husband in shock.

"What…? Oh, you sickos, I didn't mean it like that… It's why she was asking before, right?" Arnold looked at Jess. "If you're asking, then you must feel you need it?"

Jess looked at Ben, feeling ashamed. It wasn't that she couldn't remember every moment she'd spent with him. She simply wanted to live it all again. She wanted Ben to live it all again, with her.

"I need to, Ben," she said. "I need to remember everything. I think it might help with my triggering. If I can remember what it felt like to have that control, maybe I could get it back, without all this struggling."

She paused, looking at Ben shyly. "And without you and Alma having to stand so close."

***

In the two weeks since Jess initially triggered, she had been unable to gain control back, in any of her training sessions. The second time she tried, she still couldn't do it without a push. Just like her first attempt, she couldn't focus, or get angry on her own. Alma grudgingly stepped forward, on the second day of Jess's training, and walked up to Ben, rubbing his arm. This had sufficed in pulling up the jealousy and nasty feelings inside Jess, and she pulsed again.

However, she hadn't pulsed without this hot, jealous anger. In two weeks, she'd trained eight times, and each attempt, she either had to see Alma near Ben, or close her eyes and recall seeing Ben run his hands up her back, to use her ability. The control she'd mastered while inside the facility continued to elude her.

Ben closed his eyes, sighing. He was not proud of the fact that he kept putting Jess through this. The last thing he wanted to do was hurt her. The continued images of he and Alma together, tortured Jess. He knew she kept picturing it, to pulse. He also knew it was hurting her immensely. She went to sleep crying on more than one occasion after her training sessions. No amount of holding her or telling her he loved her would help. Not when she continued having to see Alma approach him, and him touching another woman, just to recall her anger.

Ben grew increasingly afraid that her trigger had now switched, and that Jess was far too dependent on the jealous feelings from seeing he and Alma together. If this kept up, she would, indeed, be unable to trigger, perhaps, without Alma by her side on Hesperia, as well as Ben. He knew this would not be possible. At the very least, he doubted it. She had never shielded two people besides herself. He didn't know if she could. He looked at Arnold, his eyes apologetic.

"Arnold?"

"It's okay, Ben," Arnold shrugged. "My son has an ability. It's meant to help people. If it's what Jess needs, I'm proud to see him help. Jen?"

Jenny smiled and nodded at Arnie. She understood this was beyond her. They all needed Jess to pulse, if they wanted to save the Graylings. Everyone had a part to play. If Mal was now being added into the mix, then so be it. Jenny loved the Graylings as much as anyone. She had relived all those feelings of being connected, only hours ago. The memories were still fresh in her mind, of when everything changed for her. They were now less than two years away from Hesperia, and their main weapon, in the form of Jess, was not running properly. If her son could help to remedy that, she would not hesitate in letting Mal use his ability. All of this, she told them.

"I'll go get Mal," Arnold said, his voice gentle and understanding.

Jess cried. She felt terrible. Ben hugged her. She cried into his shoulder.

"I'm sorry, Ben. I just can't take another session, seeing you and Alma. I know you love me, but, I just can't keep making myself see you, touching someone else."

"I know," he said, kissing her softly. "I know."

"Ben, if I do this, I need you to do it as well." She looked at him, her eyes hopeful. He loved her so much, and he understood her need.

"You know I would never leave you alone in anything," he said. She closed her eyes, grateful she didn't need to explain her feelings. He got her. He always understood. She loved him more in that moment, again, than she ever thought possible.

**

Arnold came back with his son in tow. Mal did not look nervous or scared, he just looked at Jess's tear-stained face with sympathy. He smiled and stepped forward, touching her hand with his index finger, just as he had already done twice before that day.

Jess relived everything. Her first memory began in the car, with Agent Fielding driving her up PCH, to the facility. She saw Ben, as Dr. M., when he first opened her door to beckon her into the facility. She sat in a chair, and listened to him tell her she was special, that she had a deviant gene. She met everyone inside the facility again for the first time. She met Aaron, and Hanley, and Martin. Martin kissed her. She met Jesus. She pulsed, she almost died. Ben kissed her on a plane to Nepal. He carried her in his arms. She fell in love. She and Ben made love for the first time and had a huge fight. She murdered innocent people. She found out she was pregnant. She broke Aaron's heart, and almost pulsed, killing several of her friends. Jess escaped from the facility under the incredible blanket of warmth and love that Sarah threw over everyone. They went to get Lucia. Jesus and Lucia were killed. They rescued Martin's wife. They came on board the ship. Jess almost pulsed herself out into space. She married Ben, then gave birth to Angel. She channeled into the Graylings, then later, gave birth to Alex. She met Harold and hugged him. Ramona died. Later, Harold died, and Sarah married Aaron.

Jess relived all these memories and more. Most importantly, she pulsed. In her mind, she pulsed in the orchard time and time again. She relived the moment she fell to the ground, lost, half-insane from being in isolation, unable to see Ben. She remembered when he came to her, and stood with her in the decimated field, and how happy she felt when she first saw his face. She thought her heart would burst for joy. She threw her arms around him, thinking he would push her away, afraid someone might see, but instead, he threw his own arms around her and held her tight. That was the moment she knew she wanted to be with him forever.

Jess knew at that moment, with Mal's help, that this was when everything had changed for her. She hadn't known it at the time. She was only now aware of it, while reliving it all again, with the boy's help. She knew what her new trigger was, and she cried out loud, a large, gasping wail.

Ben grew concerned. Jess's face looked so pained, so utterly shocked, and she cried out with such suddenness, Ben was afraid she'd been hurt physically, somehow, by what Mal had done to her. She snapped out of her reverie and looked down at the little boy in wonder.

"I never knew," she said. "I never realized it was that easy."

"Jess, what is it," Ben said, looking at her with such concern, she laughed. She simply couldn't help herself, bursting with joy and euphoria.

"I saw something," she said, her voice wondrous. "I remembered something I forgot. A feeling. A moment. I never knew."

"Knew what?" Ben looked desperate.

"That it was that easy," Jess said, throwing her arms around Ben. "I don't need anger, Ben."

She laughed again.

"What?" Arnold asked, looking confused. "What did you do to her, buddy?"

Mal shrugged, shaking his head. It was such a grownup reaction, from an eight-year-old, both Arnold and Jenny broke out in nervous laughter, at the same time.

"Jess, what did you see?" Jenny asked.

"A memory of me and Ben, back at the facility. I can't explain it. It was more about my feelings at the time, and everything that was going through my mind. I lived it again, and I saw it for what it really was. I never knew before," she said again, still gazing at Ben. Her eyes never left his face. "I don't need anger to trigger, Ben. I just need to remember that moment."

"What moment?" Ben asked, his face so gentle and loving, she melted.

"The moment I knew I would spend the rest of my life with you. The moment I truly knew I loved you."

"In your room that night?"

"No," she said, looking at Ben with so much love, he could hardly stand it. "That day, in the orchard. When I'd been in isolation for so long. You came to me, you'd turned the cameras off, only I didn't know. But I couldn't help myself. When I saw you, when I saw your face, I just couldn't help it. The entire world fell away, and all there was for me, in that moment, was you. And I hugged you so tight, and I thought you would push me away, so no one would see."

Ben nodded, remembering. His eyes were moist, his heart already beating faster. That had been a moment for him as well. He didn't need to relive it to remember that. Just hearing Jess describe it, from her point of view, was enough.

"You hugged me back, so tight. And all the world was inside your arms, Ben," Jess cried. "You had me then. Even if I didn't know it until now. That was the moment you had me. That was the moment I knew I couldn't do anything else in this life without you. It's all I need, Ben. To trigger. It's stronger than any anger or jealousy I could ever feel. It's the emotion I needed to know, to feel and connect with. I never did till now. I can pulse, Ben. I *know* I can. I could do it right now, even."

"No!" All three adults yelled.

Mal laughed. It was so innocent and natural. Everyone looked down at him and stared.

Ben asked Mal to touch him, and Mal did. He relived every moment with Jess. His first memory began the day she came to the facility. He remembered everything. He made love to Jess a thousand times, and each moment felt like the first; all enveloping and encompassing. He remembered the moment he learned that Jess was pregnant. He met Sarah and trained with her. He planned everyone's escape. He walked with Jess and Sarah through a hundred soldiers, who simply laid their guns down, and he boarded an alien transport ship. He carried Jesus's body back onto the ship, drenched in blood. He met all the old-boarders, and married Jess, and channeled into the Graylings. He relived the births of Angel and Alex. When his journey was done, he smiled down at Mal and thanked him.

"You have an incredible gift, young man," Ben said. He nodded at Arnold and Jenny and thanked them also.

Soon after, the three of them left the room, and Ben held Jess in his arms. They stood that way for several minutes, feeling each other's arms and heartbeat, listening to each breath flow in and out of their bodies—Feeling each other's life.

5

Sarah gave birth to a son. She and Aaron decided to name him Burne. At this point, Jemma and Rafferty had four children, ranging in age from eight, to one. Their daughter, Mara, was followed by another daughter, named Althea. Next came a son, whom they named Dorian. Finally, their son Innis was born, a year before Sarah and Aaron welcomed their first child.

On the day Burne was born, Jemma and Rafferty discovered their firstborn daughter, Mara's, ability. She was the next of the children on board the ship to manifest, following Angel and Mal.

Everyone knew about Mal, of course. A few more people, after Jess and Ben, opted to experience Mal's gift for themselves. Eileen discovered, to her great joy, that Mal's gift worked on her. She relived every moment, from the day she met Martin, through their wedding, to the day he disappeared, to coming on board the ship. She relived the birth of Eric as well. She cried and hugged Martin, who stood shell-shocked, for he had relived all her memories with her, through her thoughts.

Sarah went into labor the day after Mal's eighth birthday (and subsequent manifestation) and delivered her son in only three hours. Aaron was thrilled beyond belief. He ran around the ship, scattering rainbow-colored flowers everywhere. Jemma ran after him, picking them up, attempting to clean his mess, with her one-year-old, Innis, in tow in her arms. Mara followed behind, also helping to pick up the flowers. In a moment of distraction, however, Jemma slipped on a flower, and dropped Innis, who hit his head on the floor. A large, purple bump instantly appeared on his forehead, and Innis wailed in pain and shock.

"Dammit, Aaron!" Jemma yelled out, looking at Innis with great concern. Injuries aboard the ship were rare. The last time anyone got hurt was several months before, when Robert fell off his bike and bruised his knee. He hadn't even cried, however. He simply got back on his bike and went right on riding. Rachel and Hanley didn't even discover their son was hurt until later that night, in their quarters.

Mara knelt, looking at Innis with concern. Jemma sighed, greatly stressed. She tried to comfort Innis, but he went on crying unabated. This was also unusual, as most of the children had little reason to cry in such a way.

Mara reached out her hand and placed it over the bump on Innis's head. She held it there for several moments and Innis stopped crying, growing calm. Jemma looked down at the scene playing out in her arms, dazed. As Mara removed her hand, Jemma saw that the bump on Innis's head had vanished. Innis seemed completely fine.

Jemma blinked at Mara in shocked confusion. Hanley rushed over, looking excited.

"Did what I think just happened, happen?"

Jemma nodded hazily. Hanley looked down at Mara in awe. Then he quickly went running throughout the entire deck, yelling. Aaron still yelled as well, tossing flowers everywhere. The two grown men, running around, yelling, made quite a scene.

"We have a boy! We have a little boy! His name is Burne! Burne!" Aaron yelled. Meanwhile, Hanley attempted to out-scream him.

"We have a power! Another power! It's Mara! Mara's ability is out! She can heal!"

Several people came out of their rooms, or from the dining area, to see what all the fuss was about. Aaron drew people out from every nook and cranny of the ship, running through the library, the garden, into the gym, the observation deck, and back again, screaming about the birth of Burne. As people followed him and began to congregate in the common room, Hanley continued spreading the news about Mara, excitedly pointing at her and Jemma and Innis. The three of them still sat on the floor.

Jemma placed a hand gently on Mara's face, caressing her cheek, afraid that all the excitement would frighten her daughter. Mara, however, simply beamed. She seemed to enjoy the attention she had garnered. She looked proud, almost arrogant, in fact. However, she did give one last, worried glance down at her little brother, to make certain he was okay. Jemma saw this and finally let her own pride flow over, smiling brightly. She couldn't wait to tell Raff.

"Mara healed her brother!" Hanley yelled, still wagging a finger in the little girl's direction. Ben and Jess came out of their room to see what was happening. Ben came over to Jemma and knelt next to her, looking concerned.

"Are you okay, Jemma?" he asked. She nodded. He put out a hand and helped her to her feet. She shifted Innis in her arms, afraid she might drop him again. Aaron came running back into the common room, still yelling.

"Burne! We have a boy named Burne!!"

Aaron stopped short, staring at the crowd of people now standing in the common room. He blinked a few times, then smiled wide.

"I have a son," he gasped, now out of breath from all the exertion of running around. "I have a son, named Burne. Sarah's doing great. A son... Burne."

"We know," several people said at once.

"Mara just healed Innis with her bare hands," Hanley said.

The room fell silent for several moments.

"Are you sure?" Earl said, sounding dubious.

"I saw it with my own eyes," Jemma said, sounding defensive. "Aaron," she said, fixing him with an icy stare. "Stop throwing flowers everywhere. People are slipping on them."

"I'm sorry," Aaron said, hanging his head. He looked infinitely hurt. He walked over to Jemma and looked down at Innis, worry and shame all over his face. When Jemma saw his look, her face softened, and she immediately felt guilty.

"Congratulations, Aaron," she said. "I'm so happy for you and Sarah."

"We all are," Ben said, nodding. Everyone nodded.

"So," Earl said, sounding excited. "It's a great day, huh? We got another newbie, and another ability. What's with all the long faces? Let's celebrate this mofo!"

Everyone laughed. That night, they had a dinner celebration. Sarah brought Burne, all wrapped up in a blanket, fast asleep, and walked him around for everyone to see.

Jess looked at Burne, then up at Sarah, and felt a small pang of heartache. She couldn't believe this woman holding her baby, was the same little girl who had taken her hand and called her Aunt Jess, looking up into her face from several inches below her, on the day they all escaped from the facility. After all, she had only relived that moment the day before. Jess stood, crying, and hugged Sarah, carefully, so as not to hurt Burne.

"I love you, Sarah," she breathed into her ear.

"I love you, too, Aunt Jess." It had been a while since Sarah had called her that. She only did it on rare occasions now. She'd stopped calling her that, and only referred to her as Jess, for the most part, since channeling in with the Graylings.

Jess pulled away, swiping at her tears. She knew Sarah had called her Aunt for her benefit, the sentiment greatly appreciated.

"More like Aunt Jess to Burne, now," Jess said. She looked at Sarah, loving her. "You were never my daughter, Sarah, or my niece, but I always cared for you like you were. But somehow, today, I know you are my sister," Jess said, dissolving into tears.

Sarah's face crumbled, as the tears began to flow for her as well. Aaron came over and put his arm around his wife, winking at Jess. He kissed Sarah's cheek, taking Burne from her arms and continued parading him around to each table, proudly. Sarah, meanwhile, threw her arms around Jess and hugged her tight.

"You'll always be Aunt Jess to me," she cried. "And my sister, too."

Both women sobbed in each other's arms. All the women sighed, looking on, and several wiped away tears. Some of the men tried to hide smiles, smirking behind their hands.

"Oh, God," Hanley said, rolling his eyes. "Let me call Hallmark." Martin shook with suppressed giggles, while Eileen slapped his arm.

"You're ruining the moment," she said.

"What moment?" Earl wondered aloud. "I don't understand you women."

"We all know that," Grace said. Everyone erupted in laughter at her quip. Several people wiped away tears now, they laughed so hard.

***

Jemma stood up next, as the laughter finally died down. Rafferty remained sitting, although he still held Jemma's hand as she stood.

"Hey, everyone," she said, suddenly shy. "I know everyone's excited about Mara's ability. But," she paused, looking down at Raff, smiling. "I just wanted to announce that Rafferty and I, well, we're expecting another baby."

Everyone stared. Grace smiled, nodding. She'd confirmed the pregnancy, along with Alma only days ago. Jemma was already one month along.

"Um," Jemma said, looking nervous, as everyone continued to stare. "Raff and I have decided that this will be our last child. He or she should be born only a year before we reach Hesperia. I'm due right at the end of year nine."

She quickly sat back down again, and Rafferty kissed her cheek. It was rare for him to display such open and public affection this way. Aaron came over, still holding Burne. He smiled down at the couple, tears in his eyes.

"Congratulations, you two."

Rafferty suddenly stood and embraced Aaron. No one had ever seen him do such a thing before. Everyone looked on, quietly, in shock.

Rafferty hugged Aaron for several moments, careful not to squash Burne in his arms. Then he pulled away and looked at everyone, sheepishly. As he spoke, Aaron finally sat down, placing Burne back into Sarah's arms, taking the seat next to her.

"I just want everyone to know that I'm still giving it my all with the mission. Even as my family continues to grow."

"No one thinks otherwise, Raff," Alma said. She had delivered their last two children, and Burne. Grace now assisted her.

"Is that why you're stopping?" Jess said. "Because you think you aren't able to help? Because that's simply not true, Raff."

"No," Jemma said. "We just want to enjoy the family we have, that's all. Five is good for us. You have two, Jess. Everyone else stopped at one. Me and Raff just felt that it was right, each time. We weren't ready to say when until now. Even without the mission coming up, I think we would have still made this choice. But, Raff will be flying the transport ship with the ten people who are going, other than him. And, there's no telling what will happen. I believe we'll be successful, and that the Graylings will get their planet back, but," she paused, looking at everyone with grave eyes. "There was never any guarantee that we'll *all* come back."

Everyone sat quietly, thinking over Jemma's statements. Aaron looked at Jess.

"Jess, Harold told you he saw us triumph, right?" He stared at her. She didn't say anything, only looked down at the table.

"Jess?" Aaron repeated, frowning. "The Graylings saw a vision of you, right? They said we would succeed, and that we would live. Right?"

"Yes," she said, quietly. People could barely hear her. Martin heard her thoughts, and he chimed in, for he heard her fear, and how she did not want to say anything more. He did it for her, and she was grateful.

"The Graylings said that Jess would succeed, and that she would live," Martin said, transcribing Jess's thoughts. "They never said everyone would live. They never said anyone would die. The only guarantee they gave was that Jess would be successful. And that she would live. There are no other guarantees. In the interim between when the transport ship lands, and Jess pulses, there's no telling what events will unfold."

Everyone sat in silence taking this in. They looked at Rafferty, who gazed lovingly at Jemma, and she back at him. Martin hung his head. Jess stared at the table in front of her, while Ben held her hand, his head against hers.

"Well, we know something is going to happen, right?" Kate said, breaking the silence. "If Sarah said all these other people need to go. If other than Raff, who we know must fly the ship, and Jess, who we know must pulse are going, that still leaves nine people that Sarah says are needed. So, there will be some task, that requires those nine."

"And who knows what that task is," Hanley said, looking sad. "Or whether all nine of those people will survive."

Rachel looked at Hanley then, fear playing across her face. She was glad he wasn't going on the mission, but sad for those who were. Martin was one of them, and he was Hanley's best friend. Everyone going was leaving behind a close friend, or a spouse, or children, or in Jenny's case, a parent. No one had allowed themselves to fully think about the outcome of the mission, other than the ultimate success, which they all believed was guaranteed by the Grayling's vision. The thought that some of them might not live to see that success never entered any of their minds, until then. Except, of course, for Jemma and Rafferty, who, with their family continuing to grow, had finally entertained the thought that Rafferty might not live to see his children grow up.

"Whatever is going to happen, will happen," Rafferty said, still gazing at Jemma. "I've accepted that. We're going to carry out this mission, and we're going to succeed. The Graylings are dying. They need to be on Hesperia. We're going to get them back there. If I die while getting Jess, and everyone else who's going, down to that planet, I've accepted that, and so has Jemma. We just," Rafferty paused. Everyone realized with growing dread and shock, that he fought to keep back tears. Most had never seen Rafferty lose control of his emotions this way. They'd never even seen him come close, except a few occasions where he lost his temper.

"We've decided that this will be our last child," he finally said. "And that we want to spend our last year on the ship, enjoying the family we have. And being together, all seven of us."

Rafferty hugged Jemma then, and she silently cried into his shoulder. Innis wandered the room, quietly cruising around on the chairs and people's legs. Luckily, most of the older children had finished eating, and were not in the dining hall, except for Mara. Angel also sat quietly with her parents, as well as Robert, with Hanley and Rachel. All the other older children were off playing somewhere. Innis cruised around, and Dorian, the couples next youngest, at three, paid no attention to anything said. He sat quietly, eating, while Mara sat, looking at her parents.

"Daddy?" Mara said. "Is that why I have to come? So, I can heal you?"

"What?" Jemma pulled away from her husband and looked at her daughter in horror. "No, honey, of course not. Nothing's going to happen to your father. He's going to be just fine."

"But, if Daddy gets hurt, I can fix him," she said, beginning to cry.

"But, baby, if *you* get hurt, who's going to fix you?" Jemma cried. "Oh, Raff, I can't do it," she sobbed. "I know what I said before, but I just can't. No children are going down into a war zone. That's crazy!"

Jess stood and ran from the room. Ben quickly followed. Angel remained.

"Oh, no," Jemma sobbed. "I'm sorry."

"Sarah," Aaron said, turning back to her on his left, looking her in the eyes. "Are you certain about the people that are supposed to go?"

Sarah nodded, crying. "I'm sorry. I didn't decide this. It's just what I know."

"What if we don't send Angel?" Earl said. "Or Mara?"

"No," Sarah said, sounding panicked. "They have to go."

"Why?" Hanley said.

"I don't know why. But I feel it. I feel it so strongly. They must be on the mission."

"Jemma is right, though," Earl argued. "Why would we send any of our children down there?"

"I don't know!" Sarah yelled, visibly upset.

Meanwhile, Angel sat, quietly listening to everyone. No one seemed to notice her there, although they all talked about her. Everyone was too busy fighting their own emotions over the heated topic.

"For that matter, if we are going to send even one child, why not Mara, over Angel?" Earl continued to debate, growing agitated. "Sure, Angel can fix things, but Mara can fix *people*. She can heal someone if they get hurt, maybe even save their life. What can Angel do? Fix broken plates and bowls?"

"That's enough," Grace said. "No one's ability is better than anyone else's."

"That's not true, and you know it!" Earl yelled at Grace. They were in an out-and-out yelling match now. "You're going to sit there and tell me that my ability is just as good as Jess's? Or that Arnold snooping around is anywhere near as helpful as Mara healing a wound?!" Earl screamed.

"Hey," Arnold said, sounding hurt. But he had no further argument to make, for he happened to agree with Earl. He didn't like that fact, but it was true. His ability couldn't help to fight the war in any way.

"Every person on board this ship is equally important!" Grace spat at Earl.

"No, they're not! Woman, did you not sit in the same room I did, hearing that only one of us is going to defeat the Bailon? *Jess* is going to win the war. That makes *her* the most useful!"

"She wouldn't even be able to get down there without Rafferty!" Grace yelled. "Is he any less important?"

"No, but if he dies, it won't matter!" Earl screamed.

"What?!" Grace exclaimed in disbelief.

"Don't be a bastard, Earl!" Hanley chimed in.

"If *he* dies, the Bailon still get beat! So long as Jess lives to pulse, nothing else matters!" Earl continued.

"Stop it!" Eileen shrieked at the top of her lungs for several seconds, drawing both words out agonizingly long. Everyone turned to look at her. She stood, with fire in her eyes, her cheeks burning hot with blood.

"Stop it, all of you! Arguing won't help anything. We're all scared. We're all confused. My *husband* is going on the mission, and I'm afraid he might not come back. I already lost him once, and now I might lose him again. I don't know what part he has to play, but I know he'll do whatever needs to be done. The Graylings love us. Even *I* know that. And I'm the only one who *isn't* channeled in! But even I know that the Graylings would never put us in harms' way. They wouldn't send us on a death mission.

"I must believe that whatever happens, everyone will be all right. And if they aren't, then that's simply how it's supposed to be. Everything happens for a reason. I truly believe that. After all this time, after everything we've seen, doesn't everyone know that by now?

"We shouldn't be fighting. We have less than two years left, possibly, to be here together. To all be here as a *group*. We should spend that time, the way Jemma and Rafferty are, with their family. We should all be spending this time *together*, loving each other, and being grateful for the time we have."

"She's right," Hanley said, standing up. "That lady, standing there? She may not be a transgen, but she sure is here for a reason. No one is more important than anyone else," Hanley shot a hot look of hatred at Earl, who looked down at his table and shook his head.

"You have no idea, some of you, how much faith that woman has inspired in some of the people on board this ship. She's not even channeled into the Graylings, and she still believes in them more than we do! How is that even possible?

"Eileen has more faith than anyone else I've seen on this ship. She has never once questioned our mission, or our success. She's willing to send Martin down there, and she's never even met the Graylings!

"We're going to sit here, and argue, those of us that *are* transgens, which of us is most important? Eileen doesn't even have the gene, and she's the one fighting for us the most! The Graylings don't have the gene, and we're willing to fight, we're willing to die for them, aren't we?

"*No one* is better than anyone else. *Period.* And if I ever hear anyone say anything close to that kind of remark again, I will personally kick your arrogant, biased, prejudiced ass!" Hanley leveled this last comment directly at Earl.

Earl opened his mouth to say something, but Hanley screamed at him before he could, and he quickly shut up, not saying another word.

"Prejudiced ass!" Hanley repeated. He quickly left the room, not wanting to lose his temper further. Rachel followed him, skirting around the tables quickly. In her haste, she left Robert sitting at the table. His eighth birthday was coming up in one week.

Robert now sat at his table, alone, much the same as Angel sat alone. He gazed at Eileen, and had been, ever since his father pointed at her, making his remarks. Eileen sat down right after Hanley left the room, and held Martin's hand, crying silently. What Hanley said greatly touched her heart. He was the only one on board the ship, other than Martin, who made her feel as if she truly belonged. Hanley had been Martin's best friend long before she ever met him, but over the years, he had become her best friend, too.

Robert got up and slowly walked over to Eileen. Martin looked at him, frowning, for he could hear the oddest thoughts coming from Robert's mind.

What Martin heard was the equivalent of several different voices inside Robert's head. They all whispered, leading Robert over. They seemed to direct him, on an almost subconscious level. Martin barely heard them, because of this fact. But he recognized that although they were not Robert's thoughts, they still came from deep within his own mind. As if a radio played inside his head, and Martin could vaguely hear the broadcast, in light, static tones. He frowned, watching Robert approach them, standing next to Eileen sitting in her chair.

Eileen rested her head against Martin's shoulder and didn't even notice Robert standing next to her. Her eyes were closed. Even Martin had no idea what Robert was about to do, for he acted upon the direction of the voices inside so immediately, he had already touched Eileen, even as Martin came to hear and begin to understand what the voices said.

Robert gazed at Eileen momentarily, swaying on his feet. Then he quietly reached both hands out, and much in the same manner as Ezra did when channeling someone in, he placed both hands over Eileen's temples, gently lifting her head off Martin's shoulder.

Eileen never even opened her eyes. She sat, with Robert's hands on both sides of her head, and made no sound. Robert closed his eyes, and everyone looked on in wonder, as they saw the little boy's hands emit a bright, blue light against Eileen's head. Martin stared, dazed and frozen.

Robert's hands glowed bright, neon blue, the light emanating from his palms. The radiance sparkled and glinted, sparks of stars dancing within the blue ether. It was beautiful. Eileen gasped, her entire body jerked upright, but Robert's hands moved with her head, the contact never broken. Her face contorted in pain and suffering. In the back of his mind, Martin wondered if Robert might not be cooking her brain.

Eileen sobbed, her face shiny and beaded with sweat. Her whole body now trembled and shook, like small tremors passing through her bones.

"Somebody stop him!" Earl shouted.

No one moved. They each stayed where they were, frozen, transfixed, watching the scene, unable to move. The entire ordeal took only twenty seconds, but to everyone it felt like several minutes had passed.

Then, Robert opened his eyes and smiled at Eileen. She took in a deep gasp of air, held it, then exhaled slowly. She opened her eyes and smiled at Robert, tears slipping down her cheeks. Martin pulled in a sudden gulp of air. He looked at Eileen in shock and disbelief.

"Thank you, Robert," Eileen said.

Robert nodded and left the room, to go be with his parents. Martin now spoke to Eileen, but no one in the room knew it. She thought to him, and he heard her. More interesting, he thought to her, and *she* heard him.

Eileen? I can hear you, Martin sent. *You're with the Graylings, aren't you? I can hear them, too.*

Robert did something to me, she sent back, instantly. *He connected me, somehow. I met the Graylings, Martin. I finally met them, just like you. I saw everything. Everything that happened to them, Martin.*

"Eileen," Martin sobbed aloud.

"I know everything," Eileen said, hugging him. He hugged her back tightly, and they both sobbed.

"What the hell is going on?" Earl said.

"Robert connected Eileen with the Graylings," Grace said, putting the pieces together, sounding wondrous.

Ezra looked at Eileen, feeling disappointment. He felt as if he'd let her down.

"I'm sorry, Eileen," he said.

"For what?" she asked. "Your gift is the ability to channel in other transgens. Robert, apparently, can make a connection, somehow, in people like me. People without the gene. He still found a way to open up my mind."

"But I let you down," Ezra said, looking ashamed.

"No, you didn't. You've served your purpose. Now, it's Robert's turn. He has a different gift, meant for different people. That's all. Either way, it doesn't matter who did it. I'm with the Graylings now. And I never thought that would be possible."

"He saw a need, and his ability manifested," Arnold spoke up, looking at Jenny, nodding. "That's how it works. At least, that's the current theory. The children will only manifest their ability when the overwhelming need for it arises. Mal only manifested when he saw his mother get upset. Mara only used her power when someone got hurt, right in front of her. Angel manifested when something in the room was broken. And Robert," he paused, thinking about it. "Robert manifested his ability, after he realized Eileen wasn't connected to the Graylings. He heard Hanley say it, and then he went right over, and simply connected her. He saw the need, and his ability was pulled out. It was born." He delivered this last revelation in wonderment. Then he laughed, completely beside himself.

Everyone stared at Arnold, then back at Eileen. Martin both cried and smiled, now. He held Eileen's hand very tight.

Honey, you're hurting my hand, she thought to him. He immediately loosened his grip, and they giggled.

"Whatever he did, he didn't just connect her with the Graylings," Martin said to the group. "I can hear Eileen's thoughts and she can hear mine. We're able to speak to each other."

"Seriously?" Aaron said.

"Yeah," Eileen laughed. "He connected me to the Graylings, and, somehow, it's connected me to Martin, too. We can think back and forth to one another. It's almost like…" She looked at Martin, frowning. "It's almost as if he gave me an ability. Even if it's only being able to talk to you," she said, kissing Martin. He kissed her back.

"How is that even possible?" Earl said.

Grace sat, quietly taking the whole scene in. She thought very hard. Suddenly, she spoke, fighting to keep her voice at an even register, attempting to sound normal.

"Eileen, I'm very happy for you," Grace said. "But, you were convulsing slightly, during whatever it was that happened to you. I'd like to do a quick scan, make sure everything's okay. Maybe check your electrolyte balance? It's no big deal."

Martin looked at Grace, hearing her true thoughts, taking in her suspicions. She realized she could not fool him, at least, and quickly sent him her thoughts.

Don't say anything, Martin, please? Just go with Eileen to the infirmary. If what I think just happened, truly did, this could be quite amazing.

Martin nodded at Grace, and stood with Eileen, leading her by the hand. She followed him without question, picking up on his thoughts, from Grace, and learning of her suspicions as well. She grew excited but tried to remain calm.

"It can't hurt, honey, right?" Martin said.

"No, of course not, honey," she played along.

Grace, Martin and Eileen, left the dining hall, and the rest of the diners that remained quickly finished their meals in silence, then each left to return to their separate rooms and families.

6

In the hallway, once clear of the dining hall, Grace spoke to Martin and Eileen. They both nodded their consent.

"I'd like to stop by and bring Ben in on this, if you two don't mind?"

They knocked on Jess and Ben's door. Angel came up behind them and opened it. She'd followed the three of them, almost immediately after they left. The door opened, and Angel waved them in, smiling.

Jess and Ben were in their room. Angel knocked and then went in. Grace, Martin, and Eileen stood awkwardly inside the living room, waiting.

"Maybe we should leave and come back later," Grace said. "This was a bad idea."

The three of them turned to leave, just as Ben came out of the bedroom. Martin heard his thoughts and began turning back before the others.

"What do you need, Grace?" Ben said.

"Ben, I'm sorry. You need to be with your wife right now. I shouldn't have come."

"No," Ben said. "Jess is okay. She's calming down. You just need to understand this is very upsetting for her. Bringing Angel with us."

"Earl shouldn't have opened his mouth," Grace said, getting angry all over again.

"Jess was going to have to deal with this sooner or later," Ben said. "Better to do it now, not later. What do you need?"

"Something happened in the dining hall, after you and Jess left," Martin said.

He explained the entire event to Ben, quickly, while he listened, silently taking it all in. He looked at Grace towards the end and saw the look in her eyes. He nodded, when Martin finished, immediately agreeing to go with them to the infirmary.

Eileen talked to Grace along the way. Grace admired her greatly.

"You're going to scan my genome, aren't you?"

"Yes, if that's all right with you?"

"How long will it take for you to know?"

"With our system? Two minutes. Two minutes to scan through the entire sequence and isolate the strand we're looking for."

In the infirmary, Grace took a cotton ball and lightly swabbed Eileen's face, then dropped the material into her spectral analyzer. Eileen stared, in disbelief.

"That's all? That's all you need to do, to read me?"

"What did you think I was going to do?" Grace asked.

"I don't know, swab the inside of my cheek, or take a sample of my hair, maybe?"

Grace laughed, looking at Ben, who only shrugged.

"This isn't CSI," Grace said. "We're far beyond such limited means of analysis. Those methods take hours, even days to complete. All I need is a few cells, which are always lying loose, on the surface of the skin. You'd be amazed what a single cell can tell you about your own body."

Grace pulled up a screen on her monitor and watched as data streamed in front of her eyes. She typed in a few lines and began narrating to Ben.

"I'm pulling up the A1A sequences, on line 401," she said. Ben nodded. He also watched the screen intently.

"Is that...?" He pointed to a line near the bottom of the monitor.

"Yes," Grace said. "So, we'll be able to compare the direct change, to confirm.

Martin heard Grace and Ben's thoughts. Eileen could not. She could only hear Martin. Martin relayed what he heard instantly to Eileen, explaining that they were going to compare her original DNA markers to the new ones, to see if they had changed. They were looking specifically between two genes, where the pseudogene lay, in transgens. Anyone else simply had polymorphic genes, with no pseudogene lying between.

They all waited anxiously for the new sequence to scan and display. It felt like forever but took only one hundred and twenty seconds.

"There," Grace said, pointing at the new line as it came up. "I don't believe it. It's there, and it's coded."

Ben rubbed his chin in his hand, his eyes bright and gleaming. He thought hard. He stared at the screen for several more minutes, his mind in overdrive. Meanwhile, Martin gave Eileen the news.

"How is that even possible?"

"I don't know," Grace said. "I don't know, but it's there, plain as day. You not only have the pseudogene, it's already been coded. No Luci for you."

"What does that mean?"

"It means that you're now an active transgen, just like the rest of us," Ben said, his eyes shining bright. He looked at Grace, smiling. Tears stood in his eyes, quickly brimming over, and he wiped them away without thought.

"This is how it happens," he said.

"What?" Grace said, frowning.

"This is how humanity changes so quickly," Ben said, nodding. "It didn't make sense to me, what I saw when I channeled into the Graylings. I suddenly *knew* that humanity was going to change. *We* all changed, in one generation. Our children are all born with the sequence already coded. Because we, as a group, are comprised solely of transgens.

"But the change I saw in humanity? With only one transgen in one hundred thousand people in the general population? The change would be slow. Two inactive transgens would have to come together, to give birth to an active. The first active transgens to be born would result in, perhaps, one in one million people. Such a small percentage of the population, it didn't make sense to me, how humanity could go from what it is now, to being comprised of more active transgens than not, in only a few hundred years' time. But *this* makes sense, with what's happened to Eileen. This is how it will happen."

"Of course," Grace said. "To accelerate the change. To ensure the gene doesn't die out."

Ben nodded. Eileen looked at everyone in complete confusion.

"This is how what happens?"

"At some point, active transgens will be born, in small numbers, here and there, scattered across the globe," Ben said. "And they'll all have different abilities. Eventually, however, one will be born that's like Robert—a transgen that can convert people who don't even have the gene, into active transgens. I don't know how he did it, I wasn't there to see it, and even if I was, or I'd had you hooked up in the lab to a billion monitors, watching a person change on a molecular level would be impossible. But… he did it," Ben pondered, awestruck. "Robert, an eight-year-old child, somehow redesigned and altered your DNA, Eileen. He built the activated pseudogene sequence into your helix coding. He inserted it right smack dab in the middle of the 401-polymorphism strand.

"And if he did it, it's only a matter of time before a transgen is born on Earth who can also do it. Probably more than one. As they convert people, it will speed up the entire evolutionary process. It will increase the number of active transgens enough to slowly create a population shift, that grows exponentially, just like Arnold's models we looked at in the tactical room.

"This is how humanity will transform so quickly. This is how we will go from an aggressive, waring race, to a completely peaceful one, in only a few, very short, hundred years. It's ingenious. It's as if, whatever programmed this sequence, implanted a failsafe. A guarantee of successful conversion. It's perfect."

"Perfect?" Eileen said, blinking.

"Yes," Ben said. "It will enable us, as a society, to go from ninety percent transgenic, to a full one hundred percent, immediately. But again, in this microcosm, everything is much more accelerated. What's done in one generation here, will take two hundred years on Earth. But without an ability like Robert's, it could take twice that long, or never happen at all. But you can see the general direction of the design now, can't you?"

"Yes," Grace said. "It *is* ingenious. And again, too scary for me to even think about for too long."

"It's simply nature's way of making sure the change takes hold," Ben said. "If it's meant to happen, it will find a way, and this is the way."

"What do you mean one hundred percent?" Eileen said. "It was ninety before. You said one hundred percent."

"He means, if we let Robert change Eric," Martin said.

"No," Ben said, "I didn't mean right now. And, of course, it would be Eric's choice."

"Why, I didn't get a choice, did I?" Eileen said.

"Honey, are you upset about it? Do you regret it?" Martin asked, looking at her in concern.

"No," Eileen said, touching Martin's face. "I can hear you, and you can hear me. And I finally know and love what you know and love. I'm happy. But I don't know if I want Eric to change. Maybe he was born the way he was for a reason."

"At any rate, I wouldn't want Robert to convert a child," Grace said. "For all we know, he can't. Maybe he can only convert adults?"

"I don't know," Ben said. "Robert certainly felt that Eileen needed this. So far, none of the children have manifested unless their ability was needed. None of them have done anything other than help someone else. And back at the facility, no one manifested unless they were either defending themselves, or protecting themselves, or others."

"He must have known, somehow, how much I wanted to channel in," Eileen mused. "I mean, I did want it."

"I know," Martin said.

"I don't know about being a transgen," Eileen said. "Is this my ability, to simply hear Martin's thoughts?"

"Maybe," Grace said. "Rafferty's ability is simply that he's connected to the Graylings, without Ezra ever channeling him in. And when Hanley came on board, he realized that for some reason, he and Hanley have an open channel with one another. Now, it looks like you and Martin have developed an open channel with each other, as well as channeling into the Graylings. I wouldn't expect any other abilities to surface, but I suppose it's possible."

Grace looked to Ben for help. Ben only shrugged.

"Only time will tell, I guess. But you're coded. So, if you have an ability, it's already active. Whether it's presented itself or not, I can't say. But you were immediately able to communicate with Martin, correct?"

Eileen nodded, smiling at him. He hugged her.

"Then, I would guess that's your only ability," Ben said, sounding apologetic.

"Oh, I don't mind," Eileen said. "I actually prefer things this way. It's the only thing I ever wanted, really. I got everything I ever could have dreamed of. The only things, really, that set me apart from Martin. It's almost as if, Robert gave me exactly what I needed to finally feel like I fully belong here. Just what I needed to finally feel complete."

"Then maybe that's part of his gift as well," Ben said. "Perhaps he can grant specific abilities, if the person knows what it is they want. It's not anymore crazy than anything else that's already happened."

"What if Eric wants to be changed?" Martin said, looking at Eileen.

"You want him to change?"

"Uh-oh," Grace said, backing away, pulling on Ben's sleeve. Ben stayed where he was, watching the couple in amusement.

"No, not necessarily, but if he wants it, we should allow him to choose, honey."

"But an eight-year-old child doesn't have the mental capacity to choose, Martin."

"Then we'll wait until he's older, but honey, look at how apart he's been set from the other kids, already."

"No, not since Sarah's been with them," Eileen said, her voice rising in agitation.

"But Sarah can't always be with them, and it's still not fair to Eric. Don't you think if he could fit in with everyone, he'd jump at the chance?"

"Oh, so he should do it just to fit in? Real nice example Martin. I suppose if all the other kids wanted to jump off a bridge, you'd be okay with Eric wanting to do that too, then?"

"I told you," Grace said, through clenched teeth, her voice low. She pulled on Ben's sleeve again, but he still watched, highly amused.

"Is this what Jess and I sound like?" he said, dreamily. Grace shrugged behind his back where he didn't see.

"This is not the same thing, and you know it," Martin said. "This is something entirely different. At this point, Eric is the only human on board this ship that isn't a transgen. Now *both* his parents are. You think he'll be happy that way? Knowing he's the only regular human on board?"

"*Regular human?*" Eileen said, her voice rising considerably now. "Is that what I was to you, before this?"

"No," Martin sighed, pinching the bridge of his nose between his fingers in frustration. "That's not what I meant, and you know it."

"Really? I knew that? Because you think that now I'm a transgen, I'll just be on board with having our son genetically altered. Just like that, huh?"

"Eileen, look at the facts. There are nineteen of us on board this ship. Everyone else is active. All the children are active. We're going to an alien planet to live. Eric will grow up in a world where he's the only person who's different. What do you think is going to happen when he becomes an adult? Do you think he'll even have a hope in the world of being accepted by his peers? What about him finding a mate, hmm?"

"A mate?! You freaked out when Malcolm used that word, but now it's okay for you to use it, about our son?"

"I wasn't a father then, Eileen. My perspective has changed. Yes, I worry about my son growing up, and not being accepted by a woman. I worry about my son never having the chance to grow into a man, and know what it's like to fall in love, or even have the chance to become a father himself, one day. You realize all the children are going to grow up, and have only each other to choose from, don't you? That all these children, someday, are going to choose mates amongst one another?"

"Holy moly, he's right," Grace said. Ben looked on, frowning at Martin's statement. He hadn't thought about the future generations, after they settled on Hesperia.

"Martin, that's so far from now. How can you even worry about that?" Eileen yelled.

"It's not that far off!" Martin yelled. "We'll be on Hesperia in two years. In eight years, Eric will be well into puberty. He'll be looking at girls, in, you know… *that way*. And no one will want him, if they've got a cool transgen to pick instead."

"You don't know that!"

"Well, it's not up to either of us! If Eric wants to be converted, he'll seek out Robert and choose for himself. No one will be able to stop him."

"Fine!" Eileen yelled. "If that's how it happens, fine. But we'll deal with it then."

"Fine!" Martin yelled back.

"Then I guess everything's settled!"

"I guess so!"

Both stormed out of the infirmary together, leaving Ben and Grace alone, staring at each other. Ben raised his eyebrows. Then he lowered them into a frown.

"Martin's right," he said, still frowning. "All of our children are gonna want to, well…" he trailed off.

"Mate," Grace giggled, smiling gently at Ben. He nodded.

"And there won't be that many choices," he said.

"Well, there will be considerably more choices now, thanks to Jemma and Rafferty." Grace giggled some more.

Ben stared at Grace for several moments. Then they both broke out laughing.

***

Ben went back to his room and found Jess asleep in bed. He checked on Angel and Alex. They were already sleeping as well. They'd tucked themselves in for the night.

As Ben got into bed, attempting to be quiet, Jess stirred next to him. She rolled over, opening her eyes.

"Sorry," Ben said.

"It's okay. So, what is it? What did Grace want?"

"It's a whopper. Are you sure you're awake?"

Jess nodded. Ben told her everything, including the continuing scene in the dining hall, after they both ran out. He told her about Robert's ability manifesting, and that Eileen was now connected to the Graylings, and had the ability to mentally communicate with Martin. Jess listened to everything in silence. Then Ben told her about Martin's revelation that all their children would be coming of age in less than a decade and would be searching for mates of their own.

"Gross," Jess said.

"Why?"

"Well, all our kids will be mating with each other. Isn't that, like, incest or something?"

"None of us are related, Jess," Ben laughed. "There's nothing incestuous about it."

"But, there's not that many children. By the time they have children, won't everyone start to be related, at some point?"

"No. Because at that point, new DNA sequences will have been stranded together. As the population grows, the commonalities will become less condensed. With each new generation, the gene pool will only broaden, as new combinations come into play, with the mixing of different couples. Any common links will be removed by two and three generations. It won't ever be more related than, say, second or third cousins, at the closest generation. As the population increases, it can only move further away from that commonality level. And while there will be some common markers in certain pockets of any given generation, already the DNA sequences will be unique enough that the two combinations will only create another unique combination. Only one generation removed, which would be our children's children, the gene pool will have developed into a broad spectrum. What you're referring to is known as decreasing genetic diversity. But that only happens when the first generation born is already related, which none of us are. As our children grow and reproduce, it will only result in a larger and more variant gene pool."

"Huh," Jess said. "I guess you're right."

"You guess?" Ben laughed, kissing her forehead.

"Well, if say, Angel, and... I don't know... Mal, got married. And then, maybe Mara and Robert got married. Their children wouldn't be related."

"Nope," Ben said. "So, if those children grew up and chose each other for mates, the gene pool would continue to vary. See?"

"And eventually, we'll be a little town or something," Jess said, frowning.

"What's wrong?"

"Well, if we keep reproducing, we'll have to build our own city, away from the Graylings, since we can't be around them."

"No," Ben said. "*We* can't be around them, because we're channeled in, Jess. Our children aren't channeled in. They won't be drained the way we are. The only ones who need to live separately from the Graylings, are the nineteen adults on this ship right now."

"So, we just live, away from everyone else—exiled?" Jess said, sounding sad.

"I don't know, Jess. Maybe. But the future generations will live peacefully with and among the Graylings. It won't be any different than, say, white people and black people. Or Chinese and Latinos living together."

"Those are all still human. There's a huge difference."

"Well, not for our children's children. They'll be born, live, and grow amongst the Graylings. It won't seem strange to them at all. It's a whole new world we're going to create, Jess. For humans and the Graylings, both. Our children are growing up here, with us, and they haven't been exposed to the Graylings, because we haven't chosen to do so. Once we get to Hesperia, they'll be able to choose where they want to live and raise their children. They could even choose to move back and forth between cities. But our city will be very small, I imagine. Who knows?" Ben sighed. "Maybe we'll remain The Society till death?"

"That's scary," Jess said. Then she frowned, thinking about it. "But also, strangely comforting. We are the gap, right? Between the old and the new?"

"Yes, we are," Ben said, caressing her face.

"Then there will never be anyone else like us. No one else will ever be channeled in."

"No, they won't."

"So, to save the Graylings, we'll have to be separated from them, forever," Jess started to cry. "And be separated from all other humans, since we can't ever set foot inside the main city. We'll basically be exiled eternally, is what you're saying."

"It's the price that has to be paid, Jess, for us to save them. It's a small price, really."

"But it's still sad."

"We'll have each other, Jess. That's enough for me."

"Me, too. But I still feel so isolated. I mean, even from our own children. They're just, manifesting all these powers, with no help. Before they're even old enough to know any different. They're calm, they don't fight. They're not like us, at all."

"Jess, they're still our children, and we love them."

"Of course, I love Angel and Alex," Jess said, her voice wavery and emotional. "It's just that it hurts. Knowing we're the last of our kind."

"Maybe that's why we have each other? Maybe that's why everyone coupled up? To make living out our lives on Hesperia less isolating. The Society won't just be supporting each other here on this ship, or getting each other through the mission, or fighting the war. The Society will continue to thrive, all on our own, on Hesperia, after everything is over. Maybe we're meant to do much more than just be here for each other for ten years in space? Maybe we're meant to get each other through this whole life? I could think of worse ways to live out the rest of my days, Jess."

"Well, when you put it that way, I guess it's comforting. I mean, no one likes to change, right? When we get to Hesperia, we won't have any choice, but to *not* change. We'll have to remain together. We're all we have."

"Everything will be okay, Jess. No one said building a new world would be easy."

"No, but if I get to do it with you by my side, I think I can make it through anything," she sighed.

"Now that's my firecracker," Ben said, kissing her gently.

"No. This is your little chicken, saying please don't leave my side, Ben."

"Babe, I won't leave your side even if you order me to."

"Why would I ever do that?" Jess said, kissing the tip of his nose.

"Well, like I said, the gray hairs are coming in," Ben sighed, pulling away to look at her.

"Shut up," Jess said, groping him, attempting to start things.

"I thought you were tired?"

"Not anymore," Jess breathed. "But if you're too much of an old man, we can just go to sleep."

But even while saying this, she caressed him aggressively, and felt him responding. Pleasantly surprised, for they'd been in a dry spell the past weeks, he informed her that he was not an old man quite yet. He rolled on top of her, pinning her arms down at the wrists. She sighed in pleasure.

"This old man came rolling home," Ben breathed, and Jess laughed hysterically.

"That is the dumbest thing I've ever heard you say," she said, but he quickly shut her up with his mouth and his tongue, and they made rigorous love until they were both so worn out, Jess felt like an old woman. They fell asleep, satiated and happy, feeling complete.

7

Martin and Eileen didn't need to wait to discover Eric's choice. Angel went to see Eric and asked him to walk with her. She termed it 'play with her,' in front of the parents. Extremely astute, Angel already knew what was expected of her. Once Eric came out of the room, they walked in the hallway, and she told him everything that had happened the night before at dinner, after he and the other children had left. They'd all missed Robert's manifestation, plus all the fights that broke out.

Angel and Eric were best friends and had been for several years. She had always been more sympathetic to Eric's plight than the other children. It wasn't that she felt sorry for him, she merely saw a problem and felt the need to fix it. It was part of her personality (that Ben mused) seemed intricately linked to her ability. Angel loved to fix things. When she discovered what Robert could do, it seemed like the perfect solution to Eric's dilemma.

Eric had not even been able to play with any of the other children successfully until Angel came up with the solution of having Sarah sit with everyone, using her powers. This had been a success, but the last year or so, Sarah had pulled back, slowly, bit by bit, using her powers less, as Eric grew older.

Sarah told Angel she wanted to ween Eric from dependency on her powers. She feared if she didn't, Eric would become emotionally stunted, and never fully mature into the ability to interact on his own. She also wanted to focus now on her new husband, and soon after, the impending birth of her first child. Sarah didn't think using her power while pregnant would be a problem, but even so, she didn't want to use it as often, since it drained her energy levels and left her feeling tired, some days more than others.

The only reason the children were comfortable around Eric, however, was because of Sarah. They all enjoyed the euphoric, drugged feeling when playing with him. As Sarah pulled away, so did all the children. It wasn't long before several of them stopped playing in a large group, because without the good feelings, they reverted to viewing Eric as an outsider.

Eric was more adept at controlling his emotions by age eight, regardless of Sarah, but the children had become euphoria junkies, and they connected the experience of withdrawal to him, becoming bitter. The situation ultimately called for a more rapid emotional maturation on Eric's part, but also left Angel as his sole companion. She continued, during and after withdrawal, to seek him out and play for no other reason than she simply enjoyed his company. He was quiet and insightful. His isolation had lent to this demeanor. Angel felt drawn to his personality for this main reason, for it made him a mystery. She knew, however, that if he had the chance to be like her and all the other children, he would jump at the opportunity, much as Martin had said he would. Eric's father was right.

The moment Angel told Eric he could become a transgen and have an ability of his own, his eyes widened, shining with desire. Angel felt hot pride well up inside, happy, once again, to have fixed something. Eric immediately wanted to know how it worked. Angel said she didn't know and doubted if Robert even understood what he'd done.

"Does it matter? Your mother is a transgen now, and she can hear Martin's thoughts. They can think back and forth to one another."

"I know, they told me," Eric said. "They sat down with me this morning."

Angel nodded.

"I want to do it," he said.

"When?"

"Now."

"Maybe you should think about it for a few days."

"No." He shook his head. "You knew if you told me I'd go straight to Robert."

Angel looked at Eric, thinking his statement over. Then she nodded, looking down. Had she made this choice for him?

"Hey, it's okay, Angel."

"I knew you wouldn't resist. And I couldn't resist the chance to fix you."

"I'm not broken."

"I know," she said, looking sad. "So, maybe you're not supposed to be like us."

"I would have found out about Robert, eventually. I would have chosen this, no matter what. I can't be the only one on the ship who's different. It's *my* choice, Angel."

She nodded, a tear slipping down her cheek. He frowned.

"I thought you'd be happy for me?"

"So did I," she cried, throwing her arms around him. "But I like you the way you are."

Eric stood in shock, rigid, as Angel hugged him. He took in her statement, and let it fill him up. He closed his eyes, feeling the sincerity of what she'd said. He never forgot it, not for the rest of his life.

***

In the end, Eric had to talk Angel into being okay with the change. She nodded, wiping her tears away. They went to find Robert. He played in the garden with Mara, Althea, Mal, and Alex. When the five children saw Angel approaching with Eric, they stopped playing and stared.

Angel shyly stepped forward, eyeing Robert. She didn't need to say anything, for Robert's ability was already working again. He could hear the need, and he felt drawn to it.

Robert walked up to Eric, and all the children stood, gaping in wonder. Robert smiled at Eric, who stood frozen. He felt terrified. But deep inside, the longing still spoke. Even if Eric was not consciously aware of everything he wanted, Robert somehow knew.

He reached his hands up and placed them on Eric's temples, just as he had with Eric's mother, just the night before. Brilliant blue light emanated from his palms, so radiant, it spilled around his hands, enveloping the backs of his fingers. It looked different this time, however. It sparkled and burst with silver and light amethyst explosions. Angel looked on, her eyes wide and welling with tears.

Eric's face went slack. He showed no emotion. Unlike his mother, who had cried out in pain, he had no reaction. After twenty seconds, Robert pulled his hands away, smiled again, then walked back to rejoin the group. Everyone stared at Eric, waiting.

Eric swayed on his feet, his eyes still closed, for several moments. Then he opened his eyes, and looked at Angel, who gasped. What she saw in his look, she could not even put into words, but she sensed that he now held far more wisdom than his years should ever allow. His irises had changed from brown to periwinkle.

He decisively walked up to Angel and delivered the shock of her life. He kissed her, and she somehow knew, despite being only eight-years-old, that this was not the kiss of a child. For an instant, she also felt older. Then Eric pulled away, gently smiling. He looked at her with such love, she blushed.

"Ew. What's wrong with you?" Mal said, his face drawn down in a look of disgust.

"Nothing," Eric said. He sounded completely normal.

He looked at Mara and Althea, however, and nodded.

"Your mother is going to have another girl. She'll name her Willa."

"Huh?" Mara and Althea said together.

He smiled, shaking his head. "Nothing."

Eric turned to walk away, and Angel followed him, dazed. In the hallway, she walked silently along, glancing at him shyly. He smiled and looked at her. His assuredness completely unnerved her.

"You know things, don't you?" Her voice belied fear and trepidation.

"Yes," Eric said, matter-of-factly.

"Like what?"

"Everything."

"Everything?" Angel scoffed.

"Pretty much. But it will still be fun to watch it all happen. I can't wait for…" Eric caught himself, trailing off, but he blushed.

"What? You can't wait for what?"

"Nothing," Eric said, suddenly nervous and shy.

"*What?*"

He looked at her, his face that of an eight-year-old again. He shrugged, embarrassed, still blushing.

"Wh—why did you kiss me?" she asked, looking down at the floor.

"You don't want to know."

"I wouldn't have asked if I didn't want to know, now would I?" She looked at him, challenging.

"Are you sure?"

Angel nodded. Eric sighed, closing his eyes. Then he looked at her, fondness flaring up again, replacing timidity.

"I saw you and me, when we're older. Sarah's age, a bit younger. And…" he trailed off, blushing wildly now.

"What?"

"Well… we sort of… are… together."

"Together?" Angel frowned.

"Yeah," Eric said, flaring his eyes at her, then he looked away, turning scarlet.

"Oh," Angel said, taking his statement in, slightly surprised. Then she began to understand his full meaning. "Oh," she said, her tone changing.

"Hey," Eric said, "it's not for a while. We'll both be all grown up then."

"But you already know?"

Eric nodded. Then he smiled. "Do you want to know what we name our daughter?"

Angel looked at him in shock. She shook her head, suddenly turned, and ran away.

"Wait!" Eric yelled, running after her.

Angel slowed, but kept walking, as they rounded the hallway and entered the common room. They took no notice of anyone in there. Arnold and Jenny were there with Hanley and Rachel. Martin sat there as well. Eileen was in their room. They were still not talking. Things were about to get much worse, however.

"Angel! Wait!" Eric yelled, grabbing her shoulder, gently turning her around.

"No!" Angel yelled. "I didn't want you to change. Not like this!"

"I'm sorry. But if you didn't want me to do it, why did you even tell me about Robert at all?"

"I thought I wanted you to do it, but I was wrong," Angel cried. "You're too different."

"No, I'm not. Everything that's going to happen was going to anyway. I just happen to know about it."

"But you're not supposed to know!"

"Then, why do I?"

"Eric," Martin said, gently. He stood now, in front of everyone else. He looked at his son, his face solemn.

Eileen came out at that moment, tears streaming down her face. She'd heard Martin's thoughts. He'd been fighting hard to shield them. It was deceitful, and he wasn't proud. He had known all along what Angel came to see Eric for, of course. Eileen couldn't hear Angel's thoughts, but Martin could. He'd quickly left the room, playing anything in his head he could think of, to keep Eileen from hearing his knowledge. He knew she would try and stop Eric. He knew his son would choose to change, and he didn't want Eileen to interfere.

"Martin," Eileen cried. "How could you do this? You *knew*? You knew when it was happening? And you didn't try and stop it?"

"Mom?" Eric said, walking up to her, tears in his eyes. "It was my choice, Dad knew that. He just didn't want to take my choice away. Or you."

"But, honey," Eileen cried. She fell on her knees in front of her son, looking at his changed eyes in sadness. "I love you. You don't have to change. I loved you the way you were."

"And you'll still love me, now," Eric said, calmly hugging his mother.

"Eileen," Martin whispered, tears in his eyes. "He needed to choose. I let him. I'm sorry I didn't tell you. But I knew you'd interfere."

"Not if it's what he *really* wants. But you *lied* to me, Martin."

"No, I only shielded my thoughts," he said, looking ashamed.

"How can I trust you if you can hide your thoughts from me?"

"I won't do it again, ever. I promise. Everyone's changed now. There's nothing left to hide."

"What can you do?" Hanley asked, out of sheer curiosity, but also to try and change the subject slightly.

"He can see the future," Sarah said, coming out of her room, holding Burne.

"Really?" Rachel said. "Like what?"

"Everything," Eric said. "Everything about me."

"Only you?" Hanley said, looking disappointed.

Eric nodded, shrugging.

"What good is that?" Rachel said.

"It's good for *him*," Martin said, hearing his son's thoughts. Eric was happy. He'd seen his entire future, and he knew he had a good life in store. He saw incredible happiness, and it made him feel alive, so anxious for what lay ahead. For the first time in his life, he wasn't afraid. He knew he would belong. He knew he would be accepted. He knew he would find love.

"He got what he wanted," Martin said, smiling at his son. "He got exactly what he needed."

"Is that true, honey?" Eileen said. "Are you happier now?"

Eric nodded, then looked back at Angel, smiling. She smiled back, although, she was still frightened out of her mind at what the future held. She frowned.

"How did you know about Willa? That has nothing to do with you, does it?"

"You probably don't want to know about that right now. Trust me. You'll find out some day."

"Okay," Angel said, slowly, a bit uncertain. But she trusted Eric. "Okay," she said again, more firmly.

"Mom," Eric said, turning back to look at her. "You can't be mad at Dad. He needs you. He needs you to love him, so he can go to Hesperia."

Eileen looked at Martin, her face softening. She stood and went to her husband, hugging him tight. She sobbed.

"I love you, Eileen," Martin whispered.

"I love you, too, Martin," she cried.

Everyone went back to their daily activities after that. Eric and Angel went off to ride bikes, and Eric didn't speak any more of their future. It would happen, eventually, he reasoned. For now, they were meant to be friends, and his eight-year-old mind focused on enjoying the limited years of innocence that remained.

Nothing else changed for Eric. The children didn't suddenly begin playing with him. He didn't make new friends or become popular. Sarah didn't use her ability around him anymore, nor would she need to. From that day forward, Eric was completely calm. He didn't fight with anyone. He mainly hung out with Angel and his parents. He was quiet and read a lot. And he waited for his future, the one he'd glimpsed so brightly. He began the countdown, at eight-years-old, to the arrival of his manhood.

***

The moment Mal touched Jess, and all her memories flashed before her eyes, she was able to pulse without any trigger. All she needed was to pull up the immense relief and love that had flooded into her back on Earth at the facility that day in the orchard during her isolation and recall the feeling of complete and total release as she felt herself disappear inside Ben's arms. In that single instant, she had believed in him, trusted him, loved him completely. That was the moment she decided to be with him. She would later falter, when her mind began to work, allowing doubts to play at her thoughts. It caused she and Ben to fight. At that moment, however, in the orchard, time had fallen away, and her emotions were so pure, nothing else entered her mind, only her love for Ben. She would never feel anything so pure again, until she channeled into the Graylings, and when she hugged Harold.

The first training session after Mal used his ability, Jess stood in the middle of the floor. She closed her eyes, breathed deeply, and put herself back into the orchard, crumpled and deflated, kneeling on the ground. Then she concentrated even harder and felt the warmth of Ben's hand on her shoulder. Ben stood against the far wall, gazing at Jess, full of his own love, watching her work. He swelled with pride, knowing she recalled a memory of him. She'd told him this was her new trigger. He knew the moment well, from his own point of view.

The moment she had asked him if he could turn the cameras off in her room had stopped his heart. The tone in her voice had warmed his entire body and set his heart to racing, for her tone told him everything had changed between them. She was ready to give herself to him, and he knew it. He had been in complete shock and disbelief at this fact, but the truth remained—she stood in that orchard, his arms wrapped around her. She'd thrown herself into his embrace, into *him*, without hesitation, and he knew then that he loved her more than life itself. He always had.

He played his version of the memory, as he leaned against the wall, watching Jess. He saw her smile, and his heart broke for joy. He saw the love fill her face with sheer happiness. He saw her take in short, controlled breaths, and he knew it was his love leading her. He didn't need to hold her hand, and yet he did so all the same, for he always held her heart. He felt so connected to Jess in that moment, he thought he could die and be perfectly happy.

Jess threw her hands out and disappeared. Everyone watching gasped. They were used to the scene dissolving into a jealousy match, with Alma walking up to Ben, looking ashamed and fearful. Alma too, had reached the point where she didn't know how many more times she could do this. It hurt Kate, and it killed Alma, knowing she was hurting a friend, no matter the reason behind it.

"Well, that was unexpectedly easy," Hanley said, sitting on the far couch.

"Thank goodness," Alma breathed, hugging Kate.

"Thank Mal," Ben said, nodding to Arnold, who smiled, looking proud. "Jess found a new trigger."

"What is it?" Hanley asked.

"None of your business," Ben said, ignoring Hanley.

"Romeo and Juliet," Martin sighed, hugging Eileen.

Three minutes and forty-eight seconds later, Jess reappeared in the same spot she'd left. She stepped forward, and Ben leaned down, placing his forehead against hers.

"You did it."

"Yes," Jess said, immensely relieved.

Every training session from that day forward went flawlessly. The ship only needed to stop for ten minutes every other day. Ultimately, it added less than seven days onto the travel time to Hesperia.

8

Something odd happened near the end of year nine on board the ship. A romance developed between two unlikely members of The Society. The two people in question were Grace and Malcolm. Initially, when it became apparent to everyone that something was happening between the two, it shocked everyone, except Martin and Eileen, who told Hanley and Rachel.

Arnold had pondered, long ago, while sitting on a couch with Ezra, that some romances might not bloom for years to come, some not even developing, perhaps, until they reached Hesperia. He could not have known how right he was. It took six years for Sarah to grow into womanhood and begin noticing Aaron. It took decidedly longer for Grace and Malcolm to connect.

It didn't happen as all the other romances on board had. It wasn't sudden. There was no epiphany on either person's part. Grace and Malcolm had always been friends, same as everyone else. They were both part of the morning group that practiced meditation in the garden. Malcolm and Grace were the two closest together in age, however, so they found themselves drawn to one another more than many of the others.

Arnold and Ezra had both initially looked to Earl as a natural choice for Grace, despite the fact she was fourteen years older than him. In year one on board the ship, Grace turned forty-nine, and Earl hit thirty-five. If age was ever a factor, however, then very few of the couples would ever have formed. Ben was nineteen years older than Jess, and that did nothing to stop their love from blooming forth violently and suddenly. Aaron was eleven years older than Sarah, but this didn't stop Sarah from falling in love with him, when she was eighteen. Malcolm's own daughter had married a man ten years older.

The fact that both Grace and Earl were the only two black people on board the ship was the sole reason that anyone looked to these two as an obvious couple, plain and simple. But the two just didn't get along, at least, not for more than a few minutes at a time. Their personalities didn't match. They were simply wrong for each other.

Malcolm was fifty-six when they boarded the ship, and closest in age to Grace, other than Hanley. Malcolm was only seven years older than Grace. No one really gave this any thought, until the two became an item.

They began, slowly, over the months and years, to spend more and more time together. Walking through the hallways after meditation, sitting together at meals in the evening. Occasionally, Malcolm went to

Grace for a general checkup, citing his age. But with the healthy living and eating habits on board the ship, even Malcolm remained in excellent health.

***

Ben remarked to Grace, at one point, about the general good health of The Society. Everyone seemed in perfect shape, and had been, even back inside the facility. The only real health crises Ben had to deal with back in the facility were with Jess's caloric and nutritional needs, due to her ability. That and the issues that ensued when she became pregnant.

The Graylings had provided Grace with detailed knowledge of how to fix many of the problems that plagued mankind. She'd only needed to electrically stimulate the growth of new neural pathways in the cortical stem, to solve the simple chemical imbalances in both Rafferty and Arnold's brains. Her own addictive tendencies were solved in the same way, and Grace was cured of her drug habit.

Ben posited that the simple presence of the pseudogene, even while dormant, possibly lent to a predisposition towards better general health than the larger population back on Earth. They conversed about this for the first time in year five on board.

"After all, if you look at everyone in The Society, across the board, no one looks their age," Ben told Grace. "Take you, for example."

"Me?"

"Yes," Ben laughed. "You told everyone in year one that you were turning forty-nine. So, that would make you fifty-four now, wouldn't it?"

"Yes," Grace sighed, sounding annoyed.

Ben laughed again. "Well, you don't look a day over forty, Grace," he said, and meant it.

"It's the water, Ben. I told you that, remember?"

"Yes, and I would tend to agree with you, except I ran the facility back on Earth for ten years, and there was no Grace-purified-water to be found back then. Nor Arnold's famous smoothies."

"Arnold doesn't make those. The Graylings provide me with the necessary ingredients. Arnold is only the one who mixes things together and keeps a steady flow of the concoction going."

"Well, he certainly is proud of himself," Ben said, smirking. "The fact remains, the original members of The Society inside the facility were also in excellent health. Take Martin, for example. He was brought in while going out for a pack of cigarettes. His wife had no idea what happened to him. We brought him in and gave him a dose of Luci. No one gave things much thought after that. It flitted through my mind, but I never put it together, not till now."

"What?"

"Inside the facility, Martin never smoked. He simply went from a four-pack a week habit, to not smoking, cold turkey, in twenty-four hours' time, with no noticeable side effects."

"Maybe the Luci did something to help with that?" Grace mused. "Discovering you can hear the thoughts of everyone around you is a pretty unnerving thing, Ben. I think anyone would be preoccupied enough."

"No. Grace, you were a drug addict. You know what the physical need feels like. There's no ignoring it, am I right? There's no distraction that great, because even if your mind is preoccupied, your body still reacts to withdrawal, no matter what you think about."

"Yes," Grace said, sounding sad. "I know that feeling. I know it all too well."

"And you were cured of it, right?"

"Yes, but the Graylings stimulated the neural connections in my brain that were short circuiting my ability to withstand the urges. They built impulse control back into my brain, Ben."

"Yes, and I'm sure it helped, but I'm not so certain that part of your addiction wasn't beaten, simply by activating your gene. And I think maybe the basic coding of your pseudogene changed you, Grace, even while dormant—without Luci. I think it made you stronger, healthier. You were an addict, but you still looked healthy, even after years of abusing your body, right?"

"Yes," Grace sighed.

"Most people don't come clean with so few physical markers. So little damage," Ben said. "I think simply being a transgen, even a dormant one, makes all of us healthier. It's another marker of the evolvement of humanity. Our overall health will improve. Our lifespans will probably lengthen as well."

"You think we have longer lifespans, Ben?"

"I'm not sure," he shrugged. "The day we left the facility, Hanley was fifty-three. He didn't look a day over forty. And then, there's me."

"You?"

"Yes," he said, blushing. "I was forty-three when I met Jess. But I didn't look that old. I know I didn't. And I don't look fifty-one now, do I?"

"No," Grace said.

"And Malcolm is now sixty. If you ask me, he doesn't look a day over fifty, tops."

"Yes, he comes in here, every now and again," Grace laughed. "Wants me to check him over. He's expecting his body to fail at any time. Poor thing lost his wife to cancer." She shook her head. "If she'd been on board the ship, we could have saved her life."

Ben nodded, still thinking. He took in what Grace had said.

"So, we can fix cancer, too," Ben said, nodding. "Malcolm is the oldest person on board, and he's in perfect health?"

"Fit as a fiddle," Grace laughed again. "Which made him happy, let me tell you. And you're right, Malcolm doesn't look like he's sixty. Not even close. He's actually a fairly good-looking man." She blushed. "I mean... he's in decent shape... for his age."

"Really," Ben said, looking at Grace with amusement. She rolled her eyes.

"So, we look younger," Grace shrugged, changing the subject.

"And we're all in perfect health," Ben continued. "The women all went through labor and delivered their babies in under six hours, each, with little to no discomfort. Even the births are easier."

"So, how much longer do you think our lifespans are?"

"I have no idea. Maybe only a few years. Ten? But it could be as much as twenty or more. I'm guessing it won't be uncommon for any of us to expect to live to see a hundred, easily, and with very few health issues in between."

"Something has to end our lives," Grace reasoned.

"Yes, we'll age, and our bodies will break down, but," Ben shrugged. "If many of the common ailments have cures... then, with the Graylings' help, I don't see why any of us can't make it well into our hundreds... and still look like we're in our seventies or eighties."

"Well, it's only a theory."

"Yes, but if I'm right, then... Grace," Ben looked at her with hope. "You've only lived half your life. You could easily have another fifty-four years ahead of you."

"That's frightening," Grace laughed. Ben laughed with her.

"And you're hoping you'll get another fifty-one years with Jess," she said, her voice gentle.

Ben nodded. He looked sad. "It's not easy, aging this way, while Jess is still so young," he shrugged.

"You said it yourself, we all look younger than we are. You still don't look a day over forty-three, Ben. How do you feel?"

"Health-wise? I feel great. I don't feel like I would have expected to at my age. I keep waiting for it to kick in. I wake up every morning wondering if today I'll start having a bad back, or feel run-down, for no real reason. It has to happen at some point."

"You can't do that to yourself, Ben. If you think like that all the time, you'll drive yourself crazy. And it's not fair to Jess. If you feel great, then simply enjoy it. As you've said, we have no way of knowing how we've truly changed. How much longer our lifespans might be, if any longer at all. Just live your life, Ben. Don't worry so much."

Ben nodded, still looking insecure.

***

After their conversation that day, however, the next time Grace saw Malcolm, she couldn't help but blush. She didn't even realize she admired him physically, until she made her comments to Ben. It had surprised her. She began sneaking looks at Malcolm during the morning meditations. At her age, Grace was far too cool and collected, however, to allow her emotions to run away. At least, that's what she initially thought.

A year went by, and Malcolm came back into the infirmary for another physical. Grace chided him.

"Malcolm, you were just here."

"A year ago," he said, looking at her, his face dead serious.

"Are you feeling ill?"

"Nope," Malcolm said. "But you're supposed to have a check-up every year. That's how I did it back on Earth, and it's how I'll keep doing it here on this ship."

"Okay," Grace sighed. "Alma, would you like to do the honors this time?"

Alma came over and gave Malcolm his physical. Grace stood to the side and busied herself with other work. She found herself sneaking peeks again, however, and felt embarrassed. Not only was it immature, it was highly unprofessional, not to mention unethical. She felt ashamed of herself, and disappointed.

When the physical was complete, Malcolm left, and Grace went over to Alma.

"So, any problems?"

"No," Alma said. "He's fine. *Healthy*."

"What's wrong, Alma?" Grace detected a note in Alma's voice.

"It's nothing… Only, he's in *really* fit shape, you know?"

"What do you mean?"

"The dude's like, sixty… and he's got a *body*. Like a six-pack and everything."

"Malcolm's not sixty, Alma. He's only fifty-nine."

"So?" Alma said, dismayed. "That's only one year's difference. His body looks like… thirty."

"Huh," Grace said, dazed.

"Are you okay, Grace?"

"Yeah, why, don't I look okay?"

But she wasn't. And Martin knew it immediately, for he couldn't help it. It overlapped the same timeframe that Sarah first started noticing Aaron. She watched Aaron for over a year, before approaching him in the garden. Poor Martin spent an entire year listening to Sarah pining over Aaron, as well as Grace, wrestling with herself and her obvious physical attraction to Malcolm.

**

Nothing happened for a very long time. Eileen gained her ability to hear Martin's thoughts before Grace ever made a move on Malcolm. Martin and Eileen laughed about it in bed, often. After years of pining away, and repressing unfulfilled physical needs, every night at dinner had become a constant stream of perverted, lusty reveries inside Grace's head.

Martin heard it, and Eileen heard it in his head, by proxy. The two of them had to work very hard not to lose it half the time. It was a positive thing for the two of them to be able to share. They were still feeling a bit awkward around each other, after the incident with Eric played out. Eileen forgave Martin for hiding his thoughts from her, but she still felt hurt, nonetheless. Eric rebounded from the grownup revelations of his ability, and returned to the same quiet, insightful child he'd been before the incident. He and Angel played together more often, but nothing else changed. Except for the color of Eric's eyes, no one could tell he was any different.

Laughing about Grace's lusty crush gave Eileen and Martin a chance to heal the rift in their relationship. They found themselves, once again, laughing in bed together, as Martin reported up-to-date thoughts as they traveled throughout the ship. Only now, Martin didn't need to talk out loud. He simply thought to Eileen, and she heard. They giggled together in silence, and to any onlooker, they would have looked crazy.

Hanley was close enough to the telepathic couple, however, that he could see something was going on with Martin and Eileen and he finally got them both to spill the beans, right at the end of year eight. Once Hanley knew, the cat was out of the bag. *He* couldn't let things rest. Hanley took it upon himself to try and play matchmaker between Grace and Malcolm.

He approached Malcolm one day and asked him to go for a walk. Malcolm agreed. He had no idea what Hanley wanted.

"So," Hanley said. "Year nine is swiftly approaching."

"Yes, it is," Malcolm said.

"One year left to go," Hanley mused. "How are you feeling about the mission?"

"Fine. You?"

"Oh, I'm not going."

"Neither am I, but Jenny is. So's my son-in-law."

"That's right," Hanley said, kicking himself for opening with such a touchy subject. "I'm sorry, Malcolm, I forgot."

"It's okay. I've had a while to adjust to the idea. If Jenny needs to go, she must. And I'm grateful she has a husband who cares enough not to let her go alone."

"Yeah, it must be nice, knowing your daughter found the love of her life."

"Sure."

"It must be hard for you, though?" Hanley led, feeling awkward. He had no idea, but he felt much like Arnold had when he attempted to broach the subject of Jemma with Rafferty.

"Oh? What must be hard?"

"Being on board this ship, with so many couples, and you, not with anyone."

"Hanley, I had the love of my life. She died, more than fourteen years ago."

"I'm sorry… But, it's been fourteen years, Malcolm. Maybe it's time to consider looking around. You never know what opportunity lies in wait for you."

"Opportunity?" Malcolm laughed. "Here? On this ship? What opportunity is that?"

"Well, for love."

"With who?"

"Uh…"

Malcolm was already thinking and doing the math. "There's no one left but me, Grace, and Earl. Everyone else is together, Hanley. There's not much opportunity there."

"Yeah, I guess you're right," Hanley laughed. It was completely obvious who he was talking about, he realized. Only Malcolm hadn't bitten. So, Hanley pressed on, and decided to state the obvious.

"I guess the only one left would be Grace." He shrugged. "And her only choices are you and Earl. We all know she can't stand Earl."

"Heh, and vice-versa," Malcolm nodded. He didn't seem to get Hanley's drift. That much was obvious. Malcolm still innocently thought he and Hanley were having a hypothetical conversation. He had no idea he was being led. Hanley rolled his eyes and went a step further.

"So?" he said, eyeing Malcolm. "What do you think?"

"About what?"

"Grace!"

"Grace?"

"Yeah. You just said her only choices were you and Earl. And she can't stand Earl, so..."

"No," Malcolm said. "*You* said Grace's only choices were me and Earl. *I* never said that."

"Oh. Well, regardless, it's true, right?"

"Hanley, you can't expect someone to fall for someone else, simply because they're the only choice available."

"Why not? Give it enough time, anyone can probably fall for anyone else."

"Nope, not true. If you put Grace and Earl on a desert island, I'm almost positive they would ignore each other for fifty years, and die alone, on opposite shores."

Hanley laughed, and Malcolm joined him. Then Hanley grew quiet, thinking. He sighed.

"What?" Malcolm said. They rounded the corner to the observation deck and went inside. The view was darkness. Nonetheless, they stared at it silently for several minutes. The following morning, they would be stopped again, for Jess to train, and everyone would come to see the view. No one ever got tired of seeing that.

"Well, you keep avoiding the next obvious item," Hanley finally said.

"Which is what?"

"You put Grace and Earl on a desert island together. What about *you* and Grace?"

"*Me?*" Malcolm shook his head. "No."

"Why not?"

"Hanley. Why are you so hell-bent on fixing me up?"

"It's not *you* I'm trying to fix up." He sighed, giving Malcolm a dead stare. He was tired of playing games. Malcolm kept making things far too difficult.

"What, you want to fix Grace up with *me?*"

"Why not?"

"Well..." he frowned. "She's a doctor, and I'm a... Well, I was an accountant, before the facility."

"So?"

"So, I'm not her type."

"Why not?"

"Well, I'm…" Malcolm hesitated again. "If you put my personality inside Earl's body, I'm sure things might be different, but—"

"Oh… my… God," Hanley said. "Are you serious? You think Grace should be with Earl, just because he's black?"

"No. But, I'm *not* black."

"Well, no shit, Sherlock! So, what? You don't like black ladies?"

"What? No. That's not it at all."

"You don't think Grace is pretty? 'Cause she's colored?" Hanley said, sounding upset.

"Colored? What is this, Hanley, 1955? Of course, that's not it. I just…"

"What?"

"I'm *not black*," Malcolm said, looking at Hanley, appearing infinitely hurt.

"So?"

"So… I'm not black, Hanley. Grace wouldn't be attracted to *me*."

"So, you're ascribing prejudice to *her*, without even asking her about it?"

"I'm not saying that Grace is prejudiced," Malcolm said, growing visibly flustered. "Look, I'm just saying… Earl is this macho, virile—"

"*Virile*?!"

"Virile," Malcolm continued, ignoring Hanley. "Strong, black, handsome man, and I'm..."

"What?"

Malcolm hung his head, looking ashamed. "I'm an old, white guy, with thinning hair, and wrinkles around my eyes. Have you seen the way Grace and Earl go at it? They yell, but, underneath that, there's got to be some tension there. Even if it's only physical." He shrugged.

"Holy Jehoshaphat." Hanley slapped his own face, in mock bewilderment. "You've gotta be kidding me."

Malcolm frowned at Hanley, staring in bewildered amusement.

"Okay," Hanley said, taking a deep breath, then exhaling. "Listen up, and listen good, Mallie."

"Mallie?"

"Shut up and listen. Grace is *hot* for you. Okay? End of story. I didn't wanna just come out and say it, but, you left me no choice. Trust me. There are no thoughts about Earl going through her head. Just you. And by the way, Mallie—that old, wrinkly, white body you think is so unappealing? Well, Grace is doing laps on your pasty-ass, every night in her head."

Malcolm stared at Hanley, his mouth hanging agape. Hanley looked back at him, dead serious. Malcolm audibly swallowed.

"L—laps?" He cleared his throat.

"Yep. From what Martin's got to say about it, it's pretty heavy."

"*Grace?*" Malcolm looked completely shocked.

"You never thought about her like that?" Hanley asked. Malcolm shook his head.

"Well, do it *now*... What's the news?"

"Give me a minute," Malcolm said, closing his eyes. He thought about Grace. He shook his head. "We're friends."

"Great, it's a start."

"Hanley. Are you sure about this?"

"Apparently, this has been going on for over *two years*, now. Slowly building. It's gotten really bad over the last year... and these latest few months?" Hanley shook his head. "According to Martin, it just gets worse and worse."

"But we hang out every day."

"Uh-huh."

"We eat together all the time."

"Yep."

Malcolm frowned for several moments. Eventually, his eyes grew wide with the realization of what Hanley was saying.

"She made Alma give me my last physical... *again*," Malcolm said, his voice going up a few octaves in register. "I thought it was because she didn't want to see me naked."

"Nope, that was because she *did* want to see you naked, but didn't want you to notice her reaction," Hanley said. "Oh, and apparently, Alma thinks you're pretty hot for an old guy. Said you're ripped, or something. That got Grace all hot and bothered, apparently. Pushed things up another notch or two."

"Shit," Malcolm said. "*Really?*"

"Yep," Hanley said. "Oh, but, ah... Malcolm?"

"Yeah?" he said, still frowning.

"If you don't feel the same about Grace... If you give it some thought and realize it's not there for you... Please don't say anything to her, okay? She's a real nice lady, and I don't wanna see her get hurt."

"I don't want to hurt Grace. She's one of my closest friends."

"Yeah, well, that's how these things sneak up, sometimes, you know?"

"I guess."

"Think about it," Hanley repeated. "Give it some good thought, some time. If you conclude that being with Grace floats your boat, then go for it. If you don't, just be her friend, and she doesn't need to know we ever had this conversation, capiche?"

"Capiche," Malcolm said, nodding. Then he sighed.

"I haven't thought about being with anyone since Marie died."

"Well, after fourteen years, you're allowed, you know?" Hanley tried to sound gentle and understanding. "I never thought I'd love anyone else, after Angelique. Then me and Rachel got together, and… it was the best thing that could have happened. For both of us, I think."

Malcolm nodded. He smiled at Hanley. "How nervous were you to talk to me about this?"

"Man…" Hanley shook his head. "It seemed like a good idea in my head. Bad idea in real life."

"No. I'm pretty sure Grace would never say anything. She hasn't. I had no idea. She deserves for me to know. To give it a fair shot, thinking it through."

"Yeah, she does. You're a good friend, Mallie, you know that?"

The two of them walked out of the observation room together in silence, making their way back towards the common room.

"*Mallie*, huh?"

"You like that? It just came out."

"You know what?" Malcolm said. "I do like it, actually."

***

Malcolm went into his room and lay down on his bed, thinking. He closed his eyes and thought of Grace. He thought about her smile, and how she always looked so kind and understanding. She was highly empathic. He simply had never thought of her in a romantic way. She was very pretty, extremely attractive, in fact. He always thought so, but never let his mind go beyond that.

Malcolm stood and went into his bathroom. He removed his shirt and looked at himself in the mirror. He appeared slender and athletic, he reasoned. He looked at his abdominal muscles, wondering. He turned sideways and flexed his pecs. Then he looked at his face and laughed. He felt pathetic. All he saw when he looked at himself, was white. Pale, weak, pasty, wan skin. This was his fault, he knew. He never allowed himself to think of Grace in a romantic fashion, because he never thought she would find *him* attractive. He felt inadequate.

He left the bathroom and laid back down in bed, sighing. *Grace thinks I'm sexy? She thinks I'm good-looking? Me?* Malcolm couldn't believe it. He had always assumed the fights that erupted between Grace and Earl were laced underneath with a secret attraction, an underlying sexual tension. After all, Earl was half Malcolm's age, and the same color as Grace. Earl was a very good-looking man, but arrogant at the same time. Self-righteous. Malcolm realized, given Grace's personality, her kindness and compassion towards others, her anthropologic nature, Earl would be the last person she could ever connect with, no matter what he looked like.

Malcolm *knew* Grace. They were very good friends. He suddenly realized his idea that Grace would ever find Earl attractive in the face of a personality so juxtaposed to her own was completely ridiculous. He'd been hiding behind the false notion all this time, simply because it was easier to believe than the fact that Grace would rather be alone, than with *him*.

Except, Grace *did* want to be with him, according to Hanley and Martin. *Martin can read minds, for God's sake,* Malcolm thought. And he suddenly let it in. He realized they were perfect for one another. Not just because he was the only choice, other than Earl. He was kind, as she was. He was empathic and highly compassionate, just as she was. He cared about everyone and was endlessly impressed by Grace's interpersonal skills with the people on board the ship. He constantly stood in awe of her intellect. He was fond of her, as a friend, but it went far beyond that. Once he truly thought about it long enough to realize, it became obvious. She was the first person he went to whenever he had a thought he needed to thread out. Whenever anything bothered him, he trusted that Grace would have a competent view of the situation, and he always took her advice to heart. She was just so good with people. But more importantly, she was good with *him*. And she was in love with him, if Martin's report of her thoughts was accurate. If she hadn't felt comfortable enough talking to him about her budding attraction, then it wasn't a simple, physical issue, he reasoned.

Grace would have just told Malcolm, if she suddenly found herself attracted to him. Malcolm was certain of that. She would have told him, and most likely laughed about it. She wouldn't have been embarrassed. She had her head screwed on too straight for that kind of nonsense. In fact, Malcolm reasoned, Grace would not even have been shy, if it came to presenting Malcolm with a simple proposition of satisfying a physical need. No, the fact that she'd said nothing about her feelings to him, meant only one thing—She had deep-rooted emotions for him that went beyond physical attraction.

Malcolm felt awful now, marveling at what Grace must have endured, for he truly believed he knew her that well. Her feelings would have crossed a barrier, between simple acceptance of a possible rejection, and entered the realm of actual heartache. If Grace hadn't talked to Malcolm about her feelings, it could only mean one thing— she was afraid—and Grace would never be afraid of basic sex. Malcolm reached all these revelations as he lay there thinking about her. They'd been friends far too long for him to reach any other conclusion.

He sat up in bed. He knew what he needed to do. The simple fact of the matter was, he still felt inadequate, and the only reason he had never broached the subject of becoming romantically involved with Grace, was because *he* was afraid of being rejected. He still felt afraid, even after what Hanley told him. He decided it was time to end all the wondering. He would present himself to Grace and challenge her to fully examine her feelings for him. It was one thing to fantasize about someone in your head, another thing entirely to act upon those desires, he mused. Besides, he was starting to feel like an insecure, adolescent kid again, not a mature, fully grown adult. *I'm elderly, for Heaven's sake. That makes me an elder, not some silly teenager worrying about being rejected if I ask Suzie Q. to the dance. I'm a man, dammit! The worst that could happen is that Grace tells me 'no'. I can handle that, at my age.*

***

Malcolm left his room and headed straight for the infirmary. Hanley played cards with Martin, Eileen, and Earl, as it so happened. They all watched Malcolm go stalking off down the hallway. The direction he was headed, he could only be going to the infirmary, or the cargo bay. Three of the people watching Malcolm go, knew where he was going. Only Earl did not.

"Where's he going in such a hurry?" Earl wondered aloud. The other three people playing cards with him snickered.

"Way to go, Hanley," Eileen said.

"Nicely played," Martin added.

"Thank you," Hanley said, dealing the cards.

"What?" Earl said. "We haven't even played yet!"

Eileen, Martin, and Hanley burst out laughing. *Malcolm was afraid that Grace wanted Earl over him?* This thought was sent by Hanley, to Martin, then by Martin to Eileen. The three of them laughed even harder. Earl just shook his head, confused and annoyed.

"Man, this place is always such a nuthouse, you know?"

***

Malcolm entered the infirmary and stared at Grace and Alma. Their backs faced him, looking at a monitor on the far side of the room. He watched in awe, listening to Grace speak, not understanding a single word, and loving her for it.

"Point mutations that occur in non-coding sequences are most often without consequences, although there are exceptions. If the mutated base pair is in the promoter sequence of a gene, then the expression of the gene may change. Also, if the mutation occurs in the splicing site of an intron, then this may interfere with correct splicing of the transcribed pre-mRNA. See the difference, in the marker line, for the pseudogene?"

Alma nodded. Grace nodded back.

"Good, Alma. Then how do you identify the polymorphic marks, against point mutation?"

"In the allele sequence. It will follow a readable codon which will present itself as either a missense mutation, or a silent mutation," Alma said.

"That's right. And you got that immediately. You know, it took me months to understand all these interpolations? You get them in an instant, Alma. It makes me sick." Alma laughed.

Grace turned then, smiling, and Malcolm smiled back, seeing her face. He saw the familiar shine in her eyes, how excited she was about science, about medicine, about imparting her knowledge base to someone else, and he knew he loved her. He knew he wanted to be with her. Grace was amazing.

"Malcolm?" Grace said, looking slightly jarred by his presence. She recovered quickly, however. "I didn't even hear you come in."

She continued smiling, and crossed the room, coming over to him. Her face took on a mocking tone. She looked reproachful, but a slight smile still played at the corners of her mouth.

"I hope you're not here for another physical. I've already told you, you don't need to come in anymore, unless something is *wrong*. A pain, a symptom."

"I have a symptom," Malcolm said, too quickly, then closed his eyes, wincing at the dramatic flair in his statement.

"Oh?" Grace frowned, looking concerned. She turned away, to head over to her monitor, but stopped suddenly, her eyes flying wide.

Malcolm pulled his shirt off, raking it over his head, and stood in front of her, in pants only. His feet were bare.

Alma watched the scene unfold before her in amusement, from several feet behind Grace. She craned her neck to see around, checking out Malcolm's body. She nodded, her eyebrows raised, bemusedly appreciating the view.

"This is me," Malcolm said. He stood nervously, feeling naked. He felt stupid. His insecurities flared anew, louder than ever. It was too late now, however, so he closed his eyes, took a deep breath, and let the rest come out.

"This is what I look like. I'm old, and pale, and gray, and…" He shrugged, his entire body deflating, giving off a physical air of apology. "And white," he finished.

Malcolm opened his eyes and looked at Grace in sadness. She frowned at him, but also looked sad, her empathy always at work, he marveled.

"I know I'm not much to look at," he continued. "But this is the body I'm stuck with. This is how I was born. This is me," he said again, throwing his arms out to the air. "And you're a *goddess*. You're beautiful, Grace. You're utterly gorgeous. And next to you, I'm sickly, and disgusting. But I love you," he said, looking at her with intensity. "I love you, Grace. I love you, and—" He shook his head, thinking his next words through for a moment before going on. "And I wish you loved me, too. Because if you did, then I would say, let's just be together. If you could stand to be with *me*. A pasty, old, white guy."

"A hot, sexy, old guy," Alma said, lightly, from behind Grace. She smirked as she heard Alma exclaim almost under her breath again, "Dang, Grace, you better hit that, or you stupid, girl."

Malcolm saw Grace smirk and thought she laughed at him. He couldn't hear Alma's remarks. His heart beat so hard in his ears, it sounded like static. He felt numb and defeated, and sadly turned away to leave.

"Malcolm!" Grace called out, her voice urgent.

He turned back to look at her. She walked up to him and placed her hands on his chest, looking up into his face, her eyes shining. She looked radiant.

"You are not an old, pasty, white guy," she said. "You are a beautiful, smart, splendidly wonderful white man. But more importantly, you're simply a man. What does *white* have to do with anything? You are the man that I just happen to be in love with," she said, eyes welling with tears.

"You love me?" Malcolm said, his own eyes welling up.

"Yes, I do," she said, crying now.

"And you want to be with me?"

"Yes."

"Then, let's be together."

"Okay."

The two of them stood there, looking at each other for several moments. They both jumped when Alma yelled from across the room.

"What the heck? Kiss, for the love of all… *kiss*!" Alma shook her head. "You're ruining the moment for me, God," she complained under her breath, talking to herself.

Malcolm bent down and gently kissed Grace, timidly. He still felt afraid, but heat exploded inside, as he felt Grace press into his body, her lips eagerly kissing back. He quickly enveloped her in his arms, and the two of them spun around, locked in an embrace and a deep, passionate kiss. After a few moments, Alma skirted around them, leaving the room.

"I'll just leave you two alone, now," she said, exiting the infirmary.

Neither of them even heard her. They were in their own world.

***

It took nine years to develop, but again, love was found within The Society. At this point, no one was alone, except Earl.

Jenny was slightly surprised at her father's romance, but once she got over the initial shock (for to her, it came out of nowhere), she was happy for her father. Everyone watched Grace and Malcolm walk around, love-struck.

Year nine began with the wedding of Malcolm and Grace. It was followed, in quick succession by the birth of Jemma and Rafferty's fifth and final child—a girl, whom they named Willa. Everyone looked at Eric, when Rafferty came to deliver the news. Eric had known they would have a girl named Willa. No one knew why, but somehow, Willa would be connected to Eric's life, in the future.

9

The Society was now only one year away from landing on Hesperia and facing the Bailon. The time to focus had finally arrived. No one could any longer distract themselves with daily dramas or procrastinate.

Suddenly, there was nowhere to hide, and everyone grew extremely nervous. General anxiety bloomed on board the ship, the air rife with it.

With the atmosphere on board charged with discomfort, the couples instinctively clung to one another in bed at night, no longer making love, but simply falling asleep in the comfort of one another's arms.

People began having nightmares, the blueprint images of the Bailon coming to life inside their heads. Jess became tortured by her dreams about the mission. She woke from them, several nights in a row, screaming, crying, trembling. Martin was greatly disturbed by the terrors and couldn't mask the visions being thrust into his head. The mental agony bled from Martin's mind straight into Eileen's. The two of them began to suffer, by proxy, from the dark images that played out in Jess's dreams night after night.

***

No one had an answer for how Jess could project the horrible images from her dreams directly into Martin's head. Grace argued that it might be Martin, who had somehow connected into Jess's mind, or that somehow, in the heightened anxiety of the impending mission, everyone on board the ship had become more intricately linked with one another.

Everyone had been channeled in by Ezra, and the growing theory was that somehow, everyone became linked now by the highly charged intensity of emotions, in this case, almost overwhelming amounts of fear and trepidation. Families began isolating themselves, spending more and more time alone in their rooms. Parents clung to their children, and everyone was separated for the first time since the ship embarked from Earth.

It was now common for many people to be absent from the nightly dinners in the dining hall. When the six o'clock hour rolled around, the hall now stood sparsely populated. People came and went at random hours. Schedules that had been established for years, now thrown out the window, so to speak.

***

Rafferty finally demanded that everyone come to dinner one night. He told everyone to bring their entire families. They were only eight months away from Hesperia.

Everyone came to dinner that night, as Rafferty requested. With all the grownups, and all the children there, the dining hall overflowed. Several people had to stand. In total, there were twenty-nine souls on board now, with the birth of Willa.

Rafferty stood. He looked at everyone, his eyes grave.

"The time for secrets passed a long time ago. Everyone is walking around, scared. No one is talking about it. It's time to talk about it, now. Jemma and I have five children. I'm leaving her behind, here on this ship, in eight months, to care for four of my children, while I fly a transport ship down to Hesperia, my eldest daughter with me, to fight a war against the Bailon.

"Nine other people are going on that mission with me and Mara. If the rest of you going with me haven't spoken to your families about the mission, the time to do so is now. Go back to your rooms tonight. Talk to your children. They're old enough, now, to listen. It will be hard, but it's the only fair thing to do."

All the eldest children were now nine. The next oldest, which were Jemma and Rafferty's daughter, Althea, and Ben and Jess's son, Alex, were seven. The remaining children also belonged to Jemma and Rafferty. Dorian was five, and Innis was three. Willa was only four months old. The only other young child left, was Sarah and Aaron's boy, Burne. He was now almost two.

"All of your children are old enough to understand," Rafferty continued. "Jemma and I have the youngest. They don't all fully understand what's going on, but they know that Daddy is going on a trip, and that he might…" Rafferty wavered suddenly, taking a moment to regain his composure. He cleared his throat.

"They know that Daddy might be gone a while. Maybe even a very long time."

Jess hung her head, tears silently slipping down her cheeks. Ben put his arm around her, closing his eyes.

"Say whatever you feel is right, that part is up to you," Rafferty finished. "But you *need* to talk about it. We can't just keep walking around, not talking about it."

"So, let's talk about it, then," Arnold said, standing up. He held onto Jenny's hand. "I need to know what's going to happen on the mission." He looked directly at Rafferty. "We haven't met in the tactical room for over a year, now. What's the plan, Rafferty?"

"The plan," Rafferty said, "is to get Jess down to Hesperia, place her on the edge of the Bailon city, and let her pulse."

"That's it?" Alma said.

"That's it," Rafferty shrugged. "We have no other defense. We have no real weapons of any kind. *We are* the weapons. That's all. The Graylings can't abide anything else on board their ship. It's hard enough on them, being connected to us, and subjected to our constant emotions. Our fear, our sadness, our strife, our confusion. If they didn't love us so much, they wouldn't even be able to abide us being here. It's sped up their dying process considerably."

"We're killing them?" Alma said, her heart breaking. She had not opted to meet the Graylings in person and didn't understand the effects that human beings had on them.

"They're dying anyway," Rafferty said. "But feeling our anger, our jealousy, our negative emotions, it takes a toll. It's only those of us who are connected. Don't worry, your children don't hurt them. Only us. But we had to all connect, to commit to the mission, to truly understand and know the Graylings. It was a sacrifice they were willing to make, and they went into it, with each new connection, knowing the cost. Don't feel bad, any of you. You all care, don't you? You all love the Graylings?"

Everyone nodded. Many people cried now.

"To make a connection like that, with another species, has its costs. But it also gives each one of us an incredible gift. It's what each of us needs, to either get on that transport ship, and be brave enough to fight for them, or to watch our loved ones get on that ship and say goodbye. We all knew this was coming," Rafferty said, nodding at Hanley. "It's time to fully face it."

"I need to know details," Jess spoke up. "How will we go down there? What if they see the transport ship? What means do we have of defending ourselves, if anything goes wrong?"

"None," Rafferty said, and the room fell deadly quiet.

Jess looked at Rafferty in fear and disbelief.

"There must be some kind of plan?" Her eyes brimmed with tears and incredible fear.

"Yes," Rafferty said. "We'll land on the beach, about one mile outside the city. We'll land just before dawn, in the dark. The Bailon won't be awake to see our ship. Then we'll let you out, and you'll walk to the edge of the city, and pulse, before any of the Bailon are even awake."

"How do you know they sleep at night?" Aaron said.

"Because," Alma spoke up. "They're ectotherms. Ectotherms are animals that don't have an internal mechanism for regulating body temperature. Instead, they rely on solar energy captured by the environment. Like a reptile. Reptiles absorb heat and convert it to energy. The heat raises the metabolism of the animal which results in an active period, during daylight hours. As ambient temperature drops, the animal's metabolism slows to conserve energy. The Bailon, physically, have to be diurnal." Alma looked around at everyone. "See? I told you, you'd be surprised what you can tell about something, just by looking at it."

"Wow," Hanley said.

"So," Rafferty continued. "Jess will pulse and take out their entire city."

"What if there are more Bailon, in another city?" Rachel asked.

"No," Rafferty said. "The Graylings told Jess she would wipe them all out, with one pulse."

"No, they didn't," Aaron said, his voice high and angry. "All they said was that Jess would wipe all the Bailon out. They never said it will all happen necessarily in one pulse, did they?"

"Aaron," Rafferty sighed. "This is the plan. You just have to accept that."

"With Sarah going? No way. If you expect me to send my wife down there with you, I need way more than that."

"Aaron," Sarah said, her voice quiet and full of love. "I'll be okay."

"How do you know that?" Aaron said. He looked at Rafferty, his face pained. "Rafferty, how do you know there won't be a hundred Bailon that surround the ship, while Jess is off pulsing their city away?"

"I don't."

"Aaron, if that happens, I'll be able to use my ability," Sarah said.

"Is that why you have to go?" Aaron looked hopeful.

"I don't know."

"It makes sense," Earl piped up. "If any Bailon fail to be killed by Jess, Sarah can render them completely powerless. And then Angel can take them apart, right?"

Everyone turned to look at Angel, sitting across from Ben and Jess. Angel's eyes grew wide with concern, looking at her mother.

"Mommy? Am I going to have to take those things apart?" Angel's voice shook with fear.

"Earl, you idiot!" Hanley yelled.

"I'm sorry, I didn't realize," Earl said, looking ashamed.

"None of the children know," Hanley said.

"They do now," Arnold said, looking at Mal in concern.

"I don't want Angel to die," Mal said, his lip quivering.

"Angel is not going to die," Ben said, his voice thick with emotion.

"Angel will be fine," Eric said.

Everyone looked at Eric, trying to read his face. He only had eyes for Angel, looking at her from the table where he sat, smiling. She smiled back, feeling reassured.

"How do you know that?" Jess said, her voice soft.

"Because," Eric said, innocently shrugging. "I can see my entire future. I can't very well marry Angel, if she doesn't survive the mission, now can I?"

Somewhere in the dining hall, a fork dropped and clattered. Somebody else gasped. After that no one breathed, and dead quiet filled the room. Jess stared at Eric, her eyes wide and uncomprehending for several moments. Then she frowned, swallowing hard. She nervously grabbed her cup of water and took a drink, then quickly erupted into a series of heavy, choking coughs, her face turning bright red and desperate. Ben suppressed a laugh. Several other people did the same.

"I swallowed the wrong way," Jess choked out, continuing to cough. Ben patted her back, smiling over at Eric. Then he looked at Angel, raising his eyebrows in mock anger.

"Is there something you want to tell me, young lady?"

Angel only shrugged her shoulders, looking completely innocent. Several people shook with laughter now.

"See?" Hanley said. "Everything happens for a reason. Our dear Eric's ability, which shouldn't even be possible, allows us to know that Angel will survive the mission. Jess," Hanley said, trying to keep a straight face. "This is good news, you know?"

Jess only nodded, still attempting to clear her throat, which tickled maddeningly. She looked over at Eric, smiling sickly. He smiled back and quickly looked away, blushing. Angel also blushed now.

"Huh," Eileen said, looking at her son, then over at Martin.

"Did you know about this?" she asked.

"No way," Martin said quickly.

"Look," Rafferty said. "Everything is going to be just fine. The Graylings have felt that we will be successful."

"Yeah," Hanley said. "I mean, calling this a war, even, is really kind of a laugh."

"How do you see that?" Arnold said.

"Well, we aren't actually going to fight the Bailon," Hanley said. "Jess is going to wipe them out. There is no war, not really. We're exterminators. The whole thing sounds pretty simple to me."

"Too simple," Earl said, daring to speak once again. "I mean, does any of this sound way too easy to anyone else but me? We just traveled through space for ten years. And you're telling me that all we need to do, is drop Jess off, let her pulse, and bang, we're done? Something's not right here. If Jess is all it takes, what the hell did all the rest of us even come along for? Why are so many other people going on the mission? Why even bring anyone else but Jess? Why risk anyone else getting hurt? You realize the rest of the people, who stay behind in the transport ship, could be sitting ducks, right?"

"Not with Sarah there," Aaron said. "I know that's why she's going. It has to be."

"Then why everyone else?" Earl said, his voice rising.

"Because Sarah says they need to go," Hanley said.

"So? Again, why are we letting Sarah decide who to put in harm's way?"

"Shut up, Earl," Grace snarled. "Sarah has a gift. We're trusting Jess with her ability, aren't we? And Eric, for seeing that Angel has a future with him ahead of her. For that matter, the only choice we have is to trust everyone, with their own abilities. Sarah's gift is for a reason. We have to trust that she knows what she's talking about."

"But she doesn't know what she's talking about!" Earl screamed. "She says all these people have to go, but she can't even tell us why!"

"That's it!" Hanley screamed, launching from his chair.

Before anyone registered what had happened, Earl was knocked off his chair and onto the floor, Hanley on top of him, fists flying, along with droplets of blood. It took three grown men to pull Hanley off. They wrestled him back into his seat, where he hung his head, ashamed.

Mara immediately walked over and bent down to look at Earl's bloody face. Angel got up and went over, looking on as Mara worked, in sheer fascination.

Mara put her hands over Earl's face and covered the broken nose, split lip, and bleeding eye that made several people wince. Earl cried out in pain, as he felt sudden heat jolt through his skin. Then, in a flash, everything was done. Mara pulled her hands away, Earl's face healed. The only sign that remained that he had ever been hurt, was the blood on his skin, still bright and wet, and his soiled shirt.

Mara stood and went back to her seat. She quietly sat, staring down at her upturned palms, covered in blood. Jemma quickly stood with Mara, taking her away to get cleaned up. Rafferty stayed, smiling at his wife and daughter as they left. Then he looked around at everyone, sadness in his eyes. He didn't stand to speak this time.

"Every time someone yells, or hurts someone else, it cuts into the Graylings minds like a lightning bolt," he said, sounding sick. "If you can't feel that, I'm sorry. But I can."

"You're more connected than the rest of us," Hanley said. "Just like me. The others can't feel it as much as you or I can. We were connected through our ability. Everyone else needed Ezra. It's not their fault, Rafferty."

"I can feel it too," Ezra said. "Like you," he nodded to Hanley and Rafferty. "The Graylings are beside themselves tonight. They feel all our pain. Our nightmares," he nodded at Jess. "We're all here for a reason," Ezra said, looking at Roslyn and Vera.

Vera was nine now, but unlike many of the other children, she hadn't manifested an ability. She sat with her mother, looking scared.

"Earl, you need to stop fighting this," Ezra continued. "You need to let go. All of us do. This is how the mission is happening. It may not be the way some of you thought it would be. But how could any of us ever have known what to expect? This entire mission was always under the assumption that the Graylings have our best intentions in mind, as well as their own. Everyone is here for a reason. Everyone's ability serves a purpose. What other choice do we have, but to just follow our hearts, and follow our good intentions?"

"We have to go on faith," Hanley said. "If Jesus were here, that's what he would say. He would trust Sarah's knowledge. He wouldn't question it."

Martin shot a look over at Earl, who sat silent in his seat. He had kept quiet while Ezra and Hanley spoke, but not without great difficulty. His thoughts were not hidden from Martin, however.

Jesus is dead, Earl thought. *What good was his faith?*

"Don't," Martin said out loud, glaring at Earl with utter calm. "Don't ever say that out loud."

Hanley looked at Martin, then Earl, in complete disbelief. He could guess from Martin's face, what the other man had been itching to say.

"You know what, Earl? You're the only one making this difficult. I think everyone else is pretty much resigned to the parts they'll each play. Am I right?"

Hanley looked around, and several people nodded. Aaron nodded, putting his arm around Sarah. He trusted her. Even Jess nodded, looking at Ben, who smiled back. They both, together, turned and smiled at Angel, who looked at them, still scared, but not as much as before.

"Earl, you're the only one who's arguing. Why?" Hanley looked at him, completely baffled. "You channeled into the Graylings, just like the rest of us, and yet, you don't seem concerned with saving them. Why?"

"Because," Earl sighed. "These are my friends." His voice suddenly wavered, and to everyone's surprise, he burst into sobs. Everyone sat in shock at seeing Earl cry like this. No one said a word. He shoulders shook, face in his hands, for several minutes. Finally, he looked around at everyone, his face puffy and decimated.

"I love the Graylings, I do," he strangled out. "But there's something I never told any of you. Because I knew you'd hate me for it. As much as I love the Graylings, I still love all of you more. I do, and I'm sorry. For ten years, I've been with you people. I already lost one friend, the day we came to live here on board this ship. There are eighteen people here, besides me. Eighteen people. That's my whole world. You people. You're all I have.

"And I can't even help you. I can't protect you. I'm not going on the mission. But you expect me to just let you go? The only friends I'll ever have, for the rest of my entire life? You expect me to just let you go, not even knowing what to expect? Not even knowing if you're fully prepared? I can't lose anyone else," Earl said, shaking his head. He looked down at the table. "I can't lose anyone else," he said again, dissolving into tears once more.

"Even if we thought we knew what to expect," Ezra said, trying to sound gentle. "Things don't always turn out how we think. They never do. Do they? There's no way to be ready for this. We simply can't be ready to know what to expect, Earl."

"Earl, you're not alone in this," Jess said. "Everyone's afraid. Don't you see that? But you need to let us go. I'm sorry. You don't have any choice. Everyone who's going is ready, for whatever happens. Even if we don't know what it is. We're ready to face the unknown. I made a promise to Harold. I made a promise to all the Graylings. I won't break that."

"This coming from a woman whose nightmares are so powerful, they're bleeding over into everyone else's dreams," Earl said.

Jess looked at Earl in shock and surprise. He nodded at her, looking sad.

"Yeah, I've seen them, too. We're all connected, Jess," Earl said. "I'm just the only one, it seems, who's not quite ready to jump off into the dark, without being able to see the ground."

"Angel's coming back," Jess whispered, looking at Earl. "And so am I. Sarah will be there to protect us." Jess nodded at Aaron and Sarah. "Beyond that, I don't know what will happen. And no one else does, either. We need to just accept our parts, and let the rest unfold as it comes. Whatever is meant to happen, will happen."

"Jess," Aaron breathed, looking at her reverently. "You're there now?"

Jess nodded in her chair. She looked at Ben.

"As long as I know Angel will survive, I can do this," she said, touching Ben's face.

"You're not doing it alone," he said. "I'll be right by your side."

Jess cried, looking up into Ben's face with relief, her heart filled with happiness.

"Did you think I was going to let you stand on the edge of that city alone?" He looked at her with love. "I told you I would never leave you alone, in anything. Remember? Why else do you think Sarah put my name into the mix, hmm?"

Jess threw her arms around Ben's neck, hugging him fiercely. Angel started crying.

"Angel, your parents will be just fine," Rafferty said. "Your mom is guaranteed to succeed. Your parents will be just fine."

"Ben," Earl said. "You can't go with Jess. You can't be near her when she pulses."

"Yes, he can," Jess said. "I can shield him from the blast." She looked deep into Ben's eyes, caressing his face, and whispered. "Just like in Khardush."

Ben nodded, understanding. He knew that was how it was supposed to be. It was why things had happened the way they had back then. He felt certain of that now.

"That's right," Alma said. "Jess took me with her, once. She protected me, too."

"And she can't do it without Ben," Hanley said, looking at the two of them in awe. "What we're asking her to do, it's too big. Staring out on the edge of a city full of the most aggressive beings that ever existed, creatures with no soul, no conscience… and create a pulse as big as Rafferty says she's going to. I wondered how she could ever concentrate enough to do that. Now I know."

Jess gazed up at Ben with nothing but love. He wasn't going to leave her alone. She'd been afraid to admit she needed him there, that even after learning to pulse all over again, she still needed Ben by her side, on Hesperia. But he knew. He knew her so well. In the end, she didn't need to ask.

"Earl, now can you accept that everything's going to happen just as it's meant to?" Grace said, holding Malcolm's hand.

Earl cried but nodded his head. What other choice did he have? He looked at Ben and Jess and saw how much faith they had—faith in their own love for one another. He nodded again, then got up and walked out of the room.

10

After that night, things lightened up considerably for almost everyone. All the families went back to their separate quarters and talked things over. The oldest children were involved. Everything was explained to them. Many of them already knew, by this point. Those who had parents going on the mission were understandably more upset, but even they accepted that their parents had a crucial role to play in reclaiming the Grayling's planet. After all, Hanley reasoned to Robert, they weren't just winning Hesperia back for the Graylings.

"It's going to be our new home, too," Hanley said. "We can't just live on a ship our whole lives, now can we?"

***

Jess and Ben talked with Angel and Alex, briefly. Angel understood and was not afraid. Alex was only seven, but he seemed to understand. His entire family was going on the mission. He was being left behind. Jess worried about this. She was afraid it might be too difficult for a child his age to handle, but he smiled at her, looking up from his bed.

"I can play with everyone, until you come back," he smiled.

"Yes, you can," she said. "I want you to play. That's a good idea."

Alex loved games. They played hide-and-seek for hours, running around the ship. But Alex loved to hide in their quarters the most. It was silly, because there were only a few places to hide, really. Jess always found him within a minute. Every time she located him, however, he always giggled wildly, highly amused. He never tired of it. She looked down at her son, face filled with love.

"Everything's going to be okay, kiddo," she said. Alex nodded, closing his eyes to go to sleep.

Jess went into the bedroom, where Ben stood, waiting. Everything was about to change between them, and neither knew it—about to pass beyond a barrier, and neither had any clue.

"Ben, what's wrong?"

His face set, jaw clenched, he clearly looked angry. "Jess, I wish you had told me your fears. How could you ever think I would leave you there alone? Don't you know that's why I'm going?"

"I'm sorry," Jess sighed. "I just wanted to be strong for you, Ben. I didn't want you to think I was weak."

"I would never think that. But how could you think I would let you go alone?"

"Ben, Angel is going. Of course, you're going, to be with our daughter."

"Yes," Ben said. "But she's staying behind in the transport ship. So long as Sarah is with her, I know she'll be safe. I'm walking with you to the edge of the city. How could you not realize that?"

"I don't know."

"Jess, I told you, I'm never leaving you alone. In anything. Not even if you order me away from your side, remember?"

"And I said, *'why would I ever do that?'*" Jess recalled. "I remember, Ben. I just didn't realize you were talking about the mission."

"I wasn't," he said. "I was talking about our lives. Every moment of our *lives*."

"Because you think I'm going to leave you," Jess said, shaking her head. "You think I won't want you when you're older."

"I already am older."

"Ben, stop it!" Jess yelled. "What happened to all your faith?"

"I have faith, Jess."

"Yeah, in the mission. What about me? Why can't you just accept that I love you, no matter what?"

"I know you love me, Jess," Ben said. His face contorted in a pained frown that broke Jess's heart. "I just wish…"

"What, Ben?"

"I wish I could love you forever," he said. "Someday, I will leave you alone. It's inevitable. I'll *die*, Jess. And you won't even be close to getting old. I'll leave you all alone. I'll break my promise."

"Ben, you can't stop death. That's not breaking your promise to me."

She walked over and hugged him, his body rigid. He did not put his arms around her. She pulled away and gazed into his face.

"I wish you would just be happy with me *now*."

"I am."

"There was a time when all we wanted was to be free, remember? Free to wake up every day in each other's arms, and not have to hide anything. We have that, Ben."

He nodded.

"So just be happy. I need you. I need you to stop worrying about the future. That's years from now, Ben. Years."

"Okay," he nodded. "I can do that."

"Can you?"

She stared at him, trying to discern his look. Pain still haunted his eyes.

"Whatever is meant to happen will happen," she sighed. "For all you know, I'll die first."

"No," Ben said. "No, Jessie, you won't."

"I might. Something could happen. I could get sick, or, maybe I have a disease I don't even know about, just waiting to happen."

"No. Not with the Graylings understanding of our biology. And Mara," Ben said, sounding hopeful. "She can fix people who are hurt."

"I'm just trying to make a point. Whatever time we're meant to have together, we'll have. Let's not worry about when it might end, or how long it will be. Please?"

Ben hugged her then, finally. He held her tight, afraid to let go. He could feel something building inside him. When he finally pulled away, he looked at her face with deep longing and kissed her passionately. They hadn't made love for several weeks, not since the nightmares got so bad. He didn't want to push her, and she hadn't come to him, or shown any sign she wanted that kind of contact.

It was the first time, since they'd escaped the facility—since they'd been free to be together—that Ben felt he didn't have access to Jess. She'd spent the last several weeks pulling away from him. The divide between them felt so painful for Ben, as if trapped in free-fall, his emotions on a roller coaster. He constantly worried he had lost her. She'd never gone so long without touching him. He pulled away and gazed at her, feeling unsure, trying to read her face.

"Hey. You feel like...?" he couldn't finish. He'd never had to ask before. He was afraid of her answer. She kissed him urgently, however. She'd missed being with him also.

"Are you kidding?" she breathed. "Come on, old man," she teased. She stood and looked at him expectantly. Ben couldn't help saying something.

"See, those kinds of comments aren't helpful."

"Oh yeah?" she threw back. "And you saying, *'this old man came rolling home,'* is?"

"You're not going to let me forget that one, are you?"

He frowned. Her teasing felt slightly cruel tonight.

"Nope," she said. "That, or *'the getting is good,'*" she said in a huffy voice. "Oh, or my favorite: *'Let's get crackin'.'*" She looked at him, now standing by the bed, her eyebrows raised. "I mean, really, Ben. Sometimes you can be so immature." She delivered a wicked smile.

Her eyes twinkled. She radiated energy, Ben suddenly realized. He could see it coming off her now, reaching him in slow, looping arcs. He hadn't seen anything like this since Jess was in labor, but this was still different from that.

"*'The getting is good'* was yours," he said, walking over, kissing her madly, without laying a hand on her, however. He pulled away, suddenly, making Jess sigh in frustration. He teased her painfully, now.

He looked at the energy arcs coming off her, then down at his own skin. He could see the waves connecting to him, and the hairs on his arms stood on end. He laughed. He felt giddy. Then he felt a sudden streak of meanness shoot through him. He didn't care.

"Oh, and my personal favorite: *'all I have are these scrubs. They aren't sexy.'*" He delivered this in a high, reedy voice, to mimic Jess.

"That is not what I sound like," she said, her voice feigning insult.

"Really," he smiled, his voice deep, rich, tantalizing. He took a step away from her. She took a step forward, unbelieving.

"You are driving me nuts, you know that?" She leaned up on her tip-toes to kiss him, and he went up on his toes, pulling away from her, by bare inches, still smiling.

"Ben," Jess sighed. She closed her eyes and buried her face in his chest, running her hands all over his body, and he closed his eyes, feeling her desire. The arcs of energy swirled madly around them now, and everything felt like they were inside a dream. He still hadn't put his hands on her.

Finally, she took his hands and put them on her. He didn't respond. He had no idea why he behaved this way. He wanted to make love to her so badly, had wanted to for weeks. Now he held back and didn't understand why. She moved his hands for him, desperately running them over her body, placing them where she wanted him. It drove him crazy. It had never been like this between them before.

"Touch me, Ben," Jess breathed. "Please."

Finally, Ben gave in, letting all the tension that had built up wash over him. He took her in a frenzy, and they made wild, passionate love with more energy than ever before. All the anxiety—weeks of watching Jess wake up screaming, seeing the sunken flesh below her eyes, all his desire for her held at bay—flooded to the surface.

Ben surprised himself with his actions. He made love to Jess more roughly than he'd ever dared before. She responded in kind, the entire ordeal aggressive, even violent. The act, essentially animalistic. Ben got so carried away, he forcefully flipped her onto her stomach, to take her from behind, holding Jess down with shocking force, but she seemed to enjoy it even more. At one point, he got so rough, she screamed out in pain, but never told him to stop. When it was all over, they both lay together, in total shock. Neither of them had ever behaved that way. They fell together, then laid next to each other, panting.

Jess suddenly shuddered next to Ben. He looked at her in concern, watching her shake and tremble. He panicked, for he could see wave after wave of heat energy floating off her skin, now. She radiated, glowing. He could feel his skin tingling, as the energy touched him.

Whatever he'd done to her, he'd touched off some sort of reaction. The arcs swirled faster than ever, as it escalated, getting worse, whatever it was.

"Jess! Are you okay?" He felt utterly ashamed, his heart breaking.

Jess nodded. She wouldn't look him in the eye.

"You're shaking, Jess. You're trembling."

"I'm okay," she said, her voice soft and shaky. But the energy floated off her now in even larger arcs, engulfing Ben.

"No, you're not." He sighed, then started to cry. "I hurt you, didn't I?"

She turned to him then, touching his face so gently, he wanted to rip his own heart out. She kissed him, once, smiling.

"Jess, if I hurt you, I'll die. I only wanted to love you. I don't know why I was like that with you," he frowned.

"I was like that, too," she said. "I'm okay."

"Then why are you shaking?"

"I don't know. I just feel out-of-control."

He frowned, looking at her closely, pushing through the colors that swirled around. He took in the dark circles beneath her eyes, the pale skin, and suddenly, he knew something was very wrong with Jess.

"You're sick, Jess. Tell me what you're feeling right now."

"I don't know," she repeated. Her entire body trembled turbulently. Her voice shook wildly. She looked at Ben in desperation.

"Jess, you haven't been normal for weeks now. I thought it was the nightmares, but, even before that…" he paused, thinking. "I think we need to take you to see Grace."

"No," she said, her eyes grave. She clung onto Ben and pulled him to her.

She looked desperate and wild, clawing at him. He hardly recognized her. She kissed him frantically, pulling him on top of her. He looked down at her, confused. Something inside him was building, again. He could feel it. Whatever had happened between them before, it was happening again, only this time, Ben recognized that it wasn't natural. It felt highly charged, energized, overpowering. He felt his control slipping away.

"Jess, what are you doing to me?" Ben sounded desperate. He didn't want to hurt her again, but he felt violent lust taking hold of him, as if his id took over, shutting everything else down. He recognized it this time. He pulled away, but Jess held onto him.

"Please, Ben," she said, her voice strangled and pained. "I need you."

"Not like this," Ben said, sounding heartbroken. "Not when it hurts you."

But she continued kissing him, not satiated, still needing more. He could feel it. He didn't understand what was happening to either of them. Something clicked off inside his head then, and he could no longer control himself.

He wasn't gentle, nor did he caress her. He overpowered her. He didn't ask, he took. This time, face to face. This time, Jess didn't cry out in pain, only whimpered in low, moaning sobs. He took her, hard, nothing sensuous about it. But even as she cried, she wrapped her legs around him like a vice.

When he was done, Jess grew scarily quiet, her eyes closed. She still trembled, as if chilled to the bone. Her skin radiated fluorescent arcs of energy. Ben felt awful. He was out of whatever trance he'd been in while ravishing her, once again overcome with shame.

He knew something was wrong when Jess pulled her body to him, kissing desperately, yet again. He looked at her in shock, feeling as if his world had fallen apart.

"Again," she whispered, even as her body, racked with spasms, violently seized.

"No," Ben said, his heart cracking. "Jess, there's something wrong with you. With us."

This time, he fought the feelings threatening to take him over. He quickly dressed both himself, and Jess, as she lay in bed, shaken and pale. His heart raced.

He scooped her up into his arms and carried her from their room. Luckily, Alex was fast asleep. He quickly went to Grace's room and knocked. It felt like an eternity before Malcolm answered. He stood frowning at Ben for several moments, holding Jess in his arms, before realizing what he saw.

"Grace!"

Grace came running to the door. She took one look at Jess, who now lay limp in Ben's arms, saw the look of sadness and dejection on Ben's face, and immediately walked him down the hallway to the infirmary. Malcolm followed quickly behind.

***

"She's radiating heat energy," Ben said. "It started right before we…" He didn't finish. They entered the infirmary.

"Put her on the table, quick," Grace said. "Malcolm, please go get Alma for me?"

Malcolm left. Grace scanned Jess with her hand-held, frowning. She swabbed Jess's face and analyzed it. Then she took out another gadget and ran it over Jess's body.

Ben watched all of this in dazed shame. Grace continued frowning, shaking her head, as if trying to wake herself.

"Grace, what's wrong?"

"Nothing. I just feel… confused. A bit muddle-headed."

"It's Jess. I think she's doing something to the people around her."

Jess stirred then, gasping. She looked around, desperate.

"Jess," Grace said. "Can you describe to me what you're feeling right now?"

"The orchard!" Jess yelled. "It's the orchard!"

"She's having a psychotic break," Grace said, her voice low, sad.

"No, she's not," Martin said, panting, from behind them. He walked up to the table, taking in deep, gasping breaths.

"Martin, what do you know?" Grace asked.

"I couldn't make sense of her thoughts, at first. But, she's talking about the Atrium, Ben."

Ben frowned. He didn't understand.

"Her cells are all firing off at once," Grace said, looking at her hand-held. "I've never seen anything like it. It's almost, kinetic. But they just keep firing. I don't understand where the energy is even coming from."

"Ben," Martin said. "She's talking about that day, in the hallway, after you came in from the Atrium. When she almost pulsed, but didn't, remember? She went catatonic then."

"Yes," Ben said, nodding. "She'd stored up so much energy, but instead of releasing it in a pulse, it only kept cycling through her body, through her cells. She finally released most of it in the form of a heat compression."

"It's what she's feeling now," Martin said. "She's overloading. I can hear it in her head."

Grace frowned, running her scanner over Ben, now. He didn't even notice. She quickly swabbed his face and analyzed it. She did the same thing to herself, and then Martin.

"She's been going through all the motions of pulsing," Ben said, closing his eyes. "Without actually pulsing. Her ability is being stunted, again and again."

He shook his head, looking down at her sadly. He began to cry.

"Every time she trains, she pulls tiny amounts of energy from the air around her. She can't harness gravitational mass, but that doesn't mean she doesn't still store energy. Most of it gets used up to form an energy field around her, when she travels forward in time. But not all of it. She's been storing it in her cells. That's why I couldn't see it until now. It had to be on a sub-atomic level, highly compressed. Only, now, after pulsing so many times, without releasing any of it, it's begun to super compress. It's built up too high, even she can't control it anymore. She's releasing it, because there's simply nowhere else for it to go."

Ben looked at Grace and Martin sadly. Alma came in and walked over.

"She's going into kinetic overload. It must have begun several weeks ago, when the nightmares began. It's why everyone has been able to see her dreams. It's been Jess all along. She's been projecting her nightmares into everyone's heads, in her body's attempt to release the energy. I didn't see it then, because I was asleep," Ben hung his head. "We've all been receiving small bits of her energy, over the last several weeks, and consequently storing it ourselves. It's probably only so bad now, because Jess finally regained the ability to pulse at will. This must have begun, though, from the very first time she pulsed, while she was still pregnant with Angel. And every other time she's pulsed, including when she still needed Alma's help to piss her off. But doing it effortlessly every other day, for weeks now… months… I suspect it's been affecting everyone's moods, possibly for quite a while now, without any of us even realizing it."

"Through our connection with the Graylings," Martin said, nodding. "It must be. The energy was being converted to each of us, through our shared connection."

"Then I was right about that, at least," Grace said. "The connection stems from a positive charge of energy, being shifted. I just assumed it was caused by everyone's anxiety, not all from one person. Jess is affecting everyone, making us all emotionally unstable. Anything ranging from euphoria, giddiness, giggling fits, even, all the way to the other end of the spectrum, like raging libidos and temper tantrums, even fistfights. Ben is being affected the most, I suspect, because he's in proximity. Ben, your testosterone levels are through the roof… Are you feeling violent?"

Ben hung his head, looking ashamed. Martin heard his thoughts.

"It's not your fault, Ben."

"What?" Alma asked.

"Nothing," Martin said. "Don't worry about it."

"She can't continue firing off like this," Grace said. "She'll eventually drain out, which is good. If she continued storing any more energy, she'd begin experiencing mood swings, personality shifts. Not to mention, she's affecting anyone who gets too close. My cells are showing a shift in energy, as well. I'm having trouble concentrating. Martin's testosterone is elevated also. Ben, what kicked this off?"

Ben hung his head lower, crying silently. Grace frowned.

"Something had to catalyze this process," Grace pushed.

"They were..." Martin looked at her, eyebrows raised. He put his hands together in a suggestive way.

"Oh," Grace and Alma both said, together.

"With *that* kind of energy around you?" Grace frowned at Ben. "No wonder your testosterone is so high."

"How high?" Alma asked.

"2600 nanograms per deciliter."

"Holy shit! You had sex like that?!" Alma said. She looked at Ben, impressed. "*Wow.*" Then she looked at Jess. "No wonder she's in a coma. *Damn.*"

"Alma," Grace scolded, but she struggled to hide a smirk. Martin also suppressed laughter.

"What? I'm just saying." Alma shrugged. "That must have been *something.*"

Ben sighed, still worried about Jess. He cried even harder.

"Ben, I'm sorry, it's not funny at all. It's just the effect on all of us... it's difficult to be civil or proper. I apologize." Grace sighed. "But Jess is firing off all her energy, now. It's a good thing. Whatever effects this phenomenon had on her before, they're being purged. And she's not in a coma, she's sleeping."

Grace shot another scolding glance at Alma. She ran her scanner over Jess again, nodding.

"Look, the levels are already coming down. She's returning to normal."

Grace scanned Ben again.

"So are you. Our only problem now, once Jess recovers from this episode, will be figuring out a way to avoid another build up. We'll have to find a way for her cells to be purged of the kinetic energy, instead of being stored. If she can't release it with a regular pulse, there must be another way. We can't have everyone running around having nightmares, giggling for no appropriate reason, screaming at each other, and getting into fistfights."

"You think Jess caused all that, too?" Alma asked.

"I don't know," Grace said. "I've never seen Hanley lose his temper like that. Especially when he's more than aware of the effect it has on the Graylings. And I've never seen Earl cry like a baby, or even come close. I think we've all been storing the energy Jess has been sending out, into our own cells, sub-atomically, and for quite some time. In men, it tends to raise testosterone levels. In women, it seems to suppress it."

"Is that why you haven't been in the mood, Grace?" Malcolm piped up from behind Alma.

Grace nodded, smiling. "Probably. I suspect if you ask all the women, or the men, come to think of it, they'll all say they've been less intimate lately. Jess has been unintentionally suppressing our libidos."

"Suppressing it?" Ben looked at Grace. "Then why was Jess so…"

"What?"

"She was very aggressive as well." Martin jumped in.

"I would imagine, with all that energy firing off inside her, she couldn't help but be any other way. It sent her body into crisis mode. The act of making love was a release for her. Once she experienced that release, she would be desperate to purge the rest of the energy. Ben, what happened between the two of you is nothing to be ashamed of."

"But I hurt her."

"No, Ben, you didn't. If it weren't for what you did, Jess would still be storing that energy up, and eventually, it would have led to a full psychotic break. What happened is a good thing. The two of you love each other. You're *married*. Nothing you did could have been so horrible."

"I was so rough with her."

"Damn," Alma said. "And you think that's a bad thing?"

"Alma, you're not helping." Grace shot her a disapproving look. "Ben, I'm sure you're normally a very gentle lover," Grace soothed. "But it's okay, occasionally, to be more…"

"Cave-like?" Alma threw in.

"Okay," Martin said, clapping once. "I'm going to go now. Go see Eileen." He quickly left the room.

"Yeah, me too. Geez, Ben. It's only sex," Alma said, also leaving the room.

"Ben, Jess will be fine. She should be completely purged within a few hours. She's sleeping. She's no longer shaking. The worst is past."

Ben nodded.

"Did you force her?" Grace said, her voice gentle. Ben looked at her, shocked.

"No, of course not," he said, looking highly disturbed.

"Then what's wrong? Not every time can be *sweet*, you know."

"It always has been…" Ben sighed. "Passionate."

"Passion takes many forms, Ben. It doesn't mean you love each other any less. I think the two of you have a *lot* to talk about."

Grace walked out of the room with Malcolm, leaving Ben alone with Jess. He held her hand, looking at her lovingly, watching as the waves of rainbow color slowly drifted off her skin, in smaller and smaller arcs.

***

Two hours later, Jess woke up, to find Ben sleeping on her arm. She looked around, realizing she was in the infirmary. She slowly sat up, and Ben woke, looking at her for several moments, stunned.

Jess looked radiant, the dark circles beneath her eyes, gone. Her skin still looked pale, but had a pinkish tone to it, just under the surface. Ivory, and beautiful, her eyes shone bright. She smiled at him, and his heart filled with joy. He cried, making her frown.

"What's wrong?"

Ben looked down at the table, he couldn't look her in the eye. She touched his face.

"Hey," she said. "Would you mind explaining to me why I'm in the infirmary?"

"You don't remember?"

She shook her head, frowning.

"What's the last thing you remember?"

"Well," she sighed, thinking. Then she blushed, smiling shyly. "We were… making love…" She glanced at him, now blushing wildly. She laughed nervously. "And then…" She frowned. "We were making love again…" She sighed, still frowning. "And then I woke up here."

"M—making love?" Ben looked at her, nervous, in disbelief. "That's what you remember?"

She nodded, frowning even deeper. She looked at him, confused.

"Why? What else happened?"

"N—nothing. Just, I wasn't expecting you to say that."

"Say what?"

"Jess," Ben sighed, his eyes welling up with tears. "I hurt you."

"You did? How?"

"Don't you remember? Don't you remember how—" He choked up, unable to finish.

"Ben. I don't understand. I feel fine."

"I was so rough with you," he said, taking her hand.

"Rough? Well, maybe more energetic, but…" She frowned.

"Energetic?" His voice sounded high. "You cried, Jess. You *sobbed.*"

"So? Ben, you were *wonderful.*"

She looked at him, blushing again. He blinked, taking it all in.

"You liked it?"

"You don't have to sound so appalled, Ben," she said, looking down, embarrassed.

"Hey, no." He cradled her face in his hands. "I just didn't expect you to… be like that."

"Like what?

"Nothing."

"No, Ben, like what? What, I'm not allowed to enjoy my husband?"

"No, I just didn't know you wanted me to be so… forceful."

"Forceful? Ben, I practically had to beg you to even touch me."

"I'm sorry. It was the energy, it made me all confused. I would never have been that way otherwise."

"What energy?" She frowned.

Ben explained to her everything that had happened. She sat listening to him quietly. When he finished, she looked at him shyly.

"So, what you're saying is, I made you all super-aggressive?"

He nodded. "Jess, I would never have been like that with you otherwise."

"Oh," she said, growing quiet.

"Jess?"

"I'm sorry I made you feel bad."

"Jess, I feel bad for hurting *you*."

"But you didn't hurt me. I mean, yeah, a little, but…" She looked at him shyly. "That's not necessarily a bad thing."

He blinked at her, still surprised.

"I'm not saying it has to be like that all the time," she continued. "But, it was different…" She eyed him with longing.

"Have you not enjoyed the way I make love to you?" he asked, sounding incredibly worried.

"No, Ben, of course not. I love the way you make love to me. I always do. But just because this time was different, doesn't mean it was bad."

"Grace was right," Ben laughed, shaking his head. "We do have a lot to talk about."

"What do you mean? Ben, did you still love me when you were with me last time?"

"Of course."

"Did I tell you to stop?"

"No," he said, frowning.

"Then what's the problem?"

"I just thought I hurt you, by being so rough. I've never been that way with you before. I didn't know you wanted me to be."

"Neither did I. And I *don't* want you to be like that all the time. Not even half the time."

"Then how am I going to know when?"

"I don't know. I guess, if it feels right, you'll just do whatever feels natural."

"That wasn't natural, Jess,"

"Wasn't it? Maybe you're just not used to allowing yourself to be that way. I think *you're* the one who's hung up on this whole thing, Ben."

"Me?"

"Did you sleep with someone else?"

"No, of course, not."

"Then you can't ever hurt me, Ben."

"I don't know how to make love to you now," he shrugged. "I don't know what you want."

"I want you to touch me in whatever way feels right for you."

"And I need for you to tell me, if you need more, or something different."

"Ben. Obviously, certain things upset you. You're not comfortable. That much is obvious by this point."

"Jess, all I care about is making you happy. If you want me to make love to you the way I did tonight, I will."

"Not if you don't like it."

"I did," he frowned. "I just wasn't expecting to enjoy hurting you."

"You didn't hurt me!" she cried, exasperated. "Ben! I felt so alive. I felt so... claimed. I never felt so loved before. You have no idea how you felt to me. You were so strong. I felt so safe. So... encompassed. The pain wasn't a bad thing. It was like, I could feel how much you loved me."

"And my love feels like pain?"

"Good pain," she breathed. "I'm sorry if I make you feel ashamed of me."

She looked away. He felt awful, for he realized he was hurting her *now*, for real.

"I'm not ashamed of you, Jess. I love you so much. Do you have any idea how much I love you?"

She looked at him, her face high with color, blushing madly. Suddenly, it all flooded in. She *did* know. He had made her feel it. She'd been trying to explain to him. He'd always been holding back.

He kissed her then, gently. She sighed. He could feel her trembling.

"How did this happen, Jess?" he breathed. "When did we become afraid?"

"I'm so scared, Ben," Jess breathed. "I'm so scared of what I have to do."

"I know."

"I feel like I'm losing my mind, every time I think about it."

"I know, Jessie."

"When I'm with you, like you were... I wasn't scared."

"Okay," he said. "Okay."

"How can I train now, knowing what it's doing to me?"

"If I love you the way I did, does it help?"

She nodded. "I'm sorry, Ben. It's what I need. Please don't be ashamed of me," she said, crying.

"Jess, I couldn't be ashamed of you. I simply couldn't. Ever."

"But you're still shocked."

"I'm over it," he said, and meant it.

He kissed her again, gently, feeling nervous.

"Jess?"

"Ben?"

"Do you want me to love you now?"

"Yes," she breathed.

"Like that?"

"*Please,*" she sighed.

And he did. More than once. This time, all on his own. And it was wonderful. He felt surprised and amazed at how easy it was to let go, knowing she wanted him that way. Knowing it brought her pleasure, distracted her thoughts from the fear, made her feel alive, gave her a release from her mental anguish. He also felt alive. He realized his passion for Jess truly did come in many forms. It was forceful, but this time, Ben felt the intensity rise in him in a whole new way. He allowed his male drive to take over, taking *her*, and felt no shame.

***

They had learned to love in an entirely new way, after all this time. It bonded them even closer together. He loved her even more.

The nightmares never returned. Jess resumed training, and she and Ben now knew the release for the side effects of stored energy within her cells.

Everyone else on board the ship seemed to recover almost immediately. The Society was in a better mood. Everyone slept better at night. No more yelling or fights broke out, ever again, at least not due to Jess or her pulsing issues. There were no more fistfights. All the couples returned to their own, normal intimate activities. Most of them never knew that Jess had anything to do with the depressed mood on board the ship.

Grace was the only one to ever bring it up again. She simply wanted to know if Ben had found a solution to Jess's energy problem. He told her yes, and she saw the look on his face, the blush in his cheek. She smiled and quickly dropped the subject.

Jess and Ben didn't make love like that all the time. Not even half the time. But when she needed him that way, she found she wasn't shy about it, for he always made sure she felt comfortable with him. The moment she asked, he never hesitated. And he only loved her that way when she asked. But suddenly, after a decade together, Jess and Ben fell more deeply in love than ever.

11

Six months before they reached Hesperia, they made their final jump. Everyone gathered on the observation deck. They would never make another jump again in their lifetimes. Everyone felt slightly saddened by this fact, yet relieved at the same time. Each jump brought them closer to their mission and to saving the Graylings. Each jump also brought them closer to an unknown fate, and possible tragedy. Each mile they traveled now brought them closer to their new home as well.

As the bright white flash blinded each of them and they experienced the disorienting, floating sensations for the last time, everyone felt sadness and elation, trepidation and fear, excitement and melancholy, all at once. They all experienced the distinct revelation that something had been lost. Their travels were coming to an end. Their journey was nearly complete.

Everyone kept busy, spending time with their families. They ate together at night in the dining hall. Rafferty spent much more time with Jemma and the children, and considerably less with the engineers. He even remained on deck for the entirety of the final jump, instead of coming in afterwards. Jemma felt grateful for this time with him.

Jess and Ben spent time with Angel, preparing her for the mission. They talked to her about it. They helped her through her fears. Angel wasn't very afraid, however. She told them she couldn't be, since they had no idea what to expect. After a few heart-to-heart talks with her, explaining how she would remain on the transport while both her parents left to do their work, Angel seemed fine. She needed no further explanations.

Jess spent hours playing with Alex. She also talked to him further, about being left behind, even though Angel was going on the mission. He didn't seem to mind at all, but he was still so young. Jess and Ben were perplexed by their children's easygoing attitudes, but Ben simply shrugged, telling Jess it was part of their new genetic makeup to remain calm about things and not get too upset.

Angel had gotten upset, however, when Eric changed, Jess noted. She mentioned how Angel had yelled at Eric.

"Well, Jess, Eric *is* her best friend. And he *did* suddenly change. And it's not every day you learn your eight-year-old best friend is going to be your husband someday." He smiled.

"But, how could she yell about that, and not even seem affected at all by this mission?"

"Because," Ben shrugged. "She knows she'll grow up and marry Eric and have children. She knows everything will be okay, Jess."

Jess sighed. She still felt afraid. Of everything.

"I don't even want to think about that. I don't want to think about Angel being married, when she's only just turned nine."

"She's spending all her time with Eric."

"Yeah, and not with us."

"She has to grow up sometime, Jess."

"She's nine!"

"But she *knows* the mission will be fine. And so, nothing has changed for her, Jess. She's playing with her friends. It's a good thing. She's distracting herself. At least she's not worrying so much, like us."

"I know," Jess said. But she still sounded sad. "I just thought she'd want to spend more time with us than this, is all. She's hardly ever here."

"But Alex wants to spend time with you. And with Angel going off on her own, you don't have to compete. You can give your time to Alex, without making anyone upset, or feel left out. It's all working out perfectly, Jess."

***

Later that afternoon, Jess played hide-and-seek with Alex, for the billionth time, but he never got tired of it. As usual, they ran all over the ship, but eventually, Alex wanted to hide in their quarters. There were only a handful of places to hide, but Jess agreed, again. She sat on the couch and counted to twenty, then exclaimed, "Ready or not, here I come!"

She started in Angel's room, looking on the far side, under the bed. Then she went back out into the living room and looked under Alex's bed in the far corner near the door. Next, she looked behind the couch, despite the fact it sat in the middle of the room. This was her routine. Ben came in then, and saw Jess appear over the couch back, her face looking radiant. She loved playing with Alex. She smiled at Ben, and he smiled back, loving her. Then she put her finger to her lips to shush him, and stood up, heading to their bedroom.

"Hmm, I wonder where Alex could be?" she said, sounding playful.

In the bedroom, she looked on the far side of her bed, underneath, then frowned. Alex wasn't there. This was the only place left to look. She put her hands on her hips, thinking. Then she heard the tiniest giggle from behind her, and quickly spun around, expecting to see Alex standing behind her, giving himself up. There was no one there, however.

Jess frowned again, looking around. She knew she'd heard him laugh. There was nowhere else in the room he could possibly be,

577

however. Then she heard him laugh again. Her gaze traveled to the place the sound had come from. She slowly raised her eyes to the far corner, by their door, traveling further up. Then she screamed.

Ben sat on the couch when he heard Jess cry out. He quickly ran into the bedroom, throwing the door open. It hit Jess's back, and he turned, moving the door, closing it. The scene he came upon, both shocking, yet highly amusing, in retrospect later that evening.

Jess stood in the corner, reaching up to Alex, who sat in a crouched position, near the ceiling. She craned up on her tiptoes, trying to reach him.

"Ben," she strangled out, in her effort to reach up. "Help me reach him."

Ben took several steps back, rubbing his chin in his hands, taking the scene in. Jess turned around, to look at him.

"Ben," she wailed. "Help!"

Alex laughed loudly then, in a fit of giggles. Jess turned back to look up at him, hopping, trying to reach him, still. Alex looked down at her, laughing wildly. Ben smiled.

"Mommy couldn't find me," he said.

"Honey, get down," Jess panted. "You're going to fall."

"Wait," Ben said, walking up to Jess. He gently pushed her to the side.

"Oh, thank God," Jess said. For she thought Ben was going to reach up and help Alex down.

She eagerly stepped away, watching the scene unfold. Ben stood gazing up at his son, smiling and curious.

"How'd you get up there, bud?"

"I climbed," Alex said.

"On what?"

Alex shrugged. Ben looked at his feet, squinting his eyes, thinking. His son appeared to be sitting on thin air, crouched down. Ben looked at his stance, the way Alex sat, and backed away a few feet.

"Ben?" Jess couldn't believe he wasn't getting Alex down.

"Are you standing on a shelf, Alex?"

Alex thought about his father's question for a moment, then nodded his head, slowly at first, then more emphatically.

"Huh… Can you get down? By yourself?"

Alex nodded, but didn't move.

"Ben, he'll fall."

"No, I won't, Mommy."

"No, he won't," Ben said at the exact same moment.

Jess looked at Ben in complete disbelief at his lack of support.

"Come on, bud. Show Daddy how you get down, okay?"

"Okay," Alex said. He motioned for Ben to back up, with the back of his hand. The gesture seemed so matter-of-fact, so grown up, Ben laughed, quickly backing up.

Ben glanced over at Jess, winking, but she glared at him, then returned her worried gaze to her seven-year-old son. Alex lowered one of his feet, then appeared to simply hover in midair. He looked as if he stepped down, one stair at a time, on an invisible barrier. After he'd stepped down far enough that he could stand fully erect without hitting his head on the ceiling, Alex put both feet together and jumped from one invisible step to the next, giving Jess a heart attack, watching her son freefall, then stop in midair, repeatedly. With one last jump, and a giggle, Alex no longer stood in the air, but back on the floor. He looked up at his Dad, his face shiny, happy, and proud.

Ben stepped forward and put his hand out, indicating for Alex to slap it, and he gave him five.

"All right, now up high," Ben said, and Alex slapped his hand up high.

"Now down low," he said, then quickly pulled his hand away, causing Alex to miss and giggle. This always made him laugh. It was one of Ben's rituals with his son. A small game, but his nevertheless.

"Too slow…" he drew out, and Alex laughed again.

Ben looked at Jess, still smiling wide. She shook her head, cheeks pink with anger. He immediately dropped his grin. She stormed out of the room.

Ben sighed, looking at Alex in consternation. He went out into the living room where Jess paced and waited for the yelling to begin. She looked at him, shaking her head. When she finally spoke, her voice shook with anger.

"I can't believe you, Ben. I cannot believe you."

"Jess," Ben sighed. "Come on."

"No, Ben!" She shot out. "Don't 'come on,' with me. What are you doing?"

"Uh, supporting our son," Ben said, feeling a bit angry himself.

"What about *me*, huh?"

"Jess, this isn't about *you*."

"It isn't? My *son* was on the ceiling, Ben. The *ceiling*!" Jess became too angry then, shaking her head. She turned, quickly opened the door, and left their quarters.

"Is Mommy mad at me?"

"No, Alex, she's mad at me," Ben sighed. "I better go talk to her, okay?"

Alex nodded morosely, then immediately brightened excitedly. "Can I go play in the garden?"

"Sure, kiddo. That's a good idea."

Ben opened the door, and Alex ran out, past Jess, who now paced in the common room. As usual, several people sat on the couches, while others played cards at the two tables. As soon as everyone saw Jess come out and begin pacing, they all dropped what they were doing, and waited.

Ben came out, and Jess shot a glance at him, her face now crimson.

"Jess," Ben began.

"That's great, Ben," she spat. "Just send him off to play, without setting any limitations."

"Gosh, I love it when those two fight," Arnold said.

"Jess, I'm not going to do that, and you know it. You can't limit their abilities."

"You've got to be kidding me," Jess strangled out. "Ben, it's one thing to tell Angel, sure, go ahead and fix stuff. There's no danger in that. But Alex? Ben, it's dangerous, he could get hurt. Don't you even care if he gets hurt?"

"Jess. How is he going to get hurt?"

"Are you serious? What if he falls, Ben?"

"He's not going to fall."

"How do you know that?"

"Because, Jess, his ability is manifested. If he can get up, he can get back down. It's not just going to turn off. He knows what he's doing."

"He's seven!" Jess yelled.

"Man, this is great!" Arnold exclaimed.

"Shut up!" Several people said at once.

Earl laughed, shaking his head while shuffling a deck. "Man, I love this group."

"Ben, you can't just give him the impression that climbing the air is okay. There has to be a limit."

"Why, Jess? What's the worst that could happen, even if he did fall? How tall are the ceilings, twelve feet?"

"Ah, twenty, actually," Arnold interjected.

Several people yelled or hissed, "Shut up!" again.

"Twenty feet, Ben," Jess said, pointing at Arnold in victory. "He could break his ankle. And I'm not just talking about the ship. If he gets used to just going as high as he wants, as high as he can, fine, here on the ship. He can't go any higher than the ceiling. But what about when we get to Hesperia, huh?"

Ben stared at Jess in surprise. This was the first time she'd mentioned anything about Hesperia for the last several months. He blinked at her, smiling.

"Ben, it's not funny!" she said, looking at him in disbelief. "He needs to know there are limitations. I don't want him just climbing up the air, for hundreds of feet. And no water. He's not allowed to climb over water. No climbing over the ocean, you know?"

"Okay," Ben said, sounding so gentle it drove her nuts.

"Why is this funny?"

"Jess." Ben walked up to her and gently placed his hands on her shoulders. "You're talking about our lives on Hesperia. *After* the mission. You've never done that before."

"Yes, I have," she frowned. "When we talked about where we would live, and how we'd have to be separate from the Graylings."

"That was *months* ago, Jess," Ben smiled wide. "You haven't talked about our lives on Hesperia for months. And never like this. Limitations on games? Rules for how our children can use their abilities, how they'll play on our new home planet?" Ben looked at Jess, his face full of love.

"Ben," Jess said, letting his statement in. Letting the full meaning of everything in. She smiled then, allowing the hope and joy flood into her. She rushed into Ben's arms and he held her tight.

"Why would we need to live separately?" Earl frowned.

Hanley looked at everyone wistfully. He had also reached this realization, months ago, even before Ben. He spoke to Rachel about it, so she knew. They'd also told Robert, and he told all the children, so *they* knew.

"We can't live with the Graylings, once we get to Hesperia," Hanley explained. "For the same reason we can't be with them here on the ship. We must remain distanced from them, or it will simply be too draining on all of us. We're *still* connected to them. *For life*. That won't ever change. We simply can't be too close to them, for too long. Those of us who've actually been in the same room with them, understand why."

A few people nodded. Sarah did, looking at Aaron. He smiled at her. She'd explained what the experience was like for her when she met them. Aaron understood, even without experiencing it for himself.

"So, where are we going to live?" Jenny asked.

"In our own little city, I guess," Hanley said. "Society Ville."

Everyone sat in silence, thinking about Hanley's remarks. Suddenly, Mara and Robert came running down the hallway, straight up to Jess and Ben.

"Come quick! It's Alex!"

Jess gave Ben one quick, *I-told-you-so* look, and they both went running after Mara and Robert, down the hallway. Everyone else in the common room quickly stood and ran after them.

"Society Ville is fine with me," Earl laughed. Aaron ran alongside him, holding Sarah's hand. Aaron and Earl were still best friends. He laughed heartily at Earl's remark, nodding his head.

Everyone ran into the garden, where Mara and Robert led them. In here, the ceilings went considerably higher, over eighty feet, allowing plenty of room for the tallest trees. They all followed the children into the far-right corner, behind the wildflowers, and looked up to where Mara and Robert pointed.

All eyes ranged up, and up, and still up, to the very top of the far-right corner. There, Alex sat, again crouched. He looked considerably more afraid this time, than he had in Jess and Ben's bedroom.

"It's not fair!" Mara yelled. "You're not allowed to hide places no one can get to you!"

Mara turned to Ben and Jess. She looked annoyed.

"Tell him he's cheating. No one can even tag him up there."

Ben laughed, turning to Jess. She sighed.

"Come on, Jess. Tell me you see the humor in this?"

"Humor?" she said, still sounding annoyed, but a small smile played at her lips. "This is *your* fault Ben. I said we needed to set limitations, but *no*. You said he didn't need them. Now look! You said he could only go as high as the ceiling, which wouldn't be a problem."

"Well, I forgot about the garden, okay?" Ben said, sounding defensive, yet still amused.

"Great! Have fun getting your son down from this one."

She backed up, gesturing at Alex. She crossed her arms defiantly over her chest. "Go ahead, Ben. Fix it."

"It's not fair!" Mara said again, and Ben sighed.

He walked into a stand of grass and looked up at Alex, waving. Alex waved back feebly.

"Can you hear me, bud?" Ben called up to him.

Alex nodded, the movement barely visible from so high up. Alex looked extremely small.

"Can you come down, Alex?" Ben said, growing nervous.

Alex shook his head. Ben felt a bit scared now.

"Why not?" he called up.

"She's mad at me!" Alex said, pointing to Mara. "And Mommy's mad, too!"

"No, honey, I'm not mad!" Jess yelled. "Please, just come down!"

"You're not playing by the rules!" Mara yelled up.

"Mara, please," Ben lowered his voice. "Just, shhh." Then he yelled again. "Come down now, Alex, okay? Just like you did before. You can do it, I know you can!"

"'Course I can!" Alex yelped, sounding annoyed.

Ben smiled then, loving his son more than life itself. He swelled with pride, looking on in awe and wonder, as Alex slowly stepped down on invisible shelves of air, a few feet at a time. Everyone looked on, wide-eyed and amazed. Even Mara and Robert were floored.

"Dang it." Arnold said. "Again!"

"What?" Earl said. "Come on, that can't help the Graylings."

"So?" Arnold said, sounding bitter, yet amused. "It's still friggin' awesome."

"Arnie, *you're* friggin' awesome," Jenny breathed. She leaned up and whispered something into his ear for several seconds. He looked down at her, eyes growing wide in surprise.

"Really?"

She nodded, pulling on his arm. He never looked back. He and Jenny walked out of the garden together, quickly. Earl sighed, shaking his head.

Alex jumped down the last three steps on both feet again. He walked up to his father. Ben picked him up and hugged him tightly, then carried him over to Jess and set him back down. He got down on his knees to look Alex in the face.

"We need to set some ground rules, okay bud?" He looked up at Jess, apology written all over his face. She smiled down, mouthing, 'thank you.'

"No ceilings higher than our quarters, okay?"

Mara huffed from behind Ben, and he smiled. He looked at Alex sternly. "And no using your ability to give you an unfair advantage while playing with your friends. Got that?"

Alex nodded, looking serious. He'd never really been in any trouble before. This was the worst thing he'd ever done. He'd never needed 'rules' before. His lip quivered.

"Hey, it's okay, Alex," Ben said, hugging him again.

"Alex," Jess said. "Your ability is wonderful. We just want you to be careful with it, okay? When we get to Hesperia, you're going to have a lot of open space to climb in. It won't be like the ship. You just need to be careful, okay? No climbing over water."

Alex nodded. He smiled up at his mother. She smiled down at him, feeling immense love.

"But, other than that, have at it, kiddo," she said, giving him a high five.

12

Jess continued pulsing every other day, up until the day before they went on their mission. She could do it instantaneously and had been for the last two years. It got to the point where no one bothered looking, really, for they'd begun taking this once astounding sight for granted. Many people simply went on with their conversations, their card games, without taking any notice of Jess as she disappeared and reappeared. Always, Ben waited for her, right in front of her mark. Always, he embraced her when she came back. She always came back. No one even paid attention to them anymore, the entire last eight months or so of the voyage.

Many people also didn't watch Ben and Jess because they chose to go to the observation deck every other day to look at the view in small and varying groups. They were only stopped for about ten minutes every other day, and the amazing spectacle of space was something no one ever took for granted, as breathtaking as it always appeared. The last few weeks, when everyone realized they would never see space that way again, everyone returned to look, the common room empty during Jess's training save for her and Ben, for everyone gathered to see the view, once more, together, the same way they had for every jump. They all wanted to see the view the last several times while they could, before reaching Hesperia.

***

The days were winding down. Four months out from Hesperia, Rafferty called the team into the tactical room to discuss things. Ten people sat around the long table, waiting expectantly for Rafferty to speak. It was ten in the morning.

"Here's what you need to expect," he began. "We'll reach the solar system of Hesperia in four months. We'll hide behind one of the two moons that orbit the planet. The Graylings and I will monitor the surface, make sure we're right about their living habits. We should be able to see, then, if they have expanded beyond the Grayling's city. Although, I don't see how they could, really. Most of it is mountainous. The rest of the land would be needed to grow their food, so…"

Everyone stared at Rafferty, listening. No one spoke or interrupted, and he felt grateful.

"It may sound foolish, but I'm still working on the initial assumption that the Bailon will all be in one, large city." Rafferty took a deep breath. "When we're ready, we'll all assemble in the cargo bay, early in the morning, about an hour before we need to leave. We'll all say goodbye to our families and friends. Hug each other, cry, whatever we need to do. Then, the eleven of us will get on the transport. Our families and friends will exit the cargo bay, and we'll fly off the ship.

"It will only take about ten minutes to fly down to the surface of the planet and land. As I've already told most of you before, we'll land on the beach, about one mile from the city. Jess and Ben will exit the transport."

Rafferty looked at Jess, Ben, and Angel, who sat between them. Angel glanced back and forth, between her parents, looking small and suddenly scared. They each held one of her hands.

"It will probably take about fifteen minutes for the two of you to walk the mile, in the sand, to reach the edge of the city," Rafferty continued. "Then, you'll pulse, Jess. You and Ben will disappear, then reappear about four minutes later. The city should be destroyed, and all the Bailon will be gone. The two of you will walk back to the transport, and we'll come back here, to our families."

Silence filled the room. Everyone looked at everyone else, their eyes wide. Finally, Arnold spoke.

"Ten years," he said, his voice barely audible. "Ten years, and that's all it will take? What... half an hour of our time, maybe? And according to Rafferty, him and the other eight of us on the ship will just sit there the whole time, doing nothing? It doesn't make sense."

"It's how it's supposed to be."

"Says who?" Arnold's voice grew louder. "Says you?"

"This is the same plan I outlined to you over a year ago, Arnold," Rafferty said.

"Yeah, and if I recall, Earl said it sounded way too easy." He now yelled loudly. Several people winced. "He's right! This is nuts!"

"You have a better idea, Arnold?" Martin said.

"Yeah, I do," he said, then sat quietly, his mouth working, but no sound came out. His face colored in embarrassment.

"We're not supposed to fight, remember?" Sarah said. "We're supposed to have faith. Everything's going to be okay. The Graylings told Jess she would succeed, and live. She and Ben will succeed. And Angel is going to marry Eric someday. She'll live. If she's in the transport with us, and she lives, so will the rest of us. And if there are any Bailon outside the city, they won't be able to lift a weapon to harm anyone. I'll make certain of that. I promise."

Everyone sat in silence. The minutes drew out. Finally, Rafferty spoke again.

"Who said it had to be difficult? Why is everyone expecting some huge fight, or monumental war? Maybe it really *is* this easy. It wasn't a war when the Bailon came, was it? It wasn't a fight. It was easy enough for them to come and take Hesperia away and wipe all the Graylings out. So, why shouldn't it be just as easy for us? We never knew what to expect, did we? Yet, everyone expected something different than this? That makes no sense. This is how it is. Even so, it's not really all that easy, is it? None of this has been easy."

"No, it hasn't," Jess said. "You're all forgetting that it's slightly amazing that I'm suddenly going to become the equivalent of an epic atom bomb, dropped on the Bailon's city. That's not a good plan? Would it be better if we dropped an actual bomb from a plane? Would that seem more tactical to everyone? I've been training for two years to be able to do this. You're all forgetting that I almost couldn't. This isn't easy. It's not easy at all."

"She's right," Arnold said. "I'm sorry. I'm so sorry, Jess. I was wrong. I'm just scared, that's all. I don't even know why me, or Jenny are going with you. I can't help you."

"You don't need to help me," Jess said. "I don't know why the rest of you are going. But I know I'm grateful I won't be alone. Ben will be with me when I pulse. But knowing the rest of you are waiting for us, back at the transport, it helps. It really does."

"Look, this is how it is," Martin agreed. "We're all going, because Sarah says we need to. Even she doesn't know why. Maybe it is simply for moral support. I don't know. Maybe we need to just trust everyone else's abilities. Maybe I should just shut up now," he said, shaking his head.

"So, that's it," Rafferty said. "Jess will wipe out the Bailon, and we'll return here, to the ship. We'll share the good news with everyone, that Hesperia is now safe. The Graylings will have their home back, and we'll have arrived at our new home, as well. We'll all land in this ship, and watch—from a distance, of course—as the Graylings walk back onto their home planet for the first time in over two hundred years. And *that* is a sight I would love to watch."

***

"I really couldn't do this without you, you know," Jess said. She and Ben lay in bed together. He held her in his arms.

"I know."

"No, you don't," she said, looking up into his face. "I really don't think I could walk down that beach, in the dark, alone. How are we even going to be able to see, Ben?"

"You're forgetting that there's no such thing as 'dark,' for me, Jess," Ben said. "Everything gives off energy."

"Ben, that's scary."

"I'm used to it."

"That's not what I mean. If you weren't going with me, and you didn't have the ability that you do, how would I find my way in the dark, to the city, to pulse?"

"A flashlight?" Ben shrugged.

"And risk being seen, detected by the Bailon?"

"What are you saying?"

"I'm saying, it can't be a coincidence, can it?"

"I don't know," Ben frowned. "Maybe."

"Maybe?" Jess looked at Ben, incredulous. "You don't think it all means something?"

"Sure. It means this is exactly what's supposed to happen. And if you really believe it's not a coincidence, why are you still so nervous?"

"Are you kidding?" Jess looked at Ben, feeling lost and misunderstood.

"Of course," he said, smiling at her. She slapped his arm.

"That's not funny," she said, but she smiled.

"Well, I made you smile, firecracker."

Ben quickly scooted to line his body up with her, face to face, resting his forehead against hers. She closed her eyes.

"Jess, I know you can't do this without me. It's always been you and me, from day one. Every time you pulsed, I was right there. Maybe not right by your side, but still. I was *always* with you. It's not you that has to be strong, okay? It's *us*."

She nodded.

"We're going to do this. Together, you and me," he said. This time, she kissed him.

"I love you."

"I love you back," he said. "This is going to work. You know that, right? It has to—we didn't come this far, through everything we've been through—for nothing."

"I know," she said. "I know."

She threw her arms around him and he held her tight. They held each other.

Every night for the next four months was the same. Sometimes they made love, sometimes they only held each other and fell asleep in each other's arms. But, always, they held each other up. They supported one another. And Jess was half-right in her statements to Ben. She couldn't do this without him. However, they simply couldn't do any of it without each other.

Everyone gathered in the cargo bay. It was a little after one in the afternoon, by the ship's clocks. On Hesperia, however, it was a little less than two hours before dawn. They'd been parked on the dark side of Hesperia's second moon for six days. Rafferty had been busy on the upper decks with the Graylings, observing the surface of Hesperia.

Within forty-eight hours of arriving at their destination, it was confirmed that there appeared, indeed, to be only one large city that the Bailon resided in. It was larger than the Grayling's city had been when they were forced to leave. New buildings had been erected, backing up into the steep hills inland. However, it appeared that the Bailon lived dozens to a building. They were heavily concentrated, into one large area, just as Rafferty surmised they would.

Observation was slow and difficult, the atmosphere around Hesperia thick and clouded by pollution. Rafferty had to take the transport ship down into the planet's lower atmosphere to see the city and record data. He did this on day two, after the sun had set on the Bailon city. Just as Alma guessed, the Bailon all slept, from the moment the sun set. Nevertheless, Rafferty descended in darkness. He remained high up in the sky, some three thousand feet, and recorded all the images he would need to learn of the Bailon's activities.

***

Jess and Ben were pulled into the tactical room on day four, and Rafferty told them everything they needed to know. The remaining eight coming on mission sat and listened quietly.

"The city covers over sixty-five square miles. They've built back up into the hills. There appears to be roughly a hundred thousand dwellings, with over two dozen Bailon per building. We're looking at about three million Bailon, in roughly sixty-five square miles, with an elliptical perimeter."

Rafferty pulled a schematic of the city up on the monitor above his head. It was the original Grayling city, revised to include the new buildings, ranging back up into the hills. Rafferty nodded to Ben.

"According to Ben, when Jess pulses, the energy spreads outward, equidistant to the center of gravity around her, in a semi-arc. On Earth, the arc only covered a one-mile radius directly forward, with the energy dissipating exponentially as it rings outward from Jess's body. Nothing behind her is directly affected by the compression wave, but even so, the EMP dissipates in a 180-degree pattern.

"Hesperia's gravitational field is sixty-seven times as strong as Earth's. That means, your pulse, Jess, should create a compression wave that flattens everything directly in front of you, for over sixty-seven miles."

"But, that's exactly the size of the Bailon's city, give or take," Arnold said. "How is that even possible?"

"You're questioning things now?" Martin said. "It's perfect, just deal with it. This is going to work, Jess."

Martin nodded and smiled at her. She nodded back, taking in a deep breath. Ben squeezed her hand.

"If we place you here," Rafferty pointed to the far-southern corner of the city, "and you pulse, it should take out the entire city, even back into the hills. Alma was correct in her assessment of their diurnal activities. As soon as the sun sets, they retire indoors. No electricity, no lights. Their bodies go into hibernation mode. So long as you pulse while it's still dark, or right at dawn, if you need to see, they won't even be awake. They don't come out until the sun is well above the horizon. About a half-hour after sunrise."

"They're sitting ducks," Alma said, her eyes twinkling. "And I don't feel bad about that at all. Not after what they did to the Graylings."

"Jess?" Ben looked at her with great concern. She looked back at him, her eyes solemn.

"You think I'll feel bad? You think I won't be able to do it?"

"No, of course not."

"Good," Jess said, nodding to Alma. "Because I don't feel bad at all. According to Rafferty, my pulse will cover almost exactly the number of miles of the city. Ben, we already talked about coincidences, remember? I told you there were none. Everything happens for a reason. That's why I'm here. I don't feel bad about this. I made a promise to Harold, and I'm going to keep it. This is it, everyone. We're going to bring the Graylings back home."

***

Everyone stood in the cargo bay looking at one another in silence. They'd been hiding on the dark side of the moon now for six days. Everyone went to sleep the night before, knowing their mission would be carried out the following day, in the afternoon. Most people had trouble sleeping, of course.

Now, everyone stood, dazed and disbelieving. After ten years of traveling, living, growing, and planning, they had arrived to do what they'd been brought there for. No one could believe it was time.

Rafferty stood in front of Jemma and his five children, quietly gazing at each of them. Jemma kissed him, silently crying. She couldn't help herself.

"I love you, Raff," she whispered.

Rafferty placed his forehead against Jemma's, his eyes closed. He fought back tears of his own.

"I'll do my best to bring Mara back, Jem, I promise."

"Daddy?" Mara looked up at her father, her chin quivering.

"Yes, baby?"

But Mara couldn't say anything else. She dissolved into tears. Rafferty picked her up in his arms and held her tight, his own tears now falling unabated.

"Oh, baby, I love you," he whispered. Jemma began to sob. Althea, Dorian and Innis hugged Rafferty's legs. Little Willa cruised behind Rafferty, holding onto the transport ship's ramp. She was only one. Jemma quickly walked behind Rafferty and scooped Willa up into her arms, to see her father and sister off. He smiled at Willa, then kissed Jemma desperately on the lips.

"I've been thinking," he whispered. "We make it through this, I might want five more of these." He motioned around to all their children. Jemma laughed, tears still tracking down her cheeks in fresh spurts. She nodded.

"You make it back home, and we can talk about it, definitely," she laughed.

He kissed her again, then pulled away, still cradling Mara, and looked at his remaining children.

"You mind your mother, you understand?"

They all nodded. Rafferty looked at Mara and winked.

"Everything will be okay," he said. She nodded.

Rafferty took one last look at his family. He kissed Jemma one last time, gazing into her eyes. Then he quickly turned away, holding Mara's hand. They walked up the ramp and disappeared into the transport ship.

***

Jess walked up to Hanley and hugged him tight. Hanley hugged her back, closing his eyes.

"You take care, kiddo, okay?" he said. There were tears in his eyes.

"I'm coming back, Hanley," Jess said, nodding. He nodded back.

Martin came up to Hanley next. Hanley's chin quivered.

"Oh, come on," Martin said, but his own face looked pale and haggard. He was also close to tears.

"You already know what I want to say, so…" Hanley trailed off.

"I know," Martin said, with a trademark tap to his temple. He turned his gaze to Rachel standing next to Hanley. Jess had already said goodbye to her as well.

"I want you to take care of Eileen, while I'm gone," Martin said to Rachel. She nodded. Eileen stood next to Martin, just slightly behind.

"I'm right here, Martin," she said, stepping forward.

"I know," Martin said. He turned to Eileen and kissed her urgently, thinking his thoughts to her privately.

I love you.

I know. I love you, too, she sent back.

Martin then sent Eileen something else, that his son had told him only that morning. *Eileen, you and I are both at Eric's wedding to Angel in the future. He waited to tell me till last night because he doesn't want anyone else to know. He's not sure about anyone else, he thought it might upset them, not knowing. It's only for you and me. I'm coming back, with Jess and Angel, for sure. You can tell Hanley and Rachel after I'm gone, okay? But only if they promise not to tell anyone else. It'll make the rest more worried and nervous. Our son is very smart. He didn't think it would be fair to tell everyone. We have an unfair advantage.*

Oh, Martin! She rushed forward and clasped his hand. To everyone else, it simply looked like a fretful goodbye. No one else paid any attention to the look of relief on Eileen's face. They certainly couldn't hear it in her thoughts.

Martin let go of Eileen's hand and placed it into Rachel's. He smiled, backing away, and quickly turned to board the ship.

***

Jess, Ben and Angel all took turns hugging Alex, who didn't seem scared at all. He knew his family was coming back. At least, that's what he believed with all his heart, which was the same thing. Eric came over to say goodbye to Angel. He stood alone, away from his mother. He'd already said goodbye to his father.

"Good luck, Angel," he said. Then he whispered in her ear. "We name our first daughter Jess."

Angel looked at Eric, this time not angry, but grateful. Then she frowned.

"Our first daughter? How many do we have?"

Jess and Ben both looked down at Eric, eyebrows raised. Then Jess looked at Ben and sighed. He smiled and pulled her away.

Eric hugged Angel tight. For a moment, she got the distinct impression that, once again, Eric was much older than his years. She felt comforted, however. She hugged him back. Then she pulled away and looked at Alex.

"Hey, kiddo. I'm coming back, so don't go thinking you get my room."

Alex nodded.

Jess and Ben kneeled in front of Alex last. Jess cried.

"We're *all* coming back, Alex," she said. He hugged his mother's neck, tight. She hugged him back.

Jess looked at Eric, over her son's shoulder. She nodded to him, and he nodded back.

"He likes to play hide-and-seek," she whispered. "A billion times, okay?"

Eric nodded again, his eyes brimming with tears. He took Alex's hand, and the two boys stood and watched as Ben, Jess, and Angel boarded the transport.

***

Kate and Alma said goodbye to Grace, who hugged Alma tight. She had a pack full of medical equipment with her, for the field, in case it might be needed. Malcolm hugged Kate and Alma as well.

Hanley walked up to Alma, his face already tear-streaked from saying goodbye to Martin, Ben, and Jess. He hugged her.

"I'm glad we have a doctor going down there," he said.

"Yeah, well," Alma said, her voice shaking, "I sure hope we don't need one."

"We'll see," Hanley said, looking sad. "Who knows?"

Aaron walked up to Alma and hugged her next. He also hugged Kate.

"Be careful, huh?" he said.

Soon after that, Kate and Alma boarded the transport.

***

Arnold and Jenny hugged Mal, then turned him over to Jemma for safe keeping. Mal was more than happy to go with Mara and Althea, for he played with them often. Jenny and Arnold didn't say goodbye to anyone, really, other than Malcolm and Grace. They believed they would be seeing everyone again in only a few short hours' time. They quickly boarded the transport, before leaving became any harder than it already was.

***

Sarah was the only one left who hadn't boarded the transport. She handed Burne over to Grace and Malcolm, then stood in Aaron's arms for several minutes. He whispered in her ear.

"I should be going, like Ben. Like Arnold, like Kate. I shouldn't be letting you go."

"Aaron, this is how it's meant to be," she said, looking in his eyes, her face full of love.

"Are you sure you don't see me there, with you?" He looked at her, his eyes desperate. "I could go anyway," he said, his eyes filling with tears. "This isn't right. I can't let you go alone."

"No. Eleven people. That's it. That's all I see, Aaron. You aren't supposed to be there. You have to trust me."

"I do. You know I would go, though, right? You know I'd go anywhere with you?"

"I know."

"Do you?" He looked at her, his eyes searching. "Arnold won't let Jenny go alone," he said, shaking his head.

"But I see him there. I don't see you."

"I would die for you, Sarah. I'm going."

"No!" Sarah yelled.

Those who remained in the cargo bay all looked at Sarah and Aaron, wondering.

"No," Sarah said again, her voice softer now. "Aaron, if you love me, you'll trust me. You have to stay here."

"Why?"

"Because. I can't explain it. I just know, this is how it's supposed to be."

"I'm supposed to let my wife go on a mission alone, without me?"

"Yes," Sarah said, and kissed him passionately. "I love you, Aaron," she breathed.

Then she turned and boarded the ship, as Aaron looked on, once again feeling useless and weak. As she climbed the ramp, he felt overcome with emotion and desperation. He suddenly felt as if he couldn't breathe, physical agony filling him up. His heart broke. It was simply too much, watching her walk away from him, to go on mission alone. He couldn't do it.

"Sarah!" he screamed, rushing up the ramp.

She ran down, meeting him halfway and they crashed into each other's arms, kissing madly. Everyone looking on began to cry.

"I can't," Aaron cried. "I can't let you go alone. Please understand, Sarah."

"I'm sorry! I'm sorry!" she hitched.

"So am I. I'm going with you, Sarah. I'm going with you, and you can't stop me."

"I know," she cried.

Aaron never said goodbye to anyone in the cargo bay. Jaw set, face determined, he firmly took hold of Sarah's hand and turned with her, boarding the transport.

No one knew he was going to leave, even Earl. He looked on, watching his best friend run up the ramp, to hug Sarah. Then Earl watched in shock and disbelief as Aaron disappeared onto the transport ship. He never even had the chance to say goodbye.

13

Rafferty boarded the transport and immediately placed Mara in the far-left corner seat, closest to the cockpit, securing her in. Then he went into the cockpit to power up. Soon after, Martin entered. He sat on the far-left, next to Mara. Rafferty left the door open. He turned and nodded at Martin, as he harnessed himself in. Martin shrugged, feeling silly as he buckled his seatbelt. *Old habits die hard,* he figured.

A few minutes later, Ben, Jess, and Angel entered the transport. Ben sat next to Martin. Angel sat next to her father, and Jess sat on the other side. They were in almost the same seats they sat in ten years ago, Jess realized. The only difference now was, instead of Sarah sitting with them, at age eleven, Angel sat with them. She was only nine.

"Ben," Jess said, looking wistful. "The last time we sat here, Angel was still inside me. Sarah was in her place."

Ben looked at Jess and smiled. Then he looked down at Angel and cupped her face in his hands.

"You okay, sweetie?" Angel nodded, smiling up at her father. He loved her so much.

Martin sat with his eyes closed, meditating.

Next to board the ship were Kate and Alma. Alma sat next to Jess, who smiled, taking her hand. Kate took Alma's other hand. Jess also held Angel's hand, and Angel held her father's, so everyone now held each other's hand, in a chain, except Martin and Ben. Martin took Mara's hand, however, and Rafferty watched, giving him a grateful nod.

Arnold and Jenny came next. They sat on the right side of the cabin, nearest the cockpit. Arnold took hold of Jenny's hand, and both closed their eyes.

Everyone turned to look a few minutes later, as they heard the muffled sound of Aaron's voice yell out Sarah's name from the entrance. A minute later, they all watched in surprise as both Sarah and Aaron appeared inside the cabin.

The couple sat down next to Arnold and Jenny, Aaron sitting last, on Sarah's left. His face looked grim and set with determination. Jess searched his eyes, but he looked beyond her, at the wall over her shoulder. Her eyes went to Sarah's face, next. Sarah briefly met her gaze and smiled, looking sad, but comforted, nonetheless.

A few minutes later, Rafferty stood and walked out into the cabin. He looked at Sarah, and saw Aaron sitting with her, holding her hand. He frowned. Sarah smiled, nodding.

"It's okay, Rafferty. I can keep everyone safe."

"It's not right," Earl said, appearing inside the cabin. Everyone turned to look at him. "It's not right, keeping people from going that want to."

Earl walked over to Sarah and knelt, looking at her gently. He smiled.

"Sarah, I love you. You saved my life once. You're the wife of my best friend. I love you like you were my own sister. And I know you have a gift. You know things. And you've named the people that you feel need to go. But just because you don't see certain people, doesn't mean they shouldn't go. Everyone you say needs to go, is here, right?"

Sarah nodded, smiling. Earl nodded back. He stood to address everyone now.

"Everyone Sarah said *needs* to be here, is here. So, that's good. That's how it's supposed to be, for whatever reason. But there are others who *want* to go. And this is a team effort, correct?" Earl didn't wait for an answer.

"Anyone who truly wants to go on this mission, should be able to go. So long as the people Sarah says *need* to be here are going, everything should be okay. A few extra seats being filled shouldn't matter, should it? No one should be excluded from going, if they want to be here. That ain't right."

"Earl's right," Hanley said. He now stood in the entrance to the cabin, eyes solemn. "Don't worry, I'm not going. But anyone who really wants to, should be able. Everyone should be free to choose."

"I never meant to exclude anyone," Sarah said. "I only meant for the people I feel need to be here, to go. I never meant to dictate or lay a firm hand down. I'm sorry." Sarah hung her head in shame. "I don't know everything. I see some things. But I don't see everything. I missed people's hearts." A tear slipped down her cheek.

"It's okay," Earl said. "But just because you didn't see Aaron, as someone who *needs* to be here, doesn't mean he *shouldn't* go with you. You're his *wife*. It's *his* choice. If we're supposed to go on faith, and part of that is following your heart, my heart tells me, the more people we take, and the more abilities we have at our disposal, the safer we'll be. Look, all I know is, if people are running onto the ship at the last second, then maybe *this* is how it's all supposed to be? Crazier things have happened, right? Besides, aren't we getting a little close on the time?"

He looked at Rafferty, who nodded, looking nervous. Earl went to Aaron and motioned for him to stand. He quickly did, and Earl hugged him tight, clapping his back with his hands.

"You were gonna leave without saying goodbye?" he said, over his back.

"It wasn't planned out," Aaron said, pulling away to look at him.

"I know. And I also know Sarah will keep you safe and bring you back home," he nodded. "So, I can whip your ass at poker for another ten years."

Aaron nodded, smiling. Earl quickly said goodbye and good luck to everyone, then left the ship. Hanley looked at everyone and quickly nodded, saying goodbye to the air. As he walked back down the ramp, he sent his thoughts to Rafferty, letting him know he'd clear everyone out of the cargo bay immediately.

As soon as Hanley was off the ship, he did just that, eschewing everyone out of the cargo bay, so the transport could depart without any further delay. Unbelievably, they were still right on schedule.

Rafferty looked at everyone, briefly, then nodded.

"In a few minutes, we'll exit the cargo bay. Most of you know what it feels like, when we first get underway. A little drop, no big deal. I'll be in the cockpit, you won't be able to talk to me," Rafferty looked at Mara. "It'll take about ten minutes. Then you'll feel another drop. That's us, landing. I'll come back out then, and we'll go from there. Are we ready?"

"Yes," Jess said, answering for everyone. "Let's go."

Rafferty said nothing more. He entered the cockpit and quickly closed the door. Everyone was harnessed in now. About a minute later, they felt their stomachs flop, momentarily, and their heads swam for a few seconds, feeling disoriented. Then everything felt normal again and they all knew they flew on their way down to Hesperia.

***

Everyone on the ship immediately went back to the common room and sat down on the various couches. Half of The Society was gone. The ship seemed empty. Hanley and Rachel sat on a couch with Eileen and Robert. Ezra and Roslyn sat with Vera and Jemma, and Jemma held Willa on her lap. Althea, Dorian, Mal, and Innis sat on a third couch by themselves. Grace and Malcolm sat on a fourth couch with Burne. A fifth couch had been added to the common room over a year before. Earl sat with Eric and Alex.

There was nothing to do but wait. If things went smoothly, the transport should be back within two hours, perhaps a bit longer. It wasn't so long to wait, Hanley stated. He began shuffling cards to play crazy rummy, which as many people could play as wanted to. After attempting to play for about ten minutes, however, the game was ended, as no one could concentrate.

Everyone waited in silence, each person lost in thought, desperate for the transport ship to return. No one knew that the transport would not be returning to dock in the cargo bay of the Grayling's ship for much longer than a few hours. They couldn't know it, but they would also be waiting for much longer than two hours, before seeing any of their friends again. The next two hours, however, would be the longest of all their lives.

***

Everyone sat in silence for the first several minutes. Most of the people on board couldn't help but recall their last trip on the transport. The only people sitting there who hadn't been present ten years ago, were Arnold, Mara, and Angel. Everyone else immediately relived the events of that fateful night, a decade now past, as soon as they felt the old, familiar flopping feeling inside their stomachs.

Martin remembered the horrible moment the sniper's thoughts became clear to him and the sinking feeling of dread that came over him, as he yelled for Alma and Lucia to run. He looked over at Alma and saw the look of sadness in her eyes, as he heard her also remembering that night.

Alma sat holding Kate's hand, looking down at the floor, to the spot where she'd held Lucia's lifeless body in her arms, and silently cried. Kate squeezed her hand gently.

Jess stared at the floor, to the spot where Jesus's body had lain. She could almost see the trail of blood as it spread from under his body. She sighed and shuddered, not even aware she did so. Ben looked at her, then to where her eyes looked, and he knew what she was thinking. He closed his eyes, remembering how heavy Jesus's body felt in his arms, and the warm, wet feeling as the front of his shirt became soaked in blood. His stomach flopped, despite the fact they had taken off several minutes ago.

Aaron looked at Sarah, wondering what her thoughts were. Martin spoke, suddenly, making everyone jump.

"She doesn't remember anything," Martin said, looking at Aaron. "She was sleeping the whole time."

Aaron looked at Sarah, remembering. She looked around at everyone's faces, feeling sad. Of course, she learned about everything that had happened on board the transport, once they were on board the Grayling's ship. She'd attended the funerals along with everyone else.

"She was sleeping because she'd worn herself out, getting us out of the facility, and past all those soldiers." Martin nodded to Sarah, his eyes shining with tears, full of love.

"I'm sorry," Sarah said. "I wish I'd been awake. I could have saved Jesus and Lucia."

"No," Ben said. "You couldn't. You were exhausted, Sarah."

"It wasn't your fault," Alma said. She looked at Sarah, nodding. "Is that what you've thought, all these years? That it was your fault?"

Sarah looked down at her own hands. Aaron hugged her and kissed her head. He whispered in her ear. No one knew what he said, except for Martin, who smiled. Aaron was good for Sarah. He loved her with all his heart.

"It wasn't your fault, Sarah," Ben said. "It was mine. I should have realized there would be an escape protocol."

"Ben, it wasn't your fault, either," Jess said.

"It wasn't anyone's fault, except the man who shot at us," Aaron said. "No one knew that was going to happen. Just like we don't know what might happen on Hesperia."

"Look, everyone who came, knew the risks," Arnold spoke up. "Everything that's happened over the last ten years, Hell, over the last twenty, has led to this moment—to do one simple task. All the pieces that have fallen into place to get us here were never simple. But here we are. And in about ten minutes, we'll be on Hesperia, and Jess will pulse. Everything's going to be over, in less than half an hour."

"No one's going to die, not this time," Sarah said. Her jaw was set. "I'm stronger now than I was ten years ago. I can protect everyone."

"Everyone on the transport," Arnold said, nodding. "But Jess and Ben are walking to the city. They'll be too far away for you to cover them, too."

"But we'll be fine," Jess said, looking at Angel, attempting to comfort her. "Harold told me I would succeed, and that I would live."

"He told you, *you* would live," Arnold said. He looked at Ben, then quickly looked away.

Jess frowned, looking at Ben, then back at Arnold. Arnold looked at Jenny, then closed his eyes.

"I came knowing anything could happen, anything could go wrong. But Sarah says I'm supposed to be here, for whatever reason. Even if it's just to support Jenny. But I know something could go wrong."

"Nothing is going to go wrong," Jess said, her voice rising. "Ben will be with me. I'll be shielding him along with myself. If I live through the blast, so will Ben."

"What about afterwards," Arnold said. "Did you ever think about that? When you and Ben are walking back to the transport."

"The Bailon will already be gone," Jess said, her voice even louder now.

"We don't know that," Arnold said. "I'm assuming they won't all be dead, because otherwise, why are the rest of us here?"

"For support!" Jess yelled.

"Everybody shut up!" Alma screamed. "God!"

Everyone sat quietly then. No one spoke for several moments. The silence was suffocating. Martin finally broke it.

"If there are any Bailon still alive, after Jess pulses, I'll hear them," Martin said. "Especially if they try to surround the ship."

"And I'll protect everyone, so they won't be able to use their weapons," Sarah said.

"But no one will be able to warn Ben and Jess," Arnold said, his voice still argumentative. "I'm not trying to upset anyone. I'm just trying to prepare everyone for the possibility that something could go wrong, no matter how hard we try to avoid that. We need to be ready to accept whatever outcome happens from this mission. It's possible, even, that Jess could be the *only* person to survive."

"No," Jess said, her voice shaking. "Eric and Angel get married. Angel survives, for certain, as well."

"Fine, then," Arnold said, his voice gentle, but firm. "Then you and Angel will survive. No one else on board this ship ever had that guarantee. Everyone else on board should have come, knowing there's a possibility they might not live."

"But Sarah will use her ability," Martin repeated. He didn't dare tell anyone about his son's guarantee on his own life. It wouldn't be fair to anyone else, he knew, as scared and nervous as they all now seemed. It certainly wouldn't help to counter Arnold's argument, but might spur him on even further in his rantings.

"Stop assuming everything will be okay!" Arnold yelled.

"What are you trying to do, Arnold?" Jess yelled. "Are you trying to upset everyone?"

"No, I'm just trying to make everyone realize it may not go perfectly."

"We know that already!"

"Do you?!" Arnold screamed.

"Of course! But just as you seem to want to assume everything's going to go wrong, on the converse side, everything could go perfectly, no one dies, and we return to the ship with everyone still perfectly healthy!" Jess yelled.

"Either one could happen, or anything in between!" Arnold yelled back.

"Shut up!" Alma screamed again. "For the love of God, just shut up! No one knows what's going to happen, okay? Everyone could die. Everyone could live. Maybe the Bailon are down there waiting for us and want to throw us a party. Maybe there's a three-ring circus down there, and we'll all have popcorn and dance. Just shut-the-fuck-up!" She stomped her feet to each word of her last sentence, utterly enraged.

Everyone sat in silence again, for over thirty seconds, taking in Alma's statements. Then Martin snickered. Kate laughed. Aaron shook his head, smiling. Arnold stared at Alma, his face frozen in shock. Jess saw his face and laughed. Ben hugged her and shook, laughing silently.

Jess looked at Alma, loving her. Alma always could say the right thing to lighten up the mood. Then Jess frowned.

"Alma?" she said, still frowning.

"What?" Alma still looked pissed off.

"What's your last name?"

Alma stared at Jess for several moments, then her frown broke, and a slight smile played across her lips.

"Alvarez."

Everyone sat in silence for several more moments. Then Alma spoke again.

"Lucia Maria Alvarez. Her initials were LMA. She used to say it stood for *'love my ass.'*" Alma shook her head. "I don't know what that was all about."

"What are your initials?" Aaron asked.

"Oh, you'll love this," Alma said, smiling even wider. "I'm Alma Alessandra Alvarez. Triple A, dude."

"Really?" Aaron asked.

"Yeah," Alma nodded. "So, if Rafferty breaks down, I'm all hooked up."

"What's triple A?" Mara asked. Everyone laughed.

"Wow, ten years away from Earth, and we still remember everything," Arnold said. He looked at Alma, his eyes sad and full of apology.

"I'm sorry, Alma. I didn't mean to upset you, or anyone, really. I'm just..." Arnold sighed, shaking his head. "I'm just not sure what's going to happen."

"We all came, knowing the risks," Aaron said, squeezing Sarah's hand tight. "But just because we're erring on the side of victory, doesn't mean we're not aware something could go wrong, Arnold. Everyone knows there are risks."

Arnold nodded. He looked at Jess, his eyes questioning. Jess nodded.

"I know something could go wrong," she said. "I just happen to believe that everything will be okay. Is that so wrong?"

"No," Arnold said, looking sad. "No, there's nothing wrong with that."

"Fine," Alma said. "Then everyone be quiet, now, and let Jess concentrate. She needs to be preparing to become a freakin' Atom bomb, right?"

"You okay?" Ben looked at Jess, his eyes full of concern. She nodded.

"And everyone else needs to be preparing for whatever might happen while Ben and I are gone," Jess said. "Angel, you're going to sit next to Sarah. Mara, too, okay?"

Angel and Mara both nodded.

"Okay, Sarah?" Jess asked.

"Yeah," she said, smiling at the two little girls.

"And Martin?" Jess looked at him. "You should be by the ramp, listening for anything. You'll be able to hear the Bailon, even while they're sleeping, right?"

"Theoretically," Martin said. "Although, they won't be thinking in any language I'll be able to understand."

"But you'll hear them anyway, right?" Jess looked concerned.

"Yeah," Martin said. "And theoretically, after you pulse, I should be able to hear that they're all gone. Plus, you and Ben."

"What do you mean, *'you and Ben?'*" Aaron said.

"When Jess travels through time, it's like, she simply isn't there. I can no longer hear her thoughts. I'll know the moment she pulses, because her mind will disappear from my radar. She and Ben, both. I should also know the moment they arrive back, four minutes later, because their thoughts will pop back on my radar, again."

"Right, and I'll keep you informed, as Ben and I walk back to the transport," Jess said. "And you can be listening for any stray Bailon, and Sarah can use her gift, if that happens, to protect me and Ben, and everyone on the ship. So, no offense, Arnold, but it sounds like we have our bases covered."

A few moments went by in silence again. Then Arnold frowned, opening his mouth.

I know," Jess said, interrupting Arnold, before he could speak, putting her hand up to quiet him. "I know something could go wrong, that we don't know about, but still, we have a good plan, right?"

"Right," Alma said. Sarah and Aaron nodded.

14

Everyone quieted down, suddenly, as they felt a sinking, dropping feeling in their stomachs. They were landing on Hesperia. Everyone's eyes went wide, in sudden fear, surprise, or anxiety. It was time. Already, it was time. A minute suddenly seemed like an eternity. It was only a minute from the time everyone felt their stomachs flop, to the moment the cockpit door slid open, and Rafferty appeared. In that one minute, however, everyone's mind had ample opportunity to go through a thousand different scenarios and play various outcomes through their heads.

Then Rafferty appeared, his face gaunt and pale. His eyes immediately went to Mara, to see if she was okay. She looked at her father, eyes set and solemn. God, he loved her. Everyone looked at Rafferty expectantly.

"It's still dark out," he said. "The sun won't rise for another forty minutes, and even after it does, it will be another thirty minutes or more, before the Bailon begin to venture outside. I've parked about a mile and a quarter down the beach, south of the spot where Jess will pulse. It's a bit further down than I'd originally planned, but it feels right. Safer... Just in case."

Rafferty looked at Jess, then nodded at Ben, who nodded back. Jess's heart drummed away inside her chest. Arnold could hear it. He looked at her, his face covered in worry.

"Jess?" he said, gently. "I'm sorry."

"It's not your fault," she said. "I would have felt this way no matter what anyone said or didn't."

"Everything's going to be okay," he said, smiling in reverence of her. "I was wrong. The Bailon are all asleep. You're going to pulse them all into oblivion, long before any of them ever wake up." His eyes welled with tears.

Jess nodded. Ben held her hand very tight. She thought about this, briefly. Martin smiled.

"Easy there, Ben," Martin winked. "Don't break your wife's hand, huh?"

Ben frowned at Martin, then looked down at Jess's hand. Her fingers were white.

"Oh, sorry."

"I didn't even know I'd noticed," she said, smiling at Ben.

"Okay, we're all nervous," Rafferty said. "But I suggest we just do this and get it over with."

Jess nodded, and so did Ben. Everyone sat, frozen, watching them.

"Everyone, try and clear your minds," Rafferty sighed. "Ben, Jess, and Martin will come with me. Everyone else will stay here."

Martin stood and followed Rafferty, Ben, and Jess to the ship's entrance. The ramp was still closed.

"Martin?" Rafferty motioned for him to stand in front of the ramp. "Can you hear the Bailon?"

Martin closed his eyes, concentrating. He sat for several moments, listening intently. Then he shook his head.

"We must be too far away. I don't hear anything. But that's good, on one front," he said, looking at the three people crowding him. "It means there are no Bailon within a good mile of us."

"Well, I said, we're a mile and a quarter away," Rafferty said.

"Yeah, well, that's beyond my range, you know?" Martin said, sounding annoyed.

"It's not beyond mine," Arnold said, from behind them. He walked over to the door, stood next to Martin, and closed his eyes, listening.

"It's faint, but I can hear them breathing," Arnold said. "Slow, steady breaths. Not the breathing of an animal who's aware it's about to be attacked. They're relaxed. I can hear their hearts, very faintly," Arnold whispered, drawing his words out. He stroked the ramp door, much as Martin had ten years earlier. His eyes remained closed.

"Like a little, feathery whisper, all their hearts, humming together. I can't say for certain that every single one of them is asleep, but they're all relaxed. If even one heart was beating faster, I'd hear it. Like a discord. A dissonance, if you will."

"Great," Jess said, smiling at Arnold, looking at him in awe. "Keep listening, then. You should be able to hear me and Ben, once we're in position to pulse, right?"

Arnold nodded. "I can hear your heart beating," he looked at Jess with sympathy. "I'm sorry, Jess. I'm truly sorry. I was being a jerk."

"Well, now you're being really useful, so it all worked out," she said. "Sorry, Martin."

"It's okay," Martin shrugged. "I might still be able to hear you. When you get into place, I'll probably be able to pick up on your thoughts. Keep in mind, the Bailon extend for over sixty-five miles. Even if I could hear them, I'd only be hearing the ones on the very outskirts of town. Arnold," Martin said. "I guess we just discovered why you're here."

Arnold shrugged, blushing. "It's not so useful. We already knew they'd be asleep. Alma knew that, just by looking at a diagram."

"It doesn't matter," Jess said. "You can hear their hearts, from miles away. I'm going to walk down that beach now, knowing they're asleep, because of you, Arnold. That means something. It means something to me. Thank you, Arnold."

"You're welcome," Arnold whispered, overcome with emotion.

Rafferty turned to Jess and Ben, nodding. "Are you ready?"

Jess sighed, turning to Ben. He took both her hands in his. She looked up into his face.

"Are you certain you want to go with me?"

"Jess, are you kidding?"

"You could stay here, with Angel," she whispered.

"There is no way in Hell I'm letting you walk down that beach alone," he said, his voice shaking.

"Good," Jess sighed, laughing slightly, her voice a nervous and shaky titter.

"You and me, remember?" Ben said. "We go together, Jess."

"I know."

"You have plenty of time," Rafferty said, his voice gentle. "The sun doesn't rise for another thirty minutes."

"No, let's go," she said. "We won't be able to go very fast, in the dark."

"I can see, Jess," Ben said.

"But I won't be able to," she said. "Let's get going."

Jess nodded to Rafferty. He looked at her face with concern for another long moment, then nodded back.

"Okay, I'll go lower the ramp. So long as Arnold is listening, I'll leave the door open. When you're done, just walk back. You should have ample light by then. We'll just... be here waiting. And listening," Rafferty nodded to Arnold and Martin. They both nodded back, smiling at Jess.

Rafferty walked back down the corridor, quickly disappearing. Everyone inside the cabin watched as he went into the cockpit and adjusted a few levers. Then he walked back out of the cockpit and disappeared down the corridor again.

Jess and Ben now stood at the top of the ramp, looking out into darkness. Arnold and Martin stood behind them. Rafferty came up to them, and Arnold and Martin parted for him.

"Anytime you're ready," he said. "Do you know where to go?"

"I'm guessing that heavy glow of heat energy rising from the distance is coming from the Bailon city," Ben said, winking at everyone.

"Great," Rafferty said. "There you go, Arnold. Now we know why Ben is here."

"That's not why," Jess said, gazing at Ben in complete love and rapture.

"Great," Rafferty said again, unperturbed. "Are you ready?"

"Yeah," Jess said, her voice set and strong. "Let's get this over with."

"Good luck," Arnold said.

"Jess," Martin said, "Knock 'em dead."

"Ooh," Jess said, grimacing, "That was a bad one."

"I know, I'm sorry. I'm nervous," Martin said. "Ben? Take care of her. And both of you better come back."

"We will," Ben said.

***

Ben and Jess walked down the ramp and quickly disappeared into the darkness. Arnold kept Martin and Rafferty updated, periodically, about once every minute or so.

Rafferty went back into the cabin, once Ben and Jess were on their way, to report to everyone that they'd left the ship and were on their way to the Bailon city. Everyone just looked at him, their eyes wide and scared. Rafferty nodded at Angel.

"Arnold and Martin are listening. Everything is fine. It will all be over with very soon."

Then Rafferty disappeared down the corridor yet again. He wouldn't come back into the cabin for another forty minutes, and when he did, he would be running for the control room in a panic.

***

Jess followed Ben, allowing him to lead. Everything was pitch black for her. Ben, however, had a nice, amber light to walk by. The energy coming off the Bailon city created a large, arcing dome of light, that rose out of the darkness for him, like a beacon.

***

Arnold listened intently as Jess and Ben made their way closer and closer to the Bailon city.

"I can hear their footfalls in the sand," he said. "Jess's heart is still beating fast. So's Ben's. It might just be the exercise, though," Arnold shrugged. "Still no sign, or rather, sound, of the Bailon waking up, or becoming aware that anything's wrong."

"I can't hear anything, other than Ben and Jess's thoughts," Martin said. "I still don't hear the Bailon at all. Not one single voice."

"It's okay, I can hear them," Arnold reassured Martin. "They're all breathing, all relaxed. As far as I can tell, they're all asleep, just like Alma said."

***

"I feel light," Jess said, barely above a whisper. "Do you feel light?"

"Yes," Ben said. "It's the gravitational pull of Hesperia's magnetic field. It's much stronger than Earth's."

"Shouldn't I feel heavier then?"

"No, not with the stronger electrical current. It positively charges particles. The cells in our bodies react to the ionization in the air. It's hard to explain, but it actually makes you feel like you weigh less."

"Weird," Jess said.

"Yeah, well, look how it affects the Graylings. Without it, their lifespans are cut in half, and more. The positive ionization of the air affects how their cells function. Their bodies have adapted to this environment. Without it, everything falls apart. Now let's go get their planet back for them, hmm?"

"Just keep walking," Jess said, clinging to his hand. "Remember, I can't see anything."

"I know," Ben whispered. He squeezed her hand. "I think we're about halfway there."

***

"Chatty Cathy..." Arnold mumbled. Then he noticed Martin and Rafferty staring at him. "They're almost halfway there," he said. "And they feel light."

Arnold looked at Rafferty and Martin. "Come to think of it, so do I."

"It's the magnetic field of Hesperia," Rafferty nodded. "We've got four thousand microteslas of energy swirling around our feet. It causes positive charging of the particles in the air, so they spread out further. The air feels lighter, and so do we."

"Yeah, that's sort of what Ben said," Arnold said. "That and it's what keeps the Graylings healthy and living longer."

Rafferty nodded.

***

They walked in silence for several minutes, Jess growing more and more anxious. She couldn't see anything. The only sound she could hear was the steady crashing of waves on the beach, to her left.

After about five more minutes, Ben slowed his pace. Jess's heart instinctively sped up again, in anticipation and fear. Suddenly, Ben stopped walking. He stooped down, and Jess followed suit.

"We're here," he whispered.

Jess felt like she couldn't breathe.

***

They're there," Arnold said. "They've stopped walking." He closed his eyes, listening intently. Then he opened them again, sighing.

"Still no sign of the Bailon awakening. Slow, steady breaths, that's all I hear. But Jess is close to having a heart attack, it sounds like."

"I can hear her thoughts," Martin sighed, sounding disturbed. "She's panicking. From this far away, I can still hear her mind. Come on, Ben. Calm her down," Martin whispered. "It's why you're here."

***

Jess's hand felt like ice in Ben's. He could hear her breaths, coming in short, quick bursts. She was starting to hyperventilate. She squirmed next to him in the sand, panicking.

"Jess, look at me," Ben said. Then he sighed, as he realized she couldn't see his face in the darkness.

She was a glowing ember in his eyes, however. He could see her energy, and her face. There was nothing but panic and fear written all over her features. Ben lowered his face toward Jess, until his forehead leaned against hers.

"Listen to my breathing, Jess," Ben whispered. "Listen to it, and breath with me. Remember? Match my breathing, Jess."

He felt her nod against his face, and incredible relief flooded him. At least she was responding to his commands. He took a slow, deep breath and waited for her to follow suit. She did. He held the breath in for several moments, then slowly exhaled, and Jess did the same. They did this, together, for several minutes, before her heart began to slow to a manageable rate. She felt shaky and weak.

"I could really use a Snickers, right about now," she said. Ben laughed.

***

Arnold laughed. Rafferty and Martin stared at him. He looked at them, shrugging an apology.

"She's making jokes," he said, and the two men visibly relaxed. "She did eat, before we left, right?" Arnold looked at Martin and Rafferty in concern.

"I watched her drink down four smoothies," Martin said.

"Oh, good," Arnold said. "Man, Ben is good. Calmed her right down."

Martin nodded, not looking surprised. Rafferty looked a bit concerned, however.

"The sun is beginning to rise. She needs to pulse soon. I don't want to cut it too close."

"She's almost ready, I think," Arnold said. "Ben's getting her ready."

***

"This is it, Jess," Ben said. "Last pulse."

Jess nodded. "One for the ages, right?"

"That's right. You can do this, you know?"

"I know," she said. She looked at Ben, frowning. "I can see you."

Ben looked over his shoulder, at the sun breaking over the horizon. He turned back to Jess, his face pale.

"The sun's rising, Jess. It's time."

"Ten years," she whispered, "and it all comes down to one minute."

She looked at Ben, her eyes solemn. She remembered how she felt, that day in the orchard, when Ben came to her. She remembered how much love she'd felt, seeing his face, and how the entire world fell away. It was all right here, in front of her. She looked at Ben, and felt so much love, she cried.

"Jess?" Ben looked at her in concern. "Are you okay?"

"I'm just getting ready," she said, her voice steady, strong. He loved her so much.

Jess stood then, and Ben stood with her. They quickly climbed the slight, sandy incline, and suddenly, they looked down on the Bailon city. As the first rays of sunlight illuminated the vast expanse of dwellings, both Ben and Jess saw their first real look at what lay in front of them.

It was ugly, what they saw—their view highly disturbing. They both retained the memories in their heads from the Graylings. The city in their minds was white, sparkling and beautiful. The buildings that Jess and Ben looked upon now, barely resembled the Grayling's city. The structures were the same, for the most part, the shapes similar. The buildings, however, were brown and dirty—old and rundown.

Jess and Ben stood on the very outskirts of the town, on a slight dune, looking down into a depression. They both took in the smell, together. They'd been too caught up in their own mental preparations until now, to even notice their environment, beyond each other. They grimaced, and Jess held her nose. In the far-left corner of the city, near the mountain cliffs, a thick, dark, inky column of black, oily smoke drifted up into the sky.

Jess looked around and saw with dawning horror that the sky wasn't green, as in her memories, but a thick, scuddy-brown—the city itself—difficult to see through the thick, brown haze covering it. She looked back to her left again, at the smoke column, and followed it downward, to a thick, black, sludgy line on the ground, that went from the city, directly to the beach, and flowed into the ocean.

"What is that?"

"I don't know," he said, sounding sad.

"This is disgusting. How can anything live like this?"

"I don't know," he said, again. "I thought we were bad, back on Earth."

"How can they have done so much damage, in only a few hundred years?" Jess's voice shook.

"Jess, they didn't come here thinking it was forever. Planets aren't permanent homes to them. They don't view them that way, remember? They were never here to preserve Hesperia. Why would they care?"

"You're right, they don't care," she said, angry now, turning to look him directly in the eyes. "About anything. I'm ready, Ben."

"Jess. Are you sure?"

"Yes. The way I see it, I'm not killing the Bailon." She turned her face back towards the city, no longer looking at him. "I'm putting them out of their misery."

***

"Jeezus, she's ready," Arnold whispered. "The city's a wreck, and she's pissed. She's ready to clean house."

He looked around at Rafferty and Martin. They looked back at him in total shock.

"This is it," he said, in complete wonder. "This is it."

All three men looked out into the breaking dawn, waiting.

***

"Stand behind me, Ben," Jess said. He didn't argue, immediately following her directions.

Jess took a deep breath and gathered every ounce of concentration she had. She closed her eyes and recalled the orchard. She felt her love for Ben. She also felt her love for the Graylings well up inside. Her heart began beating a bit faster, and she took a deep breath, to slow it back down. Ben looked on in wonder, watching Jess work.

The air around them began tingling. Ben noticed it first. Jess never did, her mind fixated on the task at hand. She focused with incredible strength and concentration. She felt angry, furious with the Bailon. She felt both love and anger well up inside, a new experience she'd never felt before. She also felt rage growing in tandem with sadness.

This was supposed to be her new home, for her children to grow up in, and it was decimated. This was also what Earth would become, someday, if she didn't stop the Bailon. She saw the Graylings, on the day of their extermination. She saw the Bailon, with their weapons, and the gruesome images of the Graylings, ripped to pieces, cut to ribbons. She felt sick.

Then, all at once, her mind settled on Ben's face. She saw his eyes, and she felt the strongest emotion her heart contained. She felt hope. Not love, but hope, and it was stronger than anything, for it contained the promise of love within it. Everything was inside Ben's face, inside his eyes. Jess's heart broke open and filled with love and hope, both at the same time. Then, even the hope fell away, and all she felt was love. It swallowed her hope, and love was her entire world. It burst forth, encompassing everything.

Suddenly, all Jess's energy focused, in her mind, into a tiny point of light, not unlike the glowing grain of sand that Ezra always envisioned and felt, while stumbling around inside the darkness of every mind he channeled into.

Just as that glowing point of light became encompassed and burst into shining life, so did the focus of Jess's ability. She felt energy, strong and burning hot, build from the center of her body. Her hands raged with fire, but it did not hurt. She looked out at the city that lay before her, and she could feel the air above it *moving*—roiling, swirling—with building energy.

This was different than any pulse she'd ever released on Earth. She knew that within moments. The process already set in motion, she was merely along for the ride. She channeled her energy, feeling wave after wave of hope and love fill her.

All the while, Ben looked around him, in awe and wonder. The air was thick with ozone and static. Small flashes of dry lightning, like glittering sparks, burst forth all around them, as particles in the air heated, colliding, charging higher and higher. There was no wind, the air thick and hot.

Then the atmosphere seemed to bend. The air became a seemingly solid thing, as the gravitational fields began twisting in subduction, overlapping each other, in layers of thick, transparent energy. Ben watched in amazement, as the energy field formed a visible dome around the expansive area in front of Jess, like a giant droplet of water, covering the entire Bailon city. He watched as lightning bolts arced and flashed in the immediate center of the dome—the air slowly caving inward, toward the ground—a swirling vortex developing inside the eye of a hurricane.

The center of the dome pulled further downward, forming a clear, visible image of what looked like a waterspout—an incandescent energy swirl of highly charged particles, getting ready to channel downward—kicking off a reaction, on an atomic scale. It all happened miles up in the air, away from Jess, yet, she continued channeling energy for miles all around her into that one pinpoint immediately over the center of the Bailon city.

"My God," Ben sighed, in veneration. "She's going to drop it from the center."

***

Over a mile away, Arnold heard this statement and frowned. He had no idea what Ben meant.

***

"Jeezus," Ben whispered, as the sudden reality of what was about to happen fully hit him. "Arnold, if you can hear me, tell Rafferty to close the ramp. I don't think you even have time to get airborne. Tell everyone to seatbelt themselves in!"

***

"What?!" Arnold turned and looked at Rafferty, his eyes grave. "Rafferty, something's wrong. Ben wants you to close the ramp, and tell everyone to seatbelt themselves in. He said something about not getting airborne, too, maybe, 'cause you won't have time?"

"What?" Martin looked pale.

"I don't know, he said something about, 'Jess is going to drop it from the center,' whatever that means?"

Arnold looked at Rafferty, his face full of confusion. Rafferty already squinted, thinking hard.

"Drop it from the center," Rafferty whispered. The gears inside his mind spun in overtime.

"Um, shouldn't you close the ramp, like Ben said?" Arnold looked at Rafferty in sheer panic.

"Drop it from the center… drop it from the…" Rafferty looked at Arnold, his eyes wide with sudden comprehension. His eyes then went to Martin. Martin looked at Rafferty, receiving his thoughts.

"Holy shit," Martin said.

"Shit!" Rafferty *ran*.

"Get in your seats, *now!*" Rafferty yelled over his shoulder. He ran through the cabin, past everyone, as they all watched in complete confusion.

"Put your harnesses on, *now!*" He yelled to everyone, even as he entered the cockpit, madly pulling down on a lever, then up on another one.

Arnold and Martin appeared inside the cabin, looking pale and out of breath. They both sat down in their seats. Jenny looked at Arnold, her eyes wide with fear.

"Are the Bailon coming?!"

"No, but..." Arnold harnessed Jenny in, then himself. "Something's definitely going wrong."

"What is it?!" Alma screamed.

Meanwhile, Rafferty entered the cabin. He sat down next to Mara, harnessed himself in, then took his daughter's hand.

"Uh, you know how I said that Jess sends out an energy arc from her body?" Rafferty said, his voice shaking.

"Yeah?" Several people said in unison.

"Yeah, well. Slight miscalculation. Turns out, apparently, with the increased gravitational field on Hesperia, the energy arc actually forms *away* from Jess's body."

"Huh?" Alma said.

"She's dropping a bomb on the city," Martin said. "Only this time, instead of having a 180-degree arc, it'll drop straight down."

"Like... an actual Atom bomb," Arnold slapped his own forehead ridiculously hard.

"On the center of the city, or close to it," Rafferty picked up. "It might still arc more heavily in a 180-degree pattern, but, the blunt force will send out a 360-degree compression wave."

"Wait, so, we're going to get hit by the bomb?!" Alma screamed.

"The compression wave," Rafferty nodded. "It'll be a fast moving, heated air cannon, with EMP blast. We shouldn't even attempt to get airborne. I don't want to risk losing power and crash back down to ground. We should be protected inside the transport. I've activated the energy shields. They'll be shorted out as soon as the EMP waves over us, but not before shielding us from the compression's main force. But... we'll probably feel a... jolt," Rafferty spoke falteringly.

"How good are these seatbelts, Rafferty?" Martin said. "Because, I recall you saying once, oh, about ten years ago, that they're here more for mental comfort, than any real use?"

"Well," Rafferty said, "I guess we'll find out, huh?"

"Holy shit," Aaron said. "Way to go, Arnold. You just had to say, *'hey, what if something goes wrong?'* Way to go!"

"Hey, this isn't *my* fault! How was I supposed to know she was gonna *'drop it from the center'*...?!" Arnold yelled, making quotation marks in frustration. "I mean, what the heck?!"

"Shut up!" Alma yelled, stomping her feet. "Shut up, shut up, shut up!" She turned to Arnold. "What's going on? Can you hear anything?"

Arnold closed his eyes, listening.

15

Immediately after telling Arnold to get everyone belted in and have Rafferty close the transport ramp, Ben turned his attention back to the energy dome forming over the Bailon city. He started calculating inside his head. With the energy arcing straight downward, it would spiral in a 360-degree pattern, rolling outward with incredible force. The largest amount of energy would be absorbed by the center, then transfer outward, in all directions. Ben estimated that if an arc from Jess's body traveled for over sixty-five miles forward, the same amount of energy, concentrated from the middle outward would decimate anything in its path for thirty-five miles in any direction from the center. Dropping it straight down was a dead guarantee that the entire Bailon city would be destroyed.

"Thirty-five miles should bring the blast zone right up to this hill," Ben sighed. "The EMP will hit the transport, over a mile away, and the compression wave will travel immediately behind. Probably for a good three miles or more. Even if a Bailon were to get out of the city, their weapons would be fried. They'd be completely helpless," Ben whispered to himself.

Suddenly, the air around Ben moved. He stood only a foot behind Jess, but he felt an invisible force shove its way between them, throwing him several feet, down the sandy embankment. He stood up, quickly, and ran back up the dune. He stopped several feet away from Jess. He could see her, inside what appeared to be a cocoon of air. It was solid, he realized, as he tried touching it to push his way through. Some sort of barrier had formed around Jess, and Ben was outside of it.

Jess's eyes were closed. Ben ran at the barrier again and fell. It was all around Jess, now, protecting her, and soon, Ben knew, it would move her out of time and space, to a safe distance from the blast, now surely only moments away.

"Jess!" Ben screamed.

She heard his voice—it sounded so distant—she thought she imagined it. She thought he still stood behind her. She turned to look at him and saw that he wasn't there. Her hands still lay at her sides, but they shook violently, vibrating with the force of energy built up inside, all around, miles above her.

Jess saw Ben, and her heart broke. He stood several feet away, and she could see what looked like a small dome of glass all around her. Ben was outside. The entire gravity of the situation landed upon her in mere moments.

"Ben! Why?"

"It's not your fault, Jessie," he said. A tear tracked down his cheek.

"Ben, I can't stop it," she screamed. "I can't stop it!"

"I know. It's too late. You're not supposed to stop it. This is exactly what you were always meant to do. Don't feel bad."

"Please tell me you'll be okay," she cried.

"I will," he lied. "I have to leave you now, Jessie. I have to, to get back to the transport."

"Okay!" she cried, hysterical. "Okay!"

"I love you, Jess."

"I love you, too, Ben." She locked her eyes on him. "Now, run, Ben! Please! *Run*!"

Ben turned to run, never looking back. Even as he ran, Jess turned back and put all her concentration into holding off the pulse for as long as possible. There was no stopping it now, it had built up too high, but she thought, perhaps, she could give Ben a few minutes, if she concentrated very hard.

***

All of this took place as Rafferty closed the transport ramp and made certain everyone was harnessed in. Arnold listened, once again, after Alma asked him what was going on. By now, Ben ran from the edge of the Bailon city, the mile and a quarter distance back to the transport. He never ran so fast in his entire life. He thought his lungs might burst.

Arnold was too busy with the chaos on board the ship to hear Ben at first. It wasn't until Alma asked him what was happening that he stopped to listen, and realized he could hear Ben, running. Martin, too, could now hear Ben, as he neared closer to the transport. He was still a good half-mile away, however.

"Ben?" Martin said. He looked at Arnold, his face questioning.

Arnold shrugged, shaking his head. "He's running like the wind."

"He's not with Jess," Martin said, his voice thick and sad. His heart broke. Ben talked to Martin as he ran.

Martin looked at Angel, his eyes filling with tears. Angel looked back at him, her face frightened and confused.

"What do you mean, he's not with Jess?" Aaron said, eyeing Martin with a look of dread. "I thought you said she could shield him?"

"Aaron," Sarah said, giving him a stern warning. She tried to take Angel's hand, but Angel pulled it away.

"My daddy's outside? With the blast coming?" Tears welled up and spilled down her cheeks.

Arnold closed his eyes, listening to Ben's labored breathing and pounding heart.

***

Ben spoke to Martin as he ran. He knew he wouldn't make it back to the transport before Jess released the pulse. He knew he'd be caught up in the compression wave. He'd known from the moment he was knocked away from Jess.

Martin, Ben desperately sent his thoughts. *I'm not going to make it. I only have seconds left, I'm guessing. I left Jess, so she wouldn't have to find what's left of my body, after she comes back. I'm still a quarter of a mile away from the transport. Please, don't let Angel see me, either. Please. Send Aaron, Rafferty, maybe. Or yourself. Promise me you won't let either Jess or Angel see what's left of me. Don't let them see, Martin.*

***

Martin looked at Angel, as he heard Ben's thoughts, and the full gravity of what Ben said hit him. His eyes welled with tears. Even Arnold didn't fully understand what was happening. He could hear Ben's labored breathing, as well as his heart beating away inside his chest, but he couldn't hear the gruesome, disturbing thoughts that Ben sent out. Only Martin heard and realized that Ben knew he was going to die—and exactly how—he knew what would happen to his body when the compression wave reached him. His only concern was for Jess and Angel. Ben wanted to spare them from seeing the horror about to befall him. His only thoughts were of his wife and daughter. Martin's heart broke. He buried his face in his hands and sobbed.

"No!" Angel cried, her voice cracking.

"Jeezus!" Arnold suddenly yelled. "Jess is pulsing. Now!"

Angel struggled in her seat, attempting to undo her harness and get out of her chair. Aaron held her firmly by the shoulders, looking at Sarah, his own eyes sad and sunken. Sarah cried inconsolably while trying to help him restrain the little girl.

"Let me go! I have to save my Daddy!"

"It's too late," Arnold said, in wonder and shock.

***

Jess let out a large breath. She'd held off for as long as possible. She wasn't even sure how many minutes had gone by since Ben ran from her side. It felt like an eternity. The process was already set in motion, however. There was no stopping it.

Her body shook with the incredible effort of holding off the pulse. Her mind transported back to the day in the hallway, in front of the

Atrium door, when she'd successfully held back from pulsing. She recalled, however, that she'd sent out a large heat compression, and Ben had been burned badly on his arms, while shielding his face. He'd been covered with several heat blisters that took over two weeks to heal. A few blisters had even left scars on his arms.

Jess thought of Ben, in that moment, even as she felt herself lose the small modicum of control she managed to hold onto for what had truly seemed to be an impossible amount of time. Yet, somehow, she'd managed to hold the pulse off, with the force of her love for Ben.

Now, she lost that control, not knowing whether Ben had made it to the transport or not. She had no real concept of time, or how much of it had passed since last seeing him. She was frozen in the moment, inside her own little cocoon of energy. It was time. She felt it. The sun had risen, and she could see the entire Bailon city, now bathed in sunlight. Her eyes caught sight, perhaps, of figures moving within the dwellings. She wasn't certain, but she thought she saw shadows of dark figures, beginning to emerge deep within the city. The Bailon were waking up, becoming aware that something was happening in the sky above them.

Jess did not feel fear, however. She felt anger. The energy had built up now, to the breaking point. The pulse was imminent, and there was no holding it off any longer. Jess knew this. There was no choice. She didn't throw her hands up and out, so much as they simply moved on their own, driven by the incredible force of her ability. It was the last pulse she would ever send out.

Jess never saw the pulse. She never saw any of them. She only saw what lay in the aftermath, each time. For her, each pulse happened in a moment—although several minutes passed by—for her, everything seemed instantaneous.

Every other pulse, except this one. This one was different.

Jess threw her hands out, and instantly, she was transported in time. With every other pulse, in a split second, everything that had been whole and intact, undamaged in front of her, was simply decimated in the sheer blink of an eye, and she arrived back to the same moment, despite understanding that several minutes had passed.

This time, however, Jess's view *did* change. Her hands flew up, releasing the last of her energy stores, and instead of blinking and simply viewing the decimated landscape before her, she saw nothing but white surrounding her. She floated in an ocean of liquid light— everything blinding white—and her mind swam. She felt giddy and lost.

***

At that moment, the view of the Bailon city was one of sheer oblivion. The Bailon never even knew what happened to them, everything over for their entire race in a split second. The air above the city bent and an audible break could be heard, almost like ripping, bending metal. Then, all the energy in the air above the city fell, dropped in one small point, directly from the center of the air dome. Vast amounts of energy all concentrated into one point—smaller than a molecule—tinier than an atom. White light silently flared, blinding everything. There was nothing but white, and it made no sound.

In an instant, over sixty-five square miles of city were enveloped in a round, white dome of blinding brilliance. In another instant, the flash was over, and a large white cloud of ash and debris, carried on a vast wave of heat energy, slowly fanned out from the center of a crater, straight up into the air, several miles, lazily forming into a mushroom cloud.

A fiery tempest gale rushed through the landscape, flattening every structure within the city, reducing it to ash—everything demolished. Not a single building was left to stand, up into and against the mountains. The compression wave ringed outward, in all directions, flattening trees and any life that might be within several miles of the city.

***

"Everyone hold on!" Arnold yelled. For he could hear Jess's heartbeat, all along, even within her shield. Then suddenly, he heard nothing. Jess's heartbeat didn't slow, it simply stopped.

At that same moment, Martin heard Jess's mind disappear, while listening to Ben send his thoughts, his face still buried in his hands. Only moments had gone by. He heard Jess's mind go, as Ben's last thoughts reached him.

Don't let her blame herself. I knew the risks. Tell Jess it's not her fault.

Martin looked up and over at Arnold. He could no longer hear Jess's thoughts. Arnold looked back at Martin. He could no longer hear Jess's heart.

"She released the pulse," Arnold said, his voice quaking in awe and dread. Martin nodded.

Angel still cried and Sarah and Aaron, together, held her tight. Rafferty held onto Mara. Both their eyes were closed. Arnold turned to hold Jenny. Martin sat, eyes closed, with Kate and Alma, who held each other. Everyone waited for the blast to hit.

"Here it comes," Martin said, his voice thick.

Goodbye, Martin, Ben sent. Then Martin could no longer hear Ben's thoughts—his mind—erased.

A moment later, the transport bolted, the jolt so quick and violent, they were thrown upside down in an instant, accompanied by the loud, ripping sound of bending, tearing metal.

Luckily, the harnesses managed to hold everyone in place. Those on the left side, however—Martin, Kate, and Alma—had their heads thrown violently back against the chair rests. Despite the soft cushioning, all three were knocked unconscious. Everyone on the right side found themselves hanging, suspended in midair, shell-shocked, dazed, whiplashed. The transport had rolled over twice, and spun counter-clockwise, coming to rest at a ninety-degree angle, on the left side.

It was all over so quick, everyone suspended silently for several moments, trying to gather their wits enough to understand. Seven people hung, harnessed into their seats, suspended on the new ceiling, directly over the remaining three, unconscious passengers, now lying flat on their seatbacks, on the now-floor. No one could undo their restraints, as their bodies' weight made this impossible. There was too much tension on the lines to pull the harness's latch open. Rafferty mustered every bit of strength he had and used his right arm to push Mara's body back, and up, against her seat. This loosened the weight on the line just enough, she could unlatch her harness. She fell, and Rafferty held onto her hand, his own arm yanked down by Mara's weight. He cried out in pain, as his right shoulder dislocated.

Rafferty had no choice but to let his daughter go. She still dangled several feet above the seats on the left side. She fell onto one of them now, and quickly straightened, smiling up at her father.

"I'm okay!" she yelled up to him.

Aaron repeated the process that Rafferty had performed with Mara, this time, with Angel. This time, however, Angel held onto the loosened harness line, and Mara caught her dangling feet, helping her down. Arnold helped Jenny get loose, and slowly, everyone was unharnessed.

Mara went to Martin, Kate, and Alma and immediately healed them. Martin looked at Arnold, his eyes sad. Arnold looked back, reading his thoughts, simply from the look on his face. He shook his head. He sent his thoughts to Martin.

I don't hear Ben's heart. I don't hear him at all. I don't hear Jess, either.

Martin nodded. He knew Ben was gone. He also knew that in a few short minutes, Jess would reappear and begin heading back to the transport. Ben was very clear, in his last thoughts to Martin. He didn't want Jess to see his body, to see what happened to him. He didn't want

Angel to see, either.

Alma went to Rafferty and worked his shoulder back into place, as he cried out in pain. Mara came over and placed her hand on her father's shoulder. Immediately, the pain was gone, and Rafferty hugged his daughter. She looked at him, her face full of love. She'd wanted to come, in case her father needed her healing ability, and now, she had fulfilled that action. She was happy.

Martin looked at Rafferty and motioned for him to come over, pulling him awkwardly into the askew cockpit, keeping his voice low. Arnold came to listen as well, then Aaron. The women instinctively pulled away, allowing the men to do their work, make their plans.

Kate, Alma, Jenny, and Sarah, all four, pulled Angel and Mara to the far corner, closest to the entrance corridor. Mara hugged Angel, who still cried silently. Sarah thought about using her ability to make Angel feel better, but then thought better of it. Whatever plans the men were formulating, they would need to concentrate, without feeling giddy.

***

"We need to go out, about a quarter mile from here, and get Ben's body," Martin said. "Whatever's left of it, anyhow."

"What?" Arnold looked at Martin, his eyes wide.

"Ben sent me his thoughts, before…" Martin trailed off, shaking his head. "He knew he was going to die. He knew he'd be caught in the blast. He only ran from Jess, so she wouldn't have to find his body after. He knew he wouldn't make it back to the transport in time. He wants us to get his body, and move it, so Jess won't see. He doesn't want Angel to see, either."

"He told you that?" Aaron looked like he was going to vomit.

Martin nodded. "It's his last request. We have to honor it. We can't let Jess walk back and find him. We need to get out there and find him first."

Rafferty nodded, a tear slipping down his cheek.

Martin looked at Arnold. "Arnold, can you hear the Bailon?"

Arnold listened, completely baffled and awed. He shook his head.

"No," he said, smiling. "I don't hear them at all. Not one single heartbeat. Not one single breath. I hear nothing. I can't hear a single Bailon."

"Okay, but we can't assume that means they're all dead," Aaron said. "Things have already gone wrong. We should assume the worst. If we're going to get Ben's body, we need to take Sarah, in case any Bailon come upon us."

"No, if we do that, we'll be leaving people behind on the transport without Sarah's protection," Arnold said.

Rafferty nodded emphatically. "I'm not leaving Angel and Mara without protection. Ben wouldn't want that. Whoever goes to get his body, goes without protection." Rafferty looked at the three men around him, nodding.

"Fine," Aaron said. "The men will all go, and Sarah will stay here, to keep everyone else safe."

16

Aaron, Martin, and Arnold stumbled to the transport entrance. The ramp was still closed. Rafferty went into the control room and tried the switches. Jenny watched him, a look of trepidation on her face. Rafferty shook his head, swearing a short string of expletives under his breath. He turned to look at Jenny, apologizing.

"Sorry."

"It's okay. I think the situation calls for it. The ship's broken, isn't it?"

"The EMP wiped us out. We're basically sitting inside a dead hunk of metal."

"Can Angel fix it?" Jenny asked, looking hopeful.

"No. It's not a simple matter of putting broken pieces back together. Things are *fried*. There's nothing to put back together. New pieces need to be built back in. There's no fixing it. We're stuck."

"No, we're not," Jenny said. She quickly walked to the entrance, where the other three men stood, waiting.

Arnold saw Jenny and ran, hugging her. She pushed him away, looking at Aaron and Martin.

"You guys need to move."

"Why?" Aaron asked.

"The controls are fried," Rafferty said, arriving at the entrance. "I can't get the ramp open."

"But I can," Jenny said. "Everyone needs to move back."

Everyone moved back inside the entryway to the cabin. Arnold looked on, curious. He'd never seen Jenny use her ability before. She hadn't used it in over ten years. She concentrated now, focusing. There was no other way out of the transport. She had to pull this off.

Half a second later, an explosive boom echoed down the corridor, shocking everyone into covering their eyes. Bright sunlight streamed onto everyone's face, as the ramp flew outward, landing in several pieces on the sand below.

Arnold laughed in euphoric disbelief, and rushed up to his wife, hugging her tight. This time, she hugged him back.

"Guess we know why you're here, now," Arnold said in wonder, pulling away, caressing her face. He turned and nodded at Sarah, who gazed at the two of them, smiling.

"We need to go," Martin said. "Jess should be back by now. She could be walking back, already."

Arnold let go of Jenny and turned towards the ramp opening. He looked down at the sand, several feet below, frowning. Aaron walked up to his side, curious.

"Afraid of heights, Arnold?" Aaron said, sounding doubtful.

Arnold shook his head. "How long has it been since Jess pulsed, you think?"

Rafferty shrugged. Martin shook his head.

"Way more than four minutes, though, right?" Arnold looked at everyone, his face concerned.

"It's been at least ten," Jenny said.

Everyone stood crowded at the entrance now, including the two children. Arnold took no notice of this, however. He listened intently.

"I don't hear Jess, at all," Arnold said. "No heartbeat, no breathing." He looked at Martin.

Martin listened, then shook his head. "I can't hear her thoughts. They're gone, like they are when she's traveling in time. Nothing."

Arnold shook his head again. He looked at everyone, then his eyes landed on Angel, his face falling, as she sobbed loudly, anew.

"My Mommy's gone, too?" She hitched, choking, looking like she might pass out. Mara held her up.

"She's probably still traveling," Arnold said.

"For ten minutes?" Aaron said, ignoring Angel. "She's never been gone that long before."

"Yeah, and she also never released a pulse this big before," Rafferty said. "Or dropped it from the center."

"Okay, so she's traveling for longer this time," Arnold said, nodding at Angel and looking hopeful. "She's just not back yet."

"Regardless, we need to get going," Rafferty said.

Arnold peered below once more. Aaron looked at him again. "Heights?" he repeated.

"No," Arnold sighed. "Holy Jehoshaphat, I'm gonna have a heart attack."

"What?" Aaron said, looking back at everyone else.

"Martin, do you...?" Arnold started to ask, then stopped.

Martin came up to Arnold, on his left side, while Aaron still stood on his right. Rafferty came up and stood behind them, looking infinitely confused.

"I don't... believe it...," Arnold said. He looked at Martin. "Do you hear anything?" He eyed Martin, who frowned, looking more and more confused.

"You hear Jess?" Martin asked. He heard nothing. Not a single thought from beyond the transport.

"No," Arnold sighed, swaying on his feet. "I think I hear Ben."

"What?!" Aaron said.

"I hear a heartbeat," Arnold said. "It's very faint, very slow. I think it's Ben," Arnold said, sounding sick.

"Let's go," Mara said, pulling on Rafferty's shirt. "Daddy, if he's still alive, I can heal him."

Rafferty looked down at Mara, shock spreading over his face.

"No," Martin said. "Whatever's happened to him, regardless of whether his heart is still beating or not, he made it clear, he wouldn't look suitable to be *seen*," Martin emphasized this last word, eyeing the children.

Angel now stood by Mara, looking urgent and hopeful. She violently pulled on Rafferty's shirt.

"She has to go!" Angel said. "I'm going with you!"

"Daddy, if he's alive, I know I can save him!" Mara said, starting to cry.

"No!" Martin warned. "Your father made it very clear to me that you shouldn't see him. Not like that."

"But he thought he'd be dead, right?" Angel said, her faculties so clear, Martin was taken aback.

"Yeah?" he said.

"But he's *not* dead," Angel said. "So, let's go, and save him. It's why Mara's here."

"Go!" Sarah said, her eyes wide. "I said Mara should be here and look! Ben needs her, so go! GO!"

***

Rafferty was the first to jump. Next came Arnold, then Aaron. Rafferty helped Mara down, then Angel came next. Suddenly it became a free-for-all. Sarah came next, followed by Jenny, Kate, and Alma. Martin went last.

"Well, this makes sense," he said. "No one's left behind, without Sarah's protection."

"We all go together," Sarah said.

They walked briskly. Arnold led the way. He could still hear Ben's heart beating, faintly. The group walked for several minutes, in silence.

"We're going to make it in time, I know we are," Alma said. She fidgeted with her medical equipment.

"Anything?" Kate asked.

Alma shook her head. "Everything's fried, like the transport." Then she looked, in wonder, as the screen of her handheld came to life.

"Oh, great," Alma said, her voice wry. "The analyzer works. We can see what's wrong, but we can't fix it."

"We don't need to fix it," Kate said. "We have Mara."

***

In the distance, Arnold saw something lying in the sand. He immediately knew what it was. They had all walked roughly an eighth of a mile. Ben had almost made it back to the transport. Another two minutes and he might have been able to get up the ramp. Aaron thought this, and Martin heard him.

"He was so close," Aaron said.

Martin nodded. Then he heard Rafferty's thoughts and spoke, even as they all continued towards Ben's body.

"It's not your fault, Rafferty. If we'd parked closer, the compression wave would have hit all the harder. For all you know, then it would have knocked Mara unconscious, or worse. Then we wouldn't have had her healing ability, for your shoulder, or anything else. You did what you thought was right."

Rafferty opened his mouth to argue against Martin's logic, but Martin stopped him before he could even try.

"No, Rafferty. You decided to park further away as an extra safety precaution and look what happened. Look how hard we got hit by the unexpected compression wave, even with the extra distance. You didn't do this to Ben, Rafferty. All you did was probably save the lives of all of us onboard the transport." He paused, then interjected one final time, to shut Rafferty up for good. "Besides," he leveled the mechanic with the severity of his tone. "No one had any clue that Ben wouldn't be safe inside the forcefield with Jess, so just stop your guilt, right here and now."

Rafferty sighed, but never said a word.

The entire group ran up to Ben and surrounded him. Many turned away after only a cursory glance. Martin shook his head. "I still don't hear anything. His mind is gone. Not even unconscious. Gone."

"He's probably brain-dead," Alma said, bending down and running the analyzer over his head and body. She sucked in her breath.

Several people turned away, as soon as they saw him. Ben's body was sunken into the sand, face down, pushed by the force of the compression wave. From the misshapen form of his skull, everyone could see that he'd been effectively flattened.

He looks like a human pancake, Aaron thought, and Martin heard him, turning to vomit into the sand behind him. He turned back, wiping his mouth on his sleeve. He looked at Angel and motioned to Sarah, standing next to her.

"Turn her away, Sarah," Martin said.

Angel stared down at her father, eyes wide and unblinking. Mara also stared down at him, her face pale and sickly, shaking her head.

"I can still hear his heart," Arnold said. "It's so faint. I think he's going."

"No!" Angel screamed, crying hysterically.

Alma continued running her analyzer over Ben's body, shaking her head, tears brimming over and down her cheeks. Martin heard her thoughts.

"It was the sand," he said. "When the compression hit him, it pushed him down. It would have killed him immediately, but the sand gave way, just enough. A harder surface, he would have been completely crushed."

"He still is," Alma said, crying, her voice thick. "It did enough damage, anyway. Every single bone in his body is broken. Every single one. His skull is crushed. He's brain-dead. The only reason he's not dead, is there's no internal bleeding. Somehow, the sand stopped his internal organs from being crushed, or burst open."

Sarah closed her eyes and turned her head away. She also vomited, quietly. Martin looked at her with sympathy.

"Honestly, though," Alma said, dreamily, in shock. "It's a miracle he's even still alive."

"It got us all here, though, didn't it?" Arnold said, sounding hopeful. He looked at Mara.

"Mara, you can heal him, right? You can save him?"

Mara stepped forward, falling on her knees. She shook her head.

"This isn't healing," she said, looking up at Martin and Arnold. "I can regrow tissue, cells. I can even fix a cracked bone, but..." she trailed off.

"Ben's bones aren't cracked," Alma argued. "They're broken. Not just a few fractures. They're all in pieces. He shouldn't even be *alive*."

"He's not," Arnold said, closing his eyes, tears tracking down his face. "His heart just stopped."

Mara began to cry. She looked up at Martin, in pain.

"I can't fix this," she said, rocking rhythmically. "It's not healing. It's not healing."

"No," Angel said, kneeling next to Mara. "It isn't."

Angel looked at her father's body in wonder. She could feel her ability rising within. She felt the broken pieces calling her, just as the shards of glass had done, once. They were jagged bits, and solid parts.

They didn't need to be grown anew. They were puzzle pieces, broken apart. She could solve this, she felt it, and she believed.

"I can put him back together again," Angel whispered.

Sarah knelt beside her, looking at Angel in awe and reverence. She placed her hand on Angel's shoulder, sending her ability into the young girl. Angel no longer felt afraid. She felt confident, strong, able. She felt happy and euphoric. Yet, at the same time, she felt an urgency, and she used the strength of Sarah's comfort to concentrate on the task at hand. Instead of feeling muddled, her mind felt focused and crisp.

Everyone looked on in dazed shock, as Sarah and Angel worked together. Angel gently set her hands on her father's body and sensed within. The broken pieces sang to her—organic—but also fixed, hard. They could be reattached, reassembled. Angel felt it. The pieces hummed to her, much like the glass had.

Everyone stared in wonder as they all heard a light harmonic drone emanate lightly from inside Ben's body, muffled, but audible. Several different notes reached everyone's ears. They watched in complete disbelief as Ben's body appeared to inflate, the bones restored— thousands of infinitely small pieces suddenly pulled back into one—all at once. It happened in an instant. Then the noise stopped, and Angel removed her hands.

Alma quickly ran the scanner over Ben's lifeless body again. She shook her head, laughing out loud.

"I don't believe it," Alma whispered. "She did it. Ben doesn't have a single broken bone in his body."

"But he's still dead," Arnold said. "His heart isn't beating."

"His skull was crushed," Alma said. "His skull is fixed, but his brain is still…" she trailed off.

Mara came over and knelt, next. She placed her hands lightly on Ben's head. She stayed that way for over a minute. Then she looked up at Alma, smiling, yet, still sad.

"That's okay now, too," she said. "But I can't make his heart start beating."

"Well, can't you just do CPR or something?" Aaron said.

"No," Alma said, sounding defensive. "His heart isn't beating, Aaron. My equipment isn't working. Do I look like I have a defibrillator working?"

"I can do it," Kate said. Alma stared at her for several long moments, thinking.

"Everyone's here for a reason," Arnold said, sounding wondrous. "Kate is here to help save Ben. I know it."

Arnold searched out Sarah's face and nodded, looking for support. Sarah only shrugged.

Alma looked at Kate, nodding. Kate nodded back. "Okay, you shock him," Alma said, "And I'll go in and pump his heart."

"Will that work?" Arnold said.

"I ain't got no better idea, do you?" Alma huffed. "Nothing else is wrong with him, now. We get his heart going, Ben should be as healthy as the rest of us."

"Let's go," Kate said, kneeling on the other side of Ben, looking over his body, at Alma. Together, they turned Ben over, onto his back. Alma quickly brushed the sand off his face, and tilted his chin up, breathing into his mouth twice, while plugging his nose.

Alma nodded to Kate, who laid her hands over Ben's chest, directly over his heart.

"Here?" she asked. Alma shook her head, then moved Kate's hands to the proper places. Then she pulled her own hands back as if being held up by the police.

"No one touch him!" Alma yelled.

Kate sent a shock of high voltage electricity into Ben. His entire body jumped. Angel sucked in a breath, gasping. Sarah put an arm around her, hugging Angel tight.

Alma quickly buried her right hand inside Ben's chest, up to her wrist. No one knew what was happening now. No one could see inside of Ben. Alma, however, could feel. She quickly found Ben's heart, wrapped the molecules of her right hand around, and began pumping. After thirty pumps, she pulled her hand back out and tilted Ben's head back again, plugging his nose. She breathed air into his lungs, then nodded to Kate again.

Kate shocked Ben a second time, and Alma quickly went back in. She pumped Ben's heart for thirty more beats, and again, she breathed into his mouth, while pinching his nose shut. This went on for quite a while, and everyone started to lose hope.

When Kate shocked Ben for the fifteenth time, and Alma continued breathing for him, and pumping his heart, almost everyone had turned away. Kate cried now, giving up hope. Alma, however, wouldn't give up.

"There's nothing else wrong with him!" she cried. "This has to work!"

"Al, it's too late," Kate said. She refused to shock Ben anymore.

Alma kept on pumping Ben's heart and breathing for him. Then suddenly, she stopped, raking in a short breath, her right hand still buried inside his chest. She felt a faint vibration, the smallest of movements. Then she felt it again, and her eyes welled with tears. So much emotion, happiness, and relief suddenly flooded into Alma, she felt as if her own heart might stop beating.

Arnold turned around then, for he'd heard the faint thumping noise, as Ben's heart began beating once more, on its own. He smiled wide and fell on his knees, staring at Ben in complete shock and disbelief. He clapped his hands and laughed, tears streaming down his face.

Alma removed her hand and ran her scanner over Ben. She shook her head, tears flying from her eyes.

Kate looked at her, eyes questioning. "Al?"

"He's fine," Alma said, dazed. Then she covered her face, sobbing uncontrollably. Her words now were barely discernable, as tears streamed down her cheeks. "He's perfectly fine. There's nothing wrong with him."

Ben's chest now rose and fell, as he breathed on his own. Angel walked over and stood at the front of her father's head, as this was the only place left with room for her to stand. Everyone else surrounded Ben, looking down at him, on their knees in the sand, peering at Ben with looks of love and awe. Everyone cried.

Ben slowly opened his eyes. At first, he had trouble focusing. Then he blinked and slowly took in the faces surrounding him. He was confused. He didn't know where he was. He focused, slowly, on each individual face. Then he looked up, above his head, as he lay prone on the ground. He saw the upside-down face of his daughter, peering at him. She smiled. He took in a short, quick breath, and exhaled.

"Hey, sweetie. Whatcha doin'?"

Everyone laughed, including Angel. She showered her father's face with kisses. Ben couldn't understand what was happening, but he also started laughing. He slowly sat up and looked at everyone in bewilderment. Then he took in each face, taking count. He looked at Angel, his smile fading. Angel looked at her father and frowned.

"Honey, where's your mother?"

17

Everyone sat on the sand, surrounding Ben. He looked around, tears standing in his eyes. He'd been told about everything that happened after Jess pulsed. His memory came back in a flood. He remembered being pushed away, separated from Jess. He remembered landing in the sand, looking up, and immediately knowing that he would not be shielded from the pulse. Ben relayed his memories to everyone.

"Ben," Martin said. "Once you got closer to the transport, I could hear your thoughts clearly again. But if you hadn't verbally sent the warning through Arnold, for Rafferty not to get airborne, we all might have..."

Martin grabbed Ben and hugged him tight, crying into his shoulder, overwhelmed. Ben still looked shell-shocked and confused.

"I heard you," Arnold nodded. "When you said she was going to *'drop it from the center'*. I didn't know what you were talking about, but I heard you, and I told Raff. He figured out what you meant. He got everyone into their seats. If we hadn't been harnessed in, things would have been a whole heck of a lot worse. Martin's right, Ben. You saved everyone's life."

Ben shook his head. He remembered running as fast as he could. He smiled. "I'm not sure about your sentiments, but I do believe I ran over a mile, in under six minutes."

"You were running for your life," Rafferty said.

"Yeah, well," Arnold said, "You're lucky you didn't have a heart attack. If you'd heard your own heart and how fast it was beating, you'd understand what I'm talking about."

Ben shook his head again. "I don't remember the compression wave. I just ran, and the next moment, I woke up on the beach, surrounded by everyone. I didn't remember anything at first. I couldn't figure out what was going on. Why everyone was around me. I didn't even know where I was."

"It's fugal amnesia," Alma said. "Not uncommon after a traumatic brain injury. You were brain-dead, Ben."

"Brain-dead," Arnold scoffed, "Heck, you were *dead*-dead. No heartbeat, not breathing. Brain crushed. Every bone in your body was broken, Ben. I listened to your heart stop beating. There was nothing. You were gone."

Ben looked at Angel and cradled her face in his hands. A tear slipped down his cheek. Sarah sat next to her, holding her right hand.

"Angel put you back together again," Sarah said, looking at Ben with solemn eyes. Ben nodded, unable to speak.

What about Jess? Ben looked at Martin. "She isn't back yet."

"Her pulse was different this time," Rafferty said, immediately picking up the conversation. "So maybe her time travel is different, too."

"I want to go look," Ben said, standing up. "I need to see with my own eyes."

"Ben, you need to rest," Alma said.

"Why? I'm completely healed, aren't I?"

"Yes, but you *died*."

"You told me there's nothing wrong with me now, right?" he said, already walking. Angel followed him.

"But," Alma said, and followed them. "You should rest anyway."

Everyone else followed the first three, a line slowly forming.

"Great," Martin said. "I guess we're all going, again."

"Maybe Sarah should lead?" Aaron said. "In case there are any stray Bailon."

"I'm telling you, I don't hear anything," Arnold said. "There are no Bailon. I'd hear their hearts, their breathing. Their footsteps. I hear nothing. The Bailon are gone. Finito."

Jenny held Arnold's hand. Martin walked on the other side of him, nodding.

"He's right. I don't hear anything either."

"Yeah, but you never did," Aaron argued, following behind them.

"Okay, but as we get closer to the city, I should be able to hear them, if there are any still out there," Martin countered.

"As would I," Arnold agreed.

"Fine," Aaron said. "But Sarah should still go first."

Aaron pulled on Sarah's arm and they ran to the front of the small crowd. After fifteen minutes, they started coughing. The air was thick with smoke and debris, and extremely hot. No one could go any further. Ben gasped for breath, as he motioned for everyone to move back, into clear air.

"There's too much smoke, too much debris. The air isn't safe to breathe," Ben said, coughing.

"So, she could be in there?" Martin said. "In all this?"

"No," Ben sighed. "No, her ability seemed to be a failsafe, removing her in time far enough, that the air would be safe to breathe when she returned. I'm guessing she's still traveling in time. The air isn't safe. She won't come back until it is. That's why she's still gone. This is normal."

"Are you sure?" Martin asked.

"No," Ben said, his voice sad and defeated, shaking. "But it's my best guess."

"Hey, wait a minute," Arnold said. "You said that when she pulsed, back on Earth, because she was only gone a few minutes, she hardly moved, right?"

"Yeah?" Ben said.

"So, if she's gone too long, then when she reappears, it could be miles from here, right?"

Ben stared at Arnold for several moments, thinking. Then his eyes grew wide.

"She could reappear and be lost, right?" Arnold said. "Or even, in the middle of the ocean?"

"Come on, Arnold!" Martin scolded.

"What, am I wrong?" he said, sounding defensive.

"That wouldn't make sense," Ben said. "Her ability always protects her. Why would she reappear someplace else?"

"Well, she did almost reappear in space, Ben. I mean, otherwise, then, what?" Arnold shrugged. "You think she'll just reappear right back here?"

"Only if the air is safe to breathe," Ben said, exasperated. "And I don't know how long that will take. I have to assume that her ability will bring her back here, to the same spot."

"The planet rotates every 18.3 hours," Rafferty said, walking over. "So, theoretically, if Jess were to appear back in the same spot, she wouldn't come back until the exact same moment she pulsed, a day later."

"A day?" Arnold said. "How long has it been since she pulsed?"

"Almost two hours," Rafferty said.

"Great!" Arnold exclaimed, sarcastically. "So, we just have to wait another 16.3 hours to see if Jess comes back? That's not so long. I can handle that!"

Arnold walked off in a huff, shaking his head. Jenny followed. Ben looked at Rafferty, his eyes sad. Angel looked up at him, tugging on his shirt.

"Daddy?"

"Yes, baby?"

"Look," Angel pointed up into the sky.

Ben looked in the direction Angel pointed and saw the Grayling's ship for the first time. He'd never seen it from the outside. Everyone huddled together, watching in awe, as the massive, gray ship grew larger, coming closer. It hovered high above, then moved away.

"They're leaving?" Jenny said.

"The ship is too big and heavy to land on the beach," Rafferty said. "They're landing on that bluff, overlooking the city."

Everyone looked to where Rafferty indicated. The mountains surrounding the city formed a crescent around the valley. On the very end, to the left of the range, the mountains ended in a massive, grassy bluff, overlooking the ocean. The bluff was a good two miles long, and three miles wide, with one large tree near the edge; the ground an odd shade of sickly, pale green. Everyone watched in wonder, as the ship landed.

"Let's go!" Martin yelled, lighting off, anxious to see Eileen and hold her in his arms. Rafferty lit off as well, the thought of Jemma filling his mind.

Everyone else started running, including Ben and Angel. They ran near the water's edge, skirting the worst of the smoke from the blast, but even then, everyone pulled their shirts up to cover their nose and mouth, until they cleared the thickest plumes, which drifted on the breeze, towards them, and away from the bluff and the direction they ran. It took over fifteen minutes to reach the base of the bluff, given the distance.

***

Inside, everyone waited in the cargo bay, as the ship landed. No one knew when they'd landed, until Hanley and Ezra informed everyone they'd touched down to ground. Ezra walked over to a control panel on the far wall and frowned. Hanley came over and stood next to him.

"This one, I think," Hanley pointed to a lever on the far-left.

"Are you sure?"

"No," Hanley said. "But I think so. Can't know till we try, right?"

"Uh, sure," Ezra said, pulling the lever down. "Or we could blow up the ship," he mumbled under his breath.

***

Rafferty ran with Martin by his side. He sighed, stopping at the base of the bluff, closing his eyes.

"The far-left lever, by the control panel," he panted, sounding annoyed.

Martin looked at Rafferty, frowning. Then he read his thoughts, and smiled, shaking his head. He'd been too busy thinking about Eileen to pay attention.

***

The cargo bay suddenly flooded with bright daylight. Everyone shielded their eyes. No one had seen actual sunlight in over ten years. They all stood in the far-left corner, stunned when the entire wall in front of them folded outward, till it lay on the ground, at a severe downward angle.

Everyone slowly came to investigate, peeking over the edge. They were still several dozen feet off the ground. Everyone looked at each other, confused.

"How do we get down?" Earl said. "Do we slide down the wall?"

"Too dangerous," Grace shook her head. "At that sharp an angle? People will be injured."

"Then how do we get off this thing?" Earl repeated, now sounding slightly panicked.

"Don't know," Ezra said, coming over. "We were all flown onto here, in the transport. I never needed to exit the ship before."

"Yes, but, how do we get down?" Grace pondered, sounding uncharacteristically impatient.

Malcolm held Grace's hand. He looked at her, a smile spreading over his face. "I can get us down."

***

Grace let out a tiny squawk, as Malcolm floated up off the floor, taking her with him. Earl ran up and jumped, attempting to grab Malcolm's left hand. Malcolm came back down.

"Can I come?" Earl asked.

"Sure," Malcolm said. "Anyone that wants to come, grab hold of me."

Jemma quickly ran over and threw her left arm around Malcolm's torso, hugging him from behind, while holding Willa in her other arm. She looked at Grace, smiling. Grace held Burne.

"Normally I'd be jealous, but I guess that's okay," Grace said, winking at Jemma.

"The more the merrier," Malcolm laughed. "I'm not sure how many I can actually take, though. Better make more than one trip."

Malcolm took Grace, Earl, Jemma, Willa, and Burne down to the grassy bluff, then came back. Next, he took Hanley, Rachel, and Robert, then Ezra, Roslyn, and Vera. Next came Eileen, Eric, and Alex. Finally, on the fifth trip, Malcolm brought Althea, Dorian, and Innis.

***

Everyone tried to climb the bluff, but it was too steep. All anyone could do was look on, as the faces of their families appeared, high above them, looking down. From the base of the bluff to the top, the sheer cliff stood over a mile high. The family members above looked infinitely small to those on the beach staring up, like tiny toy people. Malcolm had to transport everyone down, once again, to the beach. Slowly, everyone was brought down, and all the families reunited.

Ben and Angel sat, waiting, as Malcolm brought Alex down. As soon as his feet touched the sand, Alex ran to his father and sister, crying. The three of them hugged for a very long time.

Mal ran to Arnold and Jenny and the three of them dissolved into tears. Malcolm hugged Jenny, first thing, and shook Arnold's hand, wiping tears away. Then he had to go back up to bring everyone else down.

Grace came down and hugged Kate and Alma. Then she pulled away, looking at Alma in reverence.

"I heard you brought Ben back," she said.

"Already? News travels fast. No, not alone," Alma said, looking at Kate. "I think maybe Kate should study medicine from now on."

"No way," Kate said. "That was enough for me."

Grace walked over to Ben and hugged him. He smiled at her, crying again.

"I heard you almost left us."

"I think I did for a little while."

"Well, I'm glad you're back."

Earl came down in the last group and tackled Aaron, nearly knocking him down. Sarah laughed, crying tears of joy.

"Son-of-a-gun," Earl said. "Here you are, in one piece."

"Here I am," Aaron said. "Did you miss me?"

"Are you kidding?" Earl said. He looked at Sarah, motioning to her. "Get yourself over here, lady."

Sarah walked over, timidly, and Earl gave her a bear hug.

Mara threw herself into her mother's arms and was soon enveloped by her brothers and sisters. Jemma stood with all five of her children, frozen. Rafferty walked up to her, simply gazing for several moments.

"Are you okay?" She reached for his shoulder and he frowned.

"Mara," she said. Rafferty looked down at his daughter, who met his gaze and smiled. Rafferty smiled back, nodding. He looked back to Jemma, tears in his eyes.

"I'm okay," he said. "Are you?"

"I am now," she said, wading through the children to throw her arms around him. The children all looked away, making gagging noises, as Jemma and Rafferty kissed madly for several moments.

Eric hugged his father fiercely, then watched as Martin and Eileen hugged each other. When it became clear they were going to remain in each other's arms for a while, he turned away from his parents and made his way over to Angel.

Ben saw Eric coming. He pulled Alex away, leaving Angel free to be alone. She saw Eric coming and looked down at the ground. He walked briskly up to Angel and took her face in his hands, kissing her squarely on the lips. Several people stopped to watch. Many, including some of the oldest kids, got the distinct impression they watched a grown man kiss a grown woman, despite the fact they looked at two nine-year-old children. It only lasted a moment, however. Then Eric pulled away and gazed into Angel's eyes.

"Your mother will be back," he said. Ben came over to listen. Angel still reeled too much from the kiss to fully register what Eric said.

"When?" Ben asked.

"I'm not sure," Eric said. "I just know she must come back. She's at our wedding," Eric shrugged. "Like I said."

Angel blushed and looked down at the ground again. Ben gazed at Eric in wonder.

"Does she look okay?" he asked, rolling his eyes. "At the wedding. Does she look healthy?"

"She must be," Eric shrugged again. "She's pregnant."

Ben stared at Eric in shock. He blinked several times, trying to process this new revelation. Not only would Jess be alive, she would be pregnant. Ben frowned.

"And, you do see *me* there, too, right?" he asked, sounding nervous.

"Of course," Eric said, frowning. "How else would Jess be pregnant?"

"I don't know," Ben laughed. "I just thought I'd check."

"Great," Hanley said, coming over. "Everything's going to be fine. Now, let's get this party started. The Graylings are home. The Bailon are gone. Everything's perfect."

***

Except, everything wasn't. Nothing was perfect. Over the next several days, the sad reality of their situation began to register on everyone, human and Grayling alike.

18

Jess floated, her mind awash on a sea of dreams. Nothing felt real. A moment ago, she'd pulsed, and before a blink of an eye had registered on her mind, she was engulfed in nothing but white. There were little pinpoints and flashes of sparks, within the blinding brilliance, however. As her mind adjusted to the glaring brightness, she noticed small sparkles of translucent, iridescent color, dancing within the wash of radiance.

There was an odd familiarity in what she saw—something strangely reminiscent in what she felt. It all reminded her of something elusive.

A flash, she thought. *Traveling through space and time. The wormholes. This is what the jump looks like, within the moment.*

Then she laughed, certain she'd lost her mind. The jump only lasted a moment. How could she be inside a jump? How could her pulse bring her here?

Jess touched her own hand. She felt her fingers, confirming she still had a body. She was here. She was real. Yet, her mind swam. She felt that dropping sensation, as if she'd been caught in a free-fall, and again, she thought of the jumps she'd experienced. Her mind fell endlessly, like the moments right after every jump they'd made aboard the Grayling's ship.

Jess remembered her pulse—how different it had been—not like all the others. She'd dropped an epic bomb on the Bailon city. Everything went white. Was she dead? *No, I have a body.* Perhaps the flash had blinded her? *But I can see… something. And I saw…* The entire city had been covered in white—she'd seen it, like all the times she'd pulsed in the orchard, as time slowed to nothing, frozen—like a polaroid taken the moment her power released. In an instant now frozen, burned and embedded in her mind, Jess saw the moment of her pulse, and *knew* the whole city was gone, even as she became instantly swallowed by the light. Without any doubt in her mind, she *knew* the Bailon were all gone. *I just killed three million living beings,* she thought. *I must have died with them,* she reasoned.

Jess suddenly became aware of the fact that she wasn't alone. Someone was there, within the light—a distinct presence—she could sense it, all around her. At the same time, her mind recognized the thoughts, the *voice*, within her consciousness. Thoughts arrived, and she immediately knew who she conversed with.

Harold!

Hello, Jess, Harold sent to her.

Where are you? Why can't I see you?

We are conversing mentally. You're connected to my mind.

Jess didn't understand. She received Harold's feelings and they weren't familiar. It was as if she were meeting him for the very first time. He seemed different than when she'd first met him. She sent this to him and received his surprise.

Have we met before?

Of course, we have, Jess thought. *Don't you remember?*

I'm afraid I don't, Harold sent, and she felt his sadness. *I know who you are, but we have not yet met, in my time.*

What do you mean, in your time? Jess felt infinitely confused. *Harold, you're back from the dead.*

In your time, have I died?

In my time? What do you mean?

Jess, at this moment you are in, I am on board my ship, and you are living within the facility.

But, how can that be? Jess's mind reeled.

You must be communicating with me from your future, as your mind is channeled in. Which must mean you eventually come on board the ship, and meet Ezra, Harold sent.

But I do meet Ezra, she sent back. *We all do. Everyone channels in.*

Who is everyone? Harold said, curious. *All of you escape the facility?*

Yes, Jess said. She proceeded to name everyone who escaped from the facility and how. She told Harold about Sarah.

I must remember to let Hanley know about her, then, Harold mused.

That's how Hanley knew? Jess's mind felt overloaded.

Tell me about your pulse, Jess. The one that connected you and I, here, now?

You're the one who told me I could do it. When we meet on the ship. After I channel in. Aaron told me I had to meet you. I didn't understand why. Even he didn't know why. When I meet you, you tell me I will defeat all the Bailon. You never told me how, but Rafferty figures it out. I kill all the Bailon. I know I did. Everything was white, like it is now. I know they're all gone.

I told you that you would do this?

Yes, she thought. *You didn't tell me how, though. You said you saw a vision of me, in light...* Jess trailed off, looking around in wonder.

Yes? Harold pressed.

"It was this, wasn't it?" Jess said, amazed to have a voice. "Your vision. It was this. Our conversation, here, right now."

Perhaps, Harold thought, then sent a firm *yes* to Jess's mind, but she knew he wasn't certain, either, what was truly happening.

Is this really happening? she thought. *You told me you and all the*

Graylings had a vision of me, in light, and all the Bailon were gone. Defeated. By me.

Are all the Bailon gone? Harold thought, his heart full of hope. Jess could feel it.

Yes. Everything was white. I destroyed them all. I know I did.

Then you are successful, Harold sent. He was proud.

But, where am I? Am I dead?

No, Harold assured her. *You could not be connected to me mentally, if you were dead.*

But, where am I? Will I return to Hesperia? What about everyone else on the mission?

Others came on the mission? Who?

Jess named everyone who came on the mission, including Aaron. She told Harold about Sarah's knowledge of who would go.

So, Aaron chose to come, of his own volition?

Yes, Jess thought. *Everyone else came simply because Sarah said they had to.*

I see, Harold thought. *And did you choose to go on the mission of your own accord?*

Yes. I promised you, Harold. I told you, when I hugged you, that I wouldn't fail. I said I would die trying, if I had to. I wish you remembered.

Jess, if you already released your power, you did not die, Harold sent. *You are alive, and you already pulsed. Which means, you were successful.*

Which is why you tell me, when you meet me, that I will be successful, Jess thought, amazed. *Your vision was this. And everything you told me, is only what I told you.*

Yes, Harold sent back. *Does this bother you?*

"You said you knew," Jess said. *But really, you only knew because I told you. Why didn't you tell me this back then?*

Back then for you, is later for me, Harold sent. *Would it have made sense to you, if I had? Or would it only have confused you more?*

I'm not even sure what you mean, Jess sent. Harold laughed, and Jess laughed with him. Then she grew sad.

Harold, you die. Before we ever reach Hesperia. And Ramona dies, two years before you, even. I defeat all the Bailon, so all the Graylings can return home. Only, you don't even live long enough to see it. Jess cried.

But I die knowing you will be successful, Jess, Harold comforted her. *And knowing my people will return home again, to live in peace and comfort, is enough for me. It is more than I could have ever hoped for.*

But, it's not fair, she thought.

It is how it was meant to be. Knowing is enough. You have given me an incredible gift, Jess. You have no idea what joy you have given me, do you?

You mean, the hug?

You mentioned that. You hug me? Harold sounded truly surprised. She sensed why—how most humans feared him, upon sight. None had ever dared to go more than several feet near him. No human had ever touched him. He felt warmed and loved.

Yes, she sent. *Because you seem so sad. And I feel bad, for yelling at you. For doubting your vision. My vision, I guess. The one I'm sending you, right now.*

I shall look forward to our meeting, Harold thought, and he truly meant it. *It will be a fulfillment of our destinies, of what must be, because it already has been. You have given me much information, Jess. I now have much to impart to others. It is an incredible gift, one that you will never fully comprehend. This does not matter, however. You made a promise to me?*

Yes, Jess cried, her heart full of sorrow. *You were dying, and I wanted you to know I would do what you asked of me. I wanted you to know I would fight for you. You said I would succeed, even though I didn't believe you.*

You didn't believe me, when I told you that you would be successful?

No, Jess thought, feeling ashamed. *I had doubts.*

But, despite these doubts, you fought anyhow?

I made you a promise and I kept it, she thought. *It was the only thing I could give you.*

No, it wasn't, Harold thought to her. *Your promise was not your gift. This conversation is. Thank you, Jess. I know my people will return home and live and thrive again. Because of you. With your help. You and the rest of The Society. I can go now, in peace. Thank you, Jess.*

What do you mean, you can go now? Where are you going? Jess felt panicked.

Our time is running out, Harold thought. *I can feel it. You are arriving at your destination. Our connection is growing weaker.*

Wait! Jess sent out. *I didn't tell you to warn Hanley about our escape, from the facility.*

I'm sorry, Jess, we're losing touch, Harold sent. *I look forward to our meeting. And the hug*, Harold sent, bemused and full of love.

"But, during our escape, something goes wrong!" Jess screamed, simultaneously sending her thoughts out to Harold. She felt him rushing away from her, his mind increasingly distant, dimming, far removed.

Jesus and Lucia! There's a sniper in the park, in Palo Alto! Rachel can kill him and save them both!

But Harold was gone. Jess fell to her knees, crying hysterically. It was all her fault. She'd had the chance to tell Harold, before they even escaped from the facility, and she hadn't done it in time. She hadn't realized. No one knew that was going to happen. Now, she knew why.

Jess buried her face in her hands and sobbed. Jesus and Lucia should have been the very first thing she told Harold about. She wept inconsolably, not registering the wind that lightly blew on her face. She didn't feel the sand digging into the skin on her arms, knees beneath her, body doubled over, her back facing the sky.

***

It took three days for the dust and debris to settle over the Grayling's city. By then, the sad reality of the situation had also settled in on everyone. Discoveries were made.

Rafferty used his tools to etch stairs into the rocky side of the bluff. By late afternoon, on the first day, everyone could climb up and down the bluff using the rocky steps. Everyone slept on the ship the first night.

Ben had trouble sleeping and was up before dawn on day two. He immediately went back to the spot where Jess had pulsed, ignoring the gritty air he breathed, and simply waited for her to return. No one could get him to leave that spot after the second morning. Arnold began bringing him smoothies to drink, but Ben refused to eat or drink anything.

On day two, Rafferty brought the parts he needed to repair the transport. He had it up and flying again by the second afternoon. He flew it inland, to the fresh water table and made discovery number one. He returned to the main ship and immediately went to the Grayling's deck, to report to them.

On the second night, Ben refused to come back on board. Angel and Alex were looked after by Martin and Eileen. Arnold trekked out to the beach, covering his mouth and nose, and brought Ben a blanket.

On the morning of day three since their mission, Arnold came out to find Ben unmoved, the blanket next to him on the ground. He was unshaven and haggard looking, his eyes ringed underneath with dark, sunken flesh. Ben was beginning to lose it. Arnold went back to the ship and talked to Grace and Malcolm.

"I'm really worried," Arnold said. "Ben's practically catatonic at this point. Jess still isn't back. The air is beginning to clear now, a bit, but it's been three days, and he's been breathing all that junk. I can't even be with him for more than two minutes without hacking up a lung. You should hear his breathing, his throat, it's..." He couldn't finish speaking, just shook his head.

"We can send Mara to heal any damage to Ben's lungs," Grace said, sounding calm, but forced. "Eric said Jess is at he and Angel's wedding."

"Yeah, well," Arnold shrugged. "Things don't look so good right now, you know? No matter what Eric says he sees. Maybe he's lying, to try and make Angel feel better?"

"The children don't lie, Arnold, you know that," Malcolm said.

"Well, why isn't she back, then?" Arnold yelled in bewilderment.

"She'll come back," Grace said, hanging her head.

***

On night three, Rafferty told everyone the same thing he'd already told the Graylings. He'd been to the freshwater table and it was horribly polluted. The water would not be suitable for drinking, or bathing, or anything else.

The air was also polluted, the sky no longer a familiar shade of green, but light brown. The Bailon had burned everything. There were no trees left on the continent. The lone tree on the end of the bluff was all that remained, the grass a nauseating green shade of pale puke. Jemma looked at it in bewilderment on day two. The tree also appeared horribly withered and ailing, with pale-white edges around the languid leaves. Everything hung, limp and hopeless. Jemma used her ability to perk the poor tree up, only to discover on day three, that the tree was ailing all over again. She quickly reached a sad realization, turning her face up to the brackish sunlight filtering through the smoggy haze. She pulled Rafferty aside to tell him.

That evening, Rafferty told all the adults the horrible news. Hesperia was dying. The Bailon were gone, but the damage had been done. Everyone sat around the common room, staring at the floor. Only Ben and Jess were missing, and the children all slept in their beds for the night.

"The grass is dying," Jemma said. "There are no more trees. Whatever plants are left, up in the mountains, are also dying. The air is too polluted. The sunlight coming through is being filtered. The plants aren't photosynthesizing correctly. They can't make their food. They'll die out, long before the skies ever clear."

"What about animals?" Earl said. "Are there any animals left?"

"No," Rafferty said, holding a scanner he'd used to evaluate things. "And the freshwater marine life is all dead, too, obviously. And everything that lived off that is dead. All the animal life was killed when the Bailon burned all the trees. It polluted the sky, which killed off everything else. Anything that lived off the remaining plants also died. That, plus the Bailon ate everything, without conserving enough numbers to keep a steady population going." He threw the scanner at the wall in anger, an action so uncharacteristic and unexpected, several people jumped, a few even screamed. The scanner hit the wall and shattered, raining shrapnel and fragments in a small explosion. Rafferty stormed out of the room, Jemma quickly following.

"What about the ocean?" Earl continued, ignoring the outburst. "Is that polluted, too?"

"The ocean's still okay," Grace said, piping up. "As soon as Jess destroyed the city, the pollution, which was the Bailon's waste, stopped flowing into the water. That, at least, will be all right. It's polluted, but not enough to kill all the marine life. Hesperia's oceans are massive."

"So, we can eat fish." Earl said. "Right?"

"But there's no plant life!" Rafferty yelled, storming back into the room. He's only made it around the corner before Jemma caught up to him. He'd heard everything said from feet away, unseen. "There are no animals."

"Are you sure?" Earl said. "Everything can't be dead. What were the Bailon eating?"

Rafferty looked at everyone, his eyes angry and haunted. He looked at Jemma and she looked away, her face pale and sick.

"I'm not sure," Rafferty said. "Once all the livestock died off, which would have happened after they burned everything, after the plants died, they wouldn't be able to even keep domesticated livestock. They wouldn't have any food to feed the livestock with. They started out, however, with a lot of fresh meat."

"What meat, the animals?" Earl asked.

"No," Grace said, quietly. "He means the Grayling's bodies. Right?" Rafferty nodded.

"The Bailon lived for quite a while on that, probably," Rafferty said. "They burned out the trees, to make room for their pods, which they placed in the mountainside. As their population grew, they built new structures back into the cliffs. They burned the trees for that, too, and to drive all the animals out, to round them up, is my best guess. They killed off all the animals and lived off those for a while. When that was gone..." Rafferty trailed off. "Probably, they ran out of food... over fifty years ago, especially as their population spiked."

"So?" Earl said. "What the hell were they eating all this time, then?"

"The only thing left to eat," Aaron said, his voice thick and guttural.

"What do you think?"

"No," Earl said. "You've got to be kidding me, right?"

"No," Sarah said. "Grace once asked why only ten thousand Bailon landed on Hesperia two hundred years ago. There were enough pods for twenty thousand to escape. I told you, wars erupted, in each pod."

"But," Earl said. "Nothing can live like that, can it?"

"Only fifty Bailon were left in each pod, when they landed here on Hesperia, right Rafferty?" Sarah asked, sounding sad.

Rafferty nodded, not meeting her eyes. She nodded back.

"But each pod could hold a hundred Bailon," she finished.

Everyone sat in silence, taking in what Sarah said—coming to terms with the gruesome reality of what the Bailon truly were—what they did.

"They weren't that far away, were they?" Arnold said, looking around. "They weren't that far away from being done here."

"With only one continent to pilfer?" Rafferty shook his head. "No. They went through Hesperia like a disposable grocery bag. I'm sure Earth would have taken thrice as long, with seven continents, so much more lush, green, open land to devastate. More room to spread out. Hesperia's larger, but it's comprised mostly of water, vast oceans, like Grace said. This planet has less than half the land mass of Earth. Plus, over half the continent here is heavily mountainous, and extremely difficult to navigate. Earth would have been a paradise for the Bailon. They would have decimated it."

"Not anymore," Earl said. "Not now or ever again. They're gone, thanks to Jess. Hesperia is clear of the Bailon. So's the Universe, for that matter. A scourge bidden good riddance."

"It doesn't matter," Jenny said. "Hesperia's in ruins. What are we going to do?"

"We're going to rebuild the Grayling's city," Rafferty shrugged.

"With what?" Earl asked. "There's nothing to build with."

"Yes, there is. The Graylings can convert matter, remember?"

"So? There're no trees to build with! The Bailon burned everything, remember?" Earl yelled.

"They can convert those ugly Bailon pods, to start with," Rafferty raised his voice. "After that, they can carve out sections of the cliffside, if need be. It's what they did before, so they wouldn't have to cut down any trees. They wouldn't upset the eco systems of the mountain animals. They can convert sheer rock into buildable materials for their homes. They can rebuild their city, no problem. Now that the trees and animals are all gone, we don't even have to worry about upsetting the environment."

"But what will they eat?" Jenny said.

"The same thing they've been eating," Rafferty said. "The same thing we've been eating. We still have the fogponics greenhouse, the marine tanks, everything we need, here on this ship. We even have a giant park and gardens, which is more than the Grayling's have."

"They have their home back," Aaron said. "Eventually, the air will clear, right? Someday, things might grow again."

"We can all still live here," Rafferty nodded. "We have clean water, here on board this ship, and so do the Graylings."

"I could look at their freshwater table," Grace said with hope in her voice. "How much water is it?"

"I'm not sure," Rafferty frowned. "I can check. We can go tomorrow, if you want."

Grace nodded. Arnold looked at everyone, his eyes sad.

"This is our home? A polluted, decimated, waste of a planet? This is what we won back for our friends?"

"Arnold," Martin said, "The Graylings are back where they belong. Their lives are healthier, regardless of the environment. Their energy is where it needs to be, right?"

"That's right," Rafferty nodded. "And maybe Jemma and Roslyn will be successful at transplanting some of Earth's flora to Hesperia's environment. We simply don't know. We knew we'd be building a new world when we came here. We knew it wouldn't be easy. These things take time."

"Says the man throwing things at the wall," Earl grumbled.

"I just didn't think we'd be raising our children under a brown sky," Arnold frowned, ignoring Earl.

"Yeah, but we never knew what to expect, right, Arnold?" Grace said. Her voice was gentle. "We came here knowing things could go wrong. Knowing we had no clue what to expect, really. Right? But that was the mission. No one thought about after, did they? I didn't. Not really. I certainly never thought Hesperia would be like this. I imagined a paradise. Silly me," Grace laughed. "Building a new world from scratch takes time. It takes hard work, sacrifice."

"Look, you guys, our goal was to win Hesperia back for the Graylings," Hanley broke in. "We did that. Jess did that. The Graylings will live longer now. They won't die off anymore. They're happy. The Bailon are gone—every single one of them. So, what if the sky is brown? It's *our* sky. It belongs to us, and to the Graylings again. They *will* rebuild. We'll find a way to live here. Everything will be okay. *We won.* We succeeded. We should be celebrating right now," Hanley looked at everyone with sad, pleading eyes.

"Celebrating?" Arnold said. "Tell that to Ben, sitting on the beach.

Tell that to Jess. Oh, wait. I'm sorry, I forgot. You can't tell Jess, can you? Because she's not here!"

"Arnie, you wanted to save the Graylings, and we did," Jenny said.

"Look, I'm happy for the Graylings, okay," Arnold sighed. "I am. And I don't care how we live. We can stay on board this ship, for all I care. Brown sky? Fine. Mucky lakes? Cool. Two people from The Society not here with us right now? Not fine. Not cool. I love the Graylings. For ten years, all I could think about was helping to save them. But during that time, I got to know all of you. You're my family. And it's not complete right now. Two people are missing."

"I know how you feel," Earl said. "I get it, Arnie. But Eric says Jess is coming back. After everything we've been through, I have no choice but to believe. Everything's going to come together. I know it is. Everything's going to be okay."

19

By the afternoon of the third day, the air began to clear. Ben sat on top of the sandy dune, a few feet from the spot where Jess had pulsed. He hadn't moved in two days. He hadn't slept. He hadn't eaten. He vaguely recalled Arnold bringing him food, a blanket. He only stared at the spot where Jess had been, ignoring Arnold. Ben was in a trance, fixated, waiting. He knew Jess would come back. He wanted to be there when she did.

In the darkness, even while sitting upright, Ben did fall asleep. For a few minutes at a time, his head would loll to the side, his chin eventually coming to rest against his chest. He always snapped awake again, in a panic, looking for Jess. Even in the darkness, he could see heat energy drifting lightly off the sand, as the warmth of the day slowly dissipated. He looked briefly toward the water. Bright waves of energy drifted off the moving tide, the water ebbing and flowing. Even at high tide, when the ocean was at its calmest, the waves lightly crashing against the sand sent off translucent arcs of kinetic energy, rainbow colors swirling with silver wisps of thready lines, combined into nothing but beauty. Ben watched this, on night three and cried. He missed Jess. He needed her.

He wanted to tell her about her incredible success. He wanted to let her know that she'd done it. He knew nothing about the trees, plants, animals, or water. He knew nothing about the sky. He never looked at it. In three days of sunlight, he never once glanced at the muddy brown firmament. He only looked to the place where he believed Jess would appear and waited. Despite the sunlight filtered through filthy smog, Ben was lightly sunburned by the end of day three on the dune.

As the fourth day dawned, Ben sat, Indian style on the sand, his eyes closed, face haggard and unshaven, skin a ruddy rouge, with darker areas burnt a crisp sienna. His lips were pale and chapped, cracked and bleeding in places, his unwashed hair slicked down with oil. And despite his stubbornness, he had finally succumbed to sleep. As the first rays of sun hit his back, he awoke and took in the view of the entire valley. The air had fully cleared overnight, and he could see across the entire diameter. This morning, as he opened his eyes, he took in the expansive view, with only a thin wisp of misty clouds still hanging over the ground, several feet in the air.

Ben cried as he took in the sight. The entire city was, indeed, gone. Nothing remained in the valley but a large crater, surrounded by blackened ground, covered with white ash. The crater extended up into the mountains for several kilometers, the rock-face sheer and dark, the only colors black and various shades of gray. It was a scene of complete annihilation and destruction, but to Ben, it was the very definition of beauty. Tears slipped from his eyes, streamed down his cheeks, and dropped onto his hands, which lay limp in his lap.

"She did it. She really did it," Ben whispered.

He looked to the spot where Jess had been, once again. The sun rose now, the light cascading across the valley, as it had done the day she'd pulsed. He finally looked up into the sky, remembering the invisible dome of energy, the way the air had bent down toward the ground. Then Ben looked back to the sand again and saw something odd.

It reminded him of watching a film in a theater. For a moment, this thought glinted through his mind. It made no sense, but he thought it nonetheless.

It's a movie, his mind whispered. He was exhausted.

In front of him, in the air above the sand, he saw the outline of Jess, her body transparent. It flickered, like film on a reel, as if only every third frame contained a still of her. She quivered in and out of Ben's vision, oscillating, like some sort of malfunction. Everything looked hazy, foggy. Ben stared in wonder, as Jess slowly gleamed more solid in front of his eyes. Finally, in one last flash of light, she fully arrived.

Ben stared in disbelief. After waiting all this time, he couldn't believe she was there. It didn't seem real. Jess always appeared in the exact same position she'd been in when she left, for one.

He stared at her, confused. She lay on the ground, bent in half, her back to the sky, as if deep in prayer, her face buried in her arms. Her entire body shook. Ben realized Jess was sobbing. The sounds came to him, muffled by her arms and the ground, but he saw the sound waves escape from around her face and throat, even her torso. She wailed madly. His heart broke, seeing her that way.

***

Jess sat crying, her heart breaking. Everything was her fault. She thought she'd been dreaming. Once she realized Harold truly conversed with her, she was so surprised and moved, it never occurred to tell him about Jesus and Lucia, and the sniper. It was too much for her to even fully comprehend that the Harold she spoke with was from over ten years in the past. That somehow, she'd opened a channel, within her ability, that transcended time and space. Her thoughts came to Harold and his thoughts back, over a span of nearly eleven years. It was enough to make Jess feel insane.

As she lay, sobbing, she didn't fully comprehend what had taken place. But she felt failure, nonetheless, and responsibility, as if *she* had shot Jesus and Lucia. Why hadn't she realized the opportunity she'd been given? She managed to tell Harold all about the escape from the facility. At least, she'd imparted how Sarah's gift would free them all and named everyone who came on board the mission. She realized, in the back of her mind, that this was how Sarah knew who would go, and again, Jess felt her mind begin to slip.

It wasn't Sarah, it was *she* who had ultimately decided who went on the mission. Jess realized it was also *her* who caused Aaron to feel the urgency in telling her that she needed to meet the Graylings. Everyone walked away with something different when they channeled in. Some of those people had walked away with things, Jess realized, which had been given due to *her* conversation with Harold—a conversation which, at the time she first met him, he'd already had with her, years before. Yet, Jess would not have that conversation with Harold for years to come.

Jess recalled feeling enveloped by love, warmth, and respect from Harold when she met him. She felt as if he already knew and loved her. Now she understood why. It must have been the same feeling Harold received, during their conversation within her pulse. She already knew him then and he didn't know her. The tables would be turned, for Harold, at least, several years in the future.

Jess wondered, there in the sand, if that was not part of the initial sadness she'd felt coming from Harold, when she met him. Everything was so confusing. He'd hugged her back and thanked her for her gift. At the time, she didn't understand what Harold meant. She'd thought, perhaps, that he was thanking her for the hug—although deep within her mind, she sensed this wasn't what Harold meant—but she didn't inquire further. Something within told her, even then, that she would not, could not, understand. She left Harold that day, believing she'd only meet him—had met him—once, and with nothing but a promise. But Harold had *known*. All along—before they ever escaped the facility—he had known the entire venture would succeed. That was why he was always so certain, within his emotions. He'd known all along that Jess would prevail—they all would—except for Jesus and Lucia. Her pain flared anew, and she sobbed violently.

Jess's heart broke again and again. She wished she could go back and tell Harold about the escape and what went wrong. She could have changed everything. If only she'd known or understood sooner. Her entire world had fallen apart.

She felt a hand on her shoulder. Her mind immediately flew to her memory of the day in the orchard, when Ben came to her. It was her final thought before releasing the pulse. Once more, her mind returned to that moment, as she felt the warmth of his touch. Her mind played tricks, for when she opened her eyes and looked up, she saw Ben, but he looked different.

His face, outlined by sunlight, looked exactly as everything had years before. She wondered if she'd traveled back in time, somehow, to that very day in the orchard. She hoped it was true. She remembered everything. She thought, in a split second, that if it were true, if she had gone back in time, somehow, she could change everything.

She stood, looking at Ben, her eyes wide. He looked at her, taking in her face, her wild expression, and his heart broke.

What Ben saw was Jess—demolished—her eyes wild with agony. She appeared lost, confused, far-off someplace, not there with him—her eyes looked upon him without recognition—and he knew, immediately, that her mind was not all there. Something had happened during her pulse, while gone, that fractured her psyche. Ben's heart shattered, as Jess began babbling incoherently. She didn't even know when or where she was, he realized. He looked at her, listening, confused and full of sorrow.

"Ben, it's not too late," Jess cried. "When we escape, and we will, there will be a sniper, in the park. We can send Rachel out to kill him, before Jesus and Lucia ever get shot!"

Ben's eyes filled with tears. Jess made no sense. She talked about things that had never happened. Jess continued ranting, completely oblivious.

"It was me, Ben! I told Harold everything, including how we escape. I met him, and he'd never met me. Later, he met me again, but I'd never met him! Neither of us knew each other at the same time," she laughed. "It was me who gave Harold everything he told Aaron and Sarah. Not anyone else, but at least those two. But he wanted us to choose, so he didn't tell Sarah about Aaron. Because it was his choice. It was my choice as well, because I wanted to keep my promise!"

"Jess," Ben said, his voice quiet. "Do you know where you are?"

"The orchard!" Jess cried, throwing her arms around him.

Ben closed his eyes, his heart aching. He was right. Jess had no idea where or when she was. She thought they were back on Earth, at the facility. She clung to him, talking all the while.

"I thought it was too late, but I came back here," she said. "Now we can escape all over again and this time I can warn everyone, and Jesus and Lucia can live!"

Jess pulled away and looked at Ben, who now cried. She frowned. Then she smiled.

"That's right," she said, her voice gentle. She cupped Ben's face in her hands, smiling at him, her eyes full of love. "Ben, in your time, we haven't gotten together," she said. "I'm sorry. I know everything that will happen over the next ten years. More, in fact. Almost eleven, actually."

"Jess, we're not on Earth," Ben said. He looked at her with trepidation, afraid of her reaction.

"Of course, we are," Jess said. She looked down into the valley and saw only the blackened ground, her mind so convinced she was in the blackened orchard, it was what she saw.

"The orchard is right there," she said, waving her arm absentmindedly down at the valley.

"That's not the orchard," he said, his voice so gentle, and she loved him so much. She kissed him, overcome with feeling. Then she pulled away and saw his eyes.

"Ben?" Her own eyes welled with tears, in reaction to the sadness in his.

"We're on Hesperia, Jess," he said, voice trembling. "You pulsed, remember? Look at the valley again."

Jess frowned and looked back at the orchard. All she saw was the blackened ground, although, it looked a bit different, distorted, somehow. She shook her head.

"Ben, you're scaring me. Look, the orchard is right there," she waved at it again, then turned her face in the other direction, still waving.

"And the facility is right… there…" she trailed off.

Jess stared at the ocean in front of her eyes. She looked at the sand. She frowned. Her heart tripled its pace. She turned her face back to the orchard and saw the valley, spread out in front of her for miles, and the broken, cratered ground. She closed her eyes.

All the while, Ben stood, watching her, afraid. When she opened her eyes again, memories flooded into her, in a torrent. She raked in a deep breath, her mind replaying the events. She saw Ben standing on the outside of her shield. She remembered him speaking to her. She closed her eyes again.

"Ben! Why?" Jess whispered, remembering.

"It's not your fault," Ben said. A tear tracked down his cheek. The actions and words were almost identical to the real events. Jess relived everything. Ben played along, hoping it would bring Jess's mind back to the present.

"Ben, I can't stop it!" Jess screamed. "I can't stop it!"

"I know. It's too late. You're not supposed to stop it. This is exactly what you were always meant to do, Jess. *Don't feel bad.*"

"Please tell me you'll be okay," she cried.

"I will," he lied, again. "I have to leave you now, Jessie. I have to, to get back to the transport." This time Ben cried, knowing exactly *how* he would die.

"Okay!" she cried, hysterical. "Okay!"

"I love you, Jess," Ben said. This time he cupped her face in his hands. There was no shield separating them.

"I love you, too, Ben." Jess felt the warmth of his hands on her face and cried harder.

"Now, run, Ben. Please," she whispered. "Run."

Jess dissolved all over again. Ben held her in his arms, also crying, but his silent tears turned to loud sobs as she resumed her incoherent rambling, her mind still broken.

"I did die," she cried. "I died, and this is Heaven. That's why I could talk to Harold. He's dead, too!"

Ben pulled away and held Jess by the shoulders. He looked in her eyes, not willing to give up. He couldn't lose her.

"You're not dead, Jess. You pulsed. You pulsed, but you're not dead."

"I'm not?"

"No."

"Then how did I talk to Harold?"

"I don't know. Jess, your mind is confused. Maybe you dreamed everything?"

"No," she said, looking adamant. "No, I felt Harold's presence. He was in my mind. I felt his emotions. It wasn't my imagination!"

"Then tell me everything," Ben said. "Everything you remember."

***

Jess told Ben everything—every word exchanged between she and Harold. When she reached the end of their conversation, she cried again. She told Ben about how she realized she'd forgotten to warn Harold about Jesus and Lucia, and the sniper. She'd told him everything else and that was how everyone knew what they did. Ben began to understand why Jess was so confused. He nodded, hugging her.

"Jess, I think you're going to be very confused, for a while," Ben said.

"Why?"

He looked at her, worry filling his eyes, etching his face. He wasn't sure how to explain things to her. He'd already felt slightly mad himself, working things through his own mind. Even he was confused, maybe even a bit insane. He wasn't sure if Jess's mind could take hearing the truth. He wasn't sure if he should tell her, or just show her. After hearing her speak, relaying all her memories, it became clear to Ben that Jess wasn't crazy. But she had changed. She had different memories than the Jess he knew. A lot had changed during her pulse.

"Jess, I know this is going to sound crazy, but I don't think this is the first time you've pulsed."

"Of course not, I've pulsed a lot of times."

"No, I mean, I don't think this is the first time you released this pulse," he said. "Or maybe, that's where you went, that day, after the Atrium, when you almost lost Angel."

"What are you talking about?"

"I don't know how to tell you this."

"Then just do it."

"Jess, the events you just relayed to me, are not the events I remember. I think they're *your* events. The you from the first pulse. But I think the you I remember, is the you leading-up to the second pulse."

"What the hell? Have you gone bat-shit crazy?" Jess frowned at Ben. He smiled.

"I see Alma still managed to rub off on you, without Lucia's help."

"Ben, what are you talking about?"

"Jess, you said you didn't warn Harold in time, right?"

"No, otherwise, things would have gone differently. Hanley would have known to warn everyone. We could have sent Rachel out first thing and told Martin to listen for the sniper. If he knew to listen, I think he could have picked his thoughts out. If he'd known…" Jess sighed.

"But he *did* know," Ben said. "Everything you just described is exactly what happened."

"What are you talking about, Ben?"

"Jess, for some reason, when you pulsed and talked to Harold, you changed everything. If what you're saying is true, you did manage to warn Harold. Everything changed, only not for me. Not for any of us. But for some reason, after returning here, your mind still contains all the old memories, from the original timeline. Which is why I think the pulse happened twice.

"In the first pulse and subsequent timeline, you imparted all the knowledge to Harold you would the second time, except for the warning about Jesus and Lucia. You lived that timeline, then reached the pulse for the second time. You talked to Harold again. Only this time, you managed to warn him about the sniper. He then imparted this knowledge to Hanley, along with everything else.

"But you were still *you*, from the original pulse. Maybe within that small pocket of existence, the other... well... the *other you*, with all the different memories... overlapped. I'm not sure how you did it, but you created a second timeline, Jess. Everyone else only knows the second one, including me. Unfortunately, you seem to remember only the first. Maybe because of your ability to travel in time, skip over things, remove yourself from the time stream. I'm just not sure."

"You sound crazy, you know that?" Jess looked at Ben, frightened. "How could I pulse twice?"

"By changing things, Jess," Ben said. "You created a different timeline. I think that's where you went, in the hallway that day. I think you put yourself here, in this pulse. I think, somehow, you crossed timelines. I just don't know, Jess. But you're telling me that when we escaped the facility, Jesus and Lucia were killed?"

"Yes," Jess said, exasperated.

"Jess," Ben looked at her with the utmost concern. "Jesus and Lucia were never killed."

"What are you talking about?" Jess whispered. "They died, of course they did."

"No. Hanley knew about the snipers, because the Graylings told him. Rachel volunteered to take them all out. Martin went to the ramp to listen. He told Rachel where to release her heat. She did. She killed the sniper—before Alma even went to knock on Lucia's door—before anyone ever left the transport. Lucia boarded the ship. Rachel did the same thing at Martin's house. Everyone made it on board the ship, Jess."

"You're crazy," she repeated, tears standing in her eyes. "Jesus and Lucia *died*. I was there, I *saw* it. I remember Alma's face. I remember the blood. I remember the funerals."

Ben smiled. Jess looked at him in complete disbelief. "This isn't funny."

"No, it's not. Jess, I don't remember any funerals. I'm smiling because I remember Jesus and Lucia's wedding."

"Wedding?"

"Jesus and Lucia are married. They have four children."

"No," Jess said, shaking her head. "No."

"Yes."

"Ben," Jess looked at him in fear. "Do you remember our wedding?"

"Of course."

"What about me and you, fighting? Did I almost pulse myself out into space?"

"Yes," Ben said, not smiling. "That happened."

"What about Alex, we still have Alex, don't we?"

"Of course, Jess," he sighed.

"Well, if I have different memories, how do I know that what happened for me, also happened for you?"

"Well, this is probably why people don't generally do time travel," Ben quipped.

"You're making jokes *again*?" She stared at him.

"It's my defense mechanism, Jess. I'm at a total loss right about now." He shrugged. "Time travel is dangerous, Jessie. It gets too complicated. Too confusing. It tends to make people go crazy, obviously."

"I'm crazy?" Jess looked at Ben in fear.

"I was talking about *me*. But you have a lot of catching up to do. I'm guessing a lot of your memories of events will be the same as what really happened. I believe things tend to veer towards the inevitable. If something happened for you, it still did for us, just, a bit delayed. Or maybe earlier. I'm not sure."

"You're making no sense, Ben."

"Come on," he said, standing up. "Let's go find out what's different for you. Okay?"

"Okay," she said, sounding nervous.

They walked towards the bluff. Along the way, Jess fired off a thousand questions. He answered everything as quickly as he could.

"Do we still live in room eight?"

"Yes."

"And we still have only two children?"

"Yes."

"Did Angel manifest an ability at age seven?"

"Yes," Ben said. He swelled with pride, remembering how Angel put his broken bones together again. He hadn't even told Jess about him dying. He decided now was not the time. He was afraid Jess's mind already had more to deal with than she could handle.

"Are Arnold and Jenny married, with Mal?"

"Yes," Ben said. "Why wouldn't they be?"

"I don't know. Who knows how two people living on board, who weren't there before, might have changed things?" She sighed.

"Well, Arnold and Jenny married each other, Jess," Ben said. "Jesus and Lucia wouldn't change that. How could they?"

"Are Malcolm and Grace—"

"Yes," Ben said, cutting her off. "And Aaron and Sarah, and Roslyn and Ezra. And Rafferty and Jemma."

"Do they have five kids?"

He frowned. "No, they have twelve."

"Twelve?!"

"I'm kidding, Jessie," he said, giving her a reproachful look. "Of course, they only have five kids."

"And Rachel and Hanley, and Robert?"

"Yes," Ben sighed. This was beginning to be fun for him.

"Do I seem different to you?"

"A little, but not really."

"Did we have a fight, after I…" Jess trailed off.

"What?"

"Well, when I keep pulsing, without actually pulsing, the energy stores up and does a lot of messed up things to people," she said. "Did all that still happen?"

"And you woke up in the infirmary, and we had a talk?" Ben led, blushing.

"That still happened, too?"

Ben nodded. They smiled at each other.

"Did Alex manifest and climb the air?"

"Why would that be different, just because Jesus and Lucia are alive?"

"I don't know!" She looked up and then frowned, changing the subject. "Why is the sky brown?"

Ben looked at the sky and frowned. Then he looked at Jess and stopped walking. She stared at him, looking frightened.

"Are we still madly in love?" she whispered.

"Madly?" He winked, driving her nuts. "That's not the word I'd use."

"Oh," she said, looking at the sand, a tear tracking down her cheek.

He looked at her with devastating intensity. "I'd say, wholly, completely, torturously, all consuming, all encompassing—" He got cut off, as Jess tackled him, a cascade of kisses showering his face, and they fell to the sand. They kissed for several minutes, then Jess pulled away, looking at Ben lovingly.

"Before we came on the mission, did you tell me it was you and me, together?"

Ben closed his eyes, thinking. He had a pretty good memory. He pulled up their conversation, verbatim, repeating the words, eyes still closed. She gazed at him in awe.

"It's always been you and me, from day one. Every time you pulsed, I was right there. Maybe not right by your side, but still. I was *always* with you. It's not you that has to be strong. It's *us*. Okay?" He opened his eyes to look at her. He had no clue if what he'd said matched her memories.

Jess cried. Ben kissed her and then looked at her with great concern.

"Is that what you remember me saying?"

She nodded.

"Good," he said, kissing her again. "Are you ready to see everyone? I know Angel and Alex are miserable, waiting for you to come back."

"Let's go," Jess said. She suddenly felt awful for not thinking of her children until then. As they walked, she asked yet another question.

"Ben?"

"Hmm?"

"I know this is a different timeline, and not everything can be the same, but… why do you smell like a sewer and look like total crap?" She figured it was her turn to have some fun with him. She winked, playfully shoving her arm against his.

"There's my firecracker."

20

Rafferty saw them first. He was outside with Jemma and Aaron. He saw Ben walking with Jess and shouted up the makeshift ramp connected to the cargo bay door. Hanley stood inside, milling around.

"Hanley! Go get Angel and Alex!" Rafferty yelled.

Aaron ran to the edge of the bluff and looked down, smiling. Hanley ran into the ship to get everyone. Aaron ran down the stairs and across the sand. He hugged Jess tightly when he reached her, almost knocking her over. Ben didn't feel jealous—he laughed—watching the scene.

"Four days," Aaron sighed. "Jeezus, Jess. Four days!" He pulled away to look at her.

"I'm sorry," she said, looking at Aaron with love.

"Jess!" Hanley yelled, reappearing in the cargo bay. He ran down the ramp, down the stone steps and hurled himself at her.

"Hey, kiddo," he whispered.

"Mommy!"

Alex reached Jess first. He sobbed as he ran. She scooped him up and hugged him tight. In the back of her mind, she felt grateful he looked exactly how she remembered. Angel ran up and hugged Jess's waist, Alex still in her arms. Jess bent down and hugged her daughter with one arm.

"Mommy, I missed you," Angel cried.

"Baby, I'm never leaving you again, okay? Ever."

By now, everyone stood on the beach. Ben saw Martin and quickly sent his thoughts, explaining that Jess had different memories, of an alternate timeline. Martin frowned, looking at him.

She remembers a timeline the rest of us don't, Ben thought. *In her timeline, Jesus and Lucia were killed by a sniper during our escape.*

Martin looked at Ben, in shock, still frowning, the realization of what Ben had relayed still not hitting home. He turned to look at the couple standing on his right, and his eyes grew wide, the revelation suddenly landing.

"Holy shit," Martin sighed.

Jess stood and looked at everyone, her eyes full of tears. Then she stopped breathing. A man walked up to her, holding a woman's hand. The couple stood in front of her, smiling. The man seemed familiar, although, he looked older. It was Jesus. He nodded at her, still smiling. He spoke, and Jess felt her world begin to fade and drift away, as if she were dreaming.

"You see?" Jesus said. "I told you. Everything is as it should be."

She stared at him for several moments. She'd forgotten to breathe. Ben held onto her shoulders, in anticipation of her shock. As Jess lost consciousness, he was right there to catch her. She never even fell, merely collapsed into Ben's waiting arms.

***

Jess dreamed. She knew she dreamed. It all felt so real, however. She saw herself, sitting in the dining hall—pregnant. She was with Ben, Martin, and Eileen. Sitting at the table next to them, were Jesus, Rachel, Hanley, and Roslyn. At another table, Lucia sat with Alma, Kate, and Jemma. Jess hovered over the tables, watching. She heard the people talking, including herself. From the conversation, she learned that everyone had been on board the ship for only three months. Jesus had channeled in with the Graylings the night before. He talked about the Graylings, and how badly he wanted to help save them.

Lucia listened at the next table. She hadn't channeled in yet, Jess somehow knew. Lucia liked Jesus, however. She liked him a lot. As soon as she'd met him on board the transport, she'd felt a connection. Jess somehow, also knew this.

Then everything changed. Jess was suddenly in the garden. Again, she floated above everything. Jesus and Lucia were getting married. Jess saw herself, standing in front of the couple, smiling. She was no longer pregnant. She spoke, her words familiar.

"And the greatest of these is love," Jess heard herself say.

"And the greatest of these is love," she whispered.

She opened her eyes and saw several faces looking at her. Everyone cried. She lay on one of the couches in the common room. Then she saw Jesus and crumbled. He saw her reaction to seeing him and Jesus dissolved. He hugged her, and she held onto him, feebly. She saw Ben's face over his shoulder. He smiled, tears in his eyes.

"I was dreaming," Jess whispered. "I was in the dining hall and you were talking about the Graylings. You'd channeled in. Then I dreamed I was at your wedding." Jess cried.

Jesus pulled away and looked at Jess with great concern and love. She continued crying while talking.

"I dreamed I spoke at your wedding, instead of your funeral. But I did. I said First Corinthians at your funeral." Jess broke down into sobs.

"Jess," Jesus spoke, gently. "You did speak at my wedding. You delivered the passage about love. Just like we talked about, that night in the cafeteria."

"I did?" Jess looked at Jesus, hitching in breaths, trying to calm down. She had no memory of this event, save for her dream.

"Yes," Jesus said. "It was lovely."

"Jess."

Ben came over and sat next to Jesus. He quickly stood and switched places with Ben, who then held Jess's hand

"I think you will eventually remember everything. It did happen to you. Your mind is just confused, that's all. I think connecting to Harold in the past simply jumbled your memories when you returned to the present, here on Hesperia. Your mind is still caught up in the past. Sort of like when we jump—your mind just needs a while to catch up. I think you will eventually acquire all the memories of the new timeline, the one *you* created. I think it will just take some time. Eventually, you'll remember everything, probably in bits and pieces, like your dream just now. Maybe the mind simply can't handle remembering everything all at once? Maybe it needs to come to you, like the last few memories—in dreams—one event, or two, at a time?"

"You think my dream wasn't a dream? You think I was remembering?"

"You did speak at Jesus's wedding. You delivered that exact speech. You were whispering in your sleep," Ben said.

"Jess," Jesus said, next to Ben. "I'm so sorry. I'm sorry you have to carry the burden of a memory of my death."

"It's not your fault," she whispered. "I can't believe you're actually here. Is any of this really real?"

"Time travel's a real bitch, huh?" Alma said. "Jess, I can't believe you have memories of Lucia dying. I can't even imagine going through that."

Alma stood behind Jess's couch, holding a woman's hand. The woman was younger, by a few years. They looked alike, but Lucia was prettier than Alma, by some people's standards. She was taller, and lithe compared to Alma. Jesus was a lucky man, Jess thought.

"Are you and Kate still..." Jess trailed off.

Alma nodded. Kate stepped forward. Jess's eyes boggled. Kate looked to be at least six or seven months pregnant.

"When did *that* happen?" she asked, motioning to Kate's stomach.

"About six months ago," Kate laughed.

"Who's the father?" Jess said, her voice high.

"Me," Earl said. "You don't remember that?"

"Did Jesus or Lucia have something to do with it?" Jess asked, confused.

"I talked to Lucia about it," Alma said. "We discussed it. She gives good advice, you know?"

"Huh. So, that's changed."

"Everything is as it should be," Jesus repeated. "Maybe you just finally put things right, after all this time? Nothing's different for any of us."

"Do I seem different?" Jess looked at Ben, worried again.

"No," Ben reassured her. "You're still you."

"I am," Jess said, nodding. "Can I get up now?"

Everyone backed up as Jess got up from the couch. Arnold handed her a smoothie. She was starving.

"Arnold," Jess said, eyeing him. "Did you hear my stomach?"

Arnold nodded, sheepishly. Jess quickly gulped down the drink. Then she looked around, frowning.

"Where is everyone else?"

"Getting ready to leave," Ben said.

"To go where?"

***

The transport wasn't large enough for everyone. There were twenty-one adults and only sixteen seats. Five adults elected to stay behind. Ezra, Roslyn, Jemma, Eileen, and Kate stayed back on the ship with all the children. Everyone else went.

Rafferty landed the transport on a rocky plateau. Once the ramp was lowered, Malcolm transported everyone down to stand at the edge of a large table of water. The lake was surrounded by tall, craggy mountains. On the far side, an aqueduct connected and headed south, down the mountainside.

Everyone stood on the edge of the water, looking at the massive pool. The water smelled. Grace and Alma talked to everyone. They explained that when the sky was polluted, the algae in the water began to die. The fish that lived off the algae then began to die. The fish that lived off those fish also began to die, in a domino effect. Everything that died remained in the water, rotting. Eventually, the water became acidic and sulfurous, polluted by all the rotting organic material. That was causing the horrible stench in the air.

The water itself was a light brown. The dead organic material had broken down by this point, into particulate matter, which caused the water to look discolored.

"This is actually a good thing," Grace said. "If there were still large masses of solid, organic material floating around in there, we'd need to net it out. Clean the water with a large filter of some kind. Since everything is broken down, I think I might be able to clean this."

"Grace," Ben said. "You once told me you could purify over one billion gallons of water at a time."

"This water table holds well over two billion gallons of water," Rafferty said. "Closer to three."

"I can't purify all of it," Grace said. "Not all at once. I'll have to keep coming back, every day, and slowly, over time, I can probably get it clean. As new rain falls into the table, it will need to be re-purified daily, anyhow. But, at the base of the mountains, it cascades into a tank, correct?"

"It did," Rafferty said. "The tank is gone, along with everything else. We'll have to build a new one."

"I can purify what's in the tank, though," Grace said. "So long as we build it to hold a billion gallons or less."

"Done," Rafferty said.

"Okay," Grace said.

She walked up to the edge of the water, and everyone looked on in wonder. Grace knelt, bending her knees, and stuck her hand into the brown liquid. Almost immediately, the water surrounding her hand turned clear. It looked like an optical illusion. No one could believe their eyes. The brown water slowly turned clear, spreading in an arc around Grace's hand. The clear water continued to spread, further than anyone could see. After several minutes, Grace sighed and pulled her hand out. Her face was shiny. She looked tired.

"I'm not used to working with this much water," she shrugged. "If you walked about a mile down the edge, you'd see, the water turns murky again."

"That's okay, Grace," Ben said. "We can come back every day. We can drop you on the other edge next time, right, Rafferty?"

"Yeah," he nodded. "Besides, once we build the tank, you won't even need to come back up here anymore, right?"

"No," Grace said. "But this doesn't help Hesperia, at any rate. I can give us clean water to drink, and bathe with. This is more for the Graylings, once they get their city rebuilt. We can just keep using the water on the ship. There are enough molecules stored to keep The Society in clean water for another fifty years. Clean water's not the problem."

"Then what is the problem?" Aaron asked. "The water's clean. How does that not help?"

"Water isn't supposed to be clean," Grace said. "For us to drink, ingest, bathe in, yes. But in a natural environment like this? It won't fix anything. When I'm done with this table, the water will be one hundred percent pure. It will contain no minerals, no trace amounts of extract, or calcium buildup. No chemicals of any kind. At the same time, it will also contain no organic matter, or bacteria, or any nutrients, and no microorganisms."

"So, how is that bad?" Aaron frowned.

"Pure water can't support life," Ben sighed. He looked at Grace with sadness. She nodded.

"Grace can clean the water, but it still won't be able to support life," Ben explained. "Algae can't grow, not in pure water."

"It doesn't matter," Rafferty said. "The life in this lake is already dead. You didn't kill it, Grace."

She nodded, clearly still disappointed in herself.

"But we can still give the Graylings clean water," Rafferty finished. "Thanks to you."

"So, let's build the tank," Aaron said. His eyes looked hopeful.

Everyone got back onto the transport and returned to the ship on the bluff.

***

That night, in their room, Jess and Ben laid together in bed, after Angel and Alex went to sleep. They played with each other's hands.

"I think you should go talk to Jesus. It's not real to you yet, is it, Jess?"

"Nothing feels real. I feel like I don't belong here. The last ten years didn't happen, Ben. At least, not like I remember."

"Alma is right. Time travel is a bitch."

"This isn't time travel, Ben. This is a different life."

"I know you'll catch up," he said. "Eventually."

"Maybe."

"If you're not ready, I understand. But Jesus isn't a ghost. You can't keep avoiding him. Eventually, you'll have to talk to him. Get to know him again. You don't remember, Jess, but you and Jesus are very close friends. He was the one that convinced you to channel in."

"He was?" Jess looked at Ben in surprise.

"Why, what do you remember?"

"When did I channel in?" Jess's heart beat fast.

"After Jesus. After listening to him talk about how much he loved the Graylings."

"No, how long after we came on board?"

"I don't know, I guess, about a month after Angel was born. You didn't want to do it while pregnant," Ben laughed. Then he looked at her with concern. "Why, when did you channel in?"

"After Angel was born," Jess nodded. "But not until she was nine months old. I only did it after you did. I channeled in because of *you*."

Ben looked at Jess for several moments, thinking. Then he nodded.

"Maybe I should be jealous, then? But you know what I'm hearing, Jess? It's just as I suspected. In two different timelines, you still decided to channel in. For two separate reasons, but regardless, in my timeline, you channeled in when Angel was only one-month old. In yours, you did it eight months later. Either way, you still did it. Because it was meant to be."

Ben looked at Jess with great love and emotion. "It's just like Jesus always says. Everything is as it should be. No matter how things come about, if they were meant to go a certain way, they will. Events will find a way of happening, no matter what else changes."

Jess shook her head. She wasn't accepting things, Ben knew. He pressed on.

"Jess, think about it. In your timeline, Jesus and Lucia died. But despite that, we all came on board. Everyone channeled in, including you. We still made it to Hesperia and carried out our mission. You pulsed, and you took out all the Bailon. Everything happened that was supposed to. Either way."

"But people are back from the dead," Jess whispered. "Do you have any idea what this is like for me?"

"No," Ben said. "Yes. Both. I can only imagine how you're feeling, no matter how hard I try to put myself in your shoes. But, Jess, you wanted to warn Harold about the sniper, right? And you thought you'd failed, but you didn't. And by warning Harold, this is exactly what you wanted, isn't it?"

"Not like this," Jess said, raising her voice. She sighed, closing her eyes, and lowered her voice, reining in her emotions. "Not like this, Ben. I thought if everything changed, I would change, too. There wasn't even time, really, to think about it. I thought if I warned Harold and changed everything, I wouldn't remember. No one else does."

"But, Jess, if you didn't remember, then when you pulsed and met Harold, you wouldn't have known to warn him. Then, ultimately, nothing would have changed. Don't you see? The only way to change things was for you—the you that remembers the sniper—to retain your memories. To keep the second timeline permanent."

"This is so confusing." Jess shook her head.

"I know. It is. But you had to remain you. The Jess from timeline one. For timeline two to exist, you had to remain locked into your old memories. At least, you did, up till now. You had to remember the old timeline, up until you pulsed, to warn Harold. To change everything, you had to only remember the first timeline, to solidify this one. Now that you're past the vital events, I believe you'll get your old memories back. Or for you, rather, your new memories. Perhaps, in time, the new memories will seem more real, and your memories of timeline one will seem more like the dream? But it will take time, Jess. I truly don't think your mind could take receiving everything too quickly. It will probably trickle in, one tiny piece at a time. It might take years for you to remember everything. As far as I know, nothing like this has ever happened before. I really don't know what to expect, what to try and warn you about. I'm sorry, Jess."

"It's not your fault." She looked him in the eyes. "I'm not ready to talk to Jesus."

"I know," he said. "Let's go to sleep."

That night, Ben held Jess in his arms. They did not make love. She was still Jess, to him. He knew, however, that Jess felt out of place, as if she didn't belong in his world. He didn't want to press her. She just needed time, and space.

***

The next morning, as Jess got ready in the bathroom, there was a knock on the door. Ben answered to find Jesus standing in front of him. Ben nodded, letting him in.

Jess came out of the bathroom to find Jesus standing in her living room, looking awkward and uncomfortable. He waved at Jess, feeling shy. She stood looking at him, frozen.

"Ben took Angel and Alex to get breakfast," Jesus said. He looked down at the ground. Then he motioned to the couch and sat down on one end.

Jess slowly walked around to the front of the couch, looking down at Jesus in fear. She felt afraid of him. She wasn't sure why.

"I'm afraid of you," Jess simply said. She stood in front of Jesus and he looked up at her, surprised.

"You're back from the dead," she whispered.

"I'm not dead. But perhaps this is how people felt when they saw Lazarus walk out of the tomb?"

"God didn't do this," Jess whispered.

"No, maybe not. Who knows? I guess, Harold did it. Or, ultimately, you."

"Me?"

"You're the one who warned Harold about the sniper, didn't you?"

"But I didn't know. I didn't think he heard me."

"But you wanted to warn him, right?"

"Yeah?"

"What did you think would happen, if you did?"

Jesus motioned for Jess to sit down. She did, reluctantly, on the other side of the couch, as far from Jesus as she could get. He smiled, unhurt.

"You wanted to stop me and Lucia from being killed, didn't you?"

"But I thought it would change everything. I didn't think I'd remember you dying, only to have you sitting on my couch. Do you know how weird this is?"

"Do you know how weird it is for me?"

Jesus looked at Jess with love and concern, but also kindness. Jess felt terrible, suddenly. She saw the look in Jesus's eyes, and it was the old Jesus that she remembered from back in the facility. The warmth and understanding were abundant in his look. Her heart immediately warmed to him.

"Do you know what it's like to find out I died? And Lucia, too?" Jesus shook his head. "To learn that in some timeline, Lucia and I never existed, together. We were never married. Our children were never born. And you and I were never best friends."

"Best friends?" Jess looked at Jesus in surprise. "We were friends inside the facility, but..."

"Yes, we were," Jesus said. "But here on the ship, we spent hours talking, about everything. The Graylings, Hesperia, life, space, our children. Playing cards, going for long walks. You came to me, when I channeled in. You wanted to know what it was like. I told you. Your whole face lit up. As soon as Angel was born, and you were ready, you couldn't wait to channel in. I took you to Ezra. I wish you remembered, Jess."

"So, do I," Jess said. She started to cry. "I'm sorry, Jesus."

"Sorry?" He looked at her, frowning. "According to you, I died. The only reason I'm here is because you somehow opened a channel with Harold, while pulsing, and warned him. According to you, Jess, I'm only here because you saved my life."

"I didn't save your life!"

"You didn't?" Jesus looked at Jess in surprise. "Jess, you pulsed, took out every Bailon, and immediately traveled back in time somehow, communicated to Harold, imparting information to the past, that saved me and Lucia, then came back to the present, here to Hesperia. That's not God, Jess. That's *you*."

"I didn't mean to. I didn't know what I was doing."

"You didn't need to know. Don't you see, Jess? Your ability has allowed for so much to take place. *Your* ability, Jess. No one else's."

"But, I'm not responsible. I didn't ask for any of this. I didn't give myself an ability."

"No, you didn't. The Graylings didn't give you the gene, either."

"What are you saying?"

"We talked a lot, Jess. About everything. Including God. You never believed. No matter what happened." He laughed. "We spent hours talking about coincidences. Like when Angel manifested, with the same ability as Angelique."

"What did I say?"

"That it was just a coincidence," Jesus laughed again. "No matter what happened, you never believed."

"But I don't believe that," Jess said. "In my timeline, I believe there are no coincidences. I try to tell Ben that."

"Yet, now, you don't believe?" Jesus frowned. "I don't understand? In the timeline where I died, you had faith?"

"Sometimes. It never stayed for long. And I'm not even sure what God to believe in, out here in space. We're not even on Earth, Jesus. If this is all God, it's not the one I learned about, or the God I know. It certainly doesn't have a name. And I'm a Christian."

"The name for God doesn't have to be the same as the Christian name you call Him by, to still be the same God," Jesus said. "Does the Bible not say that God is called by many names? And even that He has a secret name that no human knows? And what does Earth ultimately have to do with anything? Does not your Bible also say that God created the *Heavens* and the Earth? I understand, Jess, truly I do, how you could be confused in your faith with everything that has happened, regarding The Society... But how could you have faith when I *died*, yet, now, when I'm *alive*, you have more doubts?"

"I don't know."

"Don't you see, Jess? This only proves my point. I told you once, everything works out, eventually, right?"

"I guess."

"I said whatever is meant to happen will happen. If it's fate, it will find a way."

"So?"

"So, obviously, I was not meant to die, or Lucia. It may have taken over ten years to set straight, but fate found a way."

"Then why is this so hard for me?" Jess cried.

"Because you're making it hard," Jesus said.

"Gee, sorry I'm not taking things more in stride," Jess sighed, raising her voice. "Sorry that seeing you walking around, talking, *living*, is so difficult, after seeing a bullet rip through your chest. After seeing you shot through the heart, bleeding all over the damn transport! Sorry that seeing you and Lucia together is so jarring, after seeing her face literally blown off! You know they had to put a cloth over her face, at the funeral? Because she had no face left!"

Jesus hung his head and silently cried. Jess immediately felt terrible, but she also still felt irate.

"You died, Jesus! So did Lucia!"

"No, we didn't!" Jesus yelled.

Jess sat in shock. She'd never heard Jesus yell before. In the facility, he'd always been calm. He was always so collected. She stared at him in disbelief.

"You… you've never yelled before," she said, her voice low and shaky.

"I've never been so angry before," Jesus said, his voice still loud, strong. "I did not die, Jess." Jesus looked at her with firmness and fire. "And neither did Lucia. You changed everything. It's what you wanted, Jess. And if you can't accept things, well, then, I'm sorry. But you act as if you preferred it when I was dead!"

"No!" Jess cried.

She felt panicked. She threw herself across the couch and hugged Jesus tight, no longer afraid. In many ways, her emotions were like the day she met Harold and hugged him. Her only concern was to comfort Jesus. To let him know she cared.

"I'm sorry," she cried.

Already, however, Jesus hugged her back. He closed his eyes and smiled. She continued talking, her face over his shoulder.

"I'm so glad you're not dead! You have no idea. You have no idea what it was like, seeing you die. Everyone was so sad. And being here, on the ship, without you. It just wasn't right. It didn't feel right at all."

Jess pulled away, looking at Jesus in desperation. Tears streamed down her face. Jesus looked at her with concern. He hated seeing her in so much pain.

"Jess, I'm so sorry you had to go through that. I wish I could take those memories away. But, I'm here. I'm not dead."

"I still can't believe it."

"You can touch me. You can feel me. You hugged me. You can hear my voice. I'm sitting here with you. You've believed more firmly of things you couldn't even see or touch, Jess. Why can't you believe this?"

"I don't know," Jess cried. "I don't know."

"Everything is as it should be," Jesus repeated. "You have to believe that, Jess. You have to accept the part you've played in all of this."

"It's just too much."

"I know," Jesus said. He smiled, however. "It is a lot for one person to handle. But you were chosen to do many incredible things. We all were. And if you're not sure who or what chose you, does it really matter? All that matters, is how you feel, Jess. Whatever this is, it's something good. You feel that. I know you do, because we talked about it, many times. Whatever timeline you remember, I know you feel that. You've channeled into the Graylings, Jess. You've felt pure kindness. You saved them. And if what I've been hearing is right, you told Harold you would do all of this. He knew before he died that you would save his people. In turn, he saved me and Lucia. He did this, Jess, for *you*. Don't you see? You gave him an incredible gift. So, he gave you a gift in return. Don't you see that?"

Jess nodded, a tear tracking down her cheek. Jesus was right. Harold only wanted to thank her. He did so the only way he knew how. He'd given her a gift, to thank her for saving his people. To thank her for returning the Graylings to their home. Harold had given Jess her friends back. He had saved Jesus, and Lucia. Jess frowned.

"Ben said… you and Lucia have four children?" She looked at Jesus in concern.

"Yes," Jesus said, smiling.

"What are their names? How old are they?"

"We have a daughter, named Ramona. She's about to turn nine. She was born after Eric. Then we had a son, who we named Harold," Jesus smiled.

"Harold?"

Jesus nodded. "He's seven. He plays with Alex a lot. Then Lucia gave birth to Alberto. This was right after Harold died. Alberto is now three. Lastly, we had Miranda. She's one now, like Willa. And…" Jesus trailed off, looking at Jess with anticipation.

"What?"

"Lucia should be giving birth to a boy, sometime around six months from now."

Jess gasped. Jesus laughed.

"She's due to give birth about three months after Kate."

"And you're okay with Kate and Alma?" Jess asked.

"Alma's my sister-in-law," Jesus said. "And she loves Kate very much. It's all love, Jess. Why would I be against love?"

"Well, in my timeline, Ezra has a little trouble accepting two women together."

"That hasn't changed," Jesus said, rolling his eyes. "But, you seemed surprised about Kate's pregnancy. That didn't happen in your time?"

"No. But, you need to remember, in my timeline, Alma is with Kate, but she loses Lucia. She doesn't have her to talk to. I guess that made all the difference."

"Well," Jesus nodded. "It was actually Lucia who talked to Earl, about the whole subject of being a donor father."

"Huh… Weird. Earl's okay with it?"

"Signed right up. Alma performed the procedure. It only took one month, and, *Boom*, Kate was pregnant."

"Boom?" Jess laughed.

"What? What'd I say?"

"Yeah," Jess shook her head. "Things have definitely changed."

"Can you accept it, Jess?" Jesus looked at her with concern.

"Yes. I guess I can accept you and Lucia coming back from the dead."

"We didn't die," Jesus sighed.

"And I guess," Jess continued. "I can accept four new children I never knew existed before. But…"

"What?"

"If it was so important for me to win Hesperia back for the Graylings, then why is it like this? If people can come back from the dead, why is Hesperia so ruined?"

"It's not ruined, Jess. We can make it beautiful again. I truly believe that. We can't question it. We were meant to be here. One way or another, everything will work out."

"We were meant to watch the Graylings—and our own children— grow up under a brown sky? On a planet where no plants can even grow?"

"Who knows?" Jesus shrugged. "Whatever is meant to happen is going to happen. Just live your life, Jess. Stop worrying so much. Just accept things. With everything that's happened so far, you're having trouble with a little pollution?"

Jess shrugged. She looked at Jesus with apology in her eyes.

"I guess I just don't understand how we could make it this far, and everything else has worked out so perfectly, including people being alive who weren't, only to be undone by sludge and muck."

"Who says we're undone? You just said that you don't understand. But perhaps understanding is simply still yet to come? Remember our very first conversation? *'For we know in part, and we prophecy in part. But when that which is perfect is come, then that which is in part shall be done away'*. We only just got here, Jessie. The story's not over yet. Who's to say things won't still work out?"

"How?"

"Who knows?" Jesus shrugged.

Suddenly Jess's stomach growled loudly. Jesus laughed. He stood up, putting his hand out to pull Jess up off the couch.

"Will you have breakfast with a dead guy?"

***

Jess and Jesus headed to the dining hall for breakfast. Almost everyone else had already eaten. The only people in the dining hall when Jess and Jesus walked in, were Kate and Alma. Jess sat with them, after getting her smoothie.

"Hey, Chica," Alma said. "How you feelin'?"

"You're still a doctor, right?"

"I hope so," Alma said. "I impregnated my wife."

"You guys got married?"

"Yeah," Alma said, looking insulted. "Why wouldn't we?"

Jess shrugged. She looked at Kate, smiling.

"Do you know what it is? A boy or a girl?"

"We're waiting to find out," Kate said, looking at Alma, her face full of love.

"You know it's going to be black, right?" Ezra said, walking into the dining hall.

"Duh," Alma said, rolling her eyes.

Ezra shrugged, sitting down at the table next to everyone, sighing. He looked at Jess, nodding. "Ben's outside. He wants you to come out there. He wants everyone to come out."

"Ezra," Alma said. "You know it's a baby, right? Not an *it*?"

"Of course."

"Well, we don't care what color the baby is."

"You think I do?"

"You said *black*, like it was a bad thing," Alma said.

"No, I didn't," Ezra said, sounding highly insulted. "I just didn't know if Jess knew who the father was. My best friend is black. Why would I care what color it is? My wife is Asian, and my child is half-Asian. I'm not a racist."

"No, but you're a homophobe," Alma continued.

"No, I'm not. I went to your wedding."

"But, you have a problem with two women being together."

"Wow, after over ten years, you guys never hashed this out until now?" Jess said.

Jesus laughed, shaking his head. Jess looked at everyone in surprise.

"This is what we care about? Two lesbians having a baby?"

"I don't care. Just because I'm a little less receptive of it, doesn't make me a bad person. Everyone's different. I'm still friends with you guys, aren't I? I didn't boycott your wedding. I didn't try to stop you from having a baby. Just because I'm not clapping you on the back, doesn't make me a bad person."

"You're right," Kate said. "It doesn't."

"What?" Alma looked at Kate in disbelief.

"No, he's right, Al. He's entitled to his beliefs. He's not trying to stop us, is he? He's not trying to change how we think. So, why are we expecting him to change his way of thinking?"

"But…" Alma said, then said nothing more.

"I already have changed my way of thinking," Ezra said. "You think I haven't changed? I may not agree with two women getting married, but I've accepted it. Who am I to tell you what you can or can't do? I went to your wedding. I thought it was beautiful. I see that you two love each other. I may not understand it, but I can still see it. I'm happy for the two of you. I'm sorry if you thought I wasn't. But I'm not going to throw you a parade. If you ever need me for anything, I'm here for you. I'm just not an advocate, that's all."

"You don't have to be an advocate," Alma said. "Just be our friend."

"I *am* your friend," Ezra said, looking hurt. "I channeled you both in, didn't I? I said, 'everyone is here for a reason.' I meant both of you, as well. Earl's going to have a baby, and he couldn't have otherwise. He's over the moon. You two did that for him. And you and Alma were two of the people who brought Ben back to life, after he *died*."

Jess raked in a breath. Ben had never told her he'd died. She had no idea what Ezra was talking about. Everyone looked at Jess in concern. Ezra hung his head, sighing, and mentally kicked himself.

"Ben didn't tell you he died, did he?" Alma said, sounding nervous.

"Ezra, you said Ben wanted everyone to go outside, didn't you?" Jess said, sounding like a stern mother. She looked at Ezra. He could barely meet her eyes. He nodded in answer to her question. Jess stood and walked out of the room. She turned back, briefly.

"Come on, if you're coming."

21

Everyone else was already outside, when Jess came rushing up to Ben, her cheeks high with color. Ezra, Jesus, Kate, and Alma quickly followed. The rest of The Society stood near the edge of the bluff, under the lone, drooping tree. The crowd parted for Jess, however, as she came trudging up the slight incline, to stand in front of Ben.

"You died?!" She stood looking at Ben, her arms crossed over her chest.

"Jess—"

"No, Ben. When were you planning on telling me, huh? Never?"

"Jess, you just pulsed, destroyed all the Bailon, traveled through time, and created an alternate timeline, where Jesus and Lucia were alive! I didn't think you could handle hearing about my death. That's number one. Number two, the topic of my death didn't quite seem relevant, given the circumstances. It wouldn't have made sense to bring it up."

"Oh, really?" Jess yelled. "So, when were you going to tell me that you died, huh?"

"Man, things never change," Arnold said, from the sidelines. His eyes sparkled with excitement. "Hey, if Jess pulses again, and talks to Harold, can you tell him this time I want a bigger room? The suites aren't exactly designed for multiple children."

"Shut up, Arnold!" several people said in unison.

Arnold shrugged, putting his arm around Jenny. No one seemed to get his reference to multiple children. Jenny had only told him that morning that she was pregnant again. Ben and Jess went right on arguing, ignoring everyone.

"I'm waiting, Ben. When were you going to tell me that you *died*?!"

"Well, I guess I'm telling you right now," Ben said, getting angry.

"Only because I found out from Ezra!"

Ben looked at Ezra, who shrugged, shaking his head. He looked down at the ground, and Ben smiled.

"It's not funny, Ben!"

"Yes, it is," he said.

"What?!"

"It's funny that you're upset I died, when I'm standing here, right in front of you, clearly alive."

Jess looked at Ben, suddenly feeling ashamed. Jesus nodded on the sidelines. Ben, however, was still upset, and this time he allowed his anger to grow, giving Jess a what-for.

"Do you have any idea what it took to bring me back?" Ben said, his voice rising slightly. "First, our daughter put all my broken bones back together again. Then Mara healed my squashed brain. Then Kate used her ability to shock me again and again, while Alma buried her hand deep inside my chest to pump my heart. Pseudogene CPR, it's really great, Jess. And still, it took over ten minutes to get my heart beating again. I was dead for over ten minutes. The only thing that kept me from having permanent brain damage was Mara, and Alma breathing oxygen into my lungs while keeping my blood flowing through my veins, by squeezing my heart with her transparent hand!"

"Ben, stop," Jess whispered.

But Ben was livid now, his voice steadily rising the last several sentences. Now he raged, louder than Jess had ever heard him yell before, even as Dr. M.

"No!" he roared, and several people watching jumped or winced. "I died, Jess! And somehow, I'm still here! And Jesus and Lucia died! But they're still here! Accept that!"

"I have!" Jess yelled back through tears. "You think I haven't? For God's sake, Ben, I just had my world turned upside down yesterday. You'd think you could give me a little more time."

"I waited for you for four days," Ben said, his voice cracking. "I sat on that beach for four days, waiting for you to come back. And the only thing I had to hold onto, was the vision of a nine-year-old child. And I believed him. He told me you'd come back, and I believed him. A child, Jess, with an impossible knowledge of the future. *Our future.* You think I don't tell you things?"

"Sometimes," Jess said, her voice low. "You didn't tell me about what Sarah said during your last exercise, until months later. You didn't tell me about the Luci. You didn't tell me you died. You always say it's not the right time, that you want to wait. If you really believe I'm as strong as you're always telling me I am, why don't you think I can handle hearing things *now*? Don't wait to tell me, Ben. *Tell me now.*"

"Fine," Ben said, looking at Jess with love. "Eric said you'd come back, because he sees you in the future, at he and Angel's wedding. He sees you, and you're pregnant."

"I'm pregnant?" Jess looked at Ben with surprise. Then her face filled with joy.

"Nine years from now," Ben nodded. "I'm sorry I waited to tell you that." He paused for dramatic effect. "I just didn't think the time was right."

"Shut up," Jess said, but she smiled wide, laughing.

She rushed up and threw herself into Ben's arms. He enveloped her, and they kissed madly while everyone looked on, smiling.

"Freaking Romeo and Juliet," Martin sighed, hugging Eileen tight.

"What the hell are we out here for, Ben?" Martin yelled, winking at him.

Of course, Martin already knew. He'd heard everything in Aaron and Jemma's thoughts, as well as Rafferty and Ben.

"You need to hear this," Ben whispered to Jess. "Aaron?"

Ben nodded to Aaron, who stepped forward, looking nervous. He glanced over at Jemma and Rafferty, and they nodded.

"It was Jemma's idea," Aaron said. "Because she remembered how I used to always kill the plants, if I didn't change them back."

"Because Aaron changed how they photosynthesized," Jemma cut in, nodding at Aaron. "When he changes the coloring of the chlorophyll, it changes how the plants photosynthesize. With regular light, it kills them if he doesn't change them back, but…"

"Show them, Aaron," Rafferty said. He had a twinkle in his eyes.

Aaron walked over to the drooping tree. He touched the bark, laying his hand flat. Everyone watched in wonder as the leaves on the tree suddenly burst into the most amazingly vibrant shade of light purple. The leaves still drooped, albeit slightly less. Aaron turned around, smiling.

"We tried it with a few patches of grass, yesterday."

Aaron motioned for everyone to follow him. He led the group around the tree, several feet further beyond, to the very edge of the bluff. Here, everyone stopped and stared at two large patches of pink-colored grass. These cotton candy swaths were slightly taller than the rest of the dry, ailing grass, and lush in appearance. Clearly, the pink grass thrived.

"Aaron's ability may have killed plants back on Earth," Jemma said. "But here on Hesperia, it seems to be helping them flourish, allowing them adaptation to the filtered sunlight."

Everyone stared at Aaron in awe and wonder. He smiled, blushing humbly. Sarah walked over and hugged him. He kissed her in return, gazing into her eyes with intense love.

"Aaron," Jess said. "You always said your ability was useless."

Aaron looked at Jess and blushed more deeply. Jess looked up at Ben, then over at Jesus, who smiled and nodded. Jess looked at Rafferty then, who also smiled and nodded.

"Everyone said my pulse seemed tailor-made for wiping out the Bailon," Jess said. "But the Bailon are gone now. And Hesperia is still broken. Aaron, your ability is tailor-made to help Hesperia thrive again. You can revive all the ailing plant life."

"Maybe," Aaron said. "It will take a while, I guess."

"But, you once told me it took almost no energy. You said you could use your ability all day long and not even break a sweat."

"That's true. I'll just have to do a lot of walking around. I have to touch everything with my hands."

"Are you sure?" Grace said, frowning. "Have you ever tried your feet? Have you ever walked around barefoot?"

Aaron frowned at Grace, thinking, then shook his head, shrugging. He looked down. Then he took his gray shoes off and walked around, barefoot, concentrating. Everyone exclaimed in wonder, as suddenly, everywhere Aaron stepped, the grass turned bright pink.

"Holy crap!" Hanley said. "Doc, how did you not know he could do that?"

"It was useless in the facility," Ben shrugged. "Why would I care what part of his body he used?" He laughed.

"It's not useless now," Jess said. "Aaron, you'd better get busy walking around. And later, I think Rafferty needs to get you up into those mountains. There are a few ailing bushes and plants up there. I saw them, when we went to the water table."

"We can transplant from our garden, on board the ship, too," Jemma said, nodding at Roslyn. "If Aaron can change the chlorophyll to adapt the plants of Hesperia, he should be able to do the same with our plants. I mean, it's worth a try, anyway."

"We'll need to move at least one of the beehives out here then, to the bluff. And another will need to be placed at the base of the mountains, at the edge of the Grayling's city," Roslyn said.

"Aaron," Grace said, looking thoughtful. "Have you ever tried reviving water plants?"

Aaron frowned at Grace, not understanding. She looked at him with hope.

"Like, Algae?" Grace said.

"Take me up to the water table, Rafferty," Aaron said. "And Jesus better come."

***

Over the next several weeks, amazing changes took place on Hesperia. The Society watched in wonder, from the edge of the bluff, as the Graylings walked off the ship, many carrying equipment. Everyone watched, over the next several days, as the Graylings removed sheer rock from the outer edge of the mountains, on the far southern side, and converted the matter, amazingly, into crystalline, white structures. They opted for this, seeming to want nothing to do with the ugly dark metal pods leftover from the Bailon. Those remained high up in the mountainous regions, where no one ever had to worry about seeing them again.

The work went amazingly fast. Rafferty reminded everyone that when the Graylings left Hesperia, the city had housed more than two million of them. Now, they only needed to build enough structures to house a little under two hundred. The city, when finished, was much smaller than it had been, two hundred years before.

All of Hesperia needed to grow. That work went more slowly. The Graylings could only slowly rebuild their population, even as the humans continued to grow in numbers, while the flora and fauna on the planet also began to slowly heal and rebuild itself.

Over the next several weeks, Aaron revived all the plant life that remained on Hesperia. Everyone had to adjust to the brightly colored plants. Green was not the norm in their new world, but rather, neon shades of pink, purple, blue, yellow, and red.

Some of the plants from the Earth gardens were also successfully transplanted, but once changed by Aaron, they were not so easily recognizable.

***

The story was related to everyone in the dining hall over dinner one night, of how Aaron, Grace, and Jesus worked together as a team, to revive the inland water table.

Once put to work, the trio discovered their abilities were tailor-made to go together. Jesus walked the pair out into the middle of the lake, using his ability. Just as Malcolm could enable others to float, Jesus discovered his ability enabled others to walk on water with him.

Once in the middle of the lake, Grace and Aaron discovered that by holding hands, and placing their other free hand in the water, their abilities, when combined, seemed to revive the very last of the ailing algae at the very bottom of the table. They only knew this due to the bright yellow color that drifted up to their eyes, from deep within the clear water.

It would not be discovered for another three weeks, however, that there were, indeed, a few surviving marine animals within the lake. They had held on long enough to be revived by the abilities of the people from The Society, with the return of healthy algae within the lakebed.

Discovered as well, was the fact that a few mountain animals had survived, far on the northern side of the continent, where the Bailon had apparently been too lazy to burn. Slowly, over time, as the southern mountainside began to thrive, it was postulated that, eventually, the animals would venture south again, and slowly repopulate their numbers.

The bees adapted well to the environment on Hesperia. Some remained on board, in the garden, however, still maintained by Jemma and Roslyn.

***

Everyone in The Society decided to remain on board the ship. They were used to their routines, their way of life. Everyone was used to their rooms, the common room, the dining hall, and their master chef's kitchen, along with everything else. With the Graylings no longer living on board, there were several more decks available. The ship was large, taking up over half the bluff in length, and twice that in width, and no one realized until seeing it from the outside, that it also stood as tall as a nine-story building. New rooms were designed on the deck directly above theirs, with multiple rooms per quarters, so Arnold soon got his wish of having separate rooms for Mal and the impending birth of Jenny's second child.

There was enough room on board the ship to house at least twenty thousand humans. Grace mused that it would take several generations before they ran out of room and had to worry about finding more space. She'd been busy, the last several weeks, studying the plants of Hesperia, as well as some of the marine life. Alma eagerly studied right along with her.

Ben was not interested in these studies. His only concern was the well-being of his family. Angel and Alex adapted well to life on Hesperia. They enjoyed playing on the beach, as well as on the grass on the bluff. All the children were taken down into the ocean at high tide, on week two, and began swimming lessons.

Alex didn't need to use the stony steps to get down to the beach. He stepped down on the air, as Malcolm floated next to him, laughing. Jess looked on at this, shaking her head. Jesus showed off his skills, as the children clumsily learned to tread water, by running around their heads, splashing them.

"Drowning's not a worry for me," Jesus laughed and sang.

"Can you even swim, Jesus?" Jess laughed.

"Of course," Jesus said, running off and away.

The first several weeks, Ben spent mostly with Jess, alone in the evenings, once the kids were fast asleep. She began, as he suspected from the very beginning, to slowly piece together the life she'd missed, in the second timeline. Her memories came to her in dreams. She awakened, almost every morning, with several new memories of events she'd previously missed. Many events were surprisingly identical, she told Ben, once she'd remembered almost half of the new timeline. Jess had accepted her 'new life', as she liked to call it, adjusting to it well. She hadn't changed, and neither had Ben, she told him one night. Neither had anyone else, for that matter.

***

Three months into their stay on Hesperia, Grace came to Ben's room. She asked him to come to the infirmary with her. She looked radiant, as if she could barely contain her excitement. Jess shrugged her consent, busy playing with Alex, who crouched near the ceiling, laughing.

"I'm not going to play with you, if you keep doing that. It still doesn't occur to me to look up, you know that," Jess said, chiding him.

"It's not cheating," Alex said. "It's not a rule."

"Well, it should be," Jess said.

Ben quickly left, smiling, and followed Grace into the infirmary. Grace smiled uncharacteristically wide the entire way.

"Please tell me you're not pregnant," Ben said.

"That's impossible," Grace said. "I already went through menopause, remember?"

Ben nodded. He couldn't think of anything else that would make Grace smile that wide, however. He was at a total loss as to the cause of her happiness.

"What is it, Grace?"

"I may have gone through menopause, but I've got a long way to go before I'm done. Remember when you told me you thought that us being transgens might extend our lifespans?"

"Yes."

"Mm hmm? And then you told me I might have only lived half my life. That I might have another fifty-four years to go."

"Yes," Ben said again, feeling anxious.

"Well, that was over five years ago. I'm fifty-nine now, Ben, soon to be sixty. But I think I can safely say, I've got at least three times that long to live, still."

"What are you talking about?"

"I'm talking about this."

Grace motioned to her work desk, littered with petri dishes filled with dead bees, a few small fish, and a couple of plant samples.

"What's all this?"

"This is my study of the cellular regeneration of several different forms of life on Hesperia. I've also taken a few samples from the

Graylings, thanks to Rafferty. He swabbed their skin for me. I compared it to everything you see here on this table."

"So?" Ben felt both suspicious and excited.

"So... We knew that before the Graylings were forced off Hesperia, they lived for over five hundred years, right? Many of them lived well over six hundred years."

"Right?" Ben raised his eyebrows.

"And once off Hesperia, their lifespans were cut well in half, sometimes more," Grace continued.

"And," Ben had grown impatient.

"And... Now that they're back on Hesperia, their cellular degeneration has slowed quite a bit. But, so has the cellular degeneration of the plants in our own garden here on board this ship. As well as the bees.... As well as us."

Ben stared at Grace, not comprehending her statement. She looked at him, frowning.

"Where's the scientist hidden inside you, Ben?"

Ben sat thinking for several minutes. Then his face lit up. A small smile played at his lips and quickly grew. He looked at Grace with a light in his eyes that made her laugh.

"The same process that slowed the Graylings aging, slows everything that lives on the planet."

Grace nodded.

"Due to the increased ionization in the air," Ben continued. "It interacts with all living things, on a nuclear level, slowing cellular degeneration, while also enabling cells to regenerate much more easily, and many more times."

"That's right," Grace said. "So not only do things live longer on Hesperia. They also age much slower. The two go together."

"How much slower?" Ben asked, barely able to contain his excitement.

"Well, the average bumblebee lives between nine and twelve weeks. I've been studying the bees since we first landed on Hesperia. The adults that were already near the end of their lifespans when we landed here... are still alive, Ben."

"So, they've already been alive for twice the length expected," Ben said, nodding.

"I've analyzed my own cells, and their degenerative properties, under a spectroscope. I did the same thing with Alma, and Malcolm," Grace said. "None of us is showing a single sign of cellular or adipose degeneration of any kind. Not one sign, Ben."

"And we already know the Grayling's lifespans were cut in half, at least," Ben mused.

"And now the bees are living at least twice as long. The oldest workers aren't even showing signs of being anywhere near death. They're not showing any signs of aging."

"And the plant life you've studied?"

"The same. With the marine samples I've taken of algae as well as aquatic vertebrates, I've found it's a universal phenomenon. Anything that lives on this planet benefits from the environment. I suspect that's also why the Bailon proliferated in such high numbers, despite their inferior anatomical traits. Their numbers swelled much higher, and much faster than they were used to, and they all lived much longer than I'm sure they ever expected. It created an increased demand for food that they were not able to compensate for. It's why the environment was devastated so quickly. There were many more Bailon in a much shorter period than there would have been on another planet with a weaker atmosphere."

Ben nodded, the full understanding of the situation hitting home. He looked at Grace with tears in his eyes. She smiled.

"We got here just in time, didn't we?"

"Yes," Grace nodded. "Another ten years, I don't think we could have brought Hesperia back. She was on the very brink. Even so, it's taken some of our own flora to regrow things. And that's a miracle all its own. None of these things would even be possible without the specific abilities of a few people, who, prior to our landing on this planet, seemed to have completely irrelevant abilities. And some of them shouldn't even be alive, according to Jess."

Ben nodded again, sitting down. He felt dizzy.

"The party is started Ben. It's been going on for a long time. We just didn't know it," Grace said, smiling. "And everyone's invited."

Ben looked at Grace, his eyes wide and solemn. "How long?"

"How long, what?"

"To live. Our lifespans. How long do you think we have?"

"I'm thinking I've got at least two hundred more years," Grace said. "And that's before I even reach over-the-hill, perhaps. I'm guessing *you've* got a good two hundred more to go, also. Maybe even more. Hesperia easily doubles any given lifespan, and I suspect it does more than that, perhaps even triples it. The bees, as I've mentioned, are already twice as old as they should be, and they were already at the end of their lifespans when we got here. They've already lived twice the time they should have, and they aren't even showing signs of slowing down yet. I suspect Hesperia, perhaps, may even quadruple any given lifespan. So, I'm guessing the average human lifespan on Hesperia can be expected to run well over two hundred and fifty years. Some may even reach three hundred years old. Which means, I'm not even close to halfway done, as you once correctly surmised. Forget halfway, I'm not even a third done with my life. Maybe only one-quarter of my ultimate age right now. And neither are you. And we won't live nearly so long as people born here, or who arrived while still very young. You and I can expect to live nearly three hundred years, but we've already aged quite a bit before reaching Hesperia. Your children, Ben, are going to live to be *over* three hundred years old. And their children, who develop even in utero under the influence of Hesperia's environment will likely live well beyond three hundred years. Future generations of human beings can probably expect lifespans similar—perhaps just slightly less—than the average Grayling… Who lives to be over five hundred years old. But, at any rate, as I've said, us old folks get the short end of the stick, at slightly less than three hundred years, give or take." She winked at Ben, smiling mischievously.

Ben hugged Grace, then ran from the room. Grace laughed at the hug, then called after Ben, in concern.

"Where are you going?"

"Jess always says I wait to tell her things for too long," Ben called over his shoulder.

***

Ben rushed into his room. Jess was just putting Alex to bed. He rushed up to her and kissed her passionately.

"What about me, Daddy?" Alex said.

Ben gently kissed his son on the forehead. Jess watched him, curious. She sent him in to say goodnight to Angel, then went to wait for him in their bedroom.

When Ben came in, a minute later, Jess paced the floor nervously. She looked at him expectantly. She knew something was going on. Ben closed their door, then rushed up and kissed her again. When he pulled away, he looked at Jess with so much love, she could hardly stand it.

"What?" she said. "What did you do this time?"

"Nothing," Ben laughed. "I was just wondering if you would marry me."

"Ben, we're already married."

"Yes, but when I asked you to marry me the first time, you probably thought you were saying yes to, oh, I don't know, about thirty years? At the most."

"So? What, you think I didn't mean it?"

"No, I'm sure you meant it. But what if I asked you to marry me for the next, say, two hundred years?"

Jess looked at Ben, frowning. She thought he'd gone off the deep end.

"Are you wondering if I'll still want to be with you, in the afterlife?" Her frown grew deeper as Ben laughed heartily.

"No." Ben continued laughing. "I want to know if you'll be my wife for the next two hundred years."

"Ben, how can I be? In two hundred years, we'll both be dead."

"No, we won't. You said I wait to tell you things for too long, Jessie. So, I'm telling you, now. Grace just told me, in a roundabout fashion, skipping the science talk, that people on Hesperia can expect to live to be well over two hundred years old. Maybe even three hundred."

Jess stared at Ben, still frowning. He smiled.

"Not only that, but we'll age much slower. You can probably expect to be looking at this face, just as it is now, for another hundred years, before I look any older."

Jess continued staring. Ben worried she'd snapped. Perhaps, after everything they'd been through, this was simply too much for Jess to take.

"Jess?" Ben looked at her with great concern. "Jess, say something."

"Y—You," Jess stammered. "You're going to live another two hundred years?"

"More or less. A bit more, perhaps. But at least another two hundred."

"And… You want *me* to be with you the whole time?" Jess looked at Ben in disbelief.

He frowned. "Do you want to be with me?"

"Are you kidding?" Jess sighed, breaking into a giant smile. She ran at Ben, throwing her arms around him, kissing him madly.

It wasn't the first time they'd made love since Jess had pulsed, but it was markedly memorable. It was the first time they made love knowing they would be doing so for at least another few hundred years.

***

The Society thrived and flourished on Hesperia. Everyone was so happy with their families, no one ever missed Earth, save for Hanley and his Big Macs. Even Aaron, who had once suggested returning to Earth, never gave any further thought to going back. Hesperia was their home now.

Kate gave birth to a little girl, whom they named Caitlyn. Earl chose the name. Three months later, Lucia gave birth to a little boy, and they named him Willard. Jenny and Arnold were the next to have another child. They had a little girl, whom they named Gwen. All the couples, eventually ended up with more children, including Rafferty and Jemma.

Some of the children grew up and moved to the Grayling's city, and many lived there, returning to the ship for visits almost daily. Many people, eventually, simply went back and forth. The only ones never to set foot inside the Grayling's city, were the original twenty-one members of The Society, who were channeled in for life. Occasionally, they connected with Albert and Paula, catching up on how everyone did and how things went. The humans and the Graylings interacted well, and lived a symbiotic life, in peaceful tranquility.

***

Eric and Angel did, indeed, get married, nine years after The Society arrived on Hesperia. They were both eighteen. Jess was pregnant at the wedding, with she and Ben's first child since arriving on their new home planet.

The ceremonies were a bit more elaborate after arriving on Hesperia. The wedding of Eric and Angel (which Hanley again happily officiated), took place in the garden on board the ship. Afterwards, everyone went outside, and a reception was held on the bluff. Tables and chairs were brought out, and everyone ate, and even danced, in the mid-afternoon sunlight.

Already, after only nine short years on Hesperia, the sky had begun to brighten a bit, with no new pollution added into the atmosphere. Hesperia purged itself, slowly healing. The sky was still brown, but a much lighter shade now. Aaron constantly had to check up on all the flora of the planet, adjusting the chlorophyll of the plants. Eventually, he wouldn't need to do this anymore, but for the time being, it was a full-time job.

Rafferty helped prepare for the reception by building an outdoor speaker system to pipe music onto the bluff for people to dance to, along with a dance floor. All the old favorites were played at everyone's request. Any music anyone ever could have wanted was in the ship's computers. Everyone watched as Eric and Angel danced, then other couples soon joined in.

Eric informed his bride, as they danced, that Alex would be getting married in another four years, to Willa.

"Is that how Willa is connected to my family?" Angel looked at Eric, her eyes wide. "She's going to be my sister-in-law?"

"Yes. And you're going to end up with five nieces, and four nephews."

"Seriously?"

"Yep. Do you want to know how many children *we're* going to have, total?"

"No," Angel said, kissing Eric gently. "You already told me we name our first daughter Jess, and that's all I want to know."

"You don't want to know when she'll be born?"

"No," Angel said. "Well, maybe. Oh, I don't know."

"Can I give you a hint?" Eric said, his eyes shining. Angel could tell he was itching to tell her. She nodded her consent.

"Eight months from today," Eric whispered in her ear.

"But that would mean…" Angel looked at Eric in surprise. "Tonight?!"

Eric nodded. He looked at Angel with nothing but love.

"I didn't think it was fair for me to know when we make her, and you not to. I'm sorry if it bothers you to know. I just… don't like feeling like I'm keeping secrets from you. You are okay with it, right?"

"Yes," Angel said, her eyes shining with tears. "I must be, if it happens. If you see it, it happens."

"Are you happy?" Eric looked at Angel with longing.

"Don't you already know?" Angel said. She reached up and kissed him again.

Jess and Ben looked on, feeling happy for their daughter. Jess was due to give birth in two months. They didn't know whether it was a boy or a girl. They had decided not to find out and be surprised.

Everyone on the bluff danced, including all the couples. Earl danced by with Vera, Ezra and Roslyn's daughter, now eighteen years old. Ben wasn't certain, but he thought something might be developing between them, despite the considerable age difference. Martin brushed by, dancing with Eileen.

"Yep. It's not your imagination, Ben."

Ben looked at Martin, then back at Earl and Vera, surprise written all over his face. Martin shrugged, tapped his temple, then winked and smiled, and went back to dancing with his wife. Hanley and Rachel swirled by, and Rachel also nodded and winked at Ben and Jess. Hanley, meanwhile, offered his trademark, lop-sided grin and a waggly-fingered wave. Ben nodded back, then looked at his wife.

"Is this a life you could live with for a bit longer?"

"Are you kidding, Ben? If you had told me, back in the facility, that *this* is how we'd end up, I don't think I would have believed you."

"Are you talking about us?" Ben frowned.

"No, I'm talking about everything. Everything that's happened. It's practically unbelievable, isn't it?" Jess said, glancing around.

"But it did happen," Ben whispered, placing his forehead against hers.

"I know," Jess sighed, closing her eyes. "And every day I feel blessed. Jesus was right. No matter how it happens, eventually, everything falls into place. Everything is as it should be."

"No more doubts?"

"What do you think?"

"I think…" Ben trailed off, whirling Jess around, making her laugh. "I could dance with you like this forever."

"Okay."

And they did. At least, they danced for the next few hours.

***

Twenty-one friends lived their lives out on Hesperia. They lived in a galaxy that had no name, on a planet named by an ex-casino worker, so far from Earth, even the stars they looked upon at night had no titles, save for what they each decided to call them. It was a new world, one they built for themselves. They chose their own terms for everything. But most importantly, as Harold would have pointed out, they all *chose*. Everyone in The Society was free to choose whatever life they wanted, and they all chose to remain together.

About the Author

Jennifer Word is an award-winning poet, novelist, fiction and non-fiction writer, editor, reviewer, and publisher. She holds a B.A. in Psychology from Pepperdine University, with minors in Education and English. She is an inactive affiliate member of the HWA. She has worked as an editor for *Dark Moon Digest*, Dark Moon Books, Perpetual Motion Machine Publishing, and Authors Large & Small. Her short stories, articles, and poetry have been printed in: *The Storyteller*, *The Klondike Sun*, *Dark Moon Digest*, *Dark Eclipse e-Magazine*, *Surreal Grotesque*, *eFiction*, *Gamut Magazine*, and multiple anthologies, including: *Slices of Flesh*; *Zombies Need Love, Too*; *Frightmares: A Fistful of Flash Fiction Horror*; and *From Beyond the Grave*. Her current novels are available through EMP Publishing—*All Because of the Cat & Other Tales*; *Once More*; *Lyrical Tales: Collected Poems and Photography,* and *The Society: Trilogy*. You can follow her on Twitter: @jenniferword.

Hupsélos

This is the unsealed wisdom of the manifestation of the Holy Spirit and the message given unto me to depart to those left behind. As prophesied in the Book of Daniel and sealed up until the appointed time of Truth be revealed, and as such, signified that the seals are now, of some, opened.

The Holy Spirit is poured out upon many, your sons and daughters prophesy, and the battle cry is sounded; the final days draw nigh. Glory be unto God, for this Truth unsealed meant for those left behind, which has been kept from the knowledge (and I from the clutches) of Satan, till the days draw short as to prevent the wicked one from perceiving or preventing.

Therefore, take heed: For the Truth sealed until those left behind will surely have need; those days arrive quickly, and the event assuring a leaving of many, and a taking of the same, are soon to be upon the earth. Let all who have eyes to see, and all who have ears to hear, gain understanding.

† I have been delivered of a dire warning within the message for today. It is of an extremely disturbing nature, so be forewarned. †

Today's lesson for 7/26 is based on the Strong's Concordance 726, which is the word harpazó: to seize, catch up, snatch away
Original Word: ἁρπάζω
Part of Speech: Verb
Transliteration: harpazó
Phonetic Spelling: (har-pad'-zo)
Short Definition: I seize, snatch, obtain by robbery.

726 harpázō – properly, seize by force; snatch up, suddenly and decisively – like someone seizing bounty (spoil, a prize); to take by an open display of force (i.e. not covertly or secretly).

The word harpázō is the Greek translation of the Latin word rapio/rapturo, which is where the English term 'rapture' comes from.

You don't have to believe in the rapture to be raptured, nor do you need to see the signs or know that it is drawing near. All you must do to be raptured is simply believe in Jesus Christ before the rapture takes place, and you won't be left behind (1 Thessalonians 4:13-18):

¹³ But I would not have you to be ignorant, brethren, concerning them which are asleep, that ye sorrow not, even as others which have no hope.

¹⁴ For if we believe that Jesus died and rose again, even so them also which sleep in Jesus will God bring with him.

¹⁵ For this we say unto you by the word of the Lord, that we which are alive and remain unto the coming of the Lord shall not prevent them which are asleep.

¹⁶ For the Lord himself shall descend from heaven with a shout, with the voice of the archangel, and with the trump of God: and the dead in Christ shall rise first:

¹⁷ Then we which are alive and remain shall be caught up together with them in the clouds, to meet the Lord in the air: and so shall we ever be with the Lord.

¹⁸ Wherefore comfort one another with these words.

*But, be warned now, that the rapture is NOT what we have been told it will be. It will not be like it has been depicted in books and movies. We will NOT all just suddenly vanish, leaving the rest of the world to wonder where we went. If that were the case, given the endless books written, movies made, documentaries, and modern day talk about exactly what the rapture will look like, if it were to happen in that exact manner, wouldn't everyone (regardless of their religious beliefs) immediately recognize the event for what it is? And wouldn't that recognition immediately spawn a whole new congregation of believers by the billions? This will NOT be the case.

In Acts 8:39, Philip is caught up in the spirit and carried away, but NOT to Heaven. He is merely transported away from where he had just baptized the eunuch, and moved to a different place, where he was immediately needed to do more work for the Lord, in Caesarea, where he could not arrive quickly enough without aid of the Holy Spirit carrying him. His physical body did not enter Heaven.

Also keep in mind that while Jesus was resurrected and is the first fruits, he was also the Son of God, even in the flesh, and the only man of the flesh to live a sinless life. Therefore, Jesus, as a man in human form, was still and always incorruptible. Hence, his body was resurrected and disappeared, when he got up and walked out of His tomb, and He was later able, still in earthly form of flesh, to enter the Kingdom of God.

Lastly, in the book of Revelation, John writes of the visions he was given, some of which transport him to Heaven, where he sees the lamb on the throne and the 24 Elders. However, this is all still a vision granted by Jesus Christ, through the angel sent to John while he sat in punishment on the isle of Patmos. John did NOT physically enter Heaven. It is possible I am misinterpreting some of Revelation, and that, in fact, part of the revelation of John is a vision, and part of it is what he sees in Heaven, but even so, John clearly states in 4:2: "And immediately I was in the spirit".

Interesting enough, he describes it as 'immediate', much as the rapture is described as occurring so quickly, it happens in an instant. But whether John's description of being immediately "in the spirit" refers to his spiritual body being instantly in Heaven, or whether it still means he is seeing Heaven in a vision (but to see a vision of actual Heaven, I would imagine you MUST be 'in the spirit'! i.e. filled with the Holy Spirit), is unknown. Either way, it lends verification to the statement by Paul in 1 Corinthians 15:50 that human beings in the flesh (corruptible) cannot inherit the Kingdom of God (nor enter), and that when we are saved, it is our spiritual bodies that are granted eternal life.

2 Corinthians 12:1-4 further touches on this mystery, of whether one can enter Heaven "whether in the body" ... "or whether out of the body". Paul is speaking of his vision/encounter with Jesus Christ, the one that transformed him from persecuting Christians, into converting to a believer in Christ himself, and becoming a disciple. It is because he is speaking of Jesus Christ, that Paul wonders on whether he saw him "in the body" or "out of the body." However, this question is moot, as it has now been established that Jesus Christ is the only man to ever live that is qualified, able and worthy of entering Heaven in the flesh (or in this case, as Paul describes it in two variances, first in verse 3: "the third heaven," and again in verse 4: "into paradise".

The fact that it remains a mystery whether the man that Paul witnessed was a physical body or a spiritual body, and he states that only "God knoweth", lends verification to the fact that belief in the acts of God must be obtained through faith alone.

But there are two other examples (at least) within the Bible, supposedly of men being 'raptured' (this is an erroneous use of the term, however, as the actual rapture referred to in 1 Corinthians 15 and 1 Thessalonians 4 (and ultimately in Revelation 12:5) is the only occurrence of this event. Since this event only takes place once, it is only spoken of in these terms for this event, i.e., The Rapture is a one-time event, and the only occurrence that can be properly referred to as the rapture, and the people involved in this event can properly be described as 'raptured' (the word harpazó is only used for this mass event; slight variances of this word, such as harpagmos and harpagé are used in other cases). All other instances in the Bible of men being 'raptured' are not of The Rapture event and should simply be referred to in terms of single events (usually 'caught up', or 'caught away' or 'taken', or that God 'took away').

But let's examine these events, which are instances of people being 'caught away', that most mistakenly believe includes a vanishing or removal of the physical, flesh and blood, body:

The first example ever (unless I am mistaken) of any man being 'taken' by God, occurs in Genesis 5:24: "And Enoch walked with God: and he was not; for God took him." Nowhere in this very brief description should we assume that Enoch's body was swept up to Heaven, as already outlined and shown in 1 Corinthians 15:50.

There is an obvious delineation here between Enoch and all the rest of the genealogy outlined in Genesis chapter 5, to be certain, as all the other sons descending from Adam, including Adam himself, are simply stated to have died: "and he died." It is also extremely vague as to exactly what Enoch did differently than the rest to be considered (verse 22 & 24) to have "walked with God".

Regardless, clearly Enoch was regarded as above other men who lived before and after him, and his behavior would seem to have been pleasing to God, and therefore, Enoch was rewarded (in the same fashion that all who are alive and in Christ at the time of the sounding of the last trump will also be rewarded with Rapture, or not having to suffer or experience the deaths of our physical bodies) with being taken by God. But the simple statement in Genesis 5:24 that Enoch "was not; for God took him" merely means that Enoch was not dead, because God took his spiritual body up to heaven, as opposed to everyone else who simply "died". This is qualified by the fact that Enoch "walked with God", the key delineation. Therefore, Enoch's spiritual body was pure enough, and untainted by sin, so to be worthy enough to enter the Kingdom of God in the spirit, incorruptible, even without the future saving Grace and Salvation of Jesus Christ. Nowhere here is there a reason to think that Enoch's body vanished.

In the context I've outlined, this would simply mean that Enoch's spiritual body was forcibly seized out of his physical body (which in all other cases is described as instantaneous, so we'll establish here that being 'caught up', by definition, must be instantaneous, to not suffer death, i.e., to not die), and so Enoch did not die like all the rest are described to have experienced in Genesis 5, and his spiritual body entered the Kingdom of God.

Lastly, there is the catching away of Elijah, which is described in 2 Kings 2: 7-17:

[7] And fifty men of the sons of the prophets went, and stood to view afar off: and they two stood by Jordan.

[8] And Elijah took his mantle, and wrapped it together, and smote the waters, and they were divided hither and thither, so that they two went over on dry ground.

[9] And it came to pass, when they were gone over, that Elijah said unto Elisha, Ask what I shall do for thee, before I be taken away from thee. And Elisha said, I pray thee, let a double portion of thy spirit be upon me.

[10] And he said, Thou hast asked a hard thing: nevertheless, if thou see me when I am taken from thee, it shall be so unto thee; but if not, it shall not be so.

[11] And it came to pass, as they still went on, and talked, that, behold, there appeared a chariot of fire, and horses of fire, and parted them both asunder; and Elijah went up by a whirlwind into heaven.

[12] And Elisha saw it, and he cried, My father, my father, the chariot of Israel, and the horsemen thereof. And he saw him no more: and he took hold of his own clothes, and rent them in two pieces.

[13] He took up also the mantle of Elijah that fell from him, and went back, and stood by the bank of Jordan;

[14] And he took the mantle of Elijah that fell from him, and smote the waters, and said, Where is the Lord God of Elijah? and when he also had smitten the waters, they parted hither and thither: and Elisha went over.

[15] And when the sons of the prophets which were to view at Jericho saw him, they said, The spirit of Elijah doth rest on Elisha. And they came to meet him, and bowed themselves to the ground before him.

[16] And they said unto him, Behold now, there be with thy servants fifty strong men; let them go, we pray thee, and seek thy master: lest peradventure the Spirit of the Lord hath taken him up, and cast him upon some mountain, or into some valley. And he said, Ye shall not send.

[17] And when they urged him till he was ashamed, he said, Send. They sent therefore fifty men; and they sought three days, but found him not.

With the presupposition that when God carries someone away, it means He takes their physical body, one is automatically set up to interpret the above events incorrectly (and all events of this nature). Notice in verses 9-10 that when Elisha asks to be granted a double portion of Elijah's spirit, Elijah says that Elisha, "hast asked a hard thing". Nevertheless, as Elijah tells him, "if thou see me when I am taken from thee, it shall be so unto thee; but if not, it shall not be so."

Herein lies another key component of the mystery. Elijah says that Elisha has asked a hard thing, and then qualifies further that it would be hard, seemingly, not only to be granted a double portion of his spirit, but also because Elisha would only receive the answer (and the double portion) if he 'sees' Elijah being taken. This key verse indicates that when one is caught up by God (an already rare event, reserved for exemplary servants, or especially godly-minded and faithful individuals), it is even more rare for any to witness it (but the prophets must witness this, or else this Truth cannot be in the Scriptures), and I am here outlining where it is, and how it has been misunderstood.

Luckily for Elisha, he does witness the spectacle of Elijah going, "up by a whirlwind into heaven." Immediately, Elisha knows that he will be granted the double portion of Elijah's spirit. If that isn't enough alone to make him emotional, he witnesses: "behold, there appeared a chariot of fire, and horses of fire, and parted them both asunder; and Elijah went up by a whirlwind into heaven."

Elisha immediately calls out in praise, overwhelmed, "My father, my father, the chariot of Israel, and the horsemen thereof." And it further says, "And he saw him no more: and he took hold of his own clothes, and rent them in two pieces." Elisha is so overwhelmed by what he has just witnessed, he rents his own clothes in two.

But what about the verse that says that Elisha, "saw him no more," and the fact that when the 'fifty strong men' searched for three days, they could not find Elijah's body? Doesn't that prove that being caught up to Heaven by God does in fact involve our physical bodies being taken up? NO.

Try to imagine the events witnessed by Elisha. This catching away is different from all others described in the Bible. No other catching away involves a chariot of fire, and horses of fire, which part from one another and go asunder, spinning violently into a vortex, or whirlwind (essentially a fire tornado), to carry Elijah away. It is easy to understand then, how and why Elisha knew the men would not find Elijah's body, for there wasn't one. Not because Elijah's body was carried into Heaven, for we must never lose sight of 1 Corinthians 15:50.

Elisha knew the body of Elijah would not be found because he witnessed Elijah's catching away. Elisha witnessed the instantaneous transformation of Elijah's spiritual body separated from his fleshly body. He witnessed Elijah's spirit being caught up to Heaven in a fiery whirlwind, that, as the events would suggest, also included the immediate immolation of Elijah's body. The fire chariot and horses of fire, forming a whirlwind, were another honor granted to Elijah, for he was given a Holy burial in the form of Divine cremation, for lack of a better description. After everything is over, and Elisha cries out to God, then rents his clothes, he recovers himself and takes up the mantle that Elijah dropped when his body (both flesh and spiritual) were taken up in the whirlwind.

The last thing to note in this instance is that it is indicated that people don't normally witness this seizing and separation of the spiritual body from the mortal body. Case in point, if this were something we could easily witness, people would report seeing spirits rising out of bodies when seeing someone die (in the hospital, or at the site of an accident, in hospice care, etc.), but we don't.

It is not something visible to human beings (save the few witnesses who must have seen these cases mentioned in the Bible), and we know that Elisha was granted the ability to see it; this is further attested to by the sons of the prophets and the fifty strong men seeing nothing of the event, not even the fiery whirlwind; they were not able to see it, they were blinded from witnessing it. Here one could argue that they were simply too far away to see it, but given the description in that passage, which doesn't indicate that Elijah and Elisha traveled so far once they left the others behind and crossed the Jordan river, and it isn't described necessarily as being too far off for the others to see, especially a fire tornado that goes up into the sky. 2 Kings 2:7:

"7 And fifty men of the sons of the prophets went, and stood to view afar off".

It's hard to imagine, no matter how far off they stood, that they all missed the fiery whirlwind tornado that went all the way up to Heaven, unless they were simply not allowed to see it. This is the case, since even Elisha, who stood right next to Elijah, had to ask to see it, and Elijah made it clear this was a hard thing to request; even he was not certain whether God would grant the request to Elisha or not. No wonder Elisha was so moved when he was gifted with seeing such an amazing sight.

One more thing of note, and perhaps the most important of all, in this event of Elijah's being caught up. It seems that this knowledge of the separation of the flesh and blood body and the spiritual body was common knowledge during the time that the book of 2 Kings was written, and during the time that Elijah the prophet lived.

This lends further credence to my message, that we have been blinded by a deception of Satan (this I can attest was given to me), and only very recently. As research would suggest, the lie may have begun to spread sometime around 1830 and may have begun with a man named John Nelson Darby (but this I cannot verify, as those facts were not revealed to me), so are not vital to the revealing of Truth of spiritual transition to enter Heaven.

Whatever the case, this deception appears to be rather new, and less than 200 years old, give or take. Previously, Christians either were aware of the instances of 'rapture' and being 'caught up' by God, but these topics weren't discussed by parishioners or churches (or if so, very rarely), and the ones who did discuss it, most likely, did not describe the future incident (or the past ones outlined in the Bible) as involving the disappearance, or vanishing of a physical body. Here is the final revealing. 2 Kings 2:16:

16 And they said unto him, Behold now, there be with thy servants fifty strong men; let them go, we pray thee, and seek thy master: lest peradventure the Spirit of the Lord hath taken him up, and cast him upon some mountain, or into some valley. And he said, Ye shall not send.

Look at what the sons of the prophets are saying here to Elisha. They know that Elijah is gone, meaning, they know he has been taken up by God. They literally say of Elijah: "the Spirit of the Lord hath taken him up." Furthermore, they bow down to Elisha, recognizing the mantle has been passed on. They know that Elijah is no more, that he is GONE. Yet, they request to go and look for his BODY. If being caught up to Heaven by the Lord was commonly accepted to include taking the flesh and blood body up into Heaven, then why when the men acknowledge that Elijah has been taken up, do they think there is a body left to go and retrieve?

It is because they know that being 'caught up' involves the removal and taking of the Spiritual Body of a person, and that this involves (in the rare cases of being 'taken up' or 'caught up') the leaving behind of the fleshly body.

The only reason they want to look for Elijah's body (and this lends significant weight to the immolation/cremation event) is because they did not witness the 'taking away', as it is a "hard thing" to witness, i.e., rare, as attested to by Elijah; and so, having not seen the nature of Elijah's particular taking away, they have no idea that it involved a fiery whirlwind. They do not realize that Elijah's body was destroyed in the whirlwind during the process of his being taken away. Hence, they think Elijah's body is abandoned up in the mountains, and they wish to retrieve it to give him a proper burial, fit for a prophet. But this honoring of Elijah's body was seen to by God with the fiery whirlwind and was the purpose for this unusual manner of taking away.

Elisha, having witnessed the destruction of Elijah's leftover body, obviously knew it was pointless for the men to look, but they insisted until he relented, and of course, after three days of searching, they found nothing.

Why did Elisha not simply tell them about the destruction of Elijah's body? Well, Elisha himself was extremely blessed to be granted witness of the sight. Out of respect for God, I doubt Elisha would have seen it proper to then go about describing it to fifty plus men immediately after the fact, especially once he came back and realized that they'd all seen nothing of the event, not even the whirlwind.

That sight was granted to Elisha only; he could not and would not have told the men, and was then left with no choice, at their insistence, to let them fruitlessly search for Elijah's body. One would wonder, however, if, had Elisha told the men what he had seen, but having not witnessed it for themselves, would any of them have truly believed it?

To sum this all up and move on: one must arrive at the belief that we live forever in spiritual bodies on faith alone, since we cannot see this transformation. And neither will anyone witness this instantaneous transformation in millions (or billions) of people when The Rapture event occurs.

So here lies the disturbing conclusion:

This is a dire warning to all those left behind: The Rapture will not be a vanishing of millions (or billions) of people. Instead, it will appear as if countless of us all just suddenly and mysteriously died. Our bodies will remain, DEAD, here on earth. Therefore, the event of the Rapture will be obscured in mystery over what will appear to be physical death, with no apparent cause, leaving the world to speculate in chaos, heartbreak and fear. Millions of bodies will NOT disappear. There simply will be millions of dead bodies. But rest assured, we will have been Raptured, having been pulled out of our mortal, physical bodies, feeling no pain, and immediately transformed into our spiritual bodies, our new form, transformed; i.e. changed, literally in a moment. Hence the simple statement in 1 Corinthians 15:51:

"We shall not all sleep, but we shall all be changed,"

or in modern layman's terms:

We won't all die, but we will all be changed (transformed) into our spiritual bodies, from out of our flesh and blood bodies.

As it states in 1 Corinthians 15:53-54:

^{53} For this corruptible must put on incorruption, and this mortal must put on immortality.

^{54} So when this corruptible shall have put on incorruption, and this mortal shall have put on immortality, then shall be brought to pass the saying that is written, Death is swallowed up in victory.

Those Raptured will not experience death, therefore, we will not actually die. We'll merely be leaving our fleshly bodies behind, like discarded layers of clothing shed on a hot, summer day. (1 Corinthians 15:50-58):

^{50} Now this I say, brethren, that flesh and blood cannot inherit the kingdom of God; neither doth corruption inherit incorruption.

^{51} Behold, I shew you a mystery; We shall not all sleep, but we shall all be changed,

^{52} In a moment, in the twinkling of an eye, at the last trump: for the trumpet shall sound, and the dead shall be raised incorruptible, and we shall be changed.

^{53} For this corruptible must put on incorruption, and this mortal must put on immortality.

^{54} So when this corruptible shall have put on incorruption, and this mortal shall have put on immortality, then shall be brought to pass the saying that is written, Death is swallowed up in victory.

^{55} O death, where is thy sting? O grave, where is thy victory?

^{56} The sting of death is sin; and the strength of sin is the law.

^{57} But thanks be to God, which giveth us the victory through our Lord Jesus Christ.

^{58} Therefore, my beloved brethren, be ye stedfast, unmoveable, always abounding in the work of the Lord, forasmuch as ye know that your labour is not in vain in the Lord.

Therefore, my brave brethren left behind, do not despair. For those of us taken up reached our destination through FAITH. As it is with us, so it must also be with you that are left to face tribulation.

You must not believe in the appearance of a staggering number of tragic deaths, a loss so horrifying on the surface, it will drive insanity into many, and you must see it for what it truly is: The Rapture. We are all safe, we are ALIVE, and alive forever, we are in Heaven with our Saviour Jesus Christ, incorruptible, having left our mortal bodies behind, and the dead with their bodies still in the grave, are risen as Jesus Christ promised, and we are all at peace, and in our new spiritual bodies; changed, transformed in the twinkling of an eye.

Those alive at the time of the Rapture (not asleep, for asleep within the Scripture listed above means physically dead and buried. This is not the same as other Scripture that refers to some Christians as sleeping, or asleep, which in that case simply means they didn't see the signs of the end approaching as such, yet, they still believed in Jesus Christ and were also saved. Those left behind are not described as sleeping, but rather, in darkness, or blind) but I digress.

Again, those alive at the time of the Rapture did not feel physical death, we suffered none, we felt no pain or fear. And when those who understand this of what would otherwise appear to be the single most terrible event in the history of humanity, you then will be able to take up your path of faith in Jesus Christ, so that you may also be brought up to Heaven and be free of sin and live forevermore.

✝ If this were not so, then how could I, a servant and chosen remnant of God, have told you of it with dire warning months before the occurrence, and in exact detail? If this were not the Truth, how could I report it through Scripture? ✝

✝ If I were wicked and set to mislead, how could I proclaim that Jesus Christ is the one and only God, that Jesus was nailed on the cross, that Jesus died for our sins, the sins of the whole world, that Jesus Christ was resurrected and is the living God, Jesus Christ is the Son of God, Jesus Christ is Holy and Divine, Jesus Christ is the first fruit of resurrection, creating the pathway for the rest of humanity, and that whosoever believes on the name of the Lord Jesus Christ shall have everlasting life in the Kingdom of God the Father, for Jesus Christ is the way, the truth, and the life. Jesus Christ is the Lord. ✝

✝ I could not proclaim those things if I were wicked and set on misleading. I have been given knowledge through the Holy Ghost (as commanded, and never to blaspheme), and if I am somehow in error or misunderstanding, then may God and Jesus Christ forgive me, for I mean no evil, but to deliver a message to keep the faith, and not be misled by the wicked who will remain on this earth, and the Beast, who is the final Antichrist, the spirit of Satan, indwelled within a man, who will rise and try to convince the world that the Rapture was a natural event, not of God, to dismiss the works of God. ✝

✝ Do not be fooled. Have faith in God, who works through prophets and servants chosen within humanity, to deliver His merciful message of faith, hope and love. ✝

✝ If you allow the world that is evil to convince you that all the deaths, in the twinkling of an eye, across the planet, are anything naturally occurring, or otherwise non-spiritual and not of God; i.e., a strange new weapon or chemical attack, aliens, a mysterious worldwide plague, etc. (I can only begin to imagine what the wicked and satanic forces will attempt to convince you of to steer you away from this truly Holy event). Or even worse, if the Antichrist tries to convince you that the Rapture WAS God (but rest assured he'll never call it 'Rapture'), but instead try to convince the remaining world that God is evil and murderous. †

† Perhaps this will be the ultimate deception, and the pathway to convincing those left behind that the Antichrist/Beast is the true God (a LIE, LIE, LIE). Perhaps the greatest deception the Devil will attempt will be to convince everyone that God is the evil one, and that he, the Beast, is the good. It would befit Satan well, to not come up with anything more creative than to simply try and reverse the Truth and pervert it, taking credit for all wondrous things, while reducing the Grace and Mercy of God into horrendous acts of mass murder. †

† You must be forewarned to recognize these lies. If you believe the first lie, you will believe them all. †

† Whatever Satan says to pervert the Truth, you must not believe him, and the first cry to battle against Satan will be to recognize the Truth and not Satan's lies. That first Truth that Satan will attempt to disguise, discredit, or otherwise dismiss or twist, will be The Rapture. But herein is the Truth, as delivered to a servant of God, at the appointed time, as known by God from the beginning of time, to thwart Satan's attempts at deceiving mankind in the end days. †

† Read the Word of God. Come to Jesus Christ. It is where the rest of us have gone. We simply left our bodies behind, including all children. We did not die. †

† Have faith in Jesus Christ, and know that He is the way, the truth, and the life, He loves you, and He is a kind, forgiving and merciful Saviour. †

† Jesus is Lord. Amen. †

Anab Enab

There's a lot I haven't told you. Our bodies will be left behind. Only our spirits will be going. However, there will be other bodies that do disappear, those of the raised dead. The bodies that disappear are the blood sacrifices that God takes in our stead, to fulfill His Holy Law and the prophecies written of this event in the Bible. God will raise up and take the most vile and wicked for this purpose, those who have already died, and chose against Him. There will be many bodies in the troposphere, and much blood, and flesh that is decimated. The leftover carcasses will fall back to the earth, discarded unceremoniously and without dignity or respect, as dung. The entire short book of Zephaniah (all three chapters) are about the days leading up to the Rapture, and the entire Rapture event, including the blood sacrifice of the resurrected bodies of those wicked who stand against Christ and reject Him.

But God, in His infinite mercy and love for us, will also provide a final chance for those left behind to come to Him and receive His saving Grace. He will also breathe His Holy Spirit into a chosen remnant left behind. They will become what is prophesied in God's Word as the 144,000: Messengers of God, filled with His Holy Wisdom and Truth. Their mission will be to find the last of God's lost sheep and gather them, by turning their hearts toward Jesus Christ with His message of love and hope.

It is proved that Zephaniah prophesies of the events of the Rapture and end times spoken of by John in the book of Revelation, for there are direct parallels that are undeniable. Revelation 14:14-16 literally describes the Rapture, as Jesus Christ comes sitting upon a cloud, and at the sounding of an Angel (this is the trumpet blown), the Son of Man thrusts his sickle into the earth and reaps the harvest of the earth. This literally is the chosen elect, who are Raptured. There is clearly a second group spoken of immediately following those Raptured, in verses 17-20, who are gathered and thrown into the great winepress of the wrath of God. This is the very sacrifice prophesied in Zephaniah 1:7-17. Zephaniah 1:14-17 specifically corresponds with the event prophesied in Revelation 14:17-20.

Zephaniah 1:7-17:

⁷ Hold thy peace at the presence of the Lord GOD: for the day of the LORD is at hand: for the LORD hath prepared a sacrifice, he hath bid his guests.

⁸ And it shall come to pass in the day of the LORD's sacrifice, that I will punish the princes, and the king's children, and all such as are clothed with strange apparel.

⁹ In the same day also will I punish all those that leap on the threshold, which fill their masters' houses with violence and deceit.

¹⁰ And it shall come to pass in that day, saith the LORD, that there shall be the noise of a cry from the fish gate, and an howling from the second, and a great crashing from the hills.

¹¹ Howl, ye inhabitants of Maktesh, for all the merchant people are cut down; all they that bear silver are cut off.

¹² And it shall come to pass at that time, that I will search Jerusalem with candles, and punish the men that are settled on their lees: that say in their heart, The LORD will not do good, neither will he do evil.

¹³ Therefore their goods shall become a booty, and their houses a desolation: they shall also build houses, but not inhabit them; and they shall plant vineyards, but not drink the wine thereof.

¹⁴ The great day of the LORD is near, it is near, and hasteth greatly, even the voice of the day of the LORD: the mighty man shall cry there bitterly.

¹⁵ That day is a day of wrath, a day of trouble and distress, a day of wasteness and desolation, a day of darkness and gloominess, a day of clouds and thick darkness,

¹⁶ A day of the trumpet and alarm against the fenced cities, and against the high towers.

¹⁷ And I will bring distress upon men, that they shall walk like blind men, because they have sinned against the LORD: and their blood shall be poured out as dust, and their flesh as the dung.

Revelation 14:14-20:

¹⁴ And I looked, and behold a white cloud, and upon the cloud one sat like unto the Son of man, having on his head a golden crown, and in his hand a sharp sickle.

¹⁵ And another angel came out of the temple, crying with a loud voice to him that sat on the cloud, Thrust in thy sickle, and reap: for the time is come for thee to reap; for the harvest of the earth is ripe.

¹⁶ And he that sat on the cloud thrust in his sickle on the earth; and the earth was reaped.

¹⁷ And another angel came out of the temple which is in heaven, he also having a sharp sickle.

¹⁸ And another angel came out from the altar, which had power over fire; and cried with a loud cry to him that had the sharp sickle, saying, Thrust in thy sharp sickle, and gather the clusters of the vine of the earth; for her grapes are fully ripe.

¹⁹ And the angel thrust in his sickle into the earth, and gathered the vine of the earth, and cast it into the great winepress of the wrath of God.

²⁰ And the winepress was trodden without the city, and blood came out of the winepress, even unto the horse bridles, by the space of a thousand and six hundred furlongs.

It is also proved that Zephaniah speaks of the events outlined in Revelation by the undeniable parallels in description between "the remnant of Israel" (the 144,000) and the direct description of this chosen and gathered group in Revelation.

Zephaniah 3:12-13:

¹² I will also leave in the midst of thee an afflicted and poor people, and they shall trust in the name of the LORD.

¹³The remnant of Israel shall not do iniquity, nor speak lies; neither shall a deceitful tongue be found in their mouth: for they shall feed and lie down, and none shall make them afraid.

Revelation 14:1-5

¹⁴ And I looked, and, lo, a Lamb stood on the mount Sion, and with him an hundred forty and four thousand, having his Father's name written in their foreheads.

² And I heard a voice from heaven, as the voice of many waters, and as the voice of a great thunder: and I heard the voice of harpers harping with their harps:

³ And they sung as it were a new song before the throne, and before the four beasts, and the Elders: and no man could learn that song but the hundred and forty and four thousand, which were redeemed from the earth.

⁴ These are they which were not defiled with women; for they are virgins. These are they which follow the Lamb whithersoever he goeth. These were redeemed from among men, being the firstfruits unto God and to the Lamb.

⁵ And in their mouth was found no guile: for they are without fault before the throne of God.

Zephaniah 3:13 specifically corresponds to Revelation 14:4, in verifying that the 144,000 are redeemed from the earth (those left behind after the Rapture) and hold the specific quality of honesty and Truth, for they will not speak lies, nor have deceitful tongues, and no

guile (lies, deceit or dishonesty) shall be found in their mouths. They will be virgins, and all male.

So, as is shown and proved in the Scriptures, within the very Word of God, which is the Truth, The Rapture involves the "taking away" of God's chosen faithful (referred to by Jesus himself as the elect), and these people are removed in tribulation, and their very removal is the mark and start of what Jesus calls the great tribulation. From the event of The Rapture, the time remaining is 3.5 years. Here is Jesus saying that the elect shall have those days of tribulation shortened:

Matthew 24:15-22:

[15] When ye therefore shall see the abomination of desolation, spoken of by Daniel the prophet, stand in the holy place, (whoso readeth, let him understand:)

[16] Then let them which be in Judaea flee into the mountains:

[17] Let him which is on the housetop not come down to take any thing out of his house:

[18] Neither let him which is in the field return back to take his clothes.

[19] And woe unto them that are with child, and to them that give suck in those days!

[20] But pray ye that your flight be not in the winter, neither on the sabbath day:

[21] For then shall be great tribulation, such as was not since the beginning of the world to this time, no, nor ever shall be.

[22] And except those days should be shortened, there should no flesh be saved: but for the elect's sake those days shall be shortened.

Not only does this passage in Jesus's words prove that there will be a Rapture of His chosen people; it also proves the Rapture occurs at mid-tribulation. It would seem silly that there was ever a debate within the Body of Christ over whether Rapture exists or not, much less whether it occurs pre- or mid, as Jesus here clearly states the answer to both. For, how can the days be shortened for the elect's sake if the days of tribulation had not already begun? This statement by Jesus immediately follows, "For then shall be great tribulation" (which Jesus also qualifies as exponentially worse than simply normal tribulation; hence the delineation between calling it tribulation or great tribulation). There is a change there, and it is at the mid-point of the total span of events. Since there is a Body of Christ that is faithful and has earned salvation, of course they will be saved, and so their days shall be shortened.

All of this verifies the first hupsélos teaching, for it corroborates that flesh and blood cannot inherit the Kingdom of God, as stated in I Corinthians 15:50. With the end of great tribulation, in the Second Coming of Jesus Christ (this time He will not come on a cloud and hover above the earth to gather His final followers, but rather, come literally down to Earth) with an army of angels on war horses, to smite with flaming swords all those remaining who chose against Him and instead took the Mark of the Beast, aligning themselves with the Antichrist and Satan. Their flesh will not be spared. These most unfortunate souls will be flung into Hell, into a lake of fire, to burn in torment forever. All left who turned to God with the aid of the 144,000 messengers, will have been put to death in the name of Jesus Christ, beheaded. At the Second Coming of Christ, those newly dead and asleep in Christ shall be raised incorruptible, just as those who were raised in the Rapture. The living 144,000 will also be reaped at that time, and the lost who are flung into eternal hellfire shall serve as their flesh and blood sacrifice, all this to parallel in the Second Coming of Jesus Christ those events that take place during the Rapture.

Now, as already outlined in the first half of this teaching, we've established that the elect who are Raptured do not simply disappear. In fact, our bodies will be left behind, and appear to have suffered a massive die-off for no apparent reason, and no discernible cause. But there will also be bodies that are taken, in sacrifice, as attested to in Zephaniah 1:7-8, already listed above. These will be the iniquitous, who lived wicked lives, focused on the love of self, money, material things. These will also be people who knew of Jesus Christ and fully understood His sacrifice for the world, and even knew that He is the Son of God and the Messiah sent to save the world. These are the very most evil, who knew that Jesus Christ is the Lord and Saviour, and still chose during their lifetimes to turn their back on Him to continue living their preferred lives of debauchery and vileness.

These are people who God has already seen into the hearts of and judged. These are the unsaved and forever lost, who did not die in Christ, but rather, died rebuking Him. These are the chosen sacrifices, the "bidden guests" (Zephaniah 1:7), who refused the invitation of Salvation from Jesus Christ. While the elect receive the reward of Rapture (instant transformation into our spiritual bodies without suffering the transition of death, i.e., the very definition of Harpazó: to seize by force, to take, as booty or a prize), our souls not having to wait for physical death to set our spiritual bodies free, but instead, having God seize our souls and pull them from our bodies, in an instant, causing the body to seemingly die (for the body cannot live without the spirit indwelled), and this is our special reward for our unfailing faith and our love of our Lord Jesus Christ, in contrast to the unsaved dead: They are resurrected for the blood sacrifice, and they will die a second time, serving the death transition, in their iniquity, that we, the righteous Raptured, will not suffer.

Again, these "chosen" sacrifices will pay the price of flesh and blood death for their unflagging rejection of Jesus Christ.

Zephaniah 1:5

[5] And them that worship the host of heaven upon the housetops; *(this is those who practice astrology, i.e., they worship the host of heaven, or the stars which are viewed from "upon the housetops", yet, they refuse to acknowledge the maker and creator of these host of heaven, nor worship Him)* and them that worship and that swear by the LORD, and that swear by Malcham; *(These people are literally demon and Satan worshippers. Observe the definition and nature of their 'Lord' Malcham: Moloch Molech / Milcom / Malcham.

Meaning: king; the name of the national god of the Ammonites, to whom children were sacrificed by fire).*

[6] And them that are turned back from the LORD; and those that have not sought the LORD, nor enquired for him. *(These are people stated to have "turned back from the Lord", and others who do know He is real and is God, but they do not seek Him, and do not wish to, nor do they enquire for Him, or attempt to develop a relationship with Him. Full rejection of the saving Grace of our Lord Jesus Christ, in other words).*

And so, now we have established that there will be those 'taken' whose bodies will disappear, but from the grave, as these are the blood sacrifice (and their bodies as 'dung'). We have also established that these are the dead without faith, who will be resurrected for the sole purpose of fulfilling the Law of God that flesh and blood must be sacrificed, for the Raptured to not suffer this punishing fate (for the Rapture is our reward for our living Faith in Jesus Christ, as opposed to the punishment of the faithless dead. This is found in the book of Daniel 12:2.

[2] And many of them that sleep in the dust of the earth shall awake, some to everlasting life, and some to shame and everlasting contempt.

But the final truth of this Scripture from the book of Daniel will resume in the conclusion to this teaching.

Conversely, we've established that there will be those Raptured and 'taken', but their bodies will remain on the earth, appearing to be dead. And so, we come to perhaps the most misunderstood Scriptures within the Bible, and they are the words spoken by Jesus Himself, concerning this dichotomy of those taken and those left behind. (this is the very deception I have warned about from the beginning of this entire teaching).

Matthew 24:38-41:

38 For as in the days that were before the flood they were eating and drinking, marrying and giving in marriage, until the day that Noe entered into the ark,

39 And knew not until the flood came, and took them all away; so shall also the coming of the Son of man be.

40 Then shall two be in the field; the one shall be taken, and the other left.

41 Two women shall be grinding at the mill; the one shall be taken, and the other left.

Here Jesus tells us that one will be left behind, and one taken. The misunderstanding is the judgment of each. What Jesus means here is that the one taken will leave behind their body (i.e., Raptured and taken to Heaven), and the other that is left (not Raptured) will be left ALIVE. Hence, one shall be taken (Raptured, with only their body left, i.e., the spirit "taken") and the other left (alive and not Raptured up to heaven). The disciples knew and understood this. They ask Jesus (in the Gospel of Luke, which I'll outline next) where the bodies of the ones taken will be found, for they understood that the taken would be Raptured, leaving their lifeless bodies behind. Jesus tells them of the remains of the Raptured in verse 28, before delivering the parable of the ones taken and the ones left:

Matthew 24:28:

28 For wheresoever the carcase is, there will the eagles be gathered together.

But wait, this seems unclear. Aren't I reaching on the meaning of that line of Scripture? NO. It is qualified with the parallel report of Luke, which is, perhaps, a bit more easily related.

Luke 17:34-37:

³⁴ I tell you, in that night there shall be two men in one bed; the one shall be taken, and the other shall be left.

³⁵ Two women shall be grinding together; the one shall be taken, and the other left.

³⁶ Two men shall be in the field; the one shall be taken, and the other left.

³⁷ And they answered and said unto him, Where, Lord? And he said unto them, Wheresoever the body is, thither will the eagles be gathered together.

And so, the disciples ask this question of Jesus to serve as the answer to the parable, proving that those taken leave a body behind. Just as we know where the bodies of those Raptured will be. Our bodies will remain where they fall, yet we are still taken, for our spiritual bodies, incorruptible, will have been taken to Heaven.

This all ties into the final confirmation that the Rapture will occur at the 'final trumpet blast'. Once the final trump is sounded, all the events outlined will happen instantaneously, and further events will immediately follow. There will be a massive earthquake, as the faithless dead are resurrected for the sacrifice, their graves broken open (while the graves of the dead in Christ will remain unharmed, as those faithful will simply rise unseen, their incorruptible spiritual bodies awakened to ascend into Heaven), and just as quickly, the alive Raptured will appear to suddenly drop lifeless, in the blink of an eye. Within minutes of the earthquake and leaving behind of mass bodies of those Raptured, there will be blood rain, along with fire and hail. This is also in the Scriptures, in Revelation, as this is the next sequence following the Rapture, when Satan and his rebel army of angels are cast down to Earth, where Satan will reign for 3.5 years, and this all marks the beginning of the period of great tribulation. The blood from the sacrifice of the wicked will literally rain down on the earth, most likely for several days, if not weeks.

Revelation 8:7:

⁷ The first angel sounded, and there followed hail and fire mingled with blood, and they were cast upon the earth: and the third part of trees was burnt up, and all green grass was burnt up.

But, wait: How can that be the "final trump" that is supposed to herald the event of the Rapture and beginning of great tribulation, when it clearly says, "The first angel sounded"?

*The first is the last and the last is the first. God is the beginning and the end, He is the Alpha and the Omega. But my telling you that won't make understanding Revelation any easier or possible. This teaching has been delivered unto me by the Holy Spirit, who has opened my eyes to see and understand the mysteries of Revelation. My eyes have been opened to it, that I may deliver the essential Truth, as needed, for those left behind.

I will tell you that the answer lies in the simple fact that most (but not all) of Revelation is written backwards to forwards, meaning, the events described as 1-7 occur in reverse order (but again, not fully). However, I can tell you that in the order of things, definitively: The last trumpet and events that occur with it, is also the FIRST trump, and vice versa. Therefore, when it says, "The first angel sounded", this is describing the events that will occur at the LAST trump. But the last trumpet shall also sound first. If the first is the last and the last is the first, there IS no first and last. The two are one and the same, meaning: The first and last trumpets will sound at the SAME TIME. Therefore, the events of the first trumpet and the last will both happen together.

Revelation 11:15-19:

[15] And the seventh angel sounded; and there were great voices in heaven, saying, The kingdoms of this world are become the kingdoms of our Lord, and of his Christ; and he shall reign for ever and ever.

[16] And the four and twenty Elders, which sat before God on their seats, fell upon their faces, and worshipped God,

[17] Saying, We give thee thanks, O LORD God Almighty, which art, and wast, and art to come; because thou hast taken to thee thy great power, and hast reigned.

[18] And the nations were angry, and thy wrath is come, and the time of the dead, that they should be judged, and that thou shouldest give reward unto thy servants the prophets, and to the saints, and them that fear thy name, small and great; and shouldest destroy them which destroy the earth.

[19] And the temple of God was opened in heaven, and there was seen in his temple the ark of his testament: and there were lightnings, and voices, and thunderings, and an earthquake, and great hail.

Sound confusing? It is, which is why it doesn't serve much purpose in focusing on. There is only one key purpose to this teaching, and that is what I have had my eyes opened to, and it is my purpose and the mission assigned to me by Jesus Christ, God my Father in Heaven, and the Holy Spirit; that I deliver this essential Truth to you, for all those who will have eyes to see and ears to hear, and the will to understand. You must have FAITH. This teaching is being delivered to you to save you from eternal damnation by making mistakes during great tribulation that you cannot ever take back.

Yes, this Wisdom has been revealed to me, as given by the Holy Spirit. This is attested to in the book of Daniel 12:1-4.

[12] And at that time shall Michael stand up, the great prince which standeth for the children of thy people: and there shall be a time of trouble, such as never was since there was a nation even to that same time: and at that time thy people shall be delivered, every one that shall be found written in the book.

[2] And many of them that sleep in the dust of the earth shall awake, some to everlasting life, and some to shame and everlasting contempt.

[3] And they that be wise shall shine as the brightness of the firmament; and they that turn many to righteousness as the stars for ever and ever.

[4] But thou, O Daniel, shut up the words, and seal the book, even to the time of the end: many shall run to and fro, and knowledge shall be increased.

I am one of the many that Daniel speaks of that shall run to and fro, with increased knowledge. This is further testament that the days of great tribulation are extremely near, as Daniel clearly states that those running to and fro with increased knowledge is the unsealing of the book of which Daniel was ordered to "shut up the words, and seal the book, even to the time of the end". This book (and the signs of the end days of great tribulation shortly arriving) is further and finally testified to in the book of Revelation by St. John.

Revelation 10:1-11:

[10] And I saw another mighty angel come down from heaven, clothed with a cloud: and a rainbow was upon his head, and his face was as it were the sun, and his feet as pillars of fire:

[2] And he had in his hand a little book open: and he set his right foot upon the sea, and his left foot on the earth,

[3] And cried with a loud voice, as when a lion roareth: and when he had cried, seven thunders uttered their voices.

⁴ And when the seven thunders had uttered their voices, I was about to write: and I heard a voice from heaven saying unto me, Seal up those things which the seven thunders uttered, and write them not.

⁵ And the angel which I saw stand upon the sea and upon the earth lifted up his hand to heaven,

⁶ And sware by him that liveth for ever and ever, who created heaven, and the things that therein are, and the earth, and the things that therein are, and the sea, and the things which are therein, that there should be time no longer:

⁷ But in the days of the voice of the seventh angel, when he shall begin to sound, the mystery of God should be finished, as he hath declared to his servants the prophets.

⁸ And the voice which I heard from heaven spake unto me again, and said, Go and take the little book which is open in the hand of the angel which standeth upon the sea and upon the earth.

⁹ And I went unto the angel, and said unto him, Give me the little book. And he said unto me, Take it, and eat it up; and it shall make thy belly bitter, but it shall be in thy mouth sweet as honey.

¹⁰ And I took the little book out of the angel's hand, and ate it up; and it was in my mouth sweet as honey: and as soon as I had eaten it, my belly was bitter.

¹¹ And he said unto me, Thou must prophesy again before many peoples, and nations, and tongues, and kings.

The 'book' that Daniel was ordered to roll up and seal is the actual book that John eats, the tiny book the Angel holds. We know that Angels are much larger than men, so in an Angel's hands, the book would look tiny. But it was the book (or 'scroll' in some Bible version translations) of Daniel that he was ordered to roll up and seal. And then later, John ate it, to further seal it up, until the end times. And this Truth sealed up, to not be unsealed or revealed until the days remaining be so short as to fool the wicked one, Satan, that old devil, into believing that he had successfully deceived the world into believing the false narrative of what the Rapture would entail, and how it would appear, so to steal the Glory of God away. Therefore, if these Truths now be revealed, the end lies extremely near.

Furthermore, I have been ordered to place this teaching, Truth and Wisdom into the back of this book, to further conceal it from both the Antichrist and Satan himself. The wicked will look to confiscate all Bibles and anything else containing the Word of God, in any form, as well as the message of faith, hope and love that God's Word contains.

What more ingenious way to hide this Wisdom, than inside the boring science fiction trilogy of an unknown indie author.

If you are reading this after the events have transpired, then you'll know that I am accurate in everything I am teaching in this document. This teaching, as stated from the very beginning, is not for those alive now, before events have occurred, but for those left behind after. You are the ones who will need to know and understand the events of the Rapture properly, and see the Truth, so that you will not be deceived.

This paper holds within it the Truth of God's Word, including the accurate understanding of the Rapture events. You must know and understand that there are two groups involved; one group comprised of the raised and iniquitous dead, whose blood will rain down, sacrificed in physical death for the second group, the Raptured, who will NOT vanish, nor their bodies disappear, but merely appear to have all dropped dead at the same moment, by the billions, across the globe. These dead ARE the Raptured. Do not let Satan deceive you. The one claiming anything else in explanation is the Antichrist. Do not follow him, and do not take his mark.

You must also understand that the true and faithful followers of Jesus Christ are the ones whose bodies were left behind, but that we did not suffer, nor even experience death, therefore, we did NOT die. We suffered no injuries, nor did we shed any blood. In the twinkling of an eye, a mere moment so small as to be immeasurable by human standards of time; a fraction of a fraction of a second, and even that would be too long. We are not dead, we just left our bodies behind. We were Raptured by the one and only true God, our Lord and Saviour Jesus Christ.

So, if you have 'lost' a loved one in this manner, meaning, they seem to have simply dropped dead from no apparent cause (no matter what the remaining wicked on earth, nor the Beast, Satan, or the Antichrist try to LIE and tell you happened), you must not believe the lies or deceptions. If you have lost a loved one (especially a child, for ALL CHILDREN will be Raptured, including unborn babies in the womb), they are not dead, they are safe and alive, up in Heaven with God. Jesus Christ is watching over them, along with the rest of us. They are safe, happy, alive, and well taken care of, and they are waiting for YOU to choose Jesus Christ and ask Him into your life, so you can come up to Heaven as well, and be reunited with your children, or any other family and friends you may have lost.

Yes, there is a reason the Bible says in Matthew 24:19:

"[19] And woe unto them that are with child, and to them that give suck in those days!"

For all children and the unborn are saved by innocence. Unborn babies will appear to have died in the womb and will have to be delivered stillborn (other pregnant mothers who are not as far along will suffer miserable miscarriages). But remember, your baby did not die, your baby was Raptured, its spiritual body taken out of its fleshly body in your womb and delivered up to Jesus Christ in Heaven.

Mothers with newborns, young infants, babies, and toddlers, your pain will be unimaginable, and my heart goes out to you. My compassion spills over for all parents with children of any age who are still young enough to be Raptured, as they are too young to be accountable for choosing for or against Jesus Christ or God.

Your children are NOT dead. I know that won't relieve the grief of being distanced from them and unable while reading this to hold them again, or have them there with you, but I do hope and pray that this message will give you hope, and the ability to seek out Jesus Christ for yourself, so that you can be reunited with your children again very soon, and then you WILL be able to hold them again and have them with you, in HEAVEN.

You now have the Truth in your hands. The Truth and Wisdom of the Holy Spirit is in front of your eyes. If you choose to listen and SEE with an open heart for God your Father in Heaven, you have a chance, still, to be saved. If you missed the Rapture, that doesn't mean it's too late for you or that you are lost.

You will have a very tough road ahead of you. There will be messengers that can help you in times of great need (this will be those of the 144,000). You may or may not even know who they are if you meet them, if or when you talk with one of them, if they cross your path. Then again, maybe you will. I am now past any Wisdom granted to me, and so, I cannot answer to further events.

My task was to deliver the Truth of the Rapture to those left behind, so that you might be able to see and understand. This is here so that you might have one last chance at everlasting life in the Kingdom of God.

If you choose God now, you will be rewarded by going to Heaven, but you will have to pay the price for only coming to God now, at the very end of times. You will be tested. You will most likely be imprisoned. They will try to force you to take the mark of the Beast. You must NOT take this mark.

If you take the mark of the Beast, you cannot be saved, and you will NOT go to heaven. You must never willingly take the mark of Satan. Show your allegiance to Jesus Christ, your Lord and King.

If needs be, you will have to DIE for your newfound faith. This death will be over momentarily, and forever awaits you in Heaven. If your faith is strong enough to be tested in the fire, to be willing to die for your beliefs, then you have a chance. And that is the last of what I can tell you.

† May God be with you all, and may Jesus Christ find His way into your hearts, if you will open your hearts to Him. Jesus Christ is the Lord and the one and only way to salvation and eternal life. You have a very big and loving family of fellow brothers and sisters in Christ eagerly waiting for you in Heaven. I believe I can speak for all of us when I say that we are very excited to meet you. Please come home to us soon. †

† Most importantly, please come home to Jesus Christ. He loves you more than you will ever understand. God your Father also waits for you, but no one can come to the Father save through His Son Jesus Christ. Call upon the name of the Lord Jesus Christ and ask Him into your heart: If you earnestly mean it, He will not forsake you; He will answer your prayer. †

† Bless you all, from a sister in Jesus Christ. I hope to see you soon. Jesus Christ is my Lord and Saviour whom I love more dearly than anything. †

† Jesus is Lord. Amen. †

For more wisdom delivered from the Holy Spirit, please visit: http://www.untothyword.com/home.html